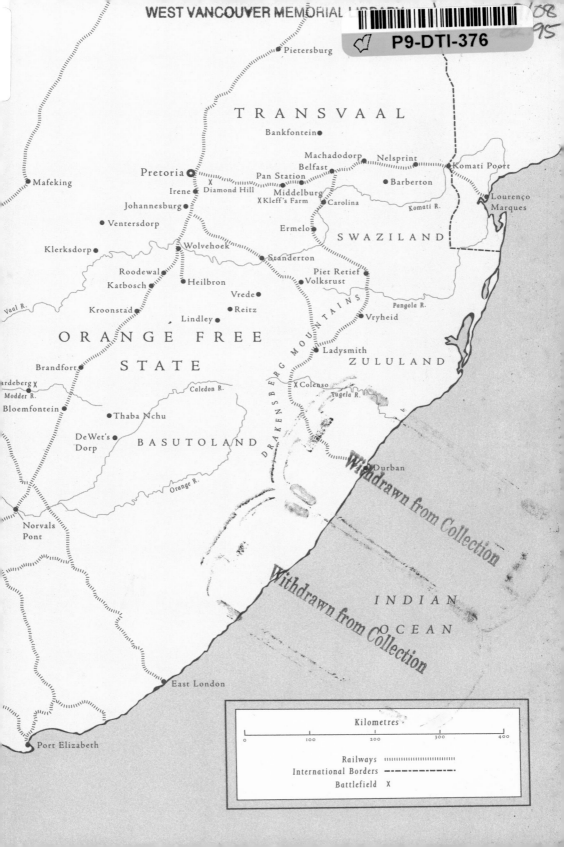

Pietersburg

T R A N S V A A L

Bankfontein

Machadodorp   Nelsprint
Belfast   Komati Poort
Pretoria   X   Pan Station   Barberton
Irene   X   Diamond Hill
Johannesburg   Middelburg   Lourenço
X Kleff's Farm   Carolina   Marques
Komati R.
Ventersdorp
Ermelo   S W A Z I L A N D
Klerksdorp
Wolvehoek
Roodewal   Standerton
Katbosch   Heilbron   Piet Retief
Volksrust
Vrede
Kroonstad   Reitz   Pangola R.
Lindley   Vryheid

O R A N G E   F R E E
Ladysmith   Z U L U L A N D
S T A T E
Brandfort   X Colenso
ardeberg X   Caledon R.   Tugela R.
Modder R.
Bloemfontein   Thaba Nchu
DeWet's   B A S U T O L A N D
Dorp   Durban
Orange R.

Mafeking

Vaal R.

Norvals
Pont

I N D I A N

O C E A N

East London

Port Elizabeth

Kilometres				
0	100	200	300	400

Railways
International Borders
Battlefield   X

D R A K E N S B E R G   M O U N T A I N S

GREAT

] THE GREAT KAROO [

Fred Stenson

THE

KAROO

DOUBLEDAY CANADA

Doubleday Canada and colophon are trademarks

LIBRARY AND ARCHIVES CANADA CATALOGUING IN PUBLICATION

Stenson, Fred, 1951–
The Great Karoo / Fred Stenson.

ISBN 978-0-385-66405-9

1. South African War, 1899–1902—Fiction. I. Title.

PS8587.T45G42 2008   C813'.54   C2008-903733-2

Book and jacket design: CS Richardson
Endpaper map: Andrew Roberts
Printed and bound in the USA

Published in Canada by Doubleday Canada,
a division of Random House of Canada Limited

Visit Random House of Canada Limited's website:
www.randomhouse.ca

BVG   10 9 8 7 6 5 4 3 2 1

FOR VERA BANTING
AND PAMELA BANTING

FORT MACLEOD
March 16, 1897

The Concorde stagecoach had been a tarry, shining black when they left the train station in Calgary. Now every surface was dull, and little drifts of yellow sat on the ledges between roof, wall, and wagon. Inside, the schoolteacher pulled back the leather window cover and looked at the Macleod Hotel, where she had reserved a room for the night. An impolite crowd jostled between the coach and the hotel's door. She slumped back in her seat.

The scald-faced drummer opposite wore a superior smile. He had his fingers stuck in his trouser pockets to the second knuckle, a posture that spread his jacket halves and exaggerated the tightness of his waistcoat. Each button strained and the shiny cloth replicated his seamed flesh in a way the schoolteacher did not want to see. Looking at the floor, she was treated to an image of his fallen socks speckled white with skin. His unshined shoes tweezed a drab carpet bag, bulging with samples.

She pulled the window blind again and the wind deflected into her face. She saw the bizarre crowd passing, moving within itself like a boiling fudge. Bow-tied storekeepers. Tradesmen in dusty jackets with hanging pockets. Bareheaded people fighting the crowd to chase a hat. The drovers, or "cowboys," the dandies of this society, wore wide-brimmed chapeaux that seemed glued to their heads. They leaned against the posts that held up the hotel's overhanging balcony, smoking cigarettes and looking amused.

And Indians! These were mostly in white-man's clothing but a few had blanket coats cinched at the waist with brass-studded belts. The wild ones had long, loose hair, slung like rags across their starved faces. Children clinging to their legs looked like little cadavers.

She turned to the smug drummer and asked, "Why are so many people here, then?"

For some reason he was holding his breath. The air escaped with a whistle. "Necktie party," he said.

She hated him, and one of the main reasons was this way of talking. Nothing clear. You had to ask and ask, thus appearing more interested than you were.

"What do you mean by that?"

"Hanging."

The drummer reached between his feet. He abruptly hoisted himself and his carpet bag, turned the handle, and let the wind slap the door open. He squeezed out through the explosion of wind. Desperately, the schoolteacher plunged after him and stayed in his wake until they were inside. In the sudden relative quiet of the hotel, she said, "And who is to be hanged?"

"Indian, Charcoal. Murdered a Mountie, Wilde."

"I don't understand you. A wild Indian?"

"Name of the Mountie he killed was Sergeant Wilde. Shot him."

A short, stout Englishman was in a cubby behind a flip-up board, keys on hooks behind him. When her turn came to sign the book, he saw her inscribe *schoolteacher* beside her name and said, "You'd be the miss for Fishburn School, then." She admitted she was. Next he asked if she was going to the hanging. Beyond his filthy front window, the mass was surging west now, heads thrust into the wind. She certainly would not be, she said. Ignoring her meaning, he told her that he'd given her the second-floor room at the rear, which had a view of the gallows. Then he flipped his counter, squeezed through, clapped on a hat, and left.

A pair of boys had brought the luggage in before running off to the hanging. Hers stood by the door. She dragged the two suitcases up through the creaking, booming hotel. It appeared she was the only person present. In her tiny room, she passed the bed and tugged the green paper blind, letting it roll to the top. The dirty little window quaked in dry putty, sprayed cold air, but did provide a fly-specked view of the gallows stage, and the crowd like a dark mat out of which the gibbet thrust.

After a while, men climbed to that stage. She counted four. The condemned man was shackled and handcuffed, and supported by the others. They took off the ankle irons and dragged a bag over his head. The priest, his dress-like garment whipping, aimed his mouth at the condemned man's ear. Then there were only two: the hangman and his victim.

It was a shocking motion that went up, not down, when the trap door fell. She thought it would be quick but it wasn't. The Indian kicked and kicked. Until finally he did hang. Deadweight. The school teacher understood the word anew.

Dinner was at two long communal tables. She sought out the drummer. After witnessing the execution, the people in the hotel were excited in a dangerous way. She felt protected against the drummer's hot, bulky flank. Had she seen the hanging, he asked. Certainly not, she said. He was waiting to be asked what he had seen. She let him wait.

Across the board and down sat a rancher and his wide-eyed son, then an old man with a long white beard like something groomed in a creek bottom, and finally a skinny, nervous youth with boils on his face. All four were bent over their stew. The young fellow with the boils filled the silence as water fills space.

"God's will. Says right in Exodus. Eye for eye. Tooth for tooth. Hand for hand. Foot for foot. Says again in Leviticus, 24:21: 'and he that killeth a man, he shall be put to death.'"

This biblical authority mopped his bowl with a sopping crust. Then the older man beside him began to unbend and rise. He rose and rose, being very tall above the waist. His beard kept coming up as well until its white tail cleared the table. He drew a long handkerchief from his shirt pocket and daintily dabbed his beard. All this unwinding and dabbing was preparation for speech, and when his mouth bloomed pink in his beard, the voice was loud and French.

"Yessir me, I ting dey hang da last wild Indian today."

The boy was poised to spout more Old Testament, but the old man was not finished.

"Yessir me, I wonder what dey'll ever do now."

Prologue (II)

—

COLENSO, NATAL
December 16, 1899

For two days, the British guns had flown their shells over the dozen brick houses of Colenso, blasting the hills on the far side of the Tugela River. The lyddite exploded yellow and the sum of the blasts was a red earth cloud tinged with green. When the smoke and dust cleared, the general's staff scoped the slopes looking for escaping men. Nothing. They threw in shrapnel rounds but, again, the effect was nil. The hills were as impassive as great turds.

On the second afternoon, Gen. Sir Redvers Buller, *Red Heifer* to the Boers, briefed his senior officers on the plan of attack. On the right, Buller would send Dundonald to fight for a hill that would be their buffer. On the left, Hart's Irishmen would advance to the river and cross. But the centre was the key. There, Hildyard's infantry brigades, with artillery support, would cross the Tugela beside the wrecked railway bridge. Then, all together, they would force their way up the hills. They would battle to the besieged town of Ladysmith and free her.

Until two days ago, there'd been a more cautious plan to go around the position. Then came word of General Methuen's defeat on the Modder River. Red Heifer had seen red. He would pussyfoot no longer. Up the Boer middle he would go. If Louis Botha got in his way, he would smash him and his farmers like so many eggs.

The attack began at daybreak. Buller stood on Naval Gun Hill with his signalmen and staff officers. It did not take long to come apart. Hart had a sketch that showed the drift where he was to cross. He'd been told it was *beside* a loop in the river, where a creek emptied. Now, for some reason, he was going into the loop. He had been told the loop was a dangerous salient and not to go there. Now a message arrived. Hart could not find the creek and was following a Native guide to some other crossing. Buller sent a galloper back: "Stay out of the loop!" But Hart's men were already surging into it.

A disturbing sound turned Buller's attention to the centre. Colonel Long's fifteen-pound guns were erupting. It was too soon and they were farther away than they should be. Stopford came riding to say that Long was ahead of Hildyard, by at least a mile.

Buller studied the hills in front of which these mistakes were being made in his name. It was not yet seven in the morning. Please, he implored, let those hills be empty. His answer was an abrupt roar of field guns and automatic rifles. Not his.

Much of what came next Buller would find out later. Hart's masterful packing of the river loop created a target a blind man could not miss. It was enfiladed by Boer trenches on three sides. A private pinned down in the grass said the Mauser bullets came so fast they looked like telegraph wire. Another called it a butcher's kitchen. The artillery, attempting to adjust to the changed plan, dropped its first shots on top of Hart's men.

In the centre, Long was wounded through the guts. A third of his men were mown down. His twelve lightest guns were abandoned to the enemy. Only the heavy naval guns, his cow guns, lagged behind enough to be saved. Going forward to survey the mess, Buller took a piece of shell to the ribs. Captain Hughes, his doctor, came to check on him, and was shot through the lungs. Hughes died a bubbling death. In the attempt to retrieve the lost guns, Tommy Roberts, General Lord Roberts' son, was killed. Buller called it off. Accepted defeat.

The next day, there was a ceasefire. Malay body snatchers hurried the wounded into ambulances. Dotted around the plain were one hundred and forty-three dead.

In the worst places, the river loop and where Long's guns had been lost, the sound was no longer warlike or even agonized. Often there was a gaping silence, so great and meditative that the occasional thrashing fight to live by horse or man seemed unmannerly, like a dish thrown on a temple floor.

The CANADIAN MOUNTED
RIFLES

BOOK ONE

The CANADIAN MOUNTED
RIFLES

Part One

—

TO AFRICA

Tommy Killam stood with the other children in the crowd on Main Street, come to see the soldiers off to South Africa. Along the hitching post in front of Charlie Beebe's livery barn, many horses stood saddled. Fred Morden's bay had a feed bag but the rest were staring miserably at the frozen ground. A Chinook meant it was windy but warm enough that the soldiers could parade without buffalo coats. It would have looked better, thought Tommy, if they all had uniforms and if the uniforms had been the same. As it was, the Mounties had Mountie ones, Fred Morden had a different kind, and the rest were in ranching and cowboy clothes.

While his teacher was not looking, Tommy stepped out of line and re-emerged at the corner. He pretended the move was so he could better hear Inspector Davidson, who was answering an earlier speech by Mr. Herron. Davidson was the Mountie in charge of the Pincher Creek detachment, and a terrible speaker who was trying to say how honoured he was to be an officer with the Canadian Mounted Rifles, Second Battalion; and how . . . honoured he was to lead such fine brave soldiers as these into the . . . honourable war for freedom in South Africa.

The real reason Tommy moved was to have a better look at Fred Morden. The Mordens were Killam's next-door neighbours on the north side of the creek, and though Tommy was only ten and Morden grown up enough to go to war, they were friends. Fred let Tommy come over and take his coyote hounds for runs in the hills. When Tommy's father gave him a .22 rifle off their store shelves at Christmas, it was Morden who took him to the canyon and taught him to hit tomato cans. Fred Morden had said many times, "Here's my good friend Tommy."

On Sundays, in good weather, Morden and his friends, including his girlfriend Trudy Black, went coyote hunting with hounds. They dressed up and pretended it was an English fox hunt. Tommy was not allowed to go but attended the punch parties afterwards, either in Morden's yard or in their front room depending on the weather. Tommy was given a glass of punch like everyone else while he fooled with the tired dogs.

For the last two months, the parties had consisted less of jokes and more of Fred Morden explaining to the others why they had to fight in South Africa.

"You can't be part of an Empire, enjoying its fruits, and not do your part."

When Canada sent its first thousand troops, they were infantry from eastern militias. Fred called it an outrage and said Canada's westerners must demand their right to fight. When the Canadian Mounted Rifles was formed, based on Mountie officers and western troopers, Tommy told Inspector Davidson to count him in. "Part of the fun," he told his friends, was that they could take their own horses.

Tommy Killam didn't try to sound like Fred Morden around his own friends. It just came out that way.

"A Boer has *nothing* to do with a pig. It's a Dutch farmer in Africa. South Africa is *on the other side of the world*. They have to cross the *Atlantic Ocean*. We *have* to fight them because the Boers won't let us vote."

Tommy was not so clear on why it was important to vote in Boer Africa, but Fred was dead certain. British Empire workers were not allowed to vote, and they must be.

Tommy was proud of Fred Morden, even though his going to war meant not seeing him for a year. Fred was good at everything he did—riding, shooting, sports—and right now he *looked* better than the other soldiers. His mother had altered the borrowed uniform to fit, and it was snappy. His squared shoulders went right to the seams. His chest filled the front. His hat was new and brushed, and the brim was straight as a razor. The Belton brothers had curled their brims, like rougher cowboys always did with hats.

Tommy watched to see where Fred's eyes went. He hoped they would look at him but they were studying Trudy Black, who was trying not to cry and failing. She had a lace handkerchief pushed to her mouth, and her friend Lily Martin, who could play a guitar, was looking sad and holding tight to Trudy's arm.

Suddenly, Inspector Davidson stopped talking. He made a helpless circling gesture with his hand, and Tommy's father, who was standing on their store porch in his apron, called for three cheers. Then a local boy did some awful bugling after which the whole street fell silent except for the wind. A wavery moment in which people didn't know if they should go or stay. The soldiers looked at their horses and were uncertain. They turned to Davidson, who was looking at the ground, probably still thinking about his speech.

A tall rancher named Lionel Brooke took a big step into the space between the soldiers and the crowd. He raised his arm and called for attention. All Brooke said was that he knew what soldiers needed at a moment like this, and he would be pleased if those who cared to would follow him to the Arlington for a stirrup-cup. Several mothers were standing behind the children. Tommy heard one say with disgust, "Drink at this hour."

The soldiers and most of the other men followed Brooke's lead to the brick hotel. It was the Arlington, but everyone called it the brick hotel. Fred Morden was with them, though his head was practically turned backwards trying to see Trudy Black. Tommy could see her clear enough. She had broken down in tears and was supported by Mrs. Morden on one side and Lily Martin on the other. The three were walking for the bridge and home.

Tommy knew he needed to be quick. He bolted from the other schoolchildren and sped by the soldiers and townsmen. He made for the back of the brick hotel, and saw a figure by the river bushes that he hoped was Young Sam. Young Sam and Tommy shared the secret that the hotel foundations were loose behind the bar. Though there was a basement under the main hotel (where Chinamen cooked and did laundry), the bar was an addition with only a crawl space beneath.

Young Sam was a Nez Perce, a kind of Indian that had fought the U.S. Cavalry. They tried to come into Canada like Sitting Bull's Sioux, but got beat first. The few who did make it were scattered. Young Sam's family lived up the canyon where a rancher let them pitch their tent, but Sam and his brother spent most of their time in town. Though Young Sam was a few years older than Tommy, they did things together, such as pull out the loose stones and crawl under the bar.

They wriggled along to the middle of the beer-smelling gloom. Thanks to crooked planks, they could see a bit. The long thin place was filled end to end. They began to smell tobacco smoke as men lit their pipes and cigars. There was the ping of someone hitting the brass spittoon with tobacco juice.

Finally, the hum of voices cut off and only Mr. Herron spoke.

"All you boys got your drinks? Good then. Let's raise a glass to these lads. It's no small thing going to a heathen country to fight for the Empire. This here *was* a heathen country when I came across the rocks from Ontario with the late Colonel Macleod to set the Red River rebels straight."

Someone interrupted. It made Tommy blush to hear his father.

"All countries were heathen if you look back that far."

"And yet, Mr. Killam—and this is my point—the Halfbreed rebellion of 1869 is tied to the present conflict in South Africa, and to our own town. General Wolseley, now senior general in the British War Office, led the British army to Red River that year. One of his officers was Redvers Buller, General Sir Redvers Buller, who has been leading the British forces in Africa."

Another voice spoke up rudely. "Until Colenso."

"Yes, that's right. There have been defeats at Colenso and Spion Kop. And when you chaps have led men into battle, you'll be free to criticize. I'm only saying that the men who cut their teeth in 1869, at Red River, are the same men leading the way in Africa. That's what Britain's Empire is all about. Every corner is involved. Nobody can say these boys are going to fight a war that has nothing to do with them."

"No one *is saying* it, Herron—except you. Can we drink or not?"

"Yes, yes. To the Canadian Mounted Rifles! May South Africa prove your bravery!"

Down below, the boys could hear the clinking and the repetition of the toasts.

"Hey, Brooke, what do you have to say to the boys about the war?"

The room went silent. Tommy's father was trying to goad Lionel Brooke into saying something funny. Brooke was English, the kind whose families send them to Canada to ranch.

"Ya, Lionel," said another, "what do you have to say about the Boers?"

"If you want me to talk, give me some space."

The men pushed back. The cleared spot was above Tommy and Young Sam, so when Brooke entered it they could see right up his sandy pant leg. There was some kind of strap holding up his sock. Past Brooke, Tommy could see Fred Morden sitting on the bar with his spurs tapping the wood. The other soldiers, the Miles brothers, the Beltons, and Robert Kerr, were probably crushed in a corner somewhere, but Fred knew how to act.

Brooke cleared his throat. "I'll require another drink."

Bill Durnham, the barman, filled Brooke's glass.

"This town has mostly Tories, and some Grits," Brooke began. "But I back no one. That's why my views on South Africa differ. Fact is, there are money grubbers in Kimberly and Johannesburg, and all they want out of this war is more diamonds and gold."

"Now, hold on, Brooke. That's not the kind of talk . . ."

"*You* hold on! You're drinking my booze. You asked me my opinion. You'll get it in full. I'm not against the Boers for British reasons, but I am against the Boers. If it was just about giving foreign workers the vote, I wouldn't leave this bar. My problem with the Boers is how they took the land from the Bantus and Zulus. Killed them and made them slaves. I say *that's* worth a war, on the assumption Britain will treat the blacks any better."

The speech brought uncomfortable silence. For once, Tommy was grateful to hear his father's voice.

"So when are you signing up, Lionel?"

Half the room laughed. Brooke laughed too.

"No, no. Me in the British army? Not any time soon. But don't count me out of Africa."

"What's that?" Tommy's father again. "A private army, like?"

"There have been many private armies. Throughout history."

"So how big an army are you thinking of?"

"A few hand-picked men. Good horses. A clear objective."

"Is it Kroo-jer you're after, Lionel?"

Another burst of laughter.

"Possibly."

"Let's hear it, fellows. Three cheers for Lionel Brooke! Empire assassin!"

"Not *Empire!*" scolded Brooke, but his voice was drowned out in all the cheering.

Someone leaned down and spit tobacco at the crack in the cleared space. Some got through and onto Tommy's neck. Young Sam started laughing.

"What the Christ? You got skunks under here, Bill?"

"Goddamn kids! You get out of there now!"

They could hear Durnham coming; saw his apron flash. First, he kicked the planks. Then he pulled down the rod he used for drawing the high window blind and started thrusting at them through the floor. Young Sam grabbed Tommy's wet collar and gave him a yank. The two crawled hard for the light.

When the soldiers filed out of the Arlington, there weren't many left to see them off. Fred Morden wore a scowl as he bent off Main Street and walked to the bridge. He stopped before the planks, and that was when Tommy jumped out.

"Ah, my good friend Tommy." Morden ruffled Tommy's hair. "Do me a favour, will you?" He pulled from his pocket some paper and a pencil stub. He turned Tommy around, and the boy felt Morden writing on his back. Then Fred folded the paper tight and printed Trudy's name on one side. He gave it to Tommy with a nickel.

"You won't read this, will you?"

Tommy shook his head.

"And you'll take care of my dogs?"

"Yes."

"Now shake hands like a man."

Tommy gripped the bigger hand. He pulled away and turned his back, waited for a count of ten, then looked and saw Fred Morden run to his horse and spring to its back. Fred's father was there and handed Fred his buffalo coat. Fred leaned down, shook his father's hand, and took something else from him. Probably money. Then all the riders backed their horses and wheeled and kicked them to a canter.

Tommy went to the middle of the bridge. Below it was ice except for where Charlie Beebe had cut a hole with an axe to water the livery horses. There was no one around so Tommy cursed aloud.

"Goddamn Boers. Goddamn Kroo-jer."

He tossed the paper at Beebe's water hole and, though his aim was good, it landed on some mush and stayed dry. He ran down the bank and slid on the ice. With his boot toe, he pressed the paper until the moving wet grabbed it and took it away.

"Goddamn Trudy Black."

Calgary, January 1900

Frank Adams woke cold and itchy in the hayloft of a Calgary livery barn. The liveryman had knocked a hole in the ice of his water barrel, and Frank washed there when he came down. He thought he should shave but the water was so cold he could not face it. Besides, it was time to go to the enlistment office. He wanted to be early.

In the frosted near darkness, the chewed street was an elaborate sculpture of iron ruts, and Frank hurried to the end and out beyond the last railway hotel. In the open space between the town and Ft. Calgary, a vicious wind spun off the bald hill to the north, gained speed across the river, and slapped him. It needled into every weakness of his clothing. Adams ran for the open fort gate and was soon inside where the wind was cut off. Within the palisade, horses were bunched along several rails. An old man leading a sullen grey pointed him to a door.

The room Frank entered was large and bare. A small fire flickered in a rock hearth on the short side wall, but the temperature had not risen much above that out of doors. A dozen benches were pulled into rows as in a church, and a surprising number of men were already sitting. Frank felt relief to see how many were cowboys. It further relaxed him to see faces he recognized. Jefferson Davis from Macleod. A cowboy named Ovide Smith from the South Fork of the Old Man. They huddled inside their full winter dress, and no one looked up or greeted him.

Other than the benches, the room had three small tables with chairs on either side. These were on the long wall opposite the outside door. Behind them was another door that led deeper into the building. To the side was the kind of screen a person might undress behind. The Cochrane Ranch's big house had one of these screens. Mrs. Billy Cochrane had shown it to Frank because it had a Chinese painting on it. This one was blank, just cotton stretched on a skinny frame.

Frank found a space on a bench and joined the others in huddling and waiting for nine o'clock. Men kept pouring in until every space was taken and a few men had to stand or sit on the floor.

At quarter to, a young Mountie with an armload of wood came in to build the fire. Five minutes later, a procession poured through the inner door. A brisk old Mountie officer led it, followed by younger Mounties and three civilians. Frank identified the civilians as doctors by the listening tubes around their necks.

Three of the youngest Mounties took seats at the tables. Each had a pile of forms he plunked down. The old Mountie, the boss one, was at the fire. He and the doctors took turns warming their hands and their asses.

Frank decided this senior Mountie must be Lieutenant-Colonel Herchmer, the Mounted Police Commissioner. Frank's father, Jim, knew Herchmer slightly from Ft. Macleod and had told Frank what he looked like: thick in the body, red-faced, bearded. Seeing him now, Frank would have said *very* red-faced and that the beard was red as well, with white splotches, as if someone had shot it with wet salt. It was coarse as a trimmed porcupine.

Frank's father was an avid reader of newspapers and had read lately that Lieutenant-Colonel Herchmer was going to command the Mounted Rifles. Jim told Frank that a lot of people would be unhappy about that, partly because Herchmer was over sixty and partly because he was a known tyrant. Frank watched Herchmer by the fire, and everything that officer did was overly vigorous, as if he knew they were thinking him old and wanted to prove it wasn't so.

When Herchmer turned and spoke to the room, his voice was several times louder than it needed to be. He yelled at them to line up at the three tables.

The Mounties at the tables asked questions and wrote down the answers. Soon, a couple of men were behind the cotton screen taking off their clothes. The doctors told them to peel to the skin and follow them through the inner door.

Frank had chosen the far right line because Jeff Davis, a slight acquaintance, was at the head of it. Now, the line was stuck as the other two lines moved. After Jeff had answered a few questions, Herchmer yelled for the clerk to stop and wait. After a while, Herchmer came over and thundered to Jeff, "Are you not aware, Mr. Davis, that this is a white man's war?"

Frank was only four back but had difficulty hearing Jeff's reply. He caught the words *school* and *treaty*. He reckoned Davis was telling Herchmer that he had a white father and had been to a white school in Ontario, and that he was part of no Indian treaty with Canada. If Frank was Jeff Davis, he would have added that his father, D.W. Davis, had been twice elected a Member of Parliament. D.W. had been a whisky trader before that, but, as an MP, he was in a way Herchmer's boss.

Herchmer's response to whatever Davis said was to yell that a telegram must be sent to Ottawa. He was yelling in the direction of one of the younger Mountie officers, and when that fellow asked, "Telegram about what, sir?" Herchmer's face went black. He shouted, "If there can be Half-breeds, of course!"

Jeff Davis was asked to stand up and step aside. He stood to the right of the table with his long arms dangling. The line of his eyes was at a window built up with ice.

Frank Adams, meanwhile, was in turmoil. He had entered this room feeling tense and excited. When he had seen other cowboys there, only the excitement remained. But now he had a heavy clevis pinching behind his breastbone. His face felt cold and hot at once. In all the talks he'd had with his father about why and how he would go to the war in South Africa, and through all the furies of his mother who hated the idea, it had never once occurred to any of them that Frank might ride all the way to Calgary and be rejected. He had thought once or twice that his excellent mare, Dunny, might be turned back for being a cayuse, but never himself. The kinds of things he imagined they would care about—health, eyesight, hearing, strength, stamina—he had in ordinary measure. How good would you have to be to be a soldier, was his reasoning.

But when he heard Herchmer say "white man's war," his notions of eligibility flipped over. It was by no means the first time he'd heard this phrase. It was often in the newspapers. But it was the first time he thought it had relevance to him. Frank had skin that freckled and burned, and his hair was a wet sand colour, same as his father's. His father was from Ontario, the very definition of a white man in Canada.

But Frank's mother was, if detail counted, a Halfbreed, the kind of person who was thought of as French or Halfbreed, depending on who was doing the looking and what kind of mood they were in.

What Frank was worried about was a possible cowboy—somewhere in this room—who had worked for the Cochrane Ranch and been fired by Frank's father. As second foreman or Segundo, Jim Adams had bossed a lot of cowboys—and fired a lot, for drunkenness, stealing, or other usual reasons. Those same cowboys would have received their bunkhouse meals from Frank's mother and seen her black hair and eyes, her brown skin.

The chair in front of Frank emptied and he sat. He could see Jeff Davis's trouser leg out the corner of his right eye. While the clerk asked questions and Frank answered them, he was struck by another thought. What if Jeff Davis, who knew Frank well enough, took it into his head to say, "If you're not taking Halfbreeds, why are you taking him?"

Frank's concentration was so murdered that the clerk had to ask him several questions twice. Frank, who was good at reading upside down, saw the fellow write *poor* in the blank for intelligence. Finally he was told to get up and go back to the cotton screen. Frank peeled off fast and dumped his clothes beside the other piles. He held his hand in front of his pecker and nuts and followed the doctor through the door. In a smaller room, he was told to stand on a scale. His chest was listened to. The doctor said he seemed to have a nervous disposition, and Frank said he was only cold.

"Well, maybe you'll be warmer in Africa," said the doctor as he signed his name at the bottom of the form.

By the time Frank was back in the main room and dressed, a new table had been brought in and placed by the fire. It held a big coffee can and a few plates of cookies. Frank drank and ate, and looked often to where Jeff Davis's tall figure still stood crucified in the air.

Frank knew that a telegram had the power to go all the way across Canada and back in one day. Whenever the one about Jeff Davis came, it could be negative. Jeff, in his disappointment, could still unmask Frank. This being possible, Frank could not relax and be cheerful like the other men. He felt more like the embarrassed few who left quickly after putting their clothes back on, having been found physically or mentally wanting.

In his nervousness, Frank needed to talk. He chose for this purpose Ovide Smith, a cowboy he had met once on a roundup near the Old Man River's South Fork. Frank chose him because Smith was not cheerful either. Ovide was older and talked very little English because he was French.

"What'd you say for next of kin?" Frank asked him, not being able to think of a more sensible question.

"Father," said Ovide.

"Where's your father from? Manitoba?"

Frank realized too late that the question might be construed as insult. With the Halfbreed business on his brain, he had asked the question many used to ascertain whether someone *was* a Halfbreed. It was possible to be white and from Manitoba, but a good many who left there for the District of Alberta or for Montana were Halfbreeds from Red River. This was roughly Frank's mother's family history.

But Ovide seemed not to notice or take offence. He said he was from Quebec. Then, after a while, in a rare volunteering of information, he added, "St. Flavie."

It was about then that Frank saw a young Mountie charge in and rush to Herchmer with a sheet of paper. Herchmer read it and marched over to Jeff Davis. He yelled in his face.

"Says here, Davis, and I shall quote, 'Yes, to Halfbreeds. Stop. If intelligent. Stop.' Would you say you are intelligent?"

In the room gone silent, Davis's low answer was heard. "Intelligent enough," he said.

Herchmer walked away chuckling, and probably most eyes followed him as he marched around the room displaying his amusement. Frank kept his eyes on Jeff Davis. Jeff answered the rest of the questions and headed behind the screen to take off his clothes. When he was half-undressed, he looked over top of the screen and right at Adams. There was nothing more, no smile or gesture, but both of them understood why he was looking.

Western District of England

The window in General Butler's small office overlooked the parade ground where a few raw militia recruits were drilling in the rain. He sat and watched his drill sergeant at work. Pith helmet recently painted; stick clutched beneath his arm; black boots stamping in the puddles. The sergeant's mouth stretched inhumanly, and his white moustache rose and fell like a gull on an ocean swell.

Butler returned his attention to his desk and stared at an envelope arrived this morning from Canada. He had not opened it and would not yet. He was holding it in reserve. Instead, he flapped open the newspaper, and there on the front page was the honest pie-face of his friend Redvers Buller. The thick-inked headline above him read DISGRACE, referring to the fiascos at Colenso and Spion Kop. If Butler looked at the matter with total selfishness, there was one good thing about Redvers Buller's miserable predicament, and that was how it had served to remove Butler's own name and face from the front pages. The gutter press and the English public had a new kicking boy.

Here in the west of England, Butler's quiet exile, he had time to think, time in excess. What he had gradually worked out was why his Government and the War Office had sent him to South Africa a year ago. When they had asked him to command their South African army and stand in for the Cape Colony governor, he had considered it an honour. He had failed to see the ambush.

Hope so often turns a man into a fool. Butler had hoped the South African appointments were the end of a long spell of minor postings—a pattern that had begun after he was in charge of transport on the Nile, in the campaign to relieve Gordon at Khartoum. During that arduous journey, his boatmen were routinely asked to do the impossible. And, still, Butler's flotilla might have done its work in time except for strange interfering orders from Wolseley and regular bureaucratic bungles. When the British reached Khartoum on January 28, 1885, two days after Gordon's death at the hands of the Mahdi's fanatics, there was a mad scramble to avoid blame. Several chose Butler as their sacrifice. The boats had caused delay, they said, critical losses of time through the Nile cataracts—and wasn't it a strange idea to begin with, bringing paddlers from Canada?

For a long time afterwards, the War Office only trusted Butler with small things—inquiries, training, tiny foreign commands—all of which made him believe that the important double command in South Africa meant absolution.

When Butler took up his twin duties in Cape Town, he could find nothing tangible in the argument for war. On the Boer side, Kruger and the other leaders did not want their people to be politically, economically, and morally swamped by a host of foreign gold miners, tradesmen, merchants, prostitutes, and what else not. The Boers were farmers and strict religionists. They governed themselves quite nicely. Naturally, they wished to continue.

On the British side, the concern over rights of foreign workers smacked of the disingenuous. A far more simple explanation was greed: Britain wanting South Africa's gold and diamonds, and to keep same out of the hands of Germany. The false piety sounded worse in the mouth of capitalists like Cecil Rhodes (who just happened to own the Cape newspapers, in which the case for war was argued shrilly most every day).

The Boers did not want the war, but neither would they be an easy enemy. When Butler began saying this in letters to the War Office and to the Government, some of it was let out to the press, and he was branded a poltroon: a duffer gone limp who was afraid to fight Billygoat Kruger and his army of farmers.

Then the War Office reeled the bait (Butler) back in. Governor Milner was reinstalled at Cape Town, full of British steel and determination. Ultimatum replaced negotiation. Armies were mobilized. Everything that was found wrong with Britain's readiness for war was blamed on Butler. The press and the public questioned nothing.

Butler could think on this only for so long before the actual crawling humiliation returned. He tossed the newspaper in the direction of the cold hearth, at the same time as he cursed his batman for letting the morning fire die. The room was as cold and moist as a morgue. In the centre of his desk blotter, he rediscovered the letter from Canada and felt an instant wash of relief. He knew what it was and that it was no threat to him. The Blood Indian Chief, Red Crow, had written with the help of his white secretary. It was a letter from a friend.

Butler found his letter knife, slit it open, and yanked out the single sheet.

Dear Butler,
My nephew tells me you are going to war. I remember when you fought the black Africans. He says it is white Africans this time. This nephew is Jefferson, son of my sister by Davis the whisky trader. Jefferson wants to fight this war. I do not know why. Years ago, he came to me wanting to be

a warrior. I did my best to teach him. He is good and will be useful. I write to ask your help. Please make sure Jefferson fights and is not some white officer's servant. It is turning cold here. We grow potatoes and grain and have more cattle, but every spring there are fewer of us. I think the whisky years when I met you were better.

Red Crow

Butler folded the letter, put it back in its envelope, pocketed it. He gave his chair a twist, stretched his legs, lowered his chin to his chest. His very deliberate intention was to reminisce about Red Crow, to think back to the long-ago time when he had met the man. If in the course of that nostalgic excursion he fell asleep, so be it. When his eyes closed, he saw brilliance: the pale naked light the Canadian prairie has in winter; a light that can literally blind you.

The Halfbreed Rebellion at Red River in 1869 was his first time in Canada's west. He'd convinced Wolseley to use him as a spy. Nights of lurking around the Halfbreed settlement after Riel and his rebels had seized it. Then Wolseley's army came (Redvers Buller was one of his officers) and the rebels fled. There was no fight. Wolseley's army harassed the remaining Halfbreeds anyway, with the rationale that beatings and terror would stanch their national ambitions. Butler remembered an old man drowning in the river as he was pelted with stones.

But, the prairie, he thought, letting his mind refill with light. While he was still in Canada, he took a commission to investigate an illegal trade in whisky near the Rocky Mountains. Americans from Montana had been debauching the Blackfoot Indians north of the border. He was supposed to find out the facts and went all the way to Rocky Mountain House. Most people from this side of the Atlantic had no understanding of the distances involved. Red River to Rocky Mountain House was like Paris to Moscow. There were buffalo herds and the sky was black with geese. It had struck the younger Butler as a kind of rigorous paradise. Land as far as the eye could see. The sky a yawning chasm. The drama of moving storms. He had tried to capture this great lone land in one of his books.

At Rocky Mountain House, Butler had consulted Hudson's Bay Company traders and visiting Indians. He did not meet Red Crow but heard of him: a once-mighty Blood chief, who had taken to trading the hide of every buffalo he shot for whisky. He had a reputation for indiscriminate violence when drunk.

Their actual meeting did not come until the winter of 1872–73. After the Red River campaign and his investigation into whisky trading, Butler had returned to Britain to find that many young puppies had bought commissions and leap-frogged him. No longer young himself, he was embarrassingly low in rank. He was placed with an unattached company at half pay. It was the low point of his career, and his response was to return to Canada—where he'd at least been happy. The address he gave to the War Office was "Carlton House, Saskatchewan."

What followed was a delicious time. He had seldom been so free and so far from recognition. His book *The Great Lone Land* was finished and published, and he went to work on a second Canadian book documenting his private winter on the Saskatchewan. In the final version, he left several adventures out, including the winter trip to the Bow River where he met Red Crow.

His goal had been to see a whisky operation first-hand. His informants at Carlton said there were drinking forts where the Elbow and Bow rivers met. Despite it being mid-winter, Butler left his hut at Ft. Carlton and rode.

The journey was full of suffering, but he made it in one piece. It was late afternoon on a blue cold day when he crossed the Bow River. He was trying to warm up before a desperate little fire when a crew of wolfers came riding. They were terrible looking men—tobacco-stained beards, long greasy hair, buffalo coats shaggy with ice, wolf skins flapping from their saddles—pirates on horseback. They were armed to the teeth and it seemed possible they meant to kill him.

They had actually ridden over to express concern. They told him he was a damn fool to be travelling alone. Only a few weeks ago, a trader named Muffraw had been killed by Indians and his fort burned down. Butler asked whose fort it was he could see from where he stood. They said it belonged to Davis. Two hundred yards from this fort were Indian tipis, and they volunteered that the tents belonged to Red Crow.

Butler remembered his thrill at the news. *A chance to interview Red Crow!* So, when the wolfers left him, Butler rode to Davis's whisky fort. Donald Watson Davis himself, a dark-bearded American, very tall, came out of the log building dressed in a dusty swallowtail coat. He helped Butler stable his horse, then led him into the trading room, with its log walls and crude plank floor. It was dominated by a stout counter behind which Davis went to pour Butler a warming whisky. Davis had no customers today, he said, but had been doing a good business with the visiting Bloods. The result was a pile of buffalo hides in the corner, the smell subdued by the frost. Though there was a firebox with a fire in it, the room was frigid.

Davis was a somewhat handsome man, perhaps a little furtive in the dark eyes. He said he was from the southern States and had fought in the Civil War. Later, in Montana, he had left the military to become an Indian trader. While he talked, he picked up a Henry rifle from behind the counter and poked some rimfire bullets into the tubular magazine. He also divulged that he was planning to marry an Indian woman from a powerful family, who would help him shake off the competition that was gathering.

It was then an Indian man entered without knocking. He was small and homely, with a big nose. His blanket coat looked as if he'd been rolling in horseshit and blood. But something in the man's eye was so challenging that Butler treated him with deference. Davis introduced the Indian as the great Blood warrior Red Crow. When Butler countered with his own military pedigree, Red Crow asked if he knew Queen Victoria. Luckily, Butler had met his monarch. After almost having died of fever in the Ashanti War, Butler had completed his recovery in England, at Netley Hospital. It was there he was visited by the Queen.

Butler told Red Crow this—Davis translating—and Red Crow at once took Butler more seriously.

Up until Red Crow's entrance, Davis had not yet asked Butler's name, and Butler had been intending to use an alias. But he found himself unable to lie to Red Crow. He sensed the Indian would know if he did.

Davis poured Red Crow and Butler a drink. Red Crow looked at his before downing it with a shudder. He nodded at Davis and the trader poured another. No payment was asked or offered. Butler was settling in, thinking what interesting insights he was about to gain, when Red Crow made to leave. "I will remember you," he said to Butler before letting himself out the door.

By then, it was dark outside, moonless and black. Davis had lit two oil lanterns. Butler had drank quite a bit of Davis's whisky and, bathed in the yellow light and the whisky's false warmth, felt in the mood to drink more. After a time, a banging on the door heralded the entrance of several more Indians: a woman leading five men. They had frost in their tangled hair and more ice glittering in the skins and blankets they wore. Intense cold emanated from them. The woman, a rough but attractive creature, approached Davis and demanded something, probably liquor. Though it was obvious they had brought nothing to trade, Davis surprised Butler by going into his backroom, pouring a can most of the way full, and giving it to them to pass around.

Possibly Butler had left this story out of his eventual book because of the shameless way he had flirted with the woman. He had smiled at her and winked, and touched her elbow when it was beside him on the bar. When Davis's gift of whisky was gone, Butler put money on the counter and told Davis to give them another round on him. Davis did so, but reluctantly. The Indian woman offered Butler the first drink from this can, and it was a shock. It was not what Davis, Red Crow, and Butler had been drinking but something raw and ghastly. He tasted Mexican peppers, maybe even coal oil.

Davis was at this point showing bad temper. He annoyed Butler by not translating a good deal of the flattery Butler was wanting to exercise on the woman. When Butler suggested another round for the Indians, Davis refused to get it. He was about to lose control of the situation, was what he said.

With no more drink forthcoming, the Indians left. They said they had a cache and would bring back skins to trade. Davis went to the door and watched them go; to ensure, he said, that they did not steal Butler's horse.

Several revelations followed, some embarrassing. The woman was called Revenge Walker and was Red Crow's sister. Two of the men with her tonight were her and Red Crow's brothers. This sister had not spoken to Red Crow since he had killed another of their brothers a year ago, for touching Red Crow's face and calling him ugly. Revenge Walker was as hard-drinking as anyone in the family, and when drunk was almost as dangerous as Red Crow. What's more, and Butler's ears burned to hear this, she was the woman Davis intended to marry.

What came next was nothing Butler could have anticipated. Outside, gunshots rang out. In the cold crisp air, they sounded very close. Davis reached down and brought up not one but two Henry rifles. He offered one to Butler and said, "Can you handle this?" His opinion of the British army was implicit. They stood together behind the counter, waiting, and it took some time before anything more occurred. When the door banged open, Revenge Walker entered, supporting one of the Indian men who'd been with her earlier. The front of his blanket was soaked in blood. Butler set his rifle down and went to help. He and the woman lowered the Indian to the floor.

All through this, Revenge Walker was talking to Davis. The wounded Indian was her brother Not Real Good. Sheep Old Man, her other brother, had mistaken him in the dark for an attacker and had shot and stabbed him before realizing his mistake. Davis translated no more after that, though the conversation went on at length.

Davis barred the door and went to his storeroom, bringing back blankets. They placed Not Real Good on two of these and covered him with more. Davis also brought whisky, a pot of boiled water off his stove, and clean cloth for bandages. He uncovered Not Real Good's wounds, carefully washed them, and tamped them with clean bandage. Butler had seen many wounds in his life and judged neither of these to be mortal.

After the doctoring was done, Davis went to his stores and brought out more blankets for Butler. None looked or smelled clean. With nothing more said, Davis went through the only other door into his quarters, and Revenge Walker followed. The door squawked shut.

Butler rolled himself in the blankets on the floor and had a miserable night. The fire died; he could find nothing with which to rebuild it. When the first grey light penetrated the room, he was up and out the door. He saddled his horse and rode for Carlton.

In his office above the parade ground, Butler got up from his chair and went to the window. It was raining so hard he could barely see, but the drill sergeant was still there and so were the sodden recruits. In the tradition of his kind, the sergeant would not stop for something as meek as rain.

Remembering the frozen night at Davis's whisky fort had given Butler a chill. Cursing his batman, he balled up Redvers Buller's picture and the rest of the newspaper and set it alight with a scoop of coal. He had transferred Red Crow's letter into his pocket. Now he drew it out and fed it to the flames.

It was possible that he could find Red Crow's nephew in the great emptiness of South Africa, and the officer in charge of him. But he would not write a letter on the fellow's behalf. Given General Butler's present reputation, Jefferson Davis was better off without him.

Regina

On the parade ground at Regina, the Canadian Mounted Rifles marched in their civilian clothes. More than half of them carried rifle-shaped pieces of wood and even broomsticks. The commissioned officers and the NCOs did their best to make the drills military through loudness and shrillness, but they were often confused, trying to remember procedures and commands they had not practised since military college or the militia drill halls of their youth.

> *Present arms. Slope arms. Shoulder arms. Change arms.*
> *Open order.*
> *By the right, quick march. Double time. Right turn. Left turn.*
> *Halt. Close order.*
> *Fix bayonets.*

Had there been a moment of forgetfulness, Frank wondered. Had someone forgotten this was a horse outfit? *Mounted* Rifles? True, they were mounted *infantry*, supposed to ride in, dismount, and fight on the ground, but when he came to that part, Frank imagined himself dug in, or firing over a big rock. When was all this shouldering and sloping of arms to take place, except on parade day?

The thermometer on the wall of the barracks was stuck at thirty below. Because of the shortage of Lee-Enfields, they had to take turns breaking them down and cleaning them, then shoving in the rounds with stiff, numb fingers, bullet by bullet into the heavy brute's magazine. Then, very important too, said the sergeant, they had to pull the bolt and run the cleaning rod through the barrel. The rifling on the Lee-Enfield was five deep grooves. These kept the barrel from being wrecked by the heat of the smokeless cordite cartridges. The same square-shouldered grooves could foul unless the men were scrupulous. And so Frank poked the giant pipe cleaner through the heavy barrel until it shone.

Once they got to the outdoor arena for horsemanship training, it was still too damn cold but things made a bit more sense. They were taught how to ride in groups, dismount, and deploy. One man in four would be a horse-holder. The rest of the time was devoted to teaching them how to ride, something Frank and most others considered themselves adept at since childhood. Whenever the sergeant was out of earshot, they would grumble. They should be getting the time off. Their horses should be back in the barn with a blanket on. Frank did not join in the talk but agreed with it. On the Cochrane Ranch, you would never work a horse hard at thirty below unless wolves were eating your calves or the cows were racing for a cliff.

For green riders who had no horse, mounts were drawn from the free pool. The Cochrane Ranch had sold horses to the army buyer, and Frank's father and Mr. Billy Cochrane had made sure the army got value. Clearly, other ranches had done otherwise. Sold as broke, some of these horses were as wild as buffalo.

Like everything else in Regina, the ground of the riding arena was frozen solid. Though the officers ordered the sharpest ruts hacked off and straw strewn around, little impact was absorbed when the flailing green-ers hit. Their training consisted of bucking off until they were banged up enough for the infirmary.

Inevitably, the boys started betting on how many jumps a fellow would last. All good fun until Lt.-Col. Sam Steele, Herchmer's second-in-command, caught them at it. It was bad luck because it was the only day Steele was in Regina. Sam gravitated to the arena and soon figured out that the seasoned riders were mocking the junior ones. He called them on it.

In that moment, Frank knew he was going to suffer. Of all the Moun-tie brass who had passed through Ft. Macleod, Frank's father insisted Steele was the toughest, tough as his fake-sounding name. He could ride all day and drink all night. Single-handed and sick with the flu, he had once bluffed a mob of miners into giving up their strike.

"This is not real soldiering," Steele began, "to come here to Regina and show off how well you can ride your own horse. Any damn fool can ride his own horse. In the deserts and mountains of South Africa, horses will die, just like men will. So, before you go any farther toward that destination, I want you to demonstrate that you can ride any horse—not just the tolerant beast who knows and permits your clumsy ways."

They were told to stable their own horses and ride a horse chosen for them by the riding sergeant. Steele and the riding sergeant kept moving them around until they got a horse that bucked. The goal was to have each man bucked off once. Some who thought themselves clever play-acted a bit and let themselves fall toward a safe landing. Frank saw the others do it and thought, why not? When everyone had bucked off once, Steele pointed at the play-actors and invited them to go up against a tougher horse.

Throughout this process, a monkey-coloured outlaw had been bucking off every man he faced. This was the horse Sam Steele wanted roped for the thespians. Frank saw a few bad wrecks, then the horse was snubbed again and it was his turn. When he was in the saddle, and the snubbers let go, the outlaw horse stood still. Its skin shuddered wherever Frank touched it. Then the beast turned its neck and considered him with a sideways eye. The rank gelding exploded upward, and the landing hurt every inch of Frank's spine. It raced to gain momentum and flung itself in a twisting buck. Lest he be taken for an actor again, Frank fought to hold on. The result was that he came off awkwardly down the horse's side, close enough to take a hoof in the ribs. A couple of fellows ran in and dragged him to the rails while two horsemen raced after the bucking horse to rope it for another.

Frank lay on the ground and waited for his breath to return. He felt along his ribs to see if any were broken. There were no juts or points of specific agony so he decided he was only bruised. He sat up among the other semi-invalids, and saw that several were faced away from the rodeo. They were looking at an Edmonton man named Albert who had arrived in Regina late, riding a dull nag. Well before Sam Steele's lesson, he had developed a leg problem and been excused from the horse work. Now, his condition seemed to have worsened. He was screwing at his kneecap like it was a loose jar lid.

When the outlaw had laid out the final rider, one of the injured called, "How's that knee, Albert? A little better, maybe?" Several did the same until they drew the horse sergeant's attention.

Before long, the ropers had the outlaw snubbed to the post again. A big fellow had the ears thumbed down while another twisted the nose. When the horse went to his knees, Albert settled himself in the saddle, poked his boot toes in the stirrups. He called for the snubbers to let the horse go.

Soon the outlaw was rocking above ground and Albert was flapping back and forth like a rag doll. A couple of high jumps and rock-hard landings, and both stirrups were lost. At times, Albert's only connection to the horse was a death grip on the saddle horn.

By now, even the badly injured were feeling guilty. The outlaw horse was infuriated to have Albert still attached. Into his next combination the horse poured so much wild energy that he shot a rear hoof into and through one of the empty stirrups. Now, he was bucking on three legs, and still it was more than Albert could handle.

Finally, it dawned on Albert that he was serving no useful purpose. He let go the horn, flew, landed, bounced, and lay still.

Military discipline was forgotten as the men charged into the arena centre and clustered around the fallen man. Limb by limb, Albert began to move. It was like a miracle to see him rise to his feet, and the boys cheered. Albert even had the aplomb to lick his fingers and twitch his moustache ends back into place.

"Well, boys," he said, "you know me, I can ride most anything with hair. But, when a horse puts his hoof in the stirrup and tries to get on behind, I reckon it's time to let him go."

They laughed so hard the riding sergeant started hitting them with his stick to make them subside.

That evening, Frank Adams sat on his bedroll on the floor of the jam-packed barracks room and probed at the purple decoration on his ribs. Though expanded and frilly, it still contained the shape of an iron-shod hood, and he would be wearing the reminder for some time.

What annoyed him about the bruise—annoyed him about all of the pains inflicted here at Regina—was how it was meant in some way to bring the men together. They had come to this war in little bunches, or alone, and were otherwise strangers. Training was supposed to change all that and weld them into a gang so unified they would back one another to the point of risking death. Frank looked around and concluded it would take more than bouncing them on the ground to make it happen.

When they'd first arrived, they had been organized into troops. Frank was in Squadron D, in a troop of Pincher Creek and Ft. Macleod men. He came from neither town but it was the closest troop to home. They had been assigned to this skinny barracks and, as soon as they were stuffed inside, had begun to divide until the Pincher herd was stacked along one side wall and the Macleod bunch along the other. Tom Scott, who had ranched near both and had enlisted in Ft. Macleod, had to choose. He had settled with the Pincher Creek men.

Frank, who took pride in belonging to neither town, bedded down on the room's midline, where eventually he was not alone. Ovide Smith had his bedroll on this line, and so did Jeff Davis, where it met the short wall.

The thing about Pincher Creek and Ft. Macleod was that, though they were both young and only thirty miles apart, they had developed a dislike of one another. Macleod was the oldest by a few years and, being the first, had a courthouse and a Mountie barracks. All Pincher had for public buildings was a small Mountie detachment and a post office desk in the corner of the hardware store. Pincher was the aggressor in the dispute, while Macleod pretended indifference.

Despite no one else in the Canadian Mounted Rifles caring less about Pincher Creek or Fort Macleod, the soldiers in the room around Frank were still thinking about who was best and how to prove it. It was almost inevitable, given the events of the day, that a contest would result involving the monkey-coloured outlaw horse.

Frank's sleeping spot in the middle of the room was ideal for eavesdropping. He heard Pincher Creek rancher Reg Redpath suggest to his best friend, Robert Kerr, that both Pincher's and Macleod's best cowboys should ride the outlaw horse for a purse. Pincher men like the Wilson brothers and Harry Gunn were asked for their thoughts.

The idea came from Pincher because they believed they had the best rider: Fred Morden. Morden was good at everything—as if God had paused in His factory and said, "Hey, let's make this one by hand." Kerr asked Morden if he was up for it, and Morden said all right, though he wasn't sure how long he could stay on the horse. All that was needed, the others assured him, was to stay on for more jumps than whoever rode for Macleod.

Frank watched Redpath cross the room's short width and deliver the challenge. Macleod accepted, because to do otherwise would have appeared frightened or uncertain. But they had no obvious candidate to go up against Morden. Though it seemed unlikely that the army would allow this test, they felt they should have a contestant in case it did.

Frank switched his attention back to the Pincher side, to see how they intended to make the riding instructor accept this event, but he seemed to have missed that part. All he heard was that Steele and the riding instructor had agreed the outlaw horse had no military use and should be sold to Regina's abattoir.

In the Macleod scrum, they were now discussing Jeff Davis. Davis was certainly a good rider. He had won bucking contests and had worked as a bronc twister in a Pat Burns beef camp. But the question was, was Davis a Macleod man? This was argued both ways. He had been born in that town and mostly raised there, but after his father and his Indian mother split up, Jeff had gone to live with the mother and his younger siblings on the Blood Reserve. Though he did not stay there, he had never returned to live in Fort Macleod.

An additional problem was that Jeff Davis was not at the barracks that night. He had been given leave to dine and stay over with family friends. In absentia, the Ft. Macleod group voted Jeff Davis to be their contestant.

Next morning, Frank stayed as near Reg Redpath as he could. He also watched for Jeff Davis but Jeff was late getting back, a fact that made the Macleod contingent anxious. When Redpath and Kerr started for the riding instructor, Frank tagged along, stopping at the edge of earshot.

Redpath and Kerr asked the riding sergeant about the outlaw horse: had a decision been made about him? The sergeant said there had: the horse would go to the abattoir. Redpath and Kerr said they thought that was a terrible waste.

How could it be a waste, the officer said. Hadn't yesterday's display been ample evidence that the horse was a man-killing savage?

Redpath said the boys had been talking about exactly that and had found themselves impressed with the horse's spirit and athletic ability. It might be the best horse in the Mounted Rifles, if it could be subdued.

The riding sergeant said this was doubtful. Redpath said he had a couple of fellows who were willing to ride the horse and put it to the test.

Finally, the idea was broached. Why not let two of the best riders have a go at the outlaw horse? Maybe, once topped, it would lose its killer streak, in which case the army would acquire a valuable animal.

The riding sergeant told them to go ahead; it was their funeral.

Shortly afterwards, Jeff Davis returned from his night of leave. The Macleod men went to him. Frank saw how the Macleod soldiers argued, and how Jeff said next to nothing. Jeff shook his head at each wave of them. Finally, they stomped away. They went to Redpath and Kerr and said they were going to forfeit. The rider they were counting on would not ride.

All that remained was to tell the riding sergeant, but when they did, Redpath and Kerr got a shock. They told him that only one of the riders was willing and so the thing must be called off, but the sergeant did not see their reasoning. Surely, one rider, if successful, served as well as two. He insisted the ride go ahead. This was an army, after all, not a rodeo.

There was nothing for it but to rope and snub the outlaw. In a brief meeting of the Pincher Creek men, Robert Kerr said it should no longer be automatic that Fred Morden ride. They should choose straws. Fred said no. He had said he would do it, and he would.

To his credit, Morden rode the outlaw better than anyone else had. But the result was the same. When Morden got to his feet after an ugly fall, he was holding his elbow and his face was white. He walked past them and straight to the infirmary. When they saw him next in barracks, he was wearing a sling. The medic thought he might have a cracked bone. Morden's training was over.

That night, Jeff Davis stayed outside until lights out. The Macleod men were happy to forget the riding contest, and the Pincher Creek fellows were mostly subdued about the disaster as well. Only Pete Belton, the older and smaller of the two Belton brothers from northwest of Pincher Creek, was in a temper. "We should beat the tar out of that damn Halfbreed right now. Stinking coward!"

Fred Morden was in a dark mood and told Belton to shut up.

"It's my arm. If there's anything to be done, I'll do it."

"So you're going to take a round out of that bastard? When you're healed? Someone sure as hell should."

"It's none of your business, so shut up about it."

Canadian Pacific Railway

The horse cars on the train were called palace cars. Four horses on each side faced into two alleys. Each car had four open doorways. That made sixteen horses per car, eight travelling across the nation facing the Atlantic, eight looking backwards at the Pacific.

The horses hated the train. The sideways rocking was foreign to their senses. The ever-present, ever-changing noise twitched their ears night and day. Every minute there was something going on that they would have bolted from on the prairie, but there they were, slotted into narrow stalls, unable to move more than a foot in any direction.

There were soldiers charged with the horses' care: tending their feed bags and offering them water from the alley barrels. But most owners visited every day. They picked their way through the packed colonist cars, then left the relative warmth to climb a ladder to the roof. In the icy wind, it was down, across, up, and along until they came to the car that held their horses, where they climbed down a side ladder to the correct door.

When the wind was in your face, you'd arrive with a frostbitten forehead you had to rub the colour back into. The hope was that your voice could contradict the strangeness of everything else. But the horses stood tense and gritted.

Frank visited, brushed, and talked to Dunny on roughly the same schedule as everyone else. He had noted that the distribution of horses was not random. The sorters placed them according to troop, but friends with pull saw that their horses stood together. Morden, Kerr, Redpath, Harry Gunn, and the Miles brothers had theirs in the forward eight of one car. Jeff, Ovide, an Irish teamster named Callaghan, the Belton brothers, and Frank had theirs in the same car's back end. The remaining stalls in Frank's end were free-pool.

Looking at his car's arrangement, Frank understood the hierarchy. Where Morden and Redpath were, that was for blooded horses. The back end was for animals that lacked breeding. Regina had been like a horse show; Frank had never seen so many. But, out of all of them, the only two he admired as much as his own dun mare were in the back end of this car. That is, if a trade was forced on him, he would only take Jeff Davis's blue mare or Casey Callaghan's big buckskin. Morden, Redpath, and the rest at the front had bays and chestnuts. They were fancy horses, no doubt, but there was something about the bone and confirmation that Frank found too elegant. In the conditions of Africa, he was betting Jeff's and his mares, and Callaghan's gelding, would prove stronger.

Much of Frank's horse knowledge was passed down to him by his Uncle Doc, a Texan who was very long-winded on the topic. Doc said Frank's dun was a descendant of old-time Spanish horses, horses that had run wild for centuries before becoming saddle stock again. Buckskins like Callaghan's and Jeff's blue also belonged in this category; a kind of horse that horse fanciers often called *cayuse* and would not ride or own.

Not all wildys were good but even the not-good ones tended to do better at picking their way over rough ground. Their eyes were set better for seeing in every direction, and that kept them from falling into badger and gopher holes. When you got a cayuse that was built pretty and had spirit, you really had something. Casey, Jeff, and Frank all had something.

The Beltons, on the other hand, had ugly horses, the kind that happens when you breed your plow horse with your saddle horse. Sometimes you get a quicker-footed workhorse. Other times, you get a saddle horse that rides like a stoneboat. The Belton horses were the latter. Frank knew a little about the Belton family from having rounded up on the Waldron range. He'd seen their dilapidated shacks off the edge of the Waldron lease.

After a day when the train had stood still for twenty hours of track fixing, they started moving again and actually got up some speed. They were enjoying the pace when a soldier came back to say the horses were freezing. The speed was sucking frozen air into the open doorways and the horses were in trouble.

They scrambled for blankets and coats, and, so burdened, climbed and crawled their way back. The horses were uneasy or dangerously far asleep, with frost growing all over their backs and faces. The sleepers had already begun to lean and hang, losing connection with the world.

In Adams' half-car, Casey Callaghan took his old buffalo coat and nailed it across the windward doorway. The men climbed onto the stalls, spreading their sleeping blankets over the horses' backs. They rubbed the frost off the faces and picked the rime out of the eyes.

Pete Belton's gelding was very nervous and making an odd noise. He stamped back and forth, as if he had sandflies on his sack. Belton said he wanted to pull the gelding out and check what was wrong. This was never done because of the open doorways. If a horse saw daylight and bolted, there would be no stopping it. But Belton said he would put his coat over the horse's eyes and direct it toward the side where Casey had the doorway covered.

The stall for Pete Belton's horse was between Davis's blue and Eddy Belton's giant. Davis's and Pete's horses had worked up a feud, and as soon as the big gelding's ass cleared its stall, he fired a kick that split The Blue's door. Davis's mare bared her teeth and lunged, hitting the end of her halter rope.

Even with Casey's buffalo coat over the light and the blanket on his head, Belton's horse almost plunged off the train. It took all of them to twist his anvil head into the wall. While three held the brute, Belton examined his horse all over and found, finally, that his tail was raw and bloody at the base. Abruptly, he turned on Davis.

"That cayuse bitch of yours bit my horse's tail bloody."

Jeff Davis had torn a board off the inside wall to patch his gate. He had borrowed a hammer from Callaghan and was pulling and straightening nails. He set the hammer down and rose. Most people match the mood of their challengers, but a few meet anger with calm. Davis did not answer but waited.

"They should never let a fucking cayuse like that with white man's horses. That's no kind of army horse."

Frank Adams felt his own hackles rise. He imagined his fist in Pete Belton's mush. Still, nothing about Davis seemed to change.

"We'll see in Africa," he said, "which horse goes farther."

"My horse's tail? You expect me to forget that?"

Davis looked at the tail. "That's not a bite."

"Course it's a fucking bite! We all saw that bitch do it! Didn't we, boys?"

The others would not meet Pete's eye. It had happened in an instant. The big horse kicking, the cayuse lunging, hitting the end of her rope. Callaghan left Frank and Eddy to hold Pete's horse while he looked at the tail. He shrugged, unconvinced.

"This is chickenshit!" said Pete Belton. "Goddamn Indian horse bites mine. Goddamn Indian says I didn't see what I saw!"

Even now, when it was personal, Davis did not rise.

"You're chickenshit, just like your uncle."

"What uncle?" asked Davis.

"That Red Crow. My Pa says, when that murdering bastard Charcoal said he wanted to kill Red Crow, your old uncle never slept once in his own bed till Charcoal was jailed."

The motion that came was more smooth than violent. Suddenly, Davis's fist was wrapped in Belton's shirt and Belton was moving backwards toward the unblocked door. Belton flailed and grabbed but could not stop himself until his boot heels hit the shallow sill. Davis pushed a little more and most of Pete Belton was outside, the ice wind thrashing his clothes. With small effort, Davis had him at the point of balance where a little shove would shoot him off, a little pull would save him. When Pete saw his giant brother come up behind Jeff, he yelled in fright, "Eddy, no!"

A few more seconds passed. Then Davis said, "You don't know Red Crow or Charcoal. You better not talk about either one again."

Then came the little tug that brought Pete back indoors. When Davis let him go, there was a comical jerk backwards and Pete almost threw himself out the door. Davis knelt down, placed the repair board, and started pounding nails and crimping their ends.

Callaghan went to the door and swung out of it to the ladder. He climbed to the next car and came back with a can of grease that he gave Pete Belton for his horse. Then, Davis threw his jacket over his blue cayuse's head, and they all worked together backing Belton's horse into its stall.

Jeff Davis finished with his stall door and put his coat back on. When he was in the open doorway, about to climb the ladder, he said to them, "You should all check your horses' tails."

Frank Adams stayed long enough to see Casey Callaghan be the first to do it. His horse was in the same front-facing four as Davis's blue and the Beltons' two. He climbed up and struck a match to see by.

"By Christ," he said, "my horse's tail is raw too."

When Callaghan finished with the grease can and climbed back out, he pointed behind Jeff Davis's blue. A bag hung behind the mare's ass, half filled with hay. A pad.

"I'll be damned," he said. "These horses facing backwards must be grinding themselves on the wall."

Frank didn't stay for the rest. He swung to the outside ladder and began the frigid journey to his car. A few days earlier, he had seen Jeff Davis place that hay pad. Though Frank's horse was facing front and was maybe not as likely to get hurt, he had half-filled a gunny sack with hay and stuck it behind Dunny's ass anyway. Frank had not figured out all that backward-forward stuff, but if a smart person did a thing, Frank did it too. It saved time and energy.

Winnipeg/Ottawa/Halifax

At Winnipeg, the Mounted Rifles were celebrated with bands and speeches, and a large cheering crowd. Because a few of their men were from St. John's College, other students from there showed up with a big farewell banner.

But when Frank looked at the local newspaper during that stop, he got a shock. The Mounted Rifles were not the lead story. Front and centre, was the news that Lord Strathcona, a wealthy part-owner of the Canadian Pacific Railway, had decided to create a mounted infantry unit for the Boer War. It was called Lord Strathcona's Horse, and the wealthy peer was outfitting and sending it at his own expense. The second shock, maybe bigger than the first, was that Maj. Sam Steele had been chosen to command Lord Strathcona's Horse, having given up his second position with the Canadian Mounted Rifles to do so.

Frank was far from the only one who read about the Strathconas and Steele's rebuff. It was in all the papers as they went along. By the time they were approaching Ottawa, the Mounted Rifles had worked up a considerable resentment for the Lord Strathconas, to whom they seemed doomed to play second fiddle. They also had a grudge against Sam Steele. His painful riding lesson at Regina had gone from a tough but proud baptism to an abuse they gravely resented.

Rolling into Ottawa's station, they were greeted by cheering crowds, brass bands, and politicians waiting with speeches. The Mounted Rifles faced them with a collective frown, knowing how much more tickled and bombastic it would have been if they were Lord Strathcona's Horse.

When they entered Quebec, and no crowds showed up at all, the Mounted Rifles did not complain. To ignore them seemed more honest than to celebrate them falsely. Frank was sitting beside Ovide Smith when they rolled past the silent station at St. Flavie, Quebec. Ovide watched out the window as his birthplace passed. Like his townsmen, he had nothing to say.

The train pulled into Halifax, bucking an ice-cold wind. It was blowing knives as they disembarked and looked upon the frozen crowd huddled in coats, and the brass band risking their lips on their instruments. It struck them that these far-from-home strangers owed them nothing, and yet here they were. The Mounted Rifles were touched and waved heartily to everyone. The crowd hustled them along the icy streets to the armouries where they would sleep.

The first day and night were solid work. They unloaded their train, got their horses into barns—fed, watered, and brushed. They themselves were turned in among great stacks of clothing and kit, and told to pick out two uniforms: one khaki for work and fighting; one dark green for parade and walking out. Tunics, trousers, shirts, greatcoats, underwear, socks, boots. They were hurried through, and hours of negotiation followed as men tried to trade their way to an acceptable fit.

As the second day tended toward evening, something like a volatile liquid flowed among them. The night would be their last in Canada, and a chafing expectancy grew more shrill the longer they were kept at work. Finally, a leave was announced, along with a list of cautions and conditions. They hit the streets in a crowd, bound for pleasure and excess. Horse cabbies drove alongside offering to take them faster for a terrible price, and the eager and the well-heeled climbed on.

In better weather, the Haligonians had helped Canada's infantrymen celebrate their final night. It was a point of pride to do the same for the Canadian Mounted Rifles, despite the cold and wind. The first priority was to get everyone indoors. Before the soldiers got their courage up to ask the local women to join them for a drink, their arms were hooked and they were dragged off to favourite taverns.

You could tell a soldier's intentions by how he dressed. If he had chosen his dress greens, it was likely a show for the ladies. If it was khaki, it suggested heavy drinking and possible fighting. No sense wearing your parade clothes if your destination was the gutter.

Ovide, Jeff, and Frank were a threesome in khaki. While others crawled the pubs, seeing how many they could drink in—or imagining prettier or less discerning women ahead—these three found a bar with a dark rear table and stayed put.

They bought beer, and in a bag under the table was a bottle of whisky that had been given to Frank in Winnipeg. A Scotsman with wild white side whiskers had thrust it through the train window, yelling, "Give those Dutchmen hell, sonny!"

It was Scotch whisky, supposedly superior to Canadian rye. It tasted like swamp water but was excellently strong. They were pleased to have it rollicking in their heads.

As for women, they were content to leave that to others. Ovide was extremely shy of women and, if truth be known, Frank only pretended to be bolder. Jeff kept his thoughts on the subject to himself.

The tavern started out empty, but eventually filled with Mounted Rifles and their women friends—and local men happy to tie one on for the Empire. Old soldiers tried to find an ear in which to pour their stories.

Then, as if it weren't loud enough, an Irish band started up: tin flute, fiddle, spoons, a drum. Some women got up to dance, and soldiers hoping to find their way under their skirts blundered around opposite.

At the table occupied by Smith, Davis, and Adams, there was little conversation. They had hardly spoken when the room was empty. Now that it was full, the din forgave them of any obligation to try. They watched the surge and flow of people until they were mesmerized, each man going somewhere deep in his head.

This quiet group of three was together for no better reason than that they were the ones who had camped along the boundary line in the Regina barracks. That had somehow led to their horses being in the same end of the same palace car. But, even if all of that was more or less happenstance, Frank wondered whether some actual friendship might result.

An only child on a ranch full of bachelor cowboys, Frank had known few people who were not adults. As he grew, he was so used to adult company he found children, well, childish. His mother was concerned about this standoffishness and forced him out to play with other children if any were on offer (community picnics; visitors to the Cochranes). A few minutes of their games and their infuriating demands, and Frank would walk off to his own pastimes: diverting a stream into a gopher hole; scooping minnows with his hat; teaching his horse to count.

When Frank thought *friend*, he thought of his parents and of Uncle Doc Windham. Doc was not his uncle but a Texan friend of his father's from their younger years. Doc was also Frank's godfather, a subject that made Frank's father laugh and his mother angry whenever it came up. Frank's mother, Madeleine, was still religious when Frank was born and had insisted there be godparents. She wanted the Billy Cochranes, but, as Doc was visiting at the time, Jim convinced her that ignoring him would be rude. Madeleine had asked Jim if Doc was religious, and Jim had said absolutely. So Doc was asked and accepted. Later, when Madeleine quizzed Doc on religion, she got an earful about theosophy, which was Doc's brand—whereby rocks and trees had spirits and men and animals used to have a common language. It had been a sore point with his mother ever since.

If Frank's father supplied history and cold analysis to Frank's life, and his mother supplied passion and ferocity, Doc had always been in charge of humour. He taught a view that life was not worth worrying about most of the time. For Frank, this was welcome news, since his father had a penchant for worry and his mother was serious to the point of fury much of the time.

Besides Doc, there had been the company of other cowboys: some permanent at the ranch; most transient. Frank would have liked their friendship but learned over and over again that cowboys were indifferent to real boys. Uncle Doc, who had been a cowboy since his own childhood, explained it to him. Cowboys were too stuck on themselves to need many other friends, he said. This also explained why their life with women was so fraught. When a cowboy seemed to love a woman (enough to make the woman think of marriage and family), the cowboy was really loving himself and the woman as a kind of reflection of his own splendour. That made the cowboy able to leave without any particular pain. He would find his girlfriend's histrionics strange and would claim not to understand her. This much was true.

Doc seldom made any allowances for Frank's being a child. Frank was ten when Doc explained about cowboys and women. He told him how cowboys tended to prefer the kinds of girls who would please them for money—because they could leave when it was over with no offence given.

Frank paused in these thoughts and again considered his tablemates. Like most people in Frank's life, Ovide was older. Pestered with the question, Ovide had divulged that he was thirty-nine, ancient for a working cowboy and maybe too old for this army. What recommended Ovide was that he was not vain like most cowboys. In fact, he seemed to lack any self at all. You had to glean what he liked from what he did, and that mainly involved horses. After Frank first engaged Ovide in conversation on recruiting day at Ft. Calgary, Ovide had welcomed him whenever they met. Frank was touched, because he imagined this was not Ovide's way with most people. Tonight's roar of noise and sea of humanity must have been unpleasant for the old cowboy but Ovide was doing his best to be a good sport.

The story was wholly different with Jeff Davis. Frank had met Jeff on the Blood Reserve years ago when an old Indian named Badger Claw had insisted on it. Frank was looking for a missing Cochrane Ranch cow when Badger Claw dragged him all the way to Red Crow's camp, where Jeff was visiting his uncle. Jeff was probably over twenty by then and Frank maybe fifteen. Davis's response to Frank was cold and almost hostile.

Bear Claw was horrified at Jeff's reaction. He scolded Jeff in Blackfoot and apologized to Frank as they rode away. But Frank was not offended, for he thought he understood. From his parents, Frank had heard the story about Davis the whisky trader–politician having an Indian wife and then parting with her to marry a white schoolteacher. Frank also knew that Jeff had left Macleod to live with his Indian mother, and sometimes with his uncle, Red Crow. What he saw in it was a fellow trying to become Indian, and having a hard time. When Badger Claw dragged Frank miles to introduce him to Jeff, it meant Badger Claw saw them both as whites who spoke some Blackfoot.

But here in the army, it was different. Frank was not certain why it had changed, but he would put his bet on when: the moment he and Davis had stared at each other after Herchmer's telegram said Jeff was in. Jeff's look had said, *You're part Indian, and I know it.* Frank's look had said, *Thanks for keeping quiet. Glad we both made it.*

Ovide had set a fresh jug of foamy beer on the cloth when Fred Morden and his Pincher Creek crew entered the bar. Morden was still wearing the sling on his left arm, and his Mounted Rifles Stetson was tipped back. Robert Kerr and the older of the two Miles brothers had found girlfriends and looked very pleased with themselves. The younger Miles, Henry, looked befuddled. The Belton brothers came last in the line.

Close to the entrance, a table had vacated and the Pincher boys grabbed it. Half sat down while the rest mined the room for chairs. Morden was the exception. He wandered around shaking hands. Frank checked and saw that Ovide and Jeff were watching Morden too.

Finally, Morden saw the three of them in their corner. His look became even brighter and pinker. He pushed through the crowd, and when he arrived he asked if they were having a good time and could he buy them a drink? Davis pointed at the jug of beer. Morden had done the polite thing and was free to leave, but before he could, Pete Belton came up behind and pushed past him. He shoved his angry face at Jeff Davis.

"I hope yer goddamn satisfied." The look slid off. His eyes were like two children trying to stay on a rolling log.

"Satisfied with what?" asked Jeff.

"My goddamn horse is dog-sick with fever. Vet might not let him on the ship. All cause-a yer goddamn cayuse."

No one spoke or looked at Pete. The three at the table knew it was untrue. Since Morden did not know, and because he was the one with the corporal's stripes, Frank decided to explain.

"Jeff's horse did nothing to Pete's."

"You shut up!" yelled Pete. "This ain't your fight!"

"This isn't a fight," said Jeff, in a mild way that made Belton worse.

"It goddamn should be and it goddamn will be!"

Pete lunged. A comical surprise loomed on his face when his hands did not reach Jeff Davis. Morden had shoved an arm in between and held him up. Now Morden got in front of Belton and gave him a square shove. Belton glanced off Ovide's chair and hit the wall. An old print of one ship blasting another fell to the floor.

"You're a soldier now," said Morden. "Act like one."

"I don't have to listen to you" was Belton's answer.

Morden was a corporal, and Pete did have to listen, but Morden let the chance to make this point go by. Belton pushed past and wrestled through to where his brother Eddy sat. Pete hauled him to his feet and pushed him outside.

Adams was feeling the Scotch like a tide of sleep rolling at him and could not bear the idea that Morden might say more, some apology or lesson. But, when Frank looked up again, Morden was gone.

Frank remembered no more than this, including how he found his way back to the armouries.

Next morning, half of Halifax was gathered at the pier. They yelled and waved handkerchiefs and the odd British flag. A line of soldiers, each leading two horses, threaded its way past the crowd and up the gangplank to be swallowed man and animal into the bowels of the ship.

It went along like the workings of a machine. Even the waving looked mechanical. The bands and cheering, the knocking sound of the unshod hooves on the pier: the sound fused into something solid, something every motion must push through.

When the marching suddenly stopped, it took a moment to see why. Then all heads turned to a commotion on the gangplank. A heavy horse rose on its hind legs and twisted in the air. It came down with such clumsy weight that the whole plank shuddered and all the other horses danced to regain their footing. One hoof on the wild horse slid sideways, stabbed through the rope sides, and pawed the air before it was jerked back. When the horse found its footing again, it kicked and struck the horse behind. It kicked again and hit a man so hard he keeled over the rope and had to be grabbed by the shirt to keep from falling. All down the plank, horses were fighting to get away, men struggling not to be trampled.

The horse at the top went up again, its back legs braced and quivering. Then came a double report from a revolver. On the third shot, the big horse bent in the air until its big head led the way down. The brown body toppled over the rope and flipped slowly upside down as it fell. The view was suddenly cut off by the pier's grey line. Hundreds waited for a splash they could not hear. Like some awkward angel, Pete Belton's horse had ceased to be in silence.

Pomeranian

When they first saw the *Pomeranian*, rock solid on her anchors and cables at the Halifax pier, the Canadian Mounted Rifles thought the ship a strong and strapping thing. By the time they boarded her to sail, on January 27, 1900, they knew from the sea-savvy people of Halifax that it was no more than a cattle boat, twice sunk and salvaged. The way a good horse trader will trim and groom an old nag until she shines, they had been gulled by a new coat of paint.

The only latrines for hundreds of men were on the top deck. There was always a lineup. Tilted boards took the offal over the edge where, depending on the day, a wind could catch it and drive it through the portholes into the steaming mess kitchen a deck below.

Out on the rolling ocean, they were sick most of the time, never having been on anything bigger than a steamboat in a river. They puked themselves lean, but the army was not satisfied. Daily drill was conducted in the sun and sea breeze of the main deck; physical exercise was taken twice daily. A funny thing to see, if it wasn't you: a man jogging on the spot or touching his toes suddenly breaking for the rail to heave.

In a moment of angry inspiration, a fellow said, "And Ottawa's fairy hand was everywhere." It became a slogan, something to say when you took a bite and tasted shit, or when you were shaving in a tin mirror a foot away from a man groaning from dysentery.

Probably the sickest man on the whole *Pomeranian* was Ovide Smith. After a while, the officers saw that he was a special case and stopped trying to get him out on deck for work and exercise. By virtue of being the only two who knew him, Frank and Jeff were his nursemaids. They brought him what he needed and took away what he'd lost. They watched him get smaller inside his already baggy uniform, and Frank made two new holes in his friend's belt with an awl.

"I won't go home by boat," Ovide would say, at his sickest, and Frank and Jeff kept it to themselves lest it become a joke on the decks above: the cowboy so ignorant he thought he could return to Canada by land.

A difference developed in how Jeff and Frank treated Ovide. When it was Jeff's turn beside Ovide's cot, he talked about how sick the horses were, how they were suffering in their winter hair, and how they were getting worse the farther south the ship went. Frank thought this was wrong and did the opposite. He told Ovide nothing about the horses, because why add depression to how sick the cowboy already was? Frank wondered if Jeff had a cruel streak.

The horses were in the ship's basement, a place stone dark and dependent for ventilation on deck sails that scooped air down the hatchways. Not much air penetrated to the lowest hold, where half the horses stood backed against the ship's outer walls and the rest stood tail to tail in the middle, facing alleys.

There could be no drainage holes into the ocean, so Frank and Jeff, and all the other soldiers except Ovide, took turns descending to hoe the shit across the cleated floor and dump it into baskets by lantern light. For the horse piss, there was a kind of drainage ditch and buckets bent to scoop into it. Everything had to be raised through the decks to the top and tossed overboard. Before they left Halifax, Ottawa's fairy hand had decreed that all horseshoes be removed. Standing unshod in shit and piss around the clock had caused the hooves to become yellow, punky, and tender to the touch.

The work was sickening in all that darkness and stench, but it was also treacherous. The horses thought they were being killed and, one time, when Frank's hoe caught a cleat and jumped sideways into Dunny's paining hoof, she kicked a pipe inches from his face. In her sickness, she did not even recognize him. When he worked around horses to whom he was a stranger, the risk was worse.

When the ship entered the tropics, conditions that seemed incapable of getting worse worsened. The horses had been pulled off the prairie with their heavy winter coats on. Now, with the hold like a wet oven, the men could do nothing about it. Ottawa had supplied no clippers, not one pair. Even the desalted water—all the horses had to drink—was hot. Many horses began to hang their heads and refuse food and water.

From the time they left Halifax until now, the Mountie veterinarian, Staff Sergeant Tracey, had been tramping the horse hold by lantern, day and night, doing everything he could for the animals. In the tropics, he worked even harder but the task began to defeat him. Angrily, he explained to whomever was present why things were so much harder on horses.

"Horses get seasick, same as men," he said. "But they can't puke."

Not a single man had before considered puking a gift from God.

Finally, it was Jeff Davis's telling Ovide every detail of the desperate lives of the horses that saved him. Hearing how seasick the horses were, and how unable they were to get rid of that sickness, Ovide sat up and turned his legs out. He grabbed the upper bunk and levered himself to his feet. He staggered onto deck and straight to the nearest rail, Jeff following closely lest Ovide meant to pitch himself off. But he only clung to the rail with both hands, and then, holding with one, hauled up his belt until it caught in the last of the new holes Frank had made.

Jeff told Frank that Ovide stood there for half an hour, the wind buffeting his empty clothes, and then he went to the ladder and started down. Frank was working in the horse hold and saw the rest himself: how Ovide came weaving down the alley headed for the yellow beacon of Tracey's lamp. Ovide told the vet he knew horses and wanted to help. Spotting his seriousness, Tracey jerked the lantern out of a young private's hands and gave it to Ovide. They moved on.

Jeff had been right all along. Working in the ghastly stench, Ovide seemed to forget to be sick. He and Tracey became a close team, and together evolved several improvements. They detected a slight relative cooling in certain hours of the tropical night. They made sure that all the next day's horse water was on deck and exposed during those hours, and that the horses received the water just before dawn. They figured out that certain stalls were better served by the wind scoops, and they moved the sickest horses there.

Beyond that, Ovide used his ability to fool a horse's mind, to wake it from its nightmare and help it remember there was something about living that it liked. To this end, he ripped away the mats of hair as they came unrooted and massaged deep into the sweating hides. He washed the horses as often as he could. He talked and he sang, and gently stroked ears, lips, and noses.

One of Ovide's and Tracey's toughest fights turned out to be Morden's gelding. The big bay had been a much admired horse back in Regina, but had taken sick almost as soon as the ship passed the first breakwater. In the heat, he had become worse and, finally, a private checking the alleys at night found the gelding down on his front knees with his back legs splayed.

The private ran for Tracey, and Tracey roused Ovide, and together the two ran their hands along every leg bone. None were broken, but when they got the horse back on his feet, there was pain in one leg, and the bay would not put weight there. He swayed three-legged. Tracey knew the bay could not last like that. He would fall again, and a splaying fall would break a leg or hip soon enough. So Tracey sent the private to wake Morden and tell him to rouse his troop. They were all to come down and move horses.

The twentieth stall in each group was left empty. They shifted the horses until the empty stall was beside Morden's bay. Then they took down the wall and moved the crown block along the roof until it was above him. They slid the slings under the horse's belly, connected them to the crown, and began winching. When the bay's back was straight, they stopped. The idea was not to lift the horse but to put the support high enough so he knew he could rest if he needed to.

But Morden's horse refused to behave in a way that would save him. He threw his whole weight on the slings and hung there. The horse had a strong personality and it was working against him now. Some horses fight to live. The bay gelding was fighting to die.

During the next night, Morden was still trying to save his horse, but Tracey and Ovide had rendered their verdict by shifting attention to other horses ailing in the heat. Morden's bay still hung in the slings, his head an iron weight on the long neck. His nose was practically on the stinking floor, snuffing circles in the putrid puddles. Eyes gone glassy; mouth slack and drooling. Morden squatted there by the hour, talking to the bay, patting him with a wet cloth, scooping the oily sweat from his face. He was still there next morning when the horse bucked in the slings, legs frantic on the floor, and died.

Tracey lost no time. He yanked out the slings, put a long rope around the neck and a front shoulder. With the power of the deck engine, routed through blocks, the horse was dragged along the alley floor until he was under the hatches. The hatches were opened so the equatorial sky was framed. At the top, the rope was switched onto a swing sheer. The knot anchoring the loop around the horse was changed to a slip knot.

Morden was rigid and sombre through all this work. Despite his arm still being weak, he insisted on taking a full portion of the weight whenever the body needed straightening. Every time the animal shifted into some undignified pose, Morden wrestled to restore a better appearance. Pulling the tail out from under. Combing the mane to the proper side. Trying and failing to close the eyes.

Then Tracey nodded and Morden nodded back. A series of shouts went up the hatches. With a low growl, the deck engine took the weight. An improbable sight: the horse rising off the alley floor and up slowly through the decks. It was the opposite of the death of Pete Belton's brute, but equally strange. Along each hatch, a row of heads moved with the ascent.

Ovide saw every moment of the drama below decks. Frank watched the horse come through the final hatch, born dead into brilliant day. The body was wet down one side from sliding on the shitted floor, but it looked like a heavy sweat more than what it was. Even with its frozen eyes and the set position of the limbs, the horse still looked alive.

"Hurry up! Get it off!"

That was the deck sergeant, wanting the body swung over the side as soon as the last hoof cleared. The sheer was bending with the weight as it swung. Corporal Griesbach was the one in place to slip the knot, and he was ready with the rope in hand.

Then there was a hesitation. Maybe Griesbach was wondering whether Morden was coming up, whether he should wait for that. The sergeant was furious, screaming, "Off! Now! Right now, damn you, corporal!"

They were on a big rolling sea. Frank understood that the sergeant's fury was because the ship had rolled just right, with the horse hanging out over the water. Finally, Griesbach yanked the rope as hard as he could—and nothing. He yanked again but the knot had bound.

"Dammit!" shrieked the sergeant. "That's what happens when you let the weight sit on the knot!"

Griesbach kept yanking but the knot would not budge. You could tell he was embarrassed. When he'd lost hope of success, he gave the rope another yank and the knot gave. The rope sprang free.

But, by now, the ship had rolled back toward the middle. At the instant when the rope fell off, the bay horse was over the hatch again. Down it went. On every deck, men saw it coming and shouted "Look out! Look out!" to the men below.

Morden appeared on deck just as his horse dropped. He ran to the hatch and saw the gelding banging down. The men below scattered clear. The horse hit bottom. By the light of lanterns, what Morden saw far below was his bay gelding lying unnaturally flat because so many bones were broken. The gelding no longer had the shape of a horse at all.

Morden flung about, his face disfigured with anger. He followed the rope that had let his horse fall, and at the end of it was Jeff Davis. Jeff had taken the rope from the sheer into his hands and was sliding it through his fingers. He was looking for the kinked spot that had caused the bind. Maybe he meant to cut that part out. Morden, gone mad in anger, saw it wrong.

"You stupid Halfbreed bastard!" he roared.

Frank was close to both men, and he felt like he himself had been slapped. Morden stared dumbly at the rope in Davis's hand.

Jeff acted as though he'd been expecting the words. He let go the rope so it swung back toward Fred. Then he turned and walked down the rail. He reached behind his ear where he had stored a cigarette. He felt in his trouser pocket for a match. He leaned his face so the cigarette pointed close to his hands, struck the match and cupped it. He reared his head back and loosed a tail of smoke.

Meanwhile, Griesbach had come hurrying to Morden, face stiff with shame and a manly determination to own up. Frank could not hear but saw the corporal mime what had happened. Over and over, he acted it out and apologized.

Frank watched for what would come next. He knew it was important. He badly wanted to see it turn out right. He watched for Morden to look around for Jeff. He poised himself to help, because, where Morden was, he probably could not see Jeff at all. But Morden did not look. He left Gries-bach, strode to the ladder, and descended to his ruined horse.

Jeff was bent deeply at the waist, with his elbows hooked over the rail. His long hands were laced at the top knuckles and drooped from his wrists. The ocean wind was smoking his cigarette for him.

Davis was looking at something in the water, and Frank looked too. Like pale slivers of moon, sharks were visible beneath the boiling surface. They had been robbed of their meat but were patiently coasting along-side. Davis pitched his cigarette among them, and a great mouth surfaced and took it casually.

Part Two

—

THE GREAT KAROO

Aldershot, February 1900

In the afternoon, General Butler burst from his brick headquarters and marched through camp. The same pressing need to walk overcame him every day. After lunch, an irritation would start, growing quickly until it was barely within his control. Before any truly embarrassing display of temper got away from him, he left to walk this practised route: through the overcrowded barracks and huts of North Camp, onto South Camp road, and along to the bridge over Basingstoke Canal.

It had been one month since the War Office had found him in his sleepy Western District office. The hand-delivered letter was long-winded and saccharine, and asked him to come immediately to take command of Aldershot. His first response had been to fashion their flattery into an arrow and fire it back.

"If I'm such a good commander, why am I not in South Africa leading troops?"

That inspired an even more servile note about his long experience (you're old) and who better to train our young men (than someone no longer trusted in the field)? Bored stiff and needing the better pay, Butler packed his bags.

Arriving at the bridge over the Basingstoke, Butler took his usual position at the downstream rail. He trained his eye on a spinach-green riffle and took several round breaths.

Aldershot was so familiar to him. He had trained here in the 1860s and had commanded infantry here in the 1890s. The parade grounds, the hoof-plowed fields, the pimple hills with their grand names. To his ears came the leather stamp of hundreds trying to be one. The halt, the whack of rifle butts; the whetstone ring of bayonets. In North Camp, cavalry recruits would be gouging their horses, wagging their sabres and swords, charging cloth dummies.

But the thing about age—something he had commiserated about with Red Crow—was the way the familiar became unfamiliar; or, if familiar, more hideous for being so.

What confounded Butler every day at Aldershot was the headlong pursuit and repetition of practices *that had never worked*. If battles were won (Sebastopol) and wars (Crimean), it was not because the strategies and generalship had made sense, it was because the enemy was even more daft than they had been. There was even a knowledge that this was so, and an acceptance. If it was tradition to do a thing badly, then, altogether now, let us continue.

In this way, South Africa was turning into a classic British war. First Redvers Buller crawled after his rabbit prey, in close order so they could always hit him. Now, General Bobs Roberts, sent to take over from Buller, was pledging to be Buller's opposite. He would race up the gut of Africa all the way to Pretoria, blinding the Boers with his speed. If Buller was too slow, Roberts would correct the flaw by being too fast. Roberts liked to outrun things—like his soldiers' medicines and bandages; their food; their ammunition and gun parts.

Butler had personally experienced this style of leadership on the Nile. The generals had goaded him for speed, so he had imported Canadian voyageurs and built Orkney boats to make better headway. He thought he had done well, but everyone in the world who watched as Britain's grand adventure failed thought he couldn't have. Too late for Chinese Gordon. Too bad for Butler, who was among the blamed.

That had been the birth of Kitchener, who Bobs Roberts had now chosen for his second-in-command in South Africa. After the failed relief of Khartoum, Kitchener had blazed in from the coast and beaten up on some of the Mahdi's fanatics: the first victory over the enemy since Gordon had been slaughtered. Hurrah!

Kitchener had also been first at Omdurman, where he killed eleven thousand dervishes and wounded another sixteen thousand. He razed the dome they had built over the Mahdi's grave and, with his ghastly sense of theatre, had tossed the Mahdi's bones into the Nile. The troops awarded Kitchener the Mahdi's handsome skull, and he kept the prize in his tent, and then on his desk—until Queen Victoria heard about it and instructed her favourite to put the poor man's head in the ground where it belonged.

The sound of boots on the bridge brought Butler's attention back. Here came two of his young staff officers, bearing papers for him to sign.

Before the young lieutenants could say anything, Butler launched into an anecdote.

"At Ladysmith, before she was besieged, it was decided to show off the town's artillery to the Boers. They arranged the guns so they were pointing at a ridge, but, at the last minute, the officer in charge decided it wasn't going to be much of a show. So they found twenty goats and led them up there, before the gunners let fly.

"You can imagine. Noise, explosions, dust. Big lyddite cloud swallowing up the ridge. After half an hour, the officer ordered the barrage stopped, and some privates were sent to see to the fate of the goats. These lads were gone a long time, and when they came back, they appeared shame-faced.

"'So, tell me. How many did you find?' asked the officer.

"'Well, sir, we counted twenty-two.'

"'Twenty-two? Nonsense! We sent twenty.'

"'Begging your pardon, sir, but the commotion caused a nanny to have twins.'"

General Butler laughed. So did his two staffers—maybe a little dutifully, a little forcedly.

Butler arrived back at his office having made a decision. It concerned Red Crow and his nephew Jefferson. Things had changed since he'd received the request to act on the nephew's behalf. The move to Aldershot, while not much of a promotion, still conferred power. Butler had sidestepped much of the public's fickle rage. Officers now in Africa, who had served with Butler in older days, were not so likely to ignore a request from him.

Butler cleared his blotter and set a clean page, unscrewed the top off the ink bottle, and dipped his pen. Jefferson Davis was likely with the Canadian Mounted Rifles. Butler wrote two letters asking that he be made a scout.

Near the end of February, the *Pomeranian* slid around the headland and entered Table Bay. It was an hour before dawn, and the massive block of Table Mountain was flooded pink. The colour of wild roses.

Like every other man on board, Frank was desperate to get off, to be delivered from the rotting stink of decks and holds; to see the horses liberated from their foul cave. The skipper cut the ship's engine and let it glide through the quiet water of the vessel-choked bay. Their anchor was lowering with a rattle of chains, and they felt it bite. Soon, the officers were among them telling them they would not get off today, as if that were obvious. They must wait their turn at the dock. They must get the holds above the horses emptied first. Tomorrow, maybe.

In moments like this one, Frank had begun to see a pattern. Whatever soldiers craved most, the army would not give them. Army logic.

They bobbed at anchor, surrounded by ships, none as scabby as their own, and they watched the mountain change, a different colour for every hour. Two small boats came to serve them, and at every level of the ship's insides, soldiers were loading pallets or raising them. Outside, more men were lowering cargo to the upturned faces of black navvies.

The day's consolation was the breaking open of the crates that held their Stetsons, crowns inside one another to make comical spires. The western hats were what would set them apart from *Tommy Atkins*, the British soldier in his metal head bucket. More crates were cracked, and they saw for the first time their Colt .45s, still slippery with factory oil.

Between trips of the cargo boats, they donned their hats and faced off like dime-novel heroes, practising their draw and trying to coax bystanders to rule on who was fastest. A crackling that sounded like pistol fire came from another ship and brought their officers running.

Finally, the profiles of Table Mountain and Devil's Peak filled with black, and the Mounted Rifles' last night on the ocean began. Frank, Ovide, and Jeff sat together on deck, on piles of coiled rope. They stared at the mountains until their shapes dissolved into the dark of sky. Then they turned their attention to the stars above.

Frank's father had told him he would be looking at a different sky down here, but only during the clear nights of the past two weeks had Frank understood this was not just a difference of perspective but a wholly different sky. How *would* Frank navigate if he were lost in this country? With no knowledge of the landmarks and, when light expired, no knowledge of the map of the sky.

Jeff, Ovide, and Frank, all three, craned their necks and stared at the stars, trying to see and remember patterns in those sparks and washes of light.

Next morning, Cape Town went mad. Cannons boomed from the hilltops and from the north flat where the city's ancient fort stood. Ships yanked their whistles open and screamed reply. It was deafening and went on and on, as the *Pomeranian* crept forward and was roped to the dock, as the disgorging of horses began. The coincidental timing made the Mounted Rifles feel like the commotion was for them.

They streamed down the plank onto the pier—stood on legs like uncooked hams. To feel that the solid world was in motion was an experience that made no sense even though they'd been told to expect it. The horses also staggered when they came to the pier, either sea wobbly or simply lame from the state of their yellow hooves.

But there was a lesson in how the horses took it, how they thrilled and preened to be ashore, despite their pain. The soldiers' whines (*Where's the damn food? Why are we standing in the sun?*) disappeared at the sight of the joyful horses. They remembered that they were on the far side of a great ocean, taking their first cold drinks of water in a month, alive and more or less healthy. In Africa.

Because the cannons kept blasting, and the steam whistles yelling, the officers could not be heard and the crowd off the ship quickly lost form and cohesion.

Frank let his horse pull him the length of the skinny pier, past the piles of cork and net, and the crowds of ugly cormorants standing on them. When the pier was only a few feet higher than the sand, Dunny jumped down and promptly rolled. She dusted herself thoroughly as she must have wanted to do for a month. Then spying green where the pier met the shore, she rolled up onto her feet and went after the grass with a wrapping tongue.

A black youth sat watching Frank and his horse, the boy's bare legs dangling below the pier. When Frank yelled, "What's the noise about?" the young fellow grinned but did not understand. Frank pointed at a cannon on the hill. Clapped his hands tight over his ears and winced in mock pain. Then he held out his arms imploringly. *Why?*

The fellow laughed at his display.

"Big battle," the youth said and mimed shooting a rifle.

"Who won?" Frank yelled.

The boy thumped himself on the chest.

Everybody higher than private was running around trying to get the Mounted Rifles together again, in formation by the ship. A corporal looked over the pier's edge and saw Frank; yelled for him to come. Dunny was hard to pull away from the sand and grass, and even harder to move along the pier in the direction of the ship. Frank knew he would never get her up the plank and into the ship again. She'd kill him first.

During the journey, each troop had been divided into fours. The number three in each four was the horse-holder. Already Jeff Davis had moved a bit away and was part of Casey Callaghan's four. Frank and Ovide were with two other cowboys, and the youngest, Gil Snaddon, was the horse-holder. They gave Gil their horses now and went to stand in line.

The battalion formed like they'd been taught to in Regina, facing Lieutenant-Colonel Herchmer and two British officers they had never seen before. An old duffer with flourishing white moustaches, a feathered hat, and a plaster of chest decoration spoke first. His voice when it came was surprisingly strong and shrill, enough to split the din. He welcomed them to Cape Colony and thanked them in advance for their sacrifice.

The old officer seemed to forget the rest, and a younger captain beside him leaned close and whispered.

"Oh, yes," the older one said. "This day, February 27, is what the Boers call Majuba Day. That was back in the first Boer War, when they attacked us on Majuba Hill. Terrific fight and we took a dusting. That was 1881. General Colley was a wonderful soldier. Boers shot him, right in the forehead."

As the old duffer pointed at his own forehead with a white-gloved finger, the younger officer cleared his throat and whispered some more.

"That's the thing, you see," said the old officer. "This very day, Majuba Day, there has been a great surrender of Boers up north. Place called Paardeburg. They surrendered to Lord Kitchener, I believe. Paardeburg means . . ."

He leaned toward the younger officer, and the younger one said, "Horse Hill."

This time the younger officer whispered longer at the old officer's ear, and more strenuously, until the older one threw up his white-gloved hands. "Captain Smithers here will tell you the rest."

Smithers raced through a description of how, nine days earlier, the British had chased down the Boer general Cronje on the Modder River, causing him to draw his wagons into a defensive circle. Lord Kitchener, having taken command of the fight, ordered several assaults. After the first attacks, Cronje was softened up for a few days with artillery, then attacked again. Finally, the Boer general could stand no more and, as of this day, had surrendered with more than three thousand of his men. It was Britain's greatest victory of the war to date. A definite turning point.

Colonel Herchmer, who had been uncharacteristically quiet so far, seemed to get angry during this last part. He made a strangled noise and asked to speak. The captain gestured for him to go ahead.

"The Royal Canadian Regiment took part in the battle of Paardeburg," Herchmer roared. "They were in the final fight that produced the surrender."

The young captain looked embarrassed. "Yes. The Canadians fought very valiantly, we are told."

The Mounted Rifles gave three cheers for the victory and another three for the Royal Canadian Regiment. Then the British officers left, and the Rifles cheered the back of them. After that, Herchmer took his hat off and put it under his arm. The Royal Canadian Regiment's contribution had not been without cost, he said. He asked for a moment of silence for the dead.

When Herchmer put his hat back on, he issued a flurry of orders. They would march through town, which, as they could hear, was in an uproar of celebration. The horses would be left on the outskirts in some shade if any could be found. He apologized to the horse-holders, who would miss the parade, but that was the nature of horse-holding.

Frank felt a rising excitement as they marched into Cape Town. It was surprisingly far and maybe an hour later they turned into Adderley Street, a main road and the centre of celebration.

The street was clogged solid for blocks with people but also with islands of tram cars, buggies, and wagons. The horses hooked to these vehicles were frustrated, dancing and jumping in their traces.

Several buildings that framed the street had covered balconies, each one lined solid with celebrants. Besides cheering, some were holding banners and waving Union Jacks, beating little tom-toms and rattling sticks on the rails. That is, they had been more or less quiet when the Mounted Rifles entered the street, but upon seeing more uniforms they roused and made noise again, as if the actual victors of Paardeburg had arrived.

Frank loved the look of the people around him, all the colours of skin and cloth. The sergeant-major marching at the head had convinced the sea to part for the Canadians, and the line of troops made a khaki rivulet through the mass. Brown children danced along beside them. Flower sellers offered the soldiers their wares for free. Frank took a couple of pink blooms that he poked in his hatband, and a couple of longer stems that he trapped crossways inside his bandolier.

Everyone in Adderley Street wore a costume, according to Frank's innocent eye: women with their heads wrapped in blue, pink, and orange cloth, knotted behind; men in puffy pantaloons; men in pillbox hats, top hats, tall cone hats with no brim; people with tattooed faces and gold rings through their ears.

When they had gone a few blocks up, turned and walked back, it was time to start for the horses.

As soon as the soldiers were no longer among the cheering crowd, Frank felt a plummet in his chest, a weight dragging, and had no clue why. He looked around him, and none of the others looked chipper either. It finally came to him that the core of this bad feeling was Paardeburg, the victory they had tried all day to celebrate, with Cape Town's eyes upon them.

Now that they were alone, except for some black children trotting alongside hoping for a penny, the truth was on display: that Paardeburg meant nothing much except a fear that the war would be over before they got there.

On the ocean, Frank had spent many hours staring at the line that divided water from sky. In his head, he was watching himself in battle. Across the sweeps of imaginary landscape, he and Dunny galloped. They scared up fantastic birds. A herd of giraffes tall as storefronts raced away. Dunny had never been keener, braver, or more sure-footed. Neither of them so much as flinched when Boer bullets floated by.

"A definite turning point," the English captain had said, and Frank, as he walked, turned that phrase around and around. Turning from what to what? From getting beat to winning something? From uncertain outcome to certain victory?

What if, in this big country on whose toe they stood, a bunch of Boer generals were sitting in the dust praying to their Dutch God for guidance. Maybe they were already in some farmhouse kitchen drafting terms of surrender.

The soldiers came to the little park where the horses stood in shade. Some murmured annoyance at having been left in such a strange place. First thing this morning, two lieutenants had left to arrange transport. A short train of high-wheeled wagons and ox carts was the result. This wagon train was already loaded high with Canadian gear, and the black drivers and bull-whackers stood ready for the order to leave for Green Point, their camp.

The soldiers arriving from downtown felt funny that there was now this layer of society beneath them: men who would shift their bale while they were off grinning at Cape Town ladies. To console this need to work, the packs they hoisted weighed like lead. With their backs to the afternoon sun, the heat came through their khaki like an iron brand.

The ocean to the right was a shade of yellow and green most had never seen. Patches of white sand showed between frothing water and black rocks. A knowledgeable type proclaimed that the Cape of Good Hope, southern end of Africa, lay beyond the cliffs ahead. He said too that the tide was coming in. A wave bigger than the rest slammed a loaf of rock and shot up spray as if to prove it.

Unique to their lives as this walk was, Paardeburg kept interrupting. The idea of being sent home without having fired their Lee-Enfields or Colt pistols in battle was humiliating even in the abstract. Frank kept imagining himself in the Fort Macleod Hotel, sipping beer. He was old, and a smart aleck from a younger generation switched a chew of tobacco into his cheek and called, "Hey, Frank Adams, tell us the one about how the turd flew through the ship's window and landed in your soup."

Would it all come down to that? An old man's protest that he had crossed the equator both ways—*so don't tell me I've never been anywhere.*

Green Point camp would be the Mounted Rifles' home until their horses were fit. It was a hot and filthy place. The point was built of sand and nary a tree. The thousands of horses and soldiers who had bivouacked here had already worn off every sprig of grass. Scrawny dogs roved the sand and fought over discarded beef tins. Pedlars came with chunks of wood carved into African animals.

The ocean tides made wind, sometimes strong wind, and the sand with nothing to hold it lifted and travelled so that no meal at Green Point lacked a sandy condiment. It was in Frank's socks and boots when he drew them on in the morning; chafed in his underwear all day. When he shook his bedroll and laid it down fresh in the tent, the sand was still there. Some days the wind blew so full of sand that goggles were issued. But somehow the flies that blackened the outsides of their tents were never scoured away.

There were other hazards. You could not walk ten yards in bare feet without cutting yourself on the rim of a drifted beef tin or sinking where a latrine crew had thrown a skim of sand over a mess. It stank too, that particular brand Frank thought he'd left on the *Pomeranian*.

The horses hated Green Point as much as the men did. The ground would not hold a picket pin, and every night in the dark, they tried to escape. The sentries roused the men to run after the horses, who were dragging their lines across the shit-mined landscape.

The horses' feet remained a problem. No one was going anywhere until a horse per man could take a nail in its hooves, so said Sergeant Tracey. Tracey decided the best course of action involved the sea—a way to exercise the horses and heal them too. He wanted volunteers to walk the horses on the beach—low tide would be best. Not only would they not hurt themselves walking and running on the sand, but the salt water would toughen the horn of their hooves and heal the tender underside, the frog.

Most fellows, when they heard the word *beach*—more sand—were determined to duck this assignment. Boer prisoners were arriving by train from up north, and most Mounted Rifles wanted to be picked to escort the enemy from the trains to the prison camp: a chance to dress up and brandish their guns.

But Frank had seen the prisoners. He and Jeff had gone over to the Boer camp one evening and stared at them through the barbed wire. Men with beards; towheaded boys. They looked defeated and depressed, and the sight of them only added to Frank's fear that the war was disintegrating. He volunteered for the beach detail.

With six horses in his grasp, Frank set out in the blooming lavender morning. The tide was out and there was a lot of beach to walk on. He led his six in front of the black rock chambers until he found a place where the stone and water made a bay. On the bay's near side, a little creek had scored a track to the sea. On the bay's far side was a protruding jut, like the foot of a stone giant. The toes were in the water even now.

At the creek's crumbling edge, every horse balked. Frank urged them through, but once past the creek there was no chance of their going back on their own. That and the rock foot made a pen in which he could give them liberty. He looped their lead ropes onto their halters and let them go.

They walked in a cluster at first, afraid of everything, but gradually began to jack around. They shied at the froth on the shallow waves, at the black rocks; at everything that rolled and scuttled. Eventually, all six were brave enough to stand where the water curled around their legs.

The situation liberated Frank to doff his boots and pocket his socks. The wet sand squished like dough between his toes. The surf rose on his shins and the bursting bubbles tickled the leg hair. Little shells rolled in the outbound waves. Tiny crabs scuttled for cover when the water unclothed them.

That night, when Frank got back to the tent he shared with Ovide, he described what he'd seen. Ovide listened with eyes closed. He had let himself be picked for duty as a shoeing smith—putting shoes back on the horses who had toughened up enough to stand it. Because horses were healing all the time, the job became heavier every day. Hot as Green Point camp was, Ovide had found the hottest place in it: pumping bellows in a black canvas cave, carrying red-hot shoes from forge to anvil.

When Frank finished telling about the beach, he urged Ovide to declare himself heat-struck come reveille tomorrow. Take a break from the infernal forge. Join him on the beach with the horses. Frank had little hope of Ovide agreeing, but, come morning, Ovide did go to his sergeant and say he wanted the day off from the forge. He wanted to exercise lamers down on the sand.

With the sun rising and banging off the mountains behind them, the two cowboys led a dozen horses. The tide was in this time, and they had to walk above the black rocks instead of below. Frank worried that they would not see any of the things he had advertised. He went scouting and found a place where a path led down through the rocks to an exposed rim of sand, then guided Ovide and the horses there. The tide had turned and every hour there was more shore to play on.

Ovide rolled his trousers to uneven heights. His thick white shins, laced with pink and purple scars, looked foreign in the water. His shirt hung out on one side. His Stetson was cockeyed. He kept picking things up and pocketing them until his pockets sagged.

Ovide glanced up and saw Frank looking, took a step onto a slippery rock, lost his balance, and fell. The horses near him pretended shock and went plunging in all directions. Ovide staggered upright, and the shells in his pockets and the ocean streaming from his pants pulled his trousers off his wide flat ass. Strangled at the ankles, he tripped again.

Frank had never seen Ovide so much as grin. Now he was laughing. Floundering in the surf and laughing. Frank looked at what he was seeing and tried to trap it in a picture. *Keep this,* he said to himself. *Take it with you when you go.*

The Great Karoo

The tracks behind the Cape Town train station swarmed with men and horses. Sergeants barked orders, trying to mask what was mere confusion. The Mounted Rifles officers took turns marching off to "sort things out," returning red-faced. Twice, they ordered the men to pick everything up and move it elsewhere on the maze of tracks—for no apparent gain or purpose.

For Frank's Squadron D, part of the problem was that their commanding officer, Maj. Gilbert Sanders, had sickened on the ship and now remained behind in a Cape Town hospital.

What broke the stalemate was a furious Brit riding into them like charging cavalry. He jerked the mouth on a wild-eyed horse, yelled and pointed. They followed his gestures to an empty length of train. Three kinds of car: high-walled open cars for the horses; a flatcar for the saddles; third-class compartments for the men.

—

When the train left the shadow of Table Mountain, Frank was one of the soldiers hanging on the outside like flies on a tent. He wanted to see where they were going and to feel the breeze. Others rode on the roof or stood on the short porches between cars.

They passed through a series of lowland farms, white houses with white fences on velvet green. In the gardens, the leaf vegetables were fleshy and fighting for space. The bushes flowered pink, purple, and yellow.

For a brief while, the train went through an orchard, and the opening tree rows gave glimpses of black pickers gathering wind-fallen fruit. Frank saw people on ladders with baskets, catching fruit that children on higher branches were throwing down.

When the country opened up, the sun-gleaming land rucked into hills, and more workers followed vineyard and garden rows in long upward sweeps.

The images fluttered through Frank's eyes and mind, something new every minute. Emotions popped inside him at the same juttering rate. All of it was so green, so rich with decorative colour: neat, gardened, groomed. Even the horses looked slicker than at home and the cattle tamer with their clunking bells. His own world, that tenderly nursed idea of prairie beauty, was in danger of being reduced for all time.

The train began to climb. The hills became steeper and the houses fewer, and the cows on the velvet hills were more beef than dairy. Through the window Frank was hanging beside, he saw an alarming rush toward him, men yapping and pointing. He twisted himself and saw a massive boil of rock swelling smooth out of an ordinary hill. Never had he seen anything so flesh-like come from the earth.

The big rock marked a frontier beyond which the land's green hide was often split to expose the rocks inside. They entered the mountains through a narrow twist of canyon that rode beside a copper-coloured creek, and the NCOs and sergeants came yelling for the men to get inside before the more rugged terrain shook or brushed them off.

Frank held on a little longer because the sun was dropping and setting the orange rocks aflame. Black birds with pink jewels on their wings sprang up and flew hard to escape the train's intrusion. Higher up, sleek rodents flowed like water.

When the sun dunked in the crags, the blackened cliffs split into rough knuckled fists whose beating had strewn a boulder field below.

Come night, Frank returned to his allotted compartment. He was the last of eight who were supposed to sleep there, an enforced intimacy worse even than the Regina barracks. A two-pound bully beef tin with a rolled-back lid was making the rounds, and Frank got to his pack and unearthed his spoon in time to catch two greasy lumps. He filled his mess tin twice with tea. Before this eating was done, four men had stretched out on bunks and a fifth on the floor, and all remaining space was taken up with gear. Frank's pack had a berth, but he did not.

He popped out and the fresher air of the corridor felt and smelled like escape. He joined a tribe of wanderers who walked and climbed the train's length in vain hope of a nook to settle in. Some said they were going to bed down with the horses, and he thought Ovide was probably doing that, and maybe Jeff too. But, before he got to the horse cars, Frank found a porch with a space he could squeeze into. Pete Belton was there, and Eddy. Pete was chewing and spitting at the clitter-clatter of tracks, while big Eddy sat cross-legged on the floor, falling asleep and then waking himself when his head banged an iron bar.

Frank looked at the crags printed black on the blue-grey sky, at a litter of stars emerging. Known only to those who did not sleep, the train stopped several times. It huffed and wheezed, and finally, straining, broke the bond between wheel and rail and stuttered forward again.

The cloudy first light had a muslin quality that would not quite reveal, but when the first long stabs of sunlight ignited vistas, the mountains were gone and replaced by a new concept of nothing. Clay slabs rolled out, looking like they had flowed from a mountain yesterday and had only just frozen into pottery. When that vision was established, the rolling train crossed into a sea of dusty sage. Then came a grey, grubby floor strewn with shards.

All around Frank, men felt called upon to comment, or just to curse, the blasted land on whose back they rode—especially here in the protection of the train. The only ones not shocked, or even surprised, were the Beltons. As their parents followed gold rushes and settlement frontiers, and always arrived too late, they had often fetched up in dry places others condemned.

"Like southern Idaho," Pete Belton proclaimed. "'Cept the sage there is bigger."

Frank hurt all over from standing through the night. He went inside and walked until he found a bench, and then watched some more through the window as sleep gained on him. He saw how rocks erupted the skin of desert, sparsely but in many forms. Like markers in abandoned graveyards. Slaggy piles whose mortar had washed away. Distant mounds of drab.

The sturdiest things in view appeared on the horizon as pyramids with their points lopped off, grey or blue. As they came closer, they turned yellow and sandy, less geometric and substantial. At close viewing, they were all seams and scars, and not much more than that.

A dry and starved kind of country, and when a goat or a sheep, or a hut with outbuildings and a water dam, floated by the window—touched into motion by motion—it was a surprise that registered as a mistake. *That should not be there*, Frank told himself, while knowing he had no experience from which to draw that conclusion.

The sage rose in height and fell, bunched and fled itself. Then for a time there was no widespread cover but a vision of flowers left separate on lifeless gravel. Each was perfectly round as a bride's bouquet. Snow-white. Pink as a forge's heart. Sunset orange.

Frank pinched his cheek and twisted, for he thought he must be asleep and dreaming. But the cheek felt pain and the flowers remained.

When a small antelope with elaborately twisted horns crept down a rocky slope, a fellow yelled out, "Where the hell are we, anyway?"

Another soldier had a map spread on his lap. He made a big circle on the sheet with his finger and yelled back, "The Great Karoo Desert!"

So at least they had a name for what bewildered them.

Frank did sleep then until awakened by the train's slowing and squealing and coming to a stop. The same blasted blankness spread to a brushed horizon, and the only sounds left were the engine's puffing and the wind's hitting the walls with fistfuls of grit. Some soldiers stuck themselves out the windows to see ahead, to detect what kind of obstacle blocked them. One remembered it was a war and thought rebels must have blown up the track. Then a sergeant came walking beside the train, rattling his stick down the metal sides, meaning they had arrived where someone meant them to be.

Frank fetched his saddle off the flatcar and saw Ovide doing the same. The old cowboy looked rumpled, even for himself, so might have slept with the horses after all. They fell in together and set their saddles on the horns in a patch of sage or gorse or heather—Frank had heard it called all those things by the plant experts on the train. Not far away was a homely scrap of town.

Ovide led Frank back to their horse car. They gave their mares turns at the water barrel before jumping them down, there being no other water in sight.

A few Boer wagons had come with them on flatcars, and the sergeants told them to load these full. Their lieutenants had gone into the Boer town and its African village to hire more wagons and blacks. Frank and Ovide's troop sergeant told them they were making camp a mile away, because the town, Victoria Roads, had a reputation for being rebel.

When they got to camp, Aussies, New Zealanders, and Derbyshire Yeomen had already made a tent town. Their own D Battery was camped among them. All total, they were the Carnarvon Field Force, and their job was to reclaim villages west of here. Boer rebels had come down from the republics to stir the Cape Boers to rebel. If the Cape Boers joined, they could attack the lowlands, maybe even Cape Town. Lord Kitchener had chased the interlopers already, pushing them across the Orange River near Britstown. But it was decided more should be done to frighten and win back the people of the desert.

Colonel Herchmer demanded they form up so he could make a speech. He repeated about the Cape Boers and going into the desert to show the flag. He added that they should not be so stupid as to think the rebels were only in the distant desert and not here. This very morning, D Battery had seen heliograph flashes in the low hills. The night previous, snipers had fired at their sentries.

Herchmer asked if there were questions. A private asked if Maj. Gilbert Sanders would be back soon. Herchmer did not care for the question.

"Do you see anywhere on me the tools of a necromancer?" he roared. "A crystal ball?" He swept his hand across the dismal Karoo desert, to emphasize what a stupid question it was, but his hand passed in front of telegraph poles that contradicted him.

During this gather and speech, Frank had seen Jeff Davis. He was standing with Casey Callaghan, the Irish teamster from Maple Creek who had stood up for Jeff against Pete Belton on the train in Canada. They had shared a tent at Green Point. They were friends now, thought Frank, with an embarrassing pang of loss.

The new arrivals were spared sentry duty that night, but Frank might as well have done the job for all the sleep he got. He sat up like a jack-in-the-box every time a hyena cried, and every time a rifle cracked. By the long spaces between the shots, it seemed the Boers wanted the British camp to fall asleep and then be awakened, to keep them all on edge.

Toward morning, there was a much bigger eruption. It started with a bucket of horse brushes being kicked. The fellow who did it dodged back and tripped on the picket rope, which touched off the horses. It looked to Frank like half the Mounted Rifles leapt up at the same time to calm the pulling horses. The instigator was a skinny black youth, one of those hired yesterday for the baggage convoy. He had snuck home overnight to celebrate and was drunk.

There was a good moon in a clear sky and, by it, Frank saw a Boer come striding in baggy trousers, his slab of chest bare. He had a whip coiled in one hand. Frank saw two soldiers draw their Colts at the sight of this big Dutchman. A D Battery lieutenant told them sharply to put them away.

"That's Case," the sergeant said. "He's *our* Boer." Wagon boss on the supply convoy.

Ovide, who had slept through the sniping and hyenas, was awake now. Frank and he stood together and watched Case jabber a weird lingo at one of the black drivers. The skinny youth was tied to a wagon wheel, then gagged, though he made no sound.

Case let go his whip beyond its handle. He took a few steps away from the wheel, dragging it behind.

"That's rhinoceros hide," said a D Battery bombardier, probably having seen it in action already.

Case barked for everyone behind him to clear away. He reared the whip back and sailed it at the skinny back. It struck and the boy stiffened. Methodically, Case continued to flog.

The light was not good enough to see what was happening to the boy's back, but Frank could hear how hard the whip laid into him and the grunt the boy made in his chest each time. It was easy to imagine red ropes of weal and blood. It went on too long, before the boy was untied and ungagged and let stumble away. Among the wagons, hands reached out to help him.

When Frank lay down again, he looked at Ovide, who was wrapping himself in his blanket. "Will they do that to us if we get out of line?"

"No."

Frank's mother, Madeleine, started up in his mind, talking angrily about how Halfbreeds and Indians were treated in ways whites never were. Frank thought about Lige Abel, one of three black people he'd ever met. Lige was a huge cowboy who worked on the Waldron; who had once carried a heavy iron bar a mile to win a bet with another cowboy. Before he slept, Frank imagined Lige ripping himself free of the wagon wheel and taking Case's whip out of his hand.

Victoria Roads / Victoria West

A train arrived next morning carrying the rest of the Canadian guns, as well as mules and more horses. Since reveille in the dark, some of the Canadians and Englishmen had been preparing to leave. Under Major Hurdman, they departed when the new train arrived.

This cavalcade, including Mounted Rifles C Squadron, was still visible as dust in the sky when D Squadron started getting ready to go. D Squadron would be led by Colonel Herchmer, and he let them know he was only doing so because Major Sanders was inconveniently sick. Sanders, their major from British Columbia, was well liked; Herchmer, less so.

Like everyone else, Frank left the saddling as late as he could. When it was time, he put his two sleeping blankets on Dunny and thumped the heavy California stock saddle on top, gave the cinch its first pull. He rolled the oil sheet and greatcoat together and tied them behind the cantle. Then he repacked his haversack. Some things you had to carry, like emergency rations and a full water bottle. The hairbrush and shaving mirror were optional, but he put them in. Frank gave the cinch another tug, swung the sack onto his back, grabbed his stupidly heavy Lee-Enfield, and clumsily mounted. Sergeant Brindle ordered them to place the rifles across their laps and hook them to their belts. Dunny looked back at Frank in disbelief. Ovide was lined up beside Frank on his small mare. Both Ovide and the mare wore looks of misery at the weight they were carrying.

Frank and Ovide stayed together as the troops were ordered into lines. Jeff and Casey had been picked as scouts and went ahead with the machine guns; then D Squadron, then some other colonials. The last Frank saw of Victoria Roads was Case dragging his rhino whip and Colonel Parsons, commander of the Carnarvon Field Force, sitting in a canopied Cape cart, having a last cup of tea.

At the start of the ride, Frank heard fellows venture that this was better than Green Point. The morning was cool and no sand was flying. Within an hour, the sun had become fierce with a light so powerful you could not look anywhere near it. As the air heated up, the wind gained velocity and the rock grit started to move. Ahead, everything swam, even the hills. They had a Cape Boer for a guide, and he told them the hills were called *kopjes* (pronounced like *copies*). Frank had studied these already and had decided they had little purpose but to shimmer and turn colour. Take that away and they were slag heaps, big and useless. Far behind them now, the train that had arrived this morning huffed a black billow and crept away. When it disappeared between hills, Frank felt lonely for it.

After the elaborate start-up, the journey was short, ending in just a few miles at a town called Victoria West. The day had been a dress rehearsal, dipping them in the Great Karoo before they were fully plunged. They camped on stony ground within sight of the Boer town and its adjacent African village.

As night came on, the sound from the sleeping camp was swallowed by the African night. A chant of insects came in waves that never stopped. The hyenas, which looked like mad dogs, had tracked them from a distance during the march. Their sound in the night was weirder than a coyote's. A big beetle entered the tent and skittered across Frank's face.

It was all just the animal world moving and calling to itself, but it was hard not to feel it was meant for you.

Victoria West was an older town that the scientists of railroad construction had bypassed. Its houses were adobe, like miniature American cavalry forts. White church, two hotels, a millinery shop. Ft. Macleod had no millinery shop. Nor had Frank expected the women to be so pretty. Part of the talk the soldiers had used to arouse their contempt was that Boer women were fat and ugly, and would be fatter and uglier the farther into the republics they penetrated. But here, already far from Cape Town, the bonneted, parasoled Boer ladies were anything but ugly.

The black women were pretty too. They wore clean pink calico like the flowers Frank had seen in the desert.

At Victoria West, the desert had no flowers and, worse yet, no grass. Sheep and goats were out among the tufts and rocks for some purpose, but whatever they were eating the horses could not find or would not eat. The horses went out in the scrub eagerly, but their heads popped up soon after they dropped. They moved on quickly to a fresh disappointment.

Ovide and Frank were leading their horses back after a failed graze when they saw Jeff coming. He had been out on another scouting chore with Casey. But, as he came closer, Frank saw that Jeff's expression was serious and troubled. He said something about how they might lose their horses. He and Frank had already discussed a rule that said officers and cavalrymen could take a trooper's horse, despite ownership, if they felt it was needed. He thought Jeff was repeating this for some reason.

"They're not getting mine," said Frank.

"No," said Jeff, and shook his head. "Listen."

What Jeff explained was something different and worse. Colonel Parsons had given Herchmer a scolding for bringing pale horses on the expedition. They would be visible at night, Parsons claimed. They would give away their position and attract sniper fire. Herchmer was stung by the rebuke, and had already gathered up six white and pale horses he intended to shoot. He would not hear of selling them, because they might fall into rebel hands.

Then Frank spotted Herchmer. He was coming in their direction with a brisk-walking entourage.

"It's this way," said Jeff, hurrying to finish. "He's got his eye on The Blue and your dun."

Frank felt light-headed and could not think. Jeff grabbed his arm and squeezed hard to get his attention back. "Don't say anything. I'll talk."

Herchmer arrived with his orderly, a sergeant, and two lieutenants. Their expressions were stern and dutiful. Herchmer said exactly what

Jeff had just explained. The blue mare and Dunny were pale and would have to go. He looked at Ovide's mare and cleared her. She had white tips on dark brown hair, but the light at the moment was showing the brown.

Jeff did what Frank could never have done. When Herchmer declared his intention to do away with the two cayuse mares, Jeff nodded as though he saw the point and the danger, and even somewhat agreed.

"But, you know, sir, these two mares came off the ship stronger than almost any other saddle horse. You could ask Sergeant Tracey."

Herchmer gave Jeff a look reserved for those slow in the head.

"If you're listening, private, I'm not talking about fitness, I'm talking about colour."

"Yes, sir. But I think, since they are solid horses, good scout horses, we might test to see if they can be seen at night or not."

Frank forgot Jeff's instruction. He blurted out a repetition of Jeff's point about consulting Sergeant Tracey.

"I will not ask Tracey! I command Tracey!"

Herchmer's face was a dangerous shade of black. Frank regretted having spoken. But some of Herchmer's colour was due to frustration over the reasonableness of Jeff's suggestion. It was reasonable, and several witnesses had heard it.

As dusk faded to night, Jeff and Frank rode their mares into the Karoo scrubland west of camp. They were to go out a mile and wait. They could choose the length of that wait, returning at any time during the next two hours. There were two sets of sentries posted on this side of camp, and both had been instructed about the plan. They were to sing out the instant they saw a pale horse. If those sentries so much as thought they saw something, Frank's and Jeff's cayuses were done for.

At the estimated mile, Jeff told Frank to dismount. The main danger, he said, was that their heads or hats would show against the sky, which was not yet solid dark. They would lead the horses back and crouch a little so everything was below the horizon. As for waiting, Jeff chose not to. He thought the best gamble was that the sentries would not expect them back directly.

Frank had hunted plenty of times with the Bloods, and he recognized

Jeff's way of walking on their return as that silent kind. Jeff led them right between the two sentry posts. After that, Frank circled around behind the left-hand post, while Jeff continued into camp.

Frank did not see anyone until he had completed most of his circle. Then two khaki backs (speaking of pale) loomed before him. The two sentries were behind a pile of rocks, peering hard into the night. Frank tied his mare to a scrub branch and came slowly forward. When he was within a few feet, he sang out, "How about it, fellas? Any luck seeing those birds?"

The sentries jumped in fright. Next they were angry. Then one of them laughed, and everybody laughed.

Meanwhile, Jeff was leading his mare into camp and up to her usual place on the picket line. He tied her, then walked to Herchmer's tent, where his orderly was sitting on a camp stool. Jeff asked whether the old boy was in and could he have a word with him? When Jeff led Herchmer over and showed him his mare on the picket line, the colonel was furious. He said he would court-martial those useless sentries. Jeff said he would be happy to try it again with different sentries. His bluff called, Herchmer stormed back to his tent and ripped the flap down.

Carnarvon Road

The idea of the Carnarvon Field Force was that it would move across the desert in three parts, the arrival of one triggering the departure of the next. E Battery's arrival at Victoria West meant it was Herchmer's time to go. There would be no easy objective this time. They were headed for Carnarvon, eighty miles away.

After two hours, they halted by a stagnant pond trapped behind a rock dam. The water was a green remnant swarming with flies. The horses wanted it, and the officers commanded that they be allowed. Frank and Ovide shared a look. Back home, only the most careless horseman would let a horse drink out of something like that.

Later in the day, they saw dust devils that they thought might be rebels. It soon turned into a sandstorm. They entered a walled room of dense grit that cancelled the sky. The suffering horses dodged their faces back and forth, looking to escape the stinging assault. Their hooves, supposedly healed, were already tender again from razor shards of rock.

Frank felt himself grow angry. What was the point, he wondered, of pampering them on the beach, if it was in preparation for this? He was thinking on behalf of the horses, but it was also a way of feeling sorry for himself. That Herchmer had come as close as he had to killing Frank's dun mare had lodged a bitterness that would not leave. Something in the way he felt about the war had changed already. He had not seen a single rebel except for the prisoners back at Green Point, but he was locked in a battle anyway. He was forced to fight for what was precious to him.

Still in the grit storm, they came upon another Boer farm. The column stopped and Frank and Ovide were in the group detached to search it. The farms they had seen so far were deserted, but this adobe contained the surprise of a Boer farmer who stood up from his table and faced them with arms stiff to his sides and his chin beard raised. There was crying below, and the searchers pulled a ring and lifted a door to see the man's wife and some girls weeping in a dirt cellar. Frank climbed down with a torch. He looked for guns and found none. The women shrank from him wherever he moved, and he saw that the wife held a big carving knife. Back on top, he did not mention the knife. In the light, he noticed a naked cross on the wall and, beside it, askew, a yellowed calendar picture of Queen Victoria.

Outside, Herchmer had a bunch of soldiers working in the empty sheep kraal. They were cutting dried dung into squares to be carried for fuel, and also checking that no rebel munitions were buried.

Ovide said "water," and he and Frank went looking. They were dreaming of a sweet well, but found another rock dam across a donga. This water looked even worse.

"Do you think they drink that shit?" asked Frank, meaning the Boer family.

Ovide did not answer, for it was evident. What else would they drink?

At seventeen miles, they bivouacked on stony ground beside more rotten water. Their own bottles had little left, and they raged with thirst after being allowed one swallow. Frank wondered if a time was coming when the green water would start to look good.

Picket pegs would not hammer into the stony ground so they tied the horses between the guns. Frank and Ovide laid their shared oil sheet and blankets on the warm drifted sand. When the moon rose full, the night shone cool.

Frank's mind was assailed by things he had seen during the day, pictures that danced weirdly in his head. It must have been like that in Ovide's head too, but almost no words had passed between them. In fact, almost nobody in the whole of D Squadron had spoken since the train. It came to Frank that the lack of talk might be because they had no words for what they were seeing. How can you talk about what you cannot name?

Frank's own search for words kept circling something Doc Windham used to say when Frank was a boy. To explain a thing, Doc would say, "It's like a moose to a horse." He would never explain beyond that, which suggested that Frank was to figure it out for himself.

That's what Frank was doing now, and he was glad not to have to explain to anyone why this thing was repeating in his brain.

Like a moose to a horse. Compared to home, the Great Karoo was *like a moose to a horse.*

Next day, reveille was at five and they were marching in an hour, taking advantage of the last of the cool. By ten, the air was hot and full of locusts that crossed the sky in a clittering cloud. When Frank was in that cloud, they struck his face like small brittle knives. While the cavalcade stopped to rest, Frank threw rocks into the locust cloud, and it made a swishing sound. The wagon drivers could slash down dozens at a time with their whips.

At noon, they were ordered to stop and sleep. They put their oil sheets over themselves to keep off the sun and locusts. At eight in the evening, they started again. The horses walked all night, surrounded by moonlit dust. Every once in a while a man asleep on his horse would fall, the sound like a box of cutlery dropped on a floor.

They followed a road, a slash of brown sand through the scrub. When the next day dawned and they were still moving, they entered a valley fertile and green. The first real grass since the Cape, and the horses woke and ran to it. In farmer's fields, mature corn stood, the ears ready for picking. Fruit trees. Thousands of sheep and goats. It was the sixteenth of March, and they had reached Carnarvon.

Carnarvon was the same kind of town as Victoria West. Flat-topped houses of unbaked brick, plastered with mud. Two white churches. A town hall. An African town, with its kraal, stood on the slope of a nearby hill.

As the Field Force rode down the dirt main street, they pointed their rifles at every building. A crowd of Boer women in bonnets and long dresses ran before them toward the town hall. Inside, a meal of tea and jam sandwiches was waiting. A nice-looking woman, maybe still in her twenties, poured tea out of a big can, and Frank went with his mess tin to get some. A C Squadron corporal was talking to her in what Frank knew was German. The woman looked embarrassed and would not answer or meet the corporal's eye.

"She can understand me," he said to Frank. "She's just trying not to. I talked German to the Boers in Cape Town. Even old Case, the wagon boss, had no trouble with it."

The woman kept on not looking at him, roses in her cheeks.

A lieutenant came along with a cup. "It's pure cussedness, you know," he said, summing up the woman's silence. "They have no grievance."

Not understanding the corporal's German had become proof of being rebel. Frank headed for a jam sandwich and tried not to think too hard.

After lunch, there was a stir of excitement because Jeff Davis and Casey Callaghan had brought in two fellows who might be rebels. They were old men, and had been caught on a kopje overlooking the town. They were skinny and long-bearded. Herchmer ordered them tied up, put in a building, and guarded.

E Battery and the supply train rolled in come evening. The sixteen-ox wagon teams looked tired and disgusted after eighty miles of desert. Each ox pair stood like statues while the black teamsters pulled the pins from the bows and lifted off the yokes.

The whole Carnarvon Field Force was together now, for at least this night. They had only been in the desert four days, but could have passed for hard-travelling pilgrims of much longer passage. Day before yesterday, Frank's bottle had emptied, and he had been forced to strain wrigglers out of green dam water. Dysentery came with remarkable swiftness, as if he had eaten gunpowder. Everyone started out with the same amount of water. Everyone ran out at the same time. Now everyone had the same case of the shits. By the night fires, they looked drained and ghastly. Bold fighters one day; fighting to keep their bungs closed the next.

There were cases of sunstroke too—what for some reason of army delicacy was called "a touch of the sun." In fact, they had been clubbed by the sun, clubbed stupid, dizzy, and sick. Ovide had sunstroke as well as the shits, and tonight he staggered wherever he walked. When Frank got their tent up and Ovide's bedroll laid, the old cowboy fell on it like a shot bird. He slept with both hands holding his head.

Next day was Sunday, and the chaplain and Herchmer had no mercy. They demanded everyone turn out for church parade. It was supposed to console and comfort them to stand in the sun and listen to scripture and sing hymns. More than a few had to flee their place in line to run for the latrine ditch. A few more toppled over, *touched by the sun*. Frank knew some were faking, having spotted a good way to get back to the tents and to sleep.

Frank saw Colonel Herchmer lurch forward and buckle at the knees. His orderly and Capt. Archie Macdonnell grabbed him and whisked him away.

Not long after church, a sandstorm rose, pouring into town on a hot wind. They took to their tents and the sand came straight through the walls, covering their bedding and leaving drifts in the corners.

When the storm stopped that afternoon, Frank felt certain he was about to see rain. A cloud raced up and lowered its ass over the town. But the drops that fell boiled in the air and never made it down.

That evening, a dispatch rider came. He climbed off his lathered horse and went to Herchmer's tent. The result was a bulletin pinned to the officers' mess tent that said Bloemfontein had fallen to General Roberts' army. Each mob of men who went to read the paper gave a feeble cheer and walked away. Bloemfontein was the capital of the Orange Free State, the closest of the two rebel republics. Another turning point.

The war was sweeping north as the Canadian Mounted Rifles were creeping west. They were farther away every day. Frank knew that some of those around him had already given up on seeing the war. Ovide had been beyond caring even before he left the ship. Frank had asked him a few times why he had ever enlisted, but got no answer. He stopped pestering when he realized his own reasons were far from clear.

Van Wyk's Vlei

The first group, now called a flying column, left Carnarvon first thing in the morning. Between that and the second group's leaving, Colonel Herchmer was loaded into a cart and given a two-soldier escort back to Cape Town. Other soldiers too sick to ride were left in town. Their next objective, Van Wyk's Vlei, was another eighty miles away.

On this weary stretch of road, the land was soon stone dry again, and the horses weakened badly. Many were humped and water-sick. No longer paying attention, they often stumbled. Their progress was slow, and this made the whole section stretch long and thin. They would have been easy meat for the rebels. Even if there were rebels, thought Frank, why should they bother to attack, when the Field Force was taking itself apart so efficiently? Dysentery, lameness, sunstroke, thirst.

Along their path, picked-clean rib cages gleamed in the scrub. A horse with a Waldron brand stood crooked on the road awaiting their approach, a still-living portent. Turned loose by the flying column, the gelding swayed on his legs, and his eyes were smoky. He stood beside one of the polished skeletons as though by a friend. Probably blind, the horse heard the other horses coming and passing. Trying to turn, he fell on his knees. The crack of a pistol, finally.

The carrion birds milled overtop the shuffling line. To the gliding birds, a smell ascended with the dust, as from a long thin kitchen. Their meat was on the grill.

The sickness and weakness of the horses told by contrast how strong Frank's dun really was. She still had her flesh and her clarity, still responded to every flicker in the bush, quick ears snapping. She probably hated this place and feared it, but that only made her more vigilant and faster to react. Frank thought of Herchmer, sick in his cart, and gave him the same lack of mercy he had shown Frank's mare. Herchmer had faltered; Dunny had not.

Out of the whole of D Squadron, the only horse doing as well as Dunny and Jeff's blue was Eddy Belton's gelding, Buck. One look at the bull's arse on Buck and you knew he was a dray, the kind that were all over the Canadian prairie now, helping pilgrims bust sod. Whatever crossbreeding produced Buck and his stoneboat gait had also made him unkillable. Stone stupid, Buck would plod through a day of scorching sun, sand, and locusts—and come out the other side unbothered. He probably didn't remember any of it.

Buck was a phenomenon, and Pete Belton, whose horse had been shot off the gangplank at Halifax, was forever mentioning that his dead gelding was the half-brother of Eddy's indestructible one. In Pete's mind, that constituted proof that his horse would have been the physical equal of Eddy's, or superior. The crime of causing the death, which Pete still attached to Jeff Davis and his blue mare, was even greater now, given the pillar of strength Eddy's Buck had proven to be.

Far less fortunate was Ovide's roan. She was a cutting horse, and the best of these are mares. A mare is more tenacious and will go into pain to get the job done. Being like that, Ovide's mare would not pace herself in the Karoo's desert heat and was growing thinner every day. Ovide had taken to walking beside her one hour in every two, telling the sergeant, when he asked, that she had a puncture from a thorn and needed time to heal.

Oliphant River

Van Wyk's Vlei was barely a town at all. They had passed some Karoo boundary on one side of which towns needed to be clean and have substance and on the other they did not. It was a loose cluster of mud-brick farms, mostly deserted. *Vlei* meant lake, said the guide, but there was no lake. Instead, there were two shrunken bits of dam water in which the foulness was reduced and intensified. The flat valley might have been a lake in some bygone time, but now looked like the bottom of a puddle gone dry.

They sat in the dirt, made fires and tea, opened tins of bully beef and soaked their hardtack biscuits until they could get their teeth in. A sandstorm erupted and suddenly none of it was edible. This was only fair, since the horses again had nothing but straw.

Frank watched new clouds boil up and lower, and expected another dribbling that would sizzle in the air. What came down was buckets, then tanks. The lake of Van Wyk's Vlei, gone for years, was returning from the sky.

The stony ground could not begin to absorb so much rain, and sudden raging rivers fed deepening pools until the horses stood half a leg deep. The guns squatted in it. The men's camp, set on higher ground, was also under water by the time the wagons carrying the tents arrived. Above the gaining lake, the few cottages had been quickly taken by the officers.

This was the last Frank saw of the disaster of Van Wyk's Vlei. Fred Morden came over and told him and Ovide to get ready to go. Lieutenant Davidson's troop had been switched into the flying column, and because of the rain, they must go instantly. To get to the final desert village of Kenhardt, they had to cross the Oliphant River while they still could.

Ovide told Morden he would not go. His horse was worn down and needed rest. Likely remembering his own horse, Morden showed annoyance. Lots of men's horses were worn out, he said. Their troop had been chosen. That was all there was to it.

The hope was that the rain at Van Wyck's Vlei was local and the flying column would travel out of it. But, when they came to the Oliphant's shore, it was raining even harder. The river was already swollen and brown, and full of brush chewed from the crumbling edges. Their officers ordered them into it, for the situation could only worsen.

One thing Frank had learned to fear was flooded rivers. He had seen stately cattle drives turn to chaos and then carnage in these kinds of muscular floods. He could too well remember being twelve and walking the wild Belly River looking for a drowned wagon driver whose Mounted Police rig and team had rolled in a flood and come back upright without him. His home country was too full of such stories.

Frank went ahead of Ovide, and when it was his and Dunny's turn to drop into the violent brown, they progressed alongside of quaking ox wagons with chin-deep black *voorlopers* trying to guide their terrified oxen. Frank could not stop imagining these giant rigs heaving into the air and twisting the yoked oxen and black teamsters over with them—their deadly bulk and mangled harness coming for him and Dunny.

] 80 [

When the river's bottom dropped away, Frank felt weightlessness, then a surge forward as Dunny swam. Her head pulsed like a pointer dog's, and though they angled downstream, there was no longer any danger between them and shore. Dunny found bottom again and bucked and fought the rest of the way. She was angry at the whole stupid business.

So powerful had Frank's visions of disaster been that he did not know, when he turned back to the river, whether what he saw was nightmare or real. Behind the veils of rain, probably at the edge of the fallaway to swimming depth, a dark horse was rearing. The river drove it over on its side and the rider, still in his stirrups and clinging, went with it. A brown wave, trimmed in yellow froth, rolled both of them under.

Frank's hair rose and his body quaked with chills. He was thinking of Ovide, who had been next in line behind him on the far shore. Frank looked around in panic, and almost overlooked his cowboy friend who was close behind him, sopping wet and squeezing water from his little mare's mane.

All around, soldiers were pointing and yelling at the wreck. Those whose horses still had strength plunged them back in. Another rider galloped downstream before he turned his horse into the water. This one had a rope unlimbered. He swung it and landed his loop in the water below where the drowning horse was rolling. Inside the floating loop, the horse's head surfaced. The rider dallied, turned, and gave it a hard enough jerk to pull the animal off the trapped soldier. Two others had put their horses in farther below, and one of them caught him by his bandolier.

Frank raced Dunny downstream and helped haul the soldier ashore. He saw that it was Lt. John McCrae, an officer from D Battery. The lieutenant was a doctor who wrote poetry. He had taken the sting out of melancholy nights on the *Pomeranian* with his singing. In Cape Town, he had led a pilgrimage to Rudyard Kipling's hotel. Now, he coughed water and showed other violent signs of life, a great relief to those around him.

Seven hours after the first riders entered the Oliphant, the last ox wagon and field gun was lifted out by thirty-two oxen. A yell of victory burst from the men on shore. In a generous mood, they clapped the black teamsters on their backs, for they were the ones who had been back and forth in the river and in its danger the longest.

The rain-dark day gave way to true night. By then, they had done nothing about camp except identify a slope on the nearest kopje where they might not drown. They tied the horses between the guns, rolled themselves into their oil sheets, and slept.

On the fourth day, the rain stopped. Frank crawled out of his and Ovide's sopping tent. Sergeant Brindle happened to be passing and he told Frank it was March 27.

"One month to the day since we set foot in Cape Town."

Watching other soldiers answer reveille, crawling out of their holes, still wet and caked in mud, gaunt from quarter-rations, it seemed remarkable to Frank that an army could be so reduced in such a short period of time. Ovide was looking like a starved tramp in his filthy oversized clothes, and even the robust Fred Morden looked down on his luck: gaunt-faced and years older. Eddy Belton had kept his weight but Pete looked ever scrawnier beside him. Jeff was one of the few who looked the same.

Sitting by a fire and starting to dry out a little, Frank decided there was some good in this, for the immediate ordeal must soon be over. The dark hungry days of rain, while not healthy, were at least good for sunstroke. Ovide's head had ceased to pain. And the horses, though starving, were in some way rested. When the river stopped rising and the swell passed, they would at least be able to cross back and be with their supplies again.

Ovide came to the fire and sat, smelling like a wet dog. He pointed, and Frank saw the NCOs and sergeants pouring from the officers' mess tent. They spread through camp, and the ones closest ordered the tents down and the wagons loaded. They would march to Kenhardt this morning. Frank asked Ovide to repeat what he had heard, because he could not believe it otherwise.

The Karoo was not built to take water and, as from a duck's wing, the flood kept sliding off, slow or fast according to the contour. The Oliphant was not finished rising and, because the desert between the kopjes was so flat, the water had swallowed the first miles of the Kenhardt road. The flying column was forced inland, travelling where there was no road, where shoals of sand and grit were stranded and must be crossed. For the horses, every step went deep and no walking rhythm was possible. An hour or two of this and they were exhausted. The gun mules could find no traction in the greasy slop. The puny strength of men was added to bring the guns through.

The first day toward Kenhardt was not worth the effort. After just a few miles, the men and beasts were too tired to continue. They stood the tents on the nearest high ground and woke early in the night to find that it was not high enough. The flood had travelled to them, and they had to drag themselves higher and camp again.

Next day and the next were repetitions of the first. The flying column struggled away from the flood and the flood followed. Though they had collected rainwater in their bottles and filled every bucket, the soldiers were running out. They looked at what the storm had left pooling around them and were afraid of it. Dysentery had only stopped sucking at their bones. In some, it had not stopped yet. They feared what would happen if they drank bad water and the dysentery came for another round.

When they saw a farm, and the scouts came back and said it had a well, Frank felt that this was justice. You could only go so long with only bad luck. Then, as the first bucket was raised and they crowded to drink, Lieutenant McCrae smelled something and knocked the bucket over. "No one drink," he said. The rebels had poisoned the well.

It had been hard for many, Frank included, to get a proper hatred going for the Boers. The poisoned well helped. Men who would fight you this way, invisibly, with poison. The farmhouse and barn were too wet to light from the outside, but under the barn's roof beam, some dry straw took the match with a nice woof. When the barn was flaming, Frank went with others into the house. They smashed chairs into kindling and set fire to a rug. They cheered when the fire burst through the thatch.

When they came to another farm and another well, also poisoned, they knew that every well from here to Kenhardt must be tainted. It went without saying that they would burn every farm.

That night, the men sat around a fire with flood water boiling in various containers. Lieutenant McCrae was there, and the boys were after him to explain how he knew it had been poison, and how the Boers would have access to poison, way out here.

Part of the answer was that McCrae was a doctor, newly graduated from the University of Toronto, but he said that poisons were not all that hard to make. The ingredients were often common. This was challenged, and Frank saw that the lieutenant did not like the contradiction.

To make his point more clear, he drew attention to their medicine chest. When they had no medic, the wicker chest was their doctor. On the underside of the lid were instructions: a list of symptoms and beside them numbers. The numbers conformed to pigeonholes in the chest's bottom where you could find a powder, a pill, or liquid in vials.

"Did you read the warning?" asked McCrae.

"Don't mix medicines except those advised," quoted a voice from the dark.

"That's so you don't accidentally mix a poison."

The fellow who had challenged McCrae earlier scoffed at this. The army might be stupid, he said, but it wasn't so stupid as to send soldiers out with a medicine box full of poison.

McCrae became more visibly irritated.

"I won't argue with your ideas on the stupidity of the army," he said, "but I assure you that you are simply wrong on the subject of poison."

Some of the other fellows laughed, and Frank saw the fellow to whom McCrae's comment was addressed flinch. Being told you were "simply wrong" by an educated man was worse than being called a goddamn fool by one your own size.

"If that's so," said the insulted man, "then you tell us how to make a poison out of that box."

Frank could see that McCrae was reluctant but also good and angry. When he did not speak, his challenger said to the others, "See? There's no poison."

McCrae stood up, thin and straight. Frank imagined him slapping the fellow with a glove.

"If you think I am full of hot air," said McCrae, "go to that chest and mix yourself a dose of five and two—with my compliments." He walked away into the dark.

The others around the fire started egging the poison expert on.

"Go on, Mickey. Have yourself a five and two. Prove him wrong."

Mickey told them to shut up and went too. The fun was over for the evening, and everybody followed.

—

As they proceeded toward Kenhardt, Ovide quit riding his mare. She was just a scrap of a horse now, struggling through the flood muck that lay in waves across the road. While Ovide worried about her, Frank worried about Ovide, who was wearing down as well. Each day, he would fall miles behind and not arrive in time for supper. In camp finally, in their tent, he would pour oil into a seashell to make a bitch lamp. Then, with awl, needle, and thread, he would go to work on his boots. Walking in the wet was making them rot and split, and he would sew them up again. Frank could see Ovide's feet looking through holes in his socks. Messed blisters. Areas of red and damp purple.

Their troop leader, Lieutenant Davidson from Pincher Creek, was also paying attention to Ovide. He would ask how Ovide's horse was doing, how the thorn puncture was healing. When Ovide lagged behind, Davidson came and asked Frank where he was. One night, Frank lied to the lieutenant and said he was asleep inside their tent.

On the fifth day on the Kenhardt road, Davidson confronted Ovide as they were about to pull out in the morning. He told him he was not fooled. He knew there was no thorn puncture. He knew the horse was worn out, like many horses were right now. He pointed to Ovide's split and patched boots.

"You will ride your horse today, private. This is a mounted infantry. You will ride until you are ordered to dismount."

The day proved red-hot. The water leaving the flooded country for the sky rose so fast the air looked liquid and everything visible through it was water-coloured and wavy. Frank rode close to Ovide and stuck with him as the cutting mare fell behind. Though Dunny hated walking behind and snorted and tossed her head, Frank held her and made her stay back.

Finally, Ovide's little mare stopped in the beaten road and sank to her knees. Ovide jumped off. The mare convulsed as if to buck, then lay over flat and died. She had burst her heart. Frank believed she was the first of their horses to die without a helping bullet. Thrifty to the end.

Ovide's face was hard to look at. The emotions all boiled over there, and the sunken eyes were deep and glaring.

That afternoon, they arrived at Kenhardt, and this made things worse. Ovide could have led the mare today and got her to the dirty little town.

She could have eaten and rested. She might have lived. Maybe she had died only to prove this was a mounted infantry; that you rode when you were told to.

Captain Meech, the British officer whom Parsons had put in charge of the flying column, led it down the street to a giant tree at Kenhardt's centre. A talkative Boer who knew English told the captain the tree was a camel thorn and five hundred years old. Asked why the town was called Kenhardt, the local said it was the tree's name, as if the tree had named itself and then the town.

The captain told this Boer ambassador to gather all the town's residents, to tell them to come to the camel thorn tree at once. When the people came, a small weathered group, the captain had a private climb up the tree and affix the Union Jack to a limb. He ordered his flying column to parade past the crowd and salute the flag. Frank imagined he was in the crowd and supposed to be awed by this. He would have laughed in his sleeve.

The officer gave a speech. The willing local translated.

"I know that you have been recently occupied by a rebel army from the north. I know these rebels took your scarce food without payment. I want to assure you, that as representatives of the British Empire and of Queen Victoria, we will not do the same."

He said they would only buy what the town could spare them.

The people returned to their homes, and the troops split up to go house to house. Not much was gleaned, either because the rebels had taken too much or because the people were unwilling to give up more. A few sacks of mealies (corncobs), a few bags of straw for the horses. Some cans of mutton fat.

In their camp, the soldiers heated the fat and drizzled it on the straw so the horses got something with strength in it. The hot fat was smelling pretty good. After the soldiers ground mealie kernels into flour for pancakes, they dribbled mutton fat on those as well.

They had been on quarter-rations for ten days. The dysentery, the work of getting here along the gummy roads—all of it had starved them. And they were as hungry after their meal as before. It made no sense. With their naked eyes, they could see sheep and goats grazing the green after the two-year rain. These animals had to belong to someone, yet no Boer had offered a one to sell. Field glasses showed more sheep and goats on the distant kopjes—while they sat here hollow.

When night came, Frank sat with Ovide in silence. They often spent evenings without speaking, but this was a thicker, heavier kind of silence. The weight was oppressive, and the arrival of Fred Morden instantly relieving. He had seen Ovide return to the column riding with Frank on Dunny. Fred knew what that meant, and he told Ovide he was sorry. He said he would do what he could to find him another mount. Ovide nodded. When Morden was gone, Frank thought what good manners he'd shown.

Frank had also thought of saying something to Ovide about a new horse, but was happy Morden had done it instead. It sounded more valid coming from him, more like something that would happen. But Frank also knew that Ovide's problems went beyond not having a horse. It was more that Lieutenant Davidson and the army had forced Ovide to be the means of his mare's destruction. In Ovide's way of thinking, there were certain things you could not forgive. Deliberately killing a horse was chief among them.

"Don't run off or something," Frank said.

Ovide's ragged lips parted. "Where would I go?"

For a fatal few seconds, Frank hovered on the edge of asking again why the hell the old cowboy had ever enlisted in the war. Given his nature (solitary, passive, fond of the familiar), what possible thing had appealed? When the fit of wanting to ask had passed, Frank was glad not to have spoken.

Here in the Great Karoo, he had been considering how the same question applied to himself. He had concluded that it had been a desire to ride a big and fenceless prairie. Further, it had been brought on by Jim's and Doc's endless stories about how fine Alberta used to be when it was wide open and innocent of the plow—when you could cut a fence if you found one and felt it was in your way, but they seldom were. Frank had wanted to ride on Dunny in such a place, so he could talk about it when he was old.

By now, Frank knew he had outfoxed himself. Like a moose to a horse, the Great Karoo was wide open all right, but was nothing like Alberta would have been in that condition. Thinking that it would be like home, but a purer version, had been a dangerous mistake. Except for Dunny's freakish vitality, Frank could have been the one dealing with his grief tonight.

Captain Meech decided overnight that his troops and their horses could have one more day and night of rest in Kenhardt. Then they would start back for Van Wyck's Vlei and, after that, Carnarvon. The duties of the Carnarvon Field Force were all but complete.

Breakfast was more mealie-flour pancakes. The mutton fat was gone and they ate them dry. Meech watched them choking the food down, and the way they stared out into the desert while they endlessly chewed made him decide another speech was needed.

"We are not an unruly mob," he began to the soldiers seated under the camel thorn tree. "As an army of the Empire, our job is to show these people that we hold to a standard higher than the rebels. The rebels invaded this town, gave brave speeches about the virtues of their rebellion, and left the citizenry hungrier and poorer than before. We must do the opposite."

Frank and the others knew in their hollow bellies what was coming.

"We have taken from these people only what they would sell. We will not coerce them to give us more. There will be no looting, and anyone thinking of such a course of action should stop now. I will not tolerate looters. If we have to suffer, we will, with dignity and discipline, because that is the Empire way."

At the end of their hungry day of rest, after the officers had retired to an abandoned mud-brick house they had commandeered, two from D Squadron and one from D Battery went among the Mounted Rifles to announce a meeting. On the side of camp closest to where the Mounted Rifles slept, the men on piquet duty were Rifles too, and the deal was they would turn a blind eye when the men went into the desert and when they came back again.

When the knock came on the tent wall, Frank sat up and Ovide rolled over. Frank had decided to go. He knew it was about food, and he was hungry. He also did not want to miss anything interesting.

On his way to the picket lines, he checked the tent Jeff Davis shared with Casey Callaghan. It was empty. Frank supposed they were out night-patrolling for rebels again. Then Frank decided he was glad they weren't here. Jeff was enjoying his scouting, and the meeting could only jeopardize that. It was a matter of Jeff having something to lose now, and Frank not.

In single file, the soldiers headed for the meeting led their horses between the sentry posts. They mounted after they were clear and aimed for the nearest kopje; stopped when the flank of it lifted them out of the scrub. There was a piece of moon in a clear sky and, by it, they could see sheep and goats.

They dismounted and let their horses graze to the length of their reins. Some sat on their heels and some on the damp ground. Frank recognized quite a few. Pete Belton, without Eddy. The Wilson brothers. Gil Snaddon. Andy Skinner. Fred Morden—which was a surprise. Morden was the only corporal, and none of his usual friends were with him. Except for Morden, those meeting were mainly cowboys.

On the ride out, someone had trotted up beside Frank and asked if the North Fork cowboy, Waldron Hank, could speak for him—meaning for the D Squadron looters. Hank was older and not given to speaking nonsense, so that was fine with Frank. Now that they were all in the circle, Frank saw Pete Belton kneeling beside Waldron Hank, acting like his assistant. Pete did not have the sense to let Hank, or whoever was going to speak for D Battery, go first.

"We're going to get some fresh meat, simple as that," Pete said belligerently, as if someone was already arguing against him. "No English captain's got the right to say we starve when the Boers don't. You can damn well bet Meech didn't go to bed hungry tonight."

Frank looked in his lap in embarrassment. He wished Pete Belton was from some other part of Canada. The Waldron cowboy asked Pete to be quiet a minute.

"This ain't a mutiny," said Waldron Hank. "It ain't about Meech or Parsons or Herchmer. All I think is that, if we play our cards right, we can rope a couple of sheep, butcher them, eat them, and be back in camp with a full belly before anybody's the wiser."

The D Battery spokesman, a gunner from Guelph, said, "I wasn't planning to eat mine raw."

It was a good point. Though the only rebels they'd seen were two old men captured at Carnarvon, some could still be out here. If the Mounted Rifles made a fire to cook their mutton, and Boer rebels saw that fire and came—if there was a fracas and the camp was attacked—it would be court martial for sure. A court martial for something that serious could mean a firing squad.

Everyone fell silent, and the Karoo's night sounds poured in. The *chant-chant* of insects pulled each man's strings tighter. If someone had said, "Quick! Let's go back!" he would not have left alone. But no one spoke or moved.

Out of this silence, Waldron Hank said, "We should go to the other side of the hill to cook the meat. I brought a Warren spade so we can dig a pit. Maybe build a wall. Sling sand on the stones so no light shows through."

"Still show above," D Battery said.

Waldron Hank continued. "Thing is, I can see a sheep from here, and I'm hungry. Anyone who wants to go back, go ahead. Password for the sentries is *Rule Britannia*."

Pete Belton said, "I don't think anyone should be let go back. Otherwise somebody'll tell, sure as hell." Frank looked at Pete and saw he was staring poisonously at Fred Morden.

Waldron Hank saw this as well. "There's no one of that low kind among us. I'll go hungry before I keep a man hostage."

Fred Morden was wearing his Stetson, the flat brim pulled tight over his eyes. The whole of his face was deep in shadow. When he spoke, the tone of voice made Frank think he was smiling.

"I'll admit I came out here to talk you out of looting. I don't think it's right to kill these farmers' sheep at the same time we're asking for their loyalty. I don't think Colonel Parsons would execute men for what you're planning to do, but he could send us home to Canada."

There was a slice of insect noise, then a different cowboy said, "Sounds good to me." They laughed. Morden did too.

"You going back to camp then, Fred?" Hank asked. They would have known each other from North Fork roundups.

"No," said Morden.

They mounted up again and discussed briefly the merits of killing a sheep here and taking it around the other side, or going to the other side and looking for a sheep there.

"The night won't last forever," said Hank. "The sheep are here."

Four ropers pulled their loops long so they hung to the ground. They walked slowly around the sheep, which only dodged a few feet before starting to graze again. Gradually, the ropers pushed them together and a few boys held the bunch while the ropers entered. There was no wild swinging of loops. They treated it like a branding, flipping the toe of the loop where a sheep would step. They dragged two out and men on foot flipped and pinned them. When the first sheep yelled, the holders on both sheep pulled their knives and cut the throats.

They hung the dead sheep over the fronts of their saddles and rode around the kopje at a trot, so the motion bled the meat.

On the far side, where a gully split the hill, they found a deep spot to work in. It was muddy in the pocket and they dug their pit on the moonshady side. While some took turns with the shovel, others built a wall. A few gathered driftwood or feathered kindling sticks. The cowboys were busy skinning the sheep and butchering them on the clean side of the hides.

It was done quickly and, once the fire was lit, they picked lumps of meat, put some on rocks and held more on branches into the hottest part of the flame. Soon the meat was sizzling and drizzling fat. The smell might have sickened them at home but made their mouths run like rivers here.

The first meat came off very rare. Pete Belton noticed that Morden's lap was bare and he speared a piece with his bayonet and carried it over, let it drip its juice just beyond Morden's boot. Frank had been watching too, to see if Morden would eat. Morden reached behind himself, felt around, and came back with a flat-sided stone. He brushed it off, opened his own knife, and stabbed the meat off Belton's bayonet. He placed it on his stone, carved off a bloody corner, and put it in his cheek.

Several more were watching this, and there was a feeling like Morden might give a speech. But the eating was the speech.

Frank was thinking how turned around things were. Cowboys, who were always bragging at home how they would hang a rustler if they ever found one, were at this moment righteously eating rustled meat. The greater crime was not taking part.

When all the best cuts on the two sheep were eaten, Waldron Hank suddenly threw the works, skins and bones, into the firepit, causing a plume of sparks to rise. He took his shovel and started throwing mud. Others pushed the rock wall over the killed fire.

They were thinking it was a job well done when a fellow threw himself flat and put his ear to the ground. "Goddamn it. Horses coming."

A few ran for their Lee-Enfields. A couple crawled into the scrub with their pistols drawn. The horses were coming from the same direction they had.

"Don't nobody shoot," said Waldron Hank.

The horsemen did not come all the way. As they'd been taught in Regina, they dismounted and gave their horses to horse-holders, then started advancing a few at a time on foot.

Hank said, and not in a whisper, "I'm betting these are ours." He stood, raised his hands, and sang out that he surrendered.

A Derbyshire sergeant yelled at them to throw their guns aside. They were to walk in the sergeant's direction with their hands on their heads. It continued like that. They were made to walk all the way back to camp, while riders led their horses, just as though they were captured Boers. Two of the riders herding them were Jeff and Casey. One of the looters got a snake bite while walking and had to be carried across Casey's horse. Back in camp, Captain Meech told them they were under arrest for looting. Their court martial would proceed tomorrow.

The jail selected was the town's library. They sat on the floor among not very many books, just enough that the room stank of old paper. Guards were posted outside. When the officers had gone, the guards looked in and said they were sorry to have to keep the boys jailed but that was the way it was. They would have to shoot them too, if anyone tried to sneak off.

Frank waited for Pete Belton to say something stupid, and he did.

"It's Fred Morden who done us. And that Halfbreed Davis. You saw him in the crowd that come for us."

Frank was surprised to find himself answering.

"Davis and Callaghan were on night patrol when this meeting was arranged. They couldn't have known about it. If Meech told them to help arrest us, they had to, didn't they? And how could Fred Morden tell anybody when he was with us?"

The night was hot and muggy, not having cooled much since day. The room was stuffy. Lizards were falling off the ceiling. Frank could not sleep after the excitement. He was beside Morden and became certain that Morden was awake too. There were things he wanted to know, so he spoke.

"How come you went out there, Fred? Or I guess you said. But why did you eat the meat?"

"I was hungry."

Frank knew that answer was a way of not saying. That did not bother him. Not saying was Morden's right. Frank went directly to imagining what the truth might be. Then Morden spoke.

"I'm a corporal, but I hope to be more than that soon. Even as a corporal, situations could arise where I was the ranking officer. I might have to ask men to do dangerous things. They would need to trust me."

Frank sat in the dark and chewed on that: the idea that Morden had tied his fate to theirs to earn their trust. It was not a thought Frank would have had. First, you would have to care about the war, which Frank was no longer sure he did. Then, you had to be a leader. Frank saw leaders as something born, something you either were or were not.

Frank and Ovide were definite followers. Morden and Jeff Davis were leaders. When Herchmer wanted to kill their horses back in Victoria West, Frank had gone straight for hopeless despair. Jeff had not seen the situation as hopeless at all. He'd made a plan and challenged Herchmer with it. A leader.

This line of thought made Frank feel weak. He rebelled against the severity of the accusation. He might not be a leader, he told himself, but he was someone you could give a job to and he'd get it done. Mr. Billy Cochrane had often picked him for jobs you did alone, like finding lost cattle on the Blood Reserve. But when Mr. Cochrane suggested once that Frank take a crew out cutting corral poles, as crew foreman, Frank had shrugged and blushed and said someone else should do it. He was not asked again.

During this thinking jag, Frank had assumed Fred Morden had fallen asleep. He jumped when Morden asked, "Why did *you* go tonight?"

"I was hungry."

Frank hoped Morden would laugh, and he did. It was a small noise but it stood for laughter. Morden had sounded depressed in their earlier conversation and did again now. Frank guessed it was because the fracas would cost him his corporal stripe.

"I like to see how things turn out," Frank said. It was the real answer.

They sat quietly. There was a crunching sound on the outside of the wall. At home, that would be a porcupine chewing low boards. Here, he couldn't say.

"You said they wouldn't shoot us," Frank said. "Why not?"

"Too far away from the front," Morden said. "If we were at the front, and they thought our actions would touch off a trend of looting, they might then."

"What *will* they do?"

"I think they'll send us back. Either to Canada or to hard labour behind the lines. Out of the war, in any case."

"You're sorry about that, I guess."

"Very sorry. I'll be ashamed before my family and before the town."

"Your father, was he a soldier, then?" Frank meant, at one time. He knew Morden's father was a rancher now.

"No. Just someone who believes in the Empire and doing the right thing by it. I was raised on that idea. Will your family be ashamed of you?"

Frank worked at not laughing. His father would not like it, but would say little and soon forget. Frank's mother would be delighted. She would bake a cake to celebrate. She hated his being in this war, for reasons that might sound treasonous if he tried to explain them to Morden.

"Not much, I guess. You'll think I'm ignorant but I don't even know why a person fights for Empire."

"You're a little late inquiring."

"But I'd like to know. If you care to tell me."

"First of all," said Morden, after he'd paused to think, "you have to believe the British Empire is good. That is, good for the part of the world it rules. Things like the right to vote. Schools. When I went to school in Pincher, there was a picture of Queen Victoria and the Union Jack over the front blackboard. We sang 'God Save the Queen' and 'Rule, Britannia' every day. Memorized poems by Tennyson. I can still recite 'Charge of the Light Brigade.' My father taught me that I wouldn't get that education in a place like Alberta if we weren't part of the British Empire. Fair trials is another thing. I went with my father to Ft. Benton, Montana, a couple of times. I had the impression that if you killed an Indian there, people would cheer."

What Morden was saying was not foreign to Frank, but caring about it was. If Pincher Creek was the edge of Empire, then the Cochrane Ranch must be just off the edge. There were two white schools, Yarrow and Fishburn, within riding distance of the ranch. At his mother's urging, Frank had gone to Fishburn. He'd seen the Union Jack and the picture of the Queen. He'd found the room stuffy, and the teacher had made him sit with the youngest children because he'd never been to school before. She never asked him if he could read, and he never told her he could. He just didn't go to school again.

As for fair trials, Frank's father had taken him to Charcoal's murder trial in Ft. Macleod and then to his execution. Charcoal had killed another Blood for fucking his wife. They chased him for a month, until he killed a Mountie called Sergeant Wilde. If they had caught Charcoal before he killed Wilde, he would have been found not guilty, since killing someone caught fucking your wife was considered justified. When his father took Frank to watch Charcoal hang in Macleod, that was what Frank was thinking: that Charcoal was there on the scaffold about to die because he had not been caught soon enough.

"If you don't mind my asking, Adams, if you don't believe in Empire, why did you enlist?"

"I don't mind, but I don't have an answer."

"Because you wanted to see how it turned out?"

If it had not been dark, Morden would have seen Frank's eyes become suddenly wet. As it was, he made a slurping sound that he turned into a cough. When he could trust his voice, he said, "That's right."

Then there was no more talk, and Frank began to feel very tired. Before his brain lost sense, he wondered why he'd cried just now and decided it was because of friendship. Morden had talked to him honestly. When he said what he'd said last, about seeing how it turned out, it meant he'd been listening too. That struck Frank as a kindness, and so he had cried.

Frank could not have been asleep long when the door yanked open with a yowling of hinges.

"Drop your peters, boys, and get out of here. You bunch of lowly sheep thieves."

It was Harry Gunn.

"What is it, Harry?" asked a private, sounding fearful. He had forgotten all his military manners, probably thinking he was about to be marched into the desert and shot.

"Put it this way: you're damn lucky to have a lieutenant like Hugh Davidson. He's been up all night pleading your case with Captain Meech. You're free to go but you'd better toe the line. There'll be no second chance."

Road to De Aar, April 1900

When the flying column staggered back into Van Wyk's Vlei, they found out many things. The Mounted Rifles trapped on the drowning vlei had gone berserk one night. Their officers had left, presumably to find a drier place to wait out the storm. So the men had formed a mob and looted the town. After that, they'd stolen whisky from their quartermaster, Jack Allan, got drunk, and fought each other. They weren't sure why they hadn't been court-martialled. Maybe because their officers had left them without much justification and with no guidance.

Greasy Griesbach was the one who told them, and Frank was one of the fellows who countered with their own story of stealing sheep. Then the group sharing stories went silent awhile, probably thinking how strange it was that this desert had turned them all into criminals. Then Greasy spoke up again to say that the driver Bradley had drowned in the dam trying to water his team. Their first casualty.

Next day, the officers broke the Carnarvon Field Force apart. Mounted Rifles D Battery was sent to garrison Victoria West. E Battery went north. Squadrons D and C were ordered to the railway junction at De Aar.

All along the march to De Aar, Frank saw flowers, the desert's answer to the rain. Brilliant flowers everywhere, the heat shaking the fanciful colours and making them rise. It was an almost unbearable beauty.

In the Native kraals they came to, the blacks were drumming and dancing. Sometimes Frank's line of march passed close and he could hear those sounds above the shrieking wagon wheels. Through the open gates, he saw lines of people moving; bobbing, jumping. But no matter how close the Mounted Rifles came or how loud they were, no one inside those kraals paused. No black faces turned toward them.

Such a clean and total shutting out reminded Frank of the Bloods at home and how their old people talked about a place in the Sand Hills where they would go when it was time to die. They said it was not far away, and not much different from their present world.

Maybe the rain had removed the screen that separated those two worlds here in the Great Karoo. Maybe the dancers were looking at other dancers in that other place.

Part Three

—

MARCHING TO PRETORIA

We are marching to Pretoria,
Pretoria, Pretoria
We are marching to Pretoria,
Pretoria, Hurrah!

An army friend had just departed General Butler's office, leaving him alone and drunk. His orderly was beyond the door, keeping people away, but there was still the problem of getting out of camp, then the problem of arriving home. This was no common occurrence for Butler. He would have been critical of any other senior officer he found drinking in the afternoon.

Butler stood and reeled, braced himself with both fists on the desk blotter. He shouted for the orderly, who slid in and closed the door quietly behind himself.

"Sir?"

"The damn coffee. Where is it?"

"On the way. Oh, and General?"

"What?"

"I've taken the liberty of ordering your carriage a half-hour later than usual. I could send a note to your wife."

"Yes. No. No note. That will be all. But do hurry with the coffee."

Butler sat back down, heavily. His thoughts churned. The visitor was an Irish-born officer with whom Butler had served in Egypt and Sudan. He had been a young chap then, a lieutenant, and had helped Butler with the system of boats on the Nile. What had walked in the door was a man much older, more so than the interval of years accounted for. His face was gullied, eroded, emptied of all freshness and optimism. Butler had failed to recognize him. Even when he said his name, the general's brain resisted.

Dumphrey. Now Major Dumphrey. Back from South Africa.

Butler stared at the empty decanter, at his and Dumphrey's glasses on the tray. The orderly should have taken it away by now. He stared at the empty chair and made Dumphrey reappear in it. The haggard face, not even shaved. The dark eyes moving in their sockets with a kind of squirm. Initially, Dumphrey had set one hand on the desk, and it hopped there of its own accord like something from a pond.

"General Butler, might we have a drink?"

"Celebrate your return, Dumphrey. Of course."

"A drink, at any rate."

Studying the man, Butler kept returning to the jacket, done up to the neck. Jackets had to fit so tightly nowadays. Officers insisted their tailors take out every bit of slack. They wanted a slender look, like a whippet, and posture like a sword. If you added anything, an undershirt even, or gained a pound, it showed. That was how Dumphrey looked: bunchy for all that he was thin. Then Butler understood: it was a cloth bandage, wrapped around him from the armpits to the waist. Torn up by shrapnel, likely, or riddled with Mauser bullets. It was no longer rare for a man to come back shot in several places.

Dumphrey threw back his first drink. Butler poured him another.

What had happened to Dumphrey was Paardeburg, followed by a stint in a Bloemfontein hospital. When enteric fever started raging there, they'd moved him to Cape Town. Then home.

Though Dumphrey still looked unhealthy in body, it was his nerves that were most acutely injured. You often saw this with younger soldiers who'd been in an attack for the first time, or who'd been left wounded on a battlefield overnight. The nerves would go, and they would chatter and cry. Getting a mess tin to their lips was like climbing the Matterhorn.

More seasoned officers were assumed to be immune, having seen so many battlefields and wounds. But here was Dumphrey, no poltroon, fluttering like an aspen leaf.

Initially, Butler had not tried to match him drink for drink, but the other's rapid imbibing caught him up. After the first three, the knot of

Dumphrey's body eased and he relaxed deeper into the chair. He had undone his jacket to make room for that relaxation, and a spot of fresh blood was revealed below the rib cage. When Butler pointed it out, Dumphrey made a *not again* face, drew his handkerchief, and pushed it between the buttons of his shirt.

That was why Butler had drank, he remembered now. He was trying to help Dumphrey relax, reasoning that a drinker was more at ease if the other fellow drank too.

Butler had inquired about the war, narrowing in on his own concern, which was how Roberts was running up the gut of Africa and distancing his supply convoys. But Dumphrey had no interest in the current state of things. His war had ended at Paardeburg. When he started to speak, compelled to speak like a freezing man trying to warm himself with words, Butler realized Dumphrey's war had also *begun* at Paardeburg. Whatever else there'd been, the nine-day battle was all that remained.

"We couldn't believe our luck when Cronje laagered up. He needn't have, you know. French's cavalry had caught him, but couldn't have held him. Cronje circled his wagons in a flat beside the Modder. Some said it was the women. Cronje should have taken his soldiers and run. Left the women. But he wouldn't."

As Dumphrey described the scene, Butler saw it. He had travelled deep inland during his two stints in South Africa; had seen with his own eyes how the Boers camped with their wagons in a circle. If threatened, they stuffed the gaps with thorn bush. It was how they had trekked inland and fended off the Africans.

Dumphrey kept on with his jittery retelling of Paardeburg. Lieutenant-General Kelly-Kenny had been in charge at the start. From a couple of little kopjes, the British had Cronje's laager in range of their guns. The thing to do was pound the Boers' kraal and trenches, and Kelly-Kenny was about to do that.

But then along came Lord Kitchener with orders from Roberts that Kelly-Kenny was to stand aside and let him run the show. The minute Kitchener had the reins, he called for an all-in attack. That was February 18. It went on all day, even after it started to pour rain.

"The Canadians and the Highlanders took an awful cutting up. Such a wide, flat space. Hardly a bush to advance behind."

Dumphrey had stiffened again. Butler poured his glass full, and the major swatted it across the room trying to grasp it. Butler drew a fresh glass and poured, waving away the apology. "Go on, Dumphrey. I want to hear."

Dumphrey was with General Kelly-Kenny, whom Kitchener had put in charge of the frontal assault. It was murder, as the Boers were dug in on the far bank of the river and could see the approach. Kelly-Kenny's men ran out onto the plain, unsupported. Cronje's Mausers took target practice on them. They faltered, threw themselves flat; crawled behind anthills. Kitchener was on a hill miles away, watching the advance falter and stop. He sent riders demanding renewed attacks, more bravery, more sacrifice.

Sometimes, Kitchener's orders were so absurd the men receiving them thought they must be a mistake or an enemy trick. Kelly-Kenny was ordered to cross the river. He refused. So many of his men were dead and wounded already.

Perhaps the saddest thing, said Dumphrey, was what happened to Colonel Hannay. Hannay commanded a unit of mounted infantry and had crossed the Modder upstream of Cronje. The order he received from Kitchener was that he and his riders must attack the laager at once and fire into it.

"Fire into their laager." Dumphrey laughed despairingly. "So good old Hannay, he sent a lot of his men away on errands before he disclosed what he was ordered to do. He finally told the remaining men about the attack. They all knew what it meant, but quite a few said they'd go. Men devoted to him. His old hands."

"Did you see it, Gerald?"

"No, no. I was shot up by then. A fellow I met in the field hospital was one of them. A lucky one, just wounded. He told me Hannay made no speech, just turned his horse and went. For a long time, Hannay wasn't hit, even as fellows were dropping behind him. But then, his horse took it in the chest. Fell and pitched Hannay over its head. He jumped up and kept advancing. The fellow in the hospital said Hannay went down for good three hundred yards from the first Boer trench."

Dumphrey's cheeks were streaming wet, rivulets riding the furrows to his chin.

"I can't imagine what I'll do, William, if they want me to go back."

"How on earth did we win that battle, Major?"

Dumphrey gathered himself, prepared to do his duty by the conversation.

It was complicated, he said. He wondered sometimes if he understood it. Somewhere along the line, De Wet had arrived and taken possession of a hill Kitchener had abandoned. He had a pom-pom, which he used to rake the field hospital.

"Got half my wounds right there under the red cross. After the first battle, Kitchener shelled Cronje's laager for days. Night, too. During that time, De Wet was signalling Cronje to come to him, but Cronje wouldn't. De Wet got disgusted and left. Nine days after it started, the white flags went up and the Boers threw their rifles out of the trenches."

Dumphrey turned his face to Butler. He tried to control his wet, squirming eyes. The effort was too much for him.

"They had us beat, William," he said. "If De Wet had stayed on that hill with his pom-pom, we might have been the ones running up the white flag. But Cronje gave up before we could. And now Kitchener is Britain's darling, again. If I could laugh, I'd laugh myself to death."

When the carriage rolled up in front of Butler's rented house, he'd had a few miles of wet wind to wash the liquor out of him. Still, he expected Elizabeth to be cool when he came through the door, as he was very late. But she sang out from somewhere in the rear. Her studio was back there. When she appeared, she was wearing her smock. She gestured with a fat brush that he was to follow.

"It's done, William. Finally."

She meant the commission. For months, she'd been struggling with a commission from the War Office. By the timing of their request, Butler had guessed they were looking for something to take the sting out of the early defeats in South Africa. But Elizabeth had been all secrecy. For the first time ever, she had not told him what her painting was about. Now she was inviting him into her studio to see it.

"I'm sorry, William, that I kept you in the dark. They wanted something inspirational, you see, something from the current war. You're so very negative about South Africa that I was certain you'd say, 'Nothing about this war is inspirational.' That would not have helped."

They were in the studio now. She was leading him to an easel, covered in a cloth. She took the cloth by one corner, pursed her lips, and made a bugle sound; whipped the veil away.

"Paardeburg!" she crowed.

Butler squinted.

"Not so close, William. I always tell you it does no good to inspect my brush strokes."

"I want to see the detail."

What he had leaned toward was the mounted figure, galloping toward two covered wagons at the centre. The rider had dropped his reins and had his rifle to his shoulder, sighting down it. The line of fire was toward a gap between the wagons. In the gap was a bearded Boer soldier whose look said he knew he was done for. Before thinking, Butler loosed an oath.

"William!"

He turned his back on the painting; stared at a pile of frames in a corner. His cheeks were burning. He felt drunk again.

"Never mind," he said.

"Oh no," she said. "You have *never* looked at one of my paintings and actually *cursed* before. I will have an explanation."

Butler continued to look at the frames, but he knew she meant it. She would not let him keep his thoughts to himself, now that he had crudely indicated their direction.

"Fine, then," he said. He turned to her painting and pointed his finger at the rider.

"That man is Colonel Hannay. That man is dead. He died three hundred yards farther back than your picture suggests. No British soldier at Paardeburg ever got this close."

Now it was night, and his wife and he were in bed. Not sleeping. Not speaking. Both angry. It would not change for the foreseeable future.

De Aar Junction

Three weeks in the Karoo desert and the Mounted Rifles finally made it back to the railway, at De Aar. A train huffed in from the south as they were approaching across the last span of waste. They cheered to see it.

Then they were cheered themselves, briefly, as they passed down De Aar's dusty main street. The people clapping and whistling were *uitlanders*, the Boer word for anyone not Boer. They could tell from the quick and desultory quality of the cheering that the locals had cheered many soldiers at this place and were tired of it. The ragged soldiers marched through and out the other side, toward a smoking town of canvas.

Major Howe, the Mountie officer who was in charge of them now, was waiting at the road entrance to camp with two black men and a cart heaped with mail. They had been half expecting Herchmer, but Howe told them the colonel was still in Cape Town, recovering. He'd sent a message to expect him farther down the road. As for Major Sanders, he was mended, but there were other plans for him, something involving Boer prisoners shipped abroad.

Howe led the way to their place in camp. The two black men hauling the mail cart trailed him, one in the handles and the other pushing from behind. They stopped at a sand-drifted spot on a windy edge, already littered with mess from bygone soldiers. Mail and newspapers fluttered in the scrub. Rags of khaki and rotten boots suggested some outfit had received new uniforms here.

They were told to set up camp and see to the horses. Mail distribution would follow.

Frank and Ovide threw up their tent in quick time. Someone watching might have thought they were hurrying to get at their mail, but what they wanted was horse detail. Minding horses was their way of avoiding latrine duty, burning litter, or manning an outpost. They were good with horses, attentive and thorough, and Lieutenant Davidson usually allowed them the choice if they got there early.

When they were watering horses in the town's dugout, they saw the mark where the water had risen to in the rain and flood, and how it was already down two feet in service of the camp. Returning to the picket line for more horses, they heard names being shouted. They could see the lucky ones running to get their letters and parcels, like children on Christmas morning.

"Think you'll get a cake, Ovide?"

That would have been cruel had there been any hope of Frank receiving mail. But he was confident he wouldn't. Frank's mother could write, but he'd never seen her write a letter. His father had a sister named Polly in Ontario who sent him a fat letter every month. Every third one, he sent a postcard back: *Nothing new here. Jim.*

Frank and Ovide kept on watering, and putting on feed bags and hay nets. They salved sore spots on the kind of horse that clips itself when it walks. There were injuries of all kinds. The work kept Frank from homesick envy and kept him from picking up some other soldier's thrown-away letter. It would be a pleasure to read one, but it would also be pathetic.

As they were finishing up, they could smell food. But instead of eating, they were ordered into formation in front of three officers, Major Howe and two British ones. Howe spoke first. The Carnarvon Field Force was disbanded, he said, as of their arrival here. Then he introduced the younger of the two British officers.

This one explained that they were now under the command of Major-General Hutton—a Canadian general, as he was sure the men knew. The Royal Canadian Dragoons were also in Hutton's brigade, as would be Lord Strathcona's Horse when that battalion arrived from Canada. All three Canadian mounted battalions were under the direct command of brevet Lt.-Col. E.A. Alderson.

The officer swung a hand toward the officer who had not yet spoken. It turned out to be Colonel Alderson himself. With some prompting from Howe, the boys saluted and Alderson saluted back.

Alderson began his speech by congratulating them for their successes in the Great Karoo. Thanks to them, he said, the rebels were back north of the Orange River. The liberation of the three Karoo towns meant people in the southern Cape could breathe more easily again. They stood there trying to believe what was said about them. There was no mention of their never having fired a shot at a Boer, or of being sheep looters and whisky thieves. Later, while eating a mutton supper, they did laugh and were stared at by men in other outfits.

After supper, a fellow came around with Young Men's Christian Association stationery and a can of sharpened pencils. He encouraged them to write to their mothers. Fred Morden was already writing. Using a book as a desk, he was scribbling fast. He had a fat package of letters from his girlfriend, and more from his parents. If he got his letters done, they could go on a southbound train before the Mounted Rifles moved on. Frank was surprised to see Jeff Davis take a pencil and sheet of paper. Jeff put the paper on his saddle seat and started printing. He went at it slowly, pausing often to think.

Frank tried to imagine doing that. He had never in his life written a letter. Printing his name at the bottom of the postcards to Aunt Pol was as close as he'd come. Now he was drawn to the idea. He composed something in his head and imagined what it would look like on paper.

We are in a camp by a railroad. We were in a desert where the horses had nothing to eat. Dunny held up good as any. Then there was rain and we almost drowned. But it's hot and dirty again. I have seen no Boer rebels except prisoners.

The sound of it was very dull. But, dull or not, he knew his parents would be proud and would show their friends, who would also be proud. They would all pretend it was the most exciting thing ever written, and this embarrassed him so much he was certain he would never do it.

What the folks at home mainly wanted to know was whether he was alive. The perfect thing would be one of those postcards his father bought at the drugstore for Aunt Pol. It was always the same postcard, showing the Macleod barracks and a Mountie beside it. The idea of having a card like that, some picture of Africa, and writing, *Still kicking. Frank,* appealed to him so much he resolved to buy one as soon as he got a chance.

During the evening, some Tommys came and asked if the Canadians would like to get up a side for a tug-of-war. Everybody called low-ranking British soldiers Tommy Atkins or Tommys, and Frank had taken to doing so too. Some of the Tommys were already kicking around a bunch of old uniform shirts tied into a ball. Just the thought of pulling on a rope for no reason made Frank weary, and the reaction of the others was the same. The Tommys went off looking for a spunkier bunch and found some willing Australians.

As it darkened, the night was clear and warm, and the wind had died. Frank and Ovide did not bother with their tent. But Frank found he could not sleep when he tried. In his head, he began a letter to Uncle Doc, which was easier and more exciting than the one to his parents. Doc and Frank's conversations had always been freewheeling and tended toward the salty and disrespectful.

Dear Doc. Both our commanding officers, Herchmer and Sanders, are laid up in Cape Town. If this keeps up, Hugh Davidson will come home a general. These officers aren't shot. They are sick. Nobody has been shot. I haven't even seen a Boer rebel except for prisoners. What's dangerous in this country is the country itself, and your own officers, and maybe yourself.

I got Ovide Smith as a tent partner. Ovide works for Jughandle Smith but isn't related. He's about perfect as he doesn't fart or snore. It's like he dies each night and rises from the dead each morning. Ovide and I hate what they do with horses here. The commander tried to have my dun mare and Jeff Davis's blue mare shot for being pale. Ovide had a pretty little cutting mare. She pushed herself too hard and blew up her heart. If I pointed at somebody and told Ovide that's the man who started this war, Ovide would blow his head off and face the firing squad with a grin. Horses are not valuable here. Men might not be either.

Three fellas in D Battery went to a hotel in Cape Town and met Rudyard Kipling. It was Lieutenant McCrae's idea. He's a gunnery officer who writes poetry and sings. Kipling asked them questions for something he might write. I was with McCrae in the Great Karoo Desert.

That Karoo was one hell of a place. What you'd call a moose to a horse. I thought it would kill us or our officers would, or we might kill them or each other. All the stops were pulled.

Frank was about to start in about how he was worried about Ovide, who had hardly spoken since his horse died—and how frightened he himself had been when it looked like he would lose Dunny. Same when they crossed that roaring river and he thought the wagon would roll over on him.

Frank stopped his imaginary writing there. He would not want Doc to know that things frightened him, and that he was especially afraid of getting pulled away from who he was. To be a stranger to yourself was an awful idea and he feared it most.

Frank thought of Jeff Davis and wondered who he could have written to. It would not be his mother, who probably could not read. He didn't know how Jeff and his father got along. It might be a brother or his sister.

Then Frank wondered if Jeff had a girlfriend. He had not mentioned one, but Jeff was the kind who might not say. Frank liked this idea best and went on imagining it: Jeff writing to a girlfriend, just like Fred Morden wrote to his.

Still not sleeping, Frank thought finally about mysteries. Jeff Davis surely was one, and Frank considered what went into that. Being quiet was not enough. Frank and Ovide could be quiet as mice and never become anybody's mystery. But Jeff's silence was mysterious. Frank wondered if it was a combination of silence and size, then, or silence and being part Indian. He rejected those ideas too.

The key to being a mystery, Frank concluded, was that people had to care what was going on behind the silence. People did care about Jeff, and wished they could see into his head. Frank knew because he wished it too.

Norvals Pont

De Aar was a junction, and its importance was that you could cross from there to the central railway, the one that went northeast toward Johannesburg and Pretoria. The central railway also went to Bloemfontein, the current front in the war—or where the war was currently stalled.

When the Mounted Rifles boarded an eastbound train, they were excited. The front beckoned to men like Fred Morden and Reg Redpath, for whom the dream of glory (or duty) still existed, but it also called to those who cared little about glory and wanted to go home. The front was where the war could be won. It was the fire you had to run through to get away.

At the central railway, they were put on another train headed north to the Orange River. That was the frontier between the Cape Colony and the first rebel republic. At the river was a high steel bridge with its middle span blown out. To replace it, the army engineers had built a pontoon bridge, a wooden floor atop a series of boats. The floating bridge sank beneath them, and they got wet. But finally, late that day, they stood on enemy soil. They were exulting about that when their officers told them they were not going any farther. They were to relieve the New Zealand garrison here at Norvals Pont and guard the bridgehead until further notice.

In that moment of being told they were stopping, Frank discovered he still had an urge to fight. Even the Karoo had not killed it. Like most everybody—everybody, that is, but Ovide—he was disappointed that the war was going to elude them again. Ovide really did not care if he ever fought. The war was just a hole in his life that he hoped would get filled somehow.

The Kiwis had their gear piled by the tracks. They did not yet have a train but there was the promise of a train. When it came, they would be heading for the war. Buoyed by this, they were keen and welcoming, and wanted to tell the glum Canadians everything there was to know about Norvals Pont. Mainly, they would have to keep a lookout at night. Some Boers were in the hills to the north, and these snuck down at night to snipe. A couple of times the Boers had faked a major attack. When the camp was roused, they faded back.

But the best thing about Norvals Pont—and they led the Mounted Rifles to the centre of the camp—was the baboon.

In the middle of a ruined sheep kraal stood a telegraph pole. Chest high from the ground, a platform had been built around the pole, about seven feet square. On that platform, a round-backed beast with a dog's face sat glowering. It was chained by the neck to the pole.

Frank knew it was a baboon. He had seen this kind of monkey loping across the Karoo. They ran in groups. It was not immediately clear to him, though, why this sour-faced thing on the platform was special. While Frank and the others stared, the ugly monkey sat with its mouth wide open, canines longer than a wolf's, occasionally flashing its crimped rope of tail.

The Kiwis said it was a male baboon that must be fed and cared for at all costs, because he was the best sentry an army could have. The slightest night movement beyond camp, and this baboon would screech and throw himself against his chain. He would even point. They had estimated that he could see (or somehow sense) disturbance at more than one hundred and fifty yards—even at night! The job here at Norvals Pont was to man a bunch of Cossack posts fanning out to the north. The New Zealanders confided that, after a while, they hadn't bothered occupying the closer posts. They slept and let the baboon do the job.

The Kiwis had caught the baboon with a net when he came into camp to steal food. They reckoned he was alone, and the theory was that he'd been separated from his gang during the recent flooding. There were several ideas about his scouting behaviour, but a favourite was that he thought every movement out on the veldt might be his friends. His fuss was an attempt to let them know where he was.

By the time the New Zealanders' train came and went, the Mounted Rifles had their camp set up and their chores done. Major Howe had decided which men would go to what outpost for the night, but since it was still just late afternoon, he did not send them. They might as well eat supper and go toward dark. Until then, they could sleep or play sports.

Frank and Ovide drifted back to the sheep kraal and the baboon. Most everybody had. Fellows were trying various kinds of foolishness to get the animal to react. Calling to him. Throwing bits of rock that hit off his hide. Making faces, as they thought another monkey might.

But the baboon was not in any mood to play. He just sat there, with his deep-socketed frown, occasionally showing his big yellow canines. A couple of young privates—Henry Miles, from north of Pincher Creek, and Gil Snaddon, a cowboy from the Willow Creek—brought long sticks and went to opposite sides of the platform. As they probed at the baboon, he stayed close to the pole in the middle, attentive and still.

Determined to get a rise out of him, the two fellows lunged so they were actually poking him. The instant their hands came within the reach of the baboon's chain, he flew through the air. He swung his head and gashed Snaddon's hand. Then he sprang the opposite way and bit Miles' finger. Both men were left bleeding.

Snaddon had drawn his Colt. Fred Morden was watching and jumped between Gil and the animal. He told Gil he would arrest him if he shot the baboon. While these two exchanged opinions on rank, Frank watched Jeff Davis work himself to the platform's edge. He began making bird and animal sounds.

Jeff did not stop at an owl, like most people would. He screeched like a hunting hawk and knocked like a woodpecker. His raven wasn't just a croak or a knock but a whole suite of complicated nonsense. Elk's bugle, moose's mating call, the howls of wolf and coyote—he really had a repertoire. He did it so well Frank was homesick.

During the fight, the baboon had been screeching, but now he fell silent. He sat back on his bony haunches and studied Jeff with a professor's intensity. After a while, the baboon started to answer him. It was like a contest, or so they thought. Gil, who had calmed down by now, stopped sucking his bleeding hand and said, "That damn monkey's trying to ape Jeff."

He meant imitation, and as soon as he said it, Frank could hear it too.

Jeff's response was to start imitating the baboon's imitations of him. Frank thought this was going in the wrong direction, because the baboon was a much poorer mimic than Jeff. But the baboon did not see it that way. He became more excited than ever, jumping and hitting the end of his chain so hard it flipped him over. He was making a brand-new sound: baboon applause. Probably, the baboon thought the human had progressed.

When the first smell of meat came off the fires, soldiers started leaving. Finally, only Frank and Ovide remained, watching and listening to the developing friendship between Jeff and the baboon. Jeff asked them to watch the baboon a minute and ran off. It did not like this despite Frank and Ovide doing their best owl hoots and wolf howls. Then Jeff returned with his oil sheet and bedroll. He said he wasn't assigned to any outpost tonight, so he was going to keep the baboon company. He made his bed outside the kraal, where the wall was broken down.

The mealtime bugle finally blew, and the three of them left to eat. The baboon had an angry fit and kept on screeching and yelling. Between bites, Jeff tried some of his sounds. Though they were seventy yards at least from the kraal, the baboon quieted. Jeff waited until it started yelling again and tried his responses in a quieter voice. The baboon stopped even then.

Lieutenant Davidson was sitting near Jeff, having his supper. He said that if Davis had been assigned to outposts tonight, he would have unassigned him. Obviously, keeping the baboon happy was central to everyone's rest.

Ovide was still dependent on a loaned horse, and tonight it was Jeff's blue. Ovide was the only rider The Blue would accept besides her owner. Frank and Ovide got their horses ready and thought they would check on the baboon kraal on the way out. Jeff was leaned over the wall, making his sounds as they approached. But right behind him—and Jeff did not know it—sat a British major on his horse. The major was watching the performance and getting angrier by the second. Frank made himself have a coughing fit until Jeff turned, and that was when the major tied into him. Was this beast his little pet? Did he think he was in a zoo? And so on.

Lieutenant Davidson heard the ruckus and came to check. The major switched his attention to him.

"This private with his baboon seems not to have noticed that we're in the middle of a war. I want him put on sentry duty immediately." Finally, he rode off.

Davidson was in a quandary. Sending Davis was now an order from a British major. But what about the baboon? As soon as Davis left, he would start screeching and keep everyone awake. And how would they know whether the baboon was screeching about Davis's absence or about Boers sneaking up?

Davidson was thinking all this aloud, and his final decision was to keep Davis close by. There was a bit of wall within sight of the camp, maybe a five-minute walk into the scrub. It was a place Jeff could stand and technically be on duty, if the major returned. Based on what had happened at supper, Davidson was guessing Jeff could keep the baboon happy at that distance.

After getting his Lee-Enfield and filling his water bottle, Jeff started out. Frank and Ovide rode beside him. Halfway to the wall, the baboon started yelling. Jeff made some of his noises, first loud, then softer, until he found the margin where the baboon started not to hear him. He kept it up out to the wall, and all was calm. It was like the baboon was a gun on a trip-wire: quiet but set to go off.

That was all Frank and Ovide saw. They were already late for their Cossack post, which was a mile farther out. The other soldiers were already there. Frank and Ovide sparked their horses to a gallop so they could get there before dark.

Pete and Eddy Belton had not been chosen for night duty, as was usual. Pete's performance in the Great Karoo had been erratic enough that no one wanted him or his brother as Cossack-post mates, especially at night. Lieutenant Davidson liked to do what his men wanted, and so saved the Beltons for daytime chores.

Pete had spent the early evening watching Jeff Davis's baboon show, and had been hiding in the shadows later when the British major came along.

Later still, when Davidson made his plan for giving Davis sentry work, Pete was listening, and he followed at a distance when Smith and Adams went out toward the wall with Davis. After that, he found Eddy and dragged his brother to a place where they could not be heard.

The fact was, Davis's celebrity in the matter of the monkey was more than Pete Belton could bear. Raised to hate Indians, Pete never thought he would see the day when a whole camp of whites would suck up to a Halfbreed. He had vowed to get back at Davis and his blue cayuse for the death of his gelding. The more he thought about it, the more he felt tonight was the right time. His plan was not refined as yet, but he was pretty sure it involved poison. He could start on that part while he thought out the rest. He would tell Eddy only the slightest bit, because the big fool seldom understood things the right way and would ask stupid questions.

What he told Eddy was that he was not feeling well, that he was sun-struck. He wanted Eddy to go get him some medicine.

"You better go, Pete. I'll get it wrong."

"You won't get it wrong. It's just two numbers: five and two. You don't even have to mix them. You just bring them."

"Why don't you go yourself?"

"Because I'm sick. Aren't you goddamn listening?"

Then he told Eddy one more thing. If he met anyone on the way, he must not tell them the numbers of the medicine he was after. He was to ask them to help him get something for sunstroke. Leave it at that.

"Why do I have to do that last part?"

"Because five and two is a secret medicine. A medicine the officers use when they get sick. If you say five and two, it'll get us in trouble. Just say you got sunstroke. They'll give you something, and that will be the end of it."

"I thought *you* had the sunstroke."

"I do, damn it! It's just simpler if you say it's you."

It took quite a while, but Eddy came back with a vial and an envelope of powder. No one had been at the medicine chest. What had taken so long was having to strike matches to find the right pigeonholes and then filling the envelope with powder in the dark.

While Eddy was gone, Pete had been thinking hard about *what* to poi-son. His first thought was to poison Davis's horse. It would certainly hurt

Davis to have his blue cayuse killed, and would neatly settle the score. But Ovide Smith had the horse tonight, so it wasn't possible.

Pete's next thought was to poison Davis himself, but there were problems there too. At mealtimes, they were just grabbing chunks of mutton off a fire or scooping mush out of a bucket. He couldn't poison Davis without killing half the squadron, and possibly himself.

Then Pete had an exciting thought. To hell with poison! Jeff Davis was out there in the dark tonight, all alone and not far away. Pete could leave the camp and sneak past that wall Davis was guarding from. He could sneak past it and then come back toward him *just like a Boer*. There wasn't much moon, but probably enough to see Davis's hat against the sky. Pete was a marksman. If he could see the hat, he could shoot Davis dead.

The problem, as usual, was Eddy. He could wait for Eddy to go to sleep, but by then it would be too dark to see Davis against the sky. And if Eddy woke and found Pete gone, he'd probably come looking for him. If Pete was out shooting Davis at the same time as Eddy was telling somebody he was missing, it could get him caught. Pete decided he had to tell Eddy about his plan.

After he finished explaining why he wanted to shoot Jeff Davis tonight, Eddy was stone still, barely breathing. He had no toughness. He never wanted to hurt anyone.

"Course you don't want to hurt Davis. 'Cause it wasn't your horse. My horse and I'm getting even."

"What about the baboon?" Eddy asked.

Pete was about to sock Eddy for never keeping his mind on one thing when he realized Eddy was right. If they started sneaking out toward Davis, and the baboon was as smart about hearing things as the New Zealanders said, the bastard would start yelling and stir up the camp. Pete could be taken for a Boer and shot.

Then Pete had it. He really had it this time! He had thought up a way to kill Davis, to quiet the baboon, and to use the poison—all three!

"First thing, Eddy," Pete said, "we'll give the baboon the medicine. The medicine puts you to sleep. It's why it works for every kind of ailment. Makes you sleep so sound you don't know you're sick."

The brothers went first to where they'd eaten supper. There'd been a box of apples for dessert. They were wormy and fellows had either left them or taken them for their horse. There were a few left, and Pete grabbed two. At their camping spot, Pete pulled his oil sheet overtop of him and Eddy, and got Eddy to strike a match. By the light, he cut a hole in the apple and poured five and two in the hole. Then he corked it with the piece he'd carved out and shook the apple hard.

"Don't forget to save some for yourself," Eddy said.

"I'm better now. Shut up."

Pete emptied the vial and envelope into the second apple.

At the platform, the baboon was a hunched shape by the centre pole. His body was pointed in the direction Davis had gone. Pete rolled the first apple across the platform toward him. The baboon grabbed it with a sudden motion, threw it in his mouth, and crunched. Same thing with the second one.

They stayed and watched until the baboon groaned and threw himself down on the platform, shuddering.

"He don't look to be sleeping very well, Pete."

"Maybe it's too strong for a baboon. Hell with it, he's quiet anyway."

Then Pete went and got his rifle and they began sneaking out of camp.

The whole night was a place of concealment. Who would stay in one place behind a wall so his enemy would know where to find him? Never assume that a hat showing behind a wall has a head in it. That was the way Red Crow had taught Jeff Davis to think.

Jeff stayed at the little wall long enough to rebuild it. The stones had been piled without mortar and had fallen. After he had repiled them, he found a dead branch and wedged it into the rocks, then set his Stetson on the branch's end. He spoke to the baboon every little while, as he did these things.

The night had a sliver of moon showing yellow through wisps of cloud. The noise of the river was distant. The insects chanted but there were no other wild sounds, of kills or kills defended. It was a quiet night for Africa. Davis walked back into camp. The baboon had been silent for some time, and he wanted to know why.

At the platform, he saw that the baboon was lying on his side. Every few seconds, his legs came up in a jerk toward his barrel gut. The baboon's teeth ground inside the grimace of his face.

Davis struck a match and hid it in his hand. He ran the light along the animal's hair. He saw bits of vomit, bits of apple with a chemical stink.

Davis left the camp. Rather than toward the pale spot that was the wall, he went fifty yards to its right. He was beyond the wall when a rifle fired from still farther out. He saw the flash and heard the bullet go toward his wall. Bent low, he ran and let the sliver of moon show him a way through the scrub. He ran for the gun flash, but wide to the right. It was the only shot. He could hear men shouting behind him in the camp. Sergeants were blowing whistles.

When Davis stopped, he heard his heart pounding. Once his heart slowed, he heard a drag of cloth through the hard brush on his left. He heard ragged breathing.

Jeff twisted his mouth and said, "Didja kill 'im, Pete?"

"Shut up, Eddy."

"I didn't say nuthin," the real Eddy said.

"I told you shut up."

The wall was about fifty yards away, between them and the camp. The smaller shape in the dark was Pete. Eddy's larger form was to Pete's right. Davis was behind Pete now and tapped the mouth of his Colt on the bone of Pete's neck.

"Rifle on the ground." He tapped again.

Pete bent and set his rifle down. Coming up, he grabbed for his revolver. The holster was empty. The Colt was already in Jeff's waistband.

"Goddamn you. Who are you?"

"The one you just killed."

"Davis? That can't be. I shot you in your goddamn head. I saw your hat fly."

"Pete?" It was Eddy calling to his brother, wanting instruction.

Pete said to be quiet.

"You've got a Colt revolver in your hand, Eddy Belton," Jeff said. "Put it away in your holster."

Davis heard this happen. More commotion was coming from the camp. Voices approaching. He could hear Lieutenant Davidson calling his name, appealing to him to answer.

"What you gonna do with us?" Pete asked.

"Come here, Eddy Belton."

The big man stepped closer, dragging himself through the brush. Davis took him by the arm and pulled him close to his brother.

"Both of you, kneel down."

"He's gonna kill us now, Pete." Eddy said it without emotion, a statement of fact.

"Shut up!"

Davis laid his rifle barrel on Pete's shoulder.

"Go on, you bastard."

"You tried to kill me, Pete Belton," Jeff said. "It didn't work. Now you're going to serve me. Both of you will do what I ask. You'll guard me all the time."

"You're letting us live?"

Davis told them to get up. He told them to take their rifle with them. They were to go twenty paces north and lie down under the scrub. They were not to move.

"I'll guide them around you."

Davidson's voice kept appealing. "Davis? Can you hear me? Answer if you can."

Davis imagined that he was a Boer, come to ambush. The next bullet would go into that voice.

When Frank and Ovide rode into camp at dawn, they were unaware of what a wild night it had been. They had heard one shot, and had assumed it was a sniper, but the whistles and the rest had not carried to them.

The story they were told over breakfast was that the sniper had come within an inch of killing Davis; had put a bullet hole in the crown of Davis's Stetson. Jeff had taken after the Boer but had not found him.

A strange part of the story was that the baboon had died in the night. They thought maybe the sniper's bullet carried into camp after going through the hat; that the baboon had been shot. But there was no blood and no hole in the animal's hide.

The baboon had been damn sick. There was vomit and shit all over the platform. Bits of apple, for some reason, though no one admitted feeding him one.

A fanciful few said they smelled poison, but why on earth would a Boer sneak into a British camp, poison a baboon, and leave without doing further damage? The ones who said poison were laughed at, and that was the end. It was too bad, though. The baboon had been an interesting animal.

Frank thought the baboon's death would bother Jeff Davis, but when Frank finally saw the scout, it was as if he did not care.

Road to Bloemfontein

The crooked beaks of the vultures were painted red but they were too sated to eat. They coiled their elastic necks and clutched their feathers around themselves; hopped on and off the gutted bodies, competing to be inside the zone of strongest stench: the roaring signature of plenty. Better this than all the droughts and plagues of history: this paradise of war.

Relieved at Norvals Pont, the Canadian Mounted Rifles were on the road to Bloemfontein. From the road itself, they learned the scale of operation they were about to enter: how many wheels and hooves it must have taken to tear this miles-wide swath and chew and pulverize this dirt to flour.

The road to Bloom reminded Frank of a cattle drive, when every rider would try to avoid the drag, the position at the rear where you lived inside your wiper and moved through never-ending dust and putridness. The road to Bloom was all drag, a dust that would lift at a whisper; a rank powder added to every minute by every form and stage of death. In the joyous intervals when Frank left the road, the smell travelled with him. It was there when he woke and after a wash. It figured in his dreams.

The land itself had changed entirely since the Orange River. There had been a subtle lifting, some change wrought of altitude and ancient events that created grass across an endless plain. Having baked in summer and endured the first strangulations of fall, the prairie was pale blond as far as the eye could see.

This was more the sort of place Frank had dreamt: a prairie like home but in sweeps more endless. But Frank had imagined it full of wild animals, and that had been wrong. This prairie was a waving silence. With the exception of some quick herds of antelope, the odd ostrich, the observable life was domestic. Sheep and goats, a few odd-looking cows.

Their new wagon-Boer liked to talk in English, and Frank asked him questions. Had this been a place of wild animals once? Did they die off gradually or in big slaughters? The Boer described and shaped with his hands all kinds of animals. He claimed they were still there, but so wary and earth-coloured only the practised eye of a Boer hunter could spot them.

And, in their extreme cleverness, they don't even shit, Frank said, but only to himself. Off in the grass and brush, there was not much variety in the scats. Sheep, goat, equine, bovine—little twists of turd from skittering creatures.

Frank was reminded of Kootenai Brown guiding Billy Cochrane into the mountains above Kootenai Lakes. They would go after mountain sheep, and, finding none, Kootenai always said it was strange, since just a week ago the slopes had been covered.

One trouble with the sparseness of wild animals was that there was no other legal thing to eat. The Orange River had proved to be a boundary beyond which supply convoys seldom moved. There were umpteen theories why the war had stopped at Bloemfontein. Some said General Roberts had pursued the enemy with such vigour he had played out his horses and men. Others said he had outraced all hope of supply, especially given the number of bridges the Boers had blown. There was also a typhoid epidemic among Roberts' troops.

Roberts and Kitchener had deemed the old way of supply—each battalion looking after itself—outmoded. They had replaced it with one big system: the smooth-functioning one that kept their army sick and hungry, and in one place.

On the march, the Mounted Rifles had no army food. On the second day of marching without, a train pulled up beside them, and the black railway crew kicked about a hundred hardtack biscuits off a flatcar onto the ground. The train moved on. That helped them make a decision. Unless they were content to eat a dirty rock-hard biscuit every couple of days, it was probably time to go back to first principles: *Feed thyself,* being one.

They limbered their ropes and honed their knives. A few rode out into the prairie and started moving sheep along until a herd was gathered.

Jeff Davis's run of scouting had ended at Norvals Pont. He was told that Hutton's brigade and Alderson's MI battalions had their own dedicated scouting troops. Casey Callaghan, who had made corporal, was picked for an Alderson scout troop, but Jeff was left behind.

Now, Frank saw that Jeff was one of those out drifting with the sheep, weaving out from time to time to steer in another one or two. Andy Skinner, Jim Fisher, Cletis Delisle, Gil Snaddon, Waldron Hank, Pete and Eddy Belton, Jeff Davis—it was all cowboys out there. The townsmen, ranchers, ranchers' sons, and everyone higher ranked than private, stayed back. Fred Morden did not cross the divide this time.

Frank took a long look at Lieutenant Davidson before he acted. Though Hugh Davidson had told them yesterday about a Tommy court-martialled for a stolen chicken, he was looking elsewhere while the cowboys worked.

Frank tapped Dunny, and they cantered out of line. Ovide still had no horse and was riding a wagon beside its black driver. Frank waved as he rode past. He also passed Fred Morden, and they touched their hats to each other.

As if Frank's arrival was the signal, the riders started corralling the sheep, and the ropers walked their horses inside the flock. In no time flat, sheep were roped, killed, and bled—and started coming apart on the insides of their hides.

The march had already stopped. Bits of wood had been gathered and fires were licking. Not one officer said boo. Everybody ate that night, and when they got up to go, many thanked the cowboys for the meal.

Norvals Pont to Bloom was just a six-day ride, but the Mounted Rifles became famous during it. Now that it was loot or starve, it came down to ability. As not everybody in Lord Roberts' army was gifted at roping and transforming sheep into mutton, the non-cowboy colonials showed up at the Mounted Rifles' night fires wanting to barter for meat. They offered all kinds of loot: liquor, tobacco, ornately carved Boer pipes, baked goods. It wasn't that they could not possibly rustle for themselves, but more that they would be awkward at it and have to use guns. That kind of display might bring the Boer rebels—or a British officer—down on everyone. Why not simply do what people had always done—start a black market where everyone got to play to his strength and no one looked a fool?

When a troop of patrolling Aussies came by not long before Bloemfontein, and paid in English pounds to eat, one of their horses, a pretty chestnut gelding, buddied up to a mare in the Rifles' free pool. When it was time to go, the Aussie owner could not find his horse in the dark. The

Canadians said, "We're going the same direction as you. Drop by tomorrow and look in daylight."

Overnight, by lantern, Jim Fisher clipped the chestnut's Queensland Mounted Infantry brand (QMI) into one that read CMR. Andy Skinner bobbed the horse's tail and roached his mane.

When the Aussie returned the next day on a borrowed horse, they invited him to have a look. He slowly rode up one side of their extended order and down the other. He entered the free pool and looked at every horse. At least three times he rode by his own horse and did not recognize him.

Right to the end, nobody was sure if it was a joke, a trick, or a theft. But they let the Aussie ride away.

Starting with the first sheep killed, Frank noticed a strange thing about the Beltons. He had gone out that first day with the idea of helping Jeff, but Jeff already had his crew. Pete and Eddy Belton were waiting for him to rope a sheep. When he dragged it in, they took care of it. They handled every other catch he made.

Each time the drovers and ropers went out to get more food, Pete and Eddy worked for Jeff and carried his meat home to the cooking fires.

Fischer's Farm

They could see the hills above Bloemfontein when a British officer on a coughing horse appeared from the dust cloud and told them to get off the main track and follow a branching trail around the town. Six miles east of Bloom they would find Fischer's Farm, where they would bivouac with other soldiers, including Royal Canadian Dragoons.

Andy Skinner was angry about the diversion. He was an American who had ridden in cattle drives north from Texas. When you came to a town on a cattle drive, he told them, your cattle boss was supposed to grant you time—to get drunk, gamble, and whore. To be diverted around a substantial town after this long a ride was an insult, and Andy would not stop talking about it. Morden tried to reason with him and so did Reg Redpath. This was a Boer town, they said. There would be a big church, probably no saloons, and certainly no whores. But Andy was convinced it was his right to go in and be disappointed.

Word of this got back to the officers, but in such a way that the officers supposed Andy had followers. After they had made camp and set their fires, a purposeful knot of lieutenants and sergeants arrived. Each lieutenant took a fire and gave the men around it a stiff talking to. It started with how lucky they were *not* to be in Bloemfontein. Typhoid was raging there, an epidemic that had started when Cronje pushed dead horses and oxen into the Modder River at Paardeburg. The Boer General, De Wet, had captured Sanna's Post, the waterworks for Bloom, and had sabotaged it, making the situation worse. The disease was killing soldiers every day, Canadian infantrymen among them. The Mounted Rifles were not likely to be at Fischer's Farm long. When they left, they would be headed for the war. They had better stop bitching and get ready.

After the lieutenants left, the sergeants took over. Frank's sergeant, Harry Brindle, an English Mountie from Macleod, let them have it. All they were known for was stealing and insubordination, he said. They probably thought that was funny, but nothing like it would be tolerated beyond this day. At the front, they would be expected to act like real soldiers.

Brindle came at them from a new angle. Though they seemed not to understand it, the Mounted Rifles were a battalion of scouts and could expect to be thrust to the front, and to the front of the front. They would be advance guards. They would guard artillery and draw fire so the artillery could spot enemy guns. Each man had better prepare his mind for that.

When Harry finally left them alone, Frank was smarting. It was true he had not thought much about being a fighting soldier, but it hardly seemed fair to let them rustle food for the camp and then give them hell for it. He was mad at Andy Skinner for bringing it on, though he suspected the lieutenants and sergeants had been waiting for an opportunity to make this speech.

Then along came Ovide, who had missed it all, grinning for the first time in weeks. An ugly horse trailed behind him. The mare looked almost green in this light, as if it had started out chestnut and gone mouldy. It was gaunt and poor in the hip. Frank kept this to himself because Ovide was delighted.

Since his arrival at Fischer's Farm, Ovide had been walking the herds of rehabilitating horses. He had found this one in an equine junk pile: horses that had been weeded out and would either be given to the black camp workers or killed. Ovide discussed the horse with the black wrangler who had taken the junk horses to graze. The man told Ovide the horse was a Basuto, named for a kind of African people who lived in the mountains east of here. They had developed this breed for the mountains, and, though not much to look at, Basutos were very hardy. The man himself had his eye on the horse, so Ovide paid him an English pound to forget about it.

Ovide gave Frank a tour of the animal, showing him the angle of the fetlock and the way the knee was set and said something about the barrel and the stifle. She still seemed like an ugly horse to Frank, but he made a fuss over her anyway, as it was good to see Ovide happy.

Then Frank left Ovide to brushing and pampering his find, and returned to brooding about whether he was a bad soldier. He certainly had not put much thought into being a good one, nor had the episode in the Karoo impressed him with army life. The more he considered the so-called Carnarvon Expedition, the more it came out as a mangle they had been turned through, for no good reason. Horses brought from Canada, like Ovide's cutting mare, had been sacrificed for nothing. The speeches tonight rankled too. Their response to the Karoo had been to find ways to stay alive in it. On the Bloemfontein road, they had found ways to eat. But here was the army saying, that's not right. They must stop using the principles of home to survive in Africa. From now on, the only sense they were allowed to make was army sense.

Brandfort

Frank was in the habit of reading whatever newspapers he found. No camp was virginal and newspapers were a staple of the trash: either papers from Cape Town or older ones that had come from Britain or the colonies, sometimes wrapped around cakes and puddings. On a good day, the news might roll right up to Frank as he lay on his bedroll: a tumbleweed of words. On the march, he would sometimes find pages stabbed on thorn bushes, rattling their whereabouts.

The habit came from home, where his father was a tireless reader and where his mother, who had taught Frank to read, could not stand for him to be in the same room as a newspaper and not read it. If he did not, she assumed he could not.

Africa was different. No one here cared whether Frank read, but he did so to get above the ant's eye view of the soldier. It was a way of finding out what was going on and what people back home might be hearing.

One thing he learned was that the folks back home weren't reading about him. Mentions of Canadians in the newspapers were rare. Now that the Mounted Rifles were in Hutton's brigade attached to General Roberts' column, Frank hoped that might change. At least, he expected the news to be about things he had seen or been part of.

What he hadn't seen yet but wanted to was General Roberts' war balloon. At the front, soldiers floated up in it and spied on Boer troop positions and gun emplacements. Frank had read about the balloon in a newspaper and had kept a page with a drawing. The reporter on the piece was Winston Churchill, who had written that the balloon was like the biblical pillar of cloud that guided the Jews to the promised land.

Another day, in a Cape Town newspaper, Frank read that Boer President Paul Kruger believed the British typhoid epidemic was the same as the plagues God sent against the Egyptians for keeping the Jews as slaves.

Both were references to the Bible story of how the Jews escaped Pharaoh, and Frank found it funny that both sides would use the same story to prove that God was with them. It seemed more likely that God liked neither side and might wipe out both before they did more damage.

When they left Fischer's Farm, it was three in the morning, black-dark and very cold. By the time dawn broke the horizon, they were beyond the hills and into another blond expanse. As the lieutenants had predicted, the Mounted Rifles were an advance guard, shepherding a battery of guns.

Except for an occasional tree or bush, there was no place for the Boers to hide, and Frank found he almost pitied them. They might as well send Lord Roberts notes. *See you on yonder hill.* Or, *When you get to the next river, we plan to give you hell.*

The uneventful day of marching ended beside the railway tracks, where they joined Hutton's brigade. The little creek of them absorbed into the great river of soldiers.

Hutton had noticed one thing about the Mounted Rifles so far: their lack of leadership. Herchmer was still in sick bay, and though Gilbert

Sanders was healthy, he was on a ship, taking Boer prisoners to St. Helena. Hutton's solution involved the Royal Canadian Dragoons, the other horse battalion that was drawn mostly from eastern Canada. Before they'd left Fischer's Farm, Hutton gave them Colonel T.B. Evans, the Dragoons second-in-command, as their temporary commander.

Mounties like Harry Brindle and Hugh Davidson grumbled. The whole idea of the Mounted Rifles was that the battalion be led by Mounted Police officers, they said, and so it should be now. Frank found he held the opposite view. If he was going to be led into battle, better it be by a soldier than by a policeman.

Colonel Evans' first act as their leader was unusual. He got them together and told them what was going on. There were three columns in this advance, he said. General Roberts' column was in the middle between Ian Hamilton's and John French's. The three together made a front too wide for the Boers to skirt. Johnny Boer was a scrappy fighter, the colonel said, smart and by no means defeated. But Paardeburg had taken a bite out of him. At the moment he was weakened and in retreat, and the British side aimed to take full advantage.

A Rifles private put up his hand and was recognized. "Where are we?" he asked.

Colonel Evans laughed. "You're at Karee Siding, private, in what the rebels call the Orange Free State."

That day, their wagon convoy and their tents did not find them. It was the coldest night Frank had experienced in Africa, with a bitter wind combing the pan they were camped on. Frank and Ovide spread their oil sheet under them, and each man wore his greatcoat and wrapped himself in his blanket. They slept cold anyway.

Next day, as they were marching, they did see the war balloon, hanging above the churned dust. The basket was trimmed with officers, their field glasses sparking. Frank thought it looked like an onion, with a striped skin and its root teat pointed down.

He jabbed Ovide, then reached in his shirt for the newspaper picture he had saved. Ovide looked back and forth from the picture to the real balloon. Frank had intended to keep the page but gave it to Ovide now. Smith folded it carefully and put it in his shirt pocket.

That evening they stopped a few miles short of Brandfort. They were told that, come morning, they would be involved in a fight to take the town and its associated kopjes. Again, they had no tents, but the general jumpiness of the camp was distraction from the cold. Frank woke up many times and saw by moonlight that men were up, either standing in their greatcoats or doing some exercise to excite warmth. Despite the general shortage of sleep, the atmosphere at their breakfast in the dark was almost giddy, as if their attack was a practical joke.

When they got on the trail, they were aimed west of Brandfort toward a couple of kopjes it would be their job to clear. Those hills were just beginning to sprout detail when the pounding of guns began. At first it was just noise but then a divide was crossed, and the first Boer shell exploded above them. Hot shrapnel shards rained down.

Beside Frank and Ovide, a heavier shell hit the ground and exploded. A wave of orange dirt came flying. Frank's eyes clamped before he asked them to. His mouth had less sense and was full of filth.

Some of the horses reared or ran, but Dunny and the Basuto held, even as dirt and stones hit them. A rabbit, frightened out of a prickly pear, ran toward them across the ruptured ground. It saw the wave of horses and zagged away. Some other fearful sight changed its mind again and it went pole-bending through the horses' legs.

They heard a repeating whine above them, like someone strumming a tight wire. Those were the rifle bullets, Mauser bullets, and the air was full of them.

In some bushes along a kopje's rise, the sergeants screamed for them to dismount and give their horses to the number threes. Frank and Ovide threw their reins to Gil Snaddon. They ran up the kopje's flank. Near the top they could make out the crack of Mausers and the high-wire sound of bullets. The Boer artillery was pounding again, trying to find their range.

At the hill's brow, a wide swale opened to the kopje's next rise. Everybody threw themselves flat while deciding what to do. A barbwire fence ran away from them at an angle and was held in place by coffin-size stones. Greasy Griesbach was the first to run and throw himself behind one. Then there was a stampede for the rest of the rocks.

Frank and Ovide got balled up. They started running but went in different directions, then tried to come back and collided. By then, the stones were all taken and second choice was an anthill. They squeezed behind one that was four feet high and three wide: blood red and hard as a helmet.

After they had been there awhile, Frank figured out he was the only one shooting. With shells exploding and bullets whizzing and whining—some hitting their anthill with a pock or singing off—Ovide had set his rifle aside and was looking at the hill in an attitude of study. Frank told him to get shooting. If an officer saw him doing nothing, he'd think him a coward. Ovide banged off a few rounds then stopped again.

He wriggled around so his feet were facing the anthill and started kicking.

"Christ sake, Ovide! That's our cover!"

Ovide kept on until a piece came off, a round of hard shell. He climbed back and put his face close to the wound, watching the ants mill about in the visible innards.

"They're green," he said.

"Damn it, Ovide, I don't give a shit if they're green. Now we'll get ants on us."

"Nope. They're not leaving."

Frank was yelling and cursing for Ovide to shoot when he heard the firing slacken, starting to his right. The Mounted Rifles on that side held back too. They swung their heads like birds on a wire, and halfway between them and where the Boers were, they saw a line of black civilians come running. Their older men were first, whipping at hollow-sided oxen. Behind the bullocks bounced humpy carts, piled with roped-down goods. Women wrapped in blankets came next, followed by children in file. Many of the women ran with baskets on their heads. They waved bits of cloth with their free hands. It was a whole African village, caught between the firing lines, trying to escape.

Close to Frank and Ovide, the villagers found a hole in the line and passed through. After they had gone, there was silence. Then, from somewhere far away, rifles started up. An artillery piece let fly and an enemy gun answered. The battle returned to its earlier tempo.

About two hours later, there was another tapering off. At first, it was just the Boers who stopped, but eventually the British did too. The Canadian sergeants started blowing their whistles, sounding the order "Stand to Your Horses." Frank and Ovide ran back and mounted. Then came the command to charge. They were soon up the rise and looking over the crest. Their officers halted them, as the Boers were already too far gone to chase. The enemy's trenches and piles of spent casings were all around them.

When it was over, Frank was amazed at how little he knew about his first battle. He could not honestly say he had seen one enemy. As they were eating tinned meat and drinking tea, Lieutenant Davidson came back from somewhere bursting with importance. As if it were self-evident, he said the strategy of the battle had been to keep adding men to the left until the British line was longer than the Boer right. This threatened the Boers with encirclement. When they saw it coming, they packed up and left.

Gossip added a little more. Apparently, things had not gone flawlessly. During the fight, a British staff officer came to tell Colonel Lessard (commander of the Royal Canadian Dragoons) to change position. A couple of soldiers who were close enough to hear thought they'd get a head start. They jumped up and ran for their horses, but had forgotten to uncock their rifles and one went off, the bullet passing between the British officer and Lessard. The Brit told Lessard he should take his stupid undertrained Canadians home.

A Dragoon private and a Mounted Rifle sergeant had been wounded in the battle, and a number of horses were hit and had to be killed. Frank heard, too, that a Dragoon private had died back at Karee Siding. Rather than face battle, he had shot himself.

Vet River, May 1900

Roused before dawn, they were hustled across the prairie in the inky dark. Come the grey light, they saw a meander of bush and trees that was the shallow valley of the Vet River. A mile closer and they could see brown lakes where the stream had overspilled.

As at Brandfort, the air began to fill with the various weights and sizes of Boer shells, lobbed invisibly from the distant kopjes. From much closer, Mauser bullets were sizzling.

For a time it was dangerous. They were pinned down and lacked cover. The Mauser fire came from the bushy green of the river's far bank. Then most of the Mounted Rifles were ordered back to their horses and out of range. They were being held in reserve, like benched hockey players, while the Dragoons moved into the battle's maw.

In their saddles, the biggest risk Frank and Ovide faced was sunstroke. While the guns shook the air from both sides and tore up distant tufts, the two of them scanned the horizons, looking for sheep and goats: something to fry up in their little pans, their dixies, come battle's end.

For Frank, the battle was another invisible thing acted out behind a curtain of coloured smoke, more noise and stink than anything visible. Though Lieutenant Davidson was looking through field glasses, he probably could not see more; but having heard the battle plan, he could at least imagine it. That was what he narrated to the men. The British were adding to their left again. Soon, the Boer flank would be turned and the enemy would have to scamper.

After a couple of hours, the noise slackened, and an order came for all remaining troops to charge. The Mounted Rifles rode across the river at Pretorius Drift. When they came out on the far side, they were apparently victorious.

In the triumphant camp that night, quite a few of the heroes were Canadian Dragoons. Two Dragoon lieutenants, Turner and Borden, both politicians' sons, had waded across the Vet River twice to fight. First time, they and their followers had shot it out with some Boers behind a stone wall. Outnumbered, the Canadians were forced back. But their lieutenants led them across again, in a place where the water was up to their faces and they had to hold their rifles over their heads.

When the Mounted Rifles had charged and crossed the drift, that was the courageous lead they had been following. A Boer gun was seized. A surprising number of Boer dead were found in the reeds and bush along the far shore. The officers said Turner and Borden were sure to be mentioned in dispatches. They might even get medals.

While this celebration went on, Frank and Ovide sat apart. Finally, they snuck off to where they would sleep. Even Ovide found Frank quiet and said so. Frank did not try to explain his thoughts, for they sounded disloyal even to him.

If it was all so damn simple, he was thinking, if the Boers were always going to be outnumbered and would always have to run when the British left extended beyond their right, then why not resign? Like you would in a hopeless game of chess.

It wasn't as if the war could not be interrupted. Back at Brandfort, the villagers had poured between their lines and the battle had stopped for them. If the war could stop then, it could stop at any time. So why, given the mismatch, did it not stop permanently?

Frank had heard various reasons: reasons of Empire, diamonds and gold; Winston Churchill and Rudyard Kipling reasons; Cecil Rhodes reasons; Paul Kruger reasons. But all Frank could imagine was his own leg blown off, or his good cayuse mare turned into one of those raddled corpses covered in vultures.

To try to slow himself down, Frank said what old cowboys were inclined to when a younger man was running off at the mouth. *So you got it all figured out, eh, sonny?*

But tonight, Frank had his mother's temper, and Madeleine could not be cooled off by any cowboy living. *Just because you're old and would trade a leg for a new story to tell, doesn't mean the rest have to hop around.* That was the sort of thing she would say.

Possessed by his mother's fury, Frank thought of Fred Morden, who would be delighted by the battles, because Pincher Creek had a school with a Union Jack and a picture of Queen Victoria.

Hair on him, Frank said to himself in his mother's voice. *Hair on all of them.*

What finally calmed Frank was Ovide. The old cowboy had made a little fire by his bedroll. He had his hat off, and the firelit dome of his head showed through his thin hair. His hat was flipped in the cross of his legs, and he was stitching along the inner band.

The sight quieted Frank because he knew that, all war long, Ovide had been thinking thoughts like Frank's tonight. He was proof you did not need to be sore about it all the time.

After Vet River, the Boers spilled across the prairie thirty miles. They were on their way to the next river, called the Zand. On the march toward that river, a Mounted Rifles private started singing. The tune was from a popular song, but he had made up new words.

Just tell them that you saw me, a mile or so behind,
With clammy brow and features drawn with pain.
He's heard the Mausers calling, he's gone supports to find,
And when the shooting stops, he'll come again.

Many laughed when they heard it, because they had observed the inspiration: a Mounted Rifles officer who had spent the Brandfort and Vet fights riding around well behind the lines. Verse by verse, the men started learning it, until dozens knew it well enough to sing. When the officer in question rode into earshot, the whole gang roared it out. The officer kept on riding, his face like plaster.

It was cruel, but Frank learned the song and sang it same as the rest. He did not plan to behave like a coward. And if he had to sit behind an anthill with red-hot metal flying around him, then it was only justice that an officer should have the courage to do the same. Even Ovide, who barely paid attention to the war, did not run from it.

The truth was that all the men around Frank had only just found out they were not cowards, that they could face enemy fire. Maybe singing the coward song was a proclamation and celebration of that fact.

Smaldeel Junction

They stopped their march at Smaldeel Junction, where General Roberts wanted them to wait for the battle at Zand River. Ovide and Frank had a little trash fire going against the cold, and Ovide was looking at his Basuto with displeasure. That is, he was happy with the mud-coloured mare, who walked with such a quick, true action, and never bottomed out, but she was losing flesh. Back at Fischer's Farm, she had begun to fatten. But the march was peeling it all off again.

Ovide's particular annoyance today was that he had asked to take his mare beyond the scoured road to graze. The request was denied. Boer patrols might be out there waiting to pick him off. For the same reason, no one was allowed to hunt, though the Roberts-Kitchener supply system had brought no food again.

Ovide, in a garrulous mood for him, said it was like coming west from Quebec with his uncle when he was ten. They had entered the wake of a huge buffalo herd and soon lost their way on that stripped and shitted ground and could not get out. They and their horses almost died. But this was worse for being deliberate.

The good news of the day was that neither Frank nor Ovide had been chosen for Curly Hutton's expedition. Hutton did not think his brigade was getting enough action and wanted to forge ahead. There'd been a squabble, and the compromise was that Hutton was allowed to mount an expedition to try to cut off Boer convoys before they crossed the Zand. Frank's theory on bravery was that you did not volunteer for extra fighting. He had also taken Ovide's advice on how to use dirt and grease to make Dunny look shabby and thin.

Frank and Ovide were not in much danger of being chosen anyway. The officers always picked fellows like Morden, Kerr, Redpath, and Griesbach—and just as automatically passed on Ovide, Frank, and the Beltons. It was the same social division that determined who got invited to a Pincher Creek oyster supper.

But Jeff had again managed to turn himself into an exception. When Hutton's expedition was forming, Casey Callaghan was there, directing the scouts. He chose Jeff to join them; to be one of his four.

Hutton's expedition dribbled back in the late afternoon. They had managed to cause an artillery duel. A private has been wounded. Some horses killed. No convoy captured. It was declared a victory, of course.

Frank and Ovide were still feeding their little fire and warming by it, anticipating a no-fires rule come dark. They stared at their dixies, which they had set to warm on the rocks at the fire's edge. They had no crumb of meat so it was a hopeful superstition: that by readying the pans, meat would come.

Then, amazingly, it did. Fists of meat flopped into their dixies. Jeff Davis coiled his long legs and sat down at the fire's open edge. He set his own dixie on the fire and placed another steak there.

Frank was marvelling at the size of the steaks. "What the hell, Jeff? Did you kill a cow?"

"Big antelope," he said. He set his fingers on his forehead, making the shape of its horns. This made Frank laugh because it was how an old man from the Blood would portray an unusual animal. Being a scout for the day had turned Jeff more Indian.

Davis's version of Hutton's expedition was that he and Casey had been well in front of it. They met the Zand downstream of the Boers, and that was where Jeff saw the eland and marked the spot for later. They had worked their way upstream to the railroad crossing where the Boers were digging trenches. An Irish wrecker had just finished blowing the first span of the bridge and was setting charges on the next one.

"So we blew him."

Irish wrecker was not part of Frank's and Ovide's vocabularies. Jeff explained that some Irish rebels who had been fighting the British in Ireland were now in Africa, making common cause with the Boers. They were ex-miners, dynamite experts, and they wrecked things the Boers wanted wrecked.

While the eland steaks sizzled, Lieutenant Davidson came carrying a small envelope. Arriving, he greeted only Davis. Frank assumed it was a dispatch that Jeff was meant to carry. Jeff thought so too.

"No, no," said Davidson. He pointed where the name was written. "It's *for* you. A dispatch *for* you. From General Roberts' staff."

Casey Callaghan had followed Davidson over. Behind him were two older men, leathery sorts. Frank knew one of them was Charlie Ross, who had been a Mountie around Macleod and Lethbridge. He was someone Frank's father knew and his mother would not let in the house, because Ross had fought against the Halfbreeds in 1885. By his uniform, Ross was not a Mounted Rifle or a Canadian Dragoon, and Frank had not seen him in Africa before.

The other fellow was a Canadian Dragoon, the top officer in their machine-gun section, but Frank had never heard his name.

Jeff opened the envelope and drew out a single sheet. The reading took but seconds, then he shrugged and held it out to Davidson. As the lieutenant read, his eyebrows rose and stuck. Casey, Charlie Ross, and the Dragoons' gunnery officer jammed in behind Davidson, trying to see.

"I'll be damned," the Dragoon gunner said.

Davidson returned the sheet to Jeff, who handed it to Frank, who turned aside and read it aloud to Ovide.

"Private Jefferson Davis, please proceed immediately to General Roberts' staff headquarters for temporary reassignment to Roberts' Scouts."

"What's it mean?" Jeff asked.

No one knew beyond the obvious. Davidson wanted to know whether Jeff had asked for a move. A corporal in C Squadron had recently asked to go to an English regiment where he had a first cousin. His wish had been granted by a similar letter.

Jeff shook his head. "I don't want to move."

The gunner leaned in. "Charlie Ross here just came from Roberts' Scouts. Maybe this private here, Davis, is the other half of a trade. They're real scouts over there, aren't they, Charlie?"

Ross neither affirmed nor denied it. Frank looked at Casey and saw his fur rise. The gunner's implication was that the Mounted Rifle scouts were not as "real" as these others.

"What do I have to do?" Jeff asked Davidson.

"No choice, Davis," Davidson said. "These are your orders. They're clear. You have to go. You should be proud."

"Can I wait until tomorrow?"

"It says immediately. You shouldn't even stay the night. I guess it's my duty to order you to go."

Jeff went to pack. The story flashed around, and several gathered where Ovide and Frank were brushing and readying Jeff's horses. To go along with The Blue, Hugh Davidson had given Jeff an Argentine to use as a pack horse. When Jeff came back, they tied his pack on the Argentine.

Frank noticed the Belton brothers standing in the shadows, looking thunderstruck. Then a bigger crowd came, and everybody wanted part of Jeff Davis. He was a sudden celebrity, the way he had been at the baboon camp. Sergeants and officers offered advice. The English ones saw a move closer to the heart of British command as a tremendous promotion. One of these had a bottle from which he gave Davis several pulls. Frank saw Fred Morden take Davis aside and whisper urgently in his ear. Frank bet it was an overdue apology for calling him a stupid Halfbreed on the *Pomeranian*.

While all this went on, Frank and Ovide withdrew to their dying fire and ate the rest of the antelope. Though burned on one side, it was excellent.

While Frank ate, he kept an eye on the Beltons and wondered again why their attitude toward Jeff had improved so dramatically. Pete had a canvas bag in his hand and Frank saw a shape inside that looked like a pistol. The hair on his neck tickled. He remembered Pete's threats on the train to Halifax and all the ones afterwards. Was there the slightest chance, he wondered, that all the recent sucking up had been a ruse: that Pete still intended to do Jeff harm? Maybe he had identified this moment as his last chance.

While the crowd fawned, Frank kept watch. If Pete had murder on his mind, he was a master actor. Both he and Eddy looked limp and sad.

The sun had by now set into the thorn trees. Jeff made a quick round shaking hands, then mounted up and turned his horse to where Frank and Ovide sat wiping eland fat off their chops. Jeff leaned down over his saddle rolls.

"Don't know where I'm going. If it's good, I'll try to get you in."

Frank doubted this was possible but appreciated his saying it. Pete Belton had followed Jeff and was again standing close. Frank got up and put himself in Pete's way. He asked what was in the bag.

"The bag ain't none of yer business," said Pete. "It's for Jeff."

"Ya, but what?"

"Never mind. Present."

Frank stayed close as Pete lifted the bag. If it was a pistol, at least he had it by the barrel end.

"What you got there?" Jeff asked.

"Mauser pistol, Jeff. What they call a broom handle. And a dozen rounds. Eddy and me found it on a corpse. Shoots good."

"Keep it, then."

"Me and Eddy be proud you take it."

Jeff reached and took it. He opened his saddlebag and stuck the pistol in, then tapped his hat and touched a spur to The Blue. She sparked forward. The Argentine lagged, and The Blue swung around and bit him on the ass.

When the two horses were swallowed whole by the falling dark, Frank's feeling of loss was out of proportion. It was how he should have felt when he'd left the Cochrane Ranch and his old parents were waving—and hadn't. He felt a deep gouge, like a hand scooping the soft pulp out of him.

Ovide hung his head and said nothing. He pulled his seldom-used tobacco plug out of his shirt pocket and offered it: a sign of distress, as he knew Frank did not chew. Ovide stuck the plug in his teeth and sawed back and forth until a piece broke off.

] 135 [

Frank was looking at Ovide, but in his mind was riding away with Jeff. He saw cactus blades reaching to his stirrup. Tree thorns clawing at the night sky. A kopje's form shouldered out of the smooth horizon, and the night insects shook like beads in a gourd.

Frank came back to the world as the crowd scattered. Again he saw Charlie Ross, Casey Callaghan, and the Dragoons' gunnery officer. The three were standing in a knot having a smoke.

"Who is that?" Frank asked. "That one beside Casey and Charlie Ross?" Frank did not expect Ovide to know but gave him the only clue he had. "He's the boss of the Dragoons' machine-gun section, but what's his name?"

Ovide sucked the tobacco ball in his cheek.

"Howard. They call him Gatling."

Arthur Gatling Howard. It was an explosive fact. Howard was one of Frank's mother's least favourite humans. In the 1885 Halfbreed rebellion, he had fired on her relatives at Batoche with a machine gun. Frank was still digesting this when Pete and Eddy Belton came to their fire.

When Frank asked their business, Pete said he and Eddy wanted to join Ovide and Frank's four. Eddy could be their horse-holder, their number three.

"Horses like Eddy," said Pete, which was true.

Frank asked him why and he said, "You're friends of Jeff Davis, and so are we."

Frank looked at Ovide, and Ovide shrugged. The fact was that their own four since Cape Town was trying to get rid of them. Andy Skinner had convinced Gil Snaddon that they should be with "real cowboys"— meaning American cowboys.

Frank nodded and Pete gave a little hop of pleasure.

Zand River

The Zand River fight had the usual elements: a feeling that the real action was elsewhere; an hour of terror; a wild charge upslope after an enemy long departed.

The Mounted Rifles were sent to the left to hook around the Boers' right and were soon under fire. They dismounted, took cover, and shot into the trees along the river's far edge, where any parting in the willow sticks might be the enemy.

Already across the river, a mixed column of British and Australians went into an African village on foot. The sheep kraals were lined inside with Boers, who gave it to them point-blank. Those who could still move ran. Their horses stampeded. The dead and wounded were left behind.

Colonel Alderson sent orders to his Canadian squadrons to relieve this crew. Together, the Dragoons and Rifles crept to the sheep kraals and found them empty. The Dragoons unslung their Lee-Enfields. The Mounted Rifles pulled their Colts. They dodged the rocks, the dead and wounded, and yelled their way to the top. From there, Frank and Ovide saw the enemy as specks in a cloud of dust, riding away. Some Scots Greys rounded the bottom of the hill on horseback and gave chase.

"Never catch 'em," Ovide said.

And they never did. The African horses were too nimble in the rocks and pulled away.

Waiting for the ambulance wagons, Ovide and Frank tied their horses and wandered the hillside. They counted fourteen corpses and not one of them Boer. Ovide found two British rifles that were still cocked and let the hammers down. He shook out the bullets and put them in his pocket. Of the wounded, some were writhing, some coughing blood. Horses tried to lift themselves, looking back at limbs that would not answer.

It was sad and sickening, but walking through it made Frank feel powerfully alive. He felt sorry every time he saw a fly on an open eye, and for the men who were suffering. But he was still happy it was not him.

Red Crow's Camp

A fine spring day. The sky was blue everywhere except for little clouds moving fast high up. Nevertheless, Red Crow brought his white secretary into the still heat of the cabin. Two letters lay on the table, side by side.

The secretary, Jean Roux, was a stout man with a black beard and very white skin. He always dressed in dark, heavy cloth. His age was hard to guess, as is the case with white men who blacken their beards with shoe polish. He had come to the Bloods long ago, in the guise of a priest. A story came with him that, back east where they make priests, Roux had been caught at some kind of sex with another boy. The priests had cast him out. That was when he came west and begged his way into the Blackfoot camps. It was also why they gave him the name Three Faces. Who knew if he understood the joke? That he was a priest, not a priest, and a mounter of men, all at once. Roux could read and write French and English, and knew the Nitsitapi language well. It was enough to earn his keep.

In the past month, Red Crow had called Three Faces to his house three times, to read his letters: the one from Butler and the one from Jefferson. Red Crow could almost recite them from memory, but he liked to hear Three Faces turn them into Blackfoot. His words were never quite the same with each reading, and Red Crow listened closely for new shades of meaning.

Red Crow did not demand that Three Faces start right away. They began by talking of other things, the latest people carried off by the blood-spitting sickness, and how the new deputy from the government's Indian office said its cause was Indians living too close together in their houses and spitting on the floor. Then Red Crow's wife came with tea and Roux filled his pipe a second time from Red Crow's tobacco bag. They smoked and drank in silence.

Finally, Red Crow turned his chair so it pointed at his one glass window. Chief Mountain, still dressed in snow on its north side, was framed by the wood around the glass. Red Crow pointed to Butler's letter. When the words started, he did not look at Three Faces, only at the holy mountain, its square head.

Butler's letter started the English way, with flattery. He called Red Crow his admired friend and a great warrior and leader. Eventually, he got to the matter of Red Crow's nephew in South Africa. Butler said he was no longer a general in Africa but was training soldiers in England for the South African war. Just locating Jefferson in such a big army was no simple thing, but he knew people of influence who might find him and ensure that he had a place of respect in battle.

One of these letters Butler had written was to Colonel Herchmer. Red Crow knew Herchmer, who became the Mountie chief after Red Crow's friend Bull Head (Colonel Macleod) became a judge. Red Crow did not think as highly of Herchmer as Bull Head. In any case, according to Butler, Herchmer now led the part of the Canadian army in South Africa to which Jefferson belonged. Butler had asked Herchmer to consider making Jefferson a scout.

In a second letter, to a British officer in Africa, Butler had described Jefferson as someone who would make a good scout. To this one, he'd said that Jefferson's uncle was a mighty warrior. The recipient of this letter worked for the biggest chief of all in Britain's African army, the one called Roberts. This Roberts had his own scouts, and, with luck, the two letters together would result in Jefferson's joining those scouts. He would then be in front of the big British army rather than behind or inside it. This might be more dangerous at times, but there would be less likelihood of his getting a disease or being shot by one of his own.

When Butler's words started to flatter again, Red Crow signalled Roux to stop and begin reading the second one: the letter from Jefferson.

Jefferson's letter was not as long as Butler's, for which Red Crow was sorry. There were so many things he must have seen and done by now that Red Crow would have liked to hear about, but his nephew did not seem to find them interesting. He had ridden the train east, the one Red Crow had also travelled on one time. Jefferson and the other new soldiers had stopped in Regina to learn things that would make them soldiers. Jefferson found these things useless and was glad Red Crow had already trained him as a warrior.

The boat ride to Africa had been long, hot, and very hard on horses. When they got to Africa, they stayed in a place beneath a mountain called Table because it had a flat top. It was like Chief Mountain, but broader. They left the coast and went inland by train and saw that the country was huge but poor. A horse could grow tired walking from one blade of grass to the next. There were many hills made of broken orange rocks. In this dry place, the water gave everyone the shits. There was a much worse sickness that killed soldiers with fever.

Jefferson said he had some friends. Frank Adams, the son of Jim Adams and his Halfbreed wife from the Cochrane Ranch, was one. A second was a French cowboy from Pincher Creek. His name was Ovide Smith and he worked for Jughandle Smith, the whisky trader turned rancher, but the two were not related. There was a third friend called Casey Callaghan who drove bull teams to and from Fort Walsh.

Jefferson told Red Crow about African animals. There were many kinds and sizes of antelope. Their horns were sometimes very large and unusually shaped. There was a buffalo too, but the black people preferred to eat the biggest antelope, which was the size of a cow and tasty. There were animals in Africa similar to a cougar. A black one was called a leopard. One even bigger was called a lion. Jefferson hoped to see a lion and was told he might, farther north.

As for the fighting, it was of a kind Red Crow would not have liked. From huge guns, both sides shot bullets big as a bannock loaf. Even when the gun was too far away to see, its bullet could still land on you. You did not see the men you were fighting most of the time. The enemy wore beards and dressed like farmers. They travelled in carts and wagons like Halfbreeds.

There were more black people in this country than white. There were brown people but no Indians. The black people were made to work for the whites and were treated poorly, as bad or worse than white people treated Indians.

Jefferson was embarrassed to say he had not yet been in a single battle when he wrote the letter. The army had given him a good rifle but with the wrong back sight. He had the correct sight now and could hit things in practice. He was hoping to kill his first Boer soon.

Then came the part that surprised Red Crow most. Jefferson wrote that he loved Bitter Water's daughter, Ran After, and hoped to make her his wife after the war.

Roux finished reading and Red Crow placed a coin on the table and told him to go. All that day until the sun went down, Red Crow stayed seated in the stuffy room and thought about his nephew.

A month ago, Red Crow had met Bitter Water at the Blood Agency, and Bitter Water had told Red Crow that some in his family had died of the blood-spitting sickness. More had the disease and were going to die. One of those was his daughter, Ran After.

As he had done every time Roux came to read him these letters, Red Crow argued with himself about his obligations. Must he tell his nephew about the girl? Would Jefferson throw his life away if he did? After a long time wrestling with it, Red Crow decided there was an important difference between telling Jefferson that the girl was sick and waiting until she died and telling him that. By splitting these two ideas, Red Crow could make a choice. He chose the path that allowed him to wait.

Kroonstad

When the war got to Kroonstad, it stalled, just as it had at Bloemfontein. The Boers had been expected to fight for the town because they had made it their Orange River capital after Bloom fell. But they did not fight for it. They continued falling back, all the way to the Vaal River: the border between the two rebel republics.

Roberts and Kitchener might have wanted to give chase but could no longer ignore their starving army and horses. They had to stop the advance to get their supply system running again; to build bridges that trains could cross. But, when they stopped at Kroonstad, a familiar camp follower caught up with them. Just as at Bloemfontein, enteric fever gathered on the morning dew and leapt into the bodies of the unsuspecting.

Many rumours went around the stalled camp, and the most prevalent said Herchmer was returning and there was a plan among the officers to get rid of him. There was also talk of a flying column that would leave Kroonstad and strike north, to surprise some rebels who had snuck back to their farms to rest.

On the third day, Frank woke to the sound of Ovide groaning. What ailed him looked more like dysentery than enteric fever, but that might only have been a wish on Frank's part. In the Karoo, he and Ovide had both had dysentery and survived. He spent the day boiling water, cooling it; urging Ovide to drink.

Between times, when water was heating, or when Ovide was staggering back and forth to the latrine, Frank brushed Dunny, and pulled her mane and tail. He trimmed her forelock so it fell between her ears and sat prettily above her arrow-shaped blaze. Ovide watched from his blankets and knew what it was about. If keeping the horses shabby was a defence against being selected for special duties, grooming the dun cayuse clearly meant the opposite.

Reasons why a man would want out of this camp were plentiful. Every day, the stretchers came in empty and walked out loaded. The sick tents were full and performing their function of hurrying sick men to their fate.

Frank was not sick at present and might avoid becoming so by leaving with Hutton's flying column.

But that was not why. Besides being dangerous, Kroonstad was tedious. Frank kept remembering how Jeff Davis had ridden off into the dark. It made him want to leave too.

In the end, Hutton did get permission for his flying column, and Frank was selected: one of fifty Mounted Rifles to go with fifty Dragoons, and a hundred and fifty other kinds of soldiers and some guns. Ovide did not even roll over for the moment of farewell.

Cantering out of town, Frank felt himself rise. Sniper bullets sang above last year's cornstalks, but neither the bullets nor Ovide's green face could drag him down today.

The column rode for several hours, then rested until dark; then rode all night and part of the next day. They kept travelling until tall trees announced a cluster of farms. Bothaville.

They split into gangs, circled and hit the farms as suddenly and simultaneously as possible. Burst through doors with Colts wagging. Shouted at terrified women and children. Stabbed bayonets into clothes closets. Threw up trap doors and shone lamps into cellars.

A couple of Boer rebels were found at table, eating their wives' pastries; another in his sitting room, smoking his pipe and reading the Bible to his children. More rebels had seen it coming in time to be in the hayloft, and one sad case they wished they had not found had squeezed himself down the hole of his outhouse.

They commandeered wagons and filled them with oat bags and mealies, sunflower seeds, root vegetables, rings of sausage. Trussed chickens and turkeys. They laid claim to enough trek oxen to haul it all. Gathered a serviceable herd of horses.

They found weapons too. Lever-action Martini-Henrys and bolt-action Mausers. Boxes of ammunition. Finding rebel guns on a farm turned it into a rebel farm. You could loot or burn a rebel farm to your heart's content.

They did not want to be ambushed at Bothaville, so they left quickly. They did not sleep, except in the saddle, all the way home.

Frank discovered that rolling into their Kroonstad camp after the Bothaville raid was a big event for the soldiers who had not gone. They lined the camp's centre road and cheered them because they had done something.

Wagons piled with booty, a herd of horses, twenty-four shuffling prisoners—those were the proof.

Frank thought of the Blood Indians riding into Crow country and coming back with scalps and horses, that this must have been how they felt—and why they went again and again, despite the wounds and the dying.

On the ground, Frank jumped and kicked until his legs would work, then hobbled to where their camp had been. Ovide had used his Wallace spade to scrape to dry ground, but he was gone and so was his greatcoat and bedroll. What remained was their oil sheet, crumpled and held down by the spade. Frank asked everyone he saw until finally one told him that Ovide was in the sick tent. Enteric fever. Quarantined.

A barbwire fence around the tent marked the quarantine line. Between that and the tent door was the cart they used to carry the dead. Frank leaned on the fence and called out. He knew they were short of nurses and doctors, but he went on calling anyway. He shouted Ovide's name. He called for help, as though he himself were sick.

Near the end of an hour, an angry nurse stepped out. She was square built and strong, maybe five years older than Frank. She had a cloth mask over her mouth and nose that had a spatter of blood across it. Her eyes were dark-rimmed. He told her he wanted to give a message to Ovide Smith, then realized he had no message.

"Just tell him Frank's back."

"That's so important you yelled at me for an hour? Do you have any idea what it's like in here? How many nurses do you think there are?"

"Five?"

"There's me."

Frank apologized. "But would you?"

She stormed back inside, and, after a very long time, came partway out. She lifted the cloth from her face. Her lips were beautiful.

"He says don't let his horse drink the dew. Now get away and stay away."

In the hole Ovide had scraped, Frank tried to sleep. The night was no colder than recent ones, but fatigue cranked him with chills and chattered his teeth. Pictures of the day flickered through his mind erratically, as if the light machine throwing them was faulty. Then one picture surprised him. He was riding into camp again, down the line of soldiers. Near the end, one of those soldiers was Colonel Herchmer.

Frank worked to see more. Herchmer was saluting the flying column. He stood straight and jutted his porcupine jaw. His greatcoat hung on him the way old coats hang on scarecrows. His cheeks burned red in a grey face. He looked like what he was: an old man who'd been sick and had rushed his recovery.

There was something else in the picture—or not in it. Herchmer was alone, except for one flunky. In all of Frank's other memories, right back to Ft. Calgary, the colonel had been surrounded by anxious officers, trying to decipher and do his bidding. Now, all but the single flunky had abandoned the wreck.

Then sleep came at Frank like an avalanche of snow.

By the time Frank awoke, the big African sun was burning a hole in an umber sky. While Frank scrounged feed and water for the horses (including a new gelding that was his share of the Bothaville loot), he kept his ears open. The talk today was mostly about the plot. The Mounted Rifles officers had gone against Herchmer.

Through morning, the story developed. Now it was a petition taken over Herchmer's head. Different versions had different complaints against him. It was on account of Herchmer's harshness. It was because of his age. It was his health. *He's had a stroke, you know.*

One story said there was no relationship between the plot and things done or not done here in Africa. The officers were settling old scores from Canada. Mounties overlooked for promotion. Contracts given out by Herchmer to his friends and family, and not to them.

Frank was still very tired and fell asleep in the afternoon by the horse lines. Fred Morden woke him, lightly kicking his boot. Fred told him that there was a meeting tonight, of D Squadron, a secret meeting after lights out. It would be held right here beside their horses.

Frank went to the sick tent but had no luck. No matter how much he called, the nurse would not come. Then Ovide himself came out. He exited the tent and crawled through the wire; caught his baggy trousers on the barbs and cursed. He looked like death but said he was better.

"Nurse put the glass thing in my mouth. No fever." It was dysentery after all, and he said that part was drying up.

Frank told him about Herchmer and the meeting, but Ovide was on his way to his horse.

That night, Frank kept himself awake. A while after the bugle sounded lights out, Fred Morden came, and they walked together in silence. Shapes converged on the horse lines, and up close Frank saw men wrapped in their blankets, looking like Indians on ration day. Everyone sat, but the meeting was slow to begin.

Frank knew why. When they'd had their secret meeting in the Great Karoo, there had been a clear problem (hunger) and a clear solution (sheep). But today the stories had gone off in all directions. Believing there would be disagreement on the facts, no one wanted to go first.

Fred Morden raised his hand and waved a piece of paper. When everyone was looking, he said, "This is a copy of what the officers gave General Hutton. It's a list of points against Colonel Herchmer."

Fred asked Tom Miles to strike a match so he could read. Tom carefully shielded the flame. Fred read, and when the match went out, he waited for Tom to light another.

Herchmer was unfit. That was the substance of the first part. It gave three pieces of evidence: staggering; cursing wildly; and forgetting what he was about to say. Frank had to admit the authors of this thing had been clever. Instead of saying there'd been a stroke or that the colonel was a lunatic, or was too old, they'd stuck to symptoms. Saying he staggered and forgot things was more diplomatic than saying he was sixty—considering that General Roberts was sixty-eight.

The letter's second part described what the men in Herchmer's command thought of him. It said Herchmer was extremely unpopular with them, so much so that they might mutiny and kill him.

That was the extent of it. Tom's match went out, and they sat in the dark. One way or another, every man present was insulted.

"I don't know about you boys," Fred Morden said, finally, "but there's at least three officers I'd kill before Herchmer."

This prompted a laugh. It loosened them up and now several wanted to talk.

"I heard that coward we had the song about is a ringleader," said one.

Morden had seen the names. He said it was true.

"Old Herchmer knows horses," said a cowboy. "We were taking better care of our horses before he got sick."

Frank thought of Herchmer shooting the pale horses and trying to get The Blue and Dunny, but didn't raise that point.

"Ever been chewed out by him, though?" said a Mountie. "He'll curse you, then your mother, then your family to the third generation of ancestors. He's hard to work for."

It sawed back and forth.

When the meeting finally broke up, Frank thought he felt a helplessness in the men drifting away. They had spoken their piece, but they knew that's where it stopped. Herchmer's fate was likely already sealed, and not by them.

Next morning, the bugler blew a long reveille. The sergeants and the NCOs told them to pack and get their horses ready to march. Though there was a sense of hurry, it also sounded like they weren't leaving until evening. A night march, for some stupid reason.

Frank and Ovide took their time. Ovide was examining the new horse: feeling along the animal's legs, touching a host of places only he knew and checking what difference it made in the gelding's eye.

Frank kept watch on the officers' tent and their mess. For a time, it was all orderlies hurrying about or standing by someone's tent waiting for an answer. Late in the morning, a slicked-up group of officers—that included the coward—headed for the British side of camp.

After the officers returned, Frank fixed his attention on Herchmer's tent. A sergeant brought him a message in the early afternoon. Herchmer and his flunky came out soon after. Herchmer's hat was brushed. His boots were newly blacked. He tucked his swagger stick under his arm, and he and the flunky marched.

After Ovide had finished examining the gelding, he turned to his Basuto and found she had a slight limp. While he'd been in the sick tent, the farrier had put on a new shoe. He'd placed one nail too high and hurt her. Ovide was angry, and he kept squinting at Frank. If Frank hadn't been away playing soldier, it would not have happened, was what the look said.

Finally, Frank was sick of it. Here they were in a whole camp buzzing with talk about their deposed commander, and he was stuck with the only person who did not care. He got up, brushed himself off, and left.

He wanted to find Fred Morden. When he did, Fred was sitting alone by the horse lines with his haversack, bedroll, and saddle beside him. He was ready to ride.

Morden was drinking cold tea out of his mess tin. Frank sat down beside him.

"So how do they get rid of a colonel?" Frank asked.

"Tell him he's not fit and offer him something he doesn't want."

"Like what?"

"Hutton offered him command of the supply depot here at Kroonstad."

"What then?"

"Herchmer said he wanted a medical board."

Morden stopped and looked at Frank for some sign that he understood what a medical board was. Frank figured it was a board to decide whether someone was sick.

"The board found him medically unfit, as Herchmer knew it would."

"So why ask for it?"

"Because it means he doesn't have to take the depot job. He can go home."

Morden did not speak for a time. Frank was about to go when Fred started up again about other events of the day. Major Howe, who had an infected eye, was leaving too. Archie Macdonnell had been promoted to major in Howe's place. Lieutenant Moodie was made captain to fill Macdonnell's old rank.

"Good promotions," said Morden.

That seemed like the end. Fred threw the last bit of his tea away and put his mess tin in the sack. Frank had come here thinking he'd tell Fred how much he'd started to hate the war. Even when he let himself be picked for Bothaville, it was just to get some fresh air—though he had unexpectedly liked the feeling of returning in triumph.

In the end, he said none of it, but Morden spoke exactly as though he had.

"Everybody's sick of the war now," he said. "I am too. We're chasing an enemy who's lost his fight. That's what today's about. Not Herchmer. Sacking him won't make any difference."

"You're disappointed, then."

"Of course I am. I'd hoped for more."

"Do you hate them?" Frank asked. "The Boers?"

Morden smiled. "Not much. I said that in a letter to a relative in Ontario and got an earful back. He used to be in the army, and he said I felt the way I did because I wasn't at Colenso or Spion Kop and lacked the imagination to put myself there."

Morden stared at his horse.

"But I'll fight them like I hate them," he said. "If I get a chance."

When the setting sun was close to the horizon, the officers blew their whistles as the signal to start. The horses were sluggish. The oxen needed the whip to pull. False starts, shouting; misunderstood orders. Everyone knew the Boers were far away, so what did it matter how smoothly or swiftly or quietly the night march began?

Major Howe came by to say his farewells. He wished them luck, and did not mention Colonel Herchmer. Reg Redpath was staying behind too and was very disappointed. Every time someone asked him why, Reg had to say the word *rupture*. The word itself made him wince. He got the injury running into an anthill at night. There were more men in the sick tent who were being left, some of whom might never be well.

Besides the sick tent, the only thing left standing on the empty ground of their camp was Colonel Herchmer's tent. All around it, newspapers and discarded letters shifted like living things. The colonel's tent sucked in and breathed out. An empty camp stool stood under the awning.

They walked their horses by it like mourners past a coffin. They were silent until Gil Snaddon said, "They didn't even leave him a horse or a servant."

Frank knew Snaddon well by now. He came from a hard-luck horse outfit south of Calgary and would never have a servant in his life. But no one laughed at the irony. It did seem shabby to leave the colonel inside his tent and alone. No horse. No flunky. No thanks.

Riding away, Frank knew why the others were moved by Herchmer's fate. It was unlucky to treat your commander badly, and in most men's minds, the war was about luck. Whether a shell landed beside you or on you. Whether a white flag meant neutrality or ambush. Whether a fever bug jumped down your throat or somebody else's.

But Frank had to risk that bad luck, because Herchmer had killed the pale horses. Herchmer'd had no mercy then, and Frank had none now.

The Doornkop

On their journey to the Vaal River, Frank wondered if the Boers hadn't done some of this on purpose. He supposed they would not give up country if they could help it, but, given that they could not help it, there was power in retreat. By seeming always to be within Curly Hutton's grasp, they could make the brigade general run wherever and however fast they wanted. Ever since the Vet River, Curly had believed he could catch the Boers and cut them off. On the way to the Vaal, he was at it again, pressing General Roberts to let him "make a dash."

For five merciless days, Frank's squadron did dash. As they approached the Vaal, the pace was frantic, and halfway through May 24, Fred Morden excitedly told Frank why. It was the Queen's birthday. Curly's brigade was racing French's cavalry to see who could cross the Vaal first and enter the Transvaal Republic on the Queen's birthday.

That night, the Mounted Rifles and Royal Canadian Dragoons were bivouacked on the Orange Free State side. Some of French's cavalry had floundered across and, thus, had won. For this victory, they had outraced their supply wagons, tired their horses, and now sat cold and exhausted in a dark camp. Frank did not tell Ovide about the Queen's birthday. He was already angry about the Basuto's sore foot and still inclined to hold Frank to blame.

Though Frank feared all big rivers, crossing the Vaal was more tedious than dangerous. Hutton's brigade went by the old ford or *drift* called Viljeon. It took all day, and allowed Frank to see the immensity of which he was part. Wherever he looked along the river, parts of the army were crossing. Like an old-time buffalo crossing, they almost plugged the river with their wagons and bodies.

Also at Viljeon's Drift was another handsome blown-up railway bridge. As for standing on the soil of the rebel Transvaal for the first time, Frank felt nothing.

For two more days, they travelled north. They saw huge heaps of coal-mine slag and shack towns like anthills where the black miners lived. Occasionally, the Boers set up shop on a ridge and fired on them, but, after a little skirmish, would retire and let them continue.

Then they came to the valley of the Klip River, beyond which a blue ridge hung across the north horizon. That six-thousand-foot plateau was the high veld, the third plateau of their climb from the sea. Black stubs along it were iron chimneys for the Rand gold mines. From one, a tail of smoke was rising. Johannesburg was somewhere beyond.

The returning scouts confirmed that the Boers intended to fight. They were dug in across the ridge. By the time Hutton's brigade came to the valley's south approach, the British artillery was in play. The duel was on.

From the smoke tufts on both sides of the fight, Frank could see that the Boer guns outranged the British ones. There was always plenty in the newspapers about field guns, and the Boers had Creusots called *Long Cecil* and *Long Tom* that could lob an eighty-eight-pound shell eleven thousand yards. To counter Long Cecil and Long Tom, the British had stripped guns from their navy ships, what they called "cow guns" because of the number of oxen it took to pull them. But even the cow guns had a shorter range and smaller shell than the Boers' longest weapons.

The Mounted Rifles had not been at the valley long when they got their orders to cross it. In the marshy middle was an intact bridge. The Canadians and some Aussies were to ride down, cross it, and take the low hills on the other side. The hills were grey and lumpish, and dwarfed by the blue ridge beyond them.

Frank studied the bridge. If the Boers had been getting ready here all week, and the bridge was still there, it had to mean that they wanted the British to use it. Before he could think more, the Mounted Rifles were given the signal to go. They swept down the slope and onto the valley's wet bottom. The Boer gunners had to see them but held fire. Ovide was beside Frank on the Boer gelding. He had left the Basuto behind.

The riders bunched at the bridge. Frank could hear the hooves of the first horses clattering the planks ahead. He imagined dynamite picking up the centre and horses and men flying. Then, it was his and Dunny's turn and the muscles in his neck and shoulders seized tight. Dunny did not like the look of the bridge either but he forced her on.

When the bridge did not explode, Frank turned to the notion that the Boer guns were aimed at the far end. It was true. While still on the bridge, Frank heard shell blasts and saw plumes of muck over the horses' ears.

Each rider jumped to the far shore with spurs digging. Each tried to design an unpredictable path across the wet plain that stretched to the hills. Frank went at it like it was a race. Put his rein hands on Dunny's neck and surged his fists. Around him, men were quirting like jockeys. Some, in fear, spurred until the blood ran. A race, but Frank made sure not to win it. He and Ovide tucked in behind the leaders and stayed there.

Fred Morden was ahead, where Frank expected him to be. When Frank saw Morden drop his reins and jerk upright, he thought he was shot, but Morden was unslinging his Lee-Enfield. He raised the rifle and popped off ten at the hill's rim.

The treed fringe at the bottom of the hills seemed very far and then came up fast. Before he reached it, Frank saw a Mounted Rifle fall from his horse in a loose heap. It was Corporal Stevens. Two riders near him pulled up, jumped off, and slung the wounded man across his saddle.

All along the hill bottom, men were running, finding each other, arranging their fours. The Beltons had stuck close to Frank and Ovide, and Frank threw his reins to Eddy. The men in Stevens' four pressed over him, holding down the hurt part as Stevens' legs galloped in the air.

The Boers were still lobbing shells, even though they sailed harmlessly above. Frank saw one hit without exploding. It dug a furrow and stopped. A dud. The live ones blew but had no one to kill. There was no more *crick-crack* of rifles. The last view of the kopje's rim showed men running away, getting a head start for the blue ridge, the real line of fire.

The lieutenants and sergeants were shouting: gathering their troops. No one was keen to leave this shelter. The sergeants told them to holster their Colts and ready their Lee-Enfields, to check that their rifle magazines were full. As for the revolvers, they were to leave the chamber under the hammer empty, so it would not fire if it fell out or the hammer caught on a branch.

Ovide was inspecting the horses. He had seen blood spots on the ground and was making sure they weren't from the Boer gelding or Dunny.

Leaving the horses with Eddy, the other three started to climb, Frank in the middle of the three. The kopje's stone was orange, and the slope of squarish rocks was like a stone fort shaken down by earthquake. They bent forward in case the Boer snipers were only pretending to have gone.

When their heads appeared above the top, the Boers cut loose the full orchestra. Shells, pom-poms, shrapnel, Mausers. Up on their blue ridge, the Boers must have loved what they saw: the enemy laid out like a buffet meal.

Frank found a knuckle of rock and cuddled behind it. He looked for Ovide and found him to his right, also in a rock's lee. Pete was scrabbling and cursing to the left. His place in the line had no upright stones, just a low-domed one not much taller than the grass. Pete bayoneted the ground. "Fucking bastards! Fucking bastards!" he yelled.

No one thought of shooting back until the sergeants came yelling. They had not come all this way to lie doggo behind a rock. Watch for a flash and fire at it. Ammunition boxes on their way. Go easy on the water.

For two hours, the barrage did not slacken. Frank fired every now and again, but there was not much to aim at. The sun was above the ridge, streaming into his eyes. Frank noticed Ovide on his back, shoulders leaned against the stone. He was looking back at the river and the valley they had crossed. When he saw Frank was watching him, Ovide pointed south, at something moving there. He swept his arm left to right, and Frank understood that the moving thing was infantry.

In the last few days, Roberts had switched Hamilton's column from east to west, and now they were headed for the Boers' right flank. Frank and Ovide and the rest were probably on these hills to keep the Boers on their ridge. If the Boers were able to come down with their guns, Hamilton's infantry would be within range.

All day long, the pounding kept on. The worst thing was a pom-pom that had their range. Pom-pom was the nickname for a Maxim-Nordenfeldt machine gun that fired a belt of one-pound shells. When a shell from a bigger gun came, you could hear it in advance and duck, but the pom-pom fired continuously. Frank could not help feeling a rising fear as the pom-pom raked toward him, no more than he could help the relief when it had passed. Pete yelled, "It's like a fucking piano!" Every once in a long while, Pete got something right.

The sun fell down the sky into the ridge's western taper. Never had they been left on a battlefield this long, and still nothing was said about going back, or about food. At dusk, Davidson came and said to eat their meat paste. Drink a small swallow every hour or two.

Then darkness. The guns slacked off, and it grew quiet. The smoke and dust separated and settled. The moon stood unshaken in its sky. The temperature had started to plummet, and continued toward certain frost. Winter on the high veldt was colder; of this they had been warned.

In each man's mind was the image of his greatcoat, his blankets and oil sheet, all on the back of his horse. They were meant to spend the night without them. Barely visible, Harry Brindle came to say, "No fires." Most men yelled some curse or question but the sergeant kept moving.

Frank thought of Eddy Belton, down at the bottom with the horses. He knew Eddy would be full of dread. Asking himself over and over if he was supposed to do something with the coats and blankets, if there was an order he'd missed or misunderstood. He would probably forget to get his own blankets and wrap himself in them; forget to eat.

Across the hill's top, the cold became awful. They had already had freezing nights, but that had been soft frost. This one was freezing solid.

"We'll freeze to fucking death!" said Pete.

When they could no longer stand it, they stood and marched. Jumped and flapped. Rubbed themselves for the shallow warmth of friction.

Frank was watching Ovide's rock when his friend stood up. He thought he would limber up or take a piss, but Ovide left. Walked away until his khaki back was absorbed by night. Frank wondered if Ovide was headed down to the horses for his bedding. They had been strictly ordered not to.

Not long after, Ovide returned. He sat behind his stone. When the old cowboy did not say anything, Frank got up and went over.

"Where'd you go?"

"Find Greaseback," Ovide said.

"Why?"

"'Cause he's smart."

Ovide had told Frank before that he thought Greasy Griesbach was the smartest soldier in the Mounted Rifles. At Van Wyk's Vlei, Ovide had seen Griesbach take his and Jameson's horses and occupy an abandoned blacksmith shed, while the rest of them stood drenched. At Brandfort, Greasy had been the first to run and flop behind a coffin stone.

Ovide had gone to see what Greasy was doing about the cold.

"He's with two other fellas. They're lying back to front. After a while, Greasy says, 'Turn!' and they roll over the other way. Later, the guy in the middle gets up and goes to the outside."

Frank yelled at Pete to come. Ovide explained it again, and Pete said he guessed so. Spooning, Frank had heard it called, normally practised by man and wife. Ovide and Frank spooned up with Pete in the middle. It was not long before Pete started squirming. His hands seemed to be moving below his belt.

"Christ sake, Pete. This is hardly the time."

"What?"

"To get friendly with yourself."

"Shut up! I'm putting my water bottle in my pants."

The others laughed at him, then realized it was wisdom. Ovide and Frank put their bottles in their pants too.

The night had an eternity to go. They turned and switched a hundred times, maybe two hundred. Every once in a while, a Boer sniper would fire down, just to keep them from getting rest. As the quality of dark finally started to change, the three got up and went to tramping and stamping, until a bullet whined off a frost-bristled rock. In the grey light, each blade of grass was in its own sheath of glass.

Frank looked as far as he could and saw men shaking their water bottles, the nut of ice banging inside. Their curses rang in the frozen morning. Together, Ovide, Frank, and Pete got up on their knees, unearthed their bottles from their trouser fronts, raised them, and drank. Took the swallow their bellies had warmed.

The Boers did not start a full bombardment at first light. Sergeant Brindle brought an order for the Mounted Rifles to go to the foot of the hill. They found Eddy and the horses. Together, they walked to the rally point, to see if there was grub. There was water but nothing to eat.

While they thought about what to do, the miracle of an old trek ox staggered out of the brush. Every man got around the bewildered beast.

Someone shot him and the rest pounced on the corpse with their bayonets. Like a starving wolf pack rending an elk. Some fellows gathered grass and twigs and lit fires. The trash burned too quickly to cook anything. They were also too hungry to wait. Finally, every man was wearing himself out, chewing trek ox raw.

Frank and Pete pushed in and got a few strings of red, gave half to Ovide and Eddy to put in their cheeks and suck on.

When the ox skeleton was more or less cleaned, it suddenly blew up. They had heard the pom-pom approaching, and a shell hit the ox smack on. The barrel of rib staves fired like spears. One flew right between Frank and Pete. They had no time to move before the Boers sent the pom-pom back the other way and hit the rally point again. Frank saw Griesbach and another man try to board Greasy's horse from opposite sides. Whether by accident or design, Greasy kicked the other right in his face. Frank saw a private named Dore, from Pincher Creek, get wounded. Another was suddenly down and bleeding.

In the panic, two horses jerked free and ran splashing into the plain. The cinch on one was loose, and Frank watched the saddle work down. The dragging bedroll snagged the horse's legs and it pitched over its own head. The cinch burst. The horse rolled up and ran free.

Everyone who could was swinging onto a horse and milling around. All of Frank's four were up, looking for someone to give them an order.

Colonel Alderson appeared out of the smoke and dust, tootling on a brass hunting horn. He lowered it and yelled, "Get out as best you can!"

The riders sprayed from the smoking hole, dodging rocks and shell holes. Everybody was trying to stay away from everyone else. Frank had Ovide twenty feet on his offside. The Beltons must be behind because he could not see them. The plain was worse footing now than yesterday, chopped to mud and slippery with frost.

Toward the bridge, the fan of riders started to funnel. Frank looked at Ovide, who bunted his head toward the river. That's where they went. They urged Dunny and the Boer gelding into the yellow water, praying for a bottom that wouldn't suck them down. Frank looked at everything that might not be water, lest a stick turn crocodile. The horses' eyes were wild, heads jerking. Then they were bucking and lunging through the ice fringe on the opposite bank, flanks streaming, trying to shake the water off beneath their loads. Frank looked back and the Beltons were coming, Eddy on his lumbering war horse, Pete on an Argentine. The four crossed the brush at the river's edge and faced the second plain. Entered it at a gallop.

They did not stop until they reached the first British cow gun. A dozen African bullwhackers were forcing dozens of oxen to turn it. A Tommy Atkins came over, a small bustling man. He was a bombardier and treated them like tourists. He explained the gun and its range, and how they aimed it.

"Now you see over there?" Because he was looking through field glasses and did not offer them, they could not see. "See that puff of smoke on the ridge? You might think that's one of Johnny Boer's. But it isn't, see? They blow up a bag of gunpowder, even flour. Hide their guns behind the hill. Move them around. To make my life difficult."

Fred Morden arrived leading his blown horse. The black's face was white with froth and ash. Fred heard the last part about how it was hard to locate the Boer guns.

"We use Canadians for that," he said.

"Good idea," said the Tommy, dropping his field glasses onto his chest. He walked off, unaware there'd been a joke.

More of Hutton's brigade gathered by the cow gun. Out of the Mounted Rifles, Stevens, Dore, and one other—the wounded men—were brought together and a red cross flag placed over them. Frank stared at Stevens, who had it worst. Likely even he would live, so the luck of the Mounted Rifles was holding. They had still not lost a man in battle. Rations were issued, and the Rifles were told to fill their water bottles from a barrel on a wagon. It suggested their day of fighting was not over.

A British major rode up. Speaking on behalf of Alderson, he explained what was next. On the west end of the Boers' ridge was a rocky feature called Doornkop. The infantry were going to take it by frontal assault. While the Boers were occupied, the cavalry and mounted artillery would hook around the Boers' right. The major pointed to where Doornkop was.

"It's the one that's smoking. The Boers have lit it on fire. Doornkop's where Dr. Jameson surrendered in '95. We must take it."

Seeing the blankness of their faces, he shrugged and rode away, his fat horse farting on every jolt.

Morden's four rode east beside Frank's. Frank asked Morden who Jameson was.

"I don't know about Jameson," said Fred, "but the Jameson Raid was something Cecil Rhodes paid for. Policemen from Rhodesia rode down to take Johannesburg. The *uitlanders* were supposed to rise up and help them. When they didn't, the Boers trapped Jameson and his raiders on the Doornkop."

When the Canadians got to where the cavalry and other MI were massing, all of the riders were facing north and studying the Doornkop. Lieutenant Davidson let his troop take turns with his field glasses.

The smoking flank was black to its rocky crest. The downhill edge was rimmed with fire. The Gordon Highlanders—"men in dresses," as the Boers called them—were climbing the burn in well-spaced lines. The Royal Canadians were at the same height, to the Highlanders' right. A soldier would pop up every once in a while, having stepped on a hot coal with a thin boot. When a soldier was shot, the others marched past as if they could not see him.

The climbers reached a necklace of stone near the top. Frank could see that the crest the infantrymen were below was not the top. Beyond it, the hill went up again and they would have to climb that to reach the Boers. Finally, the infantrymen scaled the rocks and began to spill over. They disappeared into whatever it was.

By then, the Mounted Rifles were moving again, part of a long line of riders aimed west of the Doornkop, headed for the Boers' flank. Frank questioned why they had not gone earlier, before the infantry climbed the hill. Why not turn the flank, *then* charge the Doornkop? This time he found he did not need Fred Morden to answer.

Because some mad British bugger had invaded here before and been captured. Because Roberts and Hamilton were not content to force the Boers into another retreat. Because Empire pride was involved and a show of blood was wanted.

Throw some foot soldiers on the fire. Show these Boer farmers what mad bravery Britain could summon from the ends of the earth.

The Rand was a repeating thing. At intervals not quite random stood iron chimneys and tall wooden buildings full of engines and winding gear. From the headframes, long rattling tongues of conveyor buckets descended. A maze of rails ran along the ground, and two pug engines were moving cars of ore. At one building, black men holding spades, picks, and wire-handled lunch cans waited to be wound down into the earth—while the war went on around them.

The Mounted Rifles passed through the mine works and the crushed mounds of blue and yellow reef slag. The thousand-horse thing they were part of split and reduced from time to time. They saw the Dragoons go pelting off, said to be chasing a stranded Boer convoy. Others went toward the city. Their own orders were to continue north. Johannesburg, the fabled golden city, slid by.

The long day ended at a dynamite factory. Far in the distance, Johannesburg was aglitter with bonfires, and, sitting by his troop's fire, Frank wondered how the city would celebrate its liberation. Pretty black women handing out flowers? Liquor flowing freely? It seemed doubtful given how much of the population had already left. Just today, hundreds of Boers had been streaming away along every road and trail.

After his fury at not being allowed into the plague town of Bloemfontein, Andy Skinner stared through the darkness at the lights of another Sodom and Gomorrah denied to him. Unlike last time, the cowboy faced his disappointment in silence. When the bugler blew lights out, Frank was thankful to throw his bedroll down; to try to sleep before the fire's warmth left him. In the night he woke to the sound of a horse galloping, and said to himself, "Andy." He was asleep again before he could worry about it.

Next morning's reveille was delayed, in honour of the past two days of fighting. When they rose, it was almost dawn, and Frank took a walk around the camp before chores. He remembered the horse running in the night and hoped someone might explain. When no one did, he asked Gil Snaddon, who bivouacked with Skinner. Gil's beardless face was blue from cold and wore a look of fear. Andy was gone, he said. That's all he knew.

The sergeants were soon busy, letting the camp know that today was another marching day. Sergeant Brindle returned later and said Lieutenant Davidson wanted a word with them. When they found him beside a fire, Davidson looked like he had missed sleep and was not happy. His lips moved before he spoke.

"As some of you probably know . . ." He stopped and took a sharp look around, trying to catch someone who did look like he knew.

He began again. "As some of you probably know, Andy Skinner rode into Johannesburg last night. Without permission. British MPs picked him up and threw him in jail. His court martial for desertion will take place today."

Davidson took a rest and looked at them again. Accusation. Their fault, not his.

"Good old Andy, you're probably thinking," Davidson continued bitterly. "What a wild one. I want you to know that I am 100 percent sure Andy Skinner's war is over. I am 90 percent sure he will go to jail, and not just for the duration of the war. It will be a long time before any of you see Andy Skinner again."

The men looked offended. Andy was no deserter. He wanted a piece of tail and a game of cards. He would have come back.

"I don't think most of you understand *still*. Obedience is not optional in a war. Neither is being here. You gave up your freedom when you enlisted. We insist on that because an army doesn't work if thousands of men run around doing as they please."

Frank had heard other versions of this. They all had. They were waiting for him to get to the important part. Something like, *I'll go see what can be done for him.* But Davidson wrapped up without saying it. He told them to get to their horses and be ready to move.

The horses were not much benefited by the single night's rest. They were tired when they left the dynamite factory, and they grew more tired as D Squadron pushed north. They started to falter and cripple, and to walk stupidly in ways that did not see the thorn, the rock, the hole in the path. Both the Boer gelding and Ovide's Basuto were favouring a leg, and Ovide switched back and forth between them.

The officers' attitudes toward horses had hardened. Like Ovide's cutting mare, most of the horses from Canada were dead by now. The Rifles were riding a first or second remount, some Argentine cull. It was as if the officers were saying, *Get busy and ride that thing to death. Then go fetch another.* Ovide lacked the language to curse this evil.

During the day, the Mounted Rifles joined a massive army, the one moving north toward Pretoria, driving the Boers off the hills. While French's cavalry probed ahead, the Rifles were part of his rear guard—until French's horsemen rode into a sink near the Crocodile River and were surrounded by a Boer commando. The Rifles were called forward then to help. They and several units beat the Boers back to reduce pressure on the hole, where French's horsemen were trapped and milling.

In the end, it wasn't the massacre it might have been. But while the hole was draining of cavalry, the Rifles had to stay on a ridge, even as day turned to night. Another frozen night without blankets, and by morning several men were too sick to go on. They were left coughing and with fevers for the Red Cross ambulances to find.

After that, it would have made sense to camp and let the men and horses recoup energy, but the officers, in their man-burning, horse-burning mood, said they must go on. Their orders were to be on the final hills before Pretoria by tonight.

They dragged into that camp long after dark. As soon as the horses were put up, the soldiers rolled into their blankets and slept, not bothering to eat. No one noticed that Tom Scott was missing. He had fallen behind and was stone asleep when he got to camp. His horse's abrupt stop caused him to fall, but instead of waking completely, he crawled into a bush and slept some more. The horse did what it always did: went and found its place on the line.

During the night, the Boers crept close to a Canadian outpost on the hill above and opened fire. The men in the camp were whistled awake and told to mount up and give support. They climbed the hill, and there was a dangerous fight in the dark. Though Tom Scott slept through it, his horse did not. In the moonlight, the men pursuing the Boers saw Scott's horse with an empty saddle and reins dragging, running in the thick of it.

After the Boers were chased off, the riderless horse was caught and identified as Tom's. Frank was among those who thought the worst, that Tom must by lying somewhere, shot. But a private who knew the horse said he'd seen the gelding down at the bottom of the hill, at the start. The saddle had been empty already then.

They searched for Tom closer to the camp, but were ordered to stop and get some sleep. When they started looking again at dawn, Tom came wandering out of the brush and asked them what the fuss was about.

It was a great joke and, over breakfast, everyone took his turn telling the part he'd seen. They laughed and laughed—until two military policemen appeared and put Tom under arrest. Two British officers had been in camp overnight. One, a captain, observed the fuss and heard about the riderless horse. When he inquired, he found out about Tom being asleep. It struck the captain as clear-cut dereliction of duty—asleep while under attack. Men had been shot for less.

That morning, the Mounted Rifles stood together in their greatcoats, smoking cigarettes. The officers who happened by were asked what would happen to Tom. At first, the lieutenants, and higher ranks like Moodie and Macdonnell, pooh-poohed the danger, ridiculing the men for their concern. But when these officers tried to get an audience to plead for Scott, they were refused. Proceedings were under way, the British told them. Influencing those proceedings was no longer possible. Attempting to was illegal.

Frank was watching when they pulled Tom from his prison tent and marched him to his court martial. His hands were tied behind him, as if he were dangerous and might try to run. When he saw them watching, Tom tried to fashion a plucky grin, on a face grey from lack of sleep and worry.

Scott was marched into the officers' tent. Guilty. No argument there. The question was sentence, and all around him the faces of the British officers were not reassuring. He was pushed to a table where a man sat staring at a piece of paper. On it were the known facts. This officer looked up and he and Scott stared at each other.

The last thing Tom expected in this tent was to see someone he knew, but there before him was an acquaintance. For a time when he was young, he had lived at Ft. Macleod and done barn work for the Mounties. An inspector named White-Fraser had liked how he handled horses and slipped him coins to exercise his string. Now, holding Tom's fate in his hands was the same White-Fraser.

The major recognized Tom too, though he said nothing. It was just there briefly in his eyes. He returned to examining the papers, then tore them end to end.

"Don't waste my time with this," he said.

When Scott walked out and back to the Mounted Rifles' end of camp, he was rubbing the blood back into his hands. This time, his grin was genuine.

At the end of another day of hill-sweeping, Gil Snaddon came to Frank and whispered, "Secret meeting at the horse lines. Waldron Hank says."

As before, Frank attended and Ovide did not. It was mainly Ft. Macleod and Pincher Creek cowboys. As in the Great Karoo, Fred Morden showed up and was the only man ranked higher than private. Tom Scott was there, sitting next to Waldron Hank.

"Thing is," Hank said, the minute they sat down, "if Tom here wasn't lucky enough to have White-Fraser as his judge, this could be a wake. Who else is apt to be that lucky? Now that they've done what they've done to Andy, and what they almost did to Tom, we've gotta rethink what we're doing here. The way these Brits are going at it, one wrong move—caught asleep or looting a chicken—and, hell, one of us could get shot."

"What are you saying, Hank? No more rustling grub?"

"I'm not saying that. Most days, it's rustle or starve. What I'm trying to say is going to sound like treason, so keep your damn mouths shut. Pete Belton, that means you."

After having been quiet for a couple of weeks, Pete had returned to form after Andy Skinner's arrest. He saw it as an attack on the American-born: "If the sonsabitches didn't want us, why'd they let us enlist?"

Hank continued. "All along this push, it's been our job to draw fire. We're told it's an honour. I notice few British regiments get that honour."

Hank, normally clear, was going off in all directions. Tom Scott turned to him and socked him on the shoulder.

"Come on, old son. We're listening but we don't want to be here long."

"Well, goddamn, Tom, it's that I never thought I'd have to say such a thing. But I *gotta* say it. I don't think these Brits are on our side. It's like they decided the war's almost over, they got it won, and we've got to be shown our place. If I'm right, I say we should be damn careful which orders of theirs we obey."

There was grumbling in the dark. Several present were English-born or sons of English parents. They were here based on the assumption that the British and Canadian sides were the same.

"So if they tell us to charge," said Tom Scott, "and we think it's stupid, we don't charge?"

Hank paused. In the bit of light, Frank could see he was slumped forward. "If they order it, we have to. But maybe we don't go hell for leather. Maybe, instead of trying to win a medal, we just try and survive."

The meeting had nowhere further to go. For Frank, there was not much revelation. Waldron Hank was suggesting everyone fight the war how Ovide and he had always done it.

But he knew that some did want to be heroes. For whatever reason, Jeff Davis did. If Hank was right and the British did not care as much about colonial lives as British ones, it implied that Jeff must be in danger all the time. What could be more colonial than an Indian in a troop of British scouts?

Another who wanted more stripes and maybe a medal on his chest was Morden. Fred was sitting beside Robert Kerr and seemed to be looking at Kerr's foot. His only comment was to scoop up some soil and pour it into a hole in Kerr's boot toe.

Pretoria, June 1900

The last two hills before Pretoria were giant twins flanking a deep notch. On top of one was Ft. Schanzkop; on the other, Ft. Klapperkop. Forts built by Kruger in the years after the Jameson Raid. But as the great army approached, all was quiet. Every minute, it seemed that the hilltops should explode and rain down fire, but nothing came. When they got to the forts, they were empty. All the useful guns had been taken.

Pretoria, capital of the Transvaal, was being surrendered without a fight, just as Kroonstad and Johannesburg had been. To surrender a big whorehouse like Johannesburg was one thing. To surrender your last capital, home of Oom Paul, leader of all the Boers, was quite another. It smacked of defeat.

It was doubtful that even Waldron Hank or Pete Belton could have thought up the next humiliation in store for the Canadian Mounted Rifles. On the eve of Pretoria's liberation, they were camped below Ft. Klapperkop, close enough to see the road by which Lord Roberts would enter the city. They were looking forward to taking part in that parade.

Then their lieutenants came to talk, downcast and trying hard not to be. In fake attitudes of indifference or severity, they told the men they would not be going into Pretoria tomorrow. They had orders to stay out. Talking to his troop, Hugh Davidson claimed it all made sense. The Royal Canadian Regiment was going to represent Canada in the triumphal parade, and what Canadian outfit had suffered more or lost more men? Just think of that burning hill at Doornkop.

No one begrudged the infantry, but was that the issue? Wasn't the real question how many British regiments were going to be marching the streets of Pretoria, receiving Lord Roberts' thankful salutes? A damn sight more than one.

For something to do on celebration day, Frank and some others climbed to Ft. Klapperkop. They thought they could listen to the brass bands and pipers from there. Fred Morden was with them, and Kerr and the Miles boys. Tommy Scott, who evidently held no grudge against the British war effort, came too. On the way up, Frank asked Fred Morden if he was disappointed about missing the parade. Frank assumed he would be and was surprised when he said he wasn't.

"If we'd really fought for it and won, I'd want to be there," he said.

From the top, they could hear some of the music. The brass instruments sounded tinny, but the skirl of the bagpipes, over all those miles, was clear. Some Irish Fusiliers were at the fort, looking at the guns the Boers had left behind. They were supposed to provide powder blasts for the celebration, but the guns were antiques and they were afraid to fire them. When the first helio signal came, they blew up a bag of gunpowder and called it good.

Next day was June 6, and Pretoria was ready for the mounted Canadians. Still filthy from battle and crawling with lice, the Canadian MI rode in on weary mounts. Ovide chose to lead both the Basuto and the Boer gelding. As it seemed like a long time since Frank had done anything to help his friend, he invented a problem with one of Dunny's shoes and stayed back as well. Dunny hated walking behind. Every hundred yards or so, she whacked Frank with her head.

Greasy Griesbach's horse had chosen this moment to throw a shoe, and he too was forced to the rear as they entered town. Greasy provided a tour of this place he'd never seen. When they passed between a park full of well-tended flowers and a fancy white mansion flying a flock of Union Jacks, Greasy said that must be the house Roberts had been given for a headquarters. A local merchant named Hay whose family was in Europe had offered it.

A while later, they entered Church Square, where they caught up with the men who'd ridden. The square was a few acres of grass with Pretoria's sombre law court and post office on its sides. It was already stuffed with soldiers and horses. At the centre was a plinth for a statue, but no statue.

As they stared in bushed wonderment, a dozen or so Boers entered the square from a side street and came running at them holding rifles. A few of the boys pulled their Colts, for which they were heartily jeered by a bunch of Tommy Atkins, lying on the grass.

"They're trying to surrender, you stupid gits," said the Brits.

The Canadians might have argued or offered to fight, but the Tommys looked like they'd had a tough war. They were as dirty as any Canadian, and looked far more hungry. Yet they seemed happy. Laughing at everything. Going wild every time a woman happened by.

A few black youngsters were wandering the square selling a one-page newspaper. Griesbach bought one and, after he'd read it, offered a possible explanation for the Tommys' filthy state and happy attitude.

"Prisoners of war," said Griesbach. "A bunch were just set free."

In the whole square, only the black people were actually cheering. Some danced along in big groups. They looked shabby and poor, but Frank noticed by contrast how tidy the Boers in the crowd appeared. These might look sad or angry, or afraid, but they were well fed and groomed. The *uitlanders* in the square also did not appear to have gone hungry.

"I bet *they* don't have lice," said Harry Gunn, summing up what many felt.

Tommy Scott, who was an inveterate gambler, inspired several to bet on the empty plinth. Whose statue had been there? Several put their money on Queen Victoria. They reckoned she wasn't there because the Boer rebels had pulled her down. Griesbach bet against this, and because a lot of people (not just Ovide) considered Greasy smart, there was a lot of blind money on his choice, which was that it was a Boer pioneer. The Boers had trekked in here, he said, fought the blacks, and many had died. So their pioneers were their heroes. The reason the statue wasn't there, in his version, was because British soldiers had pulled it down yesterday.

As soon as all the money was bet, Greasy scorned the silly buggers on the other side. Why would there be a statue of Queen Victoria in a Boer republic that had never in its history been governed by Britain?

But he still had to prove his contention to win, and so Greasy went around, in his confident way, stopping all the well-heeled Boers until he got his answer. They were actually all wrong. No one could win the bet because there had never been a statue on the plinth. A bronze one of Paul Kruger in a top hat had been commissioned by a coal and whisky millionaire named Sammy Marks. When the war broke out, the bronze was still in Rome.

The Mounted Rifles' orders for the day were to pass through Pretoria to a camp on the east side called Silverton. They were to stay there until further notice, screening the city from the rebels. There was no authorization from higher up for any leave in the city, but, perhaps because of yesterday's snub, the Mounted Rifles officers declared one. A two-hour leave, starting now. Because somebody had to protect the horses, the number threes did not get the leave. If they'd got off lightly in a battle or two, this was their penance. The rest could go where they wanted, but the officer said they might want to visit Paul Kruger's house, which was a couple of blocks north.

Frank spent the first twenty minutes of his leave trying to convince Ovide to vacate the square. They could buy a loaf of bread, he said; a pound of butter. Milk and an egg. Ovide said he did not care for an egg. Frank tried other arguments. Ovide parried them. It was irritating because Frank knew Ovide did not trust Eddy Belton to guard the horses. Some Pretoria sharpie would trick Eddy and make off with them. Eddy's brain power aside, this was stupid. There were probably five hundred horses stuffed into this square. Why would anybody steal a Basuto pony, a Boer gelding, or a cayuse?

Frank argued himself hoarse and was about to leave on his own when Ovide relented. He gave Eddy a litany of final instructions and presented himself to Frank.

They started on the road that had the most traffic. It was the direction in which their officer had gestured when he mentioned Kruger's house. If there had not been a bunch of soldiers already gawking at it, Frank and

Ovide might have walked by. Kruger's place was a Boer farmhouse, peculiar only for being in the city. Low and long, gables on the ends, iron roof across the middle. Two more gables on the street side framed a door and window. The only hint that it was more than a prosperous farmer's place were two stone lions on opposite sides of the path to the door. The lions were lying down: one attentive, the other half asleep.

Thinking there might be more in back, they slipped around the side. But the rear of the house was plainer still. The Krugers had some shrubs and rose bushes in winter dormancy. A black gardener was scratching debris from the lawn with a rake.

They returned to the front and stood by the gate. A British sergeant and a few Tommys were guarding the house.

"Quiet, please," the sergeant bawled every little while. "Mrs. Kruger is believed to be inside. Mr. Kruger has left for parts unknown."

The soldiers filing by the house, especially the prisoners of war, were in a rough mood. They cursed and spat. Despite the amount of spitting, Frank thought quite a few looked unsure of how they felt. They were trying on moods—angry, satirical, sly—seeing what fit. The prisoners of war put on the best performance. At least they knew why they were angry, and who at.

Ovide made a motion back toward the square and the horses, but Frank pointed across the street. There was a church there and a massive tree that threw down a patch of dark shade. Seeing Frank's intention and Ovide's resistance, the sergeant intervened.

"Your friend's right, you know," he said to Ovide. "Should go over and look at the church. Herr Kruger prayed there every day and preached on Sundays."

This extra urging got Ovide across the track, though neither of them cared where Paul Kruger prayed or preached. Frank sat on the ground in the shade. It was sweet smelling and cool and, at once, the white gleam beyond was difficult to look at. Ovide sat too, but was skittish. He had divined Frank's purpose and saw no merit in it.

"If Jeff was here, it was *yesterday*," he said.

It annoyed Frank that Ovide had figured out his thoughts. More irritating that he was right. Jeff probably had been here yesterday, if he had ever been here at all. Frank ignored him and squinted at the line of men coming up the street.

After half an hour, Morden's four came along. They looked over Oom Paul's house. Two of them cursed and spat at it. Then they spotted Frank and Ovide under the tree and came to share the shade. They had gone shopping. Kerr had a loaf of rye bread, half-eaten. He offered the torn end and Frank and Ovide broke off chunks. It was dry. They asked about other kinds of food, but the Pincher boys said there wasn't much. The Boers had cleaned the place out before leaving. Particularly sad was the absence of eggs.

The shade was soporific. The Miles brothers lay down on their sides and were soon asleep. Frank was resigned to the fact that Jeff was not coming when something hove into view that was more amazing. Four riders approached and stood out, for they were not soldiers or Boers, nor anything else commonly observed in these parts. The lead horse was an appaloosa stud, snow white and chocolate brown. Its face blaze was a white triangle. On the chocolate hip was a splash of pearls, black-rimmed so they stood out like spheres dancing above.

That horse belonged to Pincher Creek rancher Lionel Brooke. There could not be another like it in the world.

Brooke sat atop his stud, looking costumed more than dressed. The brim on one side of his hat was slapped up and tied to the crown, Australian-style. His wool jacket was Civil War blue, with dark patches where insignia had been removed. Breeches baggy at hip and thighs funnelled into tight brown boots. His monocle was tweezed between a bushy white eyebrow and his cheekbone. His beard was freshly trimmed into a neat white spade.

Behind Brooke was the one in the group that Frank did not know: a pencil-thin, clean-shaven man. His jacket was a dull British red, as if weather and time had bled it of its cruelty.

The two bringing up the rear were Jimmy Whitford and Young Sam, both riding cayuses and leading pack mules.

Frank had no idea why any of them were here, but if you accepted Brooke's presence, Whitford's made equal sense. Jimmy had worked for Lionel for years, except for when Lionel's money ran out. Jim was a Montana Halfbreed like Frank's mother, except his Indian half was Crow and the rest American. He was said to have been in the U.S. Cavalry, and Frank had heard more than once that he had survived the Custer massacre, even though it was broadly known that no one had.

Young Sam was a Nez Perce whose family squatted near Pincher Creek, having come north after the Chief Joseph war. His father was in Stony Mountain Penitentiary for killing another Indian. Young Sam and his brother lived in a tent with their grandfather Old Sam, who did errands for Pincher Creek women.

The other soldiers under the tree were by now aware of the strange arrival. Those asleep had been wakened. Brooke rode by them initially and went to the Kruger house. He asked a question of the sergeant, produced a piece of paper and a pencil from his breast pocket, and made a note. Then he turned his appaloosa into the street and crossed to the shade tree. He had seen them all along.

Brooke dismounted and tied his tall horse to a branch. He took a green bottle out of his saddlebag; drew the cork and threw it away. Then he nodded to each of them, spoke their names, shook their hands, and offered a drink.

"Where's Redpath?" he asked.

Fred Morden explained about Reg Redpath's rupture, and how he had stayed in Kroonstad. Brooke huffed as if disappointed in Redpath's showing.

"This is Allan Kettle," he said, waving a long hand at the stranger. "He's English. Friend of mine from school."

Kettle shook hands all around. His hand was light-boned but callused and curiously strong. It snapped onto Frank's wider mitt and ground the bones.

Something occurred to Brooke. He returned to his horse and drew two things from the saddlebag. One was a pair of moccasins. These were for Ovide.

"From Mrs. Jughandle. Marie Rose. They're double-soled moose hide. I could not convince her that I'd never find you."

The other present was a wallet for Morden.

"From your father." Handing it over, Brooke said, "I believe there's money inside." Morden spread the wallet, thumbed the money, and poked for something else.

"Your girlfriend sends only her tears," said Brooke.

Morden had not received letters for some time. The mail had suddenly dried up and Boer sabotage was suspected.

Ovide sat on the ground. He had his rotten boots off and the moccasins on. He looked very pleased. Nothing had been said yet about Brooke's reasons for being here. Finally, Morden asked.

Brooke looked insulted. "I told you in the Arlington Hotel, the day you left, that I was coming with a small independent force. Here we are."

Fred laughed. He looked both amused and delighted, but Robert Kerr, standing beside him, was in a darker mood.

"A few things have happened since," said Kerr, his tone unfriendly.

Frank thought things over and decided he was irked too. A lot *had* happened, and Brooke's acting like he was here to save the situation *was* annoying.

Tom Miles wanted to know if Brooke had come by train from Cape Town. He was trying to make sense of the good condition of the horses.

"Durban, actually," said Brooke. "From there, I hired a private boat to bring us to Lourenço Marques."

Lourenço Marques, in Portuguese Mozambique, was the Boers' main source of supply. None of them had ever heard of a non-Boer coming through it.

"I've pretended to be pro-Boer. A journalist from England. I have a letter from one of the more liberal rags in Britain, saying I work for them. Actually, it's the truth. I intend to scribble something and send it off once in a while to maintain the deception."

"But *why?*" It was Kerr again.

"I've been studying the war since you left," Brooke said. "I've concluded that General Roberts' army is useless—no offence. He marched right past De Wet, failing to understand that De Wet is the head that must be struck off if there is ever to be a victory. It's what we've come to do."

Kerr's anger multiplied. Red spots showed above his patchy beard. Frank saw Fred put a hand around Kerr's arm.

Brooke yawned. He turned his head and squinted in the direction of the street and Kruger's house. He looked suddenly tired or bored. The bottle had come back to him and he took a drink and thrust it at Kerr, his usual response when he had caused annoyance.

"You won't find De Wet here," said Kerr, unappeased.

Brooke continued to look away. "I realize that. I expect to find him in the

Orange Free State. We'll collect more intelligence here, rest our horses, then head south."

This was more than Kerr could bear. He shook off Morden's hand and walked behind the tree. Its girth eclipsed him.

Morden shrugged for Brooke's benefit. "It's about Redpath," he said. "Kerr and Redpath are close."

"What on earth did I say about Redpath? I asked where he was."

"It's the rupture business. People tend to think it's, well, less of a real problem than a wound. You appeared to think that."

Brooke made a face that caused his monocle to drop. He caught it expertly. "I suppose I might have. Oh well."

Frank and Ovide went to visit with Jimmy and Young Sam. The two were loosing cinches and checking under saddles and packs for rub. Ovide asked Jim questions about horses back home. Which of Jughandle's had foaled? Had he sold any? Were there race results?

Then Jim Whitford turned to Frank. This was a surprise, for Frank was not sure the old scout even knew who he was. Frank knew Whitford by sight and name, because everyone did. He was a legend.

"Your mother's mad at you," Whitford said. He dug in the pocket of his coat and pulled out something that Frank would have recognized at twenty paces: a pair of knitted socks, designed the way his mother knitted everything. The sight, then the feel of the socks, made his eyes wet.

Brooke and Morden had drifted back to the appaloosa stallion. They looked like they might be talking about the horse. Then Brooke untied his stud and drew him into the sunshine. He grabbed the saddle horn and fished high for the stirrup with his boot toe. He stood to his full height in the stirrup and stayed that way, theatrically, before he swung over.

Kettle mounted too. Frank saw how he jumped up without effort, hit the stirrup in flight. Though not young, the fellow was an athlete.

"Boys?" called Brooke. Whitford and Young Sam were already moving. Yanking cinches. Mounting.

The strange suite of riders was soon around the corner and gone. Had it not been for the socks in his hand, and the green bottle lying empty in the sand, Frank might have thought he'd had a dream—the kind you wake from admiring the strangeness of the mind.

In their camp at Silverton, the Mounted Rifles could not help but believe the war was over. They had seen so many Martini-Henrys and Mausers piled up on Pretoria's Church Square. So many fawning Boers wanting to surrender. Right now, if they chose to, they could ride a few miles east to Sammy Marks' fancy country estate and capture most of the Transvaal leaders. But an order from on high had told them to leave them alone. General Roberts wanted the Boer brass to have all the time they needed, over at Sammy's, to contemplate their hopeless situation. Meanwhile, tucked in front of a big fireplace at Melrose House, with a comfortable rug over his knees, Lord Roberts awaited news of his victory.

But other kinds of stories floated around, ones contrary to the notion that the Boers were done. Rumour had it a big British convoy had been captured in the Orange Free State. The rumour said it was Christiaan De Wet, and that he had turned a mountain of their mail into ash. Another version added wagons full of winter clothing that the Boers were now wearing. What everyone did know for certain was that no mail or winter clothes had shown up here.

Despite the rumours, Frank believed the war was close to over. Maybe it was the leisure that convinced him. He was allowed to sleep to the slothful hour of six. Breakfast at seven. Muster parade at nine. Wood and coal were plentiful, and so were commandeered metal tubs and fuel. Frank had boiled his uniform and skimmed off a rich cream of dead lice. When the water was just the right temperature between boiling and cool, he jumped in himself and had a scrub. For a couple of hours after that, while his uniform and smalls dried on a bush, he stretched out on his oil sheet, naked in the winter sunshine, and felt louse-free.

Ovide was absorbed in watching the horses eat and coming up with new ways to soothe their feet and legs. That was his excuse for not cleaning up. There was also his fatalism. The lice would come back anyway, so what was the point of getting rid of them? Finally, Frank boiled the water and demanded Ovide's clothes. Later on, when he and his clothes were washed and he was back in uniform, Ovide admitted to Frank that he felt better.

Part of the reason the men felt so comfortable at Silverton was that their horses were clapped out. A great many had died between Kroonstad and Pretoria, and hardly a one of the living was what you'd call fit. The exceptions were Eddy's monstrosity and Frank's Dunny. Via the grapevine, Frank heard that Casey Callaghan's buckskin, The General, was still doing well; and, though there was never a word about him or his horse, Frank felt confident that Jeff Davis's blue mare would still be going strong.

When Frank looked along the horse lines, nowadays, what he saw most of were knackered Argentines. Overworked, lame, ribs hanging out of them, covered in rubs and sores. They were a lazy horse to begin with but had become legitimately feeble. The opinion among the men was that the Mounted Rifles could go nowhere until a batch of remounts was found.

On June 11, the bugler blew the long reveille at 3 A.M. Hardly a man moved, thinking it was a mistake. Then the sergeants were among them, blowing whistles, shouting, poking at them with sticks. The message was to ride. Something about a battle.

In less than an hour, Frank had Dunny saddled and was standing beside her in the dark. She was sick of this camp and keen to go. Ovide was on his way to complain to Lieutenant Davidson that neither the Basuto nor the Boer gelding were fit to carry him, but Sergeant Brindle intercepted him and told him it was a bad time to plead with the lieutenant. Fact was, both the Basuto and the Boer gelding *had* to go. Ovide must pick one and let the other be taken by another soldier. Everywhere, soldiers were complaining, and sergeants and officers were telling them to shut up and get moving. The orders were to take oat bags and man rations for two days, but otherwise nothing was said about their mission or destination.

Travelling by moonlight, they started south. When they crossed the first ridge, an army appeared, flowing like a silver sludge below them. They absorbed into its near edge, with more of Hutton's brigade.

By dawn, they were six miles east, moving at the double. They crossed the Pienaars River. From behind a slant ridge that rose before them came a fearsome roar and the incoming whine of shells. An ammunition wagon flipped in a donga and all six mules were turned on their back, hoof irons churning. The Boer gunners aimed for the wagon, hoping to explode it inside the passing army.

The order came to gallop. French's cavalry raced to the fore, aimed at the ridge's heart. The Mounted Rifles were headed for the hill's north flank.

They left their horses and climbed. The order was for an extended firing line on top, well spaced.

On his way up through the brush and stones, Frank saw Ovide on his right and Pete on his left. He waved at them, as if they were surprise acquaintances in a hockey crowd. The Boer barrage was louder than ever but nothing was hitting the slope around them. It meant the shells and bullets were going overhead. It meant that, when they got to the top, they would be in the thick of it.

At the crest, Frank did not wait for evidence. He threw himself flat. It did not take long for bullets to rip the grass around him. He crawled like a mad thing, worming forward, clawing with his elbows. He was looking for a nice stout stone, and there were none. All he could find was a scatter of smaller rocks that he pulled in and piled as fast as his hands could move. In the din, he could make out the mechanical chug of a pom-pom—Pete's fucking piano, walking the keys toward them.

When his little wall was built and there were no more stones, Frank peeked through a gap and saw the bigger ridge the Mounted Rifles were facing. There was a vale between and a screen of trees. Besides higher, the Boer ridge was rockier and thickly matted with gorse and thorn. The Boers had chosen the ground and it was to their advantage. Their guns were invisible in the hill folds. Their snipers were somewhere in that brush and rock, impossible to see.

Because the barrage never stopped, time became indecipherable, immeasurable. It held Frank's attention like some everlasting song, and all he could do was fire back into the hill's bland face and dream of doing damage.

He decided four hours had gone by when the officers started bringing up reserves and piling them on the left. They were going for their tried-and-true method of extending the British flank until it went around the Boer flank. But Frank heard and felt an alteration and addition to the clamour attacking them. On the Boer side, a fresh gun and maybe another pom-pom had cut loose, aimed at that stretch of hill where the reserves were forming and scratching their holes. Frank saw shells explode among them. He saw the reserves abandon their position and peel back. There would be no turning of the Boer flank today.

As the afternoon moved along, the ironic heat of the winter sun drilled into Frank's back. When it looked like there would never be anything to do but stay put and hope not to die, an opportunity presented itself. Into a grassy interval on the opposite hillside, a Boer gun team came racing. A pom-pom on its limber bounced behind the horse. Some sharpie in the Canadian battery laid a shell right in the gun horse's face. Frank had just put ten in his magazine and he donated them to the cause of driving the Boer gunners back. Fifty others must have done the same. The gun horse was shot several times, and its team had barely unhooked the corpse from the pom-pom when they had to run for their lives. The gun was stranded, and all the Mounted Rifles had to do to keep it like that was fire at anyone who dared approach.

For twenty minutes, this was successful and fulfilling sport. Frank imagined the officer congratulating them: *Let's be honest, it was not our day, but through your quick thinking, good shooting, and pluck . . .*

Then the pom-pom moved backwards. As if it had come to life, the gun and limber lurched up the rise and disappeared over its rim.

A while later, Fred Morden came to tell Frank that it was his group's turn to go for rations. The rally point was directly below, and Ovide and Pete got there first. The talk below was of the miraculous pom-pom, and the cook dispensing meat paste said the majority opinion was that the gun's limber must have had a rope on its tail. When the gun was stranded, some Boer must have crawled forward and tied more rope to that rope, until they could pull it in from cover. Everybody hated it when the Boers were clever.

Back in the firing line, the descending sun spilled light that jewelled the cratered ridge ahead. If the Rifles were going to move, now was the time, when the light was square in the Boers' eyes. No such order came. After the flank-turning gambit had failed, the brass were out of ideas.

The Rifles stayed put and the sun vanished; the air began to fill with darkness and cold. An icy wind was blowing in their faces. It was Klip River and Crocodile Pass all over again. Another cold night without blankets.

Fred Morden and Tom Miles came with a bucket of water for their bottles and to tell them to stay in their holes. If they wanted out of the wind, they should dig themselves deeper. No visiting. No fires.

The barrage of guns had left a din between Frank's ears. The flickering pictures that filled his mind were out of kilter. The people and animals did everything too fast, a madcap pace that Frank did not want to look at. Finally, above his head's roar, he shouted a string of questions.

Why had General Roberts extended his velvet glove to the Boers again? Letting the Joburg ones leave, probably with their gold and guns? Maybe the field guns he so generously let them keep were the ones trying to plaster Frank all of today? The ones he had to hide from by keeping his face jammed in the dirt.

And where were all those wizards who sat naked in their bathtubs at Silverton, patiently explaining why the war was over? The Boers were so clearly broken, so pathetically demoralized they would never rouse themselves to fight again.

All this did not seem so clear or certain tonight, and Frank cursed himself for a gull that he had drank it up and even spouted it back. Amazing what you could tell yourself when you wanted it to be true.

In that cold and angry moment, a fellow wanted to do something to show how sick he was of Empire bombast and flummery; something the high-up types like Curly Hutton could see and know was protest. And, just as Frank was thinking it, he saw a little plume of wavering light far to his right. A soldier, thinking like Frank, had scratched together a pile of grass and struck a match to it.

Whistles blew and men yelled at the maker of the fire to put it out. Instead, another fire popped up in another place.

Frank looked around himself. Ovide's spot stayed dark but a flame bloomed where Pete Belton was. For a few seconds, Frank could see Pete's lunatic face aglow. From lower on the hill, Sergeant Brindle's whistle shrilled.

"Douse that fire, damn you!"

From the Boers' place above, it must have looked like a religious event: the Mounted Rifles' firing line suddenly mapped out in tiny dots of light. The Boer pom-pom leapt back to life, thudding the frozen walls of night. Frank saw Pete knocking out his fire with his rifle butt. Men were calling him names. He was cussing them back.

But the pom-pom was coming, and it seemed to Frank it was coming straight for him. He crushed his face against the freezing ground, clasped his hands on the back of his head, and pushed so he breathed frosty muck and smothered. He felt the blast through the ground and through himself. The one-pound shell blew his rock wall on top of him.

Frank yelled at Ovide until he replied. He yelled at Pete and Pete cussed. Frank sucked the blood off his knuckles and rocked like a child.

When the first gloomy light found him, Frank saw whiskers of frost on his shoulders and arms; down his legs. When he tried to shake it off, none of his joints worked. He had to fight himself to break their locks. Then the crystals shattered and flew.

When the first ray of sunlight sprayed from their ridge, the Boers resumed their barrage. The British reply was a fraction as loud. To Frank, the difference was a dialogue.

The British were saying, *We are conserving ammunition. We are running out.*

The Boers were replying, *We've got plenty and we're coming for you.*

Just past noon, the Boers made their push, their attempt to win the thing outright. Their firing had seemed heavy all day but was suddenly redoubled. They must have rearranged their guns and positions, for the pattern of everything was suddenly not as it had been. Their firing was dangerously aslant and unpredictable.

It was then that Private Walter Frost was killed. Whether he stood up out of cover to go for water or meat paste, or just to flex away some stiffness, or had not moved at all, he was shot and the Mauser bullet that hit him killed him. English-born cowboy. Isle of Wight. Ruddy-faced, stocky, average height. Just shy of thirty-four. A bachelor who enlisted at Calgary, same day Frank had. The first Canadian Mounted Rifle killed in battle. The dam of luck had broken.

Soon after Frost was killed, Major Macdonnell was helping some men build a rock wall. Those around him heard a pistol bark. They knew it was close and expected to see some crazy Boer standing there. But it was just themselves, and Macdonnell down, crouched over a wound in his guts. They saw his holster empty, his Colt pistol on the ground. When he had bent for a rock, the pistol had fallen; had fired when it hit. The .45 calibre bullet entered at an angle such that it went a long way and was still in Macdonnell. They laid him out and waved for the Red Cross.

In the middle of the following night, relief finally came. Reserves had been scraped together, and they found the Mounted Rifles in their holes and replaced them. When Pete, Ovide, and Frank reached Eddy and the horses, a story was making the rounds that something had given in the Boer line, something near its centre.

At dawn, when the British started probing that centre, there was no response. During the night, the middle of the Boer line had retreated; no one knew why. When the middle fell away, the beefed-up flanks were in danger of being turned from within and had to follow. Now, Roberts' army was sweeping into that cavity. The three-day battle of Diamond Hill was over. A victory.

Frank Adams would remember four things about Diamond Hill. First was the appearance of the little wall he spent the daylight hours contemplating. It was like a shrine in which Our Lady might decide to appear. Second, he remembered Pete Belton's face glowing above his trash fire, and how that brought on the pom-pom. Third was the soldier who had borrowed the Boer gelding for the fight coming to say that the horse had been blown up when the Boers made their push.

Last of all, he remembered Greasy Griesbach sucking the sole of his dirty foot. At their bivouac the night after the Boer retreat, Greasy had been kicking down an outhouse for firewood and ran a nail through his foot. He yanked his boot and sock off, and his trousers too, so he could flex his leg enough to get the foot in his mouth. He sucked the injured part pink and was ready to ride again the next day.

Part Four

—

KATBOSCH

Aldershot, June 1900

General Butler sat on a bench bolted to the wall in the court-martial shed. A window streaked from yesterday's rain looked out on a rare beautiful day. If you brought a man from the moon today, and sent him home tomorrow, he would say Aldershot was paradise.

Butler wanted no part of it. He preferred to be alone in the dark, in a place where many had paid a high price for their indiscretions and outright crimes. Not in this shed but in others like it, Butler had presided over such proceedings; had meted out jailings, floggings, years at hard labour—stripped a great many soldiers of rank. A wonder no one had dragged him into an alley and beaten him to death.

What he had never done at a court marital was pronounce a sentence of death. He had always found a way around it, some gap in the evidence, some mitigating circumstance. The day he'd stepped off the ship in Cape Town to be proxy colony governor was the closest he ever came. All they'd wanted was his signature on the document to execute a man already found guilty and sentenced. He no longer remembered how he'd ducked it, but he had.

It was all about squaring things with his exacting Catholic God. On the final day, he would much rather stand behind his military record than his personal one. For how could Butler even begin to explain to the Almighty his inability to make his one true wife happy? How to justify his failures to control his temper in the face of her antics?

It was Elizabeth, queen of his private existence, who had sent him to the court-martial shed today, looking for ghosts of suffering to moan with, but also looking for memories of happier times. In the early 1890s, when he'd been in charge of infantry at Aldershot, this shed had fallen into disuse and Elizabeth had claimed it for a studio. With horses grazing and charging about, her models were everywhere.

Her favourite thing, even then when their children were quite young, was to stand in front of a cavalry charge—see how long she could stay put with the horses thundering toward her. Butler would watch, lead-faced, determined not to show concern, but she would wait so long before bolting, he could never quite control the flutter in his guts. He barely stifled the urge to run to her. It was supposedly done for her art, to see from the enemy's perspective what it was like to face a British cavalry charge, but she also did it to show off and for the exhilaration. Afterwards, she would prance about and toss her head, somewhat *like* a horse in a moment of pride.

Butler remembered having made love to her here on just such a day—or she to him—right in this very room! Long after it had become an infrequent occurrence at home, she had taken the notion and seduced him. He had muttered about the disastrous consequences should someone walk in, but was of course pleased.

Where was any of this today? Their children liked to point out that Butler was a tyrant who would not let anyone speak on the suspicion they might disagree with him. The cruellest cut, from one of his daughters, was that he had more or less destroyed his military career by favouring the underdog, but seemed to lack any such sympathetic feelings toward his family.

Not true. If he knew what was troubling them, then he was concerned. But having had to volunteer for foreign wars in hopes of getting a reward or a promotion—in order to make his family's expensive living!—he had seldom been present during their younger years. One gets out of touch, and eventually incapable of playing with the silly young creatures. On their side, they began to treat him like an ancient grandfather or a temple statue, someone or something to be compulsorily venerated rather than loved. From there to active dislike was a short step.

But more than the children, it was Elizabeth's complaints that hurt most. She prided herself on not complaining, but somehow her grievances got out into the world. One of the most prominent notions was that marriage to Butler had been the beginning of the death of her artistic career.

Bull-necked wives of generals would directly accuse him of it.

"You must help Elizabeth find time for her wonderful art, William."

"Perhaps you are too critical, General Butler. I wouldn't *know* but it seems . . ."

What came back through friends, who did not necessarily have his best interests at heart either, was that his odd career had damaged Elizabeth by taking her away from London (the art world's pulse in London's own estimation). He had lumbered her with his strange opinions, and it showed in her work.

As for where Butler's pro-Boer, pro-Dervish, pro-Afghan sympathies showed up in her work, those who liked their war art triumphant often pointed to Elizabeth's *Remnants of an Army*, an agonized portrait of Dr. Brydon stumbling into Jalalabad on a dying horse, after the Afghans had destroyed a British army, families included, on the retreat from Kabul. Brydon had half his head missing. *There*, supposedly, was General Butler's influence, and Butler never got the opportunity to point out that he hated that bloody painting and wanted it cut up. The thing was *abject*, and whatever the British army could justly be accused of (stupidity, beastliness, obstinacy, arrogance, vainglory), *abjectness* was practically beyond it. In his opinion, *Remnants* was as wrong-headed as Elizabeth's more recent debacle on the subject of Paardeburg.

But, whether Butler had caused it or not, Elizabeth's career was in a mess, no question about that, and this very day owed its miserable beginning to her everlasting grief over it—that and her having hinted, broadly, that she really did hold Butler to blame. Sometimes Elizabeth stood up to him, such as when he had criticized her Paardeburg painting and she had erupted. That was a reaction he much preferred to what she trotted out today: sadness, blackness, bleakness—*and awful bloody sighing*.

Such had been her mood as he passed through the house to leave. She was staring out a window, as if unhappy that the sun had risen. At the end of a truly epic, cross-lifting sigh, she said just loud enough for him not to miss a syllable, "Perhaps if I had not gone with you so much. Mind you, there would always have been a household to run, wherever I was. And the children . . ."

He had already made the mistake of stopping. He felt his face burning and could imagine his red appearance. Sanguinity—bad for the health, as she liked to point out.

"Instead of reviewing the past, Elizabeth, why don't you try *painting* something in the present?"

She turned her damp eyes toward him. Her hand hung off the chair as if the arm controlling it had just been shot and killed.

"That's all fine, Will," she said in a voice without energy, the song of another sigh. "And I would almost respect you for saying it, if you did not know perfectly well that there has not been a call for my services since the Paardeburg commission. There has really been almost no interest in me since your disgrace in Africa."

"My *what*? My *disgrace*? My disparagement, you mean, surely. My dismissal. My destruction, if my enemies had their way. But I'll have you know that I have done nothing disgraceful. That is, unless trying to prevent your bloody stupid nation from bankrupting itself and sending thousands of promising young men to their death is now disgraceful in your eyes!"

"Bloody stupid nation. Isn't that what I'm talking about?"

"I meant my own country as much as yours. You're deliberately misunderstanding me."

"I suppose I am no longer sharp. Certainly those who laugh at me and call me *Roll Call Thompson* would agree with you."

He could not stand it. He had thrown on his coat, slammed the door, and made for the waiting carriage. The horses had scarcely lurched forward when he was consumed with guilt and sorrow, and the overwhelming wish to be kneeling in front of his wife, kissing her inert hands and begging her forgiveness.

And here he sat in the court-martial shed. However willing Butler was to apologize for their fight, the truth was that his disgrace, so called, was not the reason Elizabeth's career as a war artist had failed. In truth, that career had been floundering since the early 1880s, perhaps because of the layoff occasioned by the birth of their children—children who were her choice as much as his. As for his career hampering her, she had greatly enjoyed his ascent to Lieutenant-General, even if it had only happened because of his hanging on tight to Garnet Wolseley's coattails as they rose. There had been social cachet in being part of the Wolseley Ring. At the time of their marriage, a good many who dictated taste in

London had pronounced them a lovely match: the soldier-writer and his beautiful war-artist wife.

What *had* defeated Elizabeth Thompson Butler was the same thing that had defeated William Francis Butler, and that was time. Time and change. Butler did not really understand what made smokeless powder smokeless. He hated how noisy lyddite bombs were and how they painted every battlefield the same sickly colours. Nor did he care for the ever-longer howitzers, firing their fifty-pound shells for miles. What was the point of killing an enemy you could not see, who could not see you? You might as well mail him a poisoned biscuit. Eventually, would the guns get so long that the British would simply sit in London and fire at Berlin?

Butler did not like, or entirely understand, modern warfare, and it had turned him into a homebound general, soon to be an out-to-pasture general. And the same thing had turned Elizabeth Thompson Butler into Roll Call Thompson. Her pictures no longer looked like war to the people in the know. Her critics found Afghan and Ashanti and Zulu touches in what were supposed to be scenes from modern fights. They looked for the howitzers and the lyddite haze and could not find them.

Worst of all, the bastards who called her Roll Call Thompson—he'd throttle those cowards if he ever caught them—did so because Elizabeth was not jingo enough. Here again, their fates were linked. The gutter press, the war manufacturers, the financiers who owned newspapers, the bribe-taking politicians, the average British punter throwing pints into himself in a greasy pub—they were all crying for war and victories, the bloodier the better. The weaker they got, the more disgusted with themselves, the more blood and death it took to brace them.

In this shed, redolent of mouse and mildew, it could not have been more clear. Butler felt an excited desire to run home to Elizabeth and lay his findings before her; to tell her how precisely parallel their paths had run; to commiserate and plan the dignified response. But, if he did so, it would not work, and he knew exactly *why* it would not work. Butler could say all this; every bit of it could be correct; but none of it would make Elizabeth Thompson the centre of attention in the London art world again. None of it could restore her to the pinnacle she had occupied in 1877 when they had married.

Only that would do, and it did not matter that no one in the world could give her that. It only mattered that Butler could not.

Past Ovide's shoulder and out the train window, Frank watched the backward unfolding of his war. They were returning to the Orange River Colony.

At Pretoria Station, yesterday, the Mounted Rifles had been gathered into their troops, and swapped around by some formula that matched Davidson's troop with Lieutenant Ingle's troop from C Squadron. They were told to board the same car and to disembark at the same siding. They would be guarding a stretch of railway against Christiaan De Wet and his Free State saboteurs.

What intrigued Frank about the arrangement was how it left him squashed in the same half-car with men from home. They had done things as a troop before, but never to the exclusion of others. Now, except for C Squadron in the car's other half, Frank was with men who knew his landmarks and the gossip of which he was made. It was as if he *was* home, which was a good feeling, except for Eddy Belton's damp, high-smelling form wedged against his side and Pete Belton's breath a little too close behind his ear. Pete was reciting everything he saw.

"Now this here river, this is way down since we crossed it, wouldn't you say? Way down. I say it's way down."

The river was the Vaal. They crossed it on a new bridge built by army engineers to replace the blown-up one. According to Greasy Griesbach, all the railway-building in South Africa was under the orders of Maj. Percy Girouard, a Canadian friend of Lord Kitchener from the Sudan war.

Less than an hour later, the train stopped where some new track curved around a gnarl of blown steel. A sign read KROM ELM BOURG SPRUIT, and the first fifty Mounted Rifles got off, including Corporal Griesbach.

"Damn smart, him," Ovide said as he watched Griesbach disappear. "That Greaseback."

Ovide's tone was sad, and it made Frank wonder who their smartest man was, now that Greasy was gone. Who from this more local group could they rely on to think for them in a pinch? Again he wished that Jeff

Davis had never left; had resisted his urge to scout. If the trio of Ovide, Jeff, and Frank had stayed together, Jeff could have done its thinking and Frank could have followed. He never would have had to lead as he did too often with Ovide.

Without Davis, Frank decided the smartest man was Fred Morden, who probably would have been promoted by now except for oversight, and the fact that he had not had a chance to be a hero. Fred was sitting surrounded by his cronies, the Miles boys and Kerr, and all the attention was toward him, not because he was talking but because he might start.

More sets of fifty got off at Wolvehoek, Vredefort, and Roodewal. Next came Honing Spruit (Honey Creek), where no one got off because it was already defended by British ex-POWs. Quickly thereafter came Katbosch, and Ingles, seeing the sign, jumped up and said, "Okay, boys, this is us!"

Katbosch was not inspiring; the scenery had barely a ripple, except for one hazy kopje off to the east. The prairie was almost white, bleached by the winter frosts.

Beside the Katbosch sign, a shack town already existed. Frank thought it might be Africans, miners maybe, but it was actually the handiwork of two companies of Shropshires, and a battery with two fifteen-pound Armstrong guns. A telegraph line passed through the camp, and on a pole near the middle they'd hammered ladder steps up to a platform. It was so flat here, a fifteen-foot crow's nest commanded a view.

There was not much choice but to claim ground and start gathering rubbish for a suburb of their own. After a parley with the Shropshires' commander, Davidson and Ingles sent patrols to abandoned farms, where an outhouse or chicken coop might still yield a board. As for water, they would have to go to Honing Spruit and haul it back.

The Shropshire captain told them to be careful while they scavenged. Though nothing much had happened here, the thorn trees and winter grass could still harbour a Boer. A Shropshire scout had found horse tracks of late, and a Boer sniper had offended one of their sleeps.

Frank found himself perversely fond of Katbosch. The feeling he had on the train of being home stayed with him in the camp, and the feeling of being unsafe without Jeff Davis faded. If he blurred his eyes and did not look at the kopje, the country looked like places he and his father had traversed with cattle, when driving them to market in Lethbridge or Medicine Hat.

No matter how often Ingles and Davidson lectured them about Christiaan De Wet's predations, Frank's thoughts ranged beyond the war. The fact was that whole nights went by with no more disturbance than a hyena's yell. Every day they set up Cossack posts on the ends of the horseshoe kopje, and two more north and south on the railway—and nothing happened. If they saw a springbok or a family of baboons, it was a big day.

From time to time, they were visited by the Mounted Rifles scouts. These were led by Casey Callaghan and Charlie Ross, and sometimes by Capt. Tommy Chalmers. Chalmers and Gilbert Sanders had been young Mounties together at Ft. Macleod. Chalmers had very long legs and was nicknamed Scizzors, a title that had travelled with him to this day. A vivid childhood memory of Frank's was Scizzors and Sanders playing tennis at Ft. Macleod, on a court they had built themselves.

Being truthful men, the scouts admitted there was not much action right now from De Wet's rebels. The thing to remember, though, was that De Wet's favourite target was the railway, so he had to return eventually.

Frank and Ovide's days were spent with the Beltons. Frank had been selected acting corporal of their four. After a couple of days in the railway Cossack posts, they were sent on patrol, officially to search for the enemy but unofficially to scavenge.

Their first find was a patch of Boer graves, soldiers' graves that had either been dug in a hurry by the Boers or carelessly and shallowly dug by the British. The animals had been at them and the arm and leg bones stuck from the ground like signposts to hell.

Frank was stunned when Pete jumped down with his bayonet and began to dig.

"Pete! What the hell are you doing?"

"This is how Eddy and me found the Boer pistol we gave Jeff."

In a trouser pocket, Pete found a Boer coin and some matches. He had hoped for at least a knife or some bullets and was disappointed.

Farther along was a farm, from which every stick of wood had been stripped. But Ovide found the family root cellar and inside were two bags of oats and one of mealies. There were some sad root vegetables, withered and mouse-chewed. Because their biggest problem would be sustaining a fire to cook these things, Frank figured out a way to bring back wood. The root cellar was built like a mine with timbers holding up its roof. He put his rope on these and let Dunny pull them out, even the last one which brought the roof down as it was leaving. They dragged it all back to camp and were heroes.

The fuel problem was chronic, and Fred Morden went to visit the Shropshire side of camp late in the first week. He wanted to know how the Shropshires managed to have fire when the Canadians spent most evenings shivering in their greatcoats. Fred saw actual coal being burned and, after polite conversations about horses and lice, he asked how they came by it. No one spoke, and the soldiers looked at each other in a way that suggested a secret. Finally, their lieutenant said, *What the hell? Weren't they all in the same boat here?* He told Fred to grab some men and come running next time there was a train.

A day later, one came. Fred's Pincher Creek four ran for the siding and found the Shropshire lieutenant and several of his men lined along the track. The lieutenant told Fred to gather stones, throwing size, and to put them at his feet. His friends should do the same.

The train wasn't stopping but did slow down. The Shropshires waved at the engineer and stokers, and at the soldiers perched on the tender. It was a loaded coal train and the rest was open cars with black labourers riding on top.

The Englishmen picked up their stones and started pelting the black men. Though unsure why, Fred and his bunch did too. The black men, having no rocks at hand, picked up lumps of coal and fired back. When the train was gone, there was quite a bit of coal on the ground. Fred thanked the lieutenant for the lesson, and his group brought home their share. The fuel problem was greatly relieved.

After the first week, men started decorating their shacks. They took their horses off the line and tied them outside their doors. The Shropshires loved cricket, and every evening it was Englishmen against Canadians. Frank took part though he barely understood the rules. Fred Morden was a whiz at it, and Harry Gunn, who was a renowned North Fork polo player, picked it up fast.

Unfortunately for everyone, a cricket game was in process—and not in the evening but at noon—when Maj. Gilbert Sanders rode in, escorted by Scizzors Chalmers, Charlie Ross, and Casey Callaghan. The major was back in health, back from St. Helena, and back in command of D Squadron; but if Frank's troop was glad to see him, he was not glad to see them. They ran from the cricket pitch and gathered before him. He had asked Ingles for permission to address C Squadron as well. He said nothing before all were present.

He began by praising Chalmers' scouts, who in short order had produced an accurate picture, not just of what De Wet was doing now, but of what he had done over the last month.

Since General Roberts had left the Orange River Colony, De Wet had been showing his Boers a new way to fight. Battles that pitted five thousand Boers against twenty thousand British were never going to work. What made better sense was to go after the enemy's greatest weakness: its extended lines of communication and supply.

"As well, why not ambush lazy garrisons like this one?"

De Wet, with six hundred burghers, had surrounded a British convoy on the Rhenoster River.

"Do you remember crossing that river on the train down? Not far, is it?"

Two hundred Gordon Highlanders and fifty-six wagons full of loot were taken. Then, De Wet hit the rail station at Roodewal. The garrison surrendered, putting De Wet in possession of bales of British winter clothing, hundreds of cases of ammunition, and stacks of mailbags.

"If you're wondering why you haven't received mail for some time, imagine Boer soldiers rooting through it. Eating your cakes and cookies. Reading your sweetheart's love notes."

Frank looked at Morden, whose face had two bright red spots on the cheekbones. Major Sanders fell silent, so their minds could fill with pictures of what the Boers might have done. A Boer winding your birthday watch. A Boer pissing on a letter from your old mum. Since Frank did not get mail, his thoughts were of Boers putting on clean long underwear and donning a winter greatcoat.

Then Sanders completed the imagery. Whatever mail the Boers did not want, they consigned to a bonfire. In that fire, they also destroyed ammunition they could not carry. It was said that De Wet did one million British pounds' worth of damage that day.

And did they happen to know how many British and colonial prisoners De Wet's Orange Free State Boers had taken since May? More than a thousand.

"I have been told by soldiers who have been through this camp that it is utterly without discipline. You seem to feel you have no need to be careful; that, because nothing has happened, nothing will happen. Why not have a cricket game in the noonday sun?"

He let that sit with them, then continued. Did they actually think Christiaan De Wet would stop his sabotage and his raids along this railroad when they had been so successful? Wouldn't a good general go on attacking until something stopped him—something like a *wide-awake, prepared, and vigilant enemy?*

Every man's head was down, staring at his dusty boots. Nobody wanted to meet Major Sanders' eyes. But Frank found old questions poking through his shame.

Why the hell was Christiaan De Wet having all this success anyway, when, according to Lord Roberts, the war had ended weeks ago? How, in such a short period of time, had the war changed from a walkover to a thing they were being beaten at?

Frank looked up, and Major Sanders was looking maybe not at him, but in his direction. When the major continued, his tone had changed. Now he was speaking to them as if they really were soldiers, and as if they could be trusted to understand what he was saying.

"Now that Britain controls Johannesburg and both Boer capitals, it is a different war. Diamond Hill was probably the last big fight you'll see. The Boers have broken into small units and are making good use of their mobility and their knowledge of the country—the two things they have that we don't. Rather than be sorry, let's be grateful it did not happen months ago, when there were twice as many Boers in action as there are today."

That was it. Sanders had said what he'd come to say. He rode out with his escort, probably to deliver the same speech to other slack camps.

The major had not wanted Frank to feel good, and Frank did not. For two days, he went around with touchy skin. Particularly when he was on patrol or standing at a Cossack post, he felt itchy between the shoulder blades, sure that someone's field glasses were focused there, or that he was wedged in the sights of a marksman's gun.

But it did not last. The gigantic prairie skies, silent save for the frosty wind, washed the lesson from his head. The nights, ice cold and starry, froze his mind and kept all thoughts from moving. The struggle to stay warm and fed and not overrun by lice sifted his wariness under.

When they were so busy scouring from an empty land, working hard to make it emptier, it was simply difficult to conceive of the place as crawling with Boers.

On June 22, at a frigid stand-to in the black dark, they were told that firing had been reported from the direction of Honing Spruit station. No word yet as to what kind of attack or if there were casualties, but it was clear the Cossack posts must be extra vigilant today.

Ingles' C Squadron was again responsible for the posts on the horseshoe kopje. D Squadron's job was to man the railway posts. There had been grumbling of late because the kopje posts had shade and the railway posts had nothing. The railway posts' defence and shelter was the railroad embankment: one foot high, sometimes rising to the immensity of two feet.

Though picked for railway duty, Frank felt good. He and Ovide and the Beltons had drawn the north post, and it had a thorn tree. Winter naked, the tree still made a spot of porous shade if the sun got hot and was something to stand behind if the wind was sharp. Morden, Kerr, and the Miles boys had the southern post, which Frank knew from experience was bare.

Before they left, Frank sidled over to Morden and teased him. As always, Fred had an answer. He reminded Frank that the north post was miles closer to last night's firing. Though a joke, it made Frank's nerves shimmer.

Ingles with his eight pulled out for the kopje. Hugh Davidson led his eight toward the northern railway post. This choice of taking all of them north before he took half south was in case the Boers were still lurking.

When they got to the thorn tree, Davidson reminded Frank, as acting corporal, to take extra care and not to let his men and horses go to the creek. Then Davidson and Morden's four rode off. It was still dark, the idea being to have all of the Cossack fours in place by first light.

For the first half-hour, Frank's four hopped around in their greatcoats trying to get warm. Pete argued for a fire and Frank said no. They mustn't give the Boers a target.

"Whatever you say, Acting Corporal Adams," said Pete.

"Thank you, Private Belton."

"What if I say hell with you and light a fire anyway?"

"I'll order Eddy to sit on you."

When the world started to reveal itself, the prairie was a sea of hoarfrost. Even the thorn tree was dressed in white fur. Then they heard guns. After some quarrelling, they agreed it was not from the north but from the direction of the kopje. Rifles.

Frank's acting rank suddenly meant something. He told Pete and Ovide to lie five feet part on the west side of the rails, aiming east. He told Eddy to get a firm hold on the horses' reins and stretch out flat beside his brother. Frank stayed on the east side of the rails looking north and west.

The horses ripped up tufts of grass that grew from under the rails and were soon dragging on Eddy's arms trying to expand their range. Frank told Eddy to take off his hat and keep his big stump of a head down below the steel.

Frank knocked his own hat off so it hung on his back by the stampede string. He sat on his heels and watched.

The sound changed. Rather than random rifles, it was now artillery. Two guns shelling in a long-beat rhythm, and a sharper crashing sound. Frank knew what that crashing meant. Boer riflemen would bunch up and point high, firing together on signal. The bullets would go much farther that way than they would straight. Near the Klip River, Frank had seen an English cavalryman, trotting along, drop off his horse stone dead. When they searched his body, they found him punctured by half a dozen Mauser bullets.

The regular rhythm of the artillery meant only one side was firing. The British gunners were holding off until the man in the crow's nest said there were Boers close enough to hit. It also meant the Boer guns outranged the Armstrongs.

Later, the drumming of the Boer guns was torn into by opposing sounds. The guns of Katbosch had finally kicked in. A solid cloud of smoke and dust hung over top of the camp. Out on the prairie, the lyddite plumes were all over the place. The Shropshire battery had no target and was firing by guess.

Eddy squirmed on the ground. He was shifting away from the rails to allow the horses more grass. They were getting thirsty and yearned toward the creek. To keep from being dragged, Eddy had to sit up and brace his heels.

Eddy asked permission to take the horses to the creek, but Frank said no. They might be doing nothing here, their rifles stone cold, but at any minute the prairie could grow heads and flying manes. They could be fighting for their lives and must stay together.

In the afternoon, the artillery fire on the Boer side seemed to double. It was as if their guns had given birth. Soon, two horsemen came ripping north, tearing funnels of dust. Frank drew a bead even though he was fairly sure they were theirs. When they came close, Casey Callaghan and Charlie Ross hauled in their lathered mounts.

"Davidson says come."

Then they planted their spurs and charged north.

Frank's four got ready to ride. He told them to go quick but save a burst for the end. When they were in sight of camp, they spurred their mounts for all they had and waved their Stetsons lest they be confused for Boers and shot.

Once inside camp, they put their horses on the lines. Back at the perimeter, Frank found a trench where four would fit. The man on Frank's right was Tom Scott. Whenever he reloaded, Tom told Frank things. The Boers had been reinforced an hour ago. They had at least three more field pieces than they'd had earlier, including a pom-pom. Katbosch was badly outgunned and the Boers were making a push.

Tom yelled across Frank at Ovide and the Beltons to stop gawking and start firing. Ingles was shot and Davidson was in charge. He'd brought them back for their firepower. Then Lieutenant Davidson himself came and told Frank and Ovide to come with him. He wanted them somewhere else where his firing line was thin. They crossed a wedge of camp, Davidson walking fast and stumbling. Beyond the camp and the railway tracks, a horse was running, dragging its guts in the grass. There was a big hole in the roof of the Red Cross tent. A lineup of wounded soldiers was aimed next door, at the officers' mess.

Frank wondered if the Red Cross tent was an accident. He'd heard that De Wet had put shells into the Red Cross hospital at Paardeburg.

"Any of ours hit?" Frank asked.

"Ingles is bad," said Davidson. "It's how this mess started. Ingles ran into them on the kopje. He made a fighting retreat and was shot. Aspenall got it in a couple of places. Birney's shot through his foot. Those three came back, but five are missing."

Frank saw Henry Miles sitting in the dirt on the shade side of the mess tent. His hand was bloody.

"Is Morden back, then?" Frank asked, pointing at Henry. "Fred's four?"

Davidson shook his head and staggered. "No. Just Henry. Boers attacked them and Henry was hit early on. Fred sent him back with the horses. I've tried to get out there all day."

Davidson flung his hand at the things preventing it. Shell holes, blasted shacks, mules blown in half.

Frank was trying to see through the shack town to the horse lines. He had just spotted Dunny through a gap when a shell hit and a plume of dirt rose. The horses came racing through the tent alleys, dragging their picket line. The black horse orderlies were running in their wake.

Frank and Ovide left the lieutenant and went to help. They spread out and grabbed ends of the dragging picket line. By the time they had most of the runaways contained, Davidson was gone. They found a half-empty trench and dropped into it. Even Ovide was aiming and firing today, having identified a cause worth his effort. While reloading, he said, "Out there all day."

Frank was thinking it too. He left his rifle and scuttled to the tent wall where he'd seen Henry Miles. Henry had not moved. His bloody hand was cupped on his knee, not even bandaged. The back of the hand was torn open. It looked like the inside of a piano. But Henry wasn't looking at his hand. He was looking at nothing and with great intensity, as though, if his attention broke, something would get away.

"When'd you come in, Henry?"

"Fred saw Boers coming. He said they meant to cross the tracks and go north and hit our camp in the ass. We had to take them. I was horse-holder." He lifted and dropped his bloody hand. "I got shot, so Fred said take the horses. Told me to tell Davidson they could hold out."

Henry looked at Frank, his eyes bloodshot and afraid. "It was a lot of Boers, Frank."

Lieutenant Davidson came up with a plan against the Boer push. The Boers had a low tolerance for casualties, so Davidson reasoned that if he could wound a few, the rest might be called off. He sent the sergeants and corporals to the trenches and told each four-man group to pick an anthill they thought might have Boers behind it. They were to keep shooting at that target until the Boer flushed or the hill blew apart. By that means, they winged a few. The strategy did not end the battle but did cause a retreat.

Then, as the sun was crouching fat on the horizon, igniting the white grass and streaming in the direction of the Boers, the enemy began to peel away and run to where their horses were cached. Soon, they and their artillery were nothing but a road of dust in the sky.

A quarter of an hour later, Casey Callaghan and Charlie Ross rode in from the north at the head of a mixed regiment of scouts and MI. The Boers' own scouts must have relayed the news that they were coming, and that had been the cause of their departure.

Hugh Davidson put together a relief party for Morden. Most everyone in the troop wanted to go. The ones whose horses had been shot or blown up rode in a wagon. Henry Miles was on the wagon seat between the black driver and Harry Gunn. Harry had tied his horse behind and was holding Henry, lest he faint and fall off.

Frank's and Ovide's horses were tired from the race into camp, and they arrived at the Cossack post later than the rest. The sun was down and the sky losing colour. There was nothing, not even dust, to signify a battle. Beside the railway track, a half-circle of men stood, backs to them.

Frank and Ovide dismounted and tied their reins over the horses' necks, left them to graze. They went to where the others were and found a place to peer in. Davidson was down on one knee with his ear to Tom Miles' mouth. Miles was propped against his saddle, covered in blood. It seemed to come from high on one shoulder. His shirt and saddle were black with it. His face was an awful colour you would not associate with human. Still, he was alive and whispering.

Fred Morden was laid out on his back. He had bits of gravel and coal grit on his face, so must have pitched forward when he went down. In his forehead was a hole. Below his frowning brow, his eyes glared.

Robert Kerr was beside Morden. His side was bloody, but he had a cleaner, smaller wound in his chest that had killed him.

Except for Davidson talking with Tom, and the medic trying to stop Tom's shoulder from bleeding, nobody moved or spoke. Frank shifted to see Henry Miles. Harry Gunn was holding him up, for suddenly the boy could not stand on his own. He swayed and stared at his brother.

A face pushed in between Ovide and Frank, and Frank saw it was Jeff Davis. The first thing Frank felt was a wash of relief, as if everything would be all right now. Then he felt stupid, because obviously it was too late for things to be all right. There was a strip of animal fur tied around the crown of Jeff's hat. He locked a hand on Frank's arm, the other on Ovide's, and drew them away.

When they were distant from the group, he said, "I need your help. Right now, before it gets dark."

He pulled two sheets of paper from his pocket. On them, he'd drawn horseshoes, life-sized. He pointed at a little split on the top of one, and at a dark spot on the tail of the other.

"We'll go where the Boers were shooting and look for these."

"What's this?" Ovide asked, pointing at the dark spot.

"Lump of iron. It shows as a dent in the print."

Jeff started for The Blue, who was standing with Dunny. But Frank grabbed him. After a month and a half, and with Morden and Kerr lying dead, Davis wasn't acting right. Frank was offended by the lack of ceremony.

Jeff looked at where Frank's fist gripped his sleeve. "We've got to hurry or it'll be dark." He pulled his arm away.

They mounted their horses. Jeff rode east two hundred yards and jumped off. He ran around in the fading light and made circles and sweeps with his hands where he wanted them to look. In the course of searching, they found piles of spent cartridges and spots of blood.

Then Jeff hailed them. He'd found where the horses had been held. It was a stew of prints. He told them to go to the edges, where they'd be cleanest. Back along the railway, the wagon was leaving. Tom Miles lay in the back with the dead men. Henry rode on the wagon seat, leaning against Harry Gunn. The rest lined out behind.

It was close to dark when Ovide shouted. Jeff went down on hands and knees where Ovide was pointing. Frank left what he was doing and ran there too. Jeff slapped the ground beside the print. It was the one with the split top. He reared and smiled.

"Villamon," he said. "I knew it was him."

They waited and watched his face.

"What's a Villamon?" Frank asked.

"That split shoe's on Villamon's horse."

"Small shoe," Ovide observed.

"Basuto horse, same as yours," said Jeff.

"But who is he?" asked Frank.

"He scouts for De Wet. Villamon, Scheepers, and Danie Theron are the best Boer scouts. Villamon's a bastard. If he sees you, he'll kill you. I don't know why the Miles brothers are alive."

Frank looked closer at the split shoe print. Jeff continued to talk.

"De Wet and Froneman blew up track and trapped a train at Honing Spruit last night. Then Olivier led this attack on Katbosch. It was De Wet who brought the extra guns this afternoon. Villamon must have been circling to attack Katbosch in the back or side."

Frank was surprised at himself. Surprised that he was bristling mad. For all the relief he'd felt at seeing Jeff, he was angry at him now. Boer generals and scouts. All these strangers' names, when Morden and Kerr were dead.

Davis noted Frank's mood.

"I'll make him pay," he said. "I was after Scheepers, but I'll go after Villamon now."

The picture in Frank's head was of Jeff riding around with his bunch of scouts, every man with an animal skin on his hat, chasing enemy scouts who chased them back. Each one with a special enemy he'd vowed to kill.

In his head, Frank saw that. Then he saw Morden pitch forward on his face, the back of his skull blown off like a chunk of anthill.

Then Ovide reared out of the grass and pointed east. "They went out that way."

Jeff nodded at where the Pincher men had died. "They did well to keep Villamon away from your camp."

Frank did not like that either. It was as if Jeff was saying that Morden and Kerr's story was over; on its way to forgotten already. Their killers were what counted now. Frank turned and faced the spot where they'd died, as if that showed superior loyalty. Jeff moved so Frank had to look at him.

"Villamon's all I can do."

"You'll stay with that other bunch, then?"

"Not my say."

"Did you ask?"

"No."

That's when they noticed they were not alone. As if risen from the ground, Pete and Eddy Belton were there with their horses. They did not speak. They would not speak unless spoken to by Jeff.

That night in camp, the Mounted Rifles settled what they could. They talked of finding barnboards to build coffins. They imagined the grey ugliness of that and decided to bury the dead in their bedrolls. They rolled the corpses into the blankets; put the oil sheets on the outside. Ovide volunteered some slim horsehair ropes he'd braided. Tied at intervals, the bundles were at least human-shaped.

Burial would be in the morning, at the battle site. Wood was yanked from a wall and two crosses fashioned. Looking at the homely result, a fellow said, "Monument." He asked Hugh Davidson to take a pound from his soldier's pay toward the cost of a proper headstone. Others said to sign them up. Harry Gunn said to put Reg Redpath down for a pound. Redpath wasn't here but had been a close friend of Kerr's. Make that two pounds. The wood crosses would do for now.

The mourners were not allowed a fire because of Boer snipers, so they sat around a blackened firepit. The bundled bodies stretched beside them. Quartermaster Capt. Jack Allen produced two bottles of whisky. Each man had a few good pulls that changed out some of his hurt for anger. If they'd had trouble hating the Boers, it was no trouble tonight.

Frank found the whisky did not make much difference to him. The anger he saw around him seemed beside the point, though Frank wasn't sure what the point was.

When someone spoke, it was usually Hugh Davidson. He sounded broken as he recited what Tom Miles had said in his ear. Tom was in the temporary Red Cross tent, hopefully asleep.

"After Tom was shot and could not fire his own rifle," Davidson said, "he spotted for the other two. Kerr got hit next, in the side, but kept firing until he was shot in the heart. Fred Morden didn't stop firing even then. Not until the bullet hit him in the forehead. Tom said they killed at least two Boers, and wounded more."

"Fred did not have to do this," Davidson continued. "He could have let those Boers pass. No one would have blamed him. He could have surrendered. Many a brave soldier has surrendered in this war. The Boers would have let them go later."

It was an agony for Davidson to say these things, and an agony to listen to. The only other man who spoke was Harry Gunn. He patted Davidson's arm, and when the lieutenant paused, Gunn murmured things the others could not hear. But Davidson seemed to feel it was his obligation not just to tell what he'd been told, but to repeat it.

Davidson was the Mountie who had raised the troop in Pincher Creek, the one who had stirred the young men's interest and outrage and convinced them Britain's interests were their own. Now he felt responsible: for Kerr and Morden; for Tom Miles' ruined shoulder; for Henry Miles' hand.

There was little sound beyond Davidson's talk. Occasional pulses of wind pulled at rips in the Red Cross tent. No man said good night when he left the circle. The night had fallen clear, an icy silent dark.

For his own thoughts, Frank waited until he was alone. In his bedroll, he was still angry at Morden for his Empire heroics and at Jeff for his stupid game of scouting. If everyone had just stayed in their place, looked after their own, maybe Jeff could have figured a way to relieve Morden's four. Frank knew this was crazy thinking, that it could not have been that simple, but he went on thinking it anyway until he slept.

The Mounted Rifles went to the Cossack post at dawn. They dug the hole deep and wide a dozen yards from the tracks. Morden and Kerr were put in side by side. Those who were religious said prayers. Everyone sang "Glory Hallelujah," then Hugh Davidson gave a speech, his voice stronger this morning. Major Sanders had arrived in the night and spoke next. It was a rousing, patriotic talk, the one about heroic sacrifice. They'd heard it before but needed it now.

They filled the hole and punched the crosses in; piled rocks on the grave. Frank saw Casey and Jeff mount up and leave, headed east. The rest went back to camp.

Davidson and Harry Gunn had taken effects. Pocket watches, jack-knives; things that could be sent home. Harry found a half-written letter to Trudy Black in Fred's back pocket. He put it in a YMCA envelope and licked it shut; printed her name and address on the front.

By that afternoon, Percy Girouard had repaired enough track to get a train as far north as Katbosch. The train could go no farther, and a wagon full of wounded men was brought down from Honing Spruit. These were British ex-POWs, ones who'd been freed from Pretoria's prison camp. Now they were wounded and on their way to hospital.

Beside the huffing train, Lieutenant Davidson sat on a camp stool with a portable desk on his knees, deep in a kind of writing that spurted fast. He looked desperate when he was not writing. Letters to Morden's family and Kerr's sister. His face was composed but wet.

On the train, D Squadron crowded into the aisle of the car where Tom Miles lay and Henry sat. C Squadron was in a different car with Ingles, Aspenall, and Birney. The wounded were on their way to the hospital at Kroonstad.

The Mounted Rifles could not all fit inside the car. Some clung to the outside and stared through the windows. The talk was nervous and hearty, mostly false, because Tom Miles still did not look well enough to live, and because they remembered Canadians had died in Kroonstad's hospital. Henry Miles was not hurt badly, certainly not enough to go to hospital. Hugh Davidson was sending him to look out for his brother: to make sure they didn't put Tom in a room full of typhoid.

The steam whistle blew and the men jumped off. The train puffed away. Everyone who had been clustering together since the previous evening abruptly broke apart. No one wanted to hear what anyone else had to say. Most went to their horses. Where the horses had been clipped by shell fragments, they cleaned and anointed them. They brushed them until the oil rose and their coats gleamed.

In the days after the battle, every Katbosch morning started out the same. The Shropshire sergeants yelled in the dark. The Mounted Rifles corporals and sergeants ran around delivering Lieutenant Davidson's orders. Cossack posts; patrols; hunting for the pot; burying horses, oxen, and mules; gathering fuel for the fire; piecing together a new shantytown out of the flattened ruins of the old. Only the sick and the wounded were excused. Everything was about keeping fear and self-pity at bay.

It was not working for Frank Adams, who was neck deep in emotions he could not even name. He bunched it together and called it frustration. Even things that had never bothered him frustrated him now. Trapped in a small box was how he felt.

The start had been finding Morden and Kerr dead, but the feeling had spiralled tighter and higher when he hadn't liked Jeff Davis's talk. When Jeff and Casey had ridden away, the roof had caved in. That was the end of sleeping, so that every day was worse than the one before.

In the cold, sleepless, endless nights, Frank gummed his problem like a toothless dog, pushing the facts around the yard of his brain. But some things came clear. He remembered what Doc Windham used to say at funerals. As they walked away from the grave, he would put his hand on Frank's neck and say, "Sorrow is for the self."

When Jeff and Casey rode away, Frank had not been thinking about the dead; he'd been longing with all his heart to be on Dunny's back beside the scouts. In his tin-cold bedroll, Frank became convinced that he and Ovide had been going about this war exactly wrong, and that what they needed now was to become scouts as soon as possible.

When Frank went to breakfast, he bumped into Davidson, who ordered him to take his four and go on patrol five miles west. Frank asked whether it would be all right if he and Ovide went alone.

"Adams, sometimes I wonder if you think at all. Three days ago we lost two men. Does that strike you as reason to exercise less than normal vigilance? You will go out as four. Get moving."

The day was grey and the wind cold. In this calendar month at home, the prairie would be glittering with crocus, buffalo bean, pincushion, and wild rose, but the winter veldt here was frostbitten and stone dead. The horses barely looked at it.

None of the four talked about the attack two days ago, but as soon as the camp disappeared behind the first roll of landscape, its shadow was on them like a devil dog. Pete unslung his rifle and carried it across his saddle rolls. Eddy did the same. Pete was gouging his horse then yanking its head when it tried to answer. Ovide told him to quit it and Pete told him to shut up.

Though the other horses were still thin and weary, Dunny was sparky and insisted on pushing ahead. That put the nervous Beltons behind Frank, and he felt the itch all over his back. Out a mile, Dunny heard a snake in some rocks and kicked with both hind feet. Eddy's rifle cracked, luckily firing to the side. Frank stopped and ordered the Beltons to the front; ordered them to hook their fingers on the trigger guard and not on the damn trigger itself. When Dunny objected to going last, he wound her in a tight circle then snapped his reins on her when it was time to go straight. She looked back with chagrin and wonder, not used to such treatment.

The destination was a farmhouse. Davidson said it had been visited but not properly searched. The lieutenant had been impressed when Ovide found the root cellar at the first farm. He thought he might repeat the miracle.

They searched the house and found nothing. It had already played host to British soldiers. A Tommy bard had written on the wall.

BOOER NO FEAR
REMBER MAJUBA

The cupboard doors were off their hinges. The spaces within contained broken cups, dishes, and crockery. The Tommys had been thorough. A table stood on its legs in the middle of the room, but the chairs were spun off into corners and some smashed. The cellar below the house was alive with mice, who had eaten anything that could be eaten.

Frank asked Pete to check the barn loft and heard a rifle blast soon after. When Pete climbed the ladder and poked his head through, a cloud of doves had exploded out the hayloft. Pete had blown a hole in the roof.

They went to their saddlebags for hardtack biscuits and cold tea. They flipped the surviving chairs upright and swept the mouse dirt off the table. The room was dirty and the windows broken, but the walls kept out most of the wind.

Frank's plan for the day had been to soften Ovide up to the idea of scouting. He knew it would be a slow process and was anxious to begin.

He also knew that saying anything in front of Pete was risky, yet he could not stop himself.

"We ought to do something about Morden and Kerr," Frank said to Ovide. "Not just ordinary soldiering. Something else. Otherwise it could happen again."

The old cowboy kept chewing at the hardtack with his few good teeth. He could have been deaf and dumb.

Pete was on it in an instant. "What do you want us to do, Frank?"

Frank went on staring at Ovide.

"Ovide and I should go scouting," Frank said. "If we were scouts, this war would be less boring. Time would pass more quickly. We'd feel we were doing something and getting home sooner."

Ovide was hard to flatter, but Frank tried that too. He praised how Ovide had found the root cellar and the split horseshoe track at the battle site. That was real scouting. Ovide shook his head once in denial, causing some saliva to escape and run down the deep crease that bordered his chin.

Frank had not anticipated immediate success. He wanted to plant the idea in his old partner, like a grass spear in a sock.

Ovide turned toward Frank and opened his eyes turtle-slow. "Not me. These fellas, maybe."

"We'd go scouting," said Pete. "Go out with Jeff, eh?"

"No!" Frank said louder than he intended. "Jeff's not in this. It wouldn't be with Jeff."

"We're still interested. Aren't we, Eddy?"

The bigger Belton smiled and nodded agreeably with a piece of hard-tack packed in his cheek.

"We can track," said Pete. "We track real good. Don't we, Eddy?"

"I guess everybody can," Frank said, losing patience.

"Oh, no. I wouldn't say that. That's not true. Not good like we can."

Frank fell silent. Pete tried two more times to goad him into argument about tracking and whether the Beltons' ability was unusual, but Frank dummied up like Ovide had. Every man in Alberta believed himself a superior tracker, just like every man believed he had a special gift for riding horses.

"Well, we can," Pete said, insulted by Frank's silence.

Frank had known before he started that he would regret speaking in front of the Beltons. He was already thinking how to keep Pete's interest from spooking his plan.

That evening, before the camp went to sleep, Frank excused himself to Ovide and said he was going to the latrine. He started in that direction then veered for Davidson's tent. The canvas of the bell tent was lit dully from within. The black guard who looked after Davidson and his horse at night lay curled like a dog beside the flap.

"Talk to the lieutenant," Frank said to him.

The guard tapped the tent and said, "Bossy." He repeated it several times.

Davidson flung the flap. He was wearing his greatcoat, buttoned to the neck.

"What is it, Adams?"

"Need a word, sir. Have a request."

Davidson went back inside and Frank stood in the tent door. He had never been inside an officer's tent and was struck by its neatness. The bedroll was on the floor, made up and turned down. There was even a pillow. Beside the bed's head was a box that showed a book in its open top. A picture in a metal frame leaned against the box's side. It was of Davidson, his wife, and their three daughters.

On the tent's other side were two camp stools. Davidson sat on one. The other held his travel desk, open with a partly written letter and a pen dripping ink on the blotter. A lantern hung from a riveted hook above. Davidson did not offer to move the desk and Frank stayed standing.

"Ovide Smith and I would like to be scouts, sir."

Davidson knocked the ink out of his pen and wiped it. He wrapped it in a rag.

"You're good with horses," he said. "I'm surprised either of you has ambitions beyond that." Davidson paused. Maybe he thought he'd said enough to make Frank disappear, but Frank remained.

"You're letting the warmth out, Adams. Sit on the bed. Mind your boots." He reached behind Frank and pulled the flap closed.

Frank did not want to be on Davidson's bed. He sat in the middle and kept his boots near the door. He had to put an arm behind himself and lean on his elbow. He was closer now to the picture of the lieutenant's family. Four pretty females in formal dresses. A younger Davidson behind them in his Mountie uniform, head bare and hair slicked down. Frank knew the photographer was the fellow who worked the towns along the Crow's Nest Pass railway. Frank knew because a photograph of his parents and him, against the same painted sheet, hung on the wall of their cabin.

"Private? Your reasons, please."

"It's Morden and Kerr, sir, and the Miles brothers. As scouts, maybe Ovide and me could keep the outposts safer. Maybe Casey and Captain Chalmers could use help."

"Maybe our scouts don't need or want your help."

"I just thought since Jeff Davis left . . ."

"There's been plenty of time to fill that vacancy, if there was one." He saw that Frank wanted to say more. "Let me finish."

The lieutenant asked to be let finish but had nothing to say. Frank waited.

"Scouting, as you know, Adams, is more than wanting to scout. There are skills. A certain type of man."

"Ovide and I are good trackers, sir. We're both good riders."

Davidson fingered the letter he was writing. Tipped up its head end and stared. Frank was losing him. He could see the negative reply forming in the lieutenant's head. In desperation, he said, "Ovide and me are part Indian."

Davidson lifted his eyebrows and swung a look at Adams.

"My mother's a Montana Halfbreed. I don't know how it works with Ovide."

"Perhaps you should have said so at the time of enlistment."

"Colonel Herchmer had just passed Jeff Davis when I came up. I thought it would be the same for me. Since I look less Indian than Jeff."

Davidson laughed without humour. "I don't know what being Indian adds, frankly. Callaghan is Irish and seems to do well. Charlie Ross was born in Australia. At any rate, Private Adams, this is not a decision I can take—or want to take—immediately. I'll think about it. In the meantime, remember that patrols and outposts *are* scouting. The Canadian Mounted Rifles is a scouting battalion. Just do your work well. Good night."

The brevity of the conversation suggested Frank had been dismissed, and the guard at Davidson's door grinned as he left. But Frank was not defeated, no more than he had been by Ovide's silence. Davidson's final comment was not outright refusal. The possibility of success hung by a thread. He decided before he got to their bedding spot that he would not say anything about the conversation to Ovide, certainly not the part about Ovide's being a Halfbreed, which of course he wasn't.

Ovide was in his blanket and turned away by the time Frank arrived. Frank kicked off his boots. In his bedroll, he writhed to loosen his lice.

"That was a big shit," Ovide said.

"I went for a walk."

"Doubt it."

March to Transvaal, July 1900

At the start of July, the Mounted Rifles were ordered to leave the railway camps and proceed to Irene (pronounced I-ree-nee). They were being sent back north to fight Louis Botha's Transvaal Boers. As there were convoys in need of guarding, they were ordered to march rather than go by train.

The attack on Katbosch had left Davidson's troop touchy. If one of De Wet's burgher armies appeared from behind a kopje, or one of his guns started dropping shrapnel rounds from a hill's top, they were sure they would not have time to un-extend and form a defensive circle; that they would be defeated. Nor was running an option. Someone had calculated that C and D Squadrons had six fit horses among them.

The oxen were clapped out too. Every day, a few would stop. Unable to lie down in their yokes, they would stand still, and no amount of abuse from the drivers could move them. If the whipping went too far, the cowboys among the Rifles would force it to stop—for, like any cow, an ox can put its brain to sleep. In that state, you can beat it to death and achieve nothing.

Several times a day, a man would drag his horse off the line and shoot it. Pete Belton shot his early to get it out of the way. Eddy had been forced to give up his giant horse to a gun crew and was given a small Argentine who was no match for his weight. When the Argentine pony fell twice in an hour, Pete shot it as well, so that he would have Eddy's company on the wagon.

As so many horses faltered, it became harder for Frank to conceal the good health of his mare. One way was to lead her and claim it was due to a bad leg. He got the idea from Ovide, who was trying to save his Basuto by going on foot. Frank and Ovide walked together and tried to stay on the opposite side of the convoy from Davidson.

In fact, they could have walked where and how they pleased. The lieutenant was paying little attention to anything beyond his own mind. The fact that Morden and Kerr had died while he was in charge had made him doubt himself. Over and over, he replayed the battle, considering each Boer gambit and his response. Like a soothsayer casting bones, he hoped to see them come out in a way that would restore his faith; that would allow him to continue.

There could have been no worse time for Frank to badger Davidson about scouting. He knew that but was powerless not to end each day at the lieutenant's tent—as powerless as Davidson was not to be inside writing more letters to General Hutton and the people of Pincher Creek, insisting that the dead men's heroism must be recognized.

The second time Frank went to the tent, Davidson left him outside to figure out for himself that he wasn't wanted. To pass those hours, Frank made the acquaintance of Dakomi, Davidson's guard. Dakomi had been chosen for his few words of English, but Frank discovered he had a full deck of cards and knew the game of cribbage. As Frank waited, they played until the camp bugler blew lights out. Just before snuffing his lamp, Davidson said, "I have no further comment."

The third time Frank approached the lieutenant's tent, Davidson was waiting, arms folded, face like a rock. He told Frank to go away. He said it abruptly, as you would say *scat* to a cat. Frank obeyed, but returned once the lieutenant went inside.

To get around the need of a cribbage board, Frank and Dakomi gathered a heap of roughly uniform stones. As an evening passed, the pile would grow in front of one, then flow back toward the other. Possession of all of the stones would have ended the game, but this never seemed to happen.

The evening of the day they crossed the Vaal at Viljeon's Drift, Dakomi and Frank were playing when suddenly the lieutenant flung back the flap and stood in the tent's opening, his eyes blazing under coiled eyebrows, his mouth a miser's purse.

"The words *no* and *go away* have no meaning for you, do they, Adams? Are you waiting for me to tell someone to physically remove you? Because I will."

"It's important to me, sir."

"It certainly must be. And not just to you. Before you arrived tonight, Private Pete Belton paid me a visit. It seems he and his brother think they have a vocation for scouting too. He's very sure they'd be wonderful at it. Is there some kind of contest going on?"

Frank rose to his feet, accidentally kicking his pile of stones. He did not attempt to speak.

"This is absolutely my last word. Fred Morden and Robert Kerr were not scouts. They were merely excellent soldiers who did what was asked of them. That diligence cost them their lives. Now go away and try to be half the soldier they were. And, trust me, you'd be wise to stay out of my sight from now on."

Frank did not move when the flap slapped closed. The bugler blew lights out. The lamp inside the bell tent snuffed. Without any thought, Frank ran through the dark rows of sleeping men, stumbling over pieces of kit and tall men's legs. He knelt beside a form with an oil sheet pulled over its head. He grabbed and knew by the skinny neck that he had Pete Belton.

"What the Jesus?! Eddy! Wake up! Some bastard's killing me!"

Frank jerked Pete onto his back, jumped his knees onto his skinny arms. He saw the pale ghost of his own scrunched fist and could not say for sure if it was about to smash Pete's face.

Eddy sat up, rubbing his eyes with a huge mitt.

"What you doing, Frank?"

"Eddy, you stupid bastard! Get him offa me!"

"You better stop, Frank."

Hearing Eddy's mildness caused the fit to lessen. Frank recognized the words as good advice. Either Pete knew why Frank wanted to strangle him, or choking him would not cause him to learn. The scouting plan was ruined and would remain so regardless.

Then he felt a hand on his shoulder. He thought it was Eddy but, looking around, saw a familiar shape bent toward him. "Come. Come on now."

Frank rose off Pete's arms and followed Ovide meekly through the camp. Behind him, he heard Pete yelling.

"He jumped me! In my sleep! Choked me! Didn't he, Eddy? Frank Adams. Supposed to be our friend. Crazy sonofabitch!"

Ovide stood over Frank as Frank got his boots off. Ovide handed him his blanket, and only then began to get himself ready to sleep again. Frank lay face up and thought. He thought about how Pete got his meddling hands on the plan in the first place, the way it had stemmed from his own impatient need to tell Ovide. Frank's culpability in the matter took the rest of the heat out of him and allowed the ground to clutch him with its chill fingers. The blanket was more hole than cloth. You had to infuse such a covering with a powerful wish before it could warm you.

His plan had been like that too, he saw. A tangle of strings. A web. Imagining he could make Davidson decide something he had no wish to decide. Imagining he could turn Ovide into an ardent tracker and chaser of Boers.

"You'd never have come scouting with me, would you, Ovide?"

"No." The voice was thick with sleep.

"You like things boring."

Ovide made a noise close to a horse's mutter.

For some seconds, there was poignancy. Frank felt the quiet, good steadfastness of Ovide. Then, like everything else tonight, that impression flipped and a different picture bloomed: the old cowboy's eyes opening slowly. They were in the destroyed Boer kitchen, the second before Ovide said he had no interest in scouting but maybe Pete and Eddy did. More than anything else, that had wrecked Frank's plan.

Not me. These fellas, maybe.

Beneath his cold blanket, Frank was suddenly warm again. Heart fast, breath short. He felt like he had when Pete's scrawny neck was in his hands, but now it was all about Ovide handing Frank over to the Beltons, for no better reason than his own immediate convenience.

Frank imagined himself riding off with Jeff. He poured all the muscle of his mind into the question of whether he really could go if an opportunity arose. He understood he would have to become someone different—a fellow not as nice as he tried to be on any ordinary day. Frank considered it and decided he could be such a man if he tried.

Part Five

—

AAS VOGEL KRANZ

Irene, Transvaal, July 1900

Seen from Lord Roberts' war balloon, the temporary city of Irene would look cracked in half by railway tracks. One half was for soldiers; the other for animals and black labourers. Along the two sides of the railroad were the depots and factories upon which the camp's life depended.

In the soldiers' town, tent communities were ruled off by dusty streets. Each regimental suburb was a garden of the same tent vegetable; each group surrounding its regimental flag. Wherever a cavalry or mounted infantry regiment resided, picketed horses stood. The mounted regiments were on the downwind side, because the regiments of foot did not find horse smell as homey as horse soldiers did.

The other animals in this human town were pets and mascots: rock dassies; springbok captured in infancy; a baboon on a chain (shades of Norvals Pont); ostriches, who could fight out of any hobble but were addicted to oats. These were sometimes coerced to race.

On the other side of the railway tracks, farther down the prevailing wind, was the true animal town. Paddocks of cattle, sheep, goats, and bullocks; mules and free-pool horses. Between the paddocks, garbage carts rolled to the refuse pits, where vultures walked, fussy and unhurried, like shoppers in a market.

Near the dump was the African camp: shelters built of garbage that were home to the men who did the work of Irene and those who needed rest between convoys. For food, the Africans cooked heads, hooves, and offal cast out by the butchers.

Directly beside the railroad tracks, meat-fragrant smoke rose from the ovens behind the giant mess tents. Butchers' tent. Knackers' yard. Biltong smokers converting trek ox into dried meat.

At the edge of Irene, a British sergeant-major instructed Lieutenant Davidson's troop to dismount. A veterinary sergeant and his assistant walked along the horse lines. A firm believer in perverse army logic, Frank looked away and tried not to think as the vet looked at Dunny—her eyes, neck, legs, and feet. He tried not to display relief when the vet pointed her to the side with the stronger horses. Ovide's Basuto was sent to the other side, to stand with the exhausted cobs, their chests like birdcages, their eyes blank.

The men were to leave their horses and form a line behind the quartermaster sergeant. The promise was of new uniforms and smalls; much needed boots. Ovide ignored this and stayed by his Basuto, even as a sergeant with bulging eyes shrieked in his face. What might have looked like stupid impassivity was, Frank knew, implacable stubbornness. Ovide was staying with his horse and that was that.

Frank could do nothing about it, so he pushed to get near the quartermaster. When they walked inside the canvas cathedral, damp and close and rank with mildew, he raced for a stack he knew were tents and grabbed one. Then he went for the piles of khaki, taking a second, larger set of everything for Ovide. Most important were boots, for Ovide had walked much of the last fifty miles and had worn through both layers of moosehide on the moccasins Marie Rose had made for him.

Frank's arms were piled high and as he was trying to get out past a corporal who thought he was hoarding, Ovide appeared in the tent's mouth. Frank knew the Basuto was dead. He gave Ovide his half of the goods, and the corporal let them pass. Outside, Davidson was waiting to lead them to their place in the tent city.

At the dirty slab of ground, the lieutenant told them to pick a spot and dump their gear. Next stop was a horse corral for remounts, and they were due there in fifteen minutes.

Because he had a horse, Frank did not need to go to the corral. Dunny was over on the picket line, eating. But he bridled her, jumped on her bare back, and rode there anyway. He arrived at the empty corral as a hundred and sixty horses were released into it. Then he saw the unhorsed troopers coming at a run, swarming over the pole fence. Ovide was among them: adjusting his rope, wasting little time in making his choice.

The remounts were not Canadian horses, nor were they fresh off any boat. Boer ponies stolen from burned farms and Argentines other regiments had ridden down and then traded for something better. Even the best-looking Argentines were brainless culls, for why would a horse country like Argentina reduce its stock of good ones for the sake of a British war?

All the same, the boys fought over them. Frank watched Ovide drop his hoolihan over the head of a Boer mare as plain as mud, but one in whom he saw some quality. Ovide was simply never wrong about horses. Frank also noticed that the Beltons were only pretending to go after horses. They shared a rope, and Pete was flinging it, usually hitting between hip and shoulder. He gathered the rope quickly, lest he loop a pair of legs by accident.

When all of the horses were caught, Frank heard Pete tell Davidson that he and Eddy had been shut out.

"When'll there be another bunch?" he asked.

Davidson looked pained. "There are no more remounts, Belton. You're un-horsed, both of you. Until further notice, you're grooms and latrine diggers."

Pete's face fell. Thinking he would outwit the other men, imagining a second corral of better horses, he had fooled himself as he always did.

Pete spun away and saw Frank watching. His face was at once steely with hate. Whenever Pete damaged himself, he always fixed the blame on someone else. He did so now.

Ovide sat on his oil sheet in his new khaki uniform and boots. None of it fit well, but he seemed not to care. Before him was an almost-new Texas stock saddle, standing on its horn. He was feeling around inside the tree, for points or nicks that would rub his new horse wrong. Beyond him, the mare had her face in a hay net.

Frank had opened out the tent on the ground. He was rubbing dubbin into the frayed seams. Despite the new gear and horse, Frank knew Ovide was mourning. His Basuto mare had been shot. Ovide had told Frank how it happened; how he had walked beside the Tommy in charge while a black man led the mare. Ovide had argued as best he could that the Basuto should be left with him or turned out to recoup her strength; that she was much stronger than she looked.

The walk led to a trench. The Tommy stopped and stamped. Like something mechanical, he slapped his rifle to his shoulder, stamped again, brought the rifle down, and shot the mare through her eye. At the same time, the black servant put a shoulder into her, so she fell over and slid down the short slope, stopping against the limed pile of dead.

"Least we have a tent," Frank said now, for he had just thought of the portion of winter remaining. The smell of the tent was bad but they could live with it to be warm. Ovide looked up and his expression was as spiteful as Pete's had been earlier. He did not speak but kept feeling inside the saddle tree.

Within himself, Frank told Ovide to go to hell. He understood about the Basuto and Ovide's state, but was practising to think less, and care less, about what Ovide felt.

In Frank's new plan, his time to be a scout would come when another scout was killed or sick. When that moment arrived, Frank was prepared to do two things: go over Davidson's head, and leave Ovide behind. Frank would find Major Sanders and tell him he was ready and available, with a strong horse, to take the laid-low scout's place. This imagined conversation went smoothly, because Dunny was strong and because Frank only had to speak for himself. There would be no pointing at Ovide and trying to argue how much smarter and more capable he was than he seemed.

The success of the plan depended on Hugh Davidson's lack of vindictiveness and his instinct to protect his own reputation. Frank could not imagine Davidson going to Sanders and telling the major that Frank was annoying or had attacked Pete Belton in his sleep. Frank thought such talk would seem small, and that Davidson would only make himself small by saying it.

Another possible concern was that Major Sanders would have heard about the attack on Belton from the rank and file. The story had circulated fast once the Mounted Rifle troops were back together at Irene. Sometimes Frank saw it moving: men looking at him and talking low. Even fellows he knew were ready to throw out what they knew in favour of the novel idea that he was wild and unbalanced. But Frank could not imagine any of them using rare time with the major to talk about him.

Seeing how readily the other soldiers turned on him taught Frank an important lesson.

"If all people have for you is nothing against you," he said to himself, "don't count on them in time of trouble."

While Ovide and Frank were still at their chores in the late afternoon, the NCOs came around and ordered the men to their lieutenant's tent. There was to be an announcement from Major Sanders.

The news was that they were leaving tomorrow, first thing. They would head southeast to rejoin Hutton's column for a push against Louis Botha. The Royal Canadian Dragoons were already there.

The larger purpose was to capture the Delagoa Railway line, which connected Pretoria to the east coast. The railway was something for which the Boers would have to fight. At the moment, their president, Paul Kruger, was governing Transvaal from a railway car at Machadodorp. They must also defend their connection to the port of Lourenço Marques in Portuguese Mozambique, because their German munitions came from there. A major battle for the railway could come at any time, wherever the Boers thought they could win. Major Sanders said to expect the Boers to be desperate and to fight that way.

While Lieutenant Davidson delivered these messages, Frank saw Jeff Davis ride into Irene. He was alone, and he guided his blue cayuse to the D Squadron picket line. One glance, and Frank believed Jeff was here to stay, for there was no strip of animal skin on his hat. Frank felt weak with pleasure and was already imaging the conversation in which he would explain his need to be a scout. If anyone could understand this, it would be Jeff.

Davidson sent them away to prepare for tomorrow, and Frank ran for the horse lines where Jeff was standing. He shook Jeff's hand and burst out with his news.

"I want to be a scout. I got to get out of here. I don't have to bring Ovide. He doesn't want to anyway. But I do."

Then Casey Callaghan was there, slapping Jeff's shoulders with both hands. He stepped in front of Frank and hustled Jeff away toward the scouts' camp, where Frank supposed there would be a bottle to split.

Back at Frank's own tent, Ovide was doing farrier work on the new mare. He had procured a new shoe and was carefully pounding in the nails.

When Ovide saw Frank coming, saw how disheartened he was, the old cowboy said, "Least we got a tent."

Go to hell, thought Frank.

Rapid whumping on the tent wall woke Frank. He listened for the bugle but there wasn't one, just someone calling his name in the dark. He pulled on his boots and pushed out the flap. It was the horse orderly.

"Your horse is gone."

Frank's shoulders cranked so hard he almost fell.

"I was sleeping right beside the line," the orderly said. "I always wake up if there's a fuss. There's a second horse missing too. Big charger. The British officer who owns that one is madder than hell. Same thieves must have got both. I didn't hear a thing."

They rushed toward the picket line. Ovide caught up as they were looking at Frank's saddle standing in front of Dunny's empty spot. Ovide's new mare was lying half on her back next to it. Frank decided he hated a horse that slept like that.

"Anybody see who it was?"

"Nobody saw. But I gotta tell you, the Beltons are gone. Maybe I shouldn't say it's them, but they were working here yesterday."

"Can I borrow a horse?" Frank asked the orderly. "Ovide and me . . ."

"You and Smith will return to your tent."

They turned and saw Davidson. He had snuck up in the dark.

"This isn't a riding stable, Private Adams. You leave this camp without permission, it's a crime. I'd see you court-martialled for it."

"But, sir, that's my horse," Frank said, pointing to the space.

Davidson grabbed him roughly and pulled him away.

"Listen, private, I know it's your horse. I know it's a good horse. Frankly, I suspect there's more story here than I'm being told. I tell you to forget about scouting and you go directly to Pete Belton and try to wring his neck. Now your horse is gone and so are the Beltons."

Frank tried to compose the story in a concise way. It made no sense at any size.

"The Beltons have committed two serious crimes tonight," the lieutenant continued. "Horse theft and desertion. They could be executed for either. Because the other horse belongs to a British captain, there will be no mercy. If you know more, Adams, spit it out. I doubt even you want the Beltons shot."

"I think Pete took Dunny because I fought him."

"But fought him *why?*"

"He wouldn't stay out of my plan to scout. It put you off."

Davidson loosed a weary sigh. "For God's sake. If that's all, get back to bed. Our scouts are out. Maybe they'll find them. If the Beltons get beyond our outposts, the Boers will take care of them."

Frank returned to Ovide at the picket line. They stared at the space beside Ovide's new horse.

Frank said, "Eddy."

"Yup," said Ovide. "Dunny likes Eddy."

Ever since Canada, Dunny knew Pete was her enemy, would lay her ears flat whenever he passed. But, when the Beltons joined Frank's four, Eddy had liked to pet and nuzzle Dunny, and Frank had let him. Dunny had put up with it, the way most horses will humour a child.

That, in turn, meant Pete had stolen the charger, which made sense too. Eddy would take a horse he knew and was liked by. Pete would take a horse he could never ride any other way. That the charger would bring down British wrath on both their heads was Pete outsmarting himself again.

Back in the tent, Frank could not begin to sleep. He stared into the mildewed darkness and imagined Dunny yanking out of Eddy's hands or lying down and fighting off the hobble they used to contain her. He saw her galloping down the back trail, coming home with that eerie sense horses have for where they've been. Maybe she would be standing at the picket line, untied, come morning. It was all he could do to stay in the tent and not go there and watch for her.

In the occasional moment when he did not think of his horse, Frank thought of Ovide, snoring beside him, the friend he'd planned all week to leave behind. He thought of how, out of this whole camp, only Ovide would understand his loss or care. Frank rolled himself to the far edge of the tent and cried in sorrow and in shame.

The Mounted Rifles left Irene, headed southeast along a chain of hills. Britain's army was concentrated wherever a pass cut through the hills (at Tigerspoort, Witpoort, Hekpoort, and Koffyspruit). On the far side of those gaps, the Boers were waiting, and for now, the British goal was to keep them from breaking through.

This British army was not the monster that had rolled north a month ago. It had been whittled down by the need to protect the cities and roads the British had won. The Boers had lately discovered they could shrink Lord Roberts' army just by threatening Joburg or Pretoria. A few days ago, a feint toward Pretoria had caused French and Mahan to leave the front and scamper back, which was why the Canadian Dragoons and Mounted Rifles had been called up. To plug the hole.

General Hutton's brigade was charged with holding Witpoort Pass. He had seven hundred Mounted Infantry, a thousand cavalry, six hundred infantry, and twenty guns. The Boers on the far side of the pass were thought to have about the same. Fights at even strength were so unusual, many thought the odds automatically favoured the Boers. If Louis Botha thought so too, a challenge might come.

The Mounted Rifles' destination was a camp called Reitvlei, but Frank did not go with the horsemen. Dunny had not been waiting at the picket line at dawn, nor did she show up before the army lined out to leave. For the first time in the war, Frank was unhorsed. It was also the first time he had been so in his remembered life. It was a new element, and he felt as naked in it as a fish in a creel.

Leaving Irene, Frank took turns with the black labourers riding the baggage wagons. The rest of the time, he walked.

When the baggage convoy took a rest, the sergeant in charge chose Frank to come to the front and sit on the first wagon. He had his Lee-Enfield, and his job was to scan ahead and to the sides for snipers. Frank tried to keep his eyes running over the scenery and to not think. He looked for any clump of stones that might hide a man.

But though he did not think in words, pictures of Dunny kept coming to Frank. Dunny in countless poses, and such was his perversity that he often saw her in danger. His ass clenched and the nerves in his back were trilling. Into those pictures, he forced Jeff Davis and Casey Callaghan, for surely Jeff's purpose in returning was to protect them— even, as in this case, when that protection was from themselves. Frank imagined Jeff and Casey saving Dunny, and sometimes saving Eddy; but never Pete. Pete was on his own. Frank imagined Pete left on foot in places immense and barren.

Having pictured this so often in the first hours of the day, it was shocking for Frank to see the actual Jeff Davis, with Casey Callaghan, come riding up the road. They approached the baggage convoy when it was stopped at a spruit for water. The Blue and The General were as ridden down as Frank had seen them, crusted with dust and sweat. The two scouts looked stiff and tired as they dismounted and let the horses dust and water. They gave them oats and hay nets, and tied them to the emptiest wagon. The men crawled inside it to sleep.

Frank went to the two horses and started to brush them, and when The Blue spoke back to him, Jeff's face appeared atop the wagon's wall. His eyebrows were bushy with yellow dust. He had not even wiped his face before lying down to sleep.

"Did you find any tracks?" Frank asked, and by the look on Jeff's face he knew they had not been looking for the dun and did not know what had happened.

"I wondered where she was," Jeff said after Frank told him.

"Do you think anyone else tracked them away from Irene?" Frank asked.

Jeff shrugged and dropped down. Frank was asking things he could not know.

When the wagons rolled again, the two scouts kept on sleeping. Their horses walked in the wagon's wake. Frank was on the front wagon, staring through his rifle sights but seeing little. He'd pinned his hopes on Jeff and Casey finding his horse. With that idea blown, he had no other hope to go to. Pete and Eddy could have gone in any direction. The bush veldt. The Magaliese Mountains. Up or down the Vaal. If Pete had chosen east, the Boers had probably caught them.

The baggage convoy rolled into Reitvlei after dark. They'd had all kinds of problems and were very late, and a knot of angry Mounted Rifles were waiting, wanting their tents. They acted as though the wagon men were late through carelessness and sloth. Jeff and Casey were no longer with the convoy. They had woken up and departed, headed in some other direction.

Frank threw their tent down to Ovide. Later, when the wagons were bare, he went to find him. The tent was up, and Ovide shook his head in answer to the only question Frank had. Their part of camp was mostly empty, because the other Mounted Rifles were off visiting the Canadian Dragoons. The two squadrons had not seen each other since Diamond Hill. Ovide had heard some of their news. The Dragoons had still not lost a single man in battle.

Before Frank slept, fellows came back anxious to tell the stories they had heard. There was nothing in it about his horse or the Beltons. That was old news already.

Witpoort Pass

Louis Botha's general Ben Viljeon attacked Witpoort Pass at dawn.

Helios were blinking the news as soon as the sun broke the horizon— that the Boers were firing on the First Cavalry with three guns. That was on Hutton's right. The Royal Canadian Dragoons B Squadron and New Zealand Mounted Infantry were under similar attack on the left. Behind these outposts, Irish Fusiliers were positioned on both sides of the pass. They would be next if the outposts could not hold.

Hutton called for his reserves, and both the Mounted Rifles and Dragoons A Squadron left Reitvlei at a canter, bugles yodelling. By the time they reached Witpoort, B Squadron had retreated and the New Zealanders were overrun. The Fusiliers were holding, but as the reserves deployed, the Boers were jumping into the Irish trenches, and they were having at each other with rifle butts and rocks.

The Mounted Rifles were sent galloping to secure the left. The fresh Dragoons were told to dismount and to help the Fusiliers. As the Dragoons climbed, two of their troops were split off around the cliff's shoulder to surprise the Boers—where, by strange luck, the Boers were doing the same. The instant the Canadians rounded the cliff, they were fired upon but did not know from where. They dropped and waited. Lieutenants Borden and Burch stood up at the same time to see if they could figure out the enemy's location. The Boers were right in front of them, too close to miss.

Frank Adams spent the day in Reitvlei with a nurse herd of horses, the ones who had managed to break down on the road from Irene. Somehow he had not imagined Hutton's reserve could leave without him—until it did. He had supposed that an able-bodied man, even one on foot, would be of some use somewhere. But he was untrained for infantry or gun support, and was of less utility than the black men who whacked the oxen and mules and moved the guns around; who were up there now carrying shells to the mouths of smoking guns.

Ovide had left with the rest. In every fight since Fischer's Farm, Frank had been right beside Ovide or at the next point in the extended line. Always close enough to see the cowboy and to yell if his head was up or he was failing to shoot, or if he had missed a signal to move back or forward. Frank had wanted to leave Ovide only a few days ago. Now, he felt desperate at not being in battle beside him.

It took hours before anyone or any piece of news came back. The first thing was an ambulance in the early afternoon. Frank went to the Red Cross tent and watched the bodies being carried inside. Two were covered in blankets. Dead. An inert but living man went by, face bloody from the eyebrows to the jaw. The last one was writhing and yelling. Shot in the chest, he was fighting death and anyone who came near.

Neither living man was Ovide. Frank measured the corpses with his eye, trying to find them taller or shorter, more or less bulky, than his friend. He pushed into the tent, taking advantage of the confusion. The medic saw him and shouted to stop gawking and bring water.

"Who are the dead, sir?"

"They're both lieutenants. Canadian Dragoons. The wounded are Dragoons too. Now get moving."

The medic was wiping blood off the man with the wounded face. The soldier stiffened with each pass of the cloth. He had no eyes. The structure of his face was still there, so the bullet must have come from the side. Just deep enough into his profile to pierce both orbs.

The first riders who came back were Dragoons. They fired in the air and shouted, until the medic told them to have some respect. They were

A Squadron: the men who had left Reitvlei this morning. Now two of their lieutenants were dead, and they were trying to fashion it into a tale of bravery, worthwhile sacrifice, success.

From them, Frank learned that it was lieutenants Borden and Burch who had been killed. The blinded private was Mulloy, an Ontario schoolteacher. The other was Arthur Brown, who had been an English sailor. Hanging from the bloody operating table, Frank had seen Brown's thrashing arm. There was a tattoo: two hands clasped.

When the first Mounted Rifles came back, Frank asked but none of them knew where Ovide was. Most did not know *who* he was. The Mounted Rifles had seen less action so far and had been selected to guard the position overnight.

A full moon dodged among flowing clouds. Alone in his tent, Frank left the flap open so he could see the sky. He could not sleep. He had decided he was no longer worried about Ovide, but the smell of Dunny's saddle, the rank oil of the mare's hair, made him sad, made the light outside call to him. He left finally and went to the edge of camp, looking at the plain and the dark ripple of hills. The winter blond was like moonlit snow, and, on it, every thorn bush and tree stood out. A hyena laughed.

Frank imagined a pack of hyenas running in this underwater light, closing on an antelope. Then the fleeing animal became Dunny, and Frank could feel his mare between his knees: the fullness of her chest; her bellows that sprang the hinge of his ass on her deepest inhalation.

That she was gone carved him to the bone. It was no good to say the fault lay elsewhere. Frank had done things to Pete Belton that had caused his hatred. He had allowed things that had caused Eddy Belton to choose Dunny off the picket line. A touchier horseman would have told Eddy to back off, to not fool with Dunny. *Don't touch my horse*, old cowboys said from the distance of Frank's childhood; men who would never touch another man's horse or dog.

There is always fault, thought Frank, *and it is always yours.*

At the end of July, the Mounted Rifles pushed east into an ugly winter wind that was full of grit and streaked with snow. Then it filled with hard rain, until the high-wheeled transport wagons squelched through dongas in muck to their axles. On the steep downslopes, the men closest to the wagons screwed in the brakes but the wheels slid anyway and ran up on the startled drays.

Mules and oxen were helpless against the weather and the gruelling slippery pull. Any animal harbouring the germ of death hastened to that end. Pole-Carew's army had been through already and dead mules and oxen lay in their hundreds at the first river crossing. A cow gun had been left in the river's middle, mired and tipped, its barrel pointed at the sky. The men no longer wasted ammunition on blood-beaked vultures and ripping wild dogs. They made their eyes and noses blind; moved on.

They trekked onward until the town of Middelburg appeared in a bowl of hills: sedate, tidy, made of stone. They arrived as the main body of Lord Roberts' army readied to leave. It took time to understand that the Mounted Rifles were being left here: that all along they had been slated to go no farther and had been part of no one's plan for the fighting. Here, they would stick and guard the railway between Middelburg and Pan Station. They would patrol a triangle that included the northern point of Bankfontein.

At first, the Mounted Rifles stared with envy at the backs of the Canadian Dragoons, who continued east. The Rifles scolded and muttered that the Dragoons were the "fair-haired boys," not motley prairie gophers like themselves. But then an emissary rode back to say the Dragoons had their orders now and they were not much different. They would also be minding the railway: from Pan east to Belfast.

The Mounted Rifles' sense of grievance was restored the next day when news came that Lord Strathcona's Horse under General Buller was about to rendezvous with Roberts' army. While the Dragoons and Mounted Rifles stared at the blank railway, the Strathconas would be in the heart of the final war with Louis Botha.

Though the Strathconas were mostly westerners like themselves, and by now thoroughly bloodied by the war, the Mounted Rifles still liked to think of them as coddled wards of a rich patron. It helped somehow to think of the Strathconas as fops; to think of Sam Steele, who had left them for the Strathconas, as a turncoat.

—

At Middelburg, Frank and Ovide were on horse duty: Frank because he had no horse to ride and Ovide because he had refused to gallop his mare. Ovide had returned from the Witpoort Pass leading his horse; his only comment, that the mare had something wrong with her. This was his new mare, and she was reminding him of the Great Karoo and his cutting mare who had laboured around her ruined heart along the final miles.

Later, Frank found out that, during the Witpoort action, a corporal had ordered Ovide to charge a slope, and Ovide had refused. The corporal called it cowardice, and Ovide had answered that he didn't care what he called it. Ovide had been demoted to horse campie, alongside Frank, feeding and doctoring.

Their life as campies was not stationary. Major Sanders and Capt. Tommy Chalmers had the Mounted Rifles marching around the Pan-Middelburg-Bankfontein triangle relentlessly, as if it were packed with dangerous Boers and was the real centre of the Transvaal war. They divided up and marched in every combination, around the triangle perimeter and through its heart. They often stopped at a hump called Aas Vogel Kranz that guarded the Lydenburg Road. The scouts, led by Casey Callaghan and Charlie Ross, with Jeff Davis prominent, went farther, probing outside the triangle to see what threats lay beyond. There was never any news of the Beltons or Dunny.

If any of these activities located rebel Boers, it was usually because they announced themselves with rifle fire. If the Canadians guessed they had the Boers outnumbered, they would shell them, charge their position, and drive the enemy to another ridge.

When the Boers found them, it was usually in their outposts at night. There was no taking away the terror of bullets whizzing in the dark, even if the men knew the rifles were aimed by guess and unlikely to score. You could easily imagine yourself unlucky.

Frank and Ovide settled into the routines of marching and making camp, of soaking, salving, and poulticing horses. They were never called upon for anything else. They were part of no foursome, since the defection of the Beltons, and even if Frank got a horse or Ovide's was miraculously cured, it was unlikely they would be called upon again. To the satisfaction of Lieutenant Davidson and the sergeants and corporals, Ovide was a coward and Frank was bad news. Those who spoke to Frank at all seemed to direct their talk toward finding out whether he had been strange all along or had been made strange by the war. Even these fellows did not want him at their backs.

While Frank and Ovide became more isolated, the tendency among the majority of Mounted Rifles was exactly opposite. The constant marching and recombinations served to complete a spiderweb of connection among them. They were by now bound by countless strands of mutual success and failure. The more loyal the group became, the more the exceptions stood out. Frank and Ovide in the horse camp; the Beltons in absentia.

There was only one part of this to which Frank objected, and that was his inability to get out and look for Dunny. A normal assumption about a man who had lost his horse was that time would make him forget. It was, after all, a war of lost horses. But, if anything, Frank's sense of loss was increasing and ascending into a tight twist of obsession. No one knew this except Ovide, for Frank and Ovide went about their chores in silence, with the same assumed invisibility as the black men beside them.

As the whites stopped seeing Frank, the blacks began to. Frank was also much more aware of them. Ovide already had acquaintances among the trench diggers and horse campies. Now that Frank's eyes were opened, Ovide told him about them. The black men working for the Rifles were all of one people and mostly related. They had not come to the Canadians out of politics but to keep eating when the war destroyed their old economy. Once they were somewhere, they tended to stay. It was difficult to make whites trust them, if they had to start again.

Their names were Jim, Pete, Abraham, and Nandi. In his unblinkered state, Frank also noticed Dakomi, who had been demoted by Lt. Davidson for some perceived lapse, maybe even because of playing cribbage with Frank. Ovide and Frank were the whites that the rest of the whites treated like blacks, and the black campies welcomed them to their fire and shared the hot food their wives and relatives sometimes brought; also the occasional bottle of strong-tasting beer or fiery spirits.

Actual language was in short supply but no one cared. Struggling to converse with a handful of words was only frustrating, so they did the rest with gestures and work: the common tongue of a gall on a horse's back, the face you make when liquor is scorching your throat. The cribbage games with Dakomi resumed. The two took turns poking holes in an ox bone that would be their scoreboard.

Frank decided he liked this invisibility, for who but a fool would not want to be invisible in a war? In a place on which eyes did not focus, Frank drifted and listened. Because the scouts seemed most likely to encounter his dun mare, he made his ears especially sharp when they were around. When scouts came to camp, he went to their horses and gave them the best care he could—also the best hay, oats, and water. He brushed their horses to an oily gleam, and if the scouts themselves were nearby, Frank would break his silence and ply them with questions.

He did not get news of Dunny, but he did find out that General Hutton was dissatisfied with the uses his Canadian horsemen were being put to. He wanted them deeper in the war and had decided to create two new camps, one northeast and one southeast of Pan. The north one was Nooitgedacht and the south one Doornkop. A *nooitgedacht* in Boer Dutch was a place that was unexpected or hard to find. A *doornkop* was a hill of thorns. That was why the names repeated. Not long after, Frank heard that Mounted Rifles troops would soon head for these outposts.

Charlie Ross was another good source. Ross loved to tell of his exploits to anyone who would listen, including Frank. Charlie had made one investigative trip to Nooitgedacht and had spent time at Pan. He told Frank that their long-lost D Battery (last seen in the Great Karoo) was at Pan. Dinky Morrison, the Toronto newspaperman and gunner, told Charlie they had been wakened in the night by a sniper. When the villain was caught, he turned out to be a British adjutant who had gone mad and started firing on his own men.

Charlie had another story about some Mounted Rifles near Bankfontein who had fired in the night at what seemed to be fluttering ghosts. It was a column of black miners waving white flags, trying to get home alive after their labour in a local colliery.

In other conversations, Frank heard *about* Charlie Ross. At Reitvlei, Charlie had met a local farmer, a Boer deserter named Christiaan Anandale. This Anandale and Charlie became fast friends, and Charlie got him elevated to the top of Hutton's scouts. Anandale had a big farm at Reitvlei, and Charlie was said to have purchased a sizable chunk of land next door. Rumour said these two farms were filling up fast with livestock.

When Jeff Davis was among the scouts who came to Frank's camp, things were different, but only slightly. For the most part, Jeff acted as if he could not see Frank, and never thanked Frank for his preferential treatment of The Blue. It almost seemed as if Jeff had accepted the majority view that Frank was crazy and deserved his troubles. That is, it would have seemed so except that, during every visit, no matter how brief, Jeff always let Frank know he had not seen or heard about Dunny. If they were alone, he would say it. If not, he would look or gesture. But he got it said.

In early August, the troops were dispatched to Nooitgedacht and Doornkop. As D Squadron was leaving, Private Anderson was heard to say, "Where are we going? Night Attack?" And Nooitgedacht became Night Attack from then on.

Ovide and Frank were among those left behind, and, two days later, the remaining scouts at Aas Vogel Kranz captured a herd of horses, Boer ponies and ones stolen by the Boers from the British. When the horses streamed into camp, the soldiers dropped what they were doing and ran to see. They were still looking for that western stock horse they felt the war owed them. But Frank did not shift from his chores in the horse camp and never once supposed Dunny could be among the found herd. He was sure of this because he believed Dunny could only return to him through Jeff.

That evening, Frank declined a game of cribbage with Dakomi and passed up sitting with Ovide and the others at the campies' fire. He went and sat in the darkness to brood. From that vantage, he saw someone approach the fire with a lantern, and recognized the silhouette as Staff Sergeant Tracey, the veterinary doctor who had saved so many horses on the *Pomeranian*. Then Ovide and Tracey came walking through the dark. Tracey wanted to talk to Frank about a horse.

"I'll tell you right now, Adams," said the sergeant, "this is no great gift I'm offering. You better come along and see for yourself."

They went to where the new horses were quarantined, most of them already spoken for. Beyond this paddock was a little thorn-bush cage containing one horse: a brown-and-white pinto gelding with a mostly white face and walleyes—blue rims and brown centres.

Tracey explained that when the horses came in and were sorted, this one had tried to bite and kick everyone and every horse. That was why it was in the thorn cage. Aside from looking insane, Frank decided the gelding was nicely put together.

"I can't get close enough to say for sure, but my guess is he's a ridgling," Tracey continued. "Because of the one nut inside him, he thinks he's a stallion. That's why he's on the fight all the time. You're good with horses, so I thought you might be able to sort him out."

"What happens if I can't?"

"Oh, he'll be shot."

"Think the Boers left him on purpose?"

"Like a bomb? I wouldn't doubt it."

Tracey held the lantern to light Frank's way. He went to where the thorns were thinnest and leaned over. The ridgling flattened his ears and drew his top lip off his teeth.

"I think he likes me. He's grinning."

Tracey laughed. "Well, do with him what you want."

In the tent later, after Ovide began snoring, Frank drank rum from his water bottle. There were four rum rations, two of his own and two more purchased from Ovide, who did not like its taste. Frank had started the accumulation after Dunny was stolen but had not known for what. He recognized the occasion tonight. The deep rum burn, the blur of mind, had been reserved for the moment hope was lost—when he actually believed he would never see Dunny again. Taking on a new horse had delivered it.

A ridgling (also called a rig, a cryptorchid, a high flanker) was a colt whose nuts, one or both, stayed inside his body. In the few cases Frank had seen, it was one nut that stayed up while the other came down into the sac. The down nut was always castrated, but the horse grew up acting like a stallion anyway—and often more stallion than a real one. Herding and fighting, and trying to mount every mare he saw. According to Uncle Doc, ridglings were sterile because their bodies were too hot inside to make living jism. It was as if they knew their attempts to breed would not take, and it made them angry.

It was next morning, and Frank stared at his new horse inside the thorn corral. His head ached and buzzed from the previous night's rum splurge.

He could not see under the horse well enough to say what kind of rig he was, and was not planning to stick his head in the pinto's flank any time soon to find out. By the horse's behaviour, he took him to be the one-nut, half-castrated kind.

Ovide's first advice was to keep that high-flanking bastard the hell away from his mare. Ridglings were hard on mares, often injuring them in their crazed attempts to breed or while trying to keep any other horse from doing so.

Frank spent the day feeding and fetching water. Mostly, he fed the ridgling mealies and talked to him all the while. He told him they were in a similar fix: down to their last chance. The rig either made a horse for Frank or was headed for a .45 calibre bullet. The other side was that Frank risked being a pedestrian for the rest of the war.

It was hard to read the changes in the horse's china eyes, but Frank thought the day of doting care was producing glimmers of something beyond hatred. In the late afternoon, the pinto fell asleep with Frank only a few feet away. It signified the possible beginnings of trust.

Frank needed to push this thing along, so next day he borrowed a horse from the free pool and asked for Ovide's help. From atop the borrowed horse, Frank lassoed the ridgling's head. At the same time, Ovide looped the hind legs from his mount. They backed the two horses until the pinto stretched and flopped.

Now that it was safe, Frank probed the scrotum and found the castration scar. It was over on the left side, which meant that up inside the horse on the right side was the ball that addled his brain.

Frank tied the ropes to picket pins so he could keep the pinto stretched out. In a gentle voice he told him what they might do together if the horse could silence its urge to fuck and fight all the time. He showed his sleeping blanket and greatcoat to the ridgling's eye, dragged the blanket over him, and left it in a heap close to his snuffing nose. He fanned the pinto's head with his hat, fanned down his underbelly, and even at his asshole. Kept talking. He ran his hands over the entire horse, broke sticks behind his head, sang a night rider's howling lament.

In the course of the day, Frank's performance spooked horses in the adjacent yard, but the ridgling stopped fighting the ropes. He looked pissed off, then bored, then calm, then asleep. While he slept, Frank removed the ropes. He was able to halter the horse and walk him back to the thorn corral without assistance.

The following day, Frank approached the thorn cage with Dunny's saddle and blanket and a new bridle. Ovide was there to help and drew back a span of brush so Frank could enter. The pinto flicked his ears in confusion. He shuffled around but did not spin to kick or lunge to bite. Frank offered an oat bucket and another of cool water. While the ridgling ate and drank, he slipped a halter over the ears, buckled it, and attached the rope. He asked Ovide to swing the brush gate and led the ridgling into the larger world.

A Boer farmer's corner post with the big end in the ground had been left for a snubbing post. Frank tied the ridgling short and informed him what was coming: saddle, bridle, rider. He showed the tack to the horse's eye and nose, and there was dancing excitement when the rig smelled so much mare. Frank placed the blanket and pulled it back an inch. He thumped the saddle on. When he pulled the cinch, the ridgling coughed.

Frank was still not sure when he climbed aboard. He sat for several minutes, telling stories. Then he asked Ovide to bridle the ridgling. Ovide got him to take the bit, flipped his ears inside the bridle, gave Frank the reins. Then he unbuckled the halter and drew it out from under. Frank waited for the horse to understand that he was now untethered.

The ridgling started trembling and laid back his ears. Here we go, thought Frank, but did not let himself tense as he would for a bucking horse. When the pinto did nothing but tremble, Frank applied brief pressure on the bit. He tapped lightly with the spurs. When the horse still did not fire, Frank spurred harder and bent him in a tight circle. They walked around the yard several times. Frank dismounted, remounted, pushed the ridgling to a trot. Called it a day.

After the first ride, the ridgling let Frank scratch between his ears and along his throat latch; allowed him to pick up each of his feet in turn. Ovide shrugged and went back to his own pursuits. The horse was broke, maybe even trained by someone able and not too brutal. But, given all his tendencies taken together, it was likely he had not had many human friends.

Frank had a horse, albeit one people would laugh at. A perfect match. Why waste a good horse on Frank Adams or a good soldier on the ridgling?

The first dispatches from the new camps told of snipers and faked attacks, especially at night. Then, before dawn on August 9, Night Attack *was* night attacked. The Canadians in the main camp stood them off, but the Boers shifted to an outpost and attacked there. Scizzors Chalmers rode out with reinforcements and fought all day.

The harassment of the camps continued, and the concern in the dispatches grew more shrill. Chalmers said he might not be able to hold Night Attack unless he was reinforced.

On August 16, four more troops were assembled near Middelburg: two for Doornkop and two for Night Attack.

Frank and Ovide had assumed they would not be going out, but Lieutenant Davidson, whose troop had been chosen, sent a corporal to the horse camp to say that Adams and Smith were needed. Once chosen, Frank decided it made sense. Davidson respected their horse work, even if he was appalled by their soldiering.

The ride from Aas Vogel Kranz to Pan was the ridgling's debut. Frank kept him well back of the other lines of riders, an asymmetry the sergeant never would have allowed if the ridgling's reputation had not preceded him.

The plan was for the four troops to ride together to Pan, overnight, and split up next morning. Davidson was hoping for a social rendezvous with D Battery. It seemed doubtful they would still be there, but they were, the reason being that Lord Roberts had stalled his western push so his cavalry could chase Christiaan De Wet in the south.

Dinky Morrison was at Pan, and Lt. John McCrae, and a bunch of other familiar faces. Casey Callaghan was in the gunners' camp, having ridden a dispatch from Night Attack to Doornkop earlier that day.

Dinky negotiated an extra rum ration for his battery and its visitors, and they commenced a short but intense reunion. After numerous liquid toasts, they began singing. They started with "Goodbye Dolly Gray," which was all the rage among the Tommys.

It's the tramp of soldiers true, in their uniforms so blue,
I must say goodbye to you, Dolly Gray.

When it came to Canadian songs, they were stuck for ones everyone knew after "The Maple Leaf Forever." They were forced to sing "My Old Kentucky Home," with Canada substituted for Kentucky.

Warned that it was almost time for lights out, they called on John McCrae, and he made their eyes moist with "Drink to Me Only with Thine Eyes."

> *Or leave a kiss within the cup*
> *And I'll not ask for wine.*

Next morning dawned through a gauze of cloud and the officers finished sorting the men. Some last-minute trading evened things out. Frank's troop lost Harry Gunn to C Squadron.

As Frank's half set out north, a wind came and shoved the clouds off. It was hard and cold in their faces. The ridgling fought it like a hated enemy, arching his neck and whipping his head. He danced a flamenco, a constant spectacle for anyone who bothered to watch.

Ovide had woke up that morning feeling unwell. He was once again worried about his mare's heart and, though sick himself, insisted on walking half of every hour. The wind kept peeling his Stetson off until he left it hanging down his back, dragging like a bucksail on its string. The African sun burned his balding head and gave him a headache. Others were sick on the march, from bad food and water.

Frank was riding beside a baggage wagon. From inside its box came a groaning that was almost supernatural. The source was Casey Callaghan. Normally unstoppable, the scout had been laid low by a bad can of Chicago beef. Occasionally, Casey's grey face appeared over the wagon wall, and that was Frank's signal to spur the ridgling forward. Abraham, the bullwhacker, would see this and run up beside Nandi, the voorloper. All this was to get upwind of Casey, before he aired his ass over the wagon's gate, shouting and cursing the pain.

The troops at Night Attack were glad to see them, though they said it would probably bring on an all-out attack. The theory was that the Boers had been waiting for more enemy to show, to make another attack worthwhile.

The location was a well-named *nooitgedacht* with trees and coulees in all directions, through which the enemy could crawl. The groans of the sick did not abate through the night, and every so often some light sleeper would jerk awake and brandish his Colt.

Next morning, Jeff Davis rode in. The Blue looked fresh and dry. He found Lieutenant Davidson first, then went to Casey's sick wagon. After that, he steered his horse to Ovide and Frank's fire.

Ovide was still sick. Without enthusiasm, he was guiding a bit of mutton around his dixie with a pocket knife. He had been complaining all morning about a headache. Frank had his shirt off and held it over the fire, sizzling lice out of the seams. When he caught an escapee, he snapped it against his thumbnail. He was telling Ovide he should have thought about his head before letting his hat flap on his back all day.

"Wind," said Ovide.

"The rest of us held ours on, you might have noticed."

"My mare."

"Since when does it take both hands to lead a mare?"

"Lead a horse how I want."

From his mare's back, Jeff watched the banter.

"You said you wanted to scout," he said to Frank, finally, squinting out the low rays of the sun. "Casey's sick. I need somebody."

Frank hesitated. He looked at Ovide's grey face and his hand pushing the mutton.

"Come if you're coming," Jeff said, turning his horse and walking it away, the fetlocks snapping.

Frank looked at Ovide, who would not look at him. Then he collected a few things from the tent. Greatcoat. Rifle. Ammunition. He shoved his spare socks in a pocket and ran. Halfway to the picket line, Jeff was waiting. He pointed toward Callaghan's sick wagon, to Casey's buckskin gelding tied to the wheel.

"I asked Casey," Jeff said. "I told him your horse would get us killed."

The General looked indignant but allowed Frank to throw on Casey's saddle and adjust the stirrups. From grooming him, Frank knew the big buckskin head to toe. His only flaw was clipping his cannon with his left rear hoof. There was a dirty wrap in Casey's saddlebag, and Frank spun it over the scab. Jeff went to get rations and fill their bottles at the barrel. They left camp as the sun rose fat above the trees.

Frank had imagined this moment many times. Through the hills and gullies north of Night Attack, he and Jeff Davis were riding together. The General was a proud, powerful animal, so soft in the mouth Frank had only to tap a rein to move him. He had to be careful with his spurs, for the slightest touch would spark the buckskin. This made him long for Dunny, for he knew her so well he never had to think how to ride her.

Frank thought of asking what they were doing and why Jeff had chosen him. He thought of asking about Villamon. There was so much Frank did not know about Jeff now, including why he had returned to the Mounted Rifles. Was it that he had been on loan, and Major Sanders had called that loan? Or did it have to do with the day Frank tried to make him feel guilty for Kerr's and Morden's deaths?

Frank decided on silence. The truth was that Morden and Kerr already felt like a long-ago thing and that his own lust for scouting had been left on the other side of losing Dunny. His main reason for wanting to be out here today was to look for his horse. Instead of saying anything, Frank considered the favour Jeff was doing him. When nobody in Hutton's column would call on Frank for more than horse labour, Jeff Davis had taken him scouting.

They rode northeast to where a large valley opened, then went to the bottom where some mimosa bush flanked a stream. They stayed in that for a mile, then crossed the narrow water into a draw that split and split again. Whatever twists and turns the coulee made, Frank guessed they were still bearing northeast. He admired how Jeff kept them in cover and shadow, and never exposed them to hilltop or crag.

Around noon, Jeff stopped at a treed edge and they got down. He studied the valley but paid most attention to one rocky hilltop. Frank stared there and finally saw heads moving between man-sized rocks. Then the late morning sun sparked off field glasses. Frank moved for his rifle and Jeff stopped him. It felt wrong to have the enemy spotted and not squeeze off a few, but Frank supposed it was the difference between common soldiering and scouting.

They led their horses through a planted forest until they came to a coulee full of brush. Jeff pushed down through heavy branches, and the coulee was much deeper than it looked. Only a bit of light could fight its way to the bottom, and what grew there was gnarled and skinny like arms begging. The steep yellow ground was corrupt and putrid. Jeff got down on hands and knees to smell the brown trickle, to taste it. He nodded and they let the horses drink. The mares sucked at it for a long time, then pissed hot and rank and drank some more.

Jeff sat on his heels on the sticky yellow and stared at the place where a path led away beside the creek. He made no offer to talk.

They stayed all afternoon. When they finally led their horses out, the sun was low in the western sky. To look in their direction, the Boers on the hill would have to stare at the strong light. Jeff and Frank left cover and crossed open ground until they were in a twisting defile on the other side. For the next half-hour, they climbed and circled, until they were north of the Boers' hill and above it. They could see them clearly.

There were half a dozen, sitting on rocks and smoking pipes like old men, though they were young. Still Jeff did not raise a gun toward them. All he wanted from them was their back trail, and from here he found it easily. They were soon following the trail due east, and still following when the sun sank into the trees.

Frank had much time to think. He decided they were looking for a laager: the larger outfit to which the Boer boys belonged.

In the brevity of African dusk, Jeff hurried his pace. Frank assumed he was trying to find water and cover before darkness fell, but where they stopped was a slope among evergreens, a place likely to be dry. The trees were eucalyptus, a forest planted for wood.

Jeff tied his horse and put on his greatcoat. Frank did likewise. They walked a hundred yards and came to a slanted edge. They were on the north-facing side of a wedge of hills, and all the shadier slopes around them were patchy with dark forest like the one they were in.

Jeff stared at a coulee mouth dark with brush. When the dusk thickened to black, they brought the horses forward and tied them short near the forest edge. Jeff walked out of the trees and sat in the lee of an upright boulder. Frank followed and sat beside him. The moon was up, a slender peel rocking on its back, but it gave enough light to cast a shadow where they were. The cold became colder every minute, and Jeff pulled a skinny scarf out of a coat pocket and wrapped his neck. Frank envied the scarf and tied his extra socks together to make a scarf of his own.

For a long time, there was only one word, and that was Jeff whispering, "Sleep." Frank thought not. He could tell Jeff was not going to sleep and decided he wouldn't either. A surprise then to find himself fallen over sideways with his face in the smelly bowl of his hat and his mouth drooling. His bent knee joints were stiff. The moon was gone and some grey was invading the black. Jeff was still sitting up, his eyes trained on the coulee.

The grey light was barely allowing shapes when Jeff nudged Frank. Squinting, he saw something like a dark liquid ooze from the cut. The liquid turned into thirty horsemen and black servants on foot. A dozen Boers dismounted and led the black men into the eucalyptus. They came out dragging three Boer wagons by their tongues. More riders entered the trees and came out with trek oxen and a dozen cattle with calves at heel. There were loose horses, but none of them was Dunny.

The black men lifted yokes onto the oxen, slid in the ox bows and keyed them. They took their positions along the ox pairs, their bamboo and string whips at the ready. Everything moved when a long-bearded Boer on the lead wagon raised his arm and let it drop. The valley's trend was east, and the Boers followed it down until a hill swallowed them. It was not yet dawn.

Half an hour after the Boers left, Jeff went to the horses. They stood with their saddles on, loosely cinched, calm and confident that their riders would water them soon and not let them starve. Jeff tacked The Blue down, and Frank stripped The General. They led them out of the forest and let them loose on the slope. The men ate hardtack and biltong as the sun nudged upward and sprayed light through the trees. Then Jeff lay on his back, head on his saddle seat, and closed his eyes. He slept one hour and woke abruptly. They saddled and started. The Boers' track was obvious in the dew.

Frank had begun to worry about Ovide. He had only expected to be gone overnight. Now he had no idea how long Jeff intended them to be away. The way of scouting, he supposed, was not to give up until your horses were beat or something had been accomplished. While they rested by a quick small creek, Frank thought again of Ovide being sick. He could not prevent himself from asking how much farther they would go before they started back.

"These Boers are headed for Doornkop. We need to get there first."

"What about Night Attack?"

"Ovide's probably gone. Davidson told me he was sending the sick ones back. Casey and Ovide are probably in Middelburg."

Frank sucked on the ball of biltong in his cheek. It came to him that this moment, when he and Jeff were alone together, might not come again for some time. Before they continued on and became part of an army again, there were things that should be made clear between them.

"I don't want to scout anymore," he said. "I just want my horse back."

Jeff looked at the ground and smiled, then turned and faced Frank directly. He had something he wanted to say as well.

"I have a girlfriend on the Blood. Her father doesn't want me to have her. If I kill enough Boers, he'll change his mind."

It was the missing piece: the reason Jeff had come to Africa, the reason he had been different from Frank and Ovide from the start.

Riding again, they left the Boers' track for a straighter line south. To make time, they had to be more visible and they were fired upon, some bullets coming close enough to hear. They did not stop to fight the snipers.

They crossed the railway and kept on south, and when they approached a new height of land several hours along, Jeff dismounted. He gave The Blue to Frank and took field glasses from his saddlebag. He climbed the ridge and crawled the last ten yards.

Returning, Jeff said, "Doornkop's a couple of miles south. There's Boers here. We'll have to pass them."

They sprayed out of cover, and the horses galloped down the open flank. Jeff waved at Frank not to follow so close. Frank let The General weave through a dotting of thorn trees. Bullets yowled in the air and ripped the ground. When they came to the first Doornkop outposts, Jeff waved his Stetson but the piquet shot anyway. Closer, the piquets recognized them and let them pass.

Doornkop camp was spread through a few acres of blue gums near a Dutch farmhouse. While Jeff reported to the lieutenant, Frank talked to Harry Gunn. Harry said they were surrounded and expecting an attack. When Frank told him there were more Boers coming, Harry saw in it the reason for the Boers' delay. They were waiting until they were stronger.

Nothing happened that evening. They were roused well before dawn, and the lieutenants organized the troops for battle. They had decided to challenge the Boers by sending patrols to the ridges and kopjes. If the Boers had been thinking there weren't enough of them to carry the fight, maybe pressure would drive them off.

Jeff and Frank were teamed with Harry Gunn. After they had gone a few miles, they heard firing to the northeast. Jeff led them toward it. After half an hour's ride, they saw a cluster of khakis near a stony kopje top. As Boers often wore khaki these days and had been known to pretend to surround a fallen man, they approached cautiously. When they were closer, they saw a horse lying dead, something harder to fake.

Bernard Flynn, an English Mountie from Maple Creek, was sitting on the ground. He had been shot in the shoulder but, strangely, was already in a sling. He had been riding with Donald Morrison when a group of Boers popped up from the rocks and opened fire. They shot Morrison's horse and Flynn in the shoulder.

"The man who shot me was a gentleman," Flynn said in wonder. "He wore a checkered jacket and breeches. He said he was a doctor out for a day of birding. He patched me up, wished me good day, and left."

They got Bernard on his own horse and Morrison climbed on behind Frank. When they were almost back to camp, they heard more firing behind them. Doornkop had another outpost to the north, and when they got in, the lieutenant in charge turned them around and sent them to investigate.

Frank expected to be fired on as they got closer to this second outpost, but it did not happen. The post was a *shanz*, a dugout with stones piled around it. Inside, three men sat on the ground looking at a fourth who was badly wounded. Corporal Taylor and Private Mullen had been out a ways on horseback. It was one of those lucky hits the Boers made by pointing their rifles up and firing in a rainbow. Taylor was riddled and Mullen not even scratched. They had brought Taylor here, and now he appeared to be dying.

Frank helped Harry and Jeff lift the corporal onto The General. Jeff rode beside and held him on. Taylor was only back in camp an hour when he died. The effect on Frank was a fierce desperation to return to Ovide, a foreboding that crawled over his back like ants, but they were already digging a hole for Joe Taylor. The burial was held in the dark with lanterns. There were hymns and prayers. Harry Gunn was in the honour guard. Then a lieutenant said he wanted Jeff to escort Bernard Flynn back to Pan Station in the morning.

Jeff was sitting on his bedroll wrenching his boot off when Frank asked if he could leave. He meant leave alone and right now. Jeff jerked off the boot and climbed into his blankets. Frank said he needed to see Ovide. Ovide was sick and he wanted to make sure he got to Middelburg.

"Go to sleep."

With dawn came another delay. The camp's scouts had been out overnight and had returned with the gentleman who had shot and repaired Bernard Flynn. It was Dr. Van Erkum, who lived next door to a house full of British officers in Middelburg. Now, Van Erkum was given to Jeff and Frank to take to Pan along with Flynn. The wounded man and the prisoner rode in a light buggy. They talked amiably in English, debating who owed whom a nice meal.

The date of Taylor's death was August 19. Frank and Jeff got to Pan Station on the afternoon of August 20. The sick Mounted Rifles from Night Attack had passed through Pan three days earlier. They had stopped for a few hours to rest and then had kept on for Middelburg. Jeff and Frank asked for more information. Was the scout Casey Callaghan among them? Was there a French cowboy named Ovide Smith? Someone vouched for Casey, but no one remembered Ovide.

Frank asked Jeff if they could go to Middelburg now. Jeff said he couldn't, but that Frank had better. Casey would be wanting his horse back and was probably in a lather about it. Jeff himself had business with other Hutton scouts to the east. When an officer at Pan asked Frank to take Van Erkum to Middelburg, Frank lied and said he had an urgent dispatch, and was not allowed to travel that slowly.

Frank burst out of Pan at a gallop and rode hard along the railway line. He gave The General no rests and no water. At the British outposts along the railway, he yelled, "Dispatch!" and waved an empty bag he'd found in Casey's saddlebag.

At Middelburg, Frank was told that the sick troop he sought were mostly recovered and had continued north to Bankfontein. Frank asked the soldier, a C Squadron corporal, about Ovide Smith. The corporal looked at the ground and shook his head.

When Frank galloped The General into Bankfontein, it was dark. Some fires were lit and lanterns hung. He had by now ridden The General to the great horse's very bottom. The buckskin's mouth hung open and his rasping breath blew foam. The wrap had fallen off and the leg was black with blood at the clipped spot. From his head to his tail, he was dark with sweat.

Casey came running. When he saw the condition of his horse, he grabbed Frank by the chest of his uniform; ran him backwards and threw him to the ground. Frank jumped up and ran away. He ran through the darkness, looking for his and Ovide's tent, but could not find it.

In the dark rows of tents and bedding, Frank bumped into a private cradling a mess tin of hot tea. The private spilled tea on his hands, then danced and cursed Frank some more.

"Where's Ovide Smith?"

"Smith? Fuck. Smith's dead, you stupid ass."

Frank slowed. He walked back toward the fires. Among them, he studied the faces lit by each glow. At one, he saw Greasy Griesbach and Reg Redpath. Frank had not seen Redpath since Kroonstad. The group had rum and looked happy.

"Adams!" Griesbach cried. "Pull up a stump. You're as dirty as a soldier gets. Come and have your well-earned rum ration."

Griesbach had a bottle and extra mess tins. He poured Frank a generous splash.

"We're celebrating Reg's return. They've found him a truss."

Frank took the cup and raised it to Redpath, who grinned sheepishly and raised his back. Frank shot it into his throat, the black taste, the burn.

He waited. They were joking about Redpath's truss and the danger of anthills in the dark. Reg took it with mild good nature, saying how glad he was to be back. No one mentioned Ovide. The fire was big and bright, perhaps the largest fire Frank had sat beside since De Aar.

"I hear Ovide Smith died," Frank said mildly, as if it mattered little.

"Sunstroke," someone said. Another laughed.

Frank waited, and into that cold silence two drunk privates ventured. Smith had had a sick headache, one said. He was like that when they left Night Attack, and he got worse on the march to Pan. Puking, said the other. There was no medic at Pan but there was a medicine chest.

They described how Ovide went to the chest and was there looking at it for a long time. As other fellows came along, they helped him. One read the instructions over and told him it was a number seven he needed. But the number seven pigeonhole was empty.

The privates stopped, were giddy for some reason.

"Come on, Greasy," they begged. "You finish it. Tell it again."

Griesbach waved them off, but when the others persisted, he smoothed his moustache and began.

"Ovide had a dilemma. He's sick and there's none of what he needs. No number seven. Fellow comes up and Ovide tells him his problem. Fellow says, 'Why not try a five and a two?'"

Some could not hold back their laughter.

"So old Ovide, he thinks it over. He finds the five and he finds the two. Mixes them together, downs them, and dies. We buried him when we got here to Bankfontein."

The others groaned. "No, Greasy. Tell it right."

After a pause, Griesbach spoke again.

"I guess you're asking me to say that Ovide's approach may have got him killed, but you can't fault his arithmetic."

There was a burst of false laughter. Laughing at something that had been funny once. In the midst of it, no one paid attention as Frank stood, as he poured the last dribble of rum from the mess tin, then let it fall onto the crushed grass.

"Who?" asked Frank. It took them a while to settle down and pay attention.

"Who what, Adams?"

"Who told Ovide five and two?"

There was silence. Everyone looked somewhere other than at Adams. His presence was spoiling things. They wished he'd go.

"Who?"

Griesbach answered. "It was Eddy Belton."

"Eddy's not here."

"Eddy most assuredly is here, and he was at Pan Station too, where Smith poisoned himself. This is what happened, Adams, so you don't get it balled up. General Roberts sent Botha a trainload of women and children. Botha sent back a bunch of our prisoners of war. The Beltons were among them. But, before anyone noticed them, Eddy . . ."

Frank jumped through the fire. In a shower of sparks, he threw himself on Griesbach, toppled him backwards. Griesbach was strong, had long arms, and he clubbed Adams with his fists on both sides of the head. Frank drew back his own fist, but the others swarmed him. He managed to rise, dragging them. He threw off a pair and was trying to get back to Griesbach when they brained him with a rifle barrel. His weight was too great for his legs then. Not even his fingers would move. The fingers were right in front of his eyes but would not answer.

Bankfontein

Frank awakened in the cold daylight when a freight of pain crossed his head. He cringed in anticipation of more such trains but that was the only one. He was in a box-shaped tent with two men sitting cross-legged, one big, one small. They hunched forward with blankets over their shoulders.

Frank had thrown up and his cheek wore a crust of it. He rubbed it off with the dirty blanket but the stink remained. He sat up straight but his body would not stay that way. He put his hand into his hair and felt a tacky surface: a carapace of drying blood. The Beltons blurred when he looked at them.

"Where's my horse?"

"The Boers took Dunny when they caught us," Eddy said.

"Why'd you tell Ovide five and two?"

With a slurping sound, Eddy Belton started to cry.

"Shut up, you stupid idiot! You fucking baby!"

Pete windmilled at Eddy with his fists. Eddy raised his heavy arms to shield himself, but continued to cry.

Frank crawled to Pete and grabbed the shoulder of his filthy uniform. Where he pulled Pete's collar back, a big louse unhooked itself and ran.

"Leave your brother alone."

The guard knocked on the wall of the tent and yelled for them to be quiet. Frank was still swaying, felt as if he might fall senseless again. Pete wrenched his uniform out of Frank's weak fingers.

"I want to tell him," Eddy said.

"You shut up, you goddamn fool!"

"I'm going to tell him."

"You will tell him fucking nothing!"

"I will."

Pete slugged Eddy again, as hard as he could. Eddy accepted the blow. Then he turned and grabbed his brother's arms. Pete looked amazed, had perhaps never felt his brother's strength before. Eddy bent Pete backwards to the ground and spoke down into his face.

"I saw Ovide at the medicine box. We'd got off the train and nobody'd seen Pete and me. We weren't arrested yet. Ovide looked terrible sick. He was holding his head. He said the medicine he needed wasn't in the box."

"Stop it, Eddy," said Pete, but without force.

"One time, Pete told me to get five and a two out of the medicine box. He said five and two was secret medicine for officers. That was when we were at Norvals Pont and Pete wanted to kill Jeff Davis. We gave five and two to the baboon to make it sleep, but the medicine killed it. Pete said it was too strong for monkeys but was still the best medicine in the box for sick people. I didn't want to kill Ovide, Frank. I wanted to make him better."

This time the guard untied the tent flap and entered rifle first.

"What the hell's going on in here? Let him off the ground, Eddy. All you sit apart and be quiet. This is the last time or I'm coming with the gags and irons."

After the guard left, Frank asked Eddy again where Dunny went. Eddy said that when they took the horses and were riding them in the night, Pete wanted to find a Boer camp and rob it. He thought they could steal some horses and come back and be heroes.

"We rode up to their outpost and didn't even know it. They took us prisoner."

The last Eddy had seen of Dunny, she was tied in the Boer camp. The officer's charger was there too. Then Eddy and Pete were put on a train and sent east to where they were locked inside a big wire cage with British Tommys.

Frank could not hold himself up anymore. He fell over and closed his eyes against the swimming light.

Next day, Frank was less sick. Greasy Griesbach came and let him out of the jail tent while the Beltons stayed behind. The Beltons' court martial was to be soon, possibly today. Greasy led Frank to his own tent where he had hot tea and cooked mutton waiting.

While Frank was eating, Greasy apologized. He said he and the others had behaved badly last night. They were celebrating Redpath's return and had drank more liquor than they'd had in months.

"I'm genuinely sorry, Adams. I was drunk, and it didn't register that Ovide was your friend."

"Why make fun of him at all?"

"Yes. You're right, of course. It was a poor showing. I regret it. But I want you to know that, no matter how it must seem, Smith was buried with proper respect. The grave is north of camp. All the men turned out. Everybody sang."

"Am I free now?"

"I've explained this situation to Davidson. Yes, of course you're free. I can show you Smith's grave. Come. I would like to. I'll show you now."

Frank let himself be led. The hill sloped north, and the pile of stones was below camp on that slope. Frank asked Greasy to excuse him, and Greasy left.

Frank moved the rocks around the pile, trying to make everything fit better. Every time he set a rock, he pictured Ovide underneath, feeling the changed weight. He'd be wrapped in threadbare blankets, his floppy uniform too large because he never cared enough to trade for clothes that fit. His balding head, naked, sunburned, peeling.

Frank thought about Ovide's age. Ovide told the enlistment officer in Calgary he was thirty-nine and a half. That was in December 1899. It meant that sometime, here in Africa, Ovide had turned forty. Frank took a deep breath and choked on it. The idea of this birthday, uncelebrated, made him cry.

Frank said aloud to Ovide inside those rocks that he was sorry about the birthday, and sorry he'd gone Boer-chasing with Jeff Davis. Sorry that before he'd left they'd had an argument about Ovide's headache and not wearing his hat. He was sorry that, when he rode away, he had not looked back.

But it did no good to be sorry. Sorry came after and was too late. Ovide was dead and betrayed. That was all.

Bergendal Farm

Lord Roberts' army prepared to resume its eastern push. The effort to trap Christiaan De Wet in the Brandwater Basin had failed, and the commander-in-chief had refocused on driving Botha's Boers down the Delagoa Railway into the fever lands. General Pole-Carew would attack north of the railway while General Buller pressed up from the south.

After fighting his way north from Natal, Buller selected a three-acre crown of rocks at Bergendal Farm for his debut battle in the combined army. He began shelling the hill on August 27, eventually hurling so much lyddite at the knoll it looked like Vesuvius. The stubborn Johannesburg Zarps holding it would not quit—a hundred men holding back fifteen hundred. But, finally, when a quarter of them were dead, the rest retreated.

From there, Buller rolled east into Machadodorp. This had been Kruger's capital, but his railcar, his mobile legislature, had by now rolled east to Nelspruit. With the town to themselves, Buller's hungry soldiers went after Boer pigs and chooks, and the Boer women went after them with brooms and pitchforks.

"*Verdammt Rooineks!*" the women cried. Damn rednecks.

Lord Strathcona's Horse, among the first of Buller's army in the town, were accused of this looting, and their commander, Sam Steele, responded with outrage. His men would do no such thing, he roared. He had called them together and had personally observed there was no loot among them. In this way Sam transferred the indignity to himself. Were they calling him a liar?

As Pole-Carew and Buller continued east in combination, the phrase often used was that they were "sweeping Botha's army before them." Another metaphor was that they were punching a hole into Boer territory. But everything north and south of the broom's path, the punched hole, remained Boer and hostile.

—

The Beltons were court-martialled at Middelburg. Eddy looked like a child when they put him on a train to Pretoria; a big, sad, innocent child headed for a long stretch in jail for the crime of being Pete Belton's brother. Convicted, sentenced, manacled, Pete continued to insist that he had been attacking the Boers when captured and so should be recognized not as a traitor, but as a hero.

Frank's ridgling was returned to him. Without Ovide, Frank rode the ridgling among the various camps and slept outside at night, shivering in his greatcoat. Since Ovide's death, he could not sleep in their tent, though he hauled it along.

Abraham, Dakomi, and the rest in the horse yard continued to welcome Frank at their fire. In the daytime, they called him *bossy*, though it was stone clear he was no one's boss. He went about his horse work carefully, trying to mimic Ovide. Sometimes when his fingers were pressing among the fine bones of a horse's ankle, he would imagine they were Ovide's fingers, powered by Ovide's deft knowledge. When he listened for liquid in a horse's wheeze or deciphered the troubled flexion of a horse's joint, he was again acting out what Ovide would have heard and done.

But if Frank succeeded by this means with the horses, he never shifted his sorrow and guilt an inch. Simply, Ovide had died of a mistake Frank would never have let him make. Five and two. Frank had not been there, and Ovide was dead.

The only source of relief was rum, and rum came only on ration day. He soon understood that one ration would not do the job and so used what money he had to buy more. With three rations inside him, Frank could drift off and surround himself with people who would forgive him. Doc Windham had told Frank that he himself was responsible for at least three deaths and two disappearances, and had given up on guilt. Frank's mother would give him hell and then forgive him because he was her son.

The oddity of the Mounted Rifles was that none of them held Frank responsible for Ovide's death but most of them blamed him for his attack on Greasy Griesbach. Greasy was a great favourite, whose father had been regimental number one in the North West Mounted Police. A prairie aristocrat who everyone sucked up to. Now, they were pleading with Greasy to bring a charge against Adams for jumping him when Greasy had only offered the crazy bastard a drink.

Practically the only person in the Rifles' camp who did not hold this view was Greasy himself. A couple of times, Griesbach had come to see Frank, and though he acted bluff, there was a hint of contrition buzzing inside it. Both times, Greasy had made Frank an offer. He had promised to get him a better horse. He suggested he could arrange things so Frank was out of the horse yard and back on patrol. Frank's refusal frustrated and angered Greasy, though he tried not to let it show.

All this stemmed from Greasy Griesbach's being a good man who now felt guilty for ridiculing Ovide's death and insulting Ovide's friend. He wanted to make amends and be forgiven, and Frank was not ready to do that.

Next time Greasy came looking for absolution, Frank decided he would ask him for rum. Maybe Frank would even beg for it the way Indians did on the street in Ft. Macleod. That would be the perfect revenge because rum was a kind of poison, and Greasy would not be able to claim, even to himself, that he was doing Adams any good. The moral debt would remain unpaid.

Night Attack, September 1900

In early September, Major Sanders took a hundred Mounted Rifles and headed for the old sore spot of Nooitgedacht. The Boers were still pestering Night Attack, and the major had decided to take enough men there to sweep them off. It was a big expedition that required a full of set of camp orderlies and labourers. Frank was included and so were his black friends.

Night Attack was well developed by now, with an outer circle of Cossack posts to defend it. When the expedition arrived, Sanders packed his newcomers into the square of trees so the Boers would not know how many or how well armed they were. All along the outer perimeter, he wanted the trenches deepened and new ones added. Even the black labourers had shelter along the edge of the trees, and the only thing left in the open were the horses.

At dawn on September 5, the enemy cut loose with a pom-pom, two bigger guns, and a great many rifles. They were closer than seemed possible: within the camp's ring of outposts.

Frank was in the trench closest to the horses. Behind him, the unarmed bullwhackers and horse campies cowered in their holes with rounds of shrapnel burning down through the tree canopy above them.

The first few shells burst over the horse lines. Shrapnel balls rained down and some landed along the spine of a big toffee gelding. The horse dove for the ground, then fought with himself when he could not escape the pain. Beside him, an Argentine whipped against its rope and threw itself in a madness of fear. More shrapnel came, bouncing among the horses like hot, frisky hail.

Frank could see the white of bone shining through the wounded gelding's back. He laid his rifle atop a flat rock, drew a bead on its fine head, and shot twice.

As the battle continued, Frank kept watching the terrified horses. He paid little attention to other trenches or to the copse behind him. When a ball welded into a horse's muscle, the skin would shudder, as if it were trying to shake off a massive horsefly. Even then, the pain came as a surprise; the squeal, delayed.

Frank watched and was their god, deciding who had suffered enough and who should live to suffer more. A few times, he ran over and hauled down a rearing animal. He walked along the row of heads, retying them shorter, speaking calmly into their twitching ears.

His own bald-faced ridgling, normally so full of fight and lust, stood within the barrage with ears flat and a thick rind of white around the blue rims and dark cores of his eyes. He did not kick or rear but stood stock-still and trembled as the shells crashed.

Despite being outnumbered, the Canadians did some good shooting and forced the Boer gunners to move several times. They drove their riflemen out of cover and back. When the battle had gone on three hours, the Boer commandant must have noticed that he was farther away than when he'd started. He gave the order to withdraw.

In the relative silence that followed, the Canadians took stock of their losses. No Mounted Rifles had been killed but some were wounded. Lieutenant Moodie through the leg. Private Johnston through the shoulder. Johnston had been in the outpost that the Boers attacked before dawn. All six men there had been taken prisoner, but Johnston and Fotheringham had escaped and made it back to camp.

The third man wounded was Major Sanders, who had slivers of steel in his side.

In all, eight horses had been killed by the Boers or wounded and finished off by Frank. Frank wanted help picking steel out of the still-living ones and went to where his fellow campies had waited out the fight. They were in a tight group that split open as he came, revealing a man kneeling. It was Dakomi, and his bloody hands were knitted tight across his weeping belly.

Through the dappled and smoking tree shadow, Frank ran for the medic and found him with Major Sanders. The major was on a chair, leaning forward. Sanders' orderly held his shirt up, while the medic probed with long tweezers.

Frank said there was a man by the horse lines hit in the guts and bleeding to death.

The medic looked over his glasses. "Nobody's that bad, private."

Frank pointed to where Dakomi knelt.

"Oh," the medic said as he adjusted his glasses and took aim again with the tweezers. "When I'm done here."

By the time Frank returned, they had Dakomi on a blanket with a rolled coat under his head. The wound was uncovered, and Frank could see pieces of Dakomi's shirt driven into his flesh. His purple eyelids were fluttering and his teeth chattered.

"Him dying, bossy," said Abraham.

When the medic came, he shrugged before he knelt down, to proclaim the hopelessness.

Well after dark that evening, Corporal Griesbach came striding into the horse camp. He swung his head side to side, took in the fresh grave, then found Frank in a group sitting near the horse lines. There was a strong moon but no fires allowed, in case the Boers were lingering.

"A moment?" Greasy asked Frank. Frank followed him to one of the trenches that was now empty. Greasy sat on its edge with his long legs in the hole. He opened his tunic and produced a bottle.

"Let's try some good stuff for a change."

Frank took the brandy and drank. It caught in his throat and made him cough.

Greasy was staring back at the grave. "I didn't think we had anyone killed."

"Dakomi."

"What?"

"His name was Dakomi."

"Oh."

"We played cribbage."

"Too bad."

"How's Major Sanders?"

"Splinter in his side. He's put Evans in charge for a couple of days— which is bad luck for some. Evans wants to know how six men can lose an outpost, get taken prisoner, and never fire a shot. He grilled Johnston and Fotheringham for a half-hour each. Damn obvious they were asleep. If he can prove it, there'll be court martials."

Frank waited to hear why Greasy had come, what favour he wanted to bestow.

"Sanders and Evans are worried that our camps back east are under-manned. They think the fellows who attacked here might head that way. At any rate, they've ordered a few groups back."

"He wants me?" Frank asked.

"Not exactly. He asked me to lead a half-dozen to Aas Vogel Kranz. I had my six but Redpath pulled out on me. Today was his first battle since the rupture and he enjoyed himself. Wants to stay in case there's another. Something about avenging Kerr."

Griesbach stretched his arms above his head, then massaged the back of his neck.

"So I thought to myself, why not ask Adams? He might want a break. I figure we'll take a little holiday on the way."

Greasy waited for Frank to speak, probably expecting refusal.

"Tomorrow?"

"That's right. First thing. You'll go, then?"

The bottle was in Frank's hands when he nodded. "Mind if I take this bottle?" he asked. "I owe some drinks to these men." He nodded at the campies.

Greasy stared ruefully at the brandy.

"They're in mourning," said Frank, trying for a begging note.

"Yes, yes, fine."

Greasy got up quickly and left before Adams could embarrass him further.

Pan Station/Aas Vogel Kranz

The road from Night Attack to Pan Station was deserted. Because of the battle the previous day, Griesbach's six went carefully, expecting to be fired on at any time. It did not happen. They felt safer when they veered in the direction Greasy had chosen for their holiday. But, a half-hour later, a party of Boers spotted them and started to fire.

Their attackers were not many, about the same number as themselves. They settled into cover and had it out. It went on for an hour, and the Boers were the ones who called it off. They left toward the east, and Greasy declared it "a fine old turkey shoot."

The country southwest of Pan was undulating: spans of prairie with occasional sharp kopjes. The farms close to the railway were burned. A sign of the country's vacancy was that the wildlife had returned. Coming over a ridge, they interrupted some springbok. A lucky shot into the group felled one as they surged away. There would be a feast tonight, if they could find a place to have it.

When they were about five miles south of the railway, they changed their heading from south to west. Soon after, they spotted an unburned farm. On three sides, blue gum trees surrounded the buildings. The farmhouse—double-gabled, north-facing veranda—was not unlike Paul Kruger's home in Pretoria. On the two ends of the porch, white flags flew, attached to broom handles.

The oddest feature was a little kopje that rose practically out of the farmyard on its southwest corner. It masked most of the barn, but one of the six with good eyesight said he could see part of the barn door and the hind end of a horse standing inside it. He even ventured that the horse was piebald. They studied these things from the cover of thorn trees.

The white flags were a concern. Boers used them so often to disguise an ambush that ambush had become their meaning. They sat their horses and argued the point. About half thought it looked like a good prospect for the night. The other half said they'd prefer a deserted farm. A stalemate until Adams suddenly wheeled his horse and rode for the kopje.

The kopje had a little skirt of brush, and Adams tied the pinto there. They saw no more of him until he was high in the rocks. It was some time before Adams trotted back to them.

"Three horses in the barn," he said. "The one in the door stall is a paint. There's two mules lying in the yard. Could be crawling with Boers."

"Anybody see you?"

"Not me. You, maybe."

Adams had been silent all day, sullen and annoying. This show of interest was encouraging, especially for Greasy whose project it was to have him along.

"You think we should move on, then?" Greasy asked him.

Adams shrugged.

There was enough light left in the day. Greasy ruled that they continue.

Later, with sunset approaching, they found a farm that showed all the signs of abandonment. The house's front door was hanging on one hinge. The windows were broken. The gate on the sheep kraal was scraped back. Sheep and goats wandered the dome of grass on which the farm was built. No white flags.

Still, they took their time. They ran in turns until all six were along the base of the kraal. They jumped up on signal and aimed their guns over. The kraal was deep in dry sheep dung, but bare of rebels. They addressed the house with similar manoeuvres and found it empty and methodically ransacked. Pottery shards, furniture in kindling, bayoneted mattresses. In the drawing room, some respect for music had overtaken the marauders. A piano stood dusty but whole.

All manner of animal seemed to have been in the house. It stank like a chicken coop. They decided the dried-out kraal would be preferable for their entertainment. They loopholed the kraal and arranged piles of ammunition beside each firing station.

Then, they went inside the house and carried the piano out to the kraal. After sharing some drinks, Alex sat on the bench and played. In civilian life he was the organist at a Presbyterian church in Edmonton, but knew many rollicking tunes.

They made their fire and got the springbok roasting. They laughed and sang, and told funny stories—all except Adams, who had returned to his gloom and sat apart.

Frank took as much of the liquor—brandy again—as he reasonably could. From time to time, while the piano jangled and the boys sang, he would spot Greasy looking at him. Frank pretended it made him uncomfortable. He knew without doubt that Greasy was timing his approach, deciding when Adams had consumed enough liquor but not too much. At some point Greasy gave up for the evening and looked at Frank no more.

By evening of the second day, they had killed a sheep and had it cooking on an improvised spit. Each man took a turn revolving it over the fire. There was little liquor remaining, as they'd made pigs of themselves the night before.

The sole rum bottle belonged to Greasy, and when he came and sat with Frank, his first action was to pour Frank's mess tin half full.

"I'd like to straighten things out between us," he said as he sat down.

"Why?"

It was hard for Frank not to laugh at the instant flush on Greasy's face. His guess was that Greasy did not like him—why should he? But the business about Ovide remained and must be dealt with. Greasy did not want the story trailing behind him; did not want Frank out in the world telling it the way he was apt to.

The silence became leaden. Greasy flung his hands as if to cast it away.

"Do you remember on the *Pomeranian*, when Morden's horse died?" he asked.

"Of course."

"And I bet you remember who the ass was who couldn't get the knot to slip. The one who caused the horse to drop through the decks."

"I remember," said Frank.

"And Morden thought it was Jeff Davis, right?"

Frank nodded.

"What I had to do, right then," said Griesbach, and he held a hand out to Frank as if the thing he had to do was on his palm, "was tell Morden it wasn't Davis who'd caused his horse to fall. It was me. Do you know why I had to?"

"Because everyone saw you do it?"

Greasy flushed again, looked away. "Actually, no. I . . ."

"I'm joking. It was because you want to think well of yourself."

Griesbach grimaced at this interpretation. Frank watched him decide not to argue.

"All right, fine. What I'm getting at is that it's the same thing now. I did a foolish thing. I regret it. I wish to acknowledge my mistake and apologize. But, until you accept that apology, it doesn't mean anything. It will remain on my mind."

"It remains on mine."

"I'm not saying I want to forget it, Adams. I just want you and I to . . . to get beyond it. Between ourselves. What do you say?"

Greasy held out his hand again, ready to engulf Frank's. Frank looked at it.

"After you apologized to Morden, you should have talked to Davis."

"For God's sake, Adams. So I'm not a saint. What are you implying? That I should try to apologize to Smith?"

As Ovide might have done, Frank closed himself off. Made himself appear as a man who had ceased to listen. He stared at the fire, concentrating on the lacy lines of fat that ripped free and hit the flames with a sizzle. He kept staring until Greasy left.

Aas Vogel Kranz

By late September, the days and nights had warmed on the high veldt. The mealie fields were plowed and planted, and waiting for the spring rain.

There was less marching these days, and while some camps like Bankfontein were left deserted, Aas Vogel Kranz was acquiring the permanence of a town. On the sloping side of its main hill, tents stood in tidy rows, while on the hill's prominent points, stones were piled at guard posts and along systems of trench. From these places, the Mounted Rifles could see Lydenburg Road and the smoke rising from Middelburg.

An *aas vogel* was a vulture and a *kranz* a crown of rock or precipice. The kranz part of the name was a sheer rock face on the hill's west side. Below that cliff, the Little Oliphant River made a tight curl where a smaller creek fell in from the south. The joining of streams at the curve created a brown pool with a sand verge, that had long been a popular swimming place for Middelburgers. Now it was the Canadians' beach and swimming hole—until the day a crocodile crawled out to sun itself. The soldiers ran for their guns and fired wildly until the poor leathery beast was riddled well beyond mortality.

The aas vogel part of the name came from the cliff's top, which was a favourite place for vultures to sit. From there, the birds could study the countryside for nicely ripening cases of death. The Canadians placed their main lookout there, and, on any night, sounds of wild animals in the riverside thicket rose to the piquets' ears.

Since Frank had returned to Aas Vogel Kranz after Griesbach's holiday, it was like the world had forgotten the place—and him. Griesbach soon departed to assist officers in Middelburg, and his absence made the affair of Frank's attack on Greasy less urgent than other things, such as that two of the Rifles from the captured outpost at Nooitgedacht had been court-martialled, a Boer defector having testified that the post was sleeping when they found it. Fotheringham had received fifty-six days of hard labour.

Frank hoped for a visit from Jeff Davis, so he could tell him about Ovide's death, but it did not happen. The only regular contact with the outside world was a supply wagon driven by a portly white teamster called Fat Campbell.

A good thing for Frank was that Abraham and Nandi had returned to Aas Vogel after the Night Attack expedition. He tried a few times to ask them about Dakomi: how they were related; whether he'd had a family of his own; if all of them were angry that the medic had attended the major's minor wound while Dakomi bled to death? But the three did not have enough language for the topic. If Dakomi's name was mentioned and they had alcohol at their fire, they would toast him. Otherwise, the subject of Frank's cribbage partner was let grow silent.

Recognizing that their friend, their mild bossy, needed to drink, and recognizing as well that Griesbach's departure had cut him back, the men of the horse camp tried to get homemade beer and spirits from the nearest African village. Understanding this was done on his behalf and at some cost, Frank was grateful.

When Frank volunteered to ride shotgun on Fat Campbell's supply wagon, alcohol was again at the root of it. Frank had noticed the sweet smell of Fat's breath, no matter what time of day or night he arrived, and so began to ingratiate himself with the teamster. Fat's main fear was that his wagon would be attacked, and he welcomed this gunman aboard.

Often these trips took place at night, for Fat believed that invisibility was protection. Whenever he suspected the enemy might be present in the dark, he sang out with baritone authority:

"In a bit closer there, Mr. Jones."

"Carlson, would you dismount your troops and line that ridge, if you please?"

And so they drove—with Fat twitching his whip over the backs of his mule team and calling to imaginary troops in order to fool a mostly imaginary enemy. Rifle in hand, Frank sat beside him, bathed in Fat's sweet-smelling fear. Several times during each journey, Fat would haul in the mules and grope beneath the wagon seat. He gave Frank a swallow each time he drank.

Part of Fat's duties, beyond bully beef, hardtack, and mail, was bringing news. He asked questions in the camps he served and gathered discarded newspapers. Another virtue of having Frank along was that he could read to Fat in the daylight hours.

Frank read that Christiaan De Wet was still eluding would-be captors down south, and that his brother, Piet, had turned his coat and was scouting for the British. Danie Theron, the Boer scout Jeff Davis had admired, had been killed when the British surrounded him on a hill and shelled it to pieces.

On a trip to Pan Station, Frank and Fat were told that Sam Steele's Strathconas had run into bad luck at Badfontein. One of their officers had left a ridge above camp undefended. Steele sent a party to seize it; they got there late and six Canadians were killed.

The scrap at Badfontein was related to the dispersal of Louis Botha's army. When Pole-Carew's army dropped over the Drakenberg Escarpment, Botha conceded the railway all the way to the frontier. He broke his army into small pieces and sent them north and south, each to escape on its own. It was these dispersing pieces that Buller and the Strathconas were trying to capture in the hills north toward Pilgrim's Rest, and that General French's cavalry was trying to block southeast toward Barberton.

When Pole-Carew pressed through to Mozambique, his army found the Komati River full of exploded and drowned field pieces. They found wrecked railway cars and three thousand Boers awaiting capture. The British and pro-British papers made much of the number of prisoners, but to those inside the war it was obvious these were men Generals Botha and Viljeon had decided they could do without.

Early in October, Fat and Frank found a newspaper that contained the news that Buller's army was about to be disbanded. Buller himself, Britain's favourite scapegoat, was going home.

A week into October, Frank was ordered off Fat Campbell's wagon and sent back to the horse lines with Abraham and Nandi. Lieutenant Davidson was now in charge of Aas Vogel, and he suspected (maybe even smelled) that Frank was enjoying himself too much, and so re-demoted him. Although Frank was sad at the time, the move turned out well when, three days later, Jeff Davis rode in.

Jeff and Frank took some cold food down to the Klein Oliphant, where the strand was empty. Before they sat, Frank checked for tracks. As he hoped, there was a perfectly round, daisy-like imprint that Nandi had told him was a leopard. The pointed marks of a big antelope were nearby.

In a sunny spot among leafing trees, they sat on the sand and ate their cold mutton and biltong. They shared a raw potato like it was an apple. Then they lay back and basked in the hot, hot sun.

"Ovide," said Jeff, from under the hat resting on his face. It was the first time in this visit that the name had been spoken.

"Ya, Ovide," Frank replied.

Frank spent the next minutes looking at pictures of Ovide in his brain and imagined Jeff was doing the same. Frank was grateful that Jeff made no effort to share the blame. It saved Frank having to argue that his own culpability was greater.

While they rested, Jeff told Frank about a fight near Wonderfontein. A four-man patrol of Canadian Dragoons had been looking for cattle in the Boschpoort Valley and had seen some khakis signalling from rocks a half-mile away. When the Boers in khaki climbed into the rocks and started shooting, the Dragoons were caught in a wide-open valley and had to throw themselves flat without cover.

The Boers poured in Mauser rounds until two Dragoons were dead and another wounded. The last man, the horse-holder, had ridden for help.

The dead were Archie Ratcliffe, a butcher from St. Catharines, and Daniel Spence, a florist from Peterborough. Fred Thornton, the third man shot, managed to stay alive. When Casey and Jeff got there, Thornton told them the Boers had come down to look at them. The leader, a man with a droopy eyelid and wearing khaki, went through the pockets of the corpses, and through Thornton's pockets as well. Far from showing contrition for his treachery, this Boer said his name was Villamon and he was responsible for the attack.

Jeff talked to Thornton privately before the ambulance arrived. Thornton told him Villamon had gone in this direction when he left. West.

During Spence and Ratcliffe's funeral and burial, there'd been much talk of what to do with Boers in khaki. Some believed Kitchener had said in a telegram that they could be killed outright if captured. Roberts had never gone that far, but had said that rebels, khaki or not, should have their farms burned and their families turned out.

"Is that why you're here?" Frank asked. "To hunt Villamon?"

"Hutton's column is disbanded," Jeff said. "There's no more Hutton's Scouts."

"You're back with us, then?"

"Yup. Me and Casey."

"And Charlie Ross?"

Jeff took his hat off his face, jacked himself up on one elbow. "Charlie's a civilian."

He grinned at Frank's look of confusion. Frank did not know how you became a civilian in the middle of a war. Even the tradesmen who were out working for wages were still soldiers and could be called back. What Frank had heard, from Fat Campbell, were rumours that Charlie was rustling cattle from burned farms and grazing them on his ranch.

"Charlie's got something called a Transvaal Pass. Says he can buy and sell things anywhere in Transvaal."

"Can we get one?" Frank was only half joking.

"Charlie got the pass because he's not a Mounted Rifle. He tried to enlist at Lethbridge, but Sam Steele wouldn't have him. So Charlie said fuck you and went to England. That's how he got in Roberts' Scouts. It's why he's got the pull to get a pass."

Frank closed his eyes and watched the gold light through his eyelids. When a shadow crossed, he looked and Jeff was standing.

"You're going after Villamon, then?"

"Yup. There's an expedition. Dragoons and Rifles. Casey'll lead the scouts. He's picking me up here in the morning."

Frank led the way across the small stream, coffee-brown to the Oliphant's yellow. He started them onto the path that squeezed between the river and the cliff face, watching as they passed under two tall trees. He was looking for a big leisurely cat draped over a branch.

They entered the cleft between hills and climbed. Partway up, Jeff stopped. He was more serious.

"What I hear is that you drink too much and stay with the Africans."

"I guess I drink with whom I please. As for people saying it, I don't care what they say."

Jeff took his hat off, smoothed his hair; dished sweat off his brow.

"If you want to look after horses, why not come look after ours?"

Frank felt a disturbance in his chest. The last time Jeff had offered something and Frank had taken it, Ovide had died.

Frank pretended to laugh. "I wasn't nice to The General. Casey won't want me near him."

"Casey can look after his own horse then. You can look after The Blue."

Frank was also thinking that his part of the war was practically over. The Rifles had signed on for a year, which was up in December. He said that.

Jeff screwed his hat back on. "You're going to wait it out, then?"

"Guess so."

"They might decide we stay longer. If that happens, and you want a place to be, the offer stands."

Frank had no tent for them to sleep in. He had avoided his and Ovide's for so long, someone had claimed it. They found a place where the breeze smelled of spring buds and bivouacked.

When the bugle blew the rouse, Frank looked around and Jeff was gone. The edge of camp was swarming. The expedition in search of Villamon had just arrived. Frank went to look for Jeff but, when he did not see him, decided it made better sense that Casey and his scouts had come early and were already gone.

Frank went to the horse yard where a dozen new cripples had been turned in for remounts. Abraham joined him, and they started with a mare whose dangling shoe was threatening to crack a piece off her hoof.

] 257 [

Casey led his scouts north and they found the Boers—a roving hundred. The seven scouts held the hundred until Evans' expedition arrived. The Boers took a ridge. The Canadian gunners shelled them off it. So it went, ridge to ridge, until the Boers were driven north to their home laager. When the Boers spilled into the bush, Major Evans wisely let them go.

Frank was disappointed to see some of Evans' men return to Aas Vogel Kranz without Casey's scouts. Frank's visit with Jeff had made him feel almost good, and he wanted that feeling again. He had also been thinking about Jeff's offer. At the time, it had seemed impossible, but the great loneliness that entered Frank when Jeff left made a difference. He was not as sure he belonged here with Abraham and Nandi.

The returning soldiers told their stories of adventure that night. Frank listened for any mention of Jeff or Casey or Villamon. Casey and Jeff were part of the fight that took the trenches, but Villamon's name was never spoken.

Two days later, a special mail cart came. Sometimes mail would pile up somewhere and later be found. This cart came from Pan and entered camp behind Fat Campbell's wagon. The corporal in charge of the mail pulled up and started calling names. Sometimes, when he yelled a name, someone in the crowd would answer, "He's at Night Attack," or some other camp. The mail corporal flung those letters and parcels into a separate canvas bag with an air of exhaustion. He meant to convey that this breaking up of troops and all this marching around was no fun for him.

When he called Jeff Davis's name, Frank did not yell "Bankfontein," but pushed to the front and waited. During a lull, he said, "I know where Davis is."

"You going to tell me, or is it a secret?"

"He was scouting near Bankfontein. I'm pretty sure he's camped there."

The mail officer cursed, as if this was the sliver that made him a cross. "That's empty, that camp."

"That's where he is."

Lieutenant Davidson was standing by, hoping for a letter from his wife and girls. He heard what Adams said to the mail officer.

"How do you know those scouts are at Bankfontein?" he challenged. "They could be anywhere."

"I think they would have come back here before they went east," said Frank.

"They're scouts," said Davidson, meaning you could not hope to know where they were.

The mail corporal was studying Jeff Davis's letter. He showed it to Davidson, indicating the seal.

"It's from a general in Britain. See here? Aldershot. Says *personal and confidential.*"

Davidson looked at the letter, at Frank. "So what is it you want? To deliver this?"

Frank knew better than to admit it.

Fat Campbell had moved forward, wading through the crowd, his bulk squeezing them to the sides. He watched the standoff between Davidson and Adams. Davidson had the letter and was holding it close to his nose. Then he held it by a corner and fanned himself.

"Give it here." Fat's great paw reached in and pinched it away. "I'm making a run up to Bankfontein tomorrow."

Davidson was not ready to surrender. "How do you know there's anyone there?"

"Because they sent a rider to Middelburg to say they were hungry."

Davidson popped his mouth. "Done, then." Toward Adams, he smirked.

Frank started away, feeling forlorn, but Fat Campbell hustled up behind; reached and caught his shirt. "Whoa there, Sitting Bull."

The fat man grinned. "You ride there yourself, or you go with me? What's the difference?"

"Davidson won't let me do either."

"We leave early enough, Davidson don't know."

Frank tied the ridgling to Fat's wagon and helped Nandi harness the mules. It was before dawn, drizzly and cold, a mist over everything. When Fat and Frank were on the wagon, they drew an oil sheet across their backs.

They could barely see the greasy two-track, but they followed it north. The hilltops were smothered in mist. As the grey light came and the odd black-rocked kopje glowered out, Frank's neck hair rose. The idea of Boers lying in those rocks. Fat trusted Frank and seldom looked beyond the working haunches of his mules.

As they squelched along and the wagon yowled and bent itself to break-ing point over rock sills, Frank's mind never stopped working. He was al-ready dreaming the conversation at the trail's end. He wasn't expecting answers, news, or wisdom from Jeff; just the voice of a friend.

Jeff and Casey were not at Bankfontein when Fat and Frank pulled in. Casey's other five scouts were there, plus a few D Squadron men who'd stayed. Casey had left one of the five in charge, and this one was in a tent. The rest were without shelter in the rain and sat in the bush under their oil sheets. At sight of the wagon, they jumped up and pressed forward, anxious for bully beef.

Handing down the cans, Frank withheld each for a second while he asked about Jeff and Casey. The answers were consistent. They had gone north yesterday. They were chasing Villamon.

Frank and Fat stayed the night, sheltering under the wagon. When Fat pulled out next morning, Frank did not—even though the ridgling had kicked another horse and everyone wanted to see the back of him. Frank claimed his horse was injured. He took the pinto a distance away and hobbled him head to knee, then stood in the rain and pretended to be fixing some problem. Come night, Frank bedded down beside his horse.

The morning brought a still heavier rain that hit Frank's oil sheet like a cluster of arrows. The scout Casey had left in charge came out to Frank, who was again picking at the muck in the ridgling's hoof. The scout told Frank he should go. They were practically out of food again. They could not afford him.

Frank got ready, with all lack of haste. He put the saddle on, cinched it, then un-cinched and pulled it off. He dragged the oil sheet over himself and the saddle and did something noisy with a rasp. He was back in the open trying to think up another form of delay when Casey appeared through the drifting mist, followed by Jeff. Jeff stopped The Blue and hauled on a rope that pulled another horse into view, this one riderless, its saddle black and sopping: a neat coyote-coloured gelding.

The men in camp were intent on staying dry, and, beyond peeking out of their oil sheets, did nothing to celebrate the arrival. Casey unsheathed his rifle. He set the stock on the fat part of his thigh and fired into the air. He pointed the gun barrel at his tent, meaning they should go there. Seeing that the canopy was weighed with water, he used the rifle barrel again to spill it to the side.

Soon, everyone was present, sitting on the side of the tent best guarded against the slant rain. Their oil sheets were tented over their heads. Casey, Jeff, and the scout left in charge were bunched under the awning. Jeff had his back against an oat bag. On the shelves of his cheekbones, his eyes were resting slits.

Callaghan was as avid as Jeff was still. He perched on a camp stool like a child at a piano, his eyes darting, his thick cheeks red blossomed. He had a few things in his lap he intended to use to tell the story. When he knew he had their attention, he began.

Yesterday, in the late afternoon, in hilly country—drizzling, but with better visibility than today—he and Jeff had found a Boer laager. There was no warmth under the ashes. The head of an impala was left from their last meal, and a rack they'd used for drying biltong told of their preparations for travel.

Jeff and Casey were looking for more clues when, *bang*, a rifle cracked and the biltong rack shattered to the ground. That rack had been not six inches from Casey's elbow.

The laager was on the site of a dilapidated Boer farm, and they were standing inside the farm's sheep kraal. Casey ducked down behind the rocks and knocked out a loophole. Jeff was racing the horses away down the slope and behind an old Native hut.

When Jeff crawled back, they waited for the sniper to fire again. They could do nothing until they had some idea where he was. Jeff grabbed Casey's hat and put it on a stick. He bobbed and skimmed the hat, just barely above the rocks. Finally the sniper let go another shot, just one.

Shifting on his camp stool and winking at his audience, Casey picked his Stetson off his head. His hand disappeared inside and a finger wormed pinkly out a hole. The enemy was a marksman, the demonstration said.

It took an hour to coax enough shots out of the sniper so they actually located a muzzle flash. Jeff saw it and explained to Casey where in that treed hillside the rifleman was concealed. Then, as one, they rose and emptied their magazines on that spot, two lines of bullets converging.

The reward came quickly. Rooted out, the sniper thrashed through the gorse. One of them fired while the other loaded.

"We knew we didn't have him yet. There was a little draw and he was in it. Jeff guessed he had his horse in there, and the question was: does he come out or is there a way out behind? But he did come—like a bullet, eh, Jeff? He was hanging on the horse's other side, Comanche-style."

Jeff had already brought the horses. They mounted and galloped in pursuit. The Boer was well ahead, the gelding's hooves flinging muck.

The chase was on. All three had good horses. They were going along a pass that divided ridges. The slope to the right was open, so the Boer could not go there without opening up his downhill side. The opposite flank was the shady slope and had thick bush along the bottom and some higher. Casey saw a path into that bush and bent The General onto it. Jeff kept the pressure on behind, so the Boer had no choice really but to keep on straight and through the mouth of the gap.

The gap opened into a broad wetland held in by tapering hills. Tufted, dimpled, wet. The Boer's pony shattered the rain mirrors in the pocks.

"I yelled for Jeff to stop. Didn't I, Jeff? We both jumped off. We put the horses into cover and got in among some rocks at the bog's edge."

The Boer was slowed by the soggy ground. Then his horse broke through. The front legs shot in up to the chest. The rider flew over his horse's head.

The Boer got to his feet and ran. At times, his feet caught in the muck and tripped him. He was making for the edge of the bog. He was well within rifle range and knew it. Twice he turned, knelt, and fired. Jeff and Casey were in good cover, and the bullets skipped off the rocks.

"We were almost certain it was Villamon. He was still wearing khaki like he wore when he killed Ratcliffe and Spence. 'You take him,' I said to Jeff, because Jeff had sworn to kill Villamon long ago. But old Jeff, he said no. Said we'll take him together."

Casey had a glisten in his eye, as if surprised by this turn in the story, at the friendship it showed.

They stood out of the rocks, shoulder to shoulder. Took aim with their rifles and fired five times.

"Five hundred yards and we hit him with three," Casey bragged. "Last shot was Jeff's. Got him square in the head. Scattered that Boer's thoughts on the grass."

Casey lowered his head as if at the amen of a long prayer. The final line was composed, a bit false, and it rang in the air under the sound of the rain on the canvas.

The story begged three cheers, and the men shouted them. After that, Casey offered the proof to be examined. He had letters from the Boer's saddlebag: a couple addressed to Villamon; an unmailed one with his name in childish printing at the bottom. The saddle had a *V* branded into one fender. Each man stuck his head in under the canopy to see.

After the file-by, the men went away to redig their bivouac holes. Only Frank remained. Casey invited Jeff inside for a drink. The scout who had been living in the tent was already in there. Jeff still looked asleep and did not respond. Casey pursed his lips and blew; went inside.

Frank came in under the awning. An edge of the oat bag was open, and Frank sat beside Jeff and leaned there. He dug in his shirt and brought out the canvas dispatch bag in which he'd kept Jeff's letter. He nudged Jeff with an elbow and Jeff opened one eye and smiled. He had been feigning sleep all along.

Frank opened the bag, pulled out the stone-dry letter, let Jeff see his name and General Butler's name on the cover. He turned it over so Jeff could see the general's unbroken seal.

Frank considered not watching Jeff read it. But, finally, he did look. The movement of Jeff's eyes was rapid. The thin page quivered in his long fingers. Frank saw the blood leave his face. A sheen of sudden sweat appeared.

Jeff read it only once, then leaned his head on the sack and turned to the rain. Every few seconds, the awning on that side filled and released a lacy pour. Frank was concerned for the letter and watched the hand that held it move out along the ground. It went to the border between dry and wet, then crossed that line. The pour from the canopy doused the letter, which draped Jeff's fingers, weeping black.

Frank still had the envelope. He almost slid it back into the canvas for protection, but leaned it against Jeff's leg instead.

Nothing else happened, and the moment lengthened into a trance. Frank and Jeff stared at the rain that cabled the low sky to the ground.

Casey erupted through the tent's flap, waving a rum bottle.

"Davis, come on. Drink."

As if it were agreed upon, Jeff said he and Frank were going to see Ovide Smith's grave.

"You'll get pissed on," Casey argued.

They rose together, and Frank led the way into the downpour. He walked out of camp and toward the north-facing slope, the pile of rocks. Frank wore his oil sheet over his head, but Jeff had nothing but his tunic and hat. The letter was still pinched in his fingers, a little rag, mostly dissolved. At the grave, Jeff stepped past Frank, pulled a rock from the pile, put the letter in the hole, and pressed the rock back.

When Jeff turned, Frank tried not to have questions on his face. Jeff gave him an answer anyway.

"Red Crow's dead."

They walked away, Jeff leading. He went to Casey's tent, slapped on its door, and Casey let him in.

Frank went to where the ridgling stood in its solitary confinement, its prison of thorns. He rolled in his oil sheet and spent the next hours in a delirium of wondering. He remembered Jeff's face as he read the letter, the pallor, the waxy look. He weighed it against the reason: Red Crow's death. But wasn't Red Crow an old man? How could his death be so shocking?

He also wondered about the way he had forced himself on Jeff in that moment. Too late, he wondered whether it might imperil the friendship that had become his hope and his anchor.

Next morning, Frank was scavenging oats for the ridgling when Jeff came to saddle The Blue. Frank started tacking the ridgling, but went slow so Jeff finished first, to see what would happen then.

When Jeff switched the halter for the bridle, The Blue took the bit with a lunge. Jeff threw the knotted reins over her coarse mane and shoved his toe in the stirrup. He rose and turned the mare as he took his seat. His face was closed and stayed closed, looking only forward. Frank let him ride away.

Frank led the ridgling to Ovide's grave, undid the girth, and stripped off the saddle and blanket. He spread the oil sheet over the pieces of tack and let the ridgling graze the old yellow grass in the now more gentle rain.

Toward the end of October, the Canadian mounted infantry battalions were moved under the leadership of General Smith-Dorrien.

Looked at through the new general's eyes, the situation along the captured Delagoa line was unsatisfactory: both perilous and passive. To play cowboys and Indians with the Boers, on ground they knew, was to let the Boers choose both the game and the rules. What the British had was superior numbers. Why not use them?

Out of this came a Flying Column, an army of twelve-hundred that would sweep south from Belfast and hammer the Boer commandos in their hideouts around Carolina. These were the laagers from which the Boers were launching their guerilla attacks. Smith-Dorrien wanted them rooted out and the land scorched behind them.

Because the Canadian mounted infantry battalions were down to their last month or two in the war, the Flying Column was a source of great excitement. For anyone still wanting to make his mark or win chest decorations, this was the time. Major Sanders, whose splinter wound had healed, was to lead the Mounted Rifles in the column, and Colonel Lessard would lead the Dragoons. Wherever those two officers went in the final days before the march, men practically did somersaults to get their attention. The last thing most troopers wanted was to be left in a dull garrison while the boys rode off for a last shot at glory.

Lieutenant Davidson was furious with Frank Adams when he returned from Bankfontein. This was an army, he said, an army at war. It was not a ranch—he pronounced it *rawnch*—where a fellow could bugger off when he pleased. Davidson's portrayal of Frank as a child of privilege was so inaccurate, it was pleasing. He let it stand.

Abraham and Nandi were delighted to have Frank back. They had preserved a bottle of distillery-made rum for the occasion. The ruckus of their party after lights out did not improve Davidson's mood.

Then, everything at Aas Vogel Kranz changed. Davidson was chosen to lead a troop in Smith-Dorrien's Flying Column. He went around camp in soaring good spirits and never thought of Frank Adams again.

All of Aas Vogel's good soldiers were chosen to go. Other soldiers were sent in to replace them. It was not hard to figure out that the incoming fellows were not the cream of anyone's crop. The new camp commander was an old New Zealand lieutenant whose white moustache seemed to pour out of his drink-blackened nose. His second-in-command, who actually outranked him, was an Englishman who treasured an ostrich egg and carried it in a biscuit tin wherever he went. There was also a well-born corporal from an African tea-planting family who would not sit tailor-style. At each meal, he would dig a hole for his legs, so he could dine in the upright seated position.

If Aas Vogel Kranz lacked discipline before Smith-Dorrien's Flying Column, it became a disgrace after. The slackness verged on mutiny. Cossack posts were asleep more often than awake. Patrols went out undermanned and came back when they felt like it. The soldiers knocked off when they pleased for swims and games of cricket. Lieutenant Cropton, the Kiwi camp commander, would come out of his tent until something disgusted him. Then he would return inside for a consoling libation.

Nowadays, the beach on the Klein Oliphant was lined with men, and the pool at the curve was dense with bathers—crocodiles be damned! Someone had carved a proper cricket ball out of African hardwood, and the stock of a ruined Mauser served as the bat. Those who did not play cricket or swim often angled with bent pins where the two streams joined. A flat fish could be caught there whose size was perfect for their dixies.

The day's entertainments were occasionally disturbed by the roar of a field gun. Aas Vogel's good Armstrong had been taken for the Flying Column and only a bruised Creusot was left. The French gun had been seized from the Boers in the moment they were attempting its destruction with explosives. The only gunner left at Aas Vogel claimed the sights were buggered, and his daily shots were attempts to compensate for the gun's injuries. He thought he should be able to land his shells on the right hill at least, and had a ways to go to achieve that.

Someone made the joke that Aas Vogel Kranz should be renamed Sitting Duck, but it did not catch on because no one seriously believed the Boers would bother with this old berg. Smith-Dorrien's column was beating its way south through the rains and mists, and surely all the Boers had gone there to fight against them.

—

In his glee about leaving, Davidson had not thought to tell Lieutenant Cropton why Frank Adams should be limited to horse duty. As a result, the new commander looked at the white man working so diligently on the horse lines and considered it an error. Compared to the rabble he had inherited, Adams was one of the steadier, healthier men. He resolved to try him elsewhere.

The first attempt was not successful. The lieutenant sent Adams on a four-man patrol, and the private's pinto kicked another horse so hard a shoulder was broken and the horse had to be destroyed. After that, no one would go with Adams, and Cropton had to keep him in camp. He suggested Adams get a different horse but the private seemed wedded to the crazy one he had.

The best remaining alternative was to put Adams in an outpost close to home, and Cropton's choice was the "shanz on the kranz": the one that overlooked the curve in the Klein Oliphant. Cropton had been using three Australians at that post. Most things in the British army were done in fours, and these three had made themselves awkward by driving off a succession of fourth men. That and general insolence accounted for their being at Aas Vogel. If Adams, the even-tempered Canadian, could stick with the Australians, the safety of the camp would improve.

The minute the Aussies received Adams, they started the usual round of bullying and cruel jokes. They could not get the slightest rise out of the dull bugger and proceeded quickly to savagery and violence. But Adams' response to even the most inhumane antics was bovine passivity.

They might have beaten him to death just to end the frustration except it occurred to them that he was valuable. While they persecuted him, Adams had stuck to the morbid duties of a sentry with hilarious dedication. As they either slept or threw dice by the light of an illegal fire, Adams kept staring and listening into the dark, hour after hour. Having figured out that this willing slave was keeping them from court martial, they stopped twisting his goolies, pissing in his mess tin, and shitting on his hardtack. They let him do his duties and good riddance.

As for the private's ugly-tempered gelding, they let Adams know that one nick out of any of their horses and that ridgling's one-nut career was over. They tied their mounts close together in the trees, while Adams knee-haltered his above the cliff.

Six days into November, in cold and rainy weather, Fat Campbell rolled into Aas Vogel Kranz. He had news about the Flying Column. Its flight had been slow as a snail, weighed down with guns and supplies. It had been further impeded by searching every farm and burning the rebel ones. Another new practice was collecting Boer women and children and putting them in special camps. There was one at Irene and others planned for Balmoral and Middelburg. There had to be guards on the wagons that carried them back, to keep the Boer rebels from reclaiming their families.

As the Flying Column inched along, the rebels assembled on the ridges out of rifle range. If the officers got mad enough to call for field guns, the Boers had ample time to retreat out of range while the guns were unloaded and dug in. The only thing that could make the Boers run was if Gat Howard or Eddy Holland took a gallop at them with their machine guns.

But the biggest problem was the weather, the dense mists in which the Boers could so easily hide. It turned every place into a potential ambush. In a big meadow that was somewhat clear, a sniper felled Corporal Schell's horse. Schell tried to jump clear but the weight of the horse landed on his ankle. Sergeant Tryon and Major Sanders raced back. Tryon dismounted and put Schell on his horse; gave it a slap and sent it home.

Major Sanders opened a stirrup and told Tryon to jump on with him. Half standing, half leaning over the withers, Tryon stayed with Sanders as the horse charged back. But Charlie's weight on the stirrup was too much and turned the saddle. It spun and both men were hurled to the ground. While they tried to find their wind, Sanders took a bullet. He could not run at all now but staggered into some rocks. He waved for Tryon to run back on his own, which the sergeant finally did.

Sanders' friend Captain Chalmers was now in charge. He was getting a rescue together. A group of gallopers started out, while Sanders waved frantically for them to go back. The Boers unleashed such a barrage that Scizzors had to obey.

But Scizzors could not leave his friend out there and arranged a group to try to retrieve him on foot. They went in stages. Rock to anthill, they worked themselves across until they were in a trench not far from Sanders' rock pile.

There was some kind of dispute. Chalmers wanted Sanders to come to the trench. Sanders did not want to. They lost time. Suddenly, and it was bad luck for everyone, Cpl. Sheldon Herchmer rode into the field of battle from the side. He did not know what was going on, and was right in the line of Boer fire. Captain Chalmers jumped up and ran at the corporal, waving him back.

The Boer snipers opened up. The men who were there said old Scizzors' long arms and legs flew strangely when the bullets hit, completing their motions unmanned.

Aas Vogel Kranz, November 1900

After the Flying Column returned to Belfast, bedraggled if not completely defeated, General Smith-Dorrien insisted they go back. As quickly as possible, he wanted the Flying Column reorganized, resupplied, and sent.

That same night, the night before the Canadians in the Flying Column would fight a famous battle at Liliefontein, Frank Adams was in his post atop Aas Vogel Kranz with the three cruel Australians. The Aussies had gambled themselves to sleep, and Frank was alone with the night sounds: rain pelting on his oil sheet and the occasional howl of a hyena biting through the wet night.

An hour before daylight, the ridgling started staggering around in his knee-halter, whittering. Thinking it had to do with the hyena or maybe the leopard who'd left the flower prints in the sand below, Frank told his horse to be quiet and thought no more about it.

When the first light of morning drooled through the mists, Frank heard the sound of an incoming shell. He knew it would be close. He was watching for where it would land when it struck beside him. The explosion lifted the ground and blew the shanz wall on top of him.

Frank had no way of knowing how long he lay there, out cold. His return to sense was frightening, for his head was a blossom of pain, and his eyes could only see rough-edged blocks of dark, pierced by blazes of bloody gold. It took longer than a minute to figure out that he was not blind nor his sight deformed but that rocks were packed tight around his head. His whole body was imprisoned in rock, and he was about to panic, thinking of Ovide's final resting place, when he put his energy into thrusting one leg and it burst into the lightness of air.

Pushing with an arm, he felt a limb that gave no answering sensation. He thought he must have a dead arm, maybe a severed one. But then he moved all of his parts and they were there. He rolled back rocks until he found the staring eyes of one of the Australians. He shifted more rock, but the other Aussies were gone.

The air had a burnt smell. One of the posts bracing the shanz had been on fire and was still smoking. Frank noticed that blood was dripping through whatever he looked at. It seemed to come from a gash on his forehead and from another wound in his hair.

The shell's explosion had tossed up a shelf of sandy rock. Farther from the cliff edge, it had flipped over a tree so the clay-packed roots stood perpendicular to the earth. Tied to a branch of this felled tree was one of the Australian horses. It lay flat with a red opening in its side that gaped and closed like a gill.

Frank walked toward the horse and it thrashed at him with its hooves. He left the gelding alive because it was still acting like a horse and might survive.

Looking farther up the slow rise to the hill's crest, he saw spirals of smoke where other shells had exploded. From that direction, he realized he could still hear the *rick-rack* of a rifle battle. Each of these facts came to him slowly, like rocks skipping from a lake's far shore.

Then he thought of the ridgling. He thought the horse might have been blown off the cliff but found him on his front knees crowded into a thorn bush. The ridgling quivered as if covered in ants.

When Frank moved toward the ridgling, he saw past the packed tree root. A man was lying there dead. The Boer was face down with his arms stretched out ahead of him. Just beyond his curled fingers was a Mauser rifle. A full bandolier crossed his back, and the bloody hole of the departing bullet had cut part of the ammunition belt. The soldier's long beard folded beside his unseen face like the edge of a pillow he was sleeping on.

Frank talked to the ridgling. Once the animal's eyes cleared, he jumped onto three feet. He balanced on two and kicked out at the thorns that were piercing him. Frank went closer and untied the knee halter.

A thought was forming. Frank wasn't sure what that thought was exactly, or if he would act on it. He went looking for his rifle. It was among the rocks, and the front sights had been knocked off. The dead Australian's rifle was bent. He went over to the dead Boer and his Mauser looked unharmed. Frank unbuckled the bandolier and hauled it out from under the body. It came away with a wet red stripe along it. He buckled it onto himself.

He tightened the ridgling's girth and exchanged the halter for the bridle. The pinto took the bit greedily as if to say, *Let's get the hell out.*

Before leaving, Frank considered two things. He asked himself where the other two Australians were. They must have been well enough to leave. Maybe they had checked their friend and saw him dead. Maybe they saw Frank in the rocks and figured he was dead too. Or maybe they did not think of him at all.

The other thing Frank considered were the trails away. The main trail to the river below would have a team of black horse-holders at its bottom, and a Boer rebel left in charge. In the other direction, past the wounded brumby, was an animal trail. Frank knew it came out on the little creek and was blocked with wire. He bent low and led the ridgling into it. They went slowly and, when they came to the wire, he clipped the coils with cutters from his saddlebag.

At the little stream, curling through the turf, Frank led the pinto up-current. He stayed within the fringe of brush that tracked the water, and after they had made several crooked miles, Frank's head brought him to his knees and made him puke. He fell over sideways and had no choice but to stay like that.

The last thing he looked into was the ridgling's strange eye. He felt its nose snuffing on his shirt. The horse was loose and Frank could not do anything about that. Though each word he spoke hurt him, he said aloud to the horse that he hoped he would not run off and try to fuck something; that he hoped he would not kick him in the head for some remembered sin. For now, though, the ridgling was on his own.

Liliefontein

The Battle of Liliefontein was a rearguard action. The Canadians had been sent ahead to scout, but went from front to rear when General Smith-

Dorrien decided he must retreat again to Belfast. All the previous day, the Canadian gunners had been scoring against the Boers. Now that the Canadians were a rearguard, the Boers were looking at the same guns and meant to have them.

All day, the Boers fought them. They came at a gallop and fired from the saddle, sometimes face-on and sometimes flowing up the Canadian flanks and shooting from the side. There was no time when the Canadians controlled the fight; when they were sure what would happen.

Lieutenant Turner—the same one who had crossed the Vet River at Coetzee Drift—was already wounded in the arm when he called his men together and told them to hide in a brush-masked trench. The trench was close to Eddy Holland's machine gun and, hungry for that gun, the Boers came galloping. When the Canadians opened fire, two of the Boer leaders were shot in the head.

During the skirmish, Turner was shot again, in the throat this time. Still not felled, he rode to Lessard for reinforcements.

The Boers kept after Eddy Holland's machine gun. When it jammed, he did what Gatling Howard had done once before: grabbed the red-hot barrel in his hands, lifted the gun from its limber, and ran.

When the Battle of Liliefontein was over, two Canadians were dead, seven badly wounded, but not one gun lost. Many would call it Canada's best day of the war.

Cape Town, December 1900

After four days of farm-burning in the Steelpoort Valley, the Canadian MI battalions were in Irene, their war more or less over.

Of the eight hundred horses they had brought from Canada, fifty had survived, and the boys marvelled at this. Considering the carnage, that number seemed high. The owners of the surviving horses were told they must give them to other units who were staying on. It was said that some men signed back on rather than give up horses that had carried them through a year of war.

This story was attached to Casey Callaghan and Jeff Davis, both of whom left the Mounted Rifles to join the Canadian Scouts. A letter about the Canadian Scouts had come to camp in late November, bearing the signature of General Kitchener. Anyone wanting in had to sign right away. The Canadian Scouts would be led by Arthur Howard—promoted to major for that purpose. Despite the name, the Scouts were part of the British army. For his second-in-command, Gat Howard lured Charlie Ross out of retirement. Gat had arranged things so every scout had the rank of sergeant or higher, which meant minimum pay was $1.75 a day.

When Casey Callaghan and Jeff Davis signed up, no one heard either say it was for the sake of their horses. In Jeff's case, people may have said it because they could not believe a Halfbreed would be more patriotic than they were.

In Irene camp, the Canadians who were leaving waited for a train. Around their fires, it was natural to recap their battles and remember their dead. For the Mounted Rifles, the driver Bradley had been first: drowned in a dam on the Great Karoo. At the other end was Captain Chalmers, good old Scizzors, killed trying to save Sanders and warn off Sheldon Herchmer.

Taylor and Frost. Morden and Kerr. Ovide Smith's death was surely the strangest and most foolish.

The Canadian Dragoons were thinking about their men killed at Liliefontein. They also thought about the British infantry officer whom they asked for help that day, and who would not order a single volley in their defence.

All of them should have been thinking about the men who had died of enteric fever and dysentery, for this was a much bigger number than those killed in action. But it was hard to think of those boys and always had been. They faded from memory as you moved on, and they were not coming back to mind easily here on the lip of going home.

There were just two men missing in action. Oswald Weaver, an English-born rancher, had disappeared during an ambush in October. And Frank Adams was nowhere to be found after his Cossack post on Aas Vogel Kranz had been shelled in November. Living or dead, those men were staying in Africa.

No one even mentioned Pete and Eddy Belton, or the two Dragoons who had sold Boers back their guns. They had lost their right to be remembered.

—

When Canada's mounted infantry got back to Cape Town, they worked all day at the docks loading their ship. The Mounted Rifles stayed on board while the Dragoons returned to a camp called Maitland. The officers went for a dinner in their honour, and left orders that the men were denied leave in town.

The Dragoons were sharing Maitland with five hundred Australians, also denied leave. A thousand strong, they barged their way out. On the ship, the Mounted Rifles heard and decided to join the ruckus.

The bar owners on Adderley Street had army orders not to sell drink to the colonial soldiers. After a few refusals, the Canadians started jerking barmen from behind the mahogany and dispensing drink themselves. In the style of dime-store novels, some used their Colt revolvers to disintegrate chandeliers and mirrors.

Seeing what was coming, the manager of the Grand Hotel chose to give away what he could not sell. Free drinks for the Empire's soldiers! Instantly, the Grand's bar was packed. To show their gratitude, the soldiers passed the hat and gave the manager three Stetsons full of gold sovereigns.

Next morning, the Canadian soldiers were told to dress for a parade and final inspection. They walked downtown, and crowds of Cape Towners cheered them along. Governor Milner and the mayor of Cape Town told them what fine brave fellows they were, and thanked them on behalf of Britain and South Africa.

They marched to the dock and boarded their ship. At 4 P.M., December 13, 1900, the *Roslin Castle* glided out of Table Bay.

Aldershot, December 1900

General Butler could not remember when he had last seen the sun or taken a proper walk. He always seemed to be in this gloomy Aldershot office, or in his study at home, trying to read or write by the yellow light of a lamp.

No matter how often he had travelled to the southern half of the world, it was still hard to believe that South Africa was in the height of summer right now: a time when it often rained but when, on clear days, the close, bellicose sun would blind you. You hid from the weather there as well, but for quite different reasons.

If Butler was grateful for anything, it was that the disappointing year of 1900 would soon be over, its final knell being General Lord Roberts' thunderous homecoming. For having failed to defeat an enemy he outnumbered a hundred to one, Bobs was worshipped by the nation. For his extremes of waste and disorganization, and for his foggy generalship, he was elevated to the highest post in the War Office, general of generals, shoving half-blind Wolseley forever into the wings.

Meanwhile, with Kitchener of Khartoum in charge, the war in Africa staggered on like a bad London play, one with no idea how to end.

South Africa was very much on Butler's mind today. It had come calling in the unlikely form of a note from Red Crow's nephew, Jefferson. Butler had often wondered if his string-pulling had done the young man any good, and it seemed it had. Davis gave his present unit as the Canadian Scouts and his rank as regimental sergeant-major.

The Canadian Scouts was a new unit led by American machine-gun expert Arthur Howard. Howard was the sort one hears about. He had made the London papers in the first year of the war, for making desperate rushes at the enemy with his machine gun. In Butler's experience, such heroics were usually done against orders. And now Howard was a major in the British army. Good grief.

Still, Jefferson Davis had wanted to be a scout and was one. The fact that he was a regimental sergeant-major was remarkable. As a Half-breed in a white man's war, Butler would have assumed him stuck at private. It suggested Jefferson was something special, as Red Crow had always said.

Jefferson wrote that he had chosen to sign up with the Canadian Scouts after his original outfit returned to Canada. Regardless of the promotion to sergeant, this struck Butler as unwise. To Roberts' policy of farm-burning, Kitchener had added the gathering of homeless women and chil-dren into camps; had contributed to the English language by saying he was "concentrating them" in "concentration camps." The remainder of the war would not be pretty.

The camp idea illuminated one of Kitchener's greatest flaws. For all his campaigns, K of K did not understand hatred. He instilled it constantly but was always surprised to encounter it. *Why do they hate me so?* he would ask, and the chilling part was that he did not know the answer.

Jefferson Davis had not written to Butler to tell him about his progress in the war. His purpose was to thank Butler for the letter he had sent in Oc-tober, to inform Jefferson that his uncle, Red Crow, had died in August.

Butler had found out about the death by letter from Canada. It was a curious piece of correspondence, for there was a single page and a smaller sealed envelope inside a larger envelope. One look at the loose sheet and Butler knew it had been written by Jean L'Heureux, Red Crow's secretary, for he had often cursed the man's lacy, difficult script. But the tone and language of this letter was very different than anything previous, for the secretary was writing as himself. Freed of the curbs of dictation and trans-lation, L'Heureux was a pompous windbag—like a Catholic priest of the sort who dedicates himself to Church bureaucracy.

In his opening paragraph, L'Heureux identified himself with the titles *Personal Secretary to Red Crow, Chief of the Blood Tribe of the Blackfoot Confed-eracy of Indians,* and *Assistant to the Reverend Albert Lacombe, O.M.I.* Then he imparted the news of the death and gave his opinion that Red Crow's passing was an event of significance "far beyond the prairie confines where the Chief lived his life and met his death."

John Happy listed others who would be receiving notification: Queen Victoria; Pope Leo XIII; the Marquess of Salisbury, Prime Minister of England; Wilfrid Laurier, Prime Minister of Canada; William McKinley, President of the United States.

Butler felt puny in the company.

Looking back, it was easy to mock L'Heureux's letter, but the truth was Butler had wept while he read it. He had identified closely with Red Crow's complaints and concerns, and, reading the letter, had felt like he was grieving his own life.

Aging together, Red Crow and Butler had gone from fellow warriors to fellow diplomats. When their fires cooled, they had discovered that most warfare was wasteful and futile. Rather than protecting survival, war usually imperiled it. The letters of recent years had been commiserations about how their wisdom went ignored—though Butler felt his own star had dimmed more than Red Crow's. In one letter, Red Crow told how his young men had ridden south to take revenge on Crow horse thieves. Red Crow mounted his best horse and chased them to the border. He stopped the young warriors, turned them around, and brought them home. Contrast that with Butler's letter campaign to end the Boer War before it started: his conspicuous lack of success.

The second letter, the sealed one, was from Red Crow himself: dictated to L'Heureux and not yet mailed when Red Crow died. In that letter was nothing to suggest that Red Crow saw his death coming, except perhaps some talk about the deaths of others. The people of his tribe were dying steadily, taken off by "the blood-spitting sickness." Even Jefferson's girlfriend, Ran After, had succumbed in July. Red Crow said that he was beginning to believe the white doomsayers who said the Bloods must die out, just like the buffalo. "Maybe it is true," wrote Red Crow, "that we will live only in the Sand Hills."

The atmosphere of Red Crow's final letter was full of guilt at his inability to lead his people away from the source of their death. There was a more specific guilt for his not having informed Jefferson that his girlfriend was dying. Red Crow had kept the news from Jefferson because he feared the young man might throw his life away because of it.

There was one more detail in L'Heureux's letter that Butler would forever be grateful for. After all the tub-thumping, L'Heureux described in detail how Red Crow had died. The chief had been out riding in the valley of the Belly River, gathering his horses. When he was found dead, the rope to the mouth of his horse was still in his hand. His mount was beside him, calmly eating grass.

Butler could imagine the rest. August day. The brilliant heat. Locusts buzzing in the blond grass. Rich hot berry smell beside a river running green-clear to its cobble bottom. Through his blear of tears, Butler had made a note to go to Ireland whenever he felt his own death coming. He must try to be out among the birds.

Having read both letters, having wept, Butler saw what he must do. He had a strong feeling that he should write to Jefferson and tell him of his uncle's death. He could too easily imagine John L'Heureux not having done so, being too busy writing prime ministers and the Queen. The letter Butler penned was nothing flowery, just a few sentences giving the date and the circumstances of Red Crow's death—plus his condolences.

But Butler did not post the letter. He felt prevented.

That night he was snappish with Elizabeth and they argued about nothing. He slept badly. In a dream, Red Crow was on horseback coming at Butler with a lance. The Indian's face was painted and hideous. His teeth were bared in a snarl. The scene was theatrical, like the worst of Elizabeth's paintings. Butler woke with a jerk, sweating, pawing the air.

"Are you chasing rabbits?" Elizabeth asked dryly from beside him.

Two more days and nights of this and Butler began to equate his disturbance of mind with the unmailed letter. This was the spirit world at work, and not the benign one depicted at Sunday Mass. This was a message from the darker realm of ghosts and demons known to the Irish, and evidently to the Indians. From the haunted dark, the 'tween-world that is neither living nor dead, Red Crow was grasping at him.

For one more night, Red Crow sat on Butler's chest. The following day, Butler sat down at his desk and threw the first letter away. He wrote a second letter in which he added the death of Jefferson's girlfriend, Ran After, to the news of Red Crow's passing. He sealed the envelope and sent it to Jefferson, care of the Canadian Mounted Rifles in South Africa.

Abruptly, exhaustion entered and overcame him. He lay down on the couch in his office, drew up the blanket, and was instantly asleep.

That was the letter to which Jefferson Davis had replied, and replied only to say that he was grateful to know.

Kleff's Farm

The kopje was about a hundred and fifty feet above the flat. The black rocks on top showed orange where nature had cracked them. Tall plumes of last year's grass waved in the breeze.

Frank had been on this kopje and overlooked this farm before, during Griesbach's "holiday." Frank had told Greasy it looked like a place of ambush and they had moved on.

The white flags were still on the veranda corners, fluttering. The two mules lay flat in the yard, to receive the dawning sun on their bellies. The tall hip of a painted horse showed in the barn door. The barn was built for smaller animals, and the stall in the doorway was the only one in which the stallion would fit.

The horse's hip was chocolate brown with a casting of fist-sized pearls. Lionel Brooke's stallion Century, born of a Nez Perce stallion and a running thoroughbred mare. Whenever Frank's parents had visited Jughandle and Marie Rose Smith, he had asked if he could go down the road to Brooke's and look at this horse. He was unlikely to mistake it for another.

Except for occasional movements of these animals, the farm had remained still since Frank climbed the kopje in moonlight. Now, he heard a door and saw water burst on the ground beyond the house's back corner; a bucket of slops pitched into the morning that made the chickens run. One of the mules briefly reared its head, then let it flop.

Frank continued to wait, and Lionel Brooke came out on the veranda. He walked to the northeast corner, unbuttoned his flies, and pissed a healthy rope off the edge. He rocked while he urinated and stared into the prairie. After he replaced himself and buttoned up, he continued to study the north horizon. That was when Frank began to climb down. Halfway to the bottom, he started shouting: his own name, Brooke's name, those of

Jim Whitford, Young Sam, Pincher Creek, Remi Beauvais, Jughandle, and Marie Rose Smith. Everything he could think of that only someone from Brooke's home locale would know.

Brooke turned and peered through his monocle. He stared at the kopje without alarm and Frank kept coming until he stood before him.

"Morning, Mr. Brooke."

"Frank. I'll be damned."

Lionel led the way inside.

The house was wider and roomier than it appeared from above. One side contained a dining room and sitting room with windows looking west. The other side held the kitchen and bedrooms.

Lionel had guided Frank into a chair at the end of the dining table, a big varnished plank with carved flanks and legs. Lionel sat at the far end, while Young Sam and Jim Whitford were to Frank's left, and Brooke's English friend was to his right.

"Well, well," said Brooke, still squinting at Frank as though at an apparition. "You look like hell, I must say."

"I was in an explosion."

"Good. I mean, good you survived."

Brooke had his fingers knit and was twiddling his long thumbs.

"You know Young Sam and Jimmy. Did I introduce you to Allan Kettle, my school friend?"

"In Pretoria. By Paul Kruger's house."

"I'll introduce our hosts when they're finished making our coffee and breakfast. It's not in our interests to disturb them now."

He tilted his head to the kitchen, from which came sounds of scraping and pouring. Wood thunked into an iron stove.

Frank thought Lionel would want more explanation of his presence and his injuries, and was trying to think how to say it all. But the questions, when they came, were different.

"How's young Fred? Young Morden? Has he been promoted? He told me in Pretoria that he hoped to be."

"Fred's dead."

Brooke slammed back in his chair. His monocle fell. He stared at Frank as if waiting for him to retract the statement.

"Well, that . . . that is a damn shame. His family will be devastated. The whole town will be. How did he die?"

"In battle at Katbosch, north of Kroonstad. They said he was a hero."

"Is there more bad news, then?"

"Robert Kerr died in the same fight. Henry and Tom Miles were in it too. They were wounded. And Ovide Smith . . ."

"Christ, now, you're not going to tell me that Smith's hurt."

"Ovide's dead."

"My God. Same battle?"

"Something different. Not a battle."

"Well, goddamn it."

"That's all."

"All what?"

"All the ones from home who are dead. Reg Redpath had a rupture and was left behind. He got a truss and came back."

Brooke massaged his forehead. He became lost in the activity, then awoke to some other consideration.

"Coffee!" he yelled at the kitchen. "Where the hell is the coffee?"

A Boer woman came in with a heavy pottery jug. Her face was hidden by a bonnet and her dress fit big. When she hoisted the jug to pour into Frank's cup, he briefly saw her arms below the balloon sleeves. They were younger and more slender than he expected. Another woman followed with the cream jar and spoons. When she offered cream to Frank, he saw into her bonnet. She was younger than he was, with large blue eyes and lashes that were almost white. There was nothing kindly in her look.

"This is Mrs. Kleff and her daughter, Alma. Mrs. and Alma? Our visitor's name is Frank."

They paid no attention, and Brooke did not seem to expect them to. To Frank, he added, "They are not prisoners. I pay for the food we eat, and more for their work."

Brooke snapped a look at Allan Kettle, expecting contradiction.

"Allan, here," Brooke gestured a long hand at his friend, "begs to differ."

Allan Kettle turned his dark eyes on Frank. The look was fierce, though he was smiling.

"He does pay them, but that's somewhat different from their being free. We weren't exactly invited. I daresay they will be pleased to see us leave."

Kettle had a smooth voice. Creamy.

"Matter of opinion," said Brooke. "I think the money we give them is a boon. Many Boer women in this war would envy them. I mean, a woman in Mrs. Kleff's situation? Husband dead in the war? However handy she and Alma may be in the garden and fields, they can certainly use the cash."

"But we won't ask them if they consider us a boon, will we?"

"I would if I could."

Brooke had been looking at Kettle. Now he returned his attention to Frank.

"We speak to the Kleffs through Allan. His schoolboy German."

"I've climbed mountains in Switzerland, Germany, and Austria, with German-speaking teams and guides. My German is not *that* schoolboy."

"But it's not *Boer* either, is it? Point is, Frank, there's not much chit-chat goes on between us. That's enough about the Kleffs. You are here for some reason. Sounds like your war's gone bad. Tell us more."

Frank mumbled that he had found the farm and seen Lionel's stallion in the barn during a patrol. But he could not stop. He said he came back, not knowing if they would still be around, but hoping so.

Brooke was staring at Kettle again, as if some satirical remark had been directed at him. Frank took the opportunity to stare at Kettle himself. Brooke's friend was a fine-looking man. Lean-faced, clean-jawed. He looked a bit like an Indian or a Mexican. The eyes had fine age and weather lines all around them.

"You're probably wondering why we *are* still here," said Brooke. "I've had fever. Allan rather blames me for it, because instead of hastening through the low country between Delagoa Bay and the high veldt, I wanted a bit of hunting. The weather was hot and muggy. Steamy rain, bugs, and so on. I've been paying the price since, without benefit of quinine. We didn't get a lion either, though one roared in the night while I was sizzling and wishing I could die. At any rate, I'm better now."

Mrs. Kleff re-entered. She was carrying a full basin from which steam rose and had a towel and washcloth over her shoulder. She set the basin down beside Frank with a clump, rinsed and wrung out the cloth, and started rubbing hard at the hurt parts of his face. She also dabbed into his hair, which caused his headache to worsen.

Brooke watched the process for a while, then spoke.

"Now, Frank, I've noticed you tell us *how* you got here, as in how you found your way, but you're avoiding why. Where is your battalion? Why are you not with it? What does that mess on your head signify?"

Frank saw that he could not avoid the truth. He started by explaining how the shell had exploded beside his Cossack post, the wall blowing in on him, the rocks knocking him out. He described thinking he was blind and had lost an arm, then finding the dead Australian. Taking his horse down the animal trail and starting for here.

"You've deserted!" roared Brooke, slapping the table with the flat of his hand. He folded his torso over the table so his beard was in the steam from his coffee cup. He focused on the sugar dish, chopping a spoon into it until the grains splashed.

Allan Kettle tilted toward Frank. "I'm wondering if you have some amnesia? Do you remember how you felt when you woke up after the explosion?"

Frank understood that Kettle was trying to provide an alibi. "I felt sick. I wanted to leave."

"But do you know why?" Kettle asked. "Does it have to do with the dead men? Your Canadian friends who died earlier. Maybe you weren't thinking clearly."

In panic, Frank realized he was about to cry. He jumped up and ran out the door; ran all the way to the kopje and around it, to where he had tied the ridgling to a tree. The pinto had been jerking the rope and the knot was the size of a walnut. His eyes were red and hostile.

Frank came slowly. He talked while he pried the knot. He told the ridgling what had happened and about the horses he had seen on the farm. He asked the horse how they were going to prevent him from damaging Lionel's stud.

Finally, the fit of tears passed. Embarrassed or not, Frank knew he had to return to the house. He led the ridgling to the buildings and found an empty pole corral behind the barn. When he re-entered the dining room, the others were eating and there was a plate heaped with food beside his cup.

"Your coffee will be cold," said Brooke, waving his fork airily, "but the breakfast is only just served. Chicken eggs. I bet it's some time since you've had a breakfast of those."

Frank sat but did not eat. He had been thinking what to say.

"Ovide Smith was my best friend. My horse, Dunny, was stolen and I want to go find her."

"You do understand that desertion is a court-martial offence." This was Allan Kettle.

"Yes."

"What Allan means is they might execute you if they find you," said Brooke.

"I know."

"You have another choice," said Brooke. "Before your head heals, you can go back. As Allan is hinting, you could claim that your memory went and you lost your way."

"I don't want to."

"Well, then. In a few more days, we'll leave here. My goal is to find Christiaan De Wet. I guess you could come with us. But, if we encounter British army or Canadians—which is probably inevitable—the story will be that we found you wandering with a lump on your head, unable to remember where you came from. If they are not satisfied, or if they ask questions and find you out, all we can do is express shock. You'll be on your own. Does that seem fair? Clear?"

"Fair and clear."

"Then, please. Eat your breakfast."

By the time Frank left the house, the day had begun to warm. Discounting the headache and occasional dizzying nausea, he felt good. Young Sam took charge of him and led him to the horse barn. They climbed the ladder, and Young Sam showed him where his own and Jimmy's bedrolls were spread. Frank rolled out the blanket Mrs. Kleff had given him.

When they came down, Jimmy Whitford was untying horses from the rail and leading them outside. He said they were going to hunt, and that Frank should come. Frank explained that his pinto was a high flanker, and an extreme case. He would likely be fine with Jimmy's mare but might go after Young Sam's gelding—or Century, if he could get at him.

Jimmy considered this for a second, then led his mare and Young Sam's gelding toward the pole corral where the ridgling stood alertly watching. Jimmy led the two horses around the outside of the corral, past the ridgling's nose, three times. Then he opened the pole gate and took the two horses inside, again leading them around out of reach of the ridgling's hooves. The ridgling did not try to kick, just kept moving his head and ears to take them in.

Then Jimmy let his mare go, and she pranced in the middle of the round corral. She was a snuffy horse with a high-and-mighty bearing. She looked at times like she was going to attack the ridgling, but for now it was show. Then Jimmy set Young Sam's gelding loose. He was more timid and kept the mare between him and the new horse.

"You mind if your horse gets bit a little?" Jimmy asked.

"I guess not," said Frank.

"Let him loose, then."

With misgivings, Frank untied the ridgling. The horse did what Frank expected: sweet-talked the mare and threatened the gelding. But the mare kept dodging back and forth, pivoting on her back legs. The ridgling tried harder to get at the gelding, and the mare met the challenge with her teeth. She bit the ridgling twice, drawing blood both times. The second time, he let out a squeal. Retreating to the far side, he pressed himself against the rails.

Jimmy said, "That's it. Saddle him and let's go."

The Kleffs had a well. Frank raised a bucket of cold water and washed the ridgling's wounds. Neither bite was where the saddle or bridle would rub, so he went ahead and tacked him.

Starting into the prairie, Jim went first and Frank last. Young Sam was in the middle. The ridgling was the kind of horse that would ordinarily try to go first. It was unusual to see him in the drag and content. He never once tried to bite the gelding, and his eyes never left the haunches of Whitford's mare.

They rode south onto billowing sheets of prairie, crossed and edged by distant ridges. They saw the blue-gum trees of another farm but bent past it. They saw no animals except the little ones called meerkats, who, like gophers, stand upright by their holes, their forepaws delicately curled to their narrow chests like tiny store clerks.

Whitford aimed them at a low, flat-topped hill, and when he reached a blowout on the near side of it, slid off his mare and tossed the reins to Young Sam. Jim unsheathed his rifle. He pointed at Frank's Mauser, and beckoned him to follow. Together they climbed the cutbank sand. Where the sand met grass at the top, the edge was shaggy. They parted the grass, and Frank could see nothing but more grass and low brush. Whitford poked his rifle through, snake slow, took his time sighting, and shot. Just the once. Then he stood up and climbed over the lip to see what he'd done. He took off quickly across the flat and Frank had to trot to stay with him.

They were almost there by the time Frank saw the grey-brown shape that was not grass but feathers. As it was dying, the ostrich must have tried to get up. One short wing was still raised, with white plumes hanging underneath. The bird's long neck was laid out flat on the ground before it. The beak tightly closed; the eyes staring.

Jimmy handed Frank his still-warm rifle. He grabbed the wing and spilled the giant bird on its back. As the body rose, a treasure of giant eggs appeared.

"A hen, then," said Frank, not wanting to seem ignorant.

"Maybe not," said Whitford. "Both kind sit the eggs."

This begged the question of where the other might be, and, just then, Jimmy yelled, "Look out!" He gave Frank a violent shove and Frank careened and fell. With his carbine raised, Jimmy danced backwards. Frank turned his head and saw a wide-open beak on a whipping neck, a huge body pounding toward him, stubby wings flashing. The rifle fired twice. The beak lost aim and grazed Frank's cheek. Then the body hit him like a freight. The ostrich collapsed on top of him and died.

Frank fought to get his head out of the smother of feathers. His legs were locked down by the bird's weight.

Jim Whitford saw Frank's head emerge and the sight made him sit down laughing. Young Sam found them and, while the horses did their dance of fear at the two corpses, he laughed too. Frank could not see the joke.

"Look like a big chicken, you," Young Sam said.

"Help me out of here, damn you guys."

So they hoisted the ostrich enough to free him, and Frank climbed out and dusted off. He was itchy all over, as if the bird was lousier than he was.

Whitford chopped the heads and necks off both birds. They worked together to raise the first one, the cold-killed one, onto a rock so it could bleed. None of them had dealt with a two-hundred-pound bird before, so they based their plan on a turkey. With a turkey you would bleed it alive, but that was not an option here.

They managed to get five ostrich eggs into their saddlebags and hay sacks. As for the ostriches, they decided to drag them behind their horses. They skated them along on the ground, which worked until the feathers wore off and the exposed skin started to tear. Then they flipped them over and skated them on the other side. That did not last long either, and they were forced to leave one. They tarped the other and packed it on Young Sam's gelding. It took all three of them to lift it and two to hold it while it was tied. Then Young Sam climbed on the mare with Jimmy, and Frank rode the ridgling close and balanced the load. It was amazing to Frank that the ridgling could work so close to Young Sam's gelding and not cause trouble. The pinto was so afraid of Whitford's mare it was now trying to get the gelding's approval: to be an emissary between them.

At the farm, Mrs. Kleff was angry when she saw the maimed ostrich. They guessed it had something to do with the ruination of the feathers or the tearing of the skin. Or maybe it was for bringing an ostrich, when she wanted mutton or antelope.

Same with the eggs. They had foreseen giant omelette breakfasts. But after shaking and listening to the eggs, she threw them on the ground. Evidently they were too advanced for breakfast. The eggs bounded around like polo balls.

Preference aside, the two women were soon scalding and plucking; then rooting out the innards and cutting the bird into parts small enough for the oven. Jimmy took the opportunity to examine the contents of the stomach. The ostrich had been eating an unlikely assortment of things, woody matter included. He found little quartz stones, made smooth by the tumbling action of the bird's gut. The three hunters divided the stones and pocketed them as lucky.

When their horses were rested, they went back for the second bird. They had to drive a family of jackals off it, then cut around the areas where the scavengers had fed. With an axe, they split this bird in half so it could travel on two horses.

Back at the Kleffs', Lionel had a discussion with Mrs. Kleff about the birds. The decision was to eat whatever they could tonight, then make the rest into biltong. After they left, they could live on the dried meat when no fresher food was available.

The actual meal late that night was an anticlimax. There was something slippery about the meat that Frank's mouth did not care for; a raw texture when cooked. Still, he had eaten worse things and had higher hopes for ostrich biltong.

Next morning, the women started preparing the ostriches for the smoker. They got rid of their bonnets and donned old work dresses with shorter sleeves. This was the day Frank fell in love with Alma Kleff, in part because he could see her. Her face was beautiful and full of character for a girl of sixteen. Her arms were strong, and her sure movements with a knife seemed artful and graceful.

Jim and Young Sam were sent to hunt antelope, while Frank was assigned to help with the heavy work in the cutting room and smokehouse. Because Frank was helping Alma, Mrs. Kleff was free to supervise her black servant girls, Little Alma and Tia, in a thorough cleaning of the house. Except for Isaiah, the farm's white-haired servant, who was tending the smokehouse fire, Frank and Alma were alone.

Frank's job was twofold. He had to help Isaiah chop wood and feed the fire and, beyond that, he was to wield the heavy cleaver and cut the ostrich breast and leg meat into slabs. Off these slabs, with her small, keen knife, Alma carved strips that she jerked and folded over the smokehouse racks. The cutting took place in a separate building, one that was in the shade for part of the day. It was supposed to be a cool room, but at this time of year was not cool at all. Whenever Mrs. Kleff put in an appearance, it was to tell them to hurry before the meat spoiled. Sweat poured down both Alma's and Frank's faces as they worked, but even with salt in his eyes, Frank could not help but look at her.

He tried not to stare, because Alma obviously did not like it. But, between one self-admonition and the next, he would forget and find his eyes tracking her every movement.

In the late afternoon, Jimmy and Young Sam brought back a killed sheep for supper. They butchered it in the yard, and the Boer women and black girls prepared it and cooked the meat in an outdoor oven. When the torturing sun went down, it seemed as if the house got hotter, and while they ate the men mopped their faces and drank draught after draught of cool, sweet well-water. Mrs. Kleff brought a lantern, placed it on the table, and lit it for them: a sweet tulip leaf of fire.

The evening meal finished with little pastries, some with icing, some not. Nothing like this had passed Frank's lips for months, and he treasured each morsel. He even closed his eyes in delight, and when he opened them, saw Alma peeking from the kitchen door. She disappeared, and he heard laughter between her and her mother. It was a shocking sound. He had hardly seen either woman smile.

After this dessert, Lionel Brooke went to the bedroom he shared with Allan Kettle and came back with a brandy bottle, half full. He set it on the table and looked in a cabinet where glassware was kept. He returned them with his fingers stuck in five small glasses. He poured a little drop for Young Sam, Jim, and Frank, and larger measures for himself and Kettle. He had two cigars sticking out of his shirt pocket. These he cut for Kettle and himself. He lit a match with a long stroke down his trouser leg.

"How much longer, Lionel?" Kettle asked, puffing his cigar to bright pink life.

"How would I know, Allan? I have not seen a newspaper since Pretoria. What would you have me do? Pick a point on the compass and plunge forth like Don Quixote?"

"So you are waiting for Mr. De Wet to make a house call?"

"Don't nag me, Allan. I will go to Middelburg tomorrow or the next day. I would prefer a less hot day than today. We're nearly out of supplies. Tobacco and brandy are low. I'll take Jimmy. You can come if you like, but if we have no luck with newspapers, we must continue to Pretoria. That could easily stretch to a week. With luck, there'll be something in the papers to suggest where De Wet is. Or, as a reporter, I'll ask around. I'm betting on De Wetsdorp, the village named for his father. As I may have mentioned—"

"You have mentioned it countless times. What rather amuses me is that you came here saying your concern was for black South Africans. Now you've simply reverted to winning the Empire's war, like a good patriotic Englishman."

"That is entirely unfair! Untrue, as well. Britain abolished slavery in the Empire long ago. The blacks in the Boer republics are, in my opinion, still enslaved. The dismantling of the Boer republics will free them."

"Will it?"

The two fell into silence. After a moment, Lionel yanked his cigar from his mouth and waved it as near to Allan as he could reach.

"At least I have an objective," he said. "You strike me as still sitting on the fence."

"I told you at the outset I would make up my mind based on evidence. Because of your leisurely approach, I have mainly learned how Boer *vrouws* keep house. I'm not quite ready to enter into an assassination scheme."

Brooke took frantic puffs at his cigar. He was rewarded with a great plume of smoke that wreathed his head.

"What if you wind up on the Boer side, Kettle? What will you do then? Grow a long beard? Smoke a pipe? Then, after the war, settle down in the veldt growing mealie corn? Maybe with a nice fat frau?"

"Very funny, Lionel."

Just when Frank thought a fist fight might develop, Kettle and Brooke laughed. Lionel leaned forward and poured them more liquor. The two sat back contentedly sipping and smoking.

Taking advantage of the silence, Frank got up his nerve and asked Kettle a question he had been saving.

"Do you really climb mountains?"

"Mostly, I *did* climb mountains. I climb one every once in a while still, but just for fun. No more new summits or famous old climbs. Nothing difficult."

"Allan climbed the Matterhorn," said Brooke, "back when not many had."

Frank's face was blank. Kettle noticed and said, "Swiss mountain, on the Swiss–Italian border. A spire. Looks rather like your Mt. Assiniboine, which no one has conquered yet. Edward Whymper's group were the first to climb the Matterhorn and four men died. That added to the legend. I climbed it later, but it was still a notorious thing to do." Kettle caught himself on some point. "Let's just say there were some who were surprised I could manage it."

"Kettle came out to the ranch to see me," said Brooke. "Said he was looking for a new adventure—a new kind of mountain to climb, as he put it. So I challenged him to come to South Africa. We may not agree on approach, or even on a preferred outcome, but we do agree we're here to make a difference."

Back in the barn, in the dark, Young Sam did imitations.

"Don't *nag* me, Allan."

"Very *funny*, Lionel."

"We are *here* to make a *difference*."

When the barn cooled enough for sleep, Frank lay atop his blankets and worried that Allan Kettle's push for action might actually produce some. He thought of the biltong hanging on the racks: shrinking small, smoking, drying, becoming indestructible. In Frank's head, he could make Alma smile for him. He imagined cradling her work-worn hands in his own rough, wounded mitts. He knew her hands would have sympathy for his, for what work and war had done to them.

"Jimmy, Young Sam, get our horses ready!"

Brooke was shouting up the ladder, though the loft was still dark. Frank remembered that it was the day Lionel, Allan, and Jim were going to Middelburg. As Young Sam and Frank sat up and groped for their boots, they saw that Jimmy was gone.

"Where is he?" asked Frank.

"Don't know. Goes early, sometimes."

Jimmy's horse was in its stall downstairs, and Frank and Young Sam led it out with Brooke's stallion and Kettle's bay. They began to groom the three. The stallion was huffy and posturing, probably because it was excited to be going somewhere after days of idleness. When the breakfast call came, they stood the saddles by the gate and lay the tack on top.

Jimmy was at his place at table. Frank peeked into the kitchen and Young Sam said in a deep, fake voice, "Alma."

Kettle and Brooke entered from the hall, engaged in argument. Both had wet hair, brushed straight back. Kettle was clean-shaven as always.

"Middelburg is *closer*," Brooke was saying emphatically. "We would also excite less suspicion there. Jimmy can stay on the edge of town."

"It's a small town, Lionel, in the middle of nowhere. Why would it have recent British newspapers?"

"Because it has a British camp. Officers live there."

"But why does Jimmy have to come at all?"

"To guide us and protect us. That's what he does."

"Fine, but when we go from Middelburg to Pretoria—after we find out there are no newspapers—why not take the train? Leave our horses in a livery barn. I'm sure journalists don't ride horses *everywhere* they go."

"Churchill does—or if not a horse, a bicycle."

"Winston is a show-off. He'd do handsprings if he thought enough people were watching."

"That's harsh. And why don't you want Jimmy? I thought you liked Jimmy."

"Of course I like Jimmy. I revere him. But the Boers and British treat him like he's black. I don't see why we need to put him through it."

"Oh, very well, we'll take the train, and leave Jimmy behind. But it's not London to Brighton, you know? There'll be permissions needed. Delays. Army red tape."

"All of which you're very good at."

"You don't really think that for a moment. But I won't have some Boer looking after my horse. Jim will have to come as far as Middelburg. If we continue on, he can bring the horses back."

Before they set out, Brooke wanted to leave instructions for Young Sam and Frank. He could not think of much for them to do.

"Make sure the horses, mules, and guns are shipshape. No loose shoes. Rifles cleaned and oiled. When Jimmy returns with the horses, if that happens, do what he tells you."

As the others rode away, Young Sam stood beside Frank.

"Shipshape. No loose shoes. Cleaned and oiled."

Frank's and Young Sam's time in charge was brief. As it was getting dark next evening, Frank saw the white circles on Brooke's stallion juggling in the dark. Jimmy returned leading Century and Allan's bay. No recent English newspapers in Middelburg. Kettle and Brooke had gone to Pretoria. They would return to Middelburg in four days.

In the meat-cutting shed and smokehouse, Alma made faces at Frank that made him laugh. He decided it was progress. Finally, she smiled at him, and the smile he had fashioned for her in his imagination was greatly inferior to the real one.

At mealtimes, watching Frank rally to his slight success, Young Sam teased him without mercy, gawping open-mouthed and swivelling his head as Alma passed. It made Frank wonder whether Alma's mother noticed too. When he put his mind to that, he noticed she was chilly toward him, more so than to the others. She went out of her way to serve him last.

Still with no language between Alma and himself, Frank did not know how to heat up the romance—to get beyond the smiling point. Halfway through the four days of Lionel Brooke's and Allan Kettle's absence, it began to seem hopeless. Weren't his feelings for Alma stupid and overwrought, anyway, when he couldn't even bid her hello or goodbye? He could not even thank her properly when she brought a bucket of water for them to drink in the cutting room.

Frank was peeling the last bits of meat from the rib cage of the second ostrich, as Alma was waiting to cut these bits into strips for the smoker. Most of the meat cut when the birds were large cadavers was biltong already. Frank had tried it and found it edible. It had come down to these last few scraps: the little pile that he now pushed with the cleaver across the wood to the tip of Alma's knife.

She stared at the meat, then turned toward the door. She was looking at how the afternoon sun was pouring a dusty sash over the half-door. When Isaiah stuck his head into that light to ask something, Alma growled and shooed him away. Isaiah held up his pale palms and backed away, but before disappearing, he winked at Frank. Mrs. Kleff, meanwhile, was in the garden with Tia and Little Alma. Frank could hear her urging them up the rows.

They stood on opposite sides of the work table they had shared for days, its surface beaded with pale pink flesh and stained where the cleaver had chopped pink into the surface. Frank's hand on his cleaver and Alma's on her knife were the same colour as the board. Frank saw the instant that Alma's fingers uncurled from her knife's black handle. He released his cleaver, and it toppled off its blade.

Frank swept his eyes up Alma's bloody dress to her face. She was looking at him, at his face. It should have been awkward to be looked at so, but Frank found it wasn't. Her eyes were moving around his face and his hair, and he did the same: studied her almost-white eyebrows and noted that they looked as if they'd been groomed with a tiny comb; a sun-coaxed freckle that altered the surface of her nose; the shelves of her cheeks on which the work sweat gathered. Frank could not remember ever having looked at someone this long from this close.

Alma reached over and touched his sleeve above the elbow, tugged a bit on the rolled cloth. She turned and walked the few feet into the flecked sunbeam. She meant for him to follow and he did.

The sun had made her eyes light up gold. She ran them across his chest and out to the points of his shoulders, then down past the rolled sleeve to the cleaver arm where the veins rode on the outside of the muscle. He looked at the skin just above the square neck of her dress, at the pulse beating in the hollow of her neck. She moved her eyes down his belly to his crotch and studied the fullness there: He looked at her breasts, each one plump, then rode his eyes down the centre of her body. Her hands went behind her and she pulled the bulky pleats tight against herself, her slim form emerging.

Then a shrill cry came from Mrs. Kleff, closer than before. The sound scared them back to the table. In quick flashes, Alma cut the final bit of ostrich meat and took it to the smoker.

Late that night, in his nest of hay and blanket, Frank held nothing back. In his imagination, he took Alma's dress off and made love to her. She enjoyed it very much.

Next morning, in the dusty pre-dawn light, Jim Whitford was yelling up the barn ladder for him and Young Sam to come.

When the two pushed past the horses, stuffing their shirttails, they found Whitford with his rifle levelled at another man. It was a slim, fair-skinned Boer, somewhere around Frank's age. A bandolier crossed his chest. His beard was white-blond and thin. Blue-eyed, innocent looking— even at the wrong end of a rifle, he was smiling and looked calm.

"He was on the hill last night," said Jim. "Says he's their family."

As if on cue, the women ran out of the house. Mrs. Kleff was in the lead with Alma behind her. Mrs. Kleff hugged the young man tightly, crying a little. Then, as Alma hugged the visitor, Mrs. Kleff thrust herself at Jim Whitford. She spoke slowly and harshly, her words spaced, as if that would make Jimmy understand Boer.

Next, the women and the newcomer had a lengthy talk among themselves. The Canadians were not used to hearing so much out of the women, whose words clambered on top of each other. The Boer man drank it in, only interrupting once in a while to ask a question. Then he turned to Jim, Young Sam, and Frank, and spoke to them in good English.

"My aunt and cousin are telling me about you. They say you're English, but I wouldn't have thought you were."

"No questions," Jim Whitford said.

"As you like," said the Boer.

"How come you speak such good English?" Frank asked.

"My family is part English. The grandfather on my father's side. I'm related to the Kleffs through my mother. My name is Denny Straytor." He held out his hand to shake, and Frank was reaching for it when the barrel of Jim's rifle pressed Straytor's arm down. It seemed unnecessarily rude.

"But you're in a commando?" Frank asked.

"I don't deny it. But I still visit my relations."

At this point, Mrs. Kleff told them, through her nephew, that she wanted to take him inside and feed him. Jimmy insisted that Straytor stay outside on the veranda. Mrs. Kleff could feed him there. This dictation of the terms of her hospitality—and from a source not even white—inflamed Mrs. Kleff to rosy heat. She grabbed her dress by the sides and marched for the house. When she arrived on the veranda and found that Alma was not with her, she hurried back, grabbed her daughter's elbow, and towed her inside.

Jimmy directed Straytor to the veranda and pointed to a chair made of woven willow. Then Jim told Young Sam where the Boer's horse was tied on the opposite side of the kopje. He should bring it in, unsaddle it, and tie it in the corral. Whitford sat on the veranda's edge, with his rifle barrel across his thigh so it pointed up at the young Boer's midsection.

Frank was already taken with Denny Straytor. The fellow seemed neither false nor servile. What came off him was an infectious calm that soothed Frank in a way he needed. Because he liked Straytor, Frank was annoyed with Jimmy Whitford for taking such a hard line. Frank had ended his own war by deserting. Allan Kettle was leaning in a pro-Boer direction. Even Brooke was not necessarily in favour of killing low-ranked Boers, having decided to end the conflict by killing De Wet. Given all that, could Straytor even be described as an enemy?

Frank told Jimmy he wanted a private talk. Though Jimmy did not like the request, he handed his rifle to Young Sam when he returned from the horse corral. Jim followed Frank into the veldt a few yards and stopped.

Frank explained his thoughts on Straytor. As the words came out of his mouth, he understood his own stratagem. Just like the ridgling tried to make a friend of Young Sam's gelding, in order to curry favour with Whitford's mare, Frank was making a friend of Denny Straytor to be his advocate with Mrs. Kleff.

Jimmy folded his arms and stood as widely based as his short, bowed legs allowed. His body was frowning as much as his face was. He spat a stream of tobacco juice in the grass, then dug in his pocket and held a fist out to Frank. He rolled it over and opened it, revealing six rifle shells.

Frank did not understand. "I saw his ammunition belt," he said. "I know he's a soldier."

Jimmy shook the hand so the bullets jangled. "Dumdums," he said.

Frank looked more closely. He wasn't sure how you told a dumdum from a normal bullet. A dumdum was a kind of bullet that exploded inside you rather than sailing through, he knew that much—and that their use was illegal in the war. Jeff had said the bullets they dug out of Spence and Ratcliffe were dumdums.

Seeing the stupid look on Frank's face, Whitford set his finger on each bullet's point. Frank saw it then: how they were filed off so the lead core showed. That was what made them split apart when they hit.

"They were in his pocket," Jimmy said. He nodded at the kopje. "He was up there with field glasses all night."

Jim meant that Denny was a spy and intended to harm them, but Frank held back from these conclusions. He would have argued more but Jimmy lost interest, walked back, and took the rifle from Young Sam.

In a few more minutes, Jimmy told Frank and Young Sam to go out and hunt for an antelope and to keep their eyes peeled in case Straytor had friends. Frank said it would be better if Jim and Young Sam went, as Jimmy was more likely to find the antelope, and see the Boers if they were there. Jimmy didn't like the suggestion, but saw the truth in it. Kettle and Brooke would arrive tomorrow, and Lionel would want fresh meat. If there was only ostrich biltong, he would complain.

"I'll hold the gun on him," said Frank. "See what I can get out of him."

"See he don't get more out of you."

—

After Young Sam and Jim had left, riding west, Frank and Denny stayed on the veranda. It was still early in the day and the spot was in the shade. Frank sat on its edge like Jimmy had and let Denny have the willow chair. He had the rifle across his lap but did not point it.

They launched into conversation about the war, and Frank could detect no secrecy or trickery in what Denny was saying. It was just a river of amusing talk.

"You know the pastries Auntie's been making for you? One kind iced, one not? They're called *Smutsies* and *Hertzoggies*. The women invented them to honour two of our Boer generals, the local ones."

When Frank thought about grim-faced Mrs. Kleff baking and serving them this piece of satire every day, he laughed. He remembered how each of them thanked her for the kind treat.

Alma came out and joined them. Mrs. Kleff stayed inside, except to serve them a lunch of sandwiches and a big jug of cool well-water.

"What do Boers think of Canadians?" Frank asked.

"We barely know you exist," said Denny cheerfully. "Your uniforms are so much like British ones. Only the hats make you different. A lot of Boers didn't know about the Canadians, or the Australians and New Zealanders, until Pretoria fell. Even then, we had no idea why you would come so far to fight us."

"How about you?" Frank asked.

"What? You mean, do I understand why you fight us? No, I don't. Turn it around. Would the Boers cross the ocean to fight Canada?"

"Some say we're here to protect the blacks."

"Oh, don't make me laugh," said Straytor, laughing. "Your side sends blacks out with dispatches if it's too dangerous to send your own. They dig your trenches same as they dig ours."

"We don't whip them."

"Don't you? If some Boer hands-upper does the whipping for you, is that better? When your food runs short, you're going to tell me it's not the blacks who go hungry?"

Frank thought of Dakomi, gut shot and bleeding to death while the medic plucked slivers out of the major's side. He did not argue.

"Why are *you* here?" Denny asked Frank, and Frank remembered just in time Jimmy's warning about not giving out more than he got.

"To fight. That's all."

"What's your unit?"

"Can't say."

When Frank fell silent, Alma and Denny filled the gap with a long yap in Boer. Frank saw how readily and excitedly Alma talked to her cousin and felt jealous. Their own familiarity was thin as paper by comparison.

"Actually, I can tell you your battalion," said Denny, when he decided to speak in English again. "Canadian Mounted Rifle."

Frank looked at him in amazement and Denny made a face. "I won't tell you my job either, but recognizing enemy insignia is part of it. Alma tells me you are nice to her, and that your boss here pays them for food and work. That's unusual, no?"

Frank balked again, then decided he could tell Denny Straytor anything Lionel Brooke would tell him if he were present. He said that the two leaders were journalists, and the other two were horse wranglers. No one but Frank was a soldier.

"Pro-Boer or anti-Boer?"

"Pro-Boer horse wranglers?"

Denny smiled at Frank's joke. "The journalists."

"Pro-Boer."

"Are you pro-Boer?"

Frank said no. He told him his official lie. A knock on the head during a battle had left him confused. Made him get lost. He would return to his unit when he found them. He added (because it made it seem more true) that he had been well enough to go for a while, but had been dogging it on account of the good food.

"And the pretty daughter?"

Then Mrs. Kleff came out with dessert. A plate of Hertzoggies. Frank and Denny burst out laughing and she looked hurt. That changed the mood again, and while they ate the pastries and after, they had a more casual conversation that included Alma, via translation by Denny. Frank realized it was the first conversation he'd had with his girlfriend, and he learned several things. He found out that a British unit had threatened to burn the Kleff farm a week before Brooke arrived. It stayed whole because a scout had come and asked for help chasing a Boer patrol.

"What did the scout look like?" Frank asked, and when Denny translated that, Alma made a face and shrugged. It was a dumb question but Frank was entertaining the idea that it might have been Jeff: that Jeff had seen Frank's girlfriend before Frank had.

Frank learned that Alma knew a few words of English, having studied that language from a book in the years before the war. She had not tried them out on Frank because she was embarrassed about her accent. Also, if her mother heard her, she would be angry about Alma cozying up to the enemy.

"So Mrs. Kleff thinks of us as enemies still?"

"Oh yes!" said Denny. "You especially."

As enjoyable as the talk was, Frank had a worsening dilemma. He had forgotten to go to the outhouse before Young Sam and Jim left. Now, after several glasses of water and lunch, his condition was desperate. There were two choices. He could either tell Alma to go inside as he squatted beside the veranda, or he could go to the outhouse. The first option seemed crude under the circumstances so he opted for the outhouse. He took his rifle with him, so he would still in some sense be guarding Denny Straytor.

Frank ran for it, and once settled on the seat, left the door open a crack so he could see the veranda's corner. He finished quickly and ran back, putting his clothes in order as he went. The veranda was empty. The dining room and sitting room were empty. The kitchen door was closed. He banged it open and found Alma at the basin, washing the lunch dishes.

"Where's Denny?"

She would not look at him. Over her shoulder, framed in the tiny window, the ridgling came backing out of the barn, dragging his halter rope. He galloped west. Frank ran outside and saw Mrs. Kleff appear from the dark of the barn. She shook her skirt and walked past him.

Frank went to the horse corral knowing what he would see. The gate open. Straytor's horse gone. Even the mules were hopping west in their hobbles, following the direction of the escape.

Frank ran past the mules, past the house. He made it to the veldt in time to see the ridgling rounding the kopje's edge at a gallop, churning orange dust.

—

Frank made Alma and Mrs. Kleff stay in the sitting room. He sat outside in the willow chair so he could watch the veldt, the rifle across his lap. When Jimmy and Young Sam returned, each with a springbok across his saddle, the sun was not far above the horizon.

When Frank explained how Straytor had got away, Young Sam looked sad and Whitford angry. Mrs. Kleff must have tacked Straytor's horse, then come back to serve them dessert, then returned to the barn to be ready to let the ridgling loose. They had been waiting for their moment, and Frank had provided it by going to the outhouse.

Young Sam looked away to the kopje's top. Whitford spat juice.

Jim was disgusted, and showed it by not allowing Frank to go after his own horse. Jim and Young Sam fed and watered the two cayuses and left again. They rode into the dusk and returned two hours later with the ridgling. The pinto had tramped his halter rope to strings, and was covered in a scurf of sweat, dirt, and burrs. Though tired, he looked pleased with himself.

When Frank led the horse to the water tank, the ridgling bit him, and did so again when he put the feed bag on his nose. After Frank put him in the innermost stall of the barn, the ridgling kicked the wall for an hour.

Lionel Brooke sat at his place at the head of the table with a newspaper obscuring him from view. He snapped the paper often and shuffled the pages back and forth. Smoke was rising from the top of the paper as if it were on fire. Brooke had bought himself a pipe and tobacco in Pretoria and seemed to be making up for lost smoking time. After Brooke had returned with Kettle and Jimmy, he had asked everyone to come for a late lunch so he could catch them up on his plans. So far he had said nothing.

Finally, Allan Kettle slammed a fist down and said, "Lionel, for God's sake. You ask these men to come to the house and you sit there reading the paper in front of them."

Brooke folded the newspaper and set it down. He lifted the pipe from his mouth. "Sorry. Had to check some details."

He pulled a map out of his breast pocket and flattened it on the table's surface. Frank could see Transvaal, Orange Free State, and Cape Colony marked in big print. Brooke spun the map around to the others.

"On November 6, General Knox's army caught De Wet napping. The Orange Free State president Steyn was camped there too. Lt.-Col. Le Gallais came within an ace of capturing De Wet and Steyn, but both got away."

Brooke stabbed the map with his finger, just south of the Vaal River.

"Right here. At Bothaville. De Wet lost six Krupp guns."

Brooke dragged his thumb slowly south from Bothaville to a spot east and south of Bloemfontein.

"De Wet and Steyn took to their horses and went south. They crossed the middle veldt to a village east of Bloemfontein. There, they surprised a British garrison and took four hundred prisoners. That was November 23. The name of the town? De Wetsdorp! Remember when I told you we should go there? That De Wet would not be able to stand having a town named for his father in British hands?"

Brooke continued creeping the thumb south, driving the nail into the map so that a thin, visible trail led to the Orange River.

"The latest paper we were able to buy, the one I was just reading, suggests that De Wet went to the Cape Colony after that." The thumbnail creased over the Orange River and invaded the Cape.

"But what do you mean, Lionel?" Kettle drawled.

"What do you mean, *mean?*"

"Mean for us. You're implying some big action involving us but you're not saying what it is."

"Have you no sense of drama?"

"Please."

"We must go south. With the biltong smoked and the horses in good fettle, I think we could go as soon as tomorrow."

Frank's heart rose in his chest and choked him.

"South is a little imprecise as a plan," Kettle challenged.

"De Wetsdorp. How's that for precise? My hunch is De Wet will fail in the Cape. He will be forced to return to his own country. Somewhere he feels safe. The town of his father. We will be waiting."

Brooke's thumb had retraced its line to De Wetsdorp.

"Or, if I'm wrong and he does succeed in the Cape, or escapes to some other place, we will keep chasing him."

After that, the talk was about horses. Each horse was discussed in turn. When they got to the ridgling, Jim said it had a loose shoe, right front.

Must have caught it on a root during its escape. When Brooke wound the meeting up, he asked Frank if they could talk privately.

The talk turned into a walk. Brooke's stride was so long and quick that Frank had to put a little trot in his step to stay even. The sun was blinking off Brooke's monocle like a heliograph.

"Would you like to travel with us, tomorrow?" Brooke asked.

"I don't think so, thank you."

"You've changed your mind, then?"

"I think I should stay and guard the women. The British were here before and almost burned them out. It could happen again."

Brooke raised his eyebrows and the monocle fell. He caught it expertly.

"You're deluded, my boy."

"What?"

"Deluded. I have observed your infatuation with Miss Alma. I wasn't trying to spy but it's hard not to notice. Do you imagine that Mrs. Kleff would let you stay for one moment, without my being here with money for your keep?"

Frank tried to think of an argument. He wasn't sure there was one.

"No, son, you must come with us—or go back and try to find your unit before it embarks for Canada. That's probably best. That was the other news I meant to tell you. In one of the papers, it said the Canadian mounted infantry battalions were at Irene waiting for a train to Cape Town. They'll sail before Christmas. You could probably still tell your amnesia story. We could mess up the scab on your head."

"I don't want to go back."

"Not interested in going home?"

The way he said it stabbed Frank. The truth was, if there *was* a truth, Frank had lost too many things here. He wanted his horse. He wanted Alma. Wherever Jeff was now, he was trying to fix things so he could have a wife when he got home. Frank was doing the same.

"So what will it be, Frank? You want to go with us, or you don't?"

"If I can't stay here, I'll go with you."

"Tell you what then. Get your mad horse shod properly. I'm asking Mrs. Kleff and Alma to join us for dinner, as it's our last night. You can try to convince the missus that she needs you. Plight your troth. If you win her over, so be it. If not, your horse is ready to travel. Fair?"

Obviously, it was fair—so fair that Frank could no longer justify holding back the truth about Denny Straytor's escape. Brooke had already started for the house, but Frank ran and held his sleeve. He got through the story as fast as he could, but spared no detail about his own stupidity.

"And Jimmy did not tell me."

Frank flushed. It hadn't occurred to him that his disclosure would betray Jimmy's silence. Nor had it occurred to him that Jimmy would be silent to protect him.

"Don't worry about that," said Lionel, reading his face. "If he's keeping it from me, he probably has a reason. Jim has a theory, you know, that *Mister* Kleff is not dead. Whether or not this Straytor was a cousin, he was probably sent by the father to check on things."

"Do you still want me along?" Frank asked.

"I'm not the least troubled by your having taken a shit when you shouldn't have. I'm amazed, though, that you would consider staying for a girlfriend who betrayed you."

Frank looked at a plume of grass by his foot. By his mother's code, Alma choosing her family or her kind over a new boyfriend was entirely the right thing to do. But, by either Brooke's logic or Madeleine's, there did not seem to be much hope of convincing Mrs. Kleff.

The horses were in the barn, happily eating. Young Sam had scythed them a manger full of cured grass. In his tender mood, Frank could not imagine pulling the horses out of that happy situation so he could get at the ridgling. Instead, he took his shoeing box behind them to the ridgling's manger position, against the barn's far wall.

As Frank passed behind the ridgling, the horse flashed a china eye. He was scrunching a mouthful of grass that stuck out the corner of his lips, going round and round. He kept his feet on the floor.

The ridgling's right front shoe was closest to the manger and the wall. It was dark as a pit there. Frank found a dried knot in a board and clubbed it with the shoeing hammer until it fell out. A little braid of light spurted in, shining on the hair-oiled rail.

He slid his hand down the cannon bone; talked to the ridgling and tapped until the pinto took the weight off. Frank squeezed his thighs to make a lap and set the knuckled joint there. He cleaned the frog and pushed against its sponginess. He knew from the horse's lack of interest that there was no pain. The ridgling had not hurt himself when he'd snagged the root. Frank wiggled the shoe, saw which nail had pulled. He set the foot down, knelt, and studied where a new nail could go.

Through the wickets of the other horses' legs and below their bellies, he saw a change in the light and knew someone else was in the barn. He squinted into the gloom and saw the hem of Alma's skirt. He stood and warned her that the ridgling was dangerous. She spoke to the horse, who flicked an ear back to listen and let her pass.

Frank had the shoe nail in his fingers and the hammer in his hand. The light was spooling onto the hammer hand, and Alma looked there rather than at his face. The two were in the narrow squeeze between the ridgling's hot side and the barn wall. She pointed at the hammer and down at the hoof.

Frank knelt again, facing away from her. He found his spot, set the nail, tapped. Alma pushed the ridgling's hip to make more space, bracing her leg against Frank's back for purchase. He tapped until the nail was seated, then drove it home. The ridgling stopped chewing briefly.

Frank left the hammer on the floor and stood. He turned and she was in front of him, her face inches away in shadow. She came closer and printed the full length of herself onto him, the softness of her breasts, the roundness of her belly. Her thighs on his thighs. He reached his arm around her and pulled her tighter to him. Kissed her open lips. The click of teeth.

They could have started opening buttons, raising her skirts. Frank guessed they did not because her mother was not far away and that still mattered.

It ended when Alma's name was shouted from the direction of the house. She pulled back and said in English, "I am sorry."

She slid behind the ridgling, who grumbled at her leaving. Frank squatted and watched her feet pass behind the other horses' legs. There was a bucket of sand inside the door where last year's carrots were buried. She plunged her hand in and dug around, came up with a rubbery few, and left.

That night's celebration dinner was anointed by a special brandy Brooke had bought from a bootlegger in Pretoria. Mrs. and Alma Kleff had one sip each and let the rest sit in their glasses. Maybe they did not care for it, or, more probably, the mother wanted them to demonstrate their resistance.

Alma's face was already red from crying and new tears ran down her cheeks. When this happened, her mother shoved a cloth napkin onto her daughter's lap.

A confrontation and argument must have occurred, probably as soon as Alma entered the house with the carrots. The law had been laid down, and something in it, something just beyond the deducible facts, told Frank that there *was* a living father as Jimmy thought, probably a tyrant from whose wrath the mother was trying to protect Alma.

Frank knew that he would have to leave tomorrow.

Orange Free State

They stopped in a north–south swale of green to let the horses piss, the riders standing off their saddles and leaning forward to free the kidneys. Brooke was studying his compass to make sure the heading was still south. Jimmy left and went ahead because the low spot ended in a rise over which they could not see. The country was empty except for an occasional deserted farm. Even these they stayed away from.

Brooke came to Frank while they waited on Jimmy, and indicated that he wanted a private talk. When they had ridden far enough away, Brooke turned Century so he faced the ridgling.

"There's something you should know," he said, "if you're going with us." He picked at a loose sprig of leather on his saddle horn's wrap. "You'll think this an odd statement, but Allan Kettle is a woman. Alice Kettle, all right?"

Frank could not help but twist his head and look at Kettle. It looked like Allan, same as always.

"You're joking."

"Actually, I seldom joke. Everything else I've told you is more or less true. Alice was a university friend, if not quite a childhood one. She did do all that mountain climbing. She was one of the first women up the Matterhorn."

"But why?"

"Why masquerade as a man? Her contention is that if she were travelling here as a female, both the Boers and the British would treat her differently. I agreed from the outset to go along with it. Even this conversation is with her permission. We did not tell you earlier because we didn't know if you would stay. If you were going back, it was better you didn't know."

"Jimmy and Young Sam know?"

"Of course."

Whitford was returning from beyond the ridge. Halfway back, he stopped and signalled them to come. Moving again, Frank tried not to be obvious about Kettle. But he had to look sometimes. Once, she caught him and smiled. It was a woman's smile, and he could see that the consistently clean-shaven look should have been a giveaway. But there was no sense thinking like that. Whatever had not been obvious suddenly was, and reason didn't enter into it.

They rode all morning and into the afternoon, and came to a creek bending through a shallow coulee on its final descent to the Vaal. Brooke decided to water there and rest, while Jim Whitford went ahead to find a drift by which they could cross in the night. Lionel said they should eat biltong and Smutsies, then sleep.

The day was hot and moist because of the nearness of the big river. Lionel had paid Mrs. Kleff for Frank's blanket and Frank lay on it now, staring at the sky that had been pale all day but was now darker and rimmed with cloud. He was beside the pinto, who was knee-haltered away from the other horses. The ridgling's ambitions had been stirred when Mrs. Kleff let him out of the barn. He was after Young Sam's gelding again.

Alone, Frank looked hard at his mind's image of Alma. He was so far away in that study he did not see Alice Kettle coming until she sat down on his blanket's edge. Frank had not entirely surrendered the idea of her as a man, so it felt strange when she took his hand and laced their fingers, then set their hands on her strong climber's thigh.

"There'll be other girls, you know," she said.

"I don't want any."

"In any case, there will be, and you'll feel better then."

She gave their hands a knock on her leg, then wiggled her fingers free. She rose and walked back to her bedroll, a place denoted by Brooke's pipe smoke. Frank thought about the nights of Brooke and Kettle sharing a bedroom at Kleffs'. He wondered whether they were lovers.

He also thought about what Alice had said. She was trying to be kind but he saw the situation differently. He had already tried to think of Alma as gone, but something in him, something with a claw, would not let go. Frank was certain he would see Alma Kleff again.

De Wetsdorp

There was nothing fast about their move south. The night Jim Whitford led them to the Vaal, it was full of a British convoy crossing. The moon showed the procession of wagons into the river, rocking their way across. The teamsters' yells and whip cracks echoed in the night chill.

Next morning, it was the same. Black drivers led the oxen back into the river, to pull the wagons that were stuck. Among these were the ones carrying guns. One-eyed cow guns stared at the heavens.

It took three days for the river to empty, and not until the last night was it safe for Brooke's band to cross. The spring rains were still running off the land, and the river went over the backs of the horses and wet the mules to the tops of their packs.

After the Vaal, it was still slow, never because of the Boers but because the British had garrisoned so many towns and villages, and travelled so many roads.

The worry had been that Frank would be apprehended as a deserter, but most of these troops barely looked at them. When Lionel was called upon to explain his crew, he blathered on about being a reporter and they soon lost interest. One British lieutenant asked why there was a man in khaki among them, but he listened to Frank's story only as far as his saying he was a Canadian Mounted Rifle. The lieutenant butted in.

"Christ, man! You had better get to a railway station. Your lot are leaving."

Twice, they surprised lone-riding colonial soldiers, who said they were dispatch riders but did not look it. It gave Frank a chance to see how other deserters presented themselves; what kind of porous stories they told. If you multiplied these encounters by the size of South Africa, it implied there were hundreds like him, wandering around with cases of amnesia and claims of having been released from Boer custody only yesterday.

Brooke's crew moved west far enough to see the railroad tracks. They stayed until they had watched two trains go by, both southbound with soldiers on top and hanging on the sides.

"Headed for the Cape," Brooke said confidently. He was happy because he believed these were trainloads of soldiers sent to flush De Wet out of the Cape Colony and drive him back north. Brooke no longer thought De Wet would come to him at De Wetsdorp for assassination or capture; he believed it without question.

In the Orange Free State, the path they followed was Frank's war in reverse. Kroonstad, where Jeff had left them the first time. Honing Spruit and Katbosch, where Morden and Kerr had been killed. The Vet River, where a motion in some reeds gone still might have been the only Boer Frank had shot. Farther south, they saw the chain of big hills around Bloemfontein.

East of Bloemfontein was a west–east line of British forts. They avoided them by staying north. Every night, Jimmy looked for a way to cross, but came back talking about more forts and outposts, and massed armies. Brooke believed it was a buildup to prevent De Wet from getting back into the northern Free State.

The closer they came to the town of Thaba Nchu, the more the country rose and broke into small erosion-fluted mountains. Finally, Whitford advised Brooke to forget about passing this road in secret and to start thinking how to do so in daylight. Brooke regarded this as "unsporting" but knew Jimmy would not insist if it could be done otherwise. He allowed Jimmy to guide them to a fort called Springhaan's Nek.

Brooke managed to talk in private with the officer in charge. They soon found an old country link between them. That led to heavy drinking, the result of which was an escorted passage. The sergeant who led them through was a British man who had lived his adult life in Cape Town. He told them that the country beyond was dangerous: a place that might show as British on a general's map but was Boer if push came to shove.

As they were about to leave him, the sergeant pointed at Jim and Young Sam.

"The rebels will kill your niggers."

Brooke bristled. "These men are not blacks. They are North American Indians."

The sergeant's head made a tick-tock motion, a gesture to convey that it would make no difference to a Boer, and probably not to him either.

They travelled south-southwest, along the western shore of the boiling Caledon River. Beyond it to the east were little mountains that they'd been told led to bigger ones, and eventually into the mountain stronghold of the Basuto people. Everything on the far side of the Caledon was Basutoland. On their right, west, the broken country tamed quickly into Boer farmland where mealie stands and barley crops were tall and turning yellow.

Jimmy shot some tiny antelope off the rough slopes, ones who were not babies but adults of a pygmy breed. Their roasts and steaks were so small it was humorous, but the meat was a relief from biltong. Brooke broke out his last bottle of brandy to celebrate. After this bottle, an alcohol drought threatened, which Lionel faced grimly.

Finally, De Wetsdorp came in sight down the two-track road. They went close enough to see it was not much of a town: a church with a space for turning ox teams; a few gable-ended houses. It looked like the British had not re-garrisoned after De Wet's victory in November. Nor was there a laager to suggest it was in the hands of Boer rebels.

They discussed where to camp, and Jimmy left to search for a spot. He rode back after an hour and led them up a muddy crag with a notch below its peak. The notch looked like a shadow until they were there. Then a cave began to show. Old-time Africans had lived here and painted animals on the walls in red. The pictures showed men with spears, giving chase. The roof that jutted over the partial cave was still black from their fires.

Jimmy had done very well to find this. Its deepest part would stay shady all day, and they could see for miles, including the dorp and its surrounding farms. Up top was a place for the mules and horses to graze or be hobbled. Most important, it had water: a seep that dripped down a dark face in the deepest shadow. It took a minute for a cup to fill but no one would go thirsty.

Brooke grumbled that he would have preferred something south of town, as that was the direction from which De Wet would come. Whitford ignored him.

They established this camp in early December and settled in for a longish stay. With nothing to do, they watched cloud shadows march across the valleys and sheets of rain that cooled the baking croplands. It was a drowsy time and they seldom talked, nor moved unless it was necessary. On the night-cooled rocks, they lived like lizards in reverse, moving deeper into the cut to avoid the sun.

When they needed food, Jimmy went with Young Sam. What the English sergeant said about niggers seemed to have affected Jimmy's tactics, for he stayed in the broken country of which this crag was the western edge. He strictly avoided the Boer farmland. They brought back more pygmy antelope but never touched a farmer's sheep or goat, even if these wandered close and seemed unprotected.

The only disruption in these calm days was when Brooke argued with Jimmy about fire. Brooke pined for fire in this ancient notch, but Jimmy said it would be foolish. He had been careful to bring them here so that no one saw or followed. As long as they made no fire, they would remain invisible and could stay and watch for as long as it took. Brooke was disappointed.

When the light came in enough to see the walls, Frank looked at the drawings. He wondered if the herds of big antelope were what the painters actually saw on the plain, or if it was a kind of magic thinking by which they hoped to lure them. The voice of Madeleine in his head instructed him to consider whose country it was all these whites were fighting over. That made Frank think of Dakomi, or some ancestor of his, sitting where Jimmy liked to sit on the rock lip. He wondered what kind of thoughts such a man would have.

After more than a week had passed, Lionel tired of the routine and declared it time for the journalists to work. By work, he meant going to De Wetsdorp to interview locals. Because of her German, Alice had to go along.

Jim Whitford insisted on taking them north, rather than directly to the village. After several miles, they swung northwest down a bushy coulee that met the road that came from Springhaan's Nek. By joining the road and going to the village by it, they would look like travellers from the British forts. During the day, Jim would hide himself and the horses, watching for their return.

When Brooke, Kettle, and Jim Whitford returned to camp that evening, the ground was dark but the sky was pale near the place of sunset. Brooke was in bad temper and drinking from a bottle of colourless liquor he'd bought in town. Though he seemed inclined to quarrel with Alice, she was the one he invited to drink with him.

Brooke was after Jim again to build him a fire, but Jim would not answer. He went to his place on the rock lip and sat on his heels, watching the dark.

After Whitford left him, Brooke turned his harangue on Young Sam and Frank. Lacking Jimmy's force and status, the two were finally worn down and did as they were told. They gathered a pile of sticks and set them ablaze. The smoke curled around the rock roof by its ancient pathway.

Brooke and Kettle began to argue. They had gone into De Wetsdorp under a white flag and, to everyone he addressed, Brooke had shown his letter from the English newspaper. No matter what he did, Lionel was treated like a spy. Two Boers went as far as threatening him if he did not leave. It only got worse when he mentioned Christiaan De Wet. They claimed that no De Wets lived there at present. Nor did they know anything about the family.

"No De Wets in De Wetsdorp. Do they think I'm an idiot?"

"That was no excuse for what you did," Alice said.

"Oh, Christ, not this again."

To the others, she said, "He went to a farm just outside of town. The woman there looked half starved, and so did her children. Lionel dangles a strip of biltong in their faces and says, 'De Wet? De Wet?'"

"So what does she do?" Lionel asked them. "This old friend of mine?" Brooke pointed to a bruise on his cheek. "Punched me. Blind side. Ambush."

"You were being a brute. You deserved it."

Brooke was getting drunker all the while. Young Sam brought an armload of sticks and Lionel threw them on the fire.

"Yes indeed, let's *get* captured, if that's how they want to play."

"Go right ahead, Lionel. Risk our lives over your little disappointment."

"How could we be more at risk than you and I were in their town today?"

"That's ridiculous logic. You're being an absolute ass."

"*You* are being melodramatic."

"*You* had better not tell me what to do or how to be. You can order Young Sam and Frank around—they're too young to tell you to go to hell. It does not work on me."

"Why don't you go then, *Alice*? Go on. Right now. Jump on your horse and go to De Wetsdorp and join a commando. Also, I would remind you of the terms of our being here. Jim and Young Sam are not slaves. They are my partners. Equals, just as you are."

"What horseshit you talk, Lionel. One of your *partners* explained to you why this fire is stupid. But you went ahead and forced the others to light it. You're making *your partners*, so called, take this risk without discussion. I've climbed mountains with your kind. Germans who said we were equals, then told me what route to take. Bloody men. Bloody tyrants."

Brooke took another large drink. The bottle was almost empty. He sucked on his pipe like a starved infant and muttered to himself. Whenever the fire died down he roared for more wood. The others withdrew to their bedrolls and slept. It was Frank's turn to go above and sleep near the horses. The sparks were still rising past the stone roof when his eyelids grew heavy and closed.

A whooshing sound woke him, and he saw a sudden cloud of sparks passing the rock roof. The horses were agitated behind him, and the mules were moving in their hobbles. He sat up straight and something knocked his head, something metal. It knocked again and a hand grabbed him and ground into the muscle between his neck and shoulder. Whoever stood behind him showed him the broomhandle pistol's long barrel, then tapped his head with it a third time.

"Op-staan," the Boer said as he grabbed Frank's jacket and jerked him to his feet. The Boer pushed him to the path that led down to the notch. Maybe a dozen Boers were crowded there.

Brooke, Kettle, and Young Sam were sitting on a long rock before the fire. The Boer pushed Frank down at the far end beside Young Sam. Each of them was guarded by a Boer. When Frank saw that Jimmy was not present, he felt a release. Jimmy was out in this darkness with his rifle and pistol.

Beside Frank, Young Sam was rigid and wide-eyed. His eyes darted at every movement. Alice, who had managed to clap on her hat and transform back into a man, sat with her elbows on her knees, slowly rubbing her hands. Brooke, at the far end, was the least at ease. His eyesight, never good, was worse at night. Now, without his monocle, he squinted and his eyes watered.

A young Boer arrived with wood. When the fire was built up again, Frank had a better view of two older Boers sitting on a bulge of rock beyond the fire. Beyond them, another older Boer, a stout farmer, marched back and forth, into and out of the light, looking furious.

Of the sitting pair, the closest to Brooke was tall and starved-looking. He had his hat off and was rubbing and scratching in the wiry hair above his big ears. The rest of his peaked and bony head was bald. The face was like a skull, the eyes deep in their sockets. A living cadaver.

The man beside the cadaver had a squarish head and black beady eyes. He squinted out through slanted eyelids that gave him a sad appearance. His beard was cut short and square.

Frank decided the latter man was the true leader. The cadaver's trousers were made of animal hide with tears at every seam. His shirt was some kind of greasy skin as well. The leader had a jacket of good wool and heavy breeches that funnelled into tight boots. His hat was not the usual formless bowl but a town hat with a narrow brim and a short flat crown. Everything was filthy from riding, but you could see the quality.

The leader stared at the fire and barely bothered to look at them. Now, he groped inside his jacket and brought out a pipe and tobacco pouch. The pipe was the curled kind, with a broad bowl rimmed in copper. He hooked the horn mouthpiece in his lips while he stuffed and lit it.

"May I smoke as well?" asked Brooke.

The leader froze. He looked at Lionel as though he had only just noticed him. Brooke pointed at the pipe and mimed putting it in his mouth; pointed at his bedroll. The Boer said, "No," his voice deep and harsh.

Lionel had wanted to smoke to establish his seniority. Denied, he began to talk in a forceful way. He told the story about the newspaper in England. He called Jimmy and Young Sam his crew and Allan Kettle his partner.

Then the cadaverous Boer started talking too, in English.

"We already know your story from the people in the village. What we want to know is why you are asking about Christiaan De Wet."

Brooke squinted past the one who was talking to the one with the pipe. Lionel became excited and pointed.

"You're he! You're Christiaan De Wet!"

The cadaverous Boer half rose and slapped Brooke hard across the face.

"You shut up. You never mind who we are. Now answer me why."

"No one sent me, if that's what you mean," said Brooke, petulant and shaken by the blow. "I wanted to meet General De Wet to interview him for my newspaper. A pro-Boer newspaper."

The cadaver grumbled something in Boer and the leader laughed. When the bald one turned to Brooke again, that laugh remained as a snarl.

"To us, there is no such thing as pro-Boer. Except if the wind is pro-Boer. Or your mules are. Or your generals, especially Kitchener. But don't tell me about pro-Boers in England."

"I'm telling you the truth."

He looked like he might slap Lionel again but did not.

The other, the one who might be De Wet, said a few words to the cadaver, shrugged, and got up. He turned and walked away to where the horses were. The cadaver rose and followed. There was low talk in the dark, then the sounds of men mounting up, and of horses having trouble with their footing on the rocks. The sounds diminished as the party left.

When the cadaverous Boer returned and sat, Lionel asked him again if the man now gone was De Wet. The bald man paid no attention.

"Get your things. If we missed any of your weapons, give them to me stock-first."

Before they left, Brooke found his monocle and put it back in his eye. Carrying a torch, a Boer led them to their horses and mules and told them to put on halters. Jimmy's horse was there and the mystery of his absence deepened. The ridgling, who could have done some useful damage for once, was fearful and obedient.

The horses, mules, and prisoners were led down to a lower shelf where the rest of the Boer horses waited. There, the Boers tied Frank's hands in front of him. Two men picked him up and put him on the bare back of a pony. He wondered why there was such a long tail on the rope around his hands, but then they tied it around the horse's neck. They were making it so he could not roll off without getting trampled.

By the lit torch, he could see that the others were on horses and tied the same way.

He heard Brooke say he needed a saddle or his back would be injured. The cadaver told him to shut up. Each prisoner's horse was led by one Boer. Their own horses and mules were dispersed in the chain of riders.

They rode steady until they came to the Caledon River. Even though it was boiling with runoff, they crossed in the dark. Frank had nothing to hang on to but the pony's mane. The water slashed his face, and each time it startled him, for he could not see it coming. He was coughing water when the pony climbed out the other side. Frank worried about Brooke but saw his tall shape come ripping out of the current on the back of a little horse. Something was hurting Brooke badly and he yelled each time the horse lunged.

Soaking wet, they climbed mountain trails where the wind bent around the rock edges and chilled them deep. Whenever the trail became wider, the leaders boosted the gait and the wet riders were colder still. The Boer pony's chopping trot, and his own effort to stay balanced, gave Frank a gut wrench. Brooke was hunched forward and silent.

Finally, the tall horizon was haloed with coming light. It was enough to show them the mountains they rode among. When the morning took on colour, the valley was orange-yellow, the clothed slopes a smoky green.

Now that Frank could see them all, the Boers numbered seventeen, including the cadaver, whose bald ugliness was hidden under a slouch hat. Other than the cadaver and the stout farmer, the rest were young men. A half-dozen were boys as young as nine or ten.

The procession descended and came to a little creek toward which the horses yearned. The Boers would not let them drink, and only when the sun came over the mountains in a burst of heat were they allowed. While the horses drank greedily, the cadaver ordered his two biggest soldiers to dismount. They began to pluck the captives off their horses. When they had them on the ground, the two went back along the line and untied their hands. Frank's were dark and the rope's groove on his wrists looked permanent.

Brooke could only stand crookedly, and the cadaver came to him with a nasty smile.

"And now we will have Christmas. You will give me your clothes, and I will give you mine." Then, to the others: "All of you. Clothes off."

No one moved. The cadaver had already pulled his own skin shirt over his head. He threw it at Brooke's feet. He was all ropes of muscle and seams of scar.

Seeing they had done nothing, the cadaver snarled at Brooke.

"Listen, old man. If you don't take off your clothes, I'll take them off my way. After, I will club you and your friends like dogs."

Brooke's pain was great and his eyes had glazed with it. Alice had to help him out of his shirt and trousers. As Frank stripped, he could not help but look at Alice, wondering what she would do. She gave him a wink, then quickly undid her shirt buttons. Beneath the shirt was a tight undershirt that squashed her small breasts flat. She started on her trousers.

The cadaver did not notice because he was watching Young Sam. When the boy undid his shirt cuffs, the cadaver signalled to a soldier who grabbed the boy's arms and stopped him.

"Nobody wants your clothes, kaffir," the cadaver said.

Then he glanced at Alice and saw she was still in her undershirt and smalls. "Go on. Get it all off. And your boots."

While the cadaver watched, Alice crossed her arms and hoisted the undershirt. The cadaver gaped, swore a Boer oath, and spun around. Some of the others were laughing to see this man now standing there a woman. The cadaver looked sideways at Brooke and spat in his direction.

"You are a fool. You bring niggers to this war? And a woman? Tell her to put her clothes back on. There are children here."

Alice put the undershirt and shirt back on. The boys looked embarrassed but kept staring. Brooke was fully naked now. He looked very old and ill. He could not straighten and, besides stooping, had to lower one shoulder to loose some cord that was hitched wrong in his back. He had crushed mats of white hair on his shoulders and across his scrawny chest. His body was the colour of paper.

The cadaver walked over to Frank, who was naked and cupping his pecker and balls.

"We know about you because a Mr. Kleff followed you south. He lost you for a while until you helpfully lit a fire at night. He would like to speak to you."

The cadaver backed away and the stout farmer rushed forward. He reared and spat, and the bullet of phlegm hung on Frank's cheek. The farmer brought his face even closer and roared in Boer. Finally, he punched Frank awkwardly in the face, stalked off, and stood with his back to him.

The cadaver returned, looking amused. "What my friend tells you does our language proud. I wish I had the English to translate it correctly. What he says is you must stay away from his daughter or he'll cut off your balls. He would do so right now, except you are a white prisoner, and it's against our rules. If you disobey about his daughter, he will do it anyway."

Then the cadaver moved on to Young Sam. The two Boers who had pulled the prisoners from the horses stood beside him. The cadaver nodded upstream to a knot of willows.

Brooke forced himself straight with a yell. Standing to attention, he took a step toward the cadaver. The man behind him reached forward and grabbed his bushy hair; stopped him from going closer.

"There is a misunderstanding," said Brooke. "That young man is not what you call a black or a nigger or a kaffir. He is a North American Indian of the Nez Perce tribe. They are mountain people and famed horse breeders. That spotted stallion of mine was sired by one of their studs."

The cadaver nodded again, and the two Boers took Young Sam by the arms and walked him up the path.

When Alice and Frank started after them, their Boer guards barred their way. Alice threw her man aside and ran. The Boer chased her, and drove the stock of his gun into the middle of her back. She fell and he jammed the rifle's mouth against her head. The one guarding Frank turned his rifle around and drove the butt into his throat. Frank fell to his knees, unable to breath.

Young Sam fought the two who were dragging him. He hit one hard in the middle of the face. Then the two together threw him on the ground. They tied his hands, then picked him up like a bag of sticks. They carried him behind the screen of green-leafed willows.

"You can't do this!" Brooke yelled. "It is against the rules of war. This man is in no way your enemy."

"Save your breath, old man. You are a spy. I know one when I see one. I know a nigger when I see one too."

"I tell you, he's an Indian."

"The Basutos in these mountains are horse breeders but they're still niggers. If they help you British, we shoot them like dogs."

There were two shots and the sound echoed off the cliffs.

The leader of the Boers removed his ragged trousers and threw them toward Brooke. He picked up Brooke's shirt and put it on, then his trousers. He rolled up the legs and the sleeves to fit. Finally, he took off the crude leather flaps he wore as shoes and drew on Brooke's tall boots.

The cadaver was too thin for the clothes but strutted like a dandy. He got Frank's attention and pointed upstream to where the two gunmen were coming out of the trees.

"You'll find your new clothes up there," he said, and laughed.

Alice had already started in the direction of the willows. No one stopped her now. The Boers were mounting to leave. The cadaver shifted his saddle and bridle onto Century. The stallion flattened his ears at the foreign taste and shape of the bit.

Brooke shuffled forward until he was near his stallion's head.

"I will report this murder and theft at the first opportunity. I would like to name the man responsible."

"You say that," said the cadaver, "yet you don't expect me to tell you. But I will tell you, because I am proud of myself and what I do. Go tell your British authorities that Piet Von Roster killed a Half-Black and see how much they care. Another thing. If you see your old nigger before I do, tell him I will kill him too."

Then the cadaver dug his heels into Century's sides and jerked the stallion's mouth. He walked the horse to the packed mules and slid a short-handled spade from under the hitch ropes. He dropped it on the ground. He was about to go but had one more thought. He went to Alice Kettle's horse and untied her bedroll from its saddle. This, too, he dropped on the trail as he left.

Riding high on Century, the cadaver joined the procession near its end, followed into line by a boy of nine who might have been his son. Of the humans, only this boy looked back. Halfway up the line, the ridgling danced sideways and looked at Frank with one china eye.

Not far from the place of murder, the valley was joined by another with a stronger stream of water. This creek came in from the west and the three fugitives began to climb beside it. There were glimpses of black-streaked clouds between the peaks, but, where they were, the sun bored down with a baking heat. The yellow rocks soaked it in and poured it back.

When Brooke still had his map and cared what it said, he had told them about Basutoland. He had shown them how it bordered the Cape Colony and Orange Free State. The Basutos were neutral in the war. Now, Brooke was locked in silence, and it was left to Alice and Frank to decide whether to go higher and deeper into this country. They did so hoping the heart of Basutoland would be farther from the Boers and the war. They were hoping for someplace kinder.

As the three climbed, Frank relived the morning. When Von Roster rode away on Century, Lionel had sagged into a curled shape and let himself drop. He coiled in the dirt in this damaged shape; put a hand under his cheek and stared across it.

Frank had left him and joined Alice in the willows. The two of them sat beside Young Sam. Alice had straightened the boy so he would not go rigid in the crooked shape he had assumed while dying. A hole in his head. A hole in his heart.

Young Sam was still wearing the tan shirt and olive drab trousers that Lionel had bought him for the journey. Clothes he had been proud of. Only his feet were bare. One of the executioners had overcome his repugnance long enough to steal his boots. Beside his feet was a pair of worn-out flaps, and Frank put them on his own feet, having already hurt himself with thorns and stones.

"You have to put on Young Sam's clothes," she told him.

Frank shook his head. He would not bury Young Sam naked.

"You'll die of the sun."

Alice went back down the path to check on Brooke and saw her bedroll: the cadaver's act of chivalry. She brought one of the two blankets and the shovel to the willows and told Frank it would be Young Sam's shroud. She had put the second blanket over Brooke and asked him if he wanted to watch them bury Young Sam. Lionel made no response.

] 319 [

Frank took off Young Sam's shirt and trousers and drew them on. He put his finger through the red hole in the shirt's breast and touched his own skin above the heart. There was a broader, bloodier hole on the shirt's back. When they rolled Young Sam in the blanket and tied it twice with more willow strips, Frank felt glad to be wearing his friend's shirt with its bloody record of what the Boers had done to him.

They took turns digging with the short-handled spade and got the hole down a couple of feet in mostly rock, but could go no deeper. They covered him and went for more rocks until there was a pile.

The hardest moment came then: the part that should have been a funeral. Frank thought of Morden's and Kerr's funeral: the speeches and prayers. The hymns. What would any of that have meant to Young Sam, neither Christian nor a soldier? All Alice and Frank could offer their friend was silence.

Then Alice said in a bright, loud voice, "We are sorry, Young Sam."

Frank said he was sorry too.

The boy had been so young, and none of them had taken care of him well enough.

Before they could leave this place, they had to dress Brooke. He did not want the smelly animal skins, so Alice fashioned the blanket into a Mexican-style poncho. She insisted he wear the Boer's leather trousers, and she and Frank worked together to manoeuvre them over his bent shape. They also combined to tie the cadaver's leather flap shoes on Lionel's feet. The last thing in Alice's bedroll was an oiled cotton groundsheet. She rolled the cadaver's leather shirt in it and carried it across her shoulders.

Now, higher in the valley that was still rising to the west, they took turns helping Brooke walk, taking weight off his injured back. In the hooded poncho, with his pale glassy eyes, he looked like a Bible prophet addled by visions. He stayed silent even when Alice ordered him to talk and told him he was a poor excuse for a man. He was far beyond the reach of insult.

At night, it grew cold, and they huddled together like barn cats, Brooke the ill-fitting middle piece. When it rained in the dark, they spread the groundsheet over themselves. Frank kept expecting Jimmy to ride in with guns and horses. Sometimes, he imagined Jeff Davis coming to their rescue.

After another wet day and night, they were very hungry and barely able to move. They needed people. Alice climbed to a saddle between peaks and saw a valley that opened into a high terrace. The far side of the terrace was closed in by a steep mountain face. She saw a clot of white that she thought must be sheep.

They made for this place and, well before they arrived, a dozen children joined them. Close-shorn, almost bald, the children wore woven blankets and stayed well away from the whites. But they also led the visitors to a trail that entered the green place on which their village spread.

Some men with spears and one with an ancient flintlock took over from the children at the first field. They were ushered between round houses. The thatch on the conical roofs was precisely tailored. They walked between mud-smooth curving walls. Women watched calmly as they passed.

In the middle of the village was a sidehill of grass. They were told to sit. The men with spears went away and left the owner of the flintlock to guard them. The children played at a safe distance.

For several miles, Lionel Brooke had faltered badly. He could only move his feet if most of his weight was slumped over Frank's or Alice's back. Now he lay on his side in his snail shape, the blanket partly over him. Because he could not or would not speak, they did not know how to help him.

Along the journey, Alice and Frank had shied away from speech. Now, they talked. Both had made up their minds to leave, to get away from the people and ideas that had led to the youngest and purest of them being killed. They had the same thought about what must be done first. Brooke must be put into safe hands. Though the stupidity of his fire had cost Young Sam's life, Brooke was still too innocent to abandon.

When the village men returned, there was a new one among them: a man with no weapon who was dressed differently. He wore a round brimless hat like a Mountie pillbox. His blanket was dense with colourful geometry. He was, it turned out, a teacher and scholar, the one in the village who knew English.

"You want? What?" was his first question.

Alice said they were hungry. Children were dispatched to deal with this. The scholar asked what was wrong with Brooke. Alice explained about his back.

"No speak?"

"No speak."

At this, the man frowned, for it was left to him to wonder whether Brooke lacked the mechanism of speech, or simply would not talk.

"Soldiers?" he asked, moving on.

"No," said Alice pointing at both Brooke and Frank. "Not soldiers."

The scholar pointed at Frank and asked again: "Soldier?"

Alice pointed at the bloody hole in his shirt front and said, "Not soldier." She pointed at Frank's face. "Not soldier."

The children returned with a woman who carried a wooden platter of fruit and biltong on her head. Alice put a piece of the dried meat in Lionel's mouth and he sucked on it. Another woman brought a bladder from which she gave them each a drink.

Then the scholar asked what else they wanted.

It was around then that the sky, which had been building up with clouds, released a dense rain. They were taken into a thatched building bigger than the rest: a meeting house. They sat on a woven mat that covered the packed dirt floor.

Alice and the scholar resumed their conversation in the darkened room. By now, she understood that he knew more English than he could say. She was able to guide him through groups of questions to which he could answer yes or no. Progress became rapid.

She found out that the Basutos, while neutral, were less afraid of the British than of the Boers. She was able to tell the scholar that they needed to get to some British place, maybe the fort at Springhaan's Nek, without colliding with the Boers.

The scholar told Alice that, though his people were anxious to be rid of them, they were reluctant to go outside the mountains, especially in the company of English people. The Boers were using their trails to avoid the British forts. If they saw the Basutos helping the British, they would kill them.

What got them beyond this impasse was money that Alice had sewn into the seams of her shirt and trousers. She asked to be allowed to relieve herself and came back with English pounds. She said she needed horses: three, or at least two. Several horse owners were summoned, and what followed was the familiar routine of horse trading.

Horses paraded in the rain outside the meeting house, the quality declining as Alice cut more seams and revealed the full extent of her money.

In the end, there was only one horse in the whole village within reach of what she had. The Basutos explained that the British at the forts were short of horses and paying high prices.

Frank wished Ovide could be there to look over the one horse Alice could afford. The owner called it a Basuto, but, though Frank had only known one of that breed, he was sure it was not. More likely, it was riff-raff that had wandered in from the war: a stout old thing near the end of its energy.

Frank took Alice aside—as much as the situation allowed.

"You and Brooke can both ride that horse. If you go dead slow and rest him, he'll make it to Springhaan's Nek."

"But I don't have any more money, and the owner won't come down. He says he can get more at the forts."

"But he's afraid to go there. Tell him you can get more money and you'll bring it back. Leave me as a hostage."

"But I don't know if I *can* get more money, Frank. I'd probably have to go to Bloemfontein—maybe Cape Town."

"I'm telling you what to tell them, not what has to happen."

On this basis, the sale was made. The seller arranged for a boy to ride with Brooke and Kettle out of the mountains. When the two horses stood ready, Alice came to Frank and hugged him tight. She whispered in his ear.

"I don't know what will happen, Frank. I'll stay with Brooke until I get him to a hospital. Then I'll try to get money."

It seemed that was all, but when Frank pulled back, she would not let him go. She had him around the neck and was as strong as barbwire.

"Don't try to find Alma. When this is over and you're home, you'll find a wife. None of this will matter then. Do you understand me?"

She ground their heads together. He said he understood, but was only trying to get away.

When she released him, there were tears in her eyes. It made Frank understand that she would not be back. She was still holding his hands in hers, and he felt something poke into his fist. When she let him go, and she and Lionel were boosted onto the sway-backed horse, there was a second in which Frank was able to put what Alice had given him into a pocket—on top of Young Sam's lucky quartz stones.

—

For two weeks, Frank lived with the chickens in the horse owner's mud-walled yard. Even the children lost interest in him. At night, he was tied between two widely spaced stakes and had to stay awake to keep the chickens from pecking his eyes. When no one was watching him dig furrows in the man's field, he would lie down in the dirt and sleep. As for food, he ate what the animals ate, dry mealie kernels pounded with a post.

Two weeks to the day after Alice and Lionel left, the seller decided he'd had enough of feeding Frank. He put him on a mule that he led behind his own Basuto pony. They walked down several valleys until the sun was setting golden brown.

"Caledon," he said, pointing and making a wavy motion with one hand. He signalled for Frank to get down. Then he turned his horse around and led the mule away.

BOOK TWO

The CANADIAN SCOUTS

Prologue

—

PINCHER CREEK

December 1900

Tommy Killam's work these days was in his father's store, decorating it for Christmas, designing the holiday ad for the *Rocky Mountain Echo*, and handing out leaflets of the same design on main street. It was his father's campaign to keep the local shoppers from going to Ft. Macleod. The leaflet read: SHOP HERE FIRST AND YOU MAY NOT NEED TO GO FARTHER.

But, in truth, the citizens of Pincher Creek, the ones with good teams and buggies—the ones with money—enjoyed going to Macleod for a few days around Christmas. The women shopped in the better-supplied stores. The men went to Kamoose Taylor's Macleod Hotel to meet friends for a drink and a smoke. Wagered on a few hands of cards, a few games of billiards.

The people who came to Killam's were the ones without horses, the sick and the poor. The only ones with money who did their Christmas shopping there were the old people who could no longer stand the rough road east and did not want to risk the weather. There were also the Indians, who came to beg more than to buy.

Tommy knew that the leaflets and his father's newspaper ad wouldn't change any of it. It was just his father wasting money while dreaming of making some.

By coincidence, the *Echo* that carried their Christmas ad also had the biggest front-page headline Tommy had ever seen.

OUR BOYS ARE COMING HOME

As far as Tommy was concerned, the only fellows who mattered were home already (invalided out) or never coming home (dead). The fact that Inspector Davidson might show up in a month or two, or Mr. Redpath later on, did not interest him.

Tommy's surviving connection to the African war was in his pocket: a couple of columns cut out of the August 15 *Echo* and folded tightly inside the secret pocket of his wallet. It was a letter written by Hugh Davidson to the Morden family, which the Mordens had allowed the *Echo* to print so the whole town could read it. The clipping was smudged and broken at every fold, but that did not matter because Tommy had long ago committed it to memory.

> *My Dear Morden,*
> *I don't know how I should manage to write you and tell you about Fred's*
> *sad ending, were it not that I know that long before you get this letter, the*
> *newspapers as well as the telegram to Canon Middleton . . .*

Sometimes when Tommy was out with his .22 and Fred Morden's wolfhounds, up the canyon, he would recite this letter in different voices and accents, emphasizing the words that he pulled the trigger on.

> *I know what your sorrow is and what a void is left in your family circle.*
> *God grant you all His consolation.*

When Canon Middleton's buggy had rolled up to the Mordens' gate, and the clergyman strode to the door holding a telegram, Tommy had been watching from his own yard next door. He had heard the loud wail inside the Morden house. A few minutes later, Mrs. Morden had come to his mother. Just inside the door, the two women held on to each other, rocking and weeping for a long time.

In the days and weeks afterwards, the town filled with things: sorrow, indignation, hatred, Empire pride. But what happened inside Tommy was the exact opposite: an emptying of all the same things.

People noticed the difference in him and, even within his own family, mistook it for maturity.

"He grew up just like that," he heard his mother say to a customer in the store. She snapped her fingers to show how quick it had been.

Others came right up to him, women usually, and said, "You're so much more of a man now, Tommy Killam."

What would they think if they heard him in the hills above the town singing Hugh Davidson's letter?

I knows wot sorra is
And wot a woid it leaves
Yer fammm-lee circle, she is broken.
Gaaawwwd give His consolation to yuz all.

Part Seven

—

ALONE

Caledon River, January 1901

The Caledon River was high and galloping. Frank gripped his leather flap shoes tight and threw himself in. He was weak from too many raw mealies and could not swim well at the best of times. He flew and ducked like a fleck of debris, and on a tight S-turn the roaring Caledon spat him onto the sand and gravel, half drowned and eye to eye with a bloated ox who had perhaps come to shore on the same muscular water screw.

To his surprise, the map in his shirt and the pound notes in his pocket were still there. He laid them out and pinned them with rocks and let the scorching sun dry them. The map was the last thing Alice Kettle had given him. After she snuck the pound notes into his fist, she more publicly handed him Lionel's map. Brooke's days of needing it were over.

Looking at the map and relating it to past days, Frank believed the Basuto had set him down north of the Thaba Nchu road. The first option, then, was to follow Jim Whitford's path in reverse, which would mean going west toward Brandfort, then north beside the railway. Without gun or horse, that might not be the safest way, maybe just farther and hungrier. The other option was straight north, which had to be shorter but would be through unknown country. He knew how to find north from the cluster of stars, and the one thing he could get from the map was the order of rivers. He could keep count as he crossed them and know roughly where he was.

He decided on straight north and, to deal with the unknowns, he would travel by night. He would be out of the sun's terrible eye and out of view of his enemies—a group that consisted of most everyone.

As he began to walk, Frank decided it was best to think of himself as an animal, a wild animal that was no man's friend; the kind that enters your chicken yard at night and that you set your dogs on. He would not be a healthy animal, just a starving one. If he could think like that, he would be more vigilant and less fussy about his food.

The mealie crops were high enough now to hide him and the mealie stands also fed him, though the immature corn kernels played hell with his guts. He survived in a state of constant sickness.

Sometimes, in the moonlight, he would see springbok gliding, and the desire for their meat brought him close to tears. During the days, when he saw vultures circling, he would even envy them their food. But there was no sense looking for carrion. He lacked the beak and claw needed to challenge the scavengers.

Finally, when Frank was starving, and feared that soon he would be too weak to go on or defend himself, he found a farm. He entered its stand of blue-gum trees from the downwind side, tried not to imagine dogs bounding at him. He made it to the empty sheep kraal and tiptoed through the cakes of manure until he was close enough to watch the barn and house.

When daylight came, he looked for white men and women with guns, but all he saw was one black man, a little older than himself, doing the farm's morning work. As this one walked back and forth, and dragged and carried, he had the air of someone doing chores he had not thought up himself. Beside him walked a short, heavily muscled black dog with strong, slavering jaws. The dog wagged its tail and watched everything the black man did. The house's chimney smoked and so did an outdoor oven between the house and barn. Mostly, the farm worker stoked these fires.

Later, the worker went into the barn and led out a knackered horse. The dog ran in giddy circles and barked. The horse was dirty white. It had a ruined back and feet like cracked plates. The man threw a ragged blanket on it and then a sorry saddle. He went to the house and knocked, and a hefty *vrouw* answered with a double-barrelled shotgun in her hands. She broke it, raised it, looked through the barrels at the sky. She chucked it shut again and handed it over, then reached in her apron pocket and dumped a handful of shotgun shells into a pouch that hung from the black man's shoulder.

When the farmhand, the horse, and the dog left in a cloud of sun-flaring dust, Frank knew his best chance had come. The outdoor oven was giving off a meat smell that made him drool. Still, he forced himself away from it and into the garden, where he crawled between rows of peas and root vegetables. He stopped and picked some immature pea pods and ate them whole. When his helpless stomach cramped, he slithered out of the garden to a rain barrel for a drink of green-tasting water.

Still, he resisted the meat. He twisted the block latch of a work-shed door and entered a darkness that smelled of mouldy earth and horse leather. Spindly weeds more white than green coursed along the dirt floor.

Something sharp. Something to make fire. Something for his feet.

He had closed the door behind him, which left only needles of light through the wall. In a while, he could see to search. He found a glass jar full of nails that he dumped on the bench. He kept a few nails and forced the empty jar into a pocket of Young Sam's trousers. In the blackness of one corner, he found a hacksaw blade brown with rust. He lifted a horse collar off the wall and cut leather ovals from the bulges. From the same collar, he carved strips and nipped them at the ends for cord. His torn feet would have to wait. He could not take time now to poke holes and make sandals.

Outside, no one was waiting with a gun so he let himself be drawn to the rich smell of the oven. His plan involved a pitchfork that he had noticed standing beside a dung pile at the barn's rear door. He brought it over now to the shed corner closest to the oven but out of sight of the house.

He waited, and the *vrouw* finally came to check her oven. She opened the door and peered in, poked at the coals. When she was back inside the house, he counted to a hundred. Then he went to the oven door and opened it. The rich, greasy heat almost felled him. There were several fat chickens, almost brown, lying on a grate. He ran a pitchfork tine through two and ran.

Frank got no more than a minute's start before the Boer woman's first shout. He imagined her inside, getting a rifle down from a wall. He ran for the nearest mealie field, a hundred yards away. Sped along on his mangled feet with the chickens on the pitchfork ahead of him. He barged through the wall of mealie shafts. A rifle cracked and the bullet rattled and snicked through the corn stand.

He did not run. He knew movement in the cornstalks would help her kill him. He forced himself to go slowly, bending around each stalk, manoeuvring the chickens and the pitchfork at the same time. His weak body and dizziness were always close to betraying him, to making him lose balance and fall over. The *vrouw* was waiting for something like that to shoot at, and every once in a while she would try a shot, hoping to flush him.

He did not let himself eat one mouthful of chicken, not even when he came out the mealie field's far side. With the chickens still on the pitchfork, he left the farm's low valley and entered another. Finally, when the hunger threatened to take his consciousness away, he sat and made a rusty rip through the breast meat with his saw. As he began to chew, he closed his eyes and felt the start of tears. He wept all through his first meal of meat in he didn't know how long.

After two weeks of walking on his homemade sandals, of eating more mealies and garden vegetables, and never having the luck of another chicken, Frank realized he was getting nowhere. He had crossed the rivers of two of his battles, the Vet and the Zand, but was not even halfway to where he wanted to go. When he came to the river he believed was the Valsch, he did not cross it but set off down it. According to his map, this would bring him to Kroonstad. A British-held town. The railway.

He was pinning his hope on something that had happened when he'd travelled south with Lionel and the others. A British officer who stopped them had wanted to know who Frank was. When Frank had started his story and said he was a Canadian Mounted Rifle, the officer's only concern had been that he would miss his boat. Thinking about that and ignoring all other possibilities, Frank planned to throw himself on British mercy. He hoped that either kindness or confusion would save him.

By the time he staggered from the bush within sight of Kroonstad, Frank had not eaten for two days. He was sick and confused, and sometimes had to stop while his stomach bucked like some separate animal he had swallowed. Drinking from the river had given him dysentery. He could barely stand.

It took him an hour to go the remaining distance to town. On Kroonstad's main street, he fainted. A Boer farmer in for supplies revived him and carried him to the British hospital. There, a nurse saw the sunkenness of his eyes and the lack of resilience of his skin and started feeding him water they had boiled and cooled. It was one of the hospitals where Canadian soldiers had died of fever, but Frank was beyond caring.

Within two days, he was feeling stronger and clearer. They considered him well enough to do something. Could he read, they asked. He said he could, and they brought him a Cape Town newspaper. It was only days old, and he was astounded to find that Christmas and New Year had passed. It was January 1901 and the war, which had stopped for him, was not going well for the British. The Boers seemed to have the upper hand.

When the hospital staff saw that Frank could make sense of a newspaper, they figured it was time to make sense of him. A lieutenant was summoned to interrogate him. As this officer and Frank's nurse approached down the aisle between close-together cots, Frank pretended to be asleep, and so heard a couple of the lieutenant's questions and the nurse's answers. That the nurse knew anything at all suggested he had been talking deliriously the day the farmer carried him in.

"He's a confusing one, sir. The shirt he had on was not from any uniform, but it had a bullet hole in the front and a bloody spot on the back. There's no such marks on him. It was a well-made shirt too, something a hunter might wear. He's badly scarred in his hair, though it's healed."

The lieutenant was a light-built, astute man, who seemed misplaced in the war. When he started asking questions, Frank told him a version of what had happened. By now, he'd heard several deserters lie and knew how false they sounded when their powers of invention failed. For his own story, he stayed as close to the truth as he could. The only big lie was that he could not remember how he came to leave Aas Vogel Kranz.

When Frank finished, Lieutenant Burridge shook his head and made a few pencil marks on the pad of paper.

"Oh hell, Adams. I'm not going to write all that down. We hear some dillies around here, but yours takes the cake."

He probed his pencil stub into the loops of his pale hair and scratched. This made Frank think about his own hair and how heavily doused in louse powder it was. The poor lieutenant must be gagging at the smell.

"The way this usually works," Burridge said, "if a soldier's been hiding or doing civilian work and wants back in the army so he can go home, is that he'll be fatter than a normal soldier. They never come in looking as rough as you. I suppose you could have beaten yourself up to corroborate your story, but you're overzealous if that's your game.

"But let's say I believe you. Then what? Your battalion's gone home. Do we send you to Cape Town? See if you can find a boat that will take you?"

"What about Pretoria?"

"Pardon me, but you won't find too many boats there."

"But there's Canadians there still, aren't there? Strathcona's Horse. Maybe I could find them and go home when they do."

"That makes a sort of sense. There's something else called the Canadian Scouts you might look up. I don't know what they are, really, except they're new."

"Can I?"

"Can you what? Pretoria? Fine by me. They want fellows like you off the books. If you can take care of it yourself, why not? What about a uniform, though? You said yours was taken by the Boers, and they gave you this dead fella's clothes. We won't have a Mounted Rifle outfit to give you in its place."

"I can wear what I came in with."

"With the bullet hole?"

"I don't mind. I'd like boots, though."

"You sure as hell would. Your poor bloody feet."

They both stared at Frank's ragged feet for a moment. Then the lieutenant wished Frank better luck and left.

In two days, Frank was on a train north. He'd had a good wash and another round of louse powder. He had new boots and an address in Pretoria that he was to check into.

But, when he disembarked at Pretoria Station, Frank told an officer holding a clipboard that he was wanted at Middelburg, in spite of what his orders said. He'd met a soldier on the train who'd convinced him it was the British camp at Middelburg that would know what to do with him.

A train for Belfast was about to pull out. The officer shrugged and let him go. By evening, Frank had deserted again and was walking south through the night, on the now familiar trail to Kleff's Farm.

Grey drapes of cloud reeled in and out. The sky rumbled and a warm rain fell steadily. Frank's feet hurt, but from the old damage, not anything new.

His dysentery had slowed, thanks to boiled water at Kroonstad hospital. Though wet, he felt more at peace the closer he came to his destination.

When the wind rolled a cloud along the ground and bowled it off a shallow hillock, he briefly saw the kopje that marked Kleff's Farm. What he would do when he arrived was not clear. He supposed he would climb the kopje and look down; then figure out what might have changed. Would the furious Mr. Kleff be present? Denny Straytor?

Whatever else was false or true, Frank did not believe that Alma's affection and passion had been invented. Her saying in blurry English that she was sorry (for the trick that let Straytor get away). He believed in that and in her tears more than in Brooke's theory that she had betrayed him. Betrayals came in all sizes, as far as he was concerned.

What to do after he'd climbed the kopje was still a problem. He could not, as he had done with Brooke, walk down yelling, "It's me, Frank Adams!"

It would be perfect if Mrs. Kleff had yoked her ox to her ox cart and left for town, and if no other family were present. He imagined walking in with only Alma there. They would go to her bedroom. She would hug him, and kiss him. They would lie down, take off their clothes, and complete what they had begun those other times. Maybe a day spent like that would fire up an idea of what to do after the war. Or maybe it would fire up a baby—a being with the power to cut through Mrs. Kleff's hatred.

Whatever would happen, Frank was now affected by the nearness of it. Something rose in him at every squelching step, came lifting off his knees and went sailing up through the rain. Joy.

Frank was close now but still could not see the farm. The cloud skimming along the ground blocked the view. When he came to the first leafed-out tree, he knew he was at the kopje's base. At the top of the wet climb, he crossed to the far edge and still could see nothing; just the tops of the blue gums and a flannel fog. A sudden impatience took him, and he knew it was beyond him to wait here for the weather to change. Whether he would find Alma or her mother, or the furious, murderous father, he was headed there right now.

He climbed down through the fog, and the first thing he came to was the outhouse. It had a fan of black up the side, something he hadn't noticed before. He took a few more steps and the barn appeared, skeins of mist looped through a black armature of beams. He could see the full length of the manger rail, for the walls were gone. Now he could smell it too: the char and scorched resin.

Frank ran for the house. Because the corrugated metal roof was still there between the gables, he thought for a second that the house had been saved. But then he saw there was nothing underneath. The iron stove stood alone in the kitchen, covered in blackened boards and clinkers. He could see through to the veldt on the other side. He wanted to go in but stopped himself, aware of all the weight hanging.

When he turned, he saw that two small buildings remained: the cutting room and the smokehouse. The thatch roof was gone but the walls were standing. A tail of grey wisped from the smokehouse chimney.

Frank wrenched open the smokehouse door. Between him and the smoker was a broad shape under a blackened oil sheet. Rain was pattering there. He reached for it, and the sheet flung back. He was looking into the twin holes of a shotgun. The blue-black eyes of old Isaiah were behind the sites. Beside Isaiah, Jimmy Whitford was twisted around, looking at him with mild interest.

"Room for one more," said Jim and slid over. Isaiah lowered the gun and moved the other way.

Frank stepped in between them and sat on the warm, dry ground. For a time he could do nothing but stare at the source of heat. The door to the smoker was open and fire licked in the brickwork core. They had taken out the racks and laid a fire on the bottom.

"Good boots," Jim said, tapping one. "You been to the hospital, then?"

"Kroonstad. How do you know that?"

Jim shrugged. "Your clothes are clean. You stink of bug powder." He shrugged again.

Frank turned to the other man. "What happened here, Isaiah?"

Isaiah shook his white head. "What you see, boss. Burned him down."

"The British?"

Isaiah laughed, meaning, Frank supposed, that the Boers would not burn their own farm.

"Where's Alma?"

Jimmy took over. "I asked him before. He says they caught the women and put them in a wagon. Took Little Alma and Tia too. Left Isaiah."

"So where is she?"

"Camp."

Frank did not ask which one because he thought it must be Irene.

"That was six days ago," said Jim. "Only been here a day. Me."

"How come you're here at all?"

"Waiting on you."

There was a silence. Frank thought of how he would get to Irene. He'd try to get on the train tomorrow. Jimmy was lost in some other thought.

"I didn't wake up till it was too late," he said. He meant the night the Boers came to the rock cave. "I was by some bush. I had to roll into it fast and didn't get my guns. I went up top but they had you already. They had the horses."

Jimmy slid more dead sticks into the smoker, jammed at the coals in anger. They came brighter.

"They took my guns and my mare. I followed to the river and crossed it, but I couldn't find the track on the rocks. Had to wait. Took all day to find that grave."

Jim went silent again. He touched the fringe of the bullet hole on Frank's shirt. The stain was fainter after the hospital laundry.

"I had to take the rocks off to know it was Sam. Shoulda never let Brooke bring him. Shoulda never let Brooke have that fire."

Jimmy stopped and stared into the cherry heart of the smoker.

"Did the bald one shoot Sam?" he asked after a while.

"That Boer's name is Von Roster. He gave the order. Two others did it."

"I followed the wrong track. Saw how everyone got off their horse. How they shot Sam. The grave. I thought everyone rode away then, so I followed the horses. Missed your foot track."

Jimmy flung back the sheet. He stood and told Frank to come. They walked to the barn and started around the shell of it. Frank saw the edge of the round corral and that it had not burned. Then he saw the ridgling circling inside. He reached through the poles, and the pinto's teeth bared.

"He figures he's mine now." Whitford came beside Frank, reached through, and scratched the ridgling along his throat latch. "I was on that trail north. I kept getting farther behind. Then along comes the ridgling. All skinned up on the front legs. All he had on him was this old halter. He let me ride but wouldn't go north. That's how I figured you must be south somewhere."

"You found Brooke and Kettle after that?"

"A British patrol caught me. I told them I was a Native tracker looking for two English civilians. White beard. Monocle. They said someone like that came to Springhaan's Nek and went to the hospital in Bloom.

"So I rode over there and found Lionel. Bastard wouldn't talk. I told him I dug out Young Sam so I knew. Still wouldn't talk. I grabbed his big old English nose." Jimmy showed how with his fingers. "Twisted his nose *hard*. Told him he had no damn reason to sull on me. Woke him up. He said Alice was gone. Said he wanted to go home."

"He told you about me."

"He told me to look after you. Told me you were with the Basutos, and there was a debt owing on a horse. I figured you'd either be dead by now or here, so I came here."

"How'd you know I'd come here?"

Whitford clamped his mouth shut. Some questions were too stupid to answer.

The clouds broke up as night came on. The smokehouse was still the driest place and they slept there again. Through the little square of night sky, they could see stars. The insects were chanting.

They slept the night through and were awakened by the sun's heat already building inside the smokehouse walls. They were hungry, and Frank learned that the British had burned not just the buildings but the Kleffs' garden and mealie crop. They had taken all the animals.

Isaiah led them three hundred yards into the veldt. He pulled up a thick mat of prairie, exposing a wooden door. The pit house beneath was shallow and maybe ten feet in circumference. There were two heavy bags of root vegetables and a couple of rounds of smoked sausage, wrapped in oil cloth, hung from the roof.

Isaiah yanked a stick out of one dirt wall. He started to dig with it until an edge of white canvas showed. He exposed more, then pulled it out and gave it to Jimmy. Jim unwrapped enough to see the blue-black of a Mauser's barrel. In the hole was a wooden box of ammunition. Isaiah dug deeper and handed out a canvas-bagged Mauser pistol and rounds.

Back inside the smokehouse, they stoked the smoker and baked some beets and carrots. It tasted mushy and sweet. Bellies full, Isaiah and Jimmy lay down on the sun-dappled grass with their hats over their faces.

Frank could not stand their complacency. He decided he would go and wondered only whether to tell them or simply do it.

Jimmy rolled over and looked him in the face. The black bead eyes were not as calm as they had been.

"Isaiah followed."

"Followed what?"

"Followed the Kleffs."

"To Irene?"

"To Middelburg. New camp there. We'll go in an hour."

Isaiah stayed on the farm. The understanding was that they would return tonight or tomorrow. Jimmy left him the rifle and the box of shells, though he did not want them. Jimmy said he did not want them either. He wanted only the pistol, which he could hide when he entered the town.

Jimmy boosted Frank onto the ridgling's bare back and gave him the few strings that were left of the pinto's trampled halter rope. The pinto danced but stopped when Jimmy talked to him in Crow. Frank reached his arm down to help Whitford up, but Jimmy did not take it.

"Ridgling's not strong. I'll walk."

Instead, Jimmy ran, clicking his mouth so the ridgling matched his pace. It was a jog-trot that he seemed able to keep up forever. After an hour, he stopped and panted a little. He straightened and signalled Frank down, then replaced him on the horse. He touched up the ridgling to the same trot and Frank jogged along.

At a slender creek, they stopped to drink. Frank crawled to it and put his head in. Underwater, it came to him that this was the creek he had escaped along when he deserted.

Jimmy resumed running after the creek. He kept on until they could see Middelburg's smoke. Frank got down and they talked about what would happen next.

"Need a story," Jimmy said.

Frank said he had the one about a knock on the head and amnesia. He did not know if it would work without a uniform.

"Can you talk like Lionel?"

Frank abruptly heard Young Sam's voice in his head. Imitating that as much as Brooke, he said, "De Wet is the key."

"More like Kettle?"

"Bloody men. Bloody tyrants."

Jimmy nodded. That was the one. He reached inside his shirt and pulled out a waterproof dispatch bag; opened it and removed a square of folded paper. Frank could see the pebbles of the embossed stamp and knew it was Brooke's letter of introduction from the English newspaper.

"The only thing the Boers left in our camp."

"I can barely write," said Frank.

"Nobody's going to ask you to."

They went on, Frank riding and Jimmy on foot. Jimmy made some suggestions as they went. Things Frank should say. He should say they had been caught by the Boers. That the Boers had taken their saddles, bridles, and horses. They only had this horse because it was so mean the Boers did not want it.

Then a British outpost stood by the trail, and there was a shout to halt and state their business.

"Lionel Brooke! British journalist!" Frank yelled. They went in with their hands high and soon Frank was digging out the letter.

"Who's he?" the Australian corporal asked. He had finished reading the letter and was staring at Jimmy.

"Indian tracker."

"Christ. Where'd you get one of those?"

"Canada."

"Don't suppose he's got papers."

Frank was about to say no when Jimmy pulled something out of the canvas bag in his shirt. The sheet was old and yellow; had plenty of ink stamps and a flourishy signature. The young Aussie read it.

"So you're a U.S. Cavalry scout," the Aussie said, impressed.

Then Frank explained about being robbed by the Boers.

"Bastards!" said the Aussie and spat on the ground. He gave back their papers and nodded them through.

It was suppertime and Jimmy said they should find a place to eat. But he could see that Frank was not willing to wait. In his Brooke and Kettle voice, Frank asked a couple of British soldiers for directions to the camp. They pointed to the west side of town. After the last Boer houses, there was an open place where a dribbling creek divided two low hills. Down below, the creek pooled in a swampy bottom, and the camp was on the swamp's eastern edge: a hundred or so tents on a beaten slope. Some Boer women and kids were looking out through the fence, and a few more kids were up to their knees in the swamp trying to catch something in a can.

Frank looked at the women, but in their shabby bonnets and dresses, they all looked the same. On the hill beyond the swamp, Frank saw fresh mounds of earth. The camp, barely started, had produced some dead.

"You want to ask?" said Jimmy.

"Isaiah was sure they came here, right?"

"He saw them go in."

"Then, no. Not now."

Back on Middelburg's main street, a Boer family had erected a tent and called it a restaurant. Behind was a *braai*, a brickwork box with an iron grill where they cooked meat over coals. In the tent were benches and tables, and Frank and Jimmy sat at one. They asked what kind of meat it was, and the Boer woman led them to the braai where, sadly, there was only mutton on the grill.

When the food came, Frank and Jimmy concentrated on their eating. Afterwards, Jimmy wiped grease off his chops with a dirty cloth. Another eater had left a newspaper. Jimmy jumped up and fetched it, laid it open before Frank.

"You're a reporter," he said, in case Frank had forgotten.

After a couple of minutes, Jimmy asked, "So what's it say?"

"Reading's not as easy as you think," Frank said.

"Other fella?" Jimmy said, meaning the one who'd left the paper. "He didn't lean over and put his face close like that. He picked it up." Jimmy mimed how it was done.

Frank ignored him and read more. "Sounds like the Boers won some battles."

"De Wet?"

"De La Rey."

Frank read more.

"Kitchener's got some new plan."

"Do what?"

"Something about hustling and driving the Boers. Doesn't say more."

"Strathconas?"

"Nothing."

Frank wanted to go back to thinking about Alma in the camp, but first he considered Jimmy. Given that things had happened the way they had, it seemed to Frank that Jimmy shouldn't be here. He wondered why he wasn't with Lionel, helping his boss get home.

"You said you came here looking for me. You never said why."

"I did say. I said Lionel told me to look after you."

Jimmy's face froze. He had been looking over Frank's shoulder, but now he stared at his wiped-clean plate. He kicked Frank's boot. Turning slightly, Frank saw black shapes against the brightness of the tent door.

"Good day, sir," said one. Frank turned and looked. Blue tunics. Military police. The speaker was English.

"Same to you, corporal," said Frank.

"Can we see your papers?"

Frank dug out Brooke's letter. Handed it over. The corporal showed it to the other man, a big frowning brute with his nose on crooked.

"This isn't what we had in mind," said the corporal, shaking the fragile page. "How about some actual identification?"

"Problem, corporal. I've been captive. Boers took my clothing and my British papers. Took my horse. That letter is all I have."

"And where did that happen? The Boers?"

"Basuto side of the Caledon River."

The police corporal pointed at Frank's chest. "Looks like they not only robbed you but shot you to death." The brute beside him barked a laugh.

"They took my clothes and gave me these."

"Funny the Boers would leave you good boots."

"They stole my boots and gave me old scraps of leather. When I was in hospital at Kroonstad, the army gave me these."

"That's an odd accent."

"I've lived a lot of places."

"Ahh."

"How joo get here?" said the tough one.

"After Kroonstad? Army put me on a train to Pretoria."

"Why Middelburg?"

"You have a new camp here? For Boer women and children?"

"You planning to write about that, then?" asked the corporal.

"Might. There's interest in the camps back home."

"Hope you won't be a screamer."

"A what?"

"Screaming about how bad it is. We're only getting under way."

"I'll remember that."

The talker turned to Jimmy.

"And who's this handsome gentleman?"

Jim had his cavalry papers ready and handed them across.

"I hired this Native tracker to be my scout," said Frank.

Finally, the two policemen looked at each other and the rougher one shrugged. The corporal said, "If you're looking for a story, there's a party tonight for local soldiers. Town hall on the main square. The off-duty guards from the camp'll be there. Maybe do an interview."

Frank thanked him for the information.

Frank and Jimmy walked back to where the ridgling was tied to a hitching rail. When they stopped, Frank felt drained. Out of sight behind the pinto, he let his face show how frightened he'd been. Jimmy clapped him on the back; said it was a test of fire and he'd done well.

Jimmy untied the ridgling, who was looking backwards, studying passing horses.

"Why don't you?" Jimmy asked.

"What?"

"That party."

"Why?"

"Find out if the Strathconas are around."

Frank didn't care much about finding the Strathconas, but the party did attract him. The mention of off-duty camp guards. He could act the reporter and quiz them about the health of the women and children. Maybe set things up so he could go for a tour tomorrow.

A couple of farmers' carts were pulled up at a feed store behind drowsy oxen. Bulky sons carried bags of seed and flour and flopped them in the box. A black boy with a hard-used brush offered to groom the ridgling.

Two white women in bonnets and dresses looked down at some bright fruit on a blanket and some little things carved from wood. An African woman with her head wrapped in something like a towel sat on the blanket's corner watching with a hopeful smile.

Frank told Jimmy he would go to the party. They had already passed the town hall and the park beside it, and now they started walking the ridgling toward the livery barn. Quite a bit of Frank's money from Alice remained, and they agreed that the ridgling would enjoy a night with other horses. Provided he did not bite, kick, or fuck anything, it would be a rest for everyone. Jimmy had no interest in the party, but said he might have himself a smoke if Frank had tobacco money.

Along the way, Frank bought Jimmy a tin of coarse-cut Boer tobacco and a cheap pipe. He bought himself six sheets of paper and a pencil that the storekeeper shaved to a dangerous point. He also bought a tin mirror and a comb.

Frank waited until after dark to walk from the livery barn to the town hall. He had spent the afternoon and early evening fooling with his appearance. His hair was long and his clothes were dirty. He had not shaved since the hospital in Kroonstad. The person in the mirror did not look like Winston Churchill, Rudyard Kipling, or Banjo Patterson. He looked like a bummer. Frank had returned to the shop and bought a keen-edged knife and a bar of soap. He paid the liveryman to make a fire in his stove and to loan him a basin. A dirty, odd-smelling towel was thrown in as goodwill.

Shaving with a tiny knife had been a bloody business, and his hair did not get as clean as he'd hoped. When he was all done and had combed his locks, Jim Whitford suggested it needed greasing down. A can of horse ointment was found and put to this purpose. By now, Frank had climbed society's ladder no more than a rung—from bummer to pimp, or maybe a losing gambler. To achieve even that much, he'd had to rent a jacket from a fellow who came into the barn to sleep off a drunk. This was another of Jim's ideas.

Walking down the dark street toward the lamplit hall, Frank had little confidence. He smelled of horse ointment and would be badly outdressed by soldiers in their dress uniforms. The image of him quizzing people and writing down their answers was eclipsed by pictures of soldiers keeping their distance and some officer's batman asking him to leave.

For these reasons, when Frank got to the hall, he did not plunge in. He walked by the fan of steps and around the building's side. The hall windows above had been opened to allow in the evening's breeze. Looking up, he could see tobacco smoke escaping.

He was looking for another entrance, and he found it near the back: a few steps of raw lumber to a small landing and a door held open by a wooden wedge. The landing and steps were dense with soldiers passing a bottle. Frank had to push himself through while they made fun of him, calling him a gatecrasher, a spy, a bum. That got him to the door.

As he had feared, it was a well-dressed affair. A food table to one side, piled with sandwiches, made his stomach lurch. Some kind of German band blatted out a polka on a tiny stage. There was a punch bowl that fellows dipped into with a ladle; dainty cups.

Frank's eyes kept coming back to a clutch of men near the middle of the vacant dance floor. It was the uniform. They were wearing tapered khaki tunics, compared to everyone else's red, blue, or green dress uniforms. The khaki was tan, which suggested new because, after a dust storm or two and a couple of muddy launderings, khaki turned almost white.

They had whipcord trousers and lace-up boots to the knee. Several had left their silver spurs on for decoration.

These men were also noticeable because they laughed loud and often. British officers pinched the tiny handles on their punch glasses and cast frowns at the boisterous ones. Then one of the khakis stepped back to turn and cough, and Frank saw it was Casey Callaghan.

Frank was still on the landing. He jumped back into the dark, bumping a fellow who bumped a fellow who spilled his drink. Frank was cursed and given a shove.

"Why don't you go inside, for chrissake?"

He ignored them, held his ground, and tried to understand what he'd seen. Why was Casey here? The ships full of Canadian mounted infantry had sailed a month ago, according to Brooke's newspapers. Frank squinted at the group in khaki, trying to see the red dot on their uniforms, some kind of insignia.

As they jostled and laughed, more faces became visible. Frank saw Gat Howard and the young gunner Walter Bapty. Ed Hilliam. Charlie Ross. A man stood up straight and was half a head taller than the others. Jeff Davis.

When Jeff turned his way, it occurred to Frank to show himself. He leaned forward into the light, for a few seconds.

Right then, Davis sprang away from his crowd and clamped a hand over his mouth. He must have said something, for the others jumped back. A path cleared as he ran in an undignified gallop toward the main door.

The men in Jeff's group turned to watch him go. Every one was laughing. By now, Frank could tell they were drunk, and drunks always find a puking drunkard amusing.

Frank struggled through the bunch on the landing and steps. They blocked him. One clouted him on the ear. He made it down and hurried toward the building's front. There were spots of light cast by the windows, and he saw Jeff pass through one. He caught him before he could enter another.

Jeff took Frank by the arm and towed him into the park. There were no lamps among the trees. They passed a group of soldiers gathered around a fist fight. They didn't stop until they were on the park's farthest side. In a space of grass and flower beds lit by the half-moon, they faced each other.

Nothing was said for a minute. Jeff kept looking at Frank, then back and around for spies. Finally, he reached under the tail of his tunic, and pulled out a bottle. He held it to the moon to see the level. Two-thirds. Only when Jeff tipped the bottle up and took a couple of big swallows did Frank fully understand that Jeff's run for the door had been an act.

Jeff handed Frank the bottle, and Frank took a sizable drink. For some reason related to the fancy party, he was expecting good liquor, but the stuff was harsh. It burned and made him cough.

"What the hell do you think you're doing, coming here?" Jeff asked. He was not joking or faking now.

"I wanted to see if there were guards from the concentration camp. I wanted to ask them some questions. I didn't think there'd be anyone I knew."

"Everyone thinks you're dead or captured."

"I was captured for a while." Frank took a breath. Before he could go on, Jeff put an open hand in front of Frank's face. He was angry and wanted no tale of adventure.

"If you'd come inside and Casey had seen you?"

"I told you. I didn't think he'd be there. Or you, or anybody. Why *are* you here?"

Jeff ignored the question. "Casey doesn't like you. He thinks you're a deserter."

"I guess he's right."

"You tell anyone else that?"

"No. Nobody in the army, anyway."

Jeff took another pull from his bottle. It occurred to Frank that Jeff was different than his usual self. Frank had seen him drunk before, but he'd seemed sleepy and calm then. Tonight, he was sped up, intense. Frank did not understand at all why Jeff would be here. Why wasn't he on a boat? Or even back home by now? On the Blood with his girlfriend, telling her father he'd shot Villamon.

Jeff was talking again, in that rapid way.

"If you're caught and Casey convinces the others you've deserted, you're a dead man, you know that? It's about the only thing they'd shoot you for. Cowardice or desertion."

Jeff drank more. Downing it like water. Frank took another couple of turns. The mutton was long burned off, and not having had liquor in a while, each swallow punched him in the head.

"Why'd you do it?" Jeff asked.

"Why'd I leave? Sick of it, I guess."

"There was only a month to go. You'd have been home by now."

Frank began to feel grumpy about this interrogation. He'd had his reasons. Ovide, Dunny. Everyone treating the blacks like animals and treating him like a black.

Then Jeff seemed done talking. They stood and drank, with the insects in the trees making their ruckus and the bats careening: streaks of silver.

"I got a girlfriend now," Frank said. The garbled drunken sound of his own voice surprised him. Things were happening thick and slow, and a sadness jumped in him at the word *girlfriend*, for in truth Alma might not be his at all.

"Who is she?" asked Jeff.

"I found Lionel Brooke, Jimmy Whitford, and Young Sam on a farm south of here. They were staying with a Boer family. There was a daughter named Alma."

"Brooke, the rancher? He's here?"

"Said he was going to kill De Wet. His plan didn't work out. He's going home. What about your girlfriend? The one on the Blood?"

"She's dead."

Frank went still. Under the power of that word, the whole night began to roar. The insects barked. The bats sizzled. The roar of talk from the hall was a riot. The news fell through Frank as if he'd turned to rotten ice.

Jeff took a drink and handed over the bottle. Frank drank.

"I gotta sit down." Frank dropped where he was. Jeff sat beside him, his knees tall in the moonlight.

"I forget your girlfriend's name."

"You never knew it. Ran After."

"How'd you find out?"

"You were there. It was in the letter from General Butler."

Frank remembered. At Bankfontein, the day Jeff and Casey killed Villamon. It gave Frank a strange feeling that he'd been the one to carry the news, without knowing it. Everything made better sense now. How Jeff had looked and acted that night and next morning. That Jeff had passed up the chance to go home.

"The old people call it blood-spitting sickness," Jeff said. "Lots were dying before we left."

"I'm sorry."

"What about your girlfriend? She still at the farm?"

"We don't have to talk about her."

"Why not?"

"They burned her farm. She's here in Middelburg. In the camp. She and her mother."

"So she's a Boer."

"Ya. Boer."

"Pretty?"

"I'm sorry about Ran After."

"She pretty?"

"Ya, she's pretty."

"You drunk enough now?"

"I guess so, ya."

"Good, 'cause this soldier's dead."

"What soldier?"

Jeff flung the bottle into the dark. There was no sound. Frank kept waiting for it to land.

"Frank, you hear me?"

"Ya, I hear you."

"Can you listen and remember something?"

"Guess so."

"Try hard to listen. Casey and me, we're Canadian Scouts now. Some call it Howard's Canadian Scouts."

"I saw him in there. Gatling. And Charlie Ross."

"Howard put up the money. It's his command. Charlie's second-in-command. Fifteen Mounted Rifles signed up. Some Dragoons. Rest are from all over. We're heading out on a drive in a few days. A bunch of columns are going to sweep east to Swaziland."

"I won't see you, then."

"Frank, listen. You gotta come with us."

"How?"

"Invent some story. Join the Scouts. Can you think of a story?"

"I have a story."

"As long as you do and it makes sense, that's good. Howard isn't stupid, so don't count on that. But come in and tell Howard your story. Tell him you want to be a scout. I'll vouch for you."

"Casey'll say I deserted."

"He will, and you'll say different. I'll vouch for you. Don't do anything tonight. Just get out of here."

Jeff jumped up and was gone.

Frank thought he should stand and go, like Jeff said. The trouble was that his head would not lift. He could still think, though. He rolled onto his back. The damp night was fragrant. Half a moon stood trapped in some branches.

Besides needing to move, there were bigger questions. Should he take

Jeff's advice and join these Canadian Scouts? Wouldn't that take him farther from Alma?

When he tried to focus his spinning thoughts on her, they went out of control and landed on Jimmy. Suddenly, Frank understood what Jimmy had been up to. Being so drunk had torn up his thoughts, and what had not been visible was now obvious.

Jimmy had wanted Frank to go to the party *so he could get arrested.* Giving him horse ointment for a pomade and a drunkard's jacket to wear. Coming here to Middelburg and urging Frank to pose as a reporter with a fake English accent had been part of it too.

Twice today, Whitford had mentioned the Strathconas. He had been hoping Frank would run into someone who knew him, someone like Sam Steele, who would guess he had deserted and arrest him. But Sam had not been at the party.

Powered by this, Frank sat up. Then he stood. He was weaving badly, but he did not fall. He found that the faster he went, the straighter his steps became. To hell with Whitford, Frank thought. He was going where he wanted to go.

Soon, Frank was passing the last of Middelburg's houses. The little windows were dark, and his way was lit only by the moon, as clouds skated across it. The fast walking had changed his state and left him stranded somewhere between plastered and sane. His senses worked but not as a team, and while his fury had flown off, fear came to nest in the void. A gust of wind caused a broom to blow off its stoop and whack a wall. Frank's reaction whipped his neck and spine. He was jumpy. Jumping out of his skin.

He left the hard pan of the final street and felt the bounce and squish of the boggy ground. He was descending the swale. The camp was below. There was more than dogs to fear now, for the Brits would have guards watching for the likes of him—town relations and boyfriends with wire cutters or guns.

Despite the wet, Frank went down on all fours and proceeded like a dog. Cold water pooled darkly around his wrists and knees. Something splashed near him, hopefully a waterfowl and not a snake. The smell was rot and sweetness, a background of sewage.

He peered through the rushes at the fence. The page wire was printed on yellow lantern light. He crawled until he rose onto pocked ground.

The main gate was around a corner near the town side. When he squinted he could see two cigarette ends. The moon made shadows on the beaten ground. The prisoners' tents were pale shapes fanning irregularly up the rise.

There were two lamps, both hanging on poles. One was beside a metal building with a ripple roof, a guard hut probably. The other was toward the camp's lowest corner: the latrine at the swamp's edge.

Frank had no alternative but to wait. Finally, a little ruckus came from the tents. Something had been kicked over. Then someone small passed through the first lamp's yellow glow and into the pale moonlight. The motion was a boy's. He was headed for the latrine. When he got to the bottom and stopped, there was a little rip of liquid.

Frank went fast. He got as close to the boy as he could and whispered.

"*Wil jy kom, bitte? Here, here, kom.*" Things the Kleffs had said to their servants.

The boy ran a few steps and stopped.

"*Bitte, kom.*"

Frank dug in his pocket for a shilling. Threw it. It glimmered in the lamp's light and fell not far from the boy, who got down on his knees, groped, and found it.

Frank had a second shilling. He waggled it, made as if to throw but didn't.

"Alma," Frank said. "Alma Kleff. Alma Kleff. Okay?"

Then he threw the shilling. The boy picked it up and hurried away.

Frank imagined the boy crawling back into bed and forgetting everything. But it was all Frank could think to do.

Soon, there were new sounds. Someone else came, adult this time; dress and bonnet. She stopped well short of the fence.

"Alma, I'm here. It's Frank. I'm here."

The woman stopped. He could see nothing of her except that she was not moving. In a stout whisper, he kept calling.

Then the woman ran away. Frank reckoned it was just someone needing the latrine who was afraid to go there now. Or maybe it was the boy's mother come to discover the source of shillings. He lost sight of the woman among the tents. Kept waiting.

Something metal banged on metal. He looked at the guard hut and saw through holes in the wall that the yellow light was blinking. A woman dashed into the naked yard and pointed in Frank's direction.

"There! There!" Mrs. Kleff, he understood.

Men followed her into the open. Khaki showing white against the dark. He could see their rifles wagging. One held a lantern by its wire handle.

They were coming at Frank accurately enough. He lit out, trying to stay low. When the first rifle barked, the sound doubled against the damp air. He straightened and ran as hard as he could, splashed in the swale's ditch. In his mind, he was making for the fresh graves, beyond which he remembered forest.

More rifles cracked, several shots, and the bullet rips were so close he knew they could see him. He looked for shadow and made for it. He recognized the hill crest when the ground flattened and wondered when the graves would come. Then he tripped on one; fell across its greasy clay. He could tell by the yelling that the guards were still after him.

Then Frank heard a horse pounding out of the darkness. He stood and braced. The horse was right there. All he could do was dive sideways. The rider twisted the horse around and Frank heard it squeal. A hand gripped his collar and he was dragging, bumping along until his arms came out of the rented jacket. He fell on his face.

"Frank! It's Jim! Come on!"

Frank stood and took the offered arm. All he could do was jump across the withers. After they had galloped a ways, Jimmy pulled the ridgling to a halt and jumped off. He boosted Frank so he was astride, then clambered on behind so they were riding double on the ridgling's bare back.

Frank noticed little as they moved among trees, but when they entered the long white prairie, he felt something not right in the ridgling's gait. Each time the horse went to his front legs it was as though he were falling and catching himself.

Soon, Whitford pulled up and jumped off. Frank did too. In the relative stillness, Frank could hear a whistle in the ridgling's breath. Jimmy was hunting across the horse's near side, then spun him so the offside was visible in the moonglow. The problem showed as a black streak. At the top of it, a bullet had entered, gone between the ribs into the lungs.

After that, Jimmy led the ridgling, and as they walked, he spoke to the horse in Crow.

Frank asked Jimmy how he had found him. Had he been watching him all night?

Jimmy was silent.

"That's fine, Jimmy. You go ahead and hate me. I don't care at all. But so you know? About tonight? You didn't get me arrested and out of your hair. You almost got me killed. It wasn't old Sam Steele waiting, it was Casey Callaghan. Casey would arrest me, if he saw me. For desertion, and get me shot. So maybe you and Lionel could just go fuck yourselves and leave me alone. If I want to die, I'll go at it my way."

Jimmy went in the direction of Kleff's Farm. He was no more than a quarter of the way there when he started up the flank of a short kopje. He led the ridgling carefully through the stones, for the pinto could no longer see where to place his feet. It took a long time to get the horse up that hill, but when they did, there was a flat space and water from recent storms shining in rock hollows. Jimmy talked the ridgling into sucking water from a pool. Then he eased him down, first to his knees and then over on his side. That last part hurt and the ridgling made a human moan. Then he let his neck go flat and nudged up and down with his nose.

"Maybe he'll live," Frank said.

"I'd shoot him right now except for the noise."

"I'm sorry I got the ridgling shot."

But Jimmy wasn't listening. He lay down along the warmth of the ridgling's back, gathered his jacket tightly around himself, bunched his hat for a pillow, and slept.

The sun's first flash above the horizon drilled Frank awake. His head was painful. His mouth, dry. He got his feet under him and walked to a rock that still had water cupped. He saw he was alone.

Jim Whitford was gone. The ridgling was dead.

He went to the horse and knelt beside it. He saw the half-stallion's hip was a red hole from which flesh had been carved.

Frank stood and surveyed the plain in all directions. The light was creeping over it, but it was still full of places the flat morning sunlight could not find.

"Whitford! You son of a bitch!"

He imagined the old scout thinking: a dead horse is just dead. If you need it, eat it. But Frank shouted no more. If Jimmy was right there, he would not see him unless Jimmy meant him to.

Frank laid his hand on the ridgling's hip, beside the red crater. The hair was smooth; the flesh firm and tight. He said aloud, "I won't eat you. I won't eat a horse I've ridden."

For the next hour, the first of the day, Frank sat on a big ironstone. He watched the eye of the sun rise, how it painted the landscape prettily at first, then blasted it with fire. Finally, all the space was nothing but glare. Too brilliant to see.

The night cool of the rock surrendered, and once the sun bored into the cavity on the ridgling's hip, Frank imagined things changing and fusing there. It would not be long until the wafts of putrefaction climbed the breeze and the message travelled to the eaters of the dead. The iron-jawed and the red-hooked. Somewhere, big cats draped over tree limbs or popping their tails in a patch of shade would consider how hungry they were, how willing to compromise.

To avoid them and their work, Frank walked off the kopje, headed north.

The meat cut from the ridgling was one message, something about survival and how Frank was not tough enough. The other was about options and how Jimmy had taken most of them away.

Quite possibly, as Frank walked north to Middelburg, he was still under the eyes of the eerie old scout. The only consolation was that if Frank was doing what Jimmy wanted, and was saved, it would not be Jimmy who saved him. It would be Jeff.

Aldershot, January 22, 1901

Queen Victoria was dead. She had died at Osborne at 6:30 P.M., and the news was all over London within the hour. Word was somewhat slower getting to Aldershot but, when General Butler did hear, it touched off in him an abrupt and grinding drama: a grief so jagged he was amazed.

Butler had told countless Blacks, Arabs, and Indians (including Red Crow) that the Queen was their Mother. Apparently, one of those he had convinced was himself. Queen Victoria, mother of her nation's army, of her generals, was gone. Butler was orphaned and wracked.

The other effect was a surge of sibling hatred. A confidante (with access to the royal household) had come to Butler's home in the evening and told him that one of the Queen's last questions was about "dear Kitchener." How was the dear man managing in South Africa?

But nothing for or about Butler, the older son, once dear.

The Queen's death made Butler think of a controversy that had arisen in the British newspapers: people wondering when the twentieth century actually began. The country had celebrated the event on New Year's, 1900, but mathematicians had since pointed out that 1900 was the last year of the nineteenth century, not the first year of the twentieth. They should have celebrated in 1901.

At the time, Butler had dismissed the debate as trivial, but, of late, he had cast his vote with the mathematicians. Even if time were a mere invention to shine importance on human mortality, it still struck him that many things were closing up shop in the first month of the new century, January 1901.

For a whole generation, including Butler and his wife, Victoria's death made a sound like a mighty oaken door slamming. What opened wasn't another door but a slowly creeping dawn that lit a landscape suddenly unfamiliar. Barren, windblown rock—the new century looked to Butler like the Great Karoo Desert: a place not for planting but for burial.

The Queen was the symbol under which they had committed their lives, and she was gone. Did it not follow that Butler, Kitchener, Roberts, and the rest were now officially on their way to their own demise? However long it took, however far into the new century they lasted, the process of death was under way. Butler's only hope was that Kitchener was feeling it too. His clomping feet not so securely planted; his hair lifting from the same force that would one day snap him from the planet.

In this way of thinking, Butler could easily see how South African war had also split across the fulcrum of New Year's, 1901. The fight until then had been about winning. But they had not won, and so the Victorian part of the war had ended in failure and in the monarch's death.

The old century and the old Victorian style had died ineffectually in one another's arms. Butler feared that the new century would lack all of the old ornaments and comforts. Its history would likely be written in some undisciplined fashion, and certainly not by Imperial scribes like himself, who had always improved the story as it went along. Now, a thousand voices would clamour, each insisting on his version.

What this was, Butler saw, was democracy: what the new century would be all about. For a very long time, Britain had gone about bragging of democracy; insisting that the rest of the world should have it. *But had Britain been a democracy herself?* It could be argued that Britain had ceased to be a monarchy only with Victoria's passing. Only then and not before.

If Butler could have laughed tonight, he might have at this idea that they had gone to war in South Africa to force the rebel republics to accept British democracy—when Britain had not been a proper democracy itself. After more than a year of bloody and expensive fighting, the Boers had learned nothing, but Britain had finally knuckled under.

After Elizabeth went to bed, Butler locked himself in the library, without the bother of a candle. He thought about the new century, and about democracy and war.

It seemed likely that it would now be impossible to fight any war; certainly impossible to win one. If the people were the ones to decide, why would they ever choose war? Why commit the wealth of their nation and the lives of their sons to the flames of war? By definition, war required despotism: either a monarch or something with the power of one to put shoulder to the stone of peace and budge it. To Butler, it seemed unlikely to happen. So his kind by logical extension, must soon be extinguished.

Middelburg

The bush Frank lay under received the rain and concentrated it into fat droplets that dabbed his hat like a type of clock. He could not tell the time but he knew it was passing. In the tree above was a black bird that Isaiah called a Ha-Dee-Da, and from time to time it would lean down and laugh at him.

There was also a voice in his head goading him to walk down the slope and up to Gatling Howard's tent. *Go now*, it said, *while Casey's not here to accuse you*. Each time the voice spoke, Frank told it to shut up.

While it was true that The General and The Blue were not on the picket line, meaning their owners were away on a scout, Frank did not regard it as necessarily advantageous. What if Casey had already described Frank to Gatling Howard as a deserter? Even if he had never said a word to Howard, who was to say he hadn't poisoned the minds of other Mounted Rifles who were now Canadian Scouts? For that matter, what if Hilliam, Bapty, or Charlie Ross had read the entrails and concluded he was a deserter all on their own? One way or another, if Frank went to Howard now, he could still be accused, and without Jeff Davis to help him.

Having decided to wait was a little different than being content to, and Frank's discontent came from more than rain and hunger. The worst was the knowledge that, if he'd stayed sober last night, the ridgling would be alive and Frank might—at this moment!—be sitting in the concentration camp looking into Alma's face.

Now that the camp had been roused to chase a man calling after Alma Kleff, he could not go there. Not any time soon.

Watching Howard's camp in the rain told Frank a few things about the outfit he was hoping to join. For starters, they had many horses for the number of men. Except for the odd one messing with his horses or sitting under his oil sheet fixing tack, they were also an idle bunch. It looked like a roundup camp when the weather goes sour. If it had been a British army camp, some crazy officer would have invented a scheme to keep everyone busy: maybe spit-and-polishing boots that would be filthy again after ten steps of muddy marching.

After Frank had watched for several hours, a mail cart arrived. A dozen men got letters and parcels. Frank had not thought about mail for some time, but watching the men reading under their sheets and awnings made him remember when the YMCA man at De Aar had come around with sheets and pencils, and Frank had thought of writing the first letter of his life. It wasn't that he wanted to write a letter now, but that he wished he had written one then. If he had, Jim and Madeleine would have known he was alive. They could have gone about their lives thinking that.

Then it occurred to Frank that his parents had probably made the trip to Ft. Macleod when they heard which train the soldiers were on. They would have been looking among the dress uniforms for their son. They would have heard that he was missing and presumed dead.

In his pocket, probably sopping, were the sheets of paper he'd bought to be a reporter at the party. He vowed that if this scheme to get into the Scouts succeeded, he would write the damn letter and mail it soon. It would mean admitting to his mother that he was serving under Gatling Howard, the man who had shot her relatives with a machine gun, but, angry as that would make her, she would still have some relief.

Within the mist and rain, the light began to fade. The cooking fires bloomed in the murk, and Frank's impatience became shrill. He told it to shut up maybe twenty times as the smell of mutton came to him.

Finally, the eating and cleaning up were over, and the camp settled down for the night. That was when familiar shadows crossed the light. Jeff and

Casey stepped down from their mounts and gave the reins to the horse campies. Bowlegged from a long ride, they walked to the cook's fire, and the cook gave them coffee and started warming their supper. Cook also brought an oiled sheet to put over their heads, though they were soaked to the skin.

Frank watched them drink coffee and smoke; watched them eat. Finally, as he had hoped, Gat Howard's tent flap opened and, carrying a lantern, Howard came crookedly on his stick legs to sit beside them. Paying no more attention to the rain than a duck, he leaned in and listened to what his scouts had to say.

That was Frank's sign. He climbed out of the bush and popped his sodden hat against his pantleg. He walked in toward them, fast and businesslike, and pulled a stump between Howard and the two scouts. Said, "Good evening."

"Now who in the blazing Christ is this polecat? And what gives you the goddamn impression you can come sit your ass in this conversation when you ain't even a soldier?!"

Gat looked bristling mad, and divided in his mind over whether to hit Frank directly or to call a sergeant to do so. In that interval, Jeff started laughing and clapping Frank on the back. He shook Frank's hand in a big loopy way.

"Why, I'll be goddamned if this isn't Private Frank Adams, Gat. Canadian Mounted Rifle. He's been missing for months. How the hell are you, Frank?"

Frank said he was good. He tried not to look at Casey, in case that made him falter.

Jeff told how Aas Vogel Kranz had been attacked when no one expected it: how a shell had landed beside the Cossack post Frank was in. After the battle, the post had a dead Australian in it, but Frank was gone.

"So, what happened there, Frank? Did that first wave of Boers capture you?"

"I don't really know. I don't remember anything until I was wandering the prairie with that old ridgling horse I had."

Frank dug his hair apart and showed his scars to the lantern light.

"One of them rocks that blew in hit me, I guess. For a long time, if I tried to remember something, I'd get a terrible pain. I didn't even know my name."

Jeff helped him through the story. Gat was listening. Frank finally chanced a look at Casey, who was frowning but silent.

Frank explained how he came to a farm he was sure he'd seen before. Maybe he'd reconnoitered it once. There were civilians there, staying with a Boer family, and it turned out those people knew him. They were from Canada, his own part, and they even knew he was a Mounted Rifle. So they kept him and nursed him back to health.

Howard was frowning after this part. "Now why in hell would people from where you come from, civilians, be in South Africa?"

Frank was on secure ground. He gave forth about Brooke and how an English newspaper had backed him to come and write about the war.

Then Frank explained how they took him with when they left the farm; how they went to the Orange River Colony, out Caledon River way. That was when Casey could not stand it any longer.

"Why would they do that? Why wouldn't they just send you to the nearest army garrison? Or to Pretoria?"

"I don't know. Maybe they didn't think I was right in the head. If they'd seen a British patrol, they'd've handed me off."

"Why didn't they, then?" Casey said. He was on it now. Like a terrier.

"Their scout was a Canadian Halfbreed. He didn't know the country. The route he took turned out to be in Boer territory. That's how we got captured by General De Wet."

"Oh, for fuck sake!" Casey turned scarlet and looked away. Gat Howard let out a whoop.

"This here story's got more twists than the legend of Sheherazad," he said. "You really want me to believe you stepped into Boer country and General De Wet himself caught you and made you a prisoner?"

Frank said De Wet didn't stay long because he was being chased by the British. He left them with a commandant who took them into the Basuto mountains. That was where they killed Brooke's horse wrangler, a Nez Perce named Young Sam.

Jeff looked up sharply. He leaned his long body forward. "I knew Young Sam. He was just a kid. Did they say why they did that?"

"Brooke told them Young Sam was a North American Indian, not a black. But they shot him anyway."

Davis nodded and looked at Casey. Frank could tell there was an argument between them, something affected by this news.

Frank was starting into how he became a prisoner of the Basutos when Gat Howard put his hands up.

"Hold on, son. I haven't a clue if any damn word of this is true. It's a helluva story and it's long. We all got to get some sleep. You know this man, Jeff? You vouch for him?"

Jeff said he'd known him since before the war and, yes, he'd vouch for him. Gatling asked the same of Casey but Casey shook his head. He did not explain, simply refused to vouch.

"Hung jury," said Gatling. "Where I come from that means you walk free. But I guess you could've done that without our say-so. What is it you came here wanting?"

"I want to be a Canadian Scout."

"Whoa! Tall order. What is it you're good at?"

Frank could think of no answer. Then he thought of Ovide and said, "I'm good with horses." He expected Casey to sneer and tell how Frank had abused The General, but he kept quiet.

Gatling looked at Jeff. "This here's Solomon's solution. If you're vouching for this man, are you willing to make him your horse-holder?" Then, as clarification to Frank, "We each got three horses in this outfit."

Jeff said the arrangement suited him.

"That's it, then," said Howard, slapping his knees. He got to his feet with his lantern.

"When Jeff Davis needs you as a horse-holder, off you go. When not, you're a horse orderly in camp. All the rest of the orderlies are blacks. You can be their foreman. I don't make anyone a Canadian Scout if I don't know about him. Based on Casey's having doubts, and your story being such a tall tale, you're on probation. Perform well and, who knows, you might get to be a Scout after all."

Howard made an elaborate sideways bow.

"On the other hand, you can walk right back out of here. I won't stop you or say a thing. Find your way back to Canada or, for all I care, grab yourself a frau and go farming."

Frank agreed to be a horse-holder and horse orderly, and they broke up. Jeff took Frank to the quartermaster and got him a blanket and an oil sheet. He said he was sorry he could not give him a place in his tent, because he shared with Casey. He showed Frank where the blacks slept under wagons.

"You might as well get to know them," he said.

Eerste Fabrieken

Frank was alone under the wagon when he woke up. Jeff was kicking his foot.

"Come on. I want to show you your horse."

As they approached, Frank saw the horses' hips in a line and picked out the one that reflected blue: Jeff's indefatigable mare. As they came closer, she lunged for a clump of grass, and Frank felt an old thrill at the sight of a dun-coloured horse behind her. The Blue stepped back and eclipsed the other horse.

When Frank looked at Jeff, the scout was grinning. "Go on. Have a look."

Frank dodged through a gap among the horses, jumped the rope, and came out in front of the line of heads. He saw The Blue, and the dun beside her was Dunny.

Frank reached for his mare's nose. The Blue swung her head and struck his arm with the bone of her face. The dun was scrunching hay and did not stop. She grumbled a little in her throat and her eye was soft.

"What happened to her ear?" Frank asked. The right one was half gone.

"Didn't happen since I've had her," said Jeff. "A bullet does that. Boers must've had her in battle."

"Where was she?"

"Before the Mounted Rifles pulled out, I was scouting for them in the Steelpoort. They were burning farms, and I saw Anandale coming with a herd of horses. Dunny was among them. I told him she belonged to a friend. He wanted to sell her to me, but I told him to go to hell and took her."

Frank wanted to check Dunny's legs. He started into the gap between her and The Blue, and The Blue swung her head at him again and showed her teeth.

"It's a little different," Jeff said. "The Blue's buddied up with the dun. You've got to watch her all the time."

] 363 [

Frank went to the other side, untied Dunny and drew her into the open. The Blue whinnied and stamped. Inch by inch, Frank went over his horse. She had some new marks, the most prominent being a crease in the thick of her offside hip. Probably another bullet. She was far from fat but Frank knew what the dun looked like when she was in shape, and she had that look now. One thing he couldn't figure was why the lines in her throat latch were so deeply inscribed. Then he understood that she had aged.

"You been riding her?" he asked Jeff.

"Mostly leading her. She was pretty rough when I found her. We each get three, so I took her as my second. That dirty roan on The Blue's other side is my third. I use him to pack. You can ride Dunny when we're out. She's your horse. But we'd better not tell the army that right now."

Frank hid his face against Dunny's neck, and Jeff left him to it.

The morning was grey and damp but soon it was raining again. Man and horse, the Canadian Scouts boarded a westbound train. Frank took The Blue, Dunny, and the roan to a horse car and rode on its wall, watching Dunny among the other horses. Frank did not move for the hour it took to get to Eerste Fabrieken.

Fabrieken was the siding for a distillery owned by Sammy Marks. The siding's name meant First Factory. The distillery also had a name, *Volkshoop*, which meant Hope of the People. Jeff and Frank got a kick out of that.

Other trains were arriving in the rain. The area around the station was ever more cluttered with wagons, carts, field guns, downed tents, ammunition boxes, horses, oxen, and mules. Innumerable yoked oxen were towed around by voorlopers in wet floppy hats. It took the whole day to get it sorted and lined out, and by then it was time to make camp again.

Frank started getting to know his fellow horse campies. The most amenable was Kolo, a Zulu who had some English. Frank asked Kolo if he wasn't a long way from home. Kolo said yes, but that before the war, he had been a guide for white hunters and had worked all through the lowlands and gold rush country. He had been away from home so long it did not seem like home anymore.

The second morning of Frank's life as a Canadian Scouts horse-holder began in darkness and wet. The Scouts were supposed to leave at first light;

to go in front of the army and guard it against ambush. Frank readied The Blue and Dunny and left the roan with Kolo.

When the day was as bright as it was going to get, it was still too foggy to see what they were part of. Slumped forward on his horse, Gat Howard helped them picture it. Lord Kitchener's drive had twenty thousand soldiers, he said. This bunch at First Factory was one of several gathered at train stations south and east of Pretoria. Everybody was supposed to start today, at the same time. The whole thing would move in a big sweep, covering the ground from here to Swaziland.

"Burn the farms," Charlie Ross said. He was on his horse to the right of Howard.

"That's right," Gat continued. "Kitchener wants all the rebel farms torched, and the women and children collected and put in camps. I got no comment except that, since we're scouts and will be on the front end, we're likely to be searching those farms. But someone else can do the burning and transporting while we go ahead."

Gat and Charlie did not comment on the weather, the woolly fog they were in. The Scouts were meant to scout what they could not see. Charlie and Gat divided them into patrols and gave them directions on where to go and where to return.

Falling in behind Jeff and The Blue, Frank did not bother to think much about the Boers. He let others stare into the fog while he rocked in the familiar cradle of his dun mare's back. He felt happy in a way he hadn't since she'd been stolen. But, as they went along, Dunny became worked up. She yanked the reins with deep bows and stared at the walls of their cottony room.

About then, Mausers started barking. Carbines answered, and a machine gun rattled briefly. Jeff kicked up The Blue and rode headlong into the murk. Dunny followed at speed, keeping her buddy in sight.

More bursts of gunfire guided them in. Finally, the wheel of a machine-gun limber showed and a Canadian appeared in the milk beside it, swinging his carbine at every motion.

Two Scouts lay in the swampy grass beyond the gun. Both had sergeant's stripes. One was bloody. The other looked unhurt, save for being dead.

Come evening, the dead were buried at Eerste Fabrieken. So little progress had been made that they'd returned to their previous night's camp.

The blacks did most of the gravedigging, and the men who were religious said prayers and sang hymns. Gat Howard and Charlie Ross stood back with their heads bared and bowed, looking impatient.

When the funeral part was over, and they were taking turns throwing dirt into the hole, Gat screwed his hat back on and gave a speech. There was little in it about the hereafter.

"We're scouts," he said. "That's a proud thing. Part of what makes it proud is that it's dangerous. We're out ahead, where things are not well known. In dirty weather, it's where things aren't seen either. These boys found that out the hard way. But I'll tell you fellas, I'd damn sooner be a scout, even on a day like this, and actually fight this war, than herd women and sheep and burn farms."

They shouted like they were demented. It wasn't exactly three cheers but a constant roaring, as if they were in the middle of a fight and Gatling had told them to charge a hill rimmed with Boers. They roared in fury, and it went on longer than was comfortable.

Bethel

Through the murk of the next few days, Jeff and Frank worked alone, but were never far from others. The deaths of his two Scouts must have weighed on Howard's conscience, for his orders were that the Scouts should stay concentrated until the mists and fogs lifted. Gat went to the front with his personal machine gun. He rolled over the ridges and, if a peak divided the mist and a downslope was clear, he would rattle shots into the fog at the edges before he let anyone enter.

The patrols he sent were double-sized. They divided in half and stayed within shouting distance as they rode parallel. After the crude warning of the two deaths, the men were edgy but alert. Frank felt foolish about how he'd ridden out that first day, immersed in the pleasure of his horse. That could have gotten them killed, had Dunny not been smarter.

Frank expected scouting with Jeff to be the same wordless business it had been north of Night Attack. This was mostly true, and Frank spent much time staring between Dunny's ears at Jeff's long back. His thoughts were often about Alma and how he would find his way back to her. If he left that topic, it was to wonder what Jeff did with his mind now that Ran After was dead.

Like a dream in which he was trapped, Frank replayed the time at Bankfontein: when Casey recited the death of Villamon and Frank gave Jeff General Butler's letter and watched the hope drain from his friend's face. Each time around, he ended with Jeff setting the bled letter into the locket of Ovide's grave.

The fourth day dawned clear, winking blue through a fast-racing overcast. Jeff fetched Frank from under his wagon and said they would be scouting with Casey today. The Boers had been hiding in the grounded cloud, trying to pick them off. Now that the Scouts could see the Boers, they must make them pay. Casey wanted to team with his old partner for the taking of revenge.

"Casey wants to bring his second horse, that little bay he calls The Sergeant. He doesn't want you leading him." Jeff said it as though it contained no insult. "Is there a man in the horse camp who can ride a horse and speak English?"

Frank pointed to Kolo. Most of the horse campies did everything with horses but ride them. Kolo had told Frank that, when he used to guide white hunters, he rode every day. Kolo's plan was to own horses after the war; to take his final wages from the army in that form.

Jeff went away and returned with Casey, who sized up Kolo and signified satisfaction by telling him to tack The Sergeant. Casey had an extra bridle. As for a saddle, he said Kolo didn't need one.

They rode southeast for hours across swaley country. The clouds stayed high and it was windless and hot. Only once did they come upon a farm and, despite orders that all farms were to be searched and their occupants held, the four rode past as if blind.

In a long flat that approached a kopje, one that swept up like a bell tent and exploded in a rock minaret on top, Casey tapped The General's reins and the big buckskin halted. Casey pulled his tobacco bag from his shirt, and twisted a cigarette with real cigarette papers. He gave the first to Jeff and made another for himself. He and Jeff lit up and sat their horses, smoking quietly.

"They still there?" asked Jeff.

"Don't look back," Casey told Frank sharply. Then to Jeff: "Three of them still. They're within a mile now. You want to drop off?"

"Let them come to half a mile."

Without looking at Frank, Jeff said, "When we finish our smokes, we'll walk up toward that kopje and stop again. Then Casey looks back and acts like he's seen them for the first time."

"*Jesus Christ! They're after us!* That's how I'll look," said Casey.

"When we start galloping," said Jeff, "they'll think they've got us on the run. They'll be firing, so keep low. When I roll off my horse, don't look at me and don't slow down. The Blue'll keep going. Just follow Casey and do what he does."

They started up the kopje's flank at a walk. The minaret top began to alter into fat stones. They stopped again about a hundred yards from them. This time, Casey turned his horse and scanned the country. Frank thought he could look too without changing things, and saw the three Boers, well within a half-mile. Casey mimed his surprise, raised his Lee-Enfield to his shoulder, and took a barely aimed shot. Then he kicked his horse to a gallop and raced for the top. Jeff and the others followed. A couple of shots whined overhead.

As they were passing the rocky part, Casey reined right, just enough so the Boers wouldn't see them for a moment. In a blink, Jeff's saddle was empty. The Blue kept running straight, her reins knotted and looped on the horn.

They kept galloping. Frank would have liked to look back, to see whether the Boers had made it to the rocks. Then came three quick shots. Casey took a look over this shoulder and skidded The General to a halt. Up by the rocks, the Boer horses had already turned and were racing away. The crest of the hill swallowed them.

Frank took The Blue's reins and led her. They jogged the horses back and as they neared the top Jeff came out of the rocks and walked toward what they saw was a body in the grass. They arrived at the same time he did. They could see the Boers again, below in the distance, still running.

The body lay face down, long and slender. The slouch hat had come off and the back of the head was curly blond. The Boer was hit in the shoulder. It was hard to know how much damage was done.

Casey knelt, grabbed him with both hands, and rolled him over. When Frank first saw blond and a sparse beard, he felt a wave of dread. He thought it was Denny Straytor. But now, with the face showing, he could see the young fellow had coarser features and his hands, flopped palms up, were rough and hard-working. He was not conscious but was breathing.

"Hit anything else?" Casey asked.

"Nicked one's arm, I think." Jeff was still looking at the one on the ground. "Shit. I thought he was the leader."

"What do we do with him?" Frank asked.

"Just leave him," Jeff said.

Casey reached with his boot and touched one homemade flap on the boy's foot. The fellow's trousers were made of scabby home-tanned leather. Casey roughly yanked off the khaki tunic, bloody down one side. It belonged to a Tommy regiment. Frank did not know which one. It seemed rough justice to leave him here.

"Boers'll come back," Jeff said. "He'll be more trouble to them than good to us."

Casey had twisted another cigarette for himself. He climbed back on The General, and reached the cigarette out wide so the cinders would not land on the gelding. The others remounted too. Jeff opened his saddlebag and took out his water bottle. He drank big swallows, and some got past his lips onto his chin. Frank saw that the fluid was blackish before Jeff's wrist came up to wipe it off.

"Don't think us cruel," Casey told Frank, "Jeff and me. There's others would shoot him dead right now." He had the khaki tunic over his horse's withers and stabbed the bloody cloth with one finger. "The Boers have put a price on Captain Ross's head for killing Boers in khaki."

Casey took a few more sucks of smoke, and savoured them in his lungs. Jeff drank more from his bottle, and Frank could smell the rum. Then Casey blew the last smoky gust out his nose and flipped the stub away.

"Let's go. They're probably sneaking back by now."

As the army swept east, the weather remained poor. A hard wind drove the rain into their faces so it stung like pins. The Scouts worked defensively, hanging on to the column. It meant seeing more of Kitchener's farm work, and taking part.

The farms were hard to light in the falling weather. When thatch roofs were dry, they would go off like bombs, but these days they had to work from the inside: newspapers lit under cushioned chairs; torches held to sitting-room wallpaper.

An old, bonneted woman, weeping, took hold of Frank's arm and gripped him tight as the torchmen worked their way through her family's buildings.

"Please," she said, her sour breath against his cheek.

Out of all of them, she had chosen him, and he felt at once guilty and miserable. A bedraggled mother lifted her child to the high step of a wagon. A black servant astraddle the wagon wall swung him over. The boy's head twisted, his giant eyes never leaving the flames that devoured his world.

Frank patted the old hand on his tunic sleeve and it ripped away. The woman's look turned from supplication to hatred, as if it had been whispered in her ear that this khaki—this burner of farms—was after a daughter of her people.

Knobkerries were handed out. The order was to cudgel a field of sheep. Two wagons were already loaded with bleeding carcasses for their dinner. They had enough to eat and no team of drovers was present. The cudgels were about saving ammunition, about preventing waste.

Charlie Ross saw the reluctance on some of the faces. He gathered them together and fixed them with his wild black eyes.

"You'll be goddamn glad when the rebel who owns this farm comes home and can't get a rest or food or a fresh horse—those of you still interested in winning this war."

They went and beat in the heads of the sheep.

Later that day, a view opened and Frank and Jeff saw a Boer cart with a bonneted woman driving. The cart was loaded with chattels and covered in children; pulled by a hard-whipped running ox. Jeff let it go—even though they had been warned these fugitive women were forming laagers as they went east, well armed and every bit as dangerous as their menfolk.

Frank was grateful to Jeff for not chasing the woman; for not making Frank beg for it.

The whole drive was commanded by Gen. John French. The way it was constructed, General Smith-Dorrien's column was east of Alderson's: the one to which the Scouts belonged. Like a great fat snake, Smith-Dorrien's three thousand slid south down the eastern frontier, ready to swallow any Boers that escaped the front and broke in that direction.

In early February, Louis Botha did just that. With an army that also numbered three thousand, he started north, approaching the British in the vicinity of Chrissie Lake.

In the late afternoon of February 5, Casey came looking for Jeff. He found him with Adams, watching Frank put a new shoe on The Blue. She had lost it during an attack and chase the previous night. While Alderson's column was guarding the northern approaches to Ermelo, a Boer commando had risen up and stung them, killing one and wounding three. Jeff and Casey had been part of the subsequent chase—hopeless in the dark. The Boers had come and gone like wasps, their retreat as well prepared as their attack.

Now Casey was strutting toward them with a dispatch bag in hand. Frank understood there was something amiss between Callaghan and Davis, the argument he had noticed at the beginning. Frank still did not know what it was about, because Jeff stayed quiet, and because everything Casey said in front of Frank was coded. One result was that Davis had quit Callaghan's tent and slept in the open near Frank. Jeff and Frank usually worked alone, while Casey went with his own hand-picked four.

Seeing the dispatch bag, Frank thought Jeff was meant to carry it. But what Casey wanted was for Jeff and he to carry it together. Despite their falling out, Casey still came to Jeff if a proposition was difficult; if he wanted an expert behind him.

When he knew what was wanted, Jeff asked what the dispatch contained. The rumour about Botha's army moving north was loose in the camp, and Jeff supposed it was that. The question caused—or allowed—Casey to erupt.

"This," he shook the bag, "is stale rubbish about Ermelo. Written before Botha even started to move. But because it's Lord Kitchener's stale rubbish, we're meant to risk our lives delivering it to Smith-Dorrien before morning. Right through the middle of a battle, I expect."

Casey concluded by giving Frank a filthy look. He had revealed a confidence in Frank's presence and blamed Frank for being there to hear it.

Jeff asked how far, and Casey said forty miles. They had to go soon and ride all night. That led to a discussion of horses. They agreed they needed more horsepower than one. Casey wanted The General and The Sergeant. Jeff wanted all three of his, and he wanted Frank along to manage them. Casey did not want Frank. Jeff insisted. While the camp was having supper, the three men and five horses left together.

The weather was changing. The horizons on the east and west were choked with mats of low-lying cloud, but the sky above was clear. When the moon rose, it would be almost full, meaning they could see and be seen. Along some ridges and down some valleys were remnant loaves of fog left from wetter days.

They had gone maybe ten miles of the forty, and were navigating by the moon, when drifting fog along a ridge line blew off and exposed a stripe of Boer riders. Knowing they were revealed, the Boers came in pursuit. Casey darted out of the valley's gut, making for a deep shadow under a hanging cloud. The two groups were less than a mile apart.

Casey and Jeff had started the evening on their number-two horses, which meant that Frank was riding and leading a faster group. Casey signalled him ahead. With bullets singing, Frank and his three entered the trees and the relative dark. He slacked his pace and let the others catch up. The General and The Blue were saddled, and Casey and Jeff switched onto them and were off again, all without losing ground.

Casey found a notch dense with night, the mouth of a descending coulee. He entered and they galloped down, whipped by overhanging branches. They went as fast as they could in the coulee's twisting dark, and Dunny piled into The Blue when Casey slid The General to a halt and jumped off. He leapt across and climbed to the foot of a U-shaped tree. He pulled out his dispatch bag, scratched a hole among the roots, and buried it.

They continued to the coulee's bottom and spilled out on a dome grown over with moon-shiny sage. The new valley was broad and pocked, with a crooked serpent of black creek. Casey was riding The General. Wanting to take The Sergeant too, he jerked the reins from Frank. He pointed north, the direction he was headed. Casey signalled for Jeff to go the other way. To Frank, he gave no orders. Frank started to follow Jeff, but Jeff waved him back and galloped south on The Blue.

The moon was still high and bright. The packed roan was coughing and Frank felt the long rise and fall of Dunny's breath under his legs.

It came to him that he was likely to be captured now, and that perhaps that was the plan: that Frank and his horses would be caught and this would buy time for the others to get away. It made him angry. How could Jeff save Dunny only to give her away again so soon? Frank determined not to let it happen. He was about to strip off the roan's pack and leave him, but changed his mind. Frank's job was the horses, and the roan was his horse to look after, same as the dun.

Frank looked around for the darkest place and found it on the valley's far wall. The blackness there could be another coulee or a bunch of trees; something to hide inside, at any rate. He took his horses fifty yards up the creek until their hoof irons knocked on a shelf of stone. Then he urged them across the black-snake creek. He touched Dunny up to a canter across the pocked flat, the roan following, and didn't slow until they were inside the darkness.

The place was a steep-sided notch outside of which some evergreens fanned. Frank pushed both horses into the kloof's pocket and held them there. He watched the dome on the opposite side, the place where the coulee emptied.

Minutes later, twelve riders boiled onto the shining stage and halted. The Boer horses were spooky in the strange light and began to mill. Confusion was evident. When they split, only two went in Casey's direction; ten in Jeff's.

By the time Frank recrossed the flat and the creek, there was no sign or sound of anyone. He followed the path of the ten, easily visible on the moonlit grass. He kept on until the valley made a right turn, and there he left his horses and walked until he could see again. He could not see far, for the view was blunted where one side of the valley shadowed the rest.

The last thing visible before this darkness was a game trail climbing the north flank. When he'd retrieved the horses, he took this trail and rose along it. Everything had the smell of arid country when wet. The dun seemed to see much better in the dark than Frank did, and he let her walk at her normal pace while he himself was blind. The trail rose almost to the top of the wall, then levelled and went in and out of the hill folds. Sometimes they were deep in brush, sometimes in the open.

When the valley curved and went south again, the whole of it was in moonlight. Mausers began firing close by, and Frank ducked in his saddle, thinking they were aimed at him. All ten fired, almost at once, but there were no songs in the air near him, no snapping branches.

Frank urged Dunny forward until Frank could see the hip of a Boer horse in the bottom. He got down, tied the roan to Dunny, and left them in the cover of trees. He went on alone, screened by bush, until he came to an open hill flank down which he could see.

Jeff was still on The Blue. On his north side, the Boer horsemen had him half surrounded. It looked like a parley except that Jeff's hands were raised. A long-bearded Boer kicked his pony in the guts and stepped toward Jeff. Probably he meant to collect Jeff's guns: the carbine across his back and the two Colt revolvers shoved in his belt.

Frank had his carbine and took aim across a crumbled rock. Though everything was murky and uncertain, he thought he had the front Boer in his sights. Frank was calming his breath when he heard a shot and the Boer slumped away. A rattle of pistol fire followed. Jeff had both of his Colts in hand and was firing. The Blue bolted through the Boer line. A Boer horse darted away, its rider grabbing mane to stay on. At least two Boers were down, having jumped or fallen—or been shot.

Frank heard Dunny grumble. He looked to see what ailed her and saw that she was leaving, not urgently but tugging the roan along, the two of them crowded in the narrow trail. Without careful aim, Frank squeezed off a scatter of shots in the Boers' direction. Then he ran for the horses. Dunny had never left him before, but then he understood. She had scented The Blue. In horse helio, the two mares were planning a rendezvous.

Frank caught the stirrup and swung up. He held Dunny back long enough to get the roan trailing. Then he gave the dun her head, and she tore along as if it were day and the path wide. Frank put his arm over his face to shield against slapping branches.

Every while, when Frank relaxed around the notion that they were clear, a rifle would crack. Bullets snicked the bushes or whined overhead. The Boers were still following and maybe saw their motion through the brush. But there came a time when there were no more bullets; when the hooves on the rocky path were the only sound.

By the time Dunny and The Blue found each other, the moon had dipped into a cream of clouds along the horizon. Without its light, the sky overhead was deep purplish and pricked with stars. The mares stood nose to nose, instantly becalmed, and Jeff and Frank could only laugh at the unerring constancy of buddied horses. Compared to it, human relationships were fickle and qualified.

If he had spoken at that moment, Frank would have babbled in amazement at what Jeff had done. The bravest, most foolhardy thing he had witnessed in the entire war, or out of it. Frank had not been looking in the right place at the telling instant and therefore had not seen how Jeff drew his Colts and started firing. Frank had wondered all through the pursuit if he would find Davis whole or nursing wounds. But Jeff seemed not to have a scratch.

The only sign of any disturbance was how fast he drained his spiked water bottle. Then he reached into his saddlebag and produced a second one. This time, he offered a drink to Frank before taking any more. It was rum, as Frank thought. Frank could see how Jeff was calmed by the drink. He leaned peacefully over his saddle rolls, his forearms crossed in The Blue's stand-up mane, his long hands dangling.

"Casey probably picked up that bag," he said. "But we're close enough, we better check."

"I can't see," said Frank.

"The coulee we came down is just ahead. We'll let The Blue find her way. If the dispatch isn't there, we'll camp until morning."

When the horses' breathing had calmed, they rode on. Jeff was right, the coulee was there. They rode to the U-shaped tree. Frank would have ridden past, but Jeff stopped. There was a hole where the bag had been. After that, they climbed to a high bare place where the distant glows of a column's bivouac fires were visible. They took turns sleeping, and it was soon morning.

It was wet again, next day. As they covered the distance through a light drizzle, they could hear the deep booming of an artillery fight. By the time they found Smith-Dorrien's camp, the battle had been over for an hour. They asked around and found Casey. He led them to a fire with a coffee can in the coals and asked an orderly for some cold meat and hardtack. Then he told his story.

After picking up the dispatch, he'd gone most of the way to Chrissie Lake. He waited in a blue-gum forest for light. The battle started at dawn, and he came the rest of the way down seams between Boer commandos. He was just about to cross the space from the Boer to the British side when a Boer caught sight of him. Not just saw him but was willing to leave what he was doing to try to kill Casey.

"I got him to follow me. I led him into a kloof and got above him. Shot him when he came in." Casey threw up his hands in imitation of the shot Boer.

After that, he waited until the Boers started to withdraw. As soon as it was only Smith-Dorrien's guns firing canisters, he raced in. Smith-Dorrien could not believe a dispatch had made it to him through the battle. He said he would make sure Callaghan's feat was recorded in the day's dispatches.

"What about the message you were carrying?" asked Jeff.

"Smith-Dorrien read it, scrunched it, and put it in his pocket. What about you? Not many followed me, so I figured you'd drawn a crowd."

Jeff nodded.

"There were ten," Frank said.

Jeff looked at Frank mildly, but still as if he had done something wrong.

"But you got away," said Casey.

"I didn't," said Jeff. "They caught me."

"Go on, you bugger," said Casey. "You wouldn't be here."

"They had me but I got away."

Frank waited for Jeff to elaborate. He did not. After listening to Casey fluff his story as high as it would go, Frank could not believe Jeff would leave it at that. When he looked at Casey sitting there, assuming that the silence meant Jeff's adventure had been inferior to his own, Frank could not stand it.

"All ten were around him," Frank said. "Jeff had his hands up. One came for his guns. Jeff drew his Colts and shot him. He rode right through them, firing."

Jeff had closed his eyes. Casey's face turned dark. "How could you see that?" he challenged Frank.

"I followed him. I was above on a trail. I saw it clearly."

A few minutes earlier, Casey had given Jeff his cigarette makings. Jeff had twisted a smoke, and now he lit it. The cigarette's end was a leaf of fire. He detached it carefully from his lip and blew out the flame.

"Frank shot at them," Jeff said. "That helped me get clear."

"No," Frank said. "You were through. You were long gone."

"You helped hold them," Jeff said, looking at no one. He wasn't building the story up. He was still trying to make it smaller.

Casey was studying Jeff with bug eyes.

"That was stupid," he said.

Jeff did not react to the blunt insult. Again, Frank could not stand it.

"What do you mean, stupid?"

"Now listen, you," Casey said. He stuck his pointer finger out in Frank's face. "You stay out of this."

Then to Jeff, Casey said, "You want to get yourself killed? Is that it? Too much pride to surrender? A surrendered man in Boer hands loses his tunic and his boots. For Christ's sake!"

Jeff turned to Casey. He had his cigarette between his knuckles. He reached and touched the finger ends on Casey's shirt.

"White men."

This seemed to anger Casey even more. "Goddamn that nonsense! You don't look like any nigger to me."

Jeff leaned back, sipped his smoke. Closed his eyes. "Tell him about Young Sam again. Tell it all."

Frank did not want to. He'd already told both of them, and wasn't sure what Jeff was after. But, finally, clumsily, he did as he was told. He emphasized that Brooke had told Von Roster that Young Sam was an American Indian, a Nez Perce. The Boer said it made no difference to him. Then they took Young Sam away and shot him twice. Then Frank remembered the part about Jim Whitford.

"Von Roster said he'd kill Brooke's old nigger too, if he found him. He meant Jim Whitford. Jim's a Crow Halfbreed."

"The hell with this," said Casey when Frank was done. He stood and planted his hands on his hips, his thick arms angled like pot handles. "To make sure you don't get shot for a black, or a half-black, you're going to get yourself shot. It makes no sense."

Jeff leaned back and looked at his one-time scouting partner. "It's the difference between shot and executed. I don't want to be executed."

"Then *you*," said Casey, and he was pointing out of a fist at Frank again, "*you* can scout with him. Because I won't. Neither will anyone else."

Casey walked away in the direction of the other fires.

Frank had given their horses to Smith-Dorrien's campies. The horses were picketed where Jeff and Frank could see them, eating hay out of nosebags. When Casey was gone, Jeff stood and walked to them. He passed between Dunny and The Blue and came back with something clutched inside his tunic. He sat and checked around himself, but he and Frank were creatures of little interest in the angry celebration of the battle. They were calling it a victory, but an officer and more than twenty soldiers were dead.

Jeff moved his tunic back and pulled out a bottle. It was something clear and unlabelled. The day they'd been attacked north of Ermelo, he and Frank were first into a farmhouse. Jeff had not shown the bottle to Frank then, but said now that's where it came from. He opened it and handed it across. Frank took a long burning swallow. Jeff took it back and dropped the level a couple of inches.

"Casey doesn't like how I do things. That's why I don't tell him."

Frank apologized for saying so much, though he could not imagine having left it unsaid.

Jeff shrugged. "Would have happened anyway." He was already a little dreamy from the white liquor. "Maybe you won't be a horse orderly for long."

Frank felt slow, behind the pace of things. He did not understand.

"If Casey thinks you should be my partner, maybe he'll tell Gat to make you a Scout."

Frank had the bottle. He wondered whether it would happen, and whether he wanted it to.

"You don't have to be my partner," said Jeff. "Casey doesn't want anyone scouting with me. He thinks I'm dangerous. He doesn't like you so he doesn't care if it's you. It's true, you know. I could get you killed."

Frank and Jeff bedded down near the fire; killed the rest of the bottle after they were in their blankets. Jeff threw it onto the coals and a blue flame shot out the mouth.

Frank liked the idea of being Jeff's partner, of having days like today that passed in a minute. But, while he waited to sleep, Frank considered what it would mean to Alma. What would she think of him in the role of a scout? When he started this drive, he'd been certain he could avoid the violent things. But then they made him cudgel all those sheep. He remembered the old woman's hand gripping his sleeve. He believed Alma would be able to sense what he did while he was away from her; that she would smell however much char and death was on him.

Frank thought of Jeff too, and how Ran After was no longer part of his story; how, for all these reasons taken together, Jeff was right to warn him.

By the time his stomach settled and allowed sleep, Frank knew he would not try to become a Canadian Scout. If it was pushed on him, he would try to refuse it. Being Jeff's horse-holder was enough, maybe too much.

Piet Retief

General Alderson's column and the rest of French's huge army crawled southeast, with the town of Piet Retief near the Swaziland frontier as a rough target. No matter how many Boers spilled out of the trap (usually past Smith-Dorrien's left shoulder, as Botha had done), the idea remained that a significant number of the enemy were still in flight ahead and would be caught between the rock of the eight-column army and the hard place of Swaziland—where the Swazis were said to hate Boers and be willing to kill them.

As the British got closer, several captures and plunders proved the Boers were there in the squeeze. Smith-Dorrien captured a Boer convoy. Rimington's cavalry charged a commando at Klipfontein. Dartnell destroyed Boer supplies. French, with Knox and Pulteney, closed in on Piet Retief.

That was the good news. The bad news was that the weather had become worse, and they were hungry. The rivers were torrents, the roads quagmires, and convoys meant to feed them had left Natal and never arrived.

The country was also much rougher. Castellate and crumbling heights. Sun-baked scree. Blue-gum plantations on impossible slopes. All these planes colliding meant it was harder for the scouts to plan a route, or to guess where the enemy might hide.

When Casey, Jeff, and Frank returned to Alderson's column from Chrissie Lake, Frank was not offered a promotion to scout. Too much was going on—fog, rain, hunger, breakdowns—for anyone to think of it or care. Because Casey never scouted with Jeff, and no one else did, Frank was as good as partnered with Jeff anyway, without the curse of the official title.

When they were out scouting, Frank left the Boer-hunting to Jeff, while he himself concentrated on bringing them back safely. He never raised the subject with Jeff, or Jeff with him, but he believed they both understood.

Another such wordless understanding was about alcohol. If Jeff tracked down a rebel, captured or killed, Frank would check the man's saddlebags and confiscate any booze found there. When they were first into a house, Jeff guarded the family in one room, while Frank went through the promising places: father's and grandfather's dresser drawers; any stand or cabinet on the men's sides of bed; the meat safe—and, for some reason, the horse manger, where liquor was occasionally found under a pad of hay or straw.

Usually, they could count on at least one bottle per farm, and one time they hit a jackpot of homebrew in a root cellar that kept them for a week.

They did their drinking in the dark, in the dependable solitude of their evenings. Jeff had always been adept at slipping away from army fraternity, the bragging and singing that Casey so liked. Now that Casey would not ride with Jeff, it was even simpler. Jeff was a regimental sergeant-major and a valued scout, but when darkness fell, the other men avoided him. Frank had no effect. He was invisible.

Jeff seldom spoke when he drank. He would often lie with the back of his head on his saddle, studying the sky. Left to himself, Frank thought of Alma, and then of his parents and Doc. In equal measure, he thought of the past and of the hoped-for future, both at the foot of Chief Mountain.

Sometimes his thoughts would spread to Ovide, Young Sam, and Fred Morden; Jimmy Whitford and Lionel Brooke. He wondered if the latter two were back across the Atlantic; whether Lionel had said anything to Frank's mother, or to Marie Rose Smith.

Frank thought of Alice Kettle's advice, which he had resolutely gone against. Of her kindness.

What he seldom thought about were the other scouts, at the other fires, laughing, snoring, or silent. If he did think about them, it was the question of why they had signed on and not gone home. He reckoned not one had his reason of a Boer sweetheart. But some might have a friend to avenge, an Ovide or a Fred Morden. Possibly, one or two had missing horses they were trying to find.

Frank bet that many had no more reason than how little awaited them back home. In a sense, that was Jeff, whose loss of Ran After had stolen his future. Casey, too. Being a teamster at Maple Creek was never going to rival being a lieutenant of scouts.

For ones like Gat Howard and Charlie Ross, there was no home, and they didn't grieve it either. Fighting and so-called adventure were their lives. Even in a crack outfit like this one, full of good scouts, Gat was undisputed king and Charlie Ross his respected Segundo—with their histories of derring-do and their Distinguished Service Orders. Frank had heard the other men say they would follow them to hell and back, and they meant it.

At the end of Frank's and Jeff's evenings, the last one holding the bottle would throw it into the bushes. Each would roll into his blanket against the falling and rising wet. Sodden inside, sodden outside.

Derby, Transvaal

Mid-February placed them in even more confusing country close to the Swaziland border. It kept on raining and the rivers were all in flood.

On a particularly miserable night, Frank saw Gat Howard coming toward their smoky fire, his funny walk making him look as if both his legs were broken. His pipe was to the side, clamped in his teeth. He had his hand flat above the pipe's bowl, to keep the rain from wetting the tobacco.

Frank's heart flopped because he assumed this was his promotion. How was he going to tell Gat Howard that he wanted to pass on what Gat must think the greatest honour and privilege a human could have?

Frank thought they should at least hide their bottle, but Jeff had it strangled and did not move.

When their major arrived, he said, "It's my birthday. I'd like to buy you boys a drink at my fire—if you can interrupt your drinks long enough to have mine."

At Gat's fire, those with waterproofs were wearing them, while those without were wrapped in groundsheets. Gat had a few bottles circulating, and then he gave a speech. Mostly, it was the familiar one about the Scouts being the cream of the crop, the only soldiers on the British side who were a match for the Boer bitter-enders. Because they were more courageous than many units, more determined to get this thing over with, they caught more bullets. But there wasn't a decent officer in British South Africa who would dare say their high casualty rate was a failure and not about the bigger risks they took. Gat thanked them for being under his command.

"Those other officers, even Mike Rimington, would snap you boys up in a minute, if I let it happen," was how he concluded.

"How old are you?" yelled someone from the back.

Gat did not care for the question, but answered it.

"I'm fifty-five!"

Stone silence was the sound of astonishment: a hundred men trying not to show surprise. Gat laughed at their discomfort.

"Ya, I know. It's a hell of an age for a working soldier. But I don't feel one bit different than I did ten years ago. In fact, some days I feel younger."

Then other men started proposing toasts and giving speeches. Charlie Ross recounted the story of Gat unclipping his red-hot Colt machine gun from its limber and running with it in his hands, to save it. Eddie Holland had done the same thing at Liliefontein, proving how inspiration worked in an army.

An ex-Dragoon told about a reconnaissance north of Belfast when Gat got so far ahead he wound up fighting a whole Boer commando by himself. Lessard had to come back and drag him out.

Then there was the one about a Brit officer trying to keep Gat from charging a position, and how Gat had said to him, "What's your army here for anyway, then? To play lawn tennis?"

Finally, Gat ordered them all to bed. Tomorrow was a big day, he said. They had been pushing these Boers for the better part of a month and now they had the bastards trapped against the Swazi frontier. A lot of rifles and ammo and wagons and livestock had been confiscated, but that didn't mean a whole lot. Tomorrow they might find out how many Boer rebels the drive had contributed to Kitchener's bag.

"Damn good birthday," he said, to close. "I don't expect to have a better one."

Morning came too soon to believe, as if the bugler had made a mistake. The officers' whistles and the sergeants' yells, the usual hullabaloo, proved there was no error. It was always awful to crawl from damp blankets into cold drizzle in the dark, but that was the sort of morning it was.

As they readied themselves and their horses for travel, Gat Howard was all over camp, giving an illustration of his vigour, fifty-five years old or not. Today, he was to command a forward unit that contained, besides his Scouts, parts of two horse battalions and four guns from the Royal Horse Artillery.

The columns on either side of Alderson would be exerting pressure on the expected three hundred Boer rebels, to keep them trapped against the Swazi hills.

They moved out at 8:30 A.M., beginning a slow and miserable slog in continuous rain. The headway was so slow they had only made eight miles by noon. The mist was thick and, in places, stood like a wall. Though there was little sniping from the Boers, it was hard not to imagine them behind that milky stuff, rifles poised. When the Boers were not shooting in a situation so advantageous, it was worrisome. They might not be there, or they might be drawing you where they wanted you to go.

The passage of hours did not change the weather, and all of the colliding planes were more confusing in the fog and downpour. When the rain paused and the veils lifted, as briefly occurred, they saw ridges with bigger ridges behind, and a filling of grey in every gap.

In the middle of the afternoon, a decision was taken to make a push while there was still daylight. The Scouts left their support MI and moved forward at a trot. They came to a north–south ridge, and many dismounted and climbed it. Lined out in good cover, they thought they had command of the valley, but the shifting rain revealed a bigger kopje ahead. The bush-covered mass commanded them.

Again, patrols went out, probing the area between the ridges. These had only started when firing was heard. The Scouts on the ridge stared into the confusing murk.

Of the boys already down there, Beattie's men saw four wagons in the direction from which the firing had come. When Beattie got within three hundred yards of that spot, his horse was riddled; killed under him before it hit the ground. More MI and Scouts approached, and artillery. They shelled the hillside and raked it with machine guns until the Boers quit sniping.

At the wagons, they found Gat Howard dead. So was his Native guide. Howard's orderly, Sergeant Northway, was barely alive and told them how it happened; how they'd come up to the wagons and been shot point-blank. Then Northway died too.

It would soon be dark, and it was not possible to accommodate all of the men who wanted to look at their dead major and see where he'd fallen. Charlie Ross, now in command, wrapped the dead and got them on a cart. He ordered everybody to withdraw. No matter how many rifles and guns had fired at this kopje, it was a still a trap, a place of ambush. Two more men had already been wounded.

Before they left, they poured gunpowder on the wagons until they got them to burn. They were just decoys—useless, empty things—but no one wanted them to exist.

Back at camp, Charlie Ross took his Scouts and the dead away from other kinds of soldiers. They set up camp and made fires, and everyone who had liquor brought it. Though he did not drink himself, Charlie got a special rum ration from Alderson's staff.

When they were assembled, and the drinking men were drinking, Charlie Ross walked a track up and down. Anger filled him and spilled out with a kind of excitement that sped the fuel.

Alone with the bodies, they unwrapped them to determine how each had died. They thought there would be more wounds in Gat Howard, for already a rumour was circulating that the Boers had stood over him, filling him with lead. There were three wounds: arm, stomach, jaw. They uncovered Richard Northway and looked him over too. He had bullets in his back and stomach. Something about his stomach wounds made Charlie call a medic to dig the bullets out. As Charlie thought, the wounds had been made by dumdums.

Led by Charlie Ross, they pieced the story together.

Seeing the wagons in the fog, Gat had wondered if they were full of Boer ammunition. The wisest thing would have been to wait and call for MI and artillery support. But that could never happen in the little wedge of day remaining. If Gat didn't do something, the Boers might get away with those wagons. So he chose to go forward.

It was hard, in this story, to give Howard credit for knowing better than the Boers. He had thought what they wanted him to think. When he came ahead, they let him get nice and close, then let him have it.

Just last night they had been telling stories about Gat's famous impatience, how he loved to go at anyone who wanted a fight. Any bunch of Boers who were sitting out of rifle range, he'd charge with his machine gun. But his impetuosity had killed him today.

Charlie Ross had run his scout's eye over the place of murder. He had seen the angles at which the dead men lay. Those Boers must have been so close to the Scouts when they started shooting that they could have just as easily taken them prisoner. If you can take someone prisoner and you shoot him, said Charlie, it's the same as shooting a prisoner. The reason they did it was probably because Gat had a black man for a guide. That was their rule: shoot whites that use blacks to fight. If Gat's scout had a rifle, that would have done it for sure.

Foul murder and dumdum bullets. Northway had not said the Boers had been in khaki, but that was assumed. Maybe they were standing with their backs to Gat, in the curve of those wagons. Maybe that's how he had been lured. When he hailed them from close up, they spun and fired.

As the stories took on elaborate forms, the men grew angrier and angrier. They were full of the energy of hate. No one could bear to sit. They milled like cattle after a stampede. Spat tobacco juice into the flames. Cursed the Boers aloud. Bastards! Damn bastards!

Then Charlie Ross said he had heard of outfits, other colonials, who'd had this sort of thing done to them. Some of those outfits had sworn a bloody oath. What that oath said was they would never take another Boer rebel prisoner. Charlie looked around with his black eyes sparking.

Hadn't Lord Kitchener himself said that Boers caught wearing khaki, Boers using dumdums, Boers abusing white flags, should be executed? Why then, when it was so clear-cut as that, should they bother to wait on some tribunal that was not even present when the deeds were done?

"So how about it?" Charlie called, a scar on his forehead livid in the fire's light. He looked from one to another with his black eyes. "How about it?"

"How about what, Captain Ross?" a fellow asked. His stupidity made a few men laugh.

"How about—in Major Gat Howard's honour—the Canadian Scouts take that oath right now? That, after today, we will take no more Boer rebels prisoner. Who's got a Bible?"

A Bible was found, and Charlie took it and put his hand on it and swore the oath. Then he held the Bible out until another man took it and swore. And so on. One after another.

The men who had already sworn stood at the edges of the fire's glow, facing out to ensure that nobody approached and heard what they were doing.

Frank Adams watched the oath-swearing. He saw Regimental Sergeant-Major Jefferson Davis swear it, one of the first to do so. Frank stood back. The difference he had been trying to define in his head between him and the Scouts, the one he rehearsed most every night in some translated conversation with Alma—after tonight, it would be much easier to explain. The others had taken the oath and Frank had not.

Charlie Ross, with his scout's eye for detail, saw Frank Adams at the edge of the light. In the lull that signified everyone else had sworn, Ross took the Good Book and walked to Frank.

"You going to swear, Adams?"

"Not a Scout, sir."

"We've been losing Scouts. We lost two of the best today. I have the authority vested in me to change you from a horse boy to a Scout." He laid his hand on the Bible. "I swear I will do that."

Frank knew what would happen. By turning down this offer and refusing to swear, he would become the only one who had insulted Gat Howard's memory, with the great man's corpse just ten feet away. It was something no one would forget or forgive.

"Fine as I am, sir."

"What does that mean? Fine as you are?"

"Horse-holder for Sergeant-Major Davis."

"So you refuse to swear."

"Yes, I do."

Others had come close enough to listen. Several heard Frank Adams say it. It would be general knowledge by morning. Frank checked where Jeff Davis was. He was sitting by the fire with his eyes closed to slits, pretending to sleep.

Aldershot

General Butler had a friend at the War Office who kept him apprised of the rumours concerning Lord Kitchener, even the contents of some of his letters to Lord Roberts.

At times, it was hard to believe the antics at Melrose House, Kitchener's headquarters in Pretoria. A common starling fell from a Melrose chimney and Kitchener had it put in a cage. He became so fond of the bird that, when he returned from a foray and found that it had escaped, he insisted his entire staff stop what they were doing (running the war) to search for it. The starling was found in the park across the road, and the war was allowed to resume.

The bird was one of the responsibilities of Kitchener's ADC, Captain Maxwell. Kitchener was fond of Maxwell, whom he called The Brat. He allowed The Brat to tease him when no else could.

The Brat's serious duty was rousing Kitchener from his funks. If teasing and cajoling did not work on his depression, it was said that The Brat resorted to pageantry and costumes. To remind Lord Kitchener of happier days, Captain Maxwell would dress as a sultan or as a member of a sultan's harem.

At the end of February 1901, there was much of this cajoling to do, for Kitchener's massive Swaziland drive had failed to defeat the Transvaal Boers. It had yielded women and children for the concentration camps, a great deal of livestock, and very few actual rebels.

Fearing how long it might take to defeat his enemy, Lord Kitchener tried to make peace. He arranged a meeting with Louis Botha at Middelburg, Transvaal, at which the Boer general delivered a list of terms. When the British Government and Governor Milner saw the document, they would not accept many of its demands, and the process collapsed.

Kitchener locked himself in his room, and not even The Brat could lure him out for days.

What finally emerged from that room was Kitchener of Kaos, the general in his least merciful guise. If the British wanted victory at war, then the general would give it to them. He would grind Boer nationalism into sand.

From Melrose House, fresh decrees came daily. The blockhouse system that was presently guarding the railways would be greatly expanded. The lines would cross open country until the whole of rebel South Africa was sectioned and fenced.

He demanded new units of mounted infantry, small ones made up of his toughest scouts. Travelling light and fast, they would pounce on the enemy, *like tigers*. Lord Kitchener's very own bitter-enders.

Pongola River, April 1901

The problem with Kitchener's Swaziland drive was that it had no back wall. The Boers who killed Gat Howard were in theory trapped, but then they dissolved into the foggy landscape. The only advantage the drive had created was that many of the Boers no longer had homes and so must hide in the wildest places. This included women and children who had avoided the camps but now lived in wagons.

Even at this stage, Kitchener was not ready to call off the drive. A few columns were ordered to carry on into Swaziland and south of it, despite the flooded rivers and dissolving roads. The Assegai River had risen an astounding eighteen feet, and the Pongola was higher than a horse's head. The armies that went south and east were soon locked between these rivers. The Swazis were willing to feed the invading British army at a price. A two-hundred-pound bag of mealies cost a gold sovereign.

As the hungry British floundered in the wet, the Swazis—in sympathy or embarrassment—killed fourteen Boers with their assegai spears. It was the biggest one-battle addition to Kitchener's bag since the great summer drive of 1901 began.

—

Trapped beside the Pongola River, Frank finally heard a lion. There was no question. As they cowered in the muck, after another day spent up to their necks in the river trying to build a pontoon bridge, the Canadian Scouts woke to its awesome roars. The piquet was doubled. Some of the men surrendered to fear and fired blindly into the dark.

The following day, Charlie Ross went to the Swazis and parted with more of his dwindling mealie money to convince them to hunt the lion. When the Swazis returned, there was no lion hanging by its feet from a pole, but they assured the soldiers it was gone.

It was not far-fetched to say that Jeff and Frank and their horses survived this sickly camp because Dunny and The Blue could swim. Jeff told Charlie Ross that he and his horse-holder were willing to cross the flooded river and do some hunting and scouting in the highlands to the north. As most everyone else was afraid to cross, Ross said yes.

The mares swam the brown flood. Then they crossed the remaining fever flats and climbed out of them. The air cooled and sweetened as they lifted into the highlands. The first thing Jeff did was head for high grazing, so their horses could have a feed away from tsetse flies and other torturing bugs. Jeff and Frank rested in the open and scouted for Boers only in the sense of staying well away from them.

This was the first of several trips. They always stayed away two or three nights. Toward the end of each time, Jeff would exert himself to hunt. He would bring down a blesbok, a kudu, or a couple of impala. With the animals butchered and hanging in meat bags off their saddles, they descended and dared the river again. Coming back was not difficult. The horses were much stronger from the firm grass and clean air.

Though Jeff was supposed to be scouting on these trips, not even Charlie Ross quizzed him about Boer activity across the river. Charlie and everyone else was grateful for fresh meat and left it at that. The Boer fighters and their fugitive women were out there somewhere, in the pinch between the Swazis and the Zulus, but the British never saw them and were in no shape to chase them.

That this followed Gat Howard's death and Frank's refusal to take Charlie Ross's oath amounted to a good thing for Frank. For the moment, he was a part of what brought meat. That was more important than principle and revenge.

When the engineers finally built enough bridges and firmed enough roads for food convoys to arrive from Newcastle and Volksrust, the emptied wagons went back laden with soldiers suffering fever and dysentery. Alderson's column built a depot as its final act. It was April by the time they emerged from the bush.

A few days later, they boarded a northbound train on the Durban–Johannesburg line. The moment it jerked into motion, Frank was washed in sweet relief. Dunny and The Blue were in an open car behind him. Jeff was on the bench beside him. They were, all four, headed northeast. Frank did not know their destination but the direction suited him. North was the high veldt and Transvaal. Middelburg and Alma.

Magaliesberge, May–June 1901

All through May, the Canadian Scouts rode around the west Transvaal with divisions commanded by Colonel Hackett-Thompson. They were chasing General De La Rey but the wily Boer divided his army and had little trouble eluding them.

The majority of the Scouts had signed up with Gat Howard in December for six months, a period that was up at the end of May. A good many had decided to call it a war, and when the end of May passed, and then most of June, with no word on when they could de-enlist, frustration mounted.

Though his reasons were different, Frank Adams was as frustrated as anyone. As long as they were chasing De La Rey in West Transvaal, they were on the wrong side of Pretoria for what Frank wanted, and he had lately begun to think of leaving again, even though they might call him a deserter and even a thief for taking his own horse. Jeff Davis could read this thought off Frank's face, and he counselled him to wait. When the time to re-enlist or de-enlist came, their new assignment might take them to Middelburg. Failing that, there might be a break when Frank could do what he needed to do.

Finally, Charlie Ross could stonewall no longer. They started for Pretoria where he said the men who wanted to de-enlist could do so. Those who wanted to stay on would be headed for the Orange River Colony to renew their pursuit of Christiaan De Wet. It would be an exciting time,

Charlie said, because they were going to serve under the legendary Lt.-Col. Mike Rimington, the best commander of irregular army Charlie had ever seen.

Inside the railway station at Pretoria, men who had been together since they signed up for the Mounted Rifles or the Canadian Dragoons a year and half ago were suddenly parting. There was not much time for ceremony, because those de-enlisting had to get on trains for Cape Town, and those staying had to get on different trains that would take them to Heilbron, where Colonel Rimington was waiting.

On the platform at Pretoria, Jeff Davis cornered Charlie Ross. Charlie asked Jeff what his plans were, and Jeff shocked him by saying he wasn't sure. Charlie was counting on Jeff to stay and had not even considered that he might go. Before he could decide for sure, Jeff said, he had to know what his horse-holder, Frank Adams, was doing. The two worked so well together that Jeff might not continue if Adams quit.

Charlie still held his grudge against Adams, who had never sworn the oath, and didn't wear a black feather in his hat to honour Gat Howard. "Well, what the hell's he going to do then? Stay or go?"

"Frank's not sure. He's got a personal errand he needs to run before he can make up his mind."

"What the hell do you mean, personal?" It annoyed Charlie deeply to have to think so much about Frank Adams.

"Well, personal is personal, but it has something to do with a concentration camp he needs to visit," said Jeff. This darkened Charlie's mood even more.

Shortly after, Jeff found Frank and gave him two letters. One was scrawled by Charlie Ross and said that Frank Adams and his dun horse should be allowed on a train to Middelburg and then from Middelburg back to Pretoria. After that, they would need transport to Heilbron.

The second letter had been carefully printed and signed by Regimental Sergeant-Major Jefferson Davis and was addressed to whomever was in charge of the Middelburg concentration camp. It said that Frank Adams, Davis's orderly, needed to interview a Boer inmate named Alma Kleff and should be given every assistance to do so.

The last thing Jeff told Frank was that Charlie Ross had imposed a deadline. If Frank was not back with the Scouts in a week, Charlie would regard him as having deserted. His relationship with the Canadian Scouts would be over.

Middelburg

To make himself presentable, Frank heated a couple of buckets of water; washed, deloused, and shaved. He brushed Dunny thoroughly, cleaned her feet, and pulled her tail. This he managed in an African town beside the Hope of the People distillery at Eerste Fabrieken. He had ridden there from Pretoria, and slept there, because he thought the paperwork might be simpler in a less congested station.

What he had wanted and did not manage was a proper haircut. Maybe he could get that in Middelburg, before he went to Alma.

The British corporal in charge at Eerste Fabrieken was a surly, difficult brute. There was a train for Middelburg due any minute but the Tommy claimed he could not read Charlie Ross's writing. As Frank coached him through it, the corporal became concerned about Frank's accent.

"You're American?"

"I'm not."

"Accents are my hobby."

"People in my part of Canada sound like me."

"What part is that?"

"District of Alberta."

"Never heard of it."

The soldier said this with satisfaction. Frank's place of origin dismissed. Frank stopped himself from asking where the Tommy was from. Some centre of commerce and sophistication like Roadapple-on-Tyne?

"Why are you not in uniform, then, if your errand is military?"

Frank showed him part of Jeff's letter. Jeff had anticipated this problem at the concentration camp. Frank placed a finger where it read *uniform stolen while a prisoner of the Boers. Awaiting replacement.*

"Is that horse healthy?"

Dunny was the healthiest horse at the station.

By then, the train was at the siding. A stack of wooden boxes, probably liquor, was being loaded. When the train started getting up steam, the corporal scribbled something and ink-stamped Frank's letter from Ross. Frank hung on the wall of the horse car for the first mile, then climbed forward to a crate with humans in it. Soon they were climbing Diamond Hill, where the carrion eaters and the cycle of seasons had mostly cleaned up the battle of a year ago.

Sometimes, on a curve, Frank's face would appear in the window he was looking out. Each time, he felt sick at heart. No wonder the Tommy at the station hadn't readily believed him. When the train rocked, his long greasy hair flopped against his face. He tucked it down his collar as best he could. Still, he looked like someone you would not hire for a roundup, even if you were desperate for men.

As the train descended the final hill before the familiar town, a dam of impatience broke inside Frank that caused him to clamber along the cars while they were still moving. Inside the open horse car, he ran on the horses' backs and jumped on Dunny. He urged her until they were in front of the door. The moment the gate opened and the railway workers were clear, he jumped her out and rode her to the flatcar that held their tack. Moments later, they were headed for the swamp west of town.

At the concentration camp, another Tommy, an old one with the rank of sergeant, took Frank into the corrugated iron shack, where there was a table and a thick ledger book. The old Tommy's right arm was severed in its sleeve. He worked the book with his left hand and every action was difficult. He moved down the pages slowly, using the edge of a dirty wooden ruler.

"Kleff, Kleff."

After many pages, he rapped a line near the top with a huge-knuckled finger.

"There," he said. He stared close and ran his eyes along the ruler's edge. "Now let's see what this means."

Frank could see that there was a line through Alma's name. Other names were drawn through. The old fellow squeezed his eyes shut and flung them open before he attempted to read a fine scribble in the farthest margin.

"Line can mean several things." He had seen the colour leave Frank's face. Then he tapped again.

"See? What did I tell you? Barberton."

"What does that mean?"

"I can't make it . . ." He put his eye an inch from the paper. "No, it's just a blot. Date's a blot. But I can make out Barberton."

Frank looked at him, pleading.

"Barberton's another camp. When this one became overcrowded—it's overcrowded again now—a list was made and a hundred were sent to Barberton. Normally, you wouldn't go there for something like this, because it's fever country. Lesser of evils, I guess you'd say."

"What about her mother? Mrs. Kleff."

"Right you are. Just below. Mrs. Kleff went too."

At the Middelburg train station, Frank tried to explain why his letter was no longer in line with his needs. Barberton was an old gold rush capital, a long way east near Mozambique. Though he did not have written permission to ride the train beyond Middelburg, his other letter from Sergeant-Major Davis said to interview Miss Alma Kleff, who was now in Barberton. If you put the two letters together . . .

What came of an hour of talk was a one-way trip to Machadodorp. The officer who gave the permission had become interested in the story and stood with Frank and Dunny while they waited for the train. He explained a new device the Boers had for blowing up track. The barrel and lock from a rifle were geared to a dynamite cartridge. They'd slip this device in a hole under the sleeper and cover it. When the train came, the weight would depress the track and the sleeper enough to trigger the rifle lock and blow the dynamite. That was what had happened on the slope down to Waterval Boven. That was why Frank could go no farther than Machadodorp.

From Machadodorp, Frank started riding. At first, he went along beside the railway line as the station master at Machadodorp had instructed. But going that route meant being held up at every stubby tin fortress, every blockhouse, and having to show his papers and explain himself.

In a long gap, where a trestle crossed a donga, Frank pulled Dunny up and considered the country to the south. He rode her into the steep gully and never came out the other side. Reading the landscape as Jeff had taught him, he wove his way through brush and shadows, and stayed out of sight of the kopje tops.

Travelling southeast, Frank finally came to the high veldt's edge. Before him, a chasm had opened. Hundreds of yards straight down was a carpet of deep green bush. He rode around the escarpment's massive split knuckles until he found a trail. It was not a wagon trail but one for animals, and he hoped that meant there would be no Boers or British on it.

The descent was in switchbacks long and short, black with shadow. He could feel the air warm up as he went down. A rich scent of warmed foliage rose to his nose. The drop felt like miles and probably was, and where he and Dunny finally bottomed, the country was dense with bush. Through the green, a sluggish river meandered and bumped along the escarpment's foot. He tacked Dunny down and let her graze and water. He found a place for them to hide for the night, where he could see a trail coming to meet the river on its far side. They would cross there come morning.

What woke him was not the dawn but riders in the river. They were two Boers, decked out for war, who kicked their horses to the river's middle before they let them drink. Frank had his rifle across the brace of his knee. He had a bead on the lead Boer, and could have killed both. For Alma's sake, he would let them go if he could. The Boers sat on their horses talking and laughing. Finally, they continued on their way.

Below the Drakenberg cliffs, the broad valley ran east for miles toward a wrinkle of dusty horizon that was another set of mountains. Frank expected to find Barberton there.

When hours had passed and the far mountains changed from dusty humps to veined and fluted things, he came to a place where smoke rose over the bush and a clearing opened. It was an African kraal, somewhat like the Basuto town in which he had been pegged out. He went to a round hut and tapped its door. A handsome woman came out, looking unafraid. He said the word several ways—Barr-burr-ton, Baa-baa-tun—and finally she brightened. She gestured vigorously at the trail he was on. He motioned toward his mouth and showed some shillings. She gave him two strips of biltong for the silver and handfuls of mealie flour for his horse. He mimed his thanks and continued on.

At Barberton, a creek came toward them. Dunny was anxious to drink, and Frank drank too, for the water was almost as clear as a mountain creek at home.

He asked a few people and was soon at the gate of a wire cage full of Boer prisoners. Not one child played in that enclosure, something Frank had seen before during a starvation spring on the Blood Reserve. He was not as full of exhilaration as he had been in Middelburg and was not sure why. Was it not more likely he would see Alma here, he challenged himself.

What he felt was a pulling dread, a rope from his neck to a stone in the ground. He was desperate to cut it loose, to deny it, for he knew it was an intuition that she had died. Or, if not death, then a presage of some other calamity as negative.

When he said he had a letter of introduction to interview the prisoner Alma Kleff, the guard at the gate scowled but needed no book to know who she was or where to find her. He was a young Tommy, short and fit, with dark hair plastered across his head from a severe part on the side. He had shaved this morning. His thin moustache was neatly trimmed.

"What is it you want with her?" he asked, as they walked among the tents.

Frank tried to sound like an intelligence officer.

"Before Miss Kleff was put in the concentration camp at Middelburg, when she was still on her home farm, some shady types lived with her family. Englishmen and Canadians. At least one of the Canadians was a known deserter. I have orders to find out what she knows. Is there someone who can interpret for me?"

The Tommy ignored the question and stopped by a tent. He tapped the canvas.

"Alma," he called.

He turned and walked away a dozen paces, then stopped to watch.

The tent's flap was on the far side, out of sight of where Frank stood. Alma came around, looking at the ground. It struck Frank that she expected to know the person she was coming to see. She looked up and stopped abruptly.

Frank could not decipher the look on her face. It was not shock, not pleasure. Surprise, but not a huge surprise.

She looked past his shoulder to where the guard was waiting. She lifted her hand, palm forward, and moved it back and forth. An okay sign. Then she beckoned Frank to come with her.

In a patch of shade beside the tent wall was a bench made of two stumps overlaid with a barnboard. She sat and left room for Frank, who also sat and felt suddenly frozen with unease. Instead of looking at Alma, he studied her firepit, its neat ring of smallish stones. Blackened wire twisted around itself to make a screen. Poor woman's *braai*.

Still not looking at Alma, Frank gazed at her in his head. He had expected her to be much thinner, with a caved-in face. Too much work, too little food; not enough promise of better things to come. But Alma was ample, softer and thicker than when he had held her in the barn's deep shadows.

Now he did turn and look at her. She was staring away. Her profile looked strange, either a view of her he'd never had or the face of a stranger. Her hair was tied up into an old woman's knot, but the front strands were loose around her face. She was burned deep reddish-brown. Several new freckles had risen. Her expression was passive, almost insultingly so. His arrival did not seem to mean much to her.

"I went back to your farm. Saw it was burned. Isaiah was still there sleeping in the smokehouse. He told me you were in the Middelburg camp. You and your mother."

She nodded, as if to verify that the story was true so far.

"I was starving so I had to get back with the army. But I'm not a soldier anymore. I just look after a soldier's horses. I haven't shot at any Boers since I met you, even though some killed Young Sam. You remember Young Sam?"

She pushed out her lips and drew them back. An unattractive expression that could mean skepticism or that it did not matter to her if Young Sam was alive or dead.

Then Frank felt stupid. He was speaking English to a girl who neither spoke nor understood it. He had forgotten. After a while of silence, he said, "You don't understand me at all, do you, Alma?"

"Ya, I do," she said.

"You speak English?"

"Ya, in the camps, they teach me."

She looked at him and smiled briefly. It caused a grateful stir in his starved heart.

"I came to the Middelburg camp in January. At night. I snuck up to the wire. A boy came out and I asked him to get you. A woman came and I thought it was you. But it was your mother. She called the guards. They chased me off."

She reached over and put a hand on the arm that Frank was waving, the one that was helping him talk.

"My mother is dead," she said.

She waited awhile before she said more.

"Fever. Typhus." She pointed out the west side of the cage, to a line of crosses and some humps of newly dug earth.

Another silence, broken by flies that buzzed at their faces. Frank thought of what he could say. He said she looked good, healthy.

She smiled at the compliment. Eager suddenly, she said to him, "I am going to have a baby."

Her excitement had put a smile on Frank's face before he knew what she would say. He felt the smile become brittle and fall away. Because he saw how happy her news made her, he tried to act as if she had told him something else.

He could not say anything because he was imagining terrible things. Some man catching her in the dark by the latrine. A brutal guard. A Boer gone crazy.

It showed on his face, and she shook her head.

"No, no," she said. "Sometimes the guards here take us out. Girls like me. Buy us something to eat. Something to drink. One of the boys brought us food. Even jam for our bread. When my mother was so sick, he brought her real German brandy."

She smoothed her faded dress tight over her stomach so the rise would show.

"The guard who helped us, he is the father."

Frank looked at her shape. He remembered the time in the meat-cutting shed when she had pulled her dress tight to show him her slender body.

"Do you love him?"

A bit of the old fire entered her eyes. The skin across her cheekbones tightened. Anger at how stupid he was.

"I don't love you either," she said.

She smoothed her dress over her belly again. Said, "I love *him*." Meaning whoever lived in her belly. "When my son grows up, I hope he will kill soldiers like you. Soldiers like his father."

She patted Frank's arm again to get his attention away from all of the things that were crashing inside him.

"I must go. You must go. He's jealous." She nodded sharply in the direction of the Tommy guard.

They stood and, before they moved back into sunlight, she reached her hand and pushed it under the drape of greasy hair, onto the skin of his neck.

"Don't be so sorry, Frank."

Then the Tommy guard was strutting beside him, marching him to the gate, his face dark with fury. Frank had Alma's consolation inside him. He almost said, "Don't be so sorry, Tommy."

Then he was out of the cage, outside the dying world of its inhabitants. He was a thing dangerously free.

Belfast/Pretoria

On the back trail, Frank threaded through the bush, avoiding anything that represented people. Smoke, gunfire, squealing axles, barking dogs. Boer, British, African, it made no difference to him. Even the vultures circling over the bush veldt. He didn't want to see what was rending or being rent.

His rifle was across the saddle in front of him, his hand around the stock, his finger curled inside the trigger guard. Dunny's brisk walk, metronome to the passing day. Day four of Charlie Ross's ultimatum, and he was moving in a direction and at a pace that might possibly get him there in time. But he had not decided anything yet, except to seek things that distracted him from the pain in his chest. He did not aspire to fill the emptiness, for that was too big a project. Rather, he hoped to leave it undisturbed, like a locked room never explained to company.

When Dunny showed hesitation in her left rear leg, and stood on the other three while resting, Frank brought her back to the rail line quickly and went to the nearest station. It was Belfast, and he talked to the soldier in charge with a new and firm certainty that got them aboard a train. At Middelburg, he closed his eyes so as not to see the concentration camp. When he opened them again, the train was on a long curve wrapped in a stutter of telegraph poles.

Between Middelburg and Pretoria, there was a holdup while army engineers patched around fresh sabotage, the dynamite-triggering device having been used to good effect again. An enraged Tommy stood in the aisle of Frank's car and described how the dynamite had blown under a car full of British soldiers. They were drinking to celebrate the expiry of their time in Africa.

While he waited for the train to move, day six and much of seven passed. He let Dunny off the train and felt everything in her leg: hock, cannon, fetlock, pastern, frog. Asked her, "This one? This one?" The sensitive spot was in the pastern, and it was merely sore. Not poked by a branch, not cut by a wire, not abscessed, not even swollen enough to see with the eye. A sensitivity without cause, or solution.

In addition to the tender on the engine, the train had an extra water wagon. On the side of the latter was a tap from which Frank filled a bucket. He let Dunny drink half, then dribbled the rest over the troubled leg.

In Pretoria, day eight, there was no southbound train. He led Dunny to Pretoria's jail, since jails generally had nice trees and grass around them. She seemed to want to go further, so they visited Paul Kruger's house, where the jacaranda bushes were winter bare and a Union Jack billowed on a pole beside Oom Paul's veranda. In his tilted mental state, Frank thought he saw Sam Steele inside the house. He looked again, and the window was empty.

Frank led Dunny to the big tree, the one in front of the Dutch church. He took off the mare's bridle so she could crop grass without a bit in her mouth, then sat with his back to the scaly trunk.

Likely, he had led Dunny here so he could remember the other time. When he had insisted to Ovide that they wait in the tree's shade in case Jeff Davis came by. When Lionel Brooke had appeared instead. When Ovide and Young Sam were still alive and Alma Kleff did not exist for him yet.

There was a quality to this looking back that Frank recognized by its vagueness and distance. It was how old men try to lay claim to the past.

"Did that happen? Did it happen to me?"

That night, Frank and Dunny slept in the park across from Melrose House. They returned to the rail station next morning, just as the trains were being made up for the day. Day nine. He was well past Ross's deadline: a deserter once again.

His letters were stale-dated and losing their power, but he wrung from them one more permission to ride. Approaching Joburg, the iron stacks of the Rand were smoking. Governor Milner had told the newspapers that the most important thing about this stage of the war was to make safe zones around Pretoria and Johannesburg, so that commerce could resume.

After hours of shunting and sitting, Frank was headed south again. The train dipped into the shallow valley of the Vaal and crossed the bridge near Viljoen's Drift. Beyond it, Frank was one of several who wanted to stop at Wolvehoek Station, to connect with the train for Heilbron. The army station master at Wolvehoek told them the Heilbron train was out of service. It might come tomorrow.

A hundred yards out in the veldt, Frank let Dunny look for grass. The winter veldt was poor, worse still around the station. As he watched the mare, he wondered if he should ride, if the journey from here to Heilbron would worsen the pain in her pastern or make her fully lame. He was two days past Ross's ultimatum, and it seemed unlikely that one day less or more would make much difference.

By late afternoon, the day that had begun in frost felt truly warm, and through the dusty haze of it Frank saw a horse stagger out of the veldt, its balance so gone it walked sideways.

When the horse came closer, Frank went to look. Through the coating of dirt, he thought the horse might be a charcoal. Its belly was sucked up gaunt. You could count its ribs, or probably rattle down them with a stick. But Frank also saw that the gelding had good feet, no wounds, and was not wet with sweat or frothing at the mouth. It might be a good horse, just in terrible need of feed and water.

From the tank at the station, Frank filled a green bucket. The bucket's staves were loose and it leaked over his feet as he crossed to the horse. He called Dunny so she could have her say about the gelding. She seemed more disinterested than disgusted. Frank let the grey drink, then let him eat a bit from Dunny's oat bag. He fed and watered him in small helpings, watching to see if the clouds would recede from his eyes. In two hours, the horse was clearer and pretending to have energy, like a man applying for a job.

After Frank swapped his saddle onto the gelding's scarred back, the horse stood still and allowed Frank to take the stirrup. Dunny insisted on leading, and he let her go in just a halter. She picked her way along beside the rails, free and bemused, as Frank rode the gelding behind her.

Frank rode in around sunset of day ten. He was still on the gelding, though the horse was exhausted and mostly asleep. Frank let Dunny lead them into camp, because he wanted to see how long it would take her to find The Blue. In less than a minute, the two horses stood glued to one another, and The Blue gave the charcoal gelding a warning look that, tired as he was, the horse did not ignore. Frank had trouble holding the gelding, so determined was he to get away to a safe distance.

Jeff heard the ruckus near his horse and came out. He held the gelding while Frank stripped off the saddle. Under the blanket was a square of deep wet. Frank appreciated the horse for sticking it out, for the chance it had offered Dunny.

Frank explained the gelding to Jeff by pointing out the sore spot on Dunny's pastern. He said Alma had not been at Middelburg, but at Barberton. The rest was conveyed by the look on his face.

Jeff might have warned Frank about Charlie Ross's mood if there'd been time, but Charlie came too quickly: his firebox full, his steam up.

"I was told you were a goddamn deserter, Adams. Just as well I gave you the chance to prove it. I musta been crazy to offer you the honour of being a Howard's Scout. I suppose I did so out of respect for your father."

The quickness and ferocity with which Charlie got on Frank suggested he'd been waiting and practising, perhaps even looking forward to it. He dipped into his bag of invective and called Frank a "yellow belly," "an undeserving sonofabitch," "a third cousin to a poisoned pup"—and a "sheep's dag," whatever that was.

Jeff let Charlie run down like a cheap alarm clock. Then he asked Frank if he still had the letter he'd given him, and could he see it? It had become delicate from overuse, and Jeff unfolded it carefully under Charlie's nose. Jeff said Charlie should read it before he called Frank too many more things. Jeff struck matches until Charlie had finished.

"What the hell's the difference? I gave him a week and it's three days past."

] 403 [

"It was my idea," said Jeff, pretending contrition. "I wanted Frank to find this girl, Alma Kleff, and ask her some questions. I'd heard she was in Middelburg. But she turned out to be in Barberton. If you ask me, Frank did well to make that trip in ten days."

"Who is this damn girl, anyway? Boer, by the sound of it."

"She is Boer."

"What's so special, then?"

"Before her family was burned out and sent to the camps, they had some foreigners living with them. Canadians and Brits. I heard they were cattle-duffing. Since General Kitchener's so mad lately about the amount of cattle-duffing going on, I thought Frank could take a few days and find out if this Alma knew about that. I thought if we could catch some civilian rustlers, it might keep Kitchener off our backs for a while."

A set of weather changes blew over Charlie Ross's face.

"Well, did he find her? Did she know anything?"

Jeff refused to answer. He butted his head in Frank's direction, meaning it was Frank's story, and he should tell it.

Charlie hated to look at Frank but finally did. "Well?"

"I found her at Barberton," said Frank.

"I know that."

"She'd learned some English, so we could talk. She didn't know anything about the cattle stealing. They just came, paid for their keep, and left."

Jeff studied Charlie. "It's not Frank's fault I sent him on a goose chase. He was just doing what he was told."

"The hell he was! I told him to be back in seven days!"

"But, that's the thing, Charlie. Is Adams my flunky or your soldier? Seems to me he's more my flunky. So when he gets two orders, and they're in each other's way, I'm not surprised he obeys me."

Jeff said good night and left them.

"I'm not happy," Charlie said. His tone was more complaining now than angry. "We been sitting in this shithole for a week. Colonel Rimington ain't here. Nobody knows where he is. I don't care for that. I like fighting. I like doing business. I do not like sitting in one goddamn spot waiting. Not for any man."

"Captain Ross?"

"What?"

"I would like to be a Canadian Scout. I'll swear the oath. I'd be proud to wear the feather."

"What the goddamn hell? Why now and not before?"

"Things are clearer now."

"Bullshit they are! You ain't getting sergeant's rank or pay, if that's what you're after."

"Not expecting it, sir."

"You desert me again, I'll see you're shot. I'll shoot you myself."

"Thank you, sir."

"Thanks me for saying I'll shoot him. You're a crazy bastard, just like they say."

Heilbron/Kroonstad/Lindley

Colonel Rimington was a whippet-thin English cavalryman; young for forty-three. Before the war, he had been a special officer in charge of scouts in Natal. When the war began, he rose until his Rimington's Guides were said to be the best scouting unit in Roberts' army.

Rimington's popularity continued into the reign of Lord Kitchener. Colonels Benson and Rimington were Kitchener's favourite masters of the "tiger spring." First, your intelligence officer located a rebel laager. Then you marched all night and pounced at dawn. It was very successful, and the Boers had been slow to get the hang of it. Maybe they could not believe the British would go to such self-punitive extents to trap them.

Rimington was late at Heilbron because he'd been involved in many drives lately. An aspect of Kitchener's system (intensified hustling of the Boers in winter) was that little police work went on. As a result, towns had to be captured over and over again. In early June, Rimington was with Knox and Plumer as they reconquered Piet Retief. From there, Rimington had gone to Utrecht and operated along the Pongola. He had resupplied at the depot the Canadian Scouts had built.

Most recently, he had been at Vrede, where a push had sent numerous Boers into his waiting arms. Finally, he had skirmished his way back to Heilbron.

After all of his public complaining, Charlie Ross felt it a matter of pride to complain directly to Rimington. He didn't care to have his time wasted, he said. But Rimington knew Ross's weaknesses. He told him about the fabulous amount of loot he had secured at Vrede and how much more the two of them were likely to collect together in this colony. Given Ross's love of plunder, it was like a nanny telling a child about Ali Baba's Cave.

Flattery also worked on Charlie, so Rimington told him how important he was to Lord Kitchener's plan: the fast-moving bands of scouts, living off their saddlebags, a match for the Boer bitter-enders. As Kitchener's big drives ground and sifted along, men like Charlie would be fighting in the oldest ways of mounted combat; finishing the war in a pure and dignified manner.

By then, Charlie was grinning.

"Give the bastards no quarter," he said. "Never have, never will."

After a day's rest, Rimington was ready to move. He gathered the new units and gave them a talk. This was a very important part of the war, he said. The Boers could collapse at any moment. A week ago, Broadwood had recaptured the town of Reitz. His men had found a letter from a Boer general to the local commandant telling him to step out of the way as the British came. When the Brits had run up their flag and moved on, the Boers should return. The British didn't garrison, just kept plunging forward, so the safest place to be was the most recently conquered town.

Broadwood did what the letter suggested he would. He raised the Union Jack and left Reitz. But, in the middle of the night, he came back with four hundred men.

The place was full of snoozing rebels and Broadwood made a fabulous grab. The only frustration was that the big fish got away. President Steyn himself was there. He was awakened by his Native cook and escaped in his nightcap. He left £11,500 in cash behind.

This was how Colonel Rimington wanted his column to think as they set out to march. Stay alert, for at any moment you could run into a Boer president or find yourself in a scrap with Christiaan De Wet himself.

Lindley/Kroonstad, July 1901

The Scouts were a different bunch now. When many had left at the end of June, Charlie Ross had filled the spaces with Tommys and all kinds of colonials. To Frank's mind, most of the new ones were not scouts at all.

Now that Frank himself was a scout, he tried to act it. Charlie Ross had not asked him to take the oath, but Frank found a guinea fowl feather and stuck it in his hat brim. When he'd been Jeff's horse-holder, he had insisted on not shooting Boers, though he robbed them of liquor. Now, he insisted he would shoot them, if there was opportunity and cause. He was anxious to illustrate, but as Rimington's column rode away from Heilbron, there were no Boer rebels on whom to display his resolve.

When Rimington had given his speech at Heilbron, Frank had been sitting on the charcoal gelding beside Jeff and The Blue. He had noticed that Jeff paid no attention; even had his eyes closed. During July and into August, as the column marched around a Kroonstad-Lindley-Heilbron triangle, Jeff slept as much as he could and drank amply whenever he had the means. Frank knew what Jeff usually did when he was scouting, and he was not doing it. Frank found it funny that his debut of scouting with Jeff felt more like soldiering with Ovide.

But as the weeks piled up, all to no effect, Frank got Jeff's point. Why use up your horses and your scouting craft looking for Boers who weren't there? As for booty, the few head of livestock they picked up could not be called plunder in any but a tribal herdsman's sense.

On a bitterly cold August day, when Frank and Jeff were riding well ahead, they stopped in a field of anthills to have tea. Frank bashed the lid off a hill, while Jeff dumped his water bottle contents (actual water today) into his blackened kettle. Frank struck a match and lit the hill's writhing innards. Jeff threw tea leaves in the kettle and set it in the fire to boil.

As Frank walked around in his greatcoat, thumping himself with his arms, Jeff warmed his bare hands on the ant fire. Frank had been trying to figure out their situation, but had never quite been able to. Now, he gave up and asked.

"Where the hell are the Boers, anyway?"

Jeff kept one hand in the fire's heat and swished the other across the pale landscape.

"Boers don't travel in winter. No grass. They'll fight when it's spring."

"But why do *we* keep travelling?"

"Lord Kitchener thinks we're driving them. He thinks we'll wear them out."

Though Frank rode the old gelding most of the time, and had a nifty Boer gelding as his third horse, he still had no way of giving Dunny a rest. He could not leave her anywhere, because he never knew where they were going and when they'd be back. What made it worse was that Rimington liked his column to move *fast*, as if to do otherwise was disrespect to Lord Kitchener.

If Frank was angry at this waste of energy and horseflesh, Charlie Ross was beside himself. After all his time in Africa, after all his avowed and disavowed dealings, Charlie felt he knew damn well where the Boers were and where their loot was apt to be. Trotting around this triangle of northwest towns was not it.

If Charlie's boil was high, and he was certain only Scouts could hear him, he would say that, as this war waned, they would all need to be on the lookout for blame. The British newspapers were having a field day depicting the rough tactics used against the Boers. The British army's image needed sprucing up, and it needed it quickly before the war ended. If the British could convince their own people that their regular army had been fair and sound to the last, and that all of the worst excesses had been the actions of undisciplined colonials, weren't they apt to try it? Charlie had a honed way of concluding this caution: "They're cleaning up the mess, boys, and they're tearing us up for rags."

Each time Frank heard this, he looked at Jeff. It was his way of pointing out that he knew Charlie's concern was mainly for himself, and why. Charlie was the one with the price on his head for shooting Boer prisoners wearing khaki. The wilder versions of that story—never refuted by Charlie—said he made them dig their own graves.

In early August, something happened that was so perfect a nettle to Charlie's sensitivities that it was hard to believe it wasn't a planned joke. Rimington sent Capt. Hugh Trenchard to the Scouts to instill in them British discipline and procedure. A couple of days into this situation, Major Ross was having an afternoon snooze when he woke to the sound of cavalry drill.

"Form fours!"

"Flank of fours, right wheel!"

Charlie came out of his tent as if stung by bees. He ran at Trenchard and looked as if he might jump at the captain in his saddle.

"Say, you! Cut that out! These are Scouts! They're not goddamn tin soldiers!"

On August 7, Lord Kitchener sent a proclamation to all Boer generals and to the presidents of Transvaal and the Orange Free State. It said that any Boer rebel still in the field on September 15 would be banished from South Africa for life.

In the Scouts' camps, the proclamation spawned argument. Some said it would lead to mass surrender and end the war. Others said it would stiffen Boer resolve and prolong the conflict. Frank wasn't sure which he thought, and Jeff was too aloof and languorous to join the discussion.

A week later, the Boers suddenly appeared. First, the Scouts blundered into a Boer convoy near Lindley, in a place they had marched several times before. Two days later, they chased two hundred Boers for eight miles, losing them across the Liebenbergsvlei. Then a tiger spring landed on a laager near Reitz, yielding them prisoners and loaded carts. Before September ended, Rimington's column hit two more commandos on the move.

In the midst of the furious action, Frank asked Jeff for an explanation. It was still winter. Frank had never seen native grass so peeled and poor. So why, according to Jeff's theory, were the Boers suddenly active?

"They're moving supplies," Jeff said patiently, as if to a child. "It proves they mean to fight when the rains come."

Now that Rimington's column had reason to march, it marched faster and farther, and there was never a chance to rest Dunny. Jeff's suggestion was that Frank start a little string of horses for himself. Rimington's growing loot included horses, and Jeff had acquired several. He paid the horse campies to give them special care. When Jeff talked like this, he sounded like Charlie Ross. In it was the assumption that Frank must look past Dunny to his next horse, but he was unwilling to do that.

On one of the last days of August, Rimington caught another convoy. This one was the jackpot. Two thousand cattle. Sixty-one loaded wagons. It took a whole day to look through, deciding what was booty and what was dross. Frank found an unopened case of British navy rum that the Boers must have stolen. He tossed it under a bush and buried it with rejected goods.

When they were done, Rimington admitted it was time to get his convoy of plunder to the railway line. Kroonstad was the closest station. Rimington loved only to raid and regarded moving booty as a boring chore.

At their first camp on the Kroonstad road, Jeff and Frank volunteered for night patrol. They left after dark and rode straight east. A Boer commando had got there before them and was laagered up for the night next to the debouched wagon train. Frank left his Boer pony with Jeff and crawled to the rum's hiding place. Quietly, he unearthed it, then returned at a crawl. He moved the rum one arm's length at a time, shinnying forward, lifting, and shinnying again.

Instead of an accusation of looting, the two returned to praise. Rimington said the laager they had found was valuable proof that the Boers meant to attack them. The Boers were not going to surrender all these goods without a fight.

Over the next two days, Rimington's rearguard battled Boers buzzing in at a gallop from several angles. Frank and Jeff were in the thick of it, as the convoy crawled toward the railway town. Frank was watching a field gun fire when a tall, thin gunner slumped onto the barrel. The gun had been firing all afternoon and had to be sizzling hot. He ran to the soldier and the body came off the gun limp and bloody. It fell from Frank's grasp and hit the ground like a sack of grain.

When they buried him that evening, Frank learned the gunner's name. James Black, from St. Catharines.

They were camped on the edge of Kroonstad and no fires were allowed. Frank and Jeff had a rum bottle each, and though Frank was already very drunk, he kept on sipping because the death of Sergeant Black had caused him a relapse. All through this month of being a scout, Frank had managed the pain over Alma like a pile of plates on a stick. If he concentrated, never slacked, the pain could be held up there away from him. Today had jostled him hard and the plates had crashed.

After Black had been killed, Frank wanted the comfort of Dunny. He wanted to ride his old friend to town. His weight made her limp from the start, but thinking how an out-of-whack ankle or knee can be walked right, he did not swap horses but kept on. The mare stepped in the mouth of an animal hole and let out a cry. Frank had never heard a sound like it come from her. He leapt off, rubbed her, spoke soothingly. But, even with no weight on her back, she limped the rest of the way.

What had come to Frank, through these two dark heralds, was the idea that he might go home with nothing. Back on the Pongola, while wading in soup to his neck and taking reprieves with Jeff in the Swazi hills, he had achieved a faith almost religious that he could bring his woman, his horse, and his friend back. All of them, safely home to Alberta.

These ideas did not chip or fray. They were blasting apart. First, there was Alma, pregnant by the Tommy guard, wishing Frank dead. Now Dunny, with a banshee yell, had announced that Frank would be leaving Africa without her.

Today, when Frank could not hold the dead weight of Sergeant Black, and the man slid to the ground on the grease of his own blood, it told Frank that he could not save Jeff Davis either. Jeff would live or die, but not through Frank's actions, or even Jeff's own skill or luck. It would be through Jeff's will—which Frank sensed was wavering.

On his return from Barberton, Frank's consolation was the idea that he and Jeff were twinned. Both had lost their women and their dreams. They would always be, in some way of the spirit, like a man with an empty sleeve, but Frank had grabbed onto the idea that they could combine their small remaining hope and limp home together.

But tonight, on the black night of Black's death, with black rum coursing in him, Frank saw the thing as Jeff probably did. Jeff did not like Frank so well that he would go on living because of him. Each morning, Jeff probably got up and weighed his life. One of these days, he might decide it did not weigh enough.

Next day, the Scouts were given leave in Kroonstad. Though he was sick from rum, Frank went downtown by himself and bought a sheet of paper, a pencil, and an envelope.

Hello Madeleine and Jim,
This is your son Frank. Somebody probably told you I'm dead. I was only
lost. Now I am a Canadian Scout. My commander is Charlie Ross from
Lethbridge. Charlie writes letters to the Lethbridge newspaper, so if you see

that, you will know what I am up to. The Boers aren't beat yet. Say hello
for me to Uncle Doc.
Your son, Frank

Though they never saw each other, Colonel Rimington and Colonel Benson were having a contest. They were Kitchener's two top tiger-springers, and each of their successful dawn raids or taking of convoys was like a goal in a polo match. No one kept score but there was the idea of competition and who was winning all the same.

In August, Rimington had the upper hand. But, as September started, Benson went on a winning streak. He tiger-sprang Boer laagers with eerie regularity. What Benson had over Rimington was Aubrey Wools-Sampson, an intelligence officer who was a veteran of the failed Jameson Raid. Imprisoned by the Boers, he had been offered amnesty by Paul Kruger and had refused it. He'd insisted on staying in jail so that no one could ever say he'd taken a favour from a Boer. In the new conflict, he was a fanatical Boer-hater and would go to any extent to outfox and defeat the Dutchmen. His ace in the hole was a network of black spies, men who went around the African kraals and asked people what they'd seen: information Wools-Sampson would piece together to set up Benson's next attack.

On September 10, a Benson night attack surprised a camp of Boers south of Middelburg. Immediately, he tiger-sprang again and landed on another Boer laager at Tweefontein. Still in the same week, Benson night-marched forty miles from Carolina and hit a laager at Middeldrift. He could do no wrong.

During the same period, Rimington was only slightly less successful. On September 14, he hit a laager at Leufontein. A week later, he overtook Strydom's commando and made a haul. Loot and thirteen prisoners. Rimington was working on his own network of black spies.

Both men knew what would win the contest: the capture of Louis Botha or Christiaan De Wet. Whatever else they did, that was the main chance they watched for.

Come September 15, the Boers wanted to do something big to show their contempt for Kitchener's proclamation of eternal banishment. Louis

Botha's choice was to march southeast and invade Natal. Along the way, Botha destroyed the British tiger-springer Major Gough and two hundred and eighty-five of his men, but the invasion plan failed nonetheless. In October, during the spring rains, Mike Rimington teamed up with Col. Sir Henry Rawlinson on a plan to attack Botha as he tried to get back into the Transvaal.

Frank and Jeff were part of the Botha expedition. For several days after they resupplied at Standerton, the combined columns marched northeast in slow and cumbersome fashion, giving the impression of the kind of flying column that always arrives too late. Then came the night march. After dark, they flew along as fast as their horses could travel, and the rumour among the men was that Rimington's spies had given him the exact farm where Botha was sleeping tonight.

In the final half-hour of night, Frank and Jeff lay on the lip of the bowl containing the farm. Black spies went down barefoot and returned to say there were many horses in the stable and many more tied outside.

In the pre-dawn light, the whistles blew. As they raced into the yard, men and horses started spilling from everywhere. The farm looked like a smoked-out anthill. Several horsemen got away under fire before the British could pull the edges of their circle tight. Their own horses were too spent to give chase.

Rawlinson and Rimington set outposts, corralled their prisoners, and began interrogations. A couple of Boer boys with guns to their heads admitted that Louis Botha had slept there. When every pile of hay and dung had been poked with bayonets, and every crevice and bush was searched, they had to admit that the prize Rimington needed to win his contest with Benson had got away.

Jeff and Frank's job was to examine the captured remuda. They were hoping to add a horse or two to their own strings. But, the look of the Boer horses was disheartening. Going to Natal and back had sapped them. They were fit for not much more than an aas vogel's dinner.

Inside the sad herd, they found one saddled horse who was much better fleshed. A compact gelding, solid brown. The initials *LB* were on the fender, and any remaining doubt was erased by the contents of the saddlebag: notes to and from Botha. Tied to the saddle by a string was Botha's hat, and Frank and Jeff knew that was on its way to a glass case in some officer's country home.

Frank and Jeff stayed with the intelligence officer, who was looking at every tiny aspect of the horse. They could not help but dream of making him their own. Then an officer's flunky led him away to the house the officers had taken for their headquarters.

After a day's searching, they camped at the farm. It rained all night. Come morning, Rawlinson and Rimington announced that the soldiers could rest another day and night before continuing. Because of the rules of tiger springing, the men had no blankets, only their sodden greatcoats. They built smoky fires on whichever side of the buildings was most out of the lashing rain. Those who could crowded into the barn, watching the house's chimney smoke.

Some general or colonel was bound to write in a memoir that their pluck was glorious to see. But Frank knew by the snake eyes around him what everyone thought: that the holiday was nothing but a chance to catch dysentery, and that they would be better off in their saddles, returning to Standerton.

After his escape from Rimington and Rawlinson, Louis Botha stepped back into the Transvaal and started west. At the same time, Colonel Benson was following orders to burn farms and gather families, livestock, and booty around Bethel. The result was a lumbering three hundred and fifty-vehicle convoy slobbering through the rain. Benson was trying to get to the Delagoa line at Balmoral.

On October 30, Benson's convoy was strung out two miles and beset by lightning. His rearguard sent a rider to say the Boers were threatening. They had been harrying the convoy for days, but the officer who sent the message thought this was something more. Benson gathered some men and rode back through the lightning flashes. When he got to his rearguard, he told them to go to higher ground. He told the gunners to deploy as fast they could.

The gunners were setting and levelling guns when eight hundred Boers galloped out of the papery mist. Botha had marched all night to tiger-spring Benson.

In the end, Benson and his men were sheltering in a field of anthills.

Shot in the knee and crawling, Benson urged his men to fight. The colonel was shot again, and then a third bullet, a ricochet off another man, killed him. Benson had brought one hundred and seventy-eight men to protect the guns; one hundred and sixty-one were killed or wounded.

Standerton, November 1901

As the calendar turned to November, Rimington's column was teamed with Lieutenant-Colonel Damant's mobile unit. Damant was a six-foot four-inch former captain in the Rimington Guides. He was a native of South Africa, born at Kimberley, who wore dundrearies to his jaws. Rimington had been brought low by the death of his running mate Benson, but the sight of his former protege restored him.

Charlie Ross was not as optimistic. For him, the deaths of Benson and Gough were part of a cloud of evil portents that, collectively, threatened him with annihilation. When Rimington's column got back to Standerton, Casey Callaghan came to Ross and said he'd accepted another assignment. This struck Charlie a powerful blow, a low blow, for Casey was his lead scout. He demanded at once to know what Casey was leaving him for; which bastard had poached him.

Casey said the bastard was the Canadian Government. A new MI contingent was coming from Canada, called the Second Canadian Mounted Rifles. Its commander was Maj. Tom Evans, and it was he who had asked Casey to be his intelligence officer at the rank of lieutenant. The rank was the same, but intelligence officer was a considerable lift in prestige. In any case, Casey was leaving for Cape Town.

"Never liked Evans," Charlie said, staring away at nothing.

Casey could see that Charlie was determined to be morose and bitter, and did not argue with him. He was packed and ready, and began his good-byes. Many attended his departure, but the important ones were ex-CMRs like Ed Hilliam and old scouting partners like Jeff Davis. The trouble between Jeff and Casey disappeared, and Casey wanted to talk to Jeff more than to any man.

"You take care of yourself, you crazy coyote," Casey said at the end.

Frank stood back with the gawkers, the troopers for whom Casey was a legend. Frank's and Casey's fence was to remain unmended and, rather than watch Callaghan, Frank spent the moment admiring The General. Despite Frank's mistreatment of him and countless other ordeals, the amazing buckskin was still sound. Not so Dunny, who Frank had just arranged to leave here at Standerton with a black Christian named Paul.

After Casey rode out, Charlie Ross turned and searched the faces behind him. His expression was desperate until his gaze lit on Jeff Davis. Charlie pointed at the scout and hooked his finger, beckoning him to his tent.

When Jeff came out a half-hour later, he was Charlie's new lead scout. At their bivouac, Frank congratulated Jeff, who shrugged and said, "It's going to make things different."

Frank thought he meant different in the sense of difficult to drink, under Charlie Ross's teetotal nose.

"I mean, Charlie doesn't want us both."

He let this soak in before he continued.

Charlie had told Jeff that he was Charlie's partner now. As far as Adams was concerned, he was still acting like a horse-holder. It would do him good to get out of Jeff's shadow.

In the middle of saying this, a different thought had struck Charlie Ross. Giving his moustache ends a twitch, he'd told Jeff to tell Frank he was a corporal. It seemed to have occurred to Charlie in the moment of criticizing Frank that he was short of corporals and that Frank was more experienced than many.

"You'll need to find another stripe," said Jeff.

What bothered Frank was not the news but that Jeff did not seem concerned. He did not act sorry to be leaving Frank behind. It reminded Frank of early in the war, when Jeff had hived off from Ovide and Frank to get on the path toward scouting. That had been about Ran After and changing the thinking of her father. What this was about Frank did not know. There had to be something that Jeff still wanted from the war, something he could pursue more easily outside Frank's company.

The resupply at Standerton took a new turn when five hundred remounts jumped off a train. Frank saw the horses in the railway corral, and there was some decent horseflesh there. He saw Jeff and Charlie standing with other officers and their ADCs. Rimington and the giant Damant were present.

It looked like an argument, and Charlie was kicking the ground and yanking his hat brim.

When Jeff came from the corral, Frank asked him what was aggravating Charlie. He also wanted to know what he should be doing now that he was a corporal.

"They gave Charlie all the renegades. They think the Canadian Scouts are roughriders."

From this, Frank could understand Charlie's temper fit. That the Scouts were bronc-twisters had never been very true, but slightly more so in the days under Gat Howard. The level of horsemanship had dropped off the table when they switched to Rimington and lost so many men. Among those who went home were the toughest riders.

"Charlie told me to give you three troopers. You're supposed to find them horses that won't kill them." Jeff nodded toward a trio leaning on the corral. "Why not take them? They look green enough."

Jeff left him to it, and Frank went over and introduced himself. He told the boys to disregard his private's stripe; he was a corporal and in charge of them today. He found a rope and led them inside the paddock.

Two were Australian; the other, a Canadian. All three said they could ride, which of course they would say. The Canadian, Danny, was from Saskatchewan District, and had worked on a ranch near Regina, so it might be true of him. He smiled most of the time and reminded Frank of himself before the war.

First, Frank showed them the hoolihan throw, the overhand toss where you didn't swing the rope and scare the horses. He demonstrated on the first horse that went by. The four of them got it snubbed and saddled. Meanwhile, Frank had caught a second horse and they snubbed it to another post. He picked the Aussies to go first.

Both were on the ground soon enough. Frank asked Danny if he liked either of the two broncs the Aussies had tried to ride. He said he liked the bay, which was the stronger, meaner horse of the two. Frank had to mount up to rope the bay gelding a second time. When they had him ready, Danny stayed on for several jumps before hitting the dirt. He apologized to Frank for falling off and said he'd like to try again. Frank helped him rope the bay a third time, but suggested they leave him fighting the post while they looked for something less mean-eyed for the Australians.

The Aussies, Bert and Toby, were no bushrangers, and Frank looked for horses that were broke at least. By the end of the day, the Aussies had horses they could ride. Danny had been up and down with the bay several times and was beginning to get the upper hand.

That evening, in the absence of Jeff, Frank went and sat with the men he knew: Ed Hilliam and some other CMR vets. He expected them to keep their distance, maybe even display some active ill feeling. After all, these were the ones who knew about his attacks on Pete and Greasy and the question mark hovering over his disappearance from Aas Vogel Kranz.

But, from the moment he sat down, it was not like that. When they told a story from some time Frank was part of, the speaker would nod at him or even ask if he remembered how certain things had gone.

It made Frank wonder if his poor reputation had been tied to Casey. With Callaghan gone, maybe the others felt Frank had been ostracized enough. It could also be that they had forgotten everything except his familiar face.

Villiersdorp

When Frank and Jeff split up so Jeff could assume his place at Charlie Ross's right hand, the unlikely truth was that Frank had drawn the better assignment. Someone found him a corporal's stripe to sew on and, since his three greenhorns liked him, they were left in his charge. They made a foursome for patrol and Cossack post duty.

On the other half of the bargain, Jeff was working for Charlie Ross in his darkest and most erratic mood. Charlie firmly believed that officers in the highest echelons of the British army were out to get him. If you asked him why he thought that, he would say, "Because they goddamn are!"

Besides enemies, there were omens, and Charlie believed in those. He classed the deaths of Gough and Benson as omens. Botha's escape at Chrissie Lake was a harbinger. Sometimes, it was hard to know the difference between an enemy and an omen. Take the desertion of Casey Callaghan. Did Casey or Tom Evans have it in for Charlie? Or had it been an act of the fates, coming at a bad time, as those always did?

Charlie Ross had lost little in the exchange. Jeff Davis was as skilful and savvy as Casey, in some ways more so. But it was not in Charlie's nature to feel uncheated.

The evening after the remount rodeo, a black spy brought news to Standerton that a Boer commando with a big herd of cattle was approaching Villiersdorp. Rimington's column, supported by Damant, set out at dusk to cover the distance in the dark. That night, the Canadian Scouts paid for the misconception that they were roughriders. At a watering stop, a scout's new horse kicked him in the lower leg and broke the bone. Later, as they approached Villiersdorp, another new horse blew up and threw its rider. The big horse kicked the young Canadian Scout in the head on his way to the ground. Everyone found it hard to believe that the young fellow was dead. Frank felt sick, imagining that this dead boy had been one of his.

That they attacked the commando at Villiersdorp and captured two thousand cattle might have pleased Rimington, but Charlie Ross was not consoled. A man kicked to death in the dark was a portent so black Charlie was frightened to think what it might lead to.

Blijdschap

Kitchener had launched a few drives since Swaziland, using his growing blockhouse system to hem in the enemy. The drives usually went in a straight line then wheeled to crush the Boers against the blockhouses and the barbed wire. But it had not worked as well as Kitchener had hoped. Often, the Boers squirted out the sides. Sometimes they weren't there in the first place.

In his latest drive, Kitchener was going after Christiaan De Wet in the Orange River Colony with fifteen thousand soldiers in fourteen columns. This drive would be more like a wheel, or a snail, with all of the columns curling in on the same preordained spot, trapping the Boers inside. As one of the fourteen columns, Rimington was given a starting point, a trajectory, and a secret end point (near Frankfort).

On this drive, Frank took his two Boer horses and only visited Dunny long enough to give Paul more money for her keep. For the first time ever, he avoided his dun mare's eye.

While they marched and converged, Jeff Davis visited Frank most every night. Frank wondered if it was triggered by Jeff's having liquor to share, because he unfailingly did. Frank joined Jeff in a drink or two, but lately had no desire for more than that. He wasn't sure why except it had to do with the three young soldiers in his command. He was enjoying them and almost enjoying the war, and did not care to have a rum-cloudy head in the morning. Whether that mattered to Jeff, Frank could not say. Jeff kept visiting and imbibing his usual measure.

One night, Jeff pulled a paper from his pocket and unfolded it.

"This is Charlie's latest letter to the *Lethbridge News*. He asked for my opinion."

Frank read the page through a couple of times. It included a description of the scout killed by his horse and the other one whose leg was broken. For no apparent reason, it jumped from there to the Pongola River and described the horses who had died and the men laid low by fever. Of himself, Charlie had written: *I've had six horses killed under me. I've had a bullet go through my tunic.*

Frank thought of Jim and Madeleine reading this sorrowful stuff. It would undo the good of his own letter. "Tell him it's sorry," Frank suggested.

On another night, Jeff told Frank about a conversation with Colonel Rimington. Rimington had a big tent where he liked to meet his officers. Most times, Charlie Ross took Jeff along.

Pinned to Rimington's tent walls were maps and sheets. In big printing on one, Jeff had read:

1. LINDLEY—SENTIMENT!
2. WOMEN—ELLIOTT!
3. PIET—TRAITOR!

At the bottom, Rimington had scrawled: *Make him come to you!!!*

At the most recent meeting, Jeff had pretended to fall asleep. He stayed that way when it was over and the others were leaving. Someone wise-cracked, "Our Indian guide appears to be missing a troop movement."

After the rest were gone, Rimington jabbed Jeff's shoulder. Jeff jumped up and apologized.

"Damn boring session, Davis. I'd have slept too if I wasn't in command."

As he put on his hat to go, Jeff made a gesture toward the maps and sheets.

"It's all about Christiaan De Wet, isn't it?"

Rimington looked abashed. "Bit of a hobby of mine. I'd like to catch him."

Jeff looked closer at a marked-up map. "So these are places you know he's been?"

"Yes. And the approximate dates."

Jeff saw several arrows pointing to Lindley, each one dated.

"Lindley was burned, wasn't it?" Jeff asked.

He had Rimington's interest now.

"I ordered the burning. As my map developed, I saw how often De Wet returned there. Went out of his way to do so."

"Do you know why?"

"Never did figure it out—what personal event, or if he had farmed in the area. But I burned it because I was sure there was sentimental attachment. I wanted him to hate me personally."

Jeff pointed at the sheet with *Lindley—Sentiment!* as number one.

"So these are things he's sentimental about?"

Rimington laughed. "I certainly hope *you're* not a spy. Yes, you've got it. Sentimental. Emotional."

Rimington stepped up to the sheet and pointed at number two.

"Do you happen to remember when Elliott captured the laager of Boer women? No? Maybe you were in Transvaal. What happened was that Elliott took the laager, and De Wet and De La Rey happened to be having a secret meeting not far away. Against all sense, the two generals abandoned their secrecy and attacked Elliott. They were getting the better of him, but our reinforcements arrived and they had to run. But do you see what a terrific risk they took? I'd never known De Wet to do that. To be so emotionally drawn."

At that point, Rimington's ADC came in with an important message, and Jeff had to leave.

Frank asked Jeff about the third thing: *Piet—Traitor!* Would he go back and ask Rimington about it?

"I don't have to. I figured it out."

Piet had to be Christiaan's brother Piet. Earlier in the war, he was a Boer commandant. A change came over him as a result of the Boers besieging a town—Lindley again, before it was burned. Several commandos, including Piet's, could not force the British garrison there to submit. Finally, British reinforcements came and chased them off.

This inability to take the Lindley garrison caused Piet to desert. He not only surrendered but asked to fight for the British against his own people. Since then, he had put together a gang of Boer turncoats and wanted the British to recognize them formally under the title National Scouts.

Frank was still unsure how Piet fit the list, since the other two were things Christiaan De Wet liked. Jeff reminded him that Rimington had said sentimental *and* emotional. Piet was on the list because Christiaan wanted him dead. Rimington believed the general could be coaxed out of his icy control for a chance to kill his brother.

Since then, Jeff had asked around among the old Rimington hands, and they said that Mike Rimington had tried several times to get Piet De Wet to join him as a permanent part of Rimington's column. Piet wasn't interested, but Rimington started rumours that Piet *was* with him. If he could convince the older De Wet, true or false wouldn't matter. *Make him come to you!*

In late November, Rimington's column was marching in a triangle formed by Reitz, Bethlehem, and the burned town of Lindley. The colonel's maps and charts had led him here, despite the fact that no one had seen Christiaan De Wet in a month.

What Rimington had learned to do was look at the grass. As the climate moved into African summer, the prairie had improved but was better in some places than others. It was a fair assumption that De Wet would know where the grass was best, and that he would have his horses there. The grass in the triangle was the best Rimington had found.

Still, the column was wandering uncertainly, until Rimington's scouts brought in a Boer prisoner who was terrified of being tortured. Rumours of British atrocities were floating around in the Boer world. Rimington's bullies did their best to act out the Boer's fears. Suddenly he blurted out that Christiaan De Wet was gathering commandos at a farm called Blijdschap. The only problem was that this Boer immediately repented his betrayal and would not tell them where Blijdschap was. After more serious goading, the Boer finally told what he knew, and it was not much. He had no idea of the exact location of Blijdschap, and the position he gave them was so approximate it was almost useless.

Rimington put the Boer under double guard and insisted his captors stay inside the tent and never take their eyes off him. The colonel gathered his unit leaders and top scouts. He told them the news and the lack in it— the unknown location of Blijdschap farm. He emphasized how important it was not to ask any Boer for help. "Where is Blijdschap?" in the wrong ear, and De Wet would be lost to them again.

Knowing what *not* to do did not translate into knowing what *should* be done, and Rimington encouraged the group to make suggestions. No one spoke, the reason being that the most important decision was whether to move independently or to wait for help, something Rimington would have to decide on his own.

The fact was that Rimington feared taking this secret to Kitchener. The Lord General was apt to organize a drive, perhaps another snail. If so, they'd be searching for Blijdschap at Christmas.

The problem of acting alone was that Rimington did not know where the farm was or how many Boers were there. He had a thousand in his column, including Damant. But what if De Wet had more?

The decision was made not by the meeting but by the sudden arrival of a patrol. It had located a women's laager.

Rimington divided his column in two. Half would chase the women. The other half would take a different route. A known location, a farm not far from Reitz, was chosen for their rendezvous. Rimington was throwing two kinds of bait at De Wet, somewhere in the vicinity of Blijdschap.

Frank was in the half that wasn't driving the women. They marched all night and were north of Reitz when Boer horsemen boiled out of the dawn, firing on them.

It turned into a running fight, and the biggest challenge was protecting their field guns. The Boers had no artillery but came in waves. Frank's half of the column was trying to reach the point of reunion, not knowing that the column's other half was also under attack. Then black clouds filled the sky and a fierce thunderstorm broke.

When the halves met, the two groups of attacking commandos also joined, and Rimington saw that he had made a serious error; perhaps as great an error as Gough's and Benson's. The farm they had been aiming for was close, with a few acres of tree cover. Rimington ordered all of his men to make for it as fast as possible. They would dig in and hope for relief.

Among the trees, every man with a shovel dug. They worked with lightning bolts striking close enough to paint them white. A bolt split one of the higher trees, and only by luck were men not crushed when stout branches fell.

The lightning was also their saviour. The Boers had no artillery and fired into the farm with Mausers. In the continuing storm, De Wet was reluctant to order a charge.

As the day waned, De Wet decided there was no hurry. He would wait out the weather. Perhaps by morning it would be clear and he would send a party under white flag to ask for the column's surrender.

When it had been dark for some time—and, because of the continuing storm, it was stone dark between lightning flashes—Jeff came looking for Frank. He found him with his troopers, bailing water from their trench. Jeff said he needed Frank to come and do some scouting. The troopers got excited, imagining themselves scampering toward the Boer lines in the dark, but Jeff told them to stay where they were. He wanted only Frank.

As they picked their way in the sucking wet, Frank asked about horses, and Jeff said they were going on foot. Rimington thought the Boers encircling them were not a unified army but the various commandos De Wet had called together. Each commando would be camped separately, behind a screen of its own outposts. His hope was that between these camps might be gaps. That was what he wanted his scouts to look for.

He told them to go in pairs and carry a compass. He gave each team a compass heading, to keep them from colliding or investigating the same place. Every once in a while as Jeff and Frank walked, Jeff pulled his greatcoat over his head and struck a match over the compass face.

It was hard not to slip or stumble in the wet darkness. All they knew was that they were walking up a slow rise, seamed with bush and studded with rock piles. The Boers would be camped beyond the hill's roof. Probably along its crest would be their outposts.

For the first half-hour, the lightning continued. It was not as rapid as earlier, but struck every minute or two. Carrying his rifle, Frank remembered a story from home about a cowboy caught in a lightning storm while hunting, how they had decided from his cooked remains that his rifle had drawn the spark.

A bloom of lightning finally did show them an outpost in a pile of rocks higher up the slope. In the flash, Frank and Jeff saw two sopping hats and two Mauser rifles. When the vision faded, Jeff gave Frank a strong shove away. This was in case the Boers had seen them too. Frank ran and so did Jeff, in opposite directions. No shots came.

Frank stopped and stood still in the dark, trying to determine how far he'd gone, and at what angle the outpost was from him now. He kept his rifle pointed there, should another plume of light expose him.

He decided that he and Jeff should pass this place and keep on looking for other outposts and how they related to the camp. Then they should move on and see if there was a wide enough gap between this camp and the next to drive the column through. This outpost had no meaning, and if they got into a shooting match here, it could give the whole show away. The Boers would figure out that Rimington was probing their perimeters. The whole Boer army would be alerted.

Frank decided to retrace his steps and find Jeff. He hurried because he did not want to be in front of the Boers when the next flash came. When he believed he had gone far enough to put him on the outpost's north side, he still had not found Jeff. He risked whispering his name into the dark, but that did not produce him either. He worried that he himself was lost.

In a moment, lightning struck, and Frank saw that he was where he meant to be. The two Boers were south of him, facing down the hill. Then Frank saw Jeff rise behind them, his rifle bayonet raised in his right hand. In that second of light, Frank saw the blade come around one Boer's throat—then nothing.

Frank stood, and his one leg was quivering. He expected gunfire or some other sound of fighting, but none came. There was just himself and the rain rattling the roof of his hat. The cold water running down his neck and back.

At the next flash, the little outpost looked forlorn and empty. No hats, no rifles. Frank felt something at his elbow that made his body wrench. In the instant of dying light, Jeff smiled not two feet from him. He grabbed Frank's arm and pulled him away.

Frank let himself be led until they were in Rimington's camp again. They went to Rimington's tent, where they drank tea with rum in it, and Jeff told Mike about the seam between outposts—where there'd been an outpost but wasn't now. He said nothing about the dead Boers, even though he had fresh blood on his coat.

Other scouting pairs returned and told their stories. Charlie Ross came last with Capt. Arthur Lewis. They described a hairy kloof, a deep narrow canyon crossed above by branches. It had a wagon trail in its bottom that went gradually down toward the river.

The kloof entrance was masked by brush, and the Boers must have decided the British would never find it in the storm. It had been left unguarded.

Once everyone was there, Rimington explained what they would do.

The kloof went down so slowly it was almost flat. It was deep in water, running off from the storm. The rain and thunder hid the sound of their clumsy progress. The first hours were terrifying. Such a long thin line, compressed and held within walls of stone, would have no defence if discovered. The Boers could line up on top and fire into the vale.

It was almost impossible to believe they had fooled De Wet, but when enough hours had passed, they did believe. They had left most of their wagons at the farm, loaded with provisions and ammunition in the trees. The only wagons with them now held their field pieces and artillery shells. More was left on the gravel strand before they crossed the river. Then it was flat out for Heilbron.

At first light, every man was imagining how Christiaan De Wet would wake up and discover they were gone. Looking up as someone came on the run to say that the trees were empty. Then the mad scamper to find their tracks. Later, the Boers would be looking at the discarded piles along the river strand. They would curse the English for being lucky enough to find a drift with a bottom that held their gun wagons.

From the river to Heilbron, Rimington kept up their speed, for he knew the Boers would be coming. When the Boers did attack, firing on the rearguard, relief troops from Heilbron were in sight. The Boers had to run. For the last fifteen miles, the column slowed and enjoyed itself. They were home and dry.

As he rode that final distance with his three giddy troopers, Frank was stuck with thoughts he'd rather not have had. He kept reliving the moments in the dark above the farm and wondering what would have happened if Jeff's act of extreme bravery had gone wrong. One awkwardly timed lightning bolt and Jeff could have been exposed ten or twenty yards from the outpost. The Boers could have emptied their magazines into him. Or Jeff would have shot them. Either way, there would have been guns going off for other outposts to hear and be alerted by.

In this version, the Boers would have stirred their camps to wakefulness, would have sent out more sentries, would have put guards at the entrance of the hairy kloof—knowing that Rimington was not waiting in the trees but trying to escape.

In that story, they did not escape, but were locked down and half drowned in their trenches when light came. Maybe, when the rain stopped, and because of their attempt to flee in the dark, De Wet would have changed his mind about asking for surrender. Prisoners were of no use to him, beyond their guns and boots. Maybe he would have decided to flourish his *sjamboek* and order an attack.

The boys riding beside Frank could hardly contain themselves. They kept bursting into laughter and trying to talk faster than they could. The Australians were trying to slap each other's hats off. It was by far their most exciting night of the war.

Tafelkop, December 1901

From Heilbron, Rimington and Damant were sent southeast to protect blockhouse builders on the Wilge River near Tafelkop. On December 19, another lightning storm erupted when the two columns were on parallel roads, three miles apart. Rimington's column was struck and suddenly three men and their horses lay dead in the rain-pocked lake of the road.

Three miles away, Damant's advance guard was looking at a group of khaki riders approaching through the rain. The men were hunched over in their saddles, looking like they'd come a long way. When they were within a few hundred yards, the riders were fired upon by some Boers on the nearest ridge. They turned in their saddles and fired back. After that, they came faster and Damant's guard opened up to receive them. When they were almost there, the riders threw up their rifles and fired at Damant's men.

The rest of the Boer commando was on the ridge that commanded the field that Damant's column was entering. In the storm, Damant had not heard the gunfire. He marched in until his whole line was exposed. Then the Boers unleashed a wall of fire.

Frank was in the column hit by lightning. After that, a rider came and told them Damant was under attack. They found Damant's riddled body in the mud, and seventy-five more dead and wounded in the battlefield. Jeff Davis had been with Damant that day, and the story was that he had ridden after the enemy alone; had charged part of the Boer rearguard. These trailing Boers were guarding an ammunition wagon stuck in the slop. A witness said Jeff had tried to take them single-handedly. Just as they were turning to defend themselves, a British patrol entered the scene and Jeff was saved.

That night, in Rimington's bewildered, demoralized camp, in the wake of many ambulances that had come and gone, Frank sat at a smoky fire with his young troopers and watched how the day affected them. The Aussies worked at being angry, and tried to convince themselves they would do something to avenge Damant and his men. Danny said nothing, and only stared at the fire that the rain kept trying to drown.

Frank guessed at Danny's thoughts. He imagined the boy was figuring out, as Frank had done, that war was a kind of arithmetic that worked only by subtraction. Even in the moments of glory and achievement, there was always less than there had been before. Horses that had been alive were dead or ruined. Men who had been perfect in their young bodies were gone or reduced in some lasting way.

There was some noise near them in the dark. A clumsy splashing as though someone or some beast was coming on all fours. It was three men, one holding a lamp. The light showed them Charlie Ross and, at the far end of his sinewy arm, Jeff Davis. Charlie was holding Jeff by the cloth of his tunic, and Jeff was leaning and weaving so that it seemed he would fall if not held. Jeff was already covered in mud down one side. He was as drunk as Frank had ever seen him.

Charlie looked half crazy with anger. He kept snuffing as if the air was full of some stink he could not stand. He slung Jeff down beside them.

"There you go," he said. "Your Indian sidekick. All yours."

He stared at Frank, as if blaming him for whatever had gone on.

"I don't want a man brave as this anywhere near me. Nothing gets you killed faster. You can tell him that from me, when he's sober enough to understand the English language. Tell him Captain Lewis is my lead scout now. His services are no longer required."

Charlie pointed a bony finger at Frank.

"So there you go, Corporal Adams. You wanted him. He wanted you. And now you're happily reunited. All yours. All yours."

Part Ten

—

KITCHENER'S MACHINE

Aldershot, January 1902

No one knew yet, especially not Elizabeth, but General Butler had decided to quit the army. He did not have the savings to retire, so his plans would cast his family into relative poverty. If he was going to be poor anyway, he intended to insist on being so in Tipperary, his lovely home county in Ireland. He would put England behind him forever.

The reason was a simple one: that Britain had gone insane. In every sense it had begun to remind him of Rome: the Rome of Caligula; the secret Rome described by Procopius; Rome at her most rotten and mentally enfeebled.

While British generals fought and floundered through another South African summer, Britain had decided it was absolutely necessary to mark the new century in some glorious fashion. Their choice was to celebrate the man who had forged the union between Anglo and Saxon and thus created the condition of being British. That is, they had decided to celebrate Alfred the Great, ninth-century Saxon king, with a bronze statue on a plinth at Winchester.

What Alfred actually looked like was a thing no one could know across a thousand years, but that wasn't stopping the people of Britain from stating their opinion. Several of these far seers had consulted the new science of eugenics, brainchild of Darwin's cousin Sir Francis Galton, so that the depiction of Alfred had slid sideways into the fabrication of The Perfect Englishman. First of all—and no one quibbled here—Alfred had to be white. He had to be free of the "effeminacy of the colonial races." He also must be tall, straight, and manly.

Even though it was a bronze statue, colouring was argued in detail. Hair colour might resolve in the direction of blond—but wouldn't that favour the Danes more than the Danes should be favoured? Even though many British men had black hair, black could give a Dago impression. So maybe brown.

The eyes should be either blue or grey or hazel; but, again, it was a controversy.

As for personality, Alfred must be honourable, brave, and God-fearing (though still able to put the nation's enemies to the sword).

On and on it went: this building of the perfect Briton, a subject the British could not get enough of—even as actual British men were rioting in the streets. In mid-December, Lloyd George, the Welsh MP, the nation's first-ranked pro-Boer, had to be rescued from a Birmingham town hall after one of his speeches so inspired the mob that they were determined to beat him to death or run him through with daggers.

Every aspect of this was inspired to idiotic heights by the South African war. A peculiar sublimation of that war. If Britain could not defeat its farmer-enemy in the battlefield with an overwhelmingly larger army, it could still imagine itself invincible and sublime through the medium of Alfred.

Butler had his own image: Alfred was tall, well over six feet. He had grey hair, brushed back. His eyes were porcelain blue, penetrating, and maudlin. His drooping moustache descended to the chin, making him look even more morose. That is, he was the spit of Horatio Herbert Kitchener. This really was what they should put on the Winchester plinth, preferably stuffed, because no one epitomized British *fin de siècle* lunacy better than K of K.

Heilbron

On New Year's Eve, 1901, Frank and Jeff were together with the three troopers and a multiple ration of the King's rum. Earlier, there had been speeches, but when the night bore down on midnight, the five of them were alone.

Danny, Toby, and Bert were acting out events from their first year in Africa. The Australians stood and gesticulated, while Danny stayed seated and told his stories in the understated cowboy way. At one point, Danny excused himself solemnly, walked out of the fire's light, and retched. Bert and Toby laughed so hard they fell to the ground and rolled in the mud.

Frank and Jeff were quiet as they drank. When Danny returned not too worse for wear, the three troopers left to check on a fight now in progress. Frank did talk then. He talked about Christiaan De Wet's attack on the Groenkop, near Elands River Bridge, in the early hours of Christmas.

Groenkop was a big lump of rock with one sheer side, and the style of attack reminded Frank of Aas Vogel Kranz. At 2 a.m., Christmas morning, De Wet's men had climbed the hill's cliff side and were detected by an outpost only as they came to the top. The British yeoman in the main camp lower down heard firing and grabbed their rifles off the centre stook. Once outside, most ran for the hill's top, thinking that was the safest place. They did not understand that the bullets were coming from there. When they figured it out, they threw themselves down and crawled for cover. Some clutched oat sacks, as if one of those had ever stopped a .317 calibre bullet.

Frank's description of this Christmas tragedy was code for what he wanted Jeff Davis to know. The message was that the three young drunkards out watching other drunkards fight were important to him now. He wanted to protect them from stupid mistakes like those that had cost lives on the Groenkop. It wasn't that he'd given up on Jeff or didn't care. He still imagined them returning to Canada together. But Frank did not intend to tolerate Jeff's heroics, any more than Charlie Ross had, or Casey Callaghan before him.

Jeff's eyes had gone to slits, but in his own drunkenness, Frank was sure Jeff heard him and understood what he meant. In this way, 1901 slid into 1902.

In January, the Canadian Scouts were still tiger-springing around the Orange River Colony with Colonel Rimington. Now that Jeff had lost his access to the men in charge, Frank knew little beyond his orders. When he needed more, he went and sat with Hilliam and the other vets.

The persistent topic was the new scheme Kitchener was about to throw at them. All through his blockhouse-building orgy, K of K had hinted at some final project that would use the blockhouse lines to crush Boer resistance. Any day now, the last two corrugated cans would be fitted together, and the soldiers were guessing what would happen. They saw themselves yoked to other columns, their daily work prescribed, their freedom curtailed. Without knowing anything for sure, they grumbled and cursed the plan.

Another set of stories that came to camp, in the mail and with the supply convoys, involved Breaker Morant, an Australian who had killed Boer prisoners in the bush veldt north of Pretoria. It was a long story involving the murder of Morant's best friend. In some ways, it was like the story of Gat Howard's death. Morant and his men had committed several acts of revenge for which they were being tried for murder. Mentions of the trial depicted Morant as cocky and contemptuous.

Then news came that Morant, Handcock, and Witton had been found guilty and were sentenced to death. The only question was whether Kitchener would send them before a firing squad.

There was a local side to this story, which was that Charlie Ross was Breaker Morant's friend. They had met on the march north, and had exchanged letters since. Things got worrisome when a supply teamster brought the news that Morant was telling his captors he had only done what others had done before him. Pressed for an example, he told of an oath taken by Charlie Ross and his Canadian Scouts. He said they had sworn never to take another Boer prisoner after the treacherous murder of their commander, Maj. Arthur Howard.

After Charlie Ross threw Jeff Davis down beside their fire, Frank had added Jeff to their foursome. The five men marched and patrolled together. But Jeff was not like Frank had ever seen him. Even in the lazy days of the past winter, when he'd slept and drank through the early marches with Rimington, Jeff had never been this quiet and removed.

Frank tried to lure Jeff back with appeals to the vanity of rank. He asked him, as ranking officer, to tell them what route to take, what strategy to employ. Jeff would only make a brushing motion with his hand. *Go on the way you're going*, it said. If he spoke, the words were usually, "You know what to do."

Frank expected Jeff to drink, for this was what he had done during dark moods in the past, but Jeff only drank his rum ration and sought no more.

When they were on patrol, Frank tried Jeff at every position in the line, lead to drag, but he would not pay any attention wherever he was. There was no choice finally but to leave him in the middle, where you'd put a flunky or a tourist.

At their night fires, Frank studied Jeff as Jeff kept his eyes closed or stared at the sky. When Jeff had readily accepted his partnering with Ross, Frank had thought he wanted something he could not get as easily with Frank. Discarded by Ross, he seemed to have given up on whatever that was. Frank tried to find the link between that and the bursts of heroism. Cutting throats. Taking a rearguard on single-handedly. What did it mean to be so dangerously brave? Though he tried to find a different answer, Frank always came back to the idea of death. Jeff Davis had been trying to die in some way he could accept. Now, he seemed empty of even that ambition.

In the third week of January, Colonel Rimington returned from a three-day trip and called a meeting of his unit leaders. The colonel had been away several times in January, and the reason was about to be revealed.

When the officers left Rimington's tent. Charlie Ross bustled through camp with a sheet of paper gripped in his hand. He shook it at any Scouts he passed, signalling everyone to his tent.

They were camped at a farm near Bethlehem, and the Scouts had to shove in tight among the fruit trees surrounding Charlie's tent. He was in front of the canvas, shunting back and forth, the page still in his fist. Frank sat on the ground, and Bert, Toby, and Danny mobbed him like dogs. Jeff stood separate, leaning on a tree.

"Listen up," Charlie said as he marched. He said it several times, even after everyone was settled.

"Spit it out, Charlie!" yelled one of the older soldiers, one of those who never called Ross by his rank or *sir*.

Finally, Ross started talking mumbo-jumbo about pistons ramming and super-columns rolling. They stared at the wiry campaigner from stone faces, and he became uneasy under their scrutiny.

"What I've got here," he shook the paper, "is a set of rules for how to operate this piston thing. At night, we'll have three lines. First one's made of fires. It's false. Second and third are real. Every man's on piquet for a third of every night."

Two men already had their hands up. Charlie was blind to them.

"This here sheet of rules? I'll post it on my tent. More copies are supposed to come. Maybe before you start fixing this plan, you should read it. You might want to remember it was made by General Kitchener and his top officers, including Colonel Rimington. I won't try and answer if you've got complaints. You can take those up with the colonel. Tell him how you want to fix things."

Copies of the rules did arrive the next day. One man in every five had one. Frank had a copy for a while. He read it aloud to his troopers. An army spread between blockhouse lines. Digging a new trench each night. No fires, not even a single lit cigarette, after dark.

The veterans who had predicted Kitchener's plan would cramp their style were staggered by the truth of it. The plan had distilled war down to the elements most hated by soldiers: marching, boredom, digging in the ground.

They had a week before the super-column rolled, and all over the Orange River Colony, leaders like Rimington saw it as a time for revenge. Rimington threw in his lot with Dawkins and Rawlinson on a plan to capture Manie Botha, one of the Boer leaders who had decoyed, trapped, and killed Colonel Damant. Aubrey Wools-Sampson, Colonel Benson's legendary intelligence officer, was with Rawlinson now, and it was his spies who had reported that Manie Botha was on his way north, leading a convoy.

They hoped to trap the Boer when his convoy crossed through a long, rugged chain of hills. Rimington was given a third of the hills to cover, and he sent his scouts to check every trail that wagons could possibly move on.

The pass that Frank's five were sent to search was one of the more remote possibilities: a high, seldom-used trail that would be extremely difficult for a heavily loaded wagon. But, given how many were out searching for the convoy, it was not impossible the Boers would resort to it.

As Frank led his men to the summit, he was full of unease. The weathered trail ran up a slope of stone and scree that stopped at a U-shape between crumbled pinnacles. Out of sight, beyond that saddle was a cliff up which the trail from the south climbed. What worried Frank more than the convoy were the scouts they would be certain to send, to ensure the pass was clear above.

As he rode, Frank felt sparks on his back and neck. These feelings came from the rocky line of a ridge above him to the left, a place where house-sized boulders were separated by deep shadow.

A half-mile from the top, Frank checked behind him, and in his keyed-up state, the sight of Jeff Davis asleep in his saddle infuriated him.

"Goddamn you, Jeff! Wake up and watch! For fuck sake!"

Davis's chin rose slowly. His eyes came even with Frank's. Frank turned away and looked forward. To hell with him. He would get in no staring contest with a useless mute. He had a job to do and men to protect.

Frank's Boer gelding started forward. Frank twisted and saw The Blue set its haunches and leap. In a succession of jumps, the mare was climbing straight up the stony slope. Frank yelled for Jeff to stop, but the scout kept digging the mare with his spurs. At the bony ridge, they slipped out of sight.

Frank started his horse up, climbing in switchbacks. Partway, he saw The Blue and Jeff come forward atop one of the boulders. Jeff shielded his eyes with one hand and looked around in mock surveillance. Skylined.

Frank continued to the top, dismounted, and tied his gelding to a bush. He took the path between boulders and saw where The Blue must have jumped from rock to rock to gain the top.

He came up on the opposite edge from The Blue. Jeff was slumped in the saddle now, his round back to Frank. Frank moved slowly, speaking The Blue's name. When he came to her, he slid his hand along her throat latch and took hold of the bridle there. Jeff lowered the mouth of his carbine and pushed against Frank's shoulder. Frank struck the rifle away and led the horse away from the edge.

When Frank climbed down, he returned to his horse and waited. He heard the collision and the grunt as The Blue jumped down, and jumped again. Horse and man came out of the shadow.

"Get down," he told Davis.

"Why, corporal? You going to arrest me? Fight me?"

Frank was ashamed of this moment. He looked down to where his troopers were dismounted, watching. There was nothing he could say to Jeff Davis now. It was fixed the way it was.

Frank untied his Boer horse and led him down. When he looked back, the place where Jeff and The Blue had been was empty. Later, he saw Jeff riding below the knuckled ridge toward the far pinnacles.

When Davis had looked over the pass and started back. Frank told the boys to stay where they were. He went to the trail and waited. Davis stopped beside him. He was smiling.

"Sorry, Frank," he said. "I'll give you no more trouble. The Boers aren't coming this way."

He tapped The Blue and went forward at a walk. Frank and the troopers fell in behind him, and they rode for the point of rendezvous Colonel Rimington had given them this morning. In the last couple of miles, Jeff lengthened his lead. When they got to the camp, it was after dark, and Frank did not see him.

Liebenbergsvlei, February 1902

An hour before dawn, the whistles blew. The order to move skipped up and down the line. When the soldiers stepped forward, thousands of oxen strained into their yokes behind them. Thousands of wagon wheels climbed out of the cups they'd pressed into the ground overnight.

The head of the piston was a line of men fifty-four miles wide. It spread from one blockhouse line to another. The piston marched early to take advantage of the cool of the day, but the white sun rose into the naked sky and heated the glistening veldt. The light and heat weighed palpably, and the straightforward march made shade a lottery. Those whose place in line did dip down a shaded slope, or carved through a farmer's blue-gum copse, were back in the sun before they had time to celebrate their luck.

They had drank their fill from the Liebenbergsvlei River before they started, but they would hunger for water all day. With so many thousands wanting to drink, the water wagon you saw was always drained and going back for more.

Though infernal, the day was not beyond endurance. Those with a talent for numbers deciphered that their twenty miles of marching hived one thousand square miles off the zone of Boer liberty. When the British stopped to build their lines and dig their trenches, the Boers began to feint at the line and to fire to the full extent of their field weapons.

The second day was so much like the first they might have felt they were marching on the spot, except for their sergeants coming with maps to show their progress. The troops saw themselves closing the distance to the central railway, and how the southern columns would meet the rails first, near Honing Spruit, and then press northward. All the columns would tighten, and the mass would squeeze into the northwest corner, where the central railway and the Heilbron line converged at Wolvehoek Station.

The sergeant who showed the map to Frank and his troopers had called the unknown quantity in front of them "the jelly." During the third night, the jelly pushed back. Caught in the shrinking cavity, the Boers made determined charges against the piquets. Each time a Boer attack was thrown back, the men in the trenches cheered with relief. It would not be their place in line that broke.

The final day's march was brief, and when it halted Frank saw a scene he could barely comprehend. Like a stockyard, zoo, and land rush, all at once. Cattle, horses, oxen, and sheep milled around for hundreds of yards in all directions. Within that animal crush, Boer wagons stood like islands with their bucksails raised. Dusty children peered out the ends.

Everything Frank set eyes on seemed terribly sad. A cow in search of her calf, bawling until the spittle flew, running so her tight bag whacked her legs—even that sight, so common in his life, seemed like something to weep over. Black voorlopers gripped oxen by their nose rings. The thirsty beasts, tongues hanging swollen and purple, tossed the handlers like puppets made of straw.

The Boer families caught in the trap trudged and hung their heads, their hope exhausted. However bravely they had run before the British machine, they were now in its clutches. Frank had seen Indians exhausted this way, hollowed out by hunger and disease, left in the dust as land boosters passed them. Whether or not this lost country was a place the Boers had stolen in the first place, Frank found them tragic.

The few actual rebels probably felt stupid for having been caught by something so cumbersome. They sat in the dirt alone or in pairs, their guns and bandoliers in piles away from them. They were being careful not to give a Tommy or colonial soldier any excuse to shoot them. Gripping their cold pipes in their teeth, they looked like Jeff Davis had in past weeks gone by: barely in touch with the world.

Frank saw many worn and injured horses wandering abandoned. Also forgotten were the wild things. Springbok and impala flung themselves at the wire, again and again. Occasionally one would clear the height, only to land in more coils of wire between the doubled fence. They would fight and then lie still, their bloody sides heaving.

Among the armoured trains huffing on the nearby sidings was one with more flags than the rest. In it were Lord Kitchener and The Brat. When everything was searched and tallied, and the Lord General was told how many rebels he'd caught, the train got up steam and huffed away.

Wolvehoek/Vrede

Frank did not see Jeff Davis during the first piston drive. Rimington and Charlie Ross did not inquire after him either, and Frank began to wonder if he would ever see Jeff again. Maybe he had been allowed to become a civilian, as Charlie Ross had. Maybe something worse.

Then, camped at Wolvehoek, and just before they got word that the super-column was about to roll again, Jeff was at their fire, looking dirty but not too worse for wear. He apologized for his disappearance and said he had carried some dispatches for Charlie Ross into the West Transvaal. He'd even seen Casey Callaghan at a railway station, waiting for his Second Canadian Mounted Rifles. Jeff spoke freely and with humour, and it seemed that his dark fit had passed.

For its second voyage, the piston was split. Half went south along the railway to a new starting point at Kroonstad. Frank's half crossed the Vaal and would start from there. Both halves were to march west to east, with the expanse they had just scoured stranded between them. Near Frankfort, the north half would pivot right and form a back door. The two pistons would mash together in the box's southeast corner.

The news was out that Christiaan De Wet had escaped the first piston drive with the aid of a pair of wire cutters. A herd of cattle had escaped through the same hole in the fence. Kitchener was disappointed with his blockhouse system. That was why the piston's second drive would come together in open country.

—

After a long march west, the north half of the army came to its turning point. The hinge was close to Standerton, and Frank had a strong urge to visit Dunny. If she was better, he might bring her back with him. When he asked Jeff if he would cover for him, Jeff advised him against going. The country they were coming to was the roughest part of the march. Even if the dun mare was better, travelling there would make her lame again. If Frank went to Standerton and found the horse still lame, it would only upset her when he left.

When the piston wheeled, Rimington's column landed on the far east edge, with its left shoulder to the Swazi frontier. The landscape rucked and roughened: rocks, cliffs, crags, defiles. To make a horse walk straight up a slope and down was bad for the legs at any time, and nonsensical here. But the officers insisted it be done that way, or the sweep would not be thorough. Only where straightline marching would drop you off a cliff or down a hole were you allowed to deviate, and then you were supposed to go back and search on foot.

South of Vrede, Frank and his troop were traversing jagged mountains. The jumbled stone was grown through with gorse. Dassies ran in the labyrinth. They came to a place where the rock suddenly divided into a ravine or kloof twenty feet wide. The riders had no choice but to follow the kloof to its end and go around.

Moving west, they descended to a lower level and found the ravine's west entrance. The rest of the cordon had passed already and, according to the rules, the notch should have been searched. Betting that no one had, Frank dismounted to do so. The chasm was black inside: cold and damp. He went forward clumsily, imagining snakes around his ankles. He cranked his neck to look upward, and saw the slice of pale sky was cross-hatched with roots and vines. He went as far as the first twist and pressed himself around the corner. Seeing nothing, he decided he had searched enough.

Once he was back and they had ridden another hundred yards, Jeff turned The Blue in front of Frank's horse and said, "There was someone in that hole."

"How do you know?"

"Smelled their tobacco."

They talked about it briefly and decided not to take it on themselves. They hurried to catch the cordon and find Charlie Ross.

—

Charlie hated Kitchener's Machine. After telling everyone they should not question it, he himself had cursed every hour he spent in the piston's thrust. Everyone near him was treated to his theory that good men forced to do dullard's work turned sour. Such a lot of business he could have done, and booty he could have found, if he had never set eyes on this machine and had remained free-roving.

So when Frank told Charlie there might be a nest of enemy in a kloof, he cheered up. It was reason to leave this moving prison and do real work. He went to select some men.

Frank had left Jeff and the three troopers south of the ravine's entrance. When the expedition reached that point, Ross stopped to outline his plan.

But first he wanted to know what had tipped Davis off.

"Smelled them," said Jeff.

"Smelled what?"

"Tobacco. On the wind coming out of the hole."

Charlie laughed aloud. "Fellow of your talent, Davis, you should be able to tell me pipe or cigarette. Rough cut or fine?"

"Maybe I can."

"We're here anyway, boys. Let's search the goddamn thing."

Charlie divided them three ways. Frank and his troopers were to stay and guard the west opening. That was where the Boers, if they existed, were mostly likely to come out. Jeff and five more would go looking to see if the kloof had an exit on the east side. Charlie would be in the middle, leading the remaining men up the sloping rock to the split.

The three groups approached the ravine at the same time. When Charlie neared the split, the drama of the occasion overtook him. He waved for the others to stop and he strutted forward alone. He went very close to the edge. Across the gap from where he was, the rock rose in a rugged cliff for another fifty feet. He cradled his carbine on his forearm and walked back and forth like a thespian on a big rock stage.

"All right, you Boer bastards! I got a little bomb in my hand."

For the benefit of his own men, Charlie bounced the imaginary bomb on his palm.

"I'm going to light it and drop it down there. If you don't want to blow up, you'd better start walking out the west end of your cranny with your hands on your heads. Anybody with a gun, I'll shoot. Get moving now."

They waited. When no one answered, and nothing moved, Charlie lifted his carbine and aimed at an animal hole in the rock face across from him. When he fired in the hole, the dassies around it scattered. A family of baboons who had been hiding on the cliff started leaping back and forth and screaming. Shattered rock fell into the hole.

There was motion below. Someone yelled up, "Don't shoot!" The accent was not Boer but from somewhere in the English-speaking world.

Frank was watching the notch when half a dozen men came out in single file, hands on their heads as instructed. Some of the faces wore threads of blood from thorns. Three wore khaki tunics.

After ordering half of his men to stay above and half to come with him, Charlie clambered down the rocks. He walked along the line of prisoners, studying each face at close range. He muttered things.

"My, my, my. What have we here? Khaki, dear me God."

Charlie went back to the kloof entrance and leaned on an orange rock embedded in one side. He had his rifle barrel lifted by his ear.

"Little birdie tells me there's more of you in there. Someone special, I bet."

The line of prisoners turned to watch. He looked at them, then looked in the kloof and grinned. He moved as if to fire his rifle into the crack, then quickly looked back. He caught one prisoner lurching.

Charlie laughed even more brightly. "Well, well. Someone thinks a bullet might come out of this hole. It's true, you know," he yelled into the notch, "if you do shoot, you won't hit me, but you'll hit your friends."

Then he called to the men above. "You fellows up there better lie down, so you don't get any of this."

Then, he fired three times into the ravine, two high, and one about head height. They could hear the bullets pinging and shattered rock falling. The baboons screamed and leapt.

"How about it? Coming out?"

"We're coming," a voice called. Frank had it now. The accent was Irish.

Two people struggled out of the notch, hands on their heads. The first was a tall man with wavy hair and a craggy face. The second was Allan Kettle.

"That everyone?" Charlie asked.

The tall man said it was. Charlie said, "Good." Then he sprayed three more shots into the chasm. Dust was rising out the top. Then Charlie ordered Frank's troopers to go in and get the weapons. After a couple of minutes, Danny and the Australians were back, heavily freighted with rifles, pistols, and bandoliers.

"So you're Irish," Charlie said to the tall man and Allan Kettle. "Are you all Irish?" he added to the group. No one answered.

"My guess is that all of you helpful folk have come from other lands to help Johnny Boer be free. I see, too, that most of you are wearing the khaki of the British and colonial armies."

He turned to Captain Lewis, his lead scout and confidant.

"What shall we do with these men, captain?"

"Make an example of them, I guess," Lewis answered.

A Canadian Scout, an older English one transferred from another regiment, piped up unbidden, "They're Irish nationalists, major. Here to make war against England. If we don't kill them in Africa, they'll be blowing up trains in London next."

"I was actually talking to my captain," said Charlie.

Not getting the point, a nervous New Zealander asked, "But aren't they prisoners?"

"Now, goddamn it! Hold on, now! Get your hand down!" he yelled at the Englishman. "This here is not a debate in a goddamn public square. I'm trying to discuss strategy with my captain, and all you boys start volunteering your opinions. Now, please, if you would be so kind, *shut your fucking mouths!*"

He marched back and forth, too quickly, like an overwound toy.

"They are not my prisoners!" he said finally, defiantly. "No sir. Not unless I say they are. And I haven't said."

He came close to the prisoner who had lurched while in line. The sun was beating down fiercely and the man was sweating. Charlie pushed his own face to within an inch.

"You should not wear khaki. Do you know that, Irishman? Makes me very sour. You've fooled good men into getting killed by that. And now, lately, a good friend of mine looks like he'll be shot by a firing squad in Pretoria for killing you bastards for wearing khaki. No, I don't like the enemy wearing my uniform, *at all!*"

The prisoner lurched again, fell against Charlie, who drove him back with his rifle.

The English scout who'd already spoken and been silenced drew himself to attention and spoke again. "Lord Kitchener said by telegram that enemies in khaki were to be executed. Why are we even discussing it?"

Charlie lifted his free hand and pointed at the Englishman. "Only reason we're discussing it is because you won't goddamn shut up. One more word and you can get on your fucking horse and go find Lord Kitchener. Is that clear?"

Then he turned to the tall Irishman, the leader. "You see, sir, except that this rabble don't understand it today, I do have the rank and the authority to deal with you any way I please." He reached up and fingered the black feather in his hatband.

Frank was nervous. Charlie was trapping himself. If he gave the order to shoot the prisoners, some scouts—the ones with feathers—might help him. Frank imagined the prisoners bloody and dead, Alice dead, and he and the others dragging them to the dark end of the kloof for jackals and aas vogels to find.

"You can't shoot them."

Charlie turned. A muscle was clenching on one side of his face. "That's it! That's one too many. On your horse and out of here, Adams. I've warned enough."

He was pointing at Frank, and Frank raised his own arm and pointed at Alice. She shook her head at him, but he kept pointing. "That one's a woman," he said.

Charlie's arm fell and whacked his side. "Oh for fuck's holy screaming Lord! Tell me, Adams, if you wouldn't mind, how you know that. Is it the smell thing? Something you learned from your Indian friend there? Or is it just you've been too long without a female and have begun to see things?"

He turned toward Alice, approached her, and laughed. "Because, to my eyes, that's one damn stringy woman."

Some of the scouts laughed.

"She's English. I travelled with her and another Englishman after I was hit on the head. They were reporters then. I know she's a woman because she told me."

"Okay," said Charlie. "Since this day has had every other form of diversion and nonsense, you—you two—" he pointed at two scouts, "go rip the shirt off this creature. Go on."

Two men approached Alice. She showed her teeth and flung her arms at them. She was very angry and started to undo her buttons. As soon as her breasts showed inside the baggy uniform, Charlie Ross held up his hands and waved.

"Okay, okay. That's enough. We don't need a show."

He turned and stared out into open country. He was muttering to himself and finally faced them.

"I am completely sick of this. Take these pro-Boer bastards, whatever sex or flag they are, I couldn't give a shit, and find where the prisoners go and stick them there. Since you're the damsel's saviour, Adams, you and Davis can do that. You and your three troopers there. The rest of us *soldiers* are going back into line."

When Charlie and the rest were gone, Frank asked the tall Irishman if they had any horses hidden. He shook his handsome head in a way that said there were horses but he was going to preserve them as rebel horses by not saying where they were. Frank looked at the prisoners' feet. Every one wore leather flaps like the ones the Boers had left Frank after they shot Young Sam. Alice's feet were a mess, and Frank had noticed that she was also lame in the leg or hip. He was angry at her noble leader for choosing to make her suffer more.

Frank offered Alice his horse, but of course she refused.

When they moved, Frank kept watching her. She no longer had a bounding stride. With every step, she had to haul her leg past a catch in her hip.

After an hour and a half, they came to a creek. Frank ordered them to stop, drink, and rest. Alice and the Irish leader sat together. Frank went to Alice and said he wanted to talk in private. She shook her head; would not speak or meet his eye. He went to his saddlebag and pulled out his Colt. Feeling foolish, he pointed it at her and said, "I want to talk."

He saw the Irishman gesture with his chin. She had been given permission—or probably an order. Alice got to her feet with difficulty. Frank walked upstream until they reached a little tree and shade. He gestured for her to sit on a black rock and he sat on a smaller one near it.

"Did Lionel go home?"

Frank did not care if Lionel had gone over the moon, but he had to start somewhere.

"I left him with Whitford in Kroonstad. My understanding was that Whitford was going to look for you."

"He found me. What did you do after?"

"I was a nurse in a concentration camp. I am no nurse, but I was there long enough to hate my country profoundly."

"So you joined the Boers."

"I have never joined the Boers. I tried to leave. I went to Lourenço Marques, but I had no money. While I was trying to arrange some, I met him." She nodded at the Irishman.

"Your boyfriend?"

Alice's dirty, leathery face creased in a smile.

"I do not have a boyfriend. I don't have boyfriends. He has a romantic partner in Ireland, an actress and a poetess who I saw perform once in London. She's lovely and spirited. I'm much more interested in her, if you can understand that."

Frank laughed. Had no intention to, but did.

Alice made one of her old movements, threw her head the way a proud horse does. She winced.

"You're hurt."

"Yes, and it's embarrassing. When we came out of the lowlands, all the passes through the Drakenbergs were blocked by troops. I offered to lead a climb up the escarpment and fell."

"You've joined an Irish brigade, then?"

"Stop it, Frank. If you play soldier and interrogate me, this conversation is over. I'll go back to my friend." She stabbed the Colt in Frank's hand with her finger. "Or you could do as they do in dime novels. Make me dance until I divulge what you want to know."

"I won't tell anything you tell me."

"I'll say this much. I don't fight for the Boers. I find them as vile as the British. I will never forget or forgive the slaughter of Young Sam. Or what they do to the blacks. Or what they do to their own families by refusing to give up when they know they are defeated. They're bastards, like the British. I fight for myself against whom I please."

"Why are you mad at me? I don't do those things."

She reached over and grabbed his cheek, gave it a hard, painful twist. "I'm angry because you're a meddling idiot. If I choose to be a man, and you can see that, why tell them? It was a breach of friendship."

"Ross was going to kill you."

"Bullshit! I doubt he has the courage. Besides which, if we go to prison, Kitchener may kill us anyway. He hates the Irish. Wearing khaki will be his excuse. My point is, *you* had no right to choose."

"I thought we were friends."

"Friends let one another decide for themselves."

"Do they let each other die? Do you want to die?"

Alice went to reply, then turned away. She looked down the ribbon of water to where some prisoners had their feet in the creek.

"What about Alma? Did you see her again?"

"Yes."

"I thought you would. And?"

"They burned her farm. Put her in a camp. Her mother's dead."

"Where did you see her, then? In the camp?"

"In Barberton. She's having a baby."

"I see," said Alice. "Not yours."

Frank did not answer.

"Does that have to matter? She's a prisoner. Surely you understand what that can mean for a woman."

"She hates me now."

Alice looked impatient, was about to argue. Frank grabbed her arm.

"I don't blame her, okay? About the baby or hating me. It just ended."

They were quiet. When Frank looked at her again, there were wet tracks in the dirt on her face.

"What's wrong?"

"When you asked me did I want to die, or however you put it, it was strange. I would have thought I knew, but it was as if there was a stone on my tongue."

She wiped her eyes with the back of her wrists, looked to where the Irishman was.

"That's quite something. To be in the middle of a war, having chosen to fight it, and I haven't actually made a clear decision about dying. What about you, Frank Adams? Are you willing to die?"

Frank looked to where Jeff was. He was lying stretched out, propped on one elbow. His carbine was on the grass beside him. He was letting the troopers guard the prisoners.

"I could have gone home twice."

"Why didn't you?"

"First time was Alma. Second time was too, I guess. Because she didn't want me."

"So you felt you had no reason to live. You were throwing yourself away?"

"For a while, I felt like that. Lots of soldiers do."

"But why do they choose war? Why don't they just kill themselves?"

"Because they'd rather *be* killed."

"One's noble and one's not?"

"I guess."

"But you're not talking about you anymore, are you?"

Now Frank's eyes were wet. He squeezed them shut to hold it back. Alice took the Colt from his hand.

With his eyes still closed, he said, "It's empty. I don't have any bullets for it." He took a long breath. "I have fellows who depend on me now."

Frank opened his blurred eyes, looked at Jeff. Alice looked there too.

"What a selfish thing war is," she said. "How many more women and children will have to die because a bunch of men would rather fight than face the rest of their lives?"

"Aren't you like that too?"

"Close," she said. She dug her fingers into his shoulder. "But I believe it is possible that this war is not the world; that it's more of a screen that hides the world. If you and I let ourselves live, we might find the real world. We might be happy."

Frank looked up and saw Jeff waving to him. One long arm, back and forth, then pointing north. He was telling Frank they should go while there was day left to find the prison camp.

When they caught up to the army, night was falling. The two lines of trenches were dug and the sham line lit, the fires rising and falling with the hills. They were eighteen miles south of Vrede.

Behind the lines, Frank and Jeff found the prison camp. It was a half-circle of wagons with a steep cliff for a back wall. Frank held Alice by the arm so she'd hear what he said to the officer in charge. He stated that Charlie Ross had sent him over with these rebels. They had been found hiding in a kloof. He was letting Alice know she was welcome to be Allan Kettle if she liked.

He walked her a few steps into the prison, where maybe fifty Boers sat glumly in the dark. There was a half moon, but the cliff was casting a deep shadow over the prison.

Frank hadn't intended there to be more conversation, but Alice spoke.

"I saw Jim Whitford. You said you'd been to Barberton. That's where I saw him."

"What are you talking about?"

"After I quit nursing, I was on my way to Lourenço Marques. It was when Kitchener's army went to Swaziland."

"That's not possible," said Frank. "He and Brooke would have been gone by then."

"Possible or not, I saw him."

That night, conditions favoured the British. Half moon and no cloud, so the Boers could not creep up in concealment. But the Boers came anyway. They galloped, and because the British artillery was blasting into the dark, the men in the trenches did not hear it. What they saw was the Boers charging through the sham line. They had hit the seam between Rimington's trenches and those of Byng, striking where only eighty New Zealanders held the crest of a hill.

For a minute, the sham line fooled the Boers. As they passed the fires, they wavered. The New Zealanders focused their fire, but the Boers kept coming. Instead of simply escaping once they'd overrun the trenches, they wheeled and attacked along the hill. They rolled up the line until a half-mile hole was torn in it.

De Wet held back in the dark, waiting for the charge to succeed. But, when he gave the command for the rest of his army and his refugees to follow him, they would not. No matter how he flailed at them with his sjamboek, most would not believe there was a hole beyond those fires. They went against De Wet, running into the quieter space to the south. De Wet could do nothing but grab his son Isaac by the hand and escape.

—

The morning after the Boers broke through the line, Frank returned to the prison camp. The Irishmen and Alice Kettle were not there. The officer into whose hands Frank had consigned them claimed not to know where they were. Eventually, Frank found an old Zulu man who had been among the guards.

With a bit of English and hand signs, the Zulu told the story. When De Wet's Boers broke through, the guards thought they would be attacked. Half of them ran away. Those who stayed, the Zulu included, were in trenches beyond the wagon circle. By the time they knew De Wet had passed by, some of the prisoners had climbed the cliff and escaped.

Wessel Wessels' Farm, March 1902

On March 4, the column commanders at Harrismith were told to reverse themselves yet again. Someone had heard that Lord Kitchener wanted to "flatten the Boers," and some wit responded that the mechanism had gone from a piston to a sad iron.

By going north to the Vaal and then west to the central railway, most believed they would catch nothing; that they would wear out thousands of horses for no purpose.

Two days into the drive, the Canadian Scouts were crossing a farm that belonged to Boer commandant Wessel Wessels. Beside a little creek descending to the Wilge River, their line was interrupted by a steep rock wall. The creek ran along its foot. One of the keener Scouts traversed the cliff. Behind a screen of creepers he saw a shadow and continued climbing until he came to it. It was the mouth of a cave, and suddenly he was in a huge room within the cliff.

Near the entrance was a Krupp field gun. Farther inside, he found a Maxim-Nordenfeldt, a pom-pom, and a heliograph system. It was only the beginning. When he picked up some papers and brought them into the sunlight, he saw they were letters addressed to Christiaan De Wet. He had found De Wet's storehouse and hiding place.

The Canadian Scouts poured up the cliff and pressed into the cave. Charlie told them not to disturb anything but they poked around anyway.

Ever since the war began, there had been a legend about Kruger's gold, a fortune from the Rand mines secreted somewhere. In this most promising of places, they could hardly keep from looking.

Charlie wanted to give a speech, and was grinning as he did so. Exactly one week ago, Morant and Handcock had been shot against a wall outside Pretoria Gaol. He had wondered, given that and other black clouds forming, if he would ever be happy again. But, being a betting man, he also did not overlook the possibility that all of his rotten luck might turn after the Breaker's execution; that better luck might be on the way.

"Whatever else they say about me, boys—pretty bad stuff, as you know—this here find of Boer treasure is what will be beside Charlie Ross's name in the history books. *Charlie Ross and his Canadian Scouts discovered the biggest Boer arsenal ever found in the war.* That's what they'll write, and every damn one of us will have that bit of fame to point to."

They could not empty the cave in a day. A pulley system had to be brought in to lower the heavy pieces to the valley floor. Many wagons were needed for transport. In the end, a pyre was built with the rest and the man who found the cave got the honour of touching it off.

Standerton

Living in the pleasant confines of the railway paddock at Standerton, Dunny's lameness had become worse. The erosion of bone in her foot had continued. Paul, whom Frank had left in charge, was heartbroken, and Frank had a tough time making him believe he was not to blame.

The problem now was what to do with the mare. The officer in charge of the railway corral had been complaining for weeks about a ruined horse taking feed and space. Part of Paul's distress was caused by the daily argument to keep the dun from being shot.

Frank had stopped in when the drive north from Harrismith swung by Standerton. After the current drive, he and his troopers were to take part in another even longer one: from the central railway to the headwaters of the Vaal. It felt like he was out of options.

Jeff and The Blue had come along for the ride. Now Jeff asked Frank, "What does your dun mare like best?"

Frank considered the question seriously. He stared at Dunny. She and The Blue were standing on opposite sides of the fence, their necks pressed together. For all of Frank's journeys with his mare, he knew the answer to Jeff's question was not himself.

"The Blue," Frank said.

"Then let her come along."

To make things easier on Dunny, Frank did not return to the central railway with Jeff. He took her out of the railway corral and pampered her in his own camp. After a dozen days had passed, Jeff returned to tell Frank that Rimington's column was close by, headed west—and that Charlie Ross was furious again.

At the British camp, Frank went straight to Charlie for his abuse.

"You take all that goddamn time because of a horse, then you turn up here and the bastard's lame? I tell you, Adams, there ain't much of this war left, but you might get court-martialled yet."

Back with the drive, Frank rode the Boer gelding and let Dunny pick her way along behind. She wore a halter for show, but no rope. Frank had two bandages in his saddlebag and some ointment, and twice a day he spun off one bandage and spun on the other. To anyone who asked how the leg was coming, he said, "Just fine."

They went to Vrede and Tafelkop and Odendal. When they made it to the Drakenbergs, the spine of South Africa, a morning came when Dunny would not get up. The Blue stood over her, coaxing, and finally the dun bucked herself onto three legs but would not touch the ground with the fourth. The slightest pressure and she jerked the hoof back in shock and anger.

Jeff tied The Blue and held the dun for Frank as he gently flexed the fetlock and set the ruined foot onto his lap. He looked for something new, a spine, a shell fragment, but there was nothing like that. Something Dunny could not walk without had simply disintegrated.

Frank let the leg go. He started for where he had left his carbine, but Jeff called him back.

"I'll do it," he said.

Frank stood and thought. Some reflex of mind wanted to say, *No, no, I can handle it,* but Frank found it to be untrue. He could not handle it, and there was no living person he trusted more than Jeff to do it properly. Frank nodded.

Jeff gave The Blue to Frank to hold. She snorted and threw her head when she saw Jeff leading the dun mare away. Jeff and Dunny passed out of sight behind some bush.

Drakenberg Escarpment

The Canadian Scouts were crowded onto one of the long knuckles of the Drakenbergs, looking down into the big green sea of the low veldt. Their new leader, Capt. Alex MacMillan, had brought them here for a drink of whisky.

Two days earlier, four military policemen had arrived from Pretoria and demanded to see Charlie Ross. They took him into his tent, and fellows hanging around heard aggressive questioning and plenty of cursing from Charlie. The policemen searched his tent and all his belongings, including his saddlebags.

Whether or not Colonel Rimington had known this was coming, it was he who came to MacMillan and asked if, as one of the original Canadian Scouts, Alex would accept command. When Alex asked what Charlie was accused of, the colonel shook his head. Either he did not know or would not say.

They confined Charlie to his tent. Alex asked Mike Rimington if he could go talk with him, because if he was going to lead the Scouts, he wanted to know everything Charlie knew. They were in there a long time and the men outside said the two were telling stories and having a good laugh.

Two guards were ordered to watch Charlie overnight. They were told to sit outside his tent, on either side of its door flap. The camp was near the escarpment, so when Charlie cut his way out the back and snuck his best horse off the line, all he had to do was find one of the game trails that snaked down into the fever lands.

Officially, Charlie had deserted and stolen an army horse. But what the hell? He was charged with stealing Boer property and government property anyway. Everybody's guess was that Charlie would soon be in Portuguese Mozambique, sitting in a Lourenço Marques café. He could catch a boat to anywhere in the pro-Boer world and be free.

As the horses stood in an arc on the escarpment's edge, Alex dug out two bottles of whisky. He opened them and held them out over the chasm. "To Charlie," he said.

It took a while for the bottles to go around, for each of a hundred men to drink to Charlie Ross.

Part Eleven
—

PEACE

Aldershot, April 1902

General Butler found it comical: watching Milner pretend to be interested in discussing peace with the Boers; watching Kitchener pretend there was any condition the Boers could ask for that he would not readily grant.

It had started with a message to Kitchener in March, from Schalk Burger, acting Transvaal president. Burger said he and other Transvaal leaders wanted to open peace negotiations and, as a first step, would need to discuss matters with their Orange Free State counterparts. Having proclaimed all Boer rebels still in the field to be criminals doomed to banishment, Kitchener could not openly welcome the suggestion. He let others convey his acceptance for him.

The result was safe conduct through the lines for the Transvaal leaders and a free train ride to Kroonstad. This happened at the same time as Britain was assembling a sixteen thousand–strong army to fight De La Rey in the west.

No wonder Tolstoy called his book *War and Peace*, not *War Then Peace* or *War Before Peace*. War was a Punch and Judy show. Judy hits Punch over the head with a club. The couple come together and kiss. Punch sneaks his club behind Judy's back and gives her another one.

Most bizarre symbol of all, Cecil Rhodes contrived to die in Cape Town on March 27, so that while the Boer generals rode the rails to discuss peace, the flowered corpse of the man who had tried harder than anyone to start the war rode by in an elaborate funeral train, en route to his burial in Rhodesia.

—

Butler was struck by recent similarities in his own household. When he stated that he could no longer be a British general, the roof had fallen in. Elizabeth collapsed in a chair and wept, then rose back up and raked him with abrasive commentary. When the drama was complete, Butler was so far from his original position he could barely see it with the naked eye. He was no longer contemplating anything as punishing to his family as immediate resignation, but was planning to wait out the war and see what crumbs fell. The aftermath of such a corrupt and divisive war should be rife with commissions of inquiry. Among the generals, Butler was a popular choice to lead these, because he could read, write, and add.

Soon the rebel delegates in South Africa would have their meeting, would emerge with their peace proposal. Its list of conditions would be unreasonable (independence for the republics, total amnesty). Milner would pop up and cry, "Preposterous!" Kitchener would rise to his wearisome height and drawl, "Now, let's not reject this too hastily." Britain as a whole would convulse and roll around the floor. The mob would bray up and down the streets.

But, though Butler could not say exactly why he believed it, he did think that, this time, the head beating on the wall would bring the wall down. Wording would be fiddled. Vagueness would be accepted as substance. That which could not be said would not be said, and the other side would pretend not to notice. In the end, it would have passed from generals and governors into the hands of those who massage such things for a living; who can make the most violently opposed statements meet in some imaginary middle.

Kitchener would have his way. Just as Elizabeth had.

Standerton, April 1902

When Rimington's column returned from the Drakenberg Escarpment, they stopped at Standerton. It was the first of April.

Their march had been too remote for news to reach them, and suddenly they were surrounded by newspapers, telegrams, and wagging tongues, all talking about peace. The Boer leaders had met at Kroonstad, then moved under British safe conduct to Klerksdorp. De Wet, Botha, Steyn—even De La Rey was there. A little match glow of peace was roving the darkness. Some tried to blow it out. Some tried to guide it to its candle.

Though Rimington was careful not to say anything about the peace negotiations, his column's "resupply day" turned into "a delay until further notice." They were moved to a well-used camping ground on the town's downwind edge. The officers talked the quartermaster out of a quantity of tents.

Frank, Jeff, and their troopers bedded down in two bad-smelling tents and did not rise until six. They were barely up when they were called together by their lieutenant and given a lecture about slackness. Colonel Rimington wanted them reminded that there had been peace negotiations before, and that previously the Boer leadership had used such delays to rest up and rearm their commandos. If the current peace effort came to nothing, the Boers would come back at them like wolves.

Frank wondered at first what the lecture was about, but then he looked around and realized there *was* a kind of carnival feel to this camp at Standerton. Though De La Rey and De Wet were still dangerous, the overall war felt spent. The Boer towns they had passed through on their way east and then west were trying desperately to get back to normal living.

If the people were sick of the war, so were the men fighting it. Most colonials wanted to get back home, wherever home was. The Tommys were dreaming of cozy pubs, plump girls, and pints of yellow beer. Probably Johnny Boer was thinking similar things. If they didn't stop soon, the bitter-enders on both sides would be fighting this war by themselves.

As Frank watched, and in spite of the dire predictions of the officers, the filthy camp at Standerton became slacker still. Acres of men boiled lice out of their uniforms and groomed each other like monkeys. Rugby scrums. Regimental tug-of-wars. Beard trims. Boot repair. Scavenging for rum.

After a few days of this, Frank started watching Jeff Davis. There was no specific reason—Jeff was calm and mild all day long—but Frank kept expecting something. He was like the man who stares at a blue sky and predicts a tornado.

If Frank knew anything about Jeff's moods, it was that inaction frustrated him and took away his hope. When they had been threatened with Kitchener's Machine, Jeff had begun drinking. On their last independent patrol before the super piston, he had stood on a boulder and sky-lined himself for the shooting.

What they faced now was even more passive than the Machine. It was the final trickling out of the war, and maybe, as Alice Kettle had suggested, peace was what Jeff Davis feared most.

So when Frank saw Jeff get up from their daytime fire and leave without a stated purpose, he assumed he was headed for a bender and would not be seen for days. In fact, Jeff came back to Frank and the troopers in a couple of hours. He had been drinking but was not drunk. He was excited.

He had been at the officers' fire, and the talk had been of renewed action in the West Transvaal. Gen. Ian Hamilton had been selected by Kitchener to command thirteen columns there: to chase and tackle General De La Rey. Far from seeing any contradiction with the peace negotiations, Kitchener felt some sharp battles in the background would keep the discussions serious and short.

They had also been talking about the Second Canadian Mounted Rifles, in Africa since February. At the end of March, there'd been a serious fight at Hart's River in which Casey Callaghan had lost two scouts and had several more wounded. The Second CMR had fifty casualties, quite a few of them killed.

Listening to Jeff, Frank guessed where the talk was going. Jeff would say the scrap between Hamilton and De La Rey might be the last big fight of the war. He would say he wanted in on it. As Jeff kept on about the various men who would be out there—Rawlinson, Kekewich, Evans, Callaghan, Charlie Tryon, Lieutenant Moodie—Frank was thinking, *This is it.* If Alice Kettle was right, and Frank thought she was, now was when he must let his friend choose.

Jeff slapped his hands down on his knees: a gesture of completion, of action about to be taken.

"So what I think I should do is talk to Alex MacMillan and Rimington. I think we should try and go there."

As soon as Frank realized that Jeff meant for all of them to go, it wasn't

Jeff's death he was weighing but that of his troopers. He felt strongly that, if he went with Jeff, the other three should stay out of it. They were too close to getting out of the war unscathed.

Danny pushed forward. His face was red. He stared Frank in the eye.

"Why not, sir?" he asked. "We aren't green anymore. You made us soldiers. You should let us act like ones."

The Australians nodded their agreement.

Jeff jabbed Frank in his shoulder.

"Come on, boss. Let's go."

Captain MacMillan agreed to a week's leave for all of them—longer, if they needed it. He offered to come with them to Colonel Rimington, who was expected to object. Rimington's orders to his officers had been to keep the men from thinking the war was over. As soon as Jeff made the request, Rimington returned to that argument.

"You have plenty of fighting ahead, right here in my column."

"We're not asking to go for long," Jeff said. "A week. Then we'll come back and fight for you some more."

"But going to do *what*, Davis?"

"See the fight. Take part in it. In case it's the last big one. We've been here a long time, colonel. We'd feel bad to miss it."

Rimington fussed but did not argue further. It was probably true that fights of any size were a bygone thing in this war.

"What if others hear about it and want to go?"

Frank thought of the cricket matches; the naked men paring their toenails while their uniforms boiled.

"Tell them we're carrying a dispatch. To General Hamilton or General Rawlinson. We'll need that to get through the blockhouse lines anyway."

"Rawlinson, then. But what am I to say to him?"

"*Please accept these representatives of Colonel Rimington's column. Best of luck, Mike.*"

Rimington barked a laugh. He wrote it just that way, sealed it, and gave it to Jeff. He said they should leave that night.

They found Hamilton's army after four days and nights of riding. As soon as they'd started, they'd been consumed with the idea that they would miss the fight and had pushed their horses harder than was wise. They had taken two horses for every man, and now all were tired.

It was April 10 when they got there, and long past dark. In front of Hamilton's twenty-mile front were sham fires. It looked like Kitchener's Machine, without blockhouse lines to work between. The fire line tracked up and down the hills and glowed beyond the west horizon.

The first order of business was to deliver the dispatch, so they asked directions to Rawlinson's section of the line. When they arrived, the area was dense with soldiers. An error of communication had dumped Kekewich's column in the middle of Rawlinson's. Thousands of soldiers and their supply wagons were plastered together in the dark.

While Frank and the others listened to the din, General Rawlinson came riding with another general, shepherded by torch-bearing guards. The second general turned out to be Commander-in-Chief Ian Hamilton.

Jeff and Frank left the troopers with the horses and tucked in behind the generals' guards. To anyone who barred his progress, Jeff said, "Dispatch for the general," and bulled forward. Frank stayed close.

When Hamilton and Rawlinson met Kekewich, they were close enough for Frank and Jeff to hear. Kekewich was complaining and Hamilton interrupted him.

"How you came to be here and whose fault it is matters little. The truth is you're going to have to move tonight."

Hamilton described a low ridge at the west end of the cordon. He wanted Kekewich to lead his column there tonight, in case the Boers got the idea they could turn the flank.

Rawlinson said, "I hope they try it. With De La Rey off talking peace, it's a first-rate opportunity to smash up his subordinates."

Hamilton added, "Actually, Kekewich, even this balls-up works in our favour. If you march by night and arrive before morning, the Boers won't know you're there. All the more chance they'll run into you."

When Kekewich left, Jeff pushed forward with his letter. Rawlinson recognized him.

"From Rimington, Davis? Is it important?"

"Mostly just wishing you luck, sir. He sent five of us, five scouts. We're to help if we can."

"Due respect, Davis, I have scouts."

Rawlinson turned, looking for someone to take them off his hands. A lieutenant was lurking. "Do something for these men, would you, Tate? They've had a long ride."

The lieutenant led them away.

"We came to see the battle," Jeff told him.

The lieutenant laughed. "If it's action you want, I'd follow Kekewich. Mess he's in, he won't notice you're there."

Colonel Kekewich was in the process of lining out his column in the dark. His sergeants were shouting themselves hoarse. The baggage column was in everyone's way. Jeff and Frank found Danny and the Australians, and Jeff led them along the line of men and wagons and past it. He went ahead and found the advance guard. There he introduced himself, saying they were scouts from Rimington, sent to help. The corporal had no opinion and let them take a place in line.

Starting from the cordon's middle, it was a ten-mile march to the flank. It took the balance of the night. When they found the end of the line, they watered their horses at the base of a long low hill, the one they were meant to fortify. Then they started digging. Frank's five took turns with the Wallace spade.

Frank and Danny took the horses back behind the line. They found a black orderly who understood them and was willing to hold the horses. By then, the sky above the horizon was showing light and the balance of the column had arrived and was trenching all around them. Farther back, across the creek, gun teams were digging in a pair of Armstrongs.

While Frank and Danny were making arrangements for the horses, Jeff left Toby and Bert in the trench and went looking for men he knew. He hoped to find Casey, but did not. From a stranger, he learned that the Boer generals and politicians were rumoured to be on a train for Pretoria this morning, delivering their peace terms to Kitchener. The same man told Jeff that, with De La Rey gone, the Boers were apt to be led in battle by Potinger or Kemp, two commandants known for their keenness to fight.

As the hill became better defined by morning light, a unit of horsemen, maybe fifty, galloped for the crest and over. They were the bait. With luck, the Boers would chase them back, into the fusillade.

The fifty-man bait had not been gone long when firing was heard. In fifteen minutes, a pair of riders sped back. They skidded their horses to a halt before Kekewich's position. Every man squirmed deeper in his trench, rebalanced his carbine on the lip. The sun had risen. The hill crest was lit and empty.

The sight when it came was shocking, barely believable. For half a mile, the hill top was suddenly lined with Boer horsemen. When the first row flowed over, four more rows came behind it, galloping knee to knee. If the Boers were surprised by what they saw, they did not show it. The horses came at a fast canter. They streamed down the slope, holding their fire.

The first round of British case shot missed the Boer formation comically wide. But the next one tore a hole in the flowing rows. They closed the gap and kept coming. They were as neat and tidy as anything Frank had seen in the war.

At three hundred yards, the Boers began firing from the saddle. Some fired one-handed, some from the shoulder. The thousands of entrenched men cut loose and poured thousands of bullets at them.

"What the hell are they up to?" a soldier yelled from Frank's right. "Don't the stupid bastards care if they die?"

From Jeff's place in the trench, Frank heard him say quietly, "They care."

Danny, Toby, and Bert stared goggle-eyed. Frank yelled at them to remember to shoot.

Many in Kekewich's line could not stand it. The force exerted by that charging, firing wall of horsemen ripped them out of their trenches, like fish on the same bait line. Once they made the decision to run, they ran like madmen. Frank saw an old officer draw his pistol and aim it in the cowards' faces. They ran past him.

When Frank looked down his own trench, he saw that Jeff had his carbine aimed but was not firing. He sat a little high in the trench, but that was all.

The troopers were doing better now. Neither sitting like stumps nor firing like fools. Just steadily picking away.

The fusillade from the trenches began to tell. The Boers were going down, horses and men. As they closed in, Frank could see their leader, could actually see his blue shirt billowing. He was at the front and kept coming, even after bullets hit and twisted him. When he was within a hundred yards, Frank checked Jeff again. He was sitting up and taking careful aim. Frank looked forward and saw the Boer leader's head kick back, saw him peel from his saddle. The charge stalled and curled. Those who could rode away.

Frank had never seen a charge as brave and foolish. Now that it was over, he was washed in sadness. Then came fear. He looked at Jeff and expected him to be dead. He looked at his troopers, fearing one of them would be staring at a hole in his body. But all four men were unharmed. Then Frank felt a speeding joy, for surely this meant all of them would leave this war alive.

The three troopers were still staring at the battlefield, as if struck blind by the immensity of what they'd witnessed. Jeff had left his carbine lying on the front of the trench and was slumped against the back. His look was sad and fathomless. Frank climbed out and looked around. It seemed as if every trench had a man suffering in it. The Boers had done much damage.

Like magpies, Tommys were already up among the fallen Boers, looking for trophies. The rumour of peace had made them avid, and Frank was angry to see them pulling weapons from beneath wounded men.

There was a high-strung singing in Frank's head, and everything he saw played to that accompaniment. Jeff was standing now, stretching as if after a heavy night's sleep. The troopers had climbed out onto their jellied legs. Frank led them down the lines of trenches.

Most wounded men were attended to by someone. Ambulances had arrived, their horses prancing. The stretcher-bearers came and went. A gut-shot man without anybody called to Frank for water. He was heavy and blond. Two dumdum tears in his belly were turning him grey. Frank gave him his water bottle and the man took a bloody drink. His teeth chattered from pain and chill. Frank told him the usual things about a medic coming and how he would be somewhere better soon.

"Like heaven?" said the pale man. His hair was dirty and plastered to his forehead. His khaki shirt was black from the ribs down.

"Hospital. There'll be a good-looking nurse for you."

The man tried to laugh and cried instead; covered his face with a meaty hand. "I can't stand this. I wish I'd die."

They left the trenches and started up the slope. A Tommy had found a kettle tied to the saddle on a dead horse. He ran away excited, yelling about tea. Frank had marked the spot where the leader in the blue shirt had fallen. He wanted to see his face, but the bullet that had killed him had made too big a mess of it. Contemptuous of the trophy seekers a minute ago, Frank suddenly wanted something that had belonged to this brave man. He unfolded his jackknife and cut a button from the blue shirt, then a second one for Jeff.

He was standing up to go when he saw Denny Straytor. He remembered thinking he'd found him another time. But this was Denny, and he was dead. For a second, Frank thought of going through his pockets, looking for something, maybe a letter from Alma. He caught himself, and instead took off the soldier's bloody coat and covered him.

Frank could not think of anything more to do. Jeff said they should find their horses and take them to water. He said he would like a bath in the creek. Frank studied Jeff's face. He'd wanted to be in this battle, and now he'd survived it. Frank thought there should be something written in his friend's expression about that, but he couldn't find it.

The man who had taken their horses had led them into some rock cover. None of their animals had been hit, though a couple of other horses were down. One of the horse orderlies, just a boy, ran back and forth holding his arm ahead of himself, his fingers dripping blood. They paid the man who had looked after their horses and led them away.

Farther along, lieutenants and sergeants were gathering troops, yelling about the retreating Boers and how they must be chased and defeated, They must not be allowed to rally. Inside that crowd, Jeff spotted Casey Callaghan. He jumped on The Blue and trotted to where Casey was holding The General. Frank watched the two men shake hands and clap each other's backs. Casey was gesturing to the top of the hill, meaning, Frank supposed, that Jeff should come along for the chase. But Jeff returned, leading The Blue. He said nothing, except to repeat that he wanted to go to the creek and wash.

When The Blue could smell water, she started bunting Jeff's back. Though she did it hard enough to make him stumble, Jeff ignored her, being lost in thought.

Frank was behind Jeff, and the three troopers were behind him. Now that they were walking away from the dead and wounded, the young men were giddy. Arguing over how many they had killed and who had come closest to being shot. Happy to have such a story to tell.

In the trees, men were sitting and lying in the dappled shade. At the creek, a few Tommys were in the water already, naked and pale, shining like saints. It was not much of a river, shallow and full of sand, and they had to sit to get the water over their laps. Downstream, Frank and Jeff watered the horses, then tied them to trees. The three troopers were on the sandy shore, yanking at their boots, when a rifle cracked and a bullet struck the water. The men in the creek floundered and threw themselves to shore; crawled for cover, cursing and yelling. They wondered if it was a Boer who'd been hiding among them all this time, or one of their own gone mad.

Jeff walked to the creek with his boots in his hands. He stood with his back to the sniper and took no cover when another shot came through the trees.

"This is what we'll do," he said.

"Who the fuck are you?" said a skinny half-dressed Tommy.

Frank answered. "He's Regimental Sergeant-Major Jefferson Davis. Canadian Scouts. You should listen."

An older English soldier, sitting naked in the grass—fat, pink, and breasted—laughed. "If he's got a plan, I don't. Let's hear him."

Jeff pointed west, in the direction of the sniper. "There's a road there. It leads to a bridge. I think the Boer is on that road, this side of the river. Corporal Adams will lead you toward him. When he stops, he'll guess where the Boer is. When he shoots, the rest of you advance. Then you shoot the same place Adams did, and he goes forward. I'll wait here."

"He waits here," said the first Tommy. "How do you tell it's his fucking plan?"

"I'll cross the river and come up the far side to the bridge. Frank, when you know where the Boer is, let the others help you flush him. He'll head for the bridge. I'll get him there."

Before they started, Jeff took Frank aside. He reached in his pocket and pulled out a spent bullet casing from a Lee-Enfield: about the most common object in Africa. He handed it over.

"If something happens, give this to Revenge Walker. Tell her it's the bullet that killed Villamon. You got anything you want me to take?"

Frank could not think of anything except the quartz stones from the ostrich's belly that he meant to give Young Sam's family. Anyway, he wasn't expecting to die. He shook his head.

Jeff went to the edge of the creek and Frank and the others went inland. He had his three troopers and two Tommys, including the fractious one. Before they started, Frank repeated the instructions about running when Frank shot, and shooting when Frank ran. He told them to be careful not to shoot him in the back.

He crouched and ran. Counted fifty and stopped. He looked for a line that went through the trees to the sunny stripe of road, then fired three times. When the Boer returned fire, Frank tried to figure out where it was coming from. Danny, Bert, and Toby were almost up to him. So were the Tommys.

He ran again. Soon the shots of his men were passing him. Some of them thunked into the trees. They were not coming close enough to the Boer, and the Boer never stopped firing at Frank. One of those bullets ripped bark near Frank's head, and the angle at which it hit the tree finally gave him a clue to the sniper's whereabouts. When Frank stopped next and shot through the light of the road, he was sure he saw the bushes shake. He had him spotted.

When the troopers and the Tommys caught up, Frank ran to them. He explained where the Boer was, then explained it a second time.

"We're not fucking stupid," said the Tommy.

On a count of five, they stood and fired at once. It wasn't the best shooting but it ripped the bushes a few times where it mattered. The Boer burst onto the road.

When Frank entered the roadway, he was blinded. He squinted and saw the Boer running with his rifle raised, firing at the bridge. Jeff was at the bridge's far end, the planks gleaming in front of him. His rifle was waist high and pointed sideways.

The others caught up, and the noisy Tommy yelled, "Fucking hell! What's wrong with your man? Why doesn't he shoot?"

Frank was running again. At the bridge, the Boer stopped. There were only thirty yards between them now. The Boer raised his rifle. He was aiming this time. Frank pounded down the road. He still had his carbine but was afraid to fire. The Boer and Jeff were too much in line.

The Boer's rifle bucked and cracked. The shoulder of Jeff's tunic burst. Frank dropped his carbine and kept going. He was thinking he could prevent the next shot. Then someone was beside him. It was Danny, running faster than Frank and about to pass him. When Frank looked forward, the Boer had turned. He was aiming at them.

Frank lunged and hit Danny on the backs of the legs. The two of them hit the hard pan of the road, skidded and rolled. There was another shot. Frank looked up through the dust and saw the Boer stagger to the bridge's edge. The plank on the edge was doubled. The Boer's feet struck it and he fell.

The noisy Tommy picked up the Boer's Mauser and carried it to the edge. He leaned over and spat. Frank got to his feet and went there too. The Boer was face down, the brown water parting around him.

"Did Sergeant Davis shoot him?" Frank asked the Tommy.

"Fucking joking, you are," said the Tommy and spat again. "Never aimed or fired his fucking rifle once. Stood there. Bloody coward."

Frank should not have hit the Tommy. He knew that even as he did so. The Tommy stumbled and came back at him, hit Frank flush below the eye.

"The fuck you do that for?" the Tommy yelled. "Crazy bastards, all of you."

"He's not a coward, that's all."

Danny, Bert, and Toby were clustered around them, wondering if they should fight the Tommy or what was correct.

Frank left the group and walked to the bridge's far end. He took Jeff's good arm and shook it. Jeff looked up, not quite there yet; not quite in his own eyes. Frank lifted his limp hand and turned it over. He placed the rifle casing on the palm.

"Give it to her yourself."

Frank towed Jeff to where he could see the Boer in the water. The Tommy was still talking.

"Who killed the fucking Boer, then? We weren't firing. Were we?"

"Someone was," said Frank.

"Well, that's fucking genius at work. I'm asking who?"

Jeff put one knee down on the plank, as if he were faint. Then he put his legs over and dropped into the water. Frank jumped down too, and together they pulled the Boer to the bank. He was tall but light. They rolled him onto his back in some shady grass. His slouch hat was still on. Jeff pulled it off and exposed some thin reddish hair.

Frank had been thinking it was the bald Boer, the one who'd given the order to kill Young Sam. He realized what a stupid thought that was.

Jeff got to his feet and they climbed back to the road where the others waited. Frank told the Tommy he was sorry he hit him.

"I hit you a damn sight harder, and I'm not sorry."

Frank felt his cheek. It was swollen. The view from one eye was pinched.

Frank found his carbine and slung it across his back. They walked away. The Tommys and troopers were ahead. Frank and Jeff were last.

"We'll go home soon," Frank said. "It'll be all right."

Of course he did not know if that was true.

Part Twelve

—

HOME

Bansha, Tipperary, 1910

Butler sat in his chair at the top of the garden, a rug across his knees and the birds chattering in the tall, ancient trees. Some days he was able to sit here and it took nothing more than the sounds of nature to make him feel busy and fulfilled. Other days—and this was one—his thoughts roved over all of his life, as if something were lost and he must find it.

He remembered how Red Crow had died, while gathering horses on the Belly River, and how, when he read that, he'd vowed to be in Ireland when his own time came, preferably out of doors. And here he was. Not that he thought today was the day, but one of these days would be, and he was proud of himself. Life was so full of compromise. A kept promise to one-self was a thing to treasure.

Butler was not a general anymore. One of his last appointments had been President of the War Office Committee investigating the War Stores Scandal. In the final report, he had accused various parties of arranging supply agreements for the benefit of their families and friends, everyone profiting unfairly and illegally. He was applauded for his felicity of phrase, and the report was buried deep with stones on top.

This kept him in the War Office until 1905, at which time he was finally put on the Retired List. As this implied a pension, he was able to move to Ireland. They had found this pleasant place at Bansha, not far from his childhood home.

Besides going for walks and sitting, there were occasional duties in Dublin as a champion of national education, a cause he had adopted as unlikely to wear out or go bad. He was also called upon occasionally for speeches, and he marvelled at his own retriever-like response to anyone's desire to hear his thoughts and stories.

His doctor was also in Dublin, and his most recent visits there had not been encouraging. After listening to his lungs and heart, the doctor would get a faraway look and begin to wax metaphysical. Massaging Butler with hound's eyes, he would say, "I wouldn't worry too much about the pain, William. Maybe one should just be thankful one's body has carried one so far."

His former doctor would never have said such stupid things, but unfortunately Butler had outlived him. If he went to the new one often enough, he really would be beyond earthly cares. One of the sawbones' bits of wisdom would choke him, or cause a vein in his head to pop. And there he'd be: speeding toward the celestial light.

Thanks to the doctor's pithy reminders, Butler had been trying to put his affairs in order. The legal part had not taken long, for there was no great fortune to disperse. Much less simple to organize was the meeting with his Maker. His beliefs had changed so much over time that his image of himself had grown increasingly murky. He had given the majority of his years to military life and the protection of the British Empire. Now, the things in which he no longer believed included the British Empire, the supremacy of British institutions, and war as a means to an end.

What hope, then, of standing before God and pleading innocence. He had to be guilty: either of what he had been or of what he had become.

Other than this minor possibility of being damned for eternity, General Butler was quite all right with the idea of leaving the world. He did rather enjoy pretty days like this one, when the sky drooled its slow honey and birds flittered happily. But if he hung around too long, another war was sure to come.

The Boer War had taught the British nothing. From the King down to the denizens of the meanest pub, the feeling was that the Empire army had punched below its weight in Africa, but that, with more practice in foreign battlefields, it would rise again to its former splendour.

In the next war, all the ghastly modern weapons would be brought to perfection. Butler's military proteges, the ones who still kept in touch, told him there would be new wonders. Armoured motor cars instead of horses.

Flying machines that would drop bombs. Oh my, but wasn't the future bright?

What no one seemed to understand about the Boer War was how lop-sided it had been; how enormously the British had outnumbered the Boers. In the next war, there might be two giant armies of roughly equal size, both with the same far-ranging guns and all the latest gear. That was what Butler did not want to live to see.

Meanwhile, the garden sloped away into the trees and down to the brook. The thunder of guns had left him just enough hearing to enjoy the birds. Sometimes what he heard was not present. The baritone mutter of a night lion in the bush veldt. Frogs chorusing on the Nile.

Today, Butler was hearing the incredible Chinook wind, shrieking out of the valleys of the Rocky Mountains. He was seeing an old Indian, wizened and small, riding in search of his horses. One more time.

Pincher Creek, 1925

Tommy Killam was still in sales, but Killam Hardware was long gone. Tommy was on his own, representing a number of lines, including Ganong Chocolates of Stephenville, New Brunswick. The Ganong family had invented milk chocolate and the five-cent chocolate bar, and were bringing chocolate and hard candy to ordinary people. That was the beauty of it, as far as Tommy was concerned. Alberta was increasingly full of ordinary people.

At present, Tommy went about the country with horse and wagon to the towns the homestead era had popped up along the railway south of Calgary, supplying his clients on a monthly basis. But he foresaw a day when he would have his own motor car and could increase his territory and the frequency of his visits. That would make him a rich man. At present, he was working on the problem that he also needed to be a rich man to buy the motor car.

Tommy believed that money is made in the mind. Understanding the changes that are going on around you is essential to success, just as inability to understand guarantees failure. He learned this from the collapse of his father's store. It happened when the country was filling with homesteaders—hundreds of new customers. But his father, who had never provided credit except on the quiet to select friends, could not comprehend why the new people, total strangers, thought they could come into his store and buy on time.

His failure was the failure to understand that homesteaders had no cash for most of the year, sometimes for years in a row. Without credit, they could buy nothing. His father's compromise was to sell coupons. You could buy them in your flush times and redeem them in your hard times. Tommy tried to tell his father that this was the opposite of credit and that people would never go for it. That, too, his father could not understand, and the store had to be sold.

By that time, Tommy was a grown man in his twenties. Timothé Lebel, who ran the biggest store in Pincher Creek and was the town's richest man, offered Tommy a job, but Tommy told him he wanted a break from store work. He had decided to be a cowboy.

The ranch that hired him was ten miles away in the Fishburn District and belonged to Frank and Eliza Adams. Adams had started his ranch using Boer War scrip. He also homesteaded and pre-empted. His father, Jim, who had been a foreman for the Cochrane Ranch, didn't want to work for the Mormons when Billy Cochrane sold to them in 1904. He homesteaded next door to Frank, and all together it made a nice little ranch. Frank had a pretty Montana wife and two small kids, a boy and a girl. Their cattle were mostly Herefords.

At first, Tommy was disappointed to find out that Frank was a Boer War veteran. One of the things he wanted to leave behind in Pincher Creek was war talk, and the endless toasts to soldiers and war veterans at fowl dinners and oyster suppers. But here he was, trapped on a ranch with a vet. Lucky for Tommy, Frank did not go in for telling his war adventures. In fact, beyond saying he had been in that war, Frank had nothing to say about it.

With one exception.

On a spring day, Tommy and Frank went into Pincher Creek for supplies. They loaded up at Lebel's, and Frank turned the rig around and pointed it home. But then he stopped the team and sat staring up the hill at the Catholic Church. This in itself was odd. Tommy was a Catholic but Frank wasn't. Finally, Frank made a decision and said he needed an hour to see somebody. He offered Tommy a dollar to go to Old Aunty's café, for a piece of pie. Or, he could come where Frank was going. Because Frank never visited anybody in town, Tommy was intrigued and said he would like to come.

Frank whipped up the Percherons and got them climbing the very steep hill. Tommy knew this was an impulse and not something Frank had planned. If it had been a plan, they would have driven the horses up here before the wagon was loaded. When they got to the top, they passed the church and Frank pulled up in front of the two-storey house next door.

This belonged to Marie Rose Smith. Marie and her husband, Jughandle, used to own a ranch higher up the Pincher Creek. The house was Marie Rose's retirement project, for she took in boarders. The location had to do with her being a fervent Catholic.

One of her tenants, an old Englishman named Lionel Brooke, was sitting on the front veranda when Frank and Tommy drove up. He had an easel in front of him and was making a picture. Brooke used to ranch beside the Smiths. Some said he was an English lord. He was tall and thin, and wore a spade-shaped beard, snow white. He also wore a monocle, which had not been fashionable eyewear for some time.

Frank excused himself to Tommy and walked to the veranda and leaned on its railing. The team of Percherons was well behaved, so Tommy left them. He walked behind Frank to where he could hear the conversation.

Brooke kept on dabbing at the little bricks of colour in the tin. He did not act happy to see Frank.

"Come to dig up some bones, Mr. Adams?" Brooke asked.

"Maybe."

"Do your worst, then."

Frank said he wanted an address for a woman named Kettle. Alice Kettle.

"You're out of luck. I sent a note to her, care of her parents in England. It was returned to me unopened from Switzerland. On the outside, she had printed, *Whereabouts unknown.* And below that, she scribbled, *This means you, Lionel.* Hurtful, but comical."

Brooke suddenly stopped painting and leaned toward Frank, staring through his monocle. "Alice Kettle is not her name. If you were British, you would know that. Kettle is a common name and Alice is anything but common."

Frank seemed disturbed by that, but held his ground. Brooke asked if there was anything else. When Tommy had worked in the store, that was how you got rid of a loitering customer.

Frank said he had questions about Jim Whitford. Brooke said Whitford wasn't around. He lived at Hobbema now, with the Cree. Frank said he knew that. It wasn't what he wanted to know.

"I want to know if he really was at the Little Bighorn."

With surprising agility, Lionel jumped up and went into the house. They could hear the stairs groaning as he climbed. He came back out with an age-yellowed letter and sat down in front of his painting.

"There was a time many years ago when my remittance from England failed—dispute with my family. I couldn't pay Jimmy and he quit. He had difficulty finding other work. I got to thinking about the time he served in the U.S. Cavalry as a scout. It seemed a pension should be owing, so I started writing letters. Eventually, I got this letter back."

He handed it to Frank. Tommy went close so that he could read it too. The letter was short, and a couple of sentences had been underlined.

There will be no pension for James Whitford, U.S. Cavalry Scout.
Mr. Whitford was killed by the Sioux at the Battle of Little Bighorn.

Brooke laughed when Frank handed the letter back. "Jimmy rather liked the idea of being dead. I had to promise not to write more letters. By that time, he was doing well and did not need the money."

A boy, ten years old or so, came walking up the hill from Main Street. He was carrying a burlap bag in one hand. When Lionel saw him, he clapped his hands and hooted. He went to the foot of the steps to greet the boy. Tommy could see that the bag was wriggling. Lionel paid the boy some money and praised him. He took the bag and started for the door of the Smith house.

"You have to go now, Adams." He held up the wriggling bag. "Baby pigeons straight from the nest. They must be cooked immediately."

He turned to the door.

"When did Jimmy come back from Africa?"

Lionel kept hold of the handle.

"In 1902. Now, goodbye."

"One more thing," said Frank. "I want to know if Jimmy was looking after me the whole time until he came home. I want to know if he ever shot a Boer who was about to shoot me."

"You know that he followed you and looked after you."

"But I don't know for how long."

"And you don't need to know."

Brooke went inside and let the screen door slap. They could hear him yelling Marie Rose's name.

On the road home that day, Frank was deep in thought. Tommy finally took the reins because Frank was letting the horses wander. Tommy had decided that the queer incident and the questions had to do with the Boer War, and though he could not understand the conversation, he could see that there was something unfinished about it for Frank. Again, Tommy admired that Frank didn't talk about the war, when men who hadn't even been in one wouldn't shut up about it.

That day also made Tommy think about Fred Morden. He asked Frank if he'd known Fred. Frank woke from his dream and said he'd known Fred well. They'd been in the same troop under Hugh Davidson. Tommy asked if he remembered the day Fred was killed, and Frank said he remembered it like it was yesterday. Fred, Robert Kerr, and the Miles brothers had been in one railway Cossack post, and Frank had been a few miles north in another. He explained the attack and how Fred's bunch had been trapped, with no way to reinforce them. He told Tommy what he saw when they got to Fred's Cossack post that evening.

"Fred was a friend of yours, then?" Frank asked Tommy when he finished.

"Good friend," Tommy said, and to his embarrassment he started to cry.

Frank paid no attention to that. He said, "Fred Morden was an admirable fellow. I liked him too. It's sad about war that sometimes that being admirable gets you killed."

For the rest of that day and for a week afterwards, Tommy kept thinking about Fred Morden and feeling tearful. He wasn't a boy anymore by any means, and such a display was embarrassing. He kept seeing Fred on his beautiful bay horse, with his wolfhounds all around, and thinking about the day Fred taught him to shoot his new .22; how he'd put his face right down beside Tommy's and told him to put the front sight in the middle of the V-sight and how to breathe and how to squeeze until the rifle fired.

And it came to Tommy, finally, that he had loved Fred Morden, plain and simple, an idea that confused and troubled him, because it was the sort of thing that would get you beat up if you ever said it aloud.

Over the years since, Tommy had continued to think about Fred and to remember that day of revelation. Even now, with a nice woman waiting for him to have enough money to marry her, Tommy remembered the kind of love he'd had for Fred, and it embarrassed him less and less, and finally not at all. Anybody with eyes could see that young boys often felt that way about older boys who were everything they wanted to be. It was a gift, really, to have that kind of feeling, and it was sad if boys were afraid of it and tried to choke it down: sad and wasteful. Nowadays, when Tommy thought about Fred, it was with joy.

The strange irony was what might have happened if Fred Morden had not been killed, and had returned to Pincher Creek a war hero. It was possible that Tommy's admiration, still flourishing, might have driven him into the great European war that had followed. Instead, remembering the grief that the Boer War had caused him, Tommy was determined not to go to the European war, even as many Pincher Creek fellows did—quite a few of them destined to die there in the trenches of France. Marie Rose Smith lost two sons on the same day in 1917.

Even when the older men of the town asked Tommy why he wasn't going to fight, in that way that suggested cowardice, he kept his mind steadfastly pointed toward the future. The truth was he never intended to go to Britain or Europe, in time of war or peace. He intended to live his life right here in Alberta.

Fishburn, May 31, 1942

The end of May and snow all night. Wet, heavy spring snow that weighed down the aspen branches and pushed the bushes flat. If I was smart, I'd be out there with a broomstick knocking that snow off. Instead, I'm sitting here at the kitchen table, where I've been all night. It's forty years to the day since the Boer War ended.

Last time we had a family dinner, my daughter asked me to write a war memoir. My son chimed in and said it was a good idea. The grandkids nodded their heads wisely. Grandpa *should* do *something*. My daughter had heard on the radio that the fortieth anniversary was approaching. Because we are in yet another war, having a father or grandfather who fought in South Africa is antique currency, like a Spanish doubloon.

The day she came up with the idea, I asked my daughter if I was look-ing peaked—because, in my experience, the memoir part of life comes just before the death part. I asked her and her brother, why the Boer War? Why not my cowboy memoir? Or, my broke-down rancher memoir? But then I quit horsing around, because the idea of a memoir already had me reliving the story in my head. Last night, I got down to it, and there it sits. *Frank Adams' Boer War Memoir.* Twelve pages.

Over the years, I've read anything I could about the Boer War, including Arthur Conan Doyle's fat book, that Uncle Doc gave me for Christmas when it came out. English writers like Conan Doyle could write a whole book about the South African War and not mention there were Canadians in it. Though to be fair, I should say that Conan Doyle did mention the day Charlie Ross and his Canadian Scouts found De Wet's cave full of booty (just like Charlie predicted some history writer would). I'm told that Dinky Morrison, the gunner from Toronto, wrote a book when he came home from Africa, but I haven't seen it. There's a rumour going around that William Griesbach is working on one, and that interests me and makes me nervous, because that one might contain more than I want known.

What I don't like about the Boer War books I've read so far is that they don't contain the feeling of being there. Mostly they're just place names and dates and how many got killed, and who won a DSO or a Victoria Cross. Now that I've written my own, I'm pretty sure it's just as bad, for the same reasons. My daughter would say I shouldn't expect to stay up for one night and pen a masterpiece. But if I took six months and wrote a hundred pages, it would be the same, because I'd still have left out all the interest-ing parts.

Pete and Eddy Belton are an example of why. There's a pair I don't care much about or see very often. They showed up in Alberta around 1910 after having served their jail time for desertion and theft. They went back into the North Fork country and squatted in some cranny, running a few cattle on other people's grass. Every fall, they go through the Livingstone Gap, to hunt for elk and the Lost Lemon Mine. If I see Pete in town, that's what he tells me: that this is the year he's going to find the Lost Lemon and become a rich man.

In my memoir, I don't mention them, because I don't want to tell how they poisoned the baboon, tried to shoot Jeff Davis, and stole my dun mare. Nobody thinks highly of Eddy and Pete, but I don't think it's my job to give people reasons to look down on them even more.

I do mention Ovide. I say that he was a friend of mine from home, and how we fought together and looked after horses, and that he died of poisoning at Pan Station. I left out how his poisoning occurred, because I don't want to be like Greasy, telling how Ovide took medicines five and two when he needed seven and died of good arithmetic. Greasy's a major-general now and Ovide's long dead. Why tell a story that makes Greasy look mean and Ovide look stupid?

Something that made me feel a little better about Ovide was when Pincher Creek built a new hospital and called it Memorial in honour of the town's Boer War dead. They could have put Fred Morden's and Robert Kerr's names on the plaque and stopped there, and no one would have been disturbed. But they put Ovide Smith's name on too. I've bought my supplies in Pincher Creek ever since.

In the part of the memoir that's about me, I've skipped a lot and did not add any bluster. From the start, I told my wife, and then my children, that I was no war hero. I said I would never take much of a risk to shoot a Boer, which was the truth. I tell them it was a stupid war from start to finish and benefited no one but the rich. The proof is that the black people of South Africa never did get the vote, just like Indians here in Canada don't have the vote to this day.

What I've left out of the memoir is that, after Ovide died and Dunny was stolen, I deserted. Nor is there a whisper of my having loved a Boer girl. I did not want my children to think of me as a coward. I did not want my wife to know I loved someone before her, in case she thought I loved her less.

I did write about Jeff Davis, but mostly about what happened after the war. Jeff and I accepted an offer from the British Government to go to

England and be part of the celebration of the new King's coronation. When we got there, Victoria's son Bertie had appendicitis and the coronation was postponed. We bummed around London the whole summer and enjoyed ourselves. Finally, we rode in the coronation parade with a few other Canadian Scouts and Alex MacMillan in the lead. The newspaper called us "very tough desperados," and I cut that out and brought it home.

Before we left Africa, Jeff had shipped The Blue to Halifax with instructions to send her to a certain Halifax livery barn. When we arrived in Halifax from England, we found the blue cayuse, not only alive but fatter and sassier than ever.

A few weeks later, Jeff and I took leave of one another at the Old Man River ford. He was going east to Ft. Macleod. I had quite a long ride yet to the Cochrane Ranch. We did not embrace or shake hands. We had a whole lifetime to meet up and shoot the breeze. That's what we told each other.

Four years later, on a hot summer day, Jeff's brother Charlie came over from the Blood Reserve to tell me Jeff was dead. He'd had a little farm on the Willow Creek, which he acquired with Boer War scrip I'd encouraged him to apply for. His hay binder was plugged and he was leaning over the canvas, pulling hay out, when his horses spooked and a tine popped up and pierced his heart. He was still on it when they found him.

I had dreams about Jeff's death for years. I would be there and trying to lift him off. But there was always a problem. I'd be caught on something or my arms would have no strength. I could never help Jeff no matter how many times I dreamed it.

By the time of his death, Jeff had a reputation around Ft. Macleod as a drunkard. "Just a Halfbreed" was what he was called in a book about the range era by a man named Kelly. Kelly also called him "shiftless, unmoral, and whisky sodden." There was a whole page devoted to running Jeff down as a war hero who came home and did nothing "with all his advantages."

I have seldom been as angry in my life. I wrote a storming-mad letter to Kelly, but I never sent it. I did not because I knew that, if Jeff were alive, he wouldn't have bothered. He would have laughed about it and had another drink.

—

When I get up from this table, I will make a fire in the wood stove. Then I will feed this memoir to that fire, every page. Back in the Great Karoo when I kept telling myself it was a moose to a horse, that was the closest I came to understanding. The whole war was like that. We travelled inside it, Ovide, Jeff, and me, but we never understood it and were never part of it. Ovide proved that the day he tried to turn five and two into seven. Jeff believed he could make the war do tricks but finally couldn't even get it to kill him. And here I am trying to make sense of it still, trying to make a horse when it never was a horse and never will be.

THE END

ACKNOWLEDGEMENTS

Many have helped me with this novel.

I thank my wife Pamela Banting for her understanding, patience, and wonderful sense of language.

Many thanks to my agent Anne McDermid for finding *The Great Karoo* a home, and to Maya Mavjee for her certainty that Doubleday Canada should be that home. The team at Doubleday Canada has been wonderful, but special thanks to Martha Kanya-Forstner for her fine editing and unfailing calm good humour.

Several times in the writing of this novel, I was given information that was simply not available in others ways. For these gifts, I thank Joyce Bonertz, Peter Redpath, Rachel Wyatt, Linda Smith, Barbara Brydges, and Hugh Dempsey.

Thanks to Elaine and Robin Phillips of Cochrane for helping prepare me for my research trip to South Africa. In Middelburg, Transvaal, Peter Dickson and Gerald Gerhardt gave me a fine tour, including the concentration camp graveyard, the military graveyard (where I found the grave of Ovide Smith), and Aas Vogel Kranz. Kate Minaar of Middelburg served me Hertzoggies and Smutzies in her home. Thanks to these Middelburg gentlefolk for their generosity to a complete stranger.

I would like to thank the friends who helped at key times: Marina Endicott, Peter Ormshaw, Caroline Adderson, Chris Fisher, Andrew Wreggitt, Don Smith, Ian Prinsloo, Steve Gobby, and George Parry. Special thanks to Greg Gerrard for the author photo.

I would like to recognize the staff of the Glenbow Museum, Library and Archives, for all the help they have given me over the years—and again with this book. Thanks as well to the National Archives of Canada. Of the many books that were profoundly useful sources, I would like to recognize *Painting the Map Red* by Carman Millar, *Our Little Army in the Field* by Brian A. Reid, *Canada's Sons on Kopje and Veldt* by T. G. Marquis, *The Boer War* by Thomas Packenham, and *Firewater* by Hugh Dempsey. The wonderful memoir *I Remember* by W. A. Griesbach provided a great deal of detail and atmosphere, and I apologize that Frank Adams took such umbrage at Mr. Griesbach's joke about Ovide Smith. Though the novel's General Butler is a fiction, the factual basis of the character came mostly from William Francis Butler's *An Autobiography*, as well as his Canadian memoirs: *The Great Lone Land* and *Wild North Land*.

Finally, my thanks to the Canada Council for the Arts for the timely grant that allowed me to imagine and frame this novel.

A NOTE ABOUT THE TYPE

The Great Karoo has been set in Adobe Jenson (commonly known as "antique" Jenson), a modern face which captures the essence of Nicolas Jenson's roman and Ludovico degli Arrighi's italic typeface designs. The combination of these two typographic icons of the Renaissance results in an elegant typeface suited to a broad spectrum of subject matter, including historical fiction.

BOOK DESIGN BY CS RICHARDSON

SOUTH AFRICA

1899 - 1902

ATLANTIC

OCEAN

Orange R.

Kenhardt ●

Prieska ●

Van Wyk's Vlei ●

Great Karoo Desert

CAPE

COLONY

Carnarvon ●

Victoria West ●

Victoria Roads ●

Kimberle

De A

N

Cape Town